TAKING THE BASTILE

"THE DISTANCE WAS TOO GREAT TO ENABLE HIM TO SEE CLEARLY"

Dumas, Vol. Nine

THE WORKS OF
ALEXANDRE DUMAS

IN THIRTY VOLUMES

❦

TAKING THE BASTILE

❦

ILLUSTRATED WITH DRAWINGS ON WOOD BY
EMINENT FRENCH AND AMERICAN ARTISTS

Fredonia Books
Amsterdam, The Netherlands

Taking the Bastile

by
Alexandre Dumas

ISBN 1-58963-238-9

Reprinted from the 1902 edition

Fredonia Books
Amsterdam, The Netherlands
http://www.fredoniabooks.com

TAKING THE BASTILE.

CHAPTER I.

On the borders of Picardy and the province of Soissons, and on that part of the national territory which, under the name of the Isle of France, formed a portion of the ancient patrimony of our kings, and in the center of an immense crescent formed by a forest of fifty thousand acres which stretches its horns to the north and south, rises, almost buried amid the shades of a vast park planted by Francis I. and Henry II., the small city of Villers-Cotterets. This place is celebrated from having given birth to Charles Albert Demoustier, who, at the period when our present history commences, was there writing his Letters to Émilie, on Mythology, to the unbounded satisfaction of the pretty women of those days, who eagerly snatched his publications from one another as soon as printed.

Let us add, to complete the poetical reputation of this little city, whose detractors, notwithstanding its royal château and its two thousand four hundred inhabitants, obstinately persist in calling it a mere village—let us add, we say, to complete its poetical reputation, that it is situated at two leagues' distance from Laferte-Milan, where Racine was born, and eight leagues from Château-Thierry, the birthplace of La Fontaine. Let us also state the mother of the author of " Britannicus " and " Athalie " was from Villers-Cotterets.

But now we must return to its royal château and its two thousand four hundred inhabitants.

This royal château, begun by Francis I., whose salamanders still decorate it, and finished by Henry II., whose cipher it bears intwined with that of Catherine de Medicis, and encircled by the three crescents of Diana of Poictiers, after having sheltered the loves of the knight-king with Mme. d'Etampes, and those of Louis Philippe of Orleans with the beautiful Mme. de Montesson, had become almost uninhabited since the death of this last prince ; his son Philippe d'Orleans, afterward called Egalité, having made it descend from the rank of a royal residence to that of a mere hunting rendezvous.

It is well known that the château and forest of Villers-Cotterets formed part of the appanage settled by Louis XIV. on his brother *Monsieur*, when the second son of Anne of Austria married the sister of Charles II., the Princess Henrietta of England.

As to the two thousand four hundred inhabitants of whom we have promised our readers to say a word, they were, as in all localities where two thousand four hundred people are united, a heterogeneous assemblage.

Firstly, of a few nobles, who spent their summers in the neighboring châteaus and their winters in Paris, and who, mimicking the prince, had only a lodging-place in the city.

Secondly, of a goodly number of citizens, who could be seen, let the weather be what it might, leaving their houses after dinner, umbrellas in hand, to take their daily walk, a walk which was regularly bounded by a deep, invisible ditch which separated the park from the forest, situated about a quarter of a league from the town, and which was called, doubtless on account of the exclamation which the sight of it drew from the asthmatic lungs of the promenaders, satisfied at finding themselves not too much out of breath, the " Ha ! ha ! "

Thirdly, of a considerably greater number of artisans, who worked the whole of the week and only allowed themselves to take a walk on the Sunday, whereas their fellow-townsmen, more favored by fortune, could enjoy it every day.

Fourthly and finally, of some miserable proletarians, for whom the week had not even a Sabbath, and who, after having toiled six days in the pay of the nobles, the citizens, or even of the artisans, wandered on the seventh day through the forest to gather up dry wood, or branches of the lofty trees, torn from them by the storm, that mower of the forest to whom oak-trees are but as ears of wheat, and which it scattered over the humid soil beneath the lofty trees, the magnificent appanage of a prince.

If Villers-Cotterets (*Villerii ad Cotiam Retiæ*) had been

unfortunately, a town of sufficient importance in history
to induce archæologists to ascertain and follow up its successive changes from a village to a town, and from a town
to a city—the last, as we have said, being strongly contested, they would certainly have proved this fact, that
the village had begun by being a row of houses on either
side of the road from Paris to Soissons ; then they would
have added that its situation on the borders of a beautiful
forest having, though by slow degrees, brought to it a
great increase of inhabitants, other streets were added to
the first, diverging like the rays of a star, and leading toward other small villages with which it was important to
keep up communication, and converging toward a point
which naturally became the center, that is to say, what
in the province is called "The Square," whatever might
be its shape, and around which the handsomest buildings
of the village, now become a burgh, were erected, and in
the middle of which rises a fountain, now decorated with
a quadruple dial ; in short, they would have fixed the
precise date when, near the modest village church, the first
want of a people, arose the first turrets of the vast château,
the last caprice of a king ; a château which, after having
been, as we have already said, by turns a royal and a
princely residence, has, in our days, become a melancholy
and hideous receptacle for mendicants under the direction
of the Prefecture of the Seine, and to which M. Marrast
issues his man dates through delegates of whom he has not,
nor probably will ever have, either the time or the care to
ascertain the names.

But at the period at which this history commences,
royal affairs, though already somewhat tottering, had not
yet fallen to the low degree to which they have fallen in
our days ; the château was no longer inhabited by a prince,
'tis true, but it had not yet become the abode of beggars ;
it was simply uninhabited, excepting the indispensable
attendants required for its preservation ; among whom
were to be remarked the doorkeeper, the master of the
tennis-court, and the house-steward ; and, therefore, the
windows of this immense edifice fronting the park, the
other on a large court which was aristocratically called
the square of the château, were all closed, which added
not a little to the gloominess and solitary appearance of
this square, at one of the extremities of which rose a small

house, regarding which the reader, we hope, will permit us to say a few words.

It was a small house, of which, if we may be allowed to use the term, the back only was to be seen. But, as is the case with many individuals, this back had the privilege of being the most presentable part. In fact, the front, which was toward the Rue de Soissons, one of the principal streets of the town, opened upon it by an awkwardly constructed gate, and which was ill-naturedly kept close eighteen hours out of the twenty-four, while that of the other side was gay and smiling ; that is to say, that on the opposite side was a garden, above the wall of which could be seen the tops of cherry, pear, and plum-trees, richly laden with their beauteous fruits, while on each side of a small gate, by which the garden was entered from the square, was a centenary acacia-tree, which in the spring appeared to stretch out its branches above the wall, to scatter their perfumed flowers over the surrounding grounds.

This abode was the residence of the chaplain of the château, who, notwithstanding the absence of the master, performed mass every Sunday in the seignorial church. He had a small pension, and, besides this, had the charge of two purses, the one to send a scholar yearly to the college of Plessis, the other for one to the seminary of Soissons. It is needless to say that it was the Orleans family who supplied these purses ; founded, that of the seminary, by the son of the regent, that for the college by the father of the prince ; and that these two purses were the objects of ambition to all parents, at the same time that they were a cause of absolute despair to the pupils, being the source of extraordinary compositions, which compositions were to be presented for approval of the chaplain every Thursday.

Well, one Thursday in the month of July, 1789, a somewhat disagreeable day, being darkened by a storm, beneath which the two magnificent acacias we have spoken of, having already lost the virginal whiteness of their spring attire, shed a few leaves yellowed by the first heats of summer. After a silence of some duration, broken only by the rustling of those leaves as they whirled against one another upon the beaten ground of the square, or by the shrill cry of the martin pursuing flies as he skimmed along the ground, eleven o'clock resounded from the pointed and slated belfry of the town hall.

Instantly a hurrah, loud as could have been uttered by a whole regiment of fusileers, accompanied by a rushing sound like that of the avalanche when bounding from crag to crag, was heard ; the door between the two acacia-trees was opened, or, rather, burst open, and gave egress to a torrent of boys, who spread themselves over the square, when instantly some five or six joyous and noisy groups were formed, the one around a circle formed to keep peg-tops prisoners, another about a game of hop-scotch traced with chalk upon the ground, another before several holes scientifically hollowed out, where those who were fortunate enough to have sous might lose them at pitch-and-toss.

At the same time that these gambling and playful scholars—who were apostrophized by the few neighbors, whose windows opened on this square, as wicked do-no-goods, and who, in general, wore trousers, the knees of which were torn, and so were the elbows of their jackets —assembled to play upon the square, those who were called good and reasonable boys, and who, in the opinion of the gossips, must be the pride and joy of their respective parents, were seen to detach themselves from the general mass, and by various paths, though with slow steps, indicative of their regret, walking, basket in hand, toward their paternal roofs, where awaited them the slice of bread and butter, or of bread and preserved fruit, destined to be their compensation for the games they had thus abjured. The latter were, in general, dressed in jackets in tolerably good condition, and in breeches which were almost irreproachable ; and this, together with their boasted propriety of demeanor, rendered them objects of derision, and even of hatred, to their less well-dressed, and, above all, less well-disciplined companions.

Besides the two classes we have pointed out under the denomination of gambling and well-conducted scholars, there was still a third, which we shall designate by the name of idle scholars, who scarcely ever left school with the others, whether to play in the square or to return to their paternal homes. Seeing that this unfortunate class were almost constantly, what in school language is termed " kept "—which means to say, that while their compan-

ions, after having said their lessons and written their
themes, were playing at top or eating their bread and jam,
they remained nailed to their school-benches or before
their desks, that they might learn their lessons or write
their themes during the hours of recreation, which they
had not been able to accomplish satisfactorily during the
class; when, indeed, the gravity of their faults did not
demand a punishment more severe than that of mere detention, such as the rod, the cane, or the cat-o'-nine tails.

And had any one followed the path which led into the
the schoolroom, and which the pupils had just used, in
the inverse sense, to get out of it, they would—after going
through a narrow alley, which prudently ran outside of
the fruit-garden and opened into a large yard which served
as a private play-ground—they would, as we have said,
have heard, on entering this courtyard, a loud, harsh
voice resounding from the upper part of a staircase, while
a scholar, whom our impartiality as historians compels us
to acknowledge as belonging to the third class we have
mentioned, that is to say, to that of the idle boys, was precipitately descending the said staircase, making just such
a movement with his shoulders as asses are wont to do
when endeavoring to rid themselves of a cruel rider, or as
scholars when they have received a sharp blow from the
cat-o'-nine-tails, to alleviate the pain they are enduring.

"Ah, miscreant! ah you little excommunicated villain!"
cried the voice, "ah, you young serpent! away with you,
off with you; *vade, vade!* Remember that for three whole
years have I been patient with you, but there are rascals
who would tire the patience of even God himself. But
now it is all over; I have done with you. Take your squir-
rels, take your frogs, take your lizards, take your silk-
worms, take your cockchafers, and go to your aunt, go to
your uncle if you have one, or to the devil if you will,
so that I never more set eyes upon you; *vade, vade!*"

"Oh! my good Monsieur Fortier, do, pray, forgive me,"
replied the other voice, still upon the staircase and in a
supplicating tone. "Is it worth your while to put yourself into such a towering passion for a poor little barbarism
and a few solecisms, as you call them?"

"Three barbarisms and seven solecisms in a theme of
only twenty-five lines!" replied the voice, in a rougher
and still more angry tone.

"It has been so to-day, sir, I acknowledge; Thursday is always my unlucky day; but if by chance to-morrow my theme should be well written, would you not forgive me my misfortunes of to-day? Tell me, now, would you not, my good abbé?"

' On every composition day for the last three years you have repeated that same thing to me, you idle fellow, and the examination is fixed for the first of November, and I, on the entreaty of your aunt Angelique, have had the weakness to put your name down on the list of candidates for the Soissons purse; I shall have the shame of seeing my pupil rejected, and of hearing it everywhere declared that Pitou is an ass—*Angelus Petovius asinus est.*"

Let us hasten to say—that the kind-hearted reader may, from the first moment, feel for him all the interest he deserves—that Ange Pitou, whose name the Abbé Fortier had so picturesquely latinized, is the hero of the story.

"Oh, my good Monsieur Fortier! oh, my dear master!" replied he, in despair.

"I, your master!" exclaimed the abbé, deeply humiliated by the appellation. "God be thanked, I am no more your master than you are my pupil. I disown you— I do not know you. I would that I had never seen you. I forbid you to mention my name, or even bow to me. *Retro*, miserable boy, *retro!*"

"Oh, Monsieur Abbé," insisted the unhappy Pitou, who appeared to have some weighty motive for not falling out with his master, "do not, I entreat you, withdraw your interest for me on account of a poor, halting theme."

"Ah!" exclaimed the abbé, quite beside himself on hearing this last supplication, and running down the first four steps of the staircase, while Ange Pitou jumped down the four bottom ones, and could thus be seen from the courtyard. "Ah! you are chopping logic when you can not even write a theme; you are calculating the extent of my patience, when you know not how to distinguish the nominative from the vocative."

"You have always been so kind to me, Monsieur l'Abbé," replied the committer of barbarisms, "and you will only have to say a word in my favor to my lord the bishop."

"Would you have me belie my conscience, wretched boy?" cried the infuriated abbé.

"If it be to do a good action, Monsieur l'Abbé, the God of mercy will forgive you for it."

"Never! never!"

"And, besides, who knows, the examiners perhaps will not be more severe toward me than they were toward my foster-brother, Sebastian Gilbert, when last year he was a candidate for the Paris purse; and he was a famous fellow for barbarisms, if ever there was one, although he was only thirteen years old, and I am seventeen."

"Ah, indeed! and this is another precious stupidity which you have uttered," cried the abbé, coming down the remaining steps, and in his turn appearing at the door with his cat-o'-nine-tails in his hand, while Pitou took care to keep at the prudent distance from his professor which he had all along maintained. "Yes, I say stupidity," continued the abbé, crossing his arms and looking indignantly at his scholar; "and this is the reward of my lessons. Triple animal that you are! it is thus you remember the old axiom—*Noli minora, loqui majora volens*. Why, it was precisely because Gilbert was so much younger, that they were more indulgent toward a child—a child of fourteen years old—than they would have been to a great simpleton of nearly eighteen."

"Yes, and because he is the son of Monsieur Honoré Gilbert, who has an income of eighteen thousand livres from good landed property, and this on the plain of Pillalen," replied the logician, in a piteous tone.

The Abbé Fortier looked at Pitou, pouting his lips and knitting his brows.

"This is somewhat less stupid," grumbled he, after a moment's silence and scrutiny. "And yet it is but specious, and without any basis: *Species non autem corpus*."

"Oh! if I were the son of a man possessing an income of eighteen thousand livres!" repeated Ange Pitou, who thought he perceived that his answer had made some impression on the professor.

"Yes; but you are not so, and to make up for it, you are as ignorant as the clown of whom Juvenal speaks—a profane citation," the abbé crossed himself, "but no less just—*Arcadius juvenis*. I would wager that you do not even know what *Arcadius* means."

"Why, Arcadian, to be sure," replied Ange Pitou, drawing himself up with the majesty of pride.

" And what besides ? "

" Besides what ? "

" Arcadia was the country of donkeys, and with the ancients, as with us, *asinus* was synonymous with *stultus.*"

" I did not wish to understand your question in that sense," rejoined Pitou, " seeing that it was far from my imagination that the austere mind of my worthy preceptor could have descended to satire."

The Abbé Fortier looked at him a second time, and with as profound attention as the first.

" Upon my word ! " cried he, somewhat mollified by the incense which his disciple had offered him ; " there are really moments when one would swear that the fellow is less stupid than he appears to be."

" Come, Monsieur l'Abbé," said Pitou, who, if he had not heard the words the abbé had uttered, had caught the expression which had passed over his countenance, of a return to a more merciful consideration ; " forgive me this time, and you will see what a beautiful theme I will write by to-morrow."

" Well, then, I will consent," said the abbé, placing, in sign of truce, his cat-o'-nine-tails in his belt, and approaching Pitou, who, observing this pacific demonstration, made no further attempt to move.

" Oh, thanks, thanks ! " cried the pupil.

" Wait a moment and be not so hasty with your thanks. Yes, I forgive you, but on one condition."

Pitou hung down his head, and as he was not at the discretion of the abbé, he waited with resignation.

" It is that you shall correctly reply to a question I shall put to you."

" In Latin ? " inquired Pitou, with much anxiety.

" In Latin," replied the professor.

Pitou drew a deep sigh.

There was a momentary silence, during which the joyous cries of the schoolboys who were playing on the square reached the ears of Ange Pitou. He sighed a second time, more deeply than the first.

" *Quid virtus, quid religio ?* " asked the abbé.

These words, pronounced with all the pomposity of a pedagogue, rang in the ears of poor Ange Pitou like the trumpet of the angel on the day of judgment ; a cloud passed before his eyes, and such an effect was p·oduced

upon his intellect by it, that he thought for a moment he
was on the point of becoming mad.

However, as this violent cerebral labor did not appear
to produce any result, the required answer was indefi-
nitely postponed. A prolonged noise was then heard, as
the professor slowly inhaled a pinch of snuff.

Pitou clearly saw that it was necessary to say something.

"*Nescio!*" he replied, hoping that his ignorance would
be pardoned by his avowing that ignorance in Latin.

"You do not know what is virtue!" exclaimed the
abbé, choking with rage; "you do not know what is religion!"

"I know very well what it is in French," replied Ange,
"but I do not know it in Latin."

"Well, then, get thee to Arcadia, *juvenis;* all is now
ended between us, pitiful wretch!"

Pitou was so overwhelmed that he did not move a step,
although the Abbé Fortier had drawn his cat-o'-nine-tails
from his belt with as much dignity as the commander of
an army would, at the commencement of a battle, have
drawn his sword from the scabbard.

"But what is to become of me?" cried the poor youth,
letting his arms fall listlessly by his sides. "What will
become of me if I lose the hope of being admitted into
the seminary?"

"Become whatever you can. It is, by Heaven! the
same to me."

The good abbé was so angry that he almost swore.

"But you do not know, then, that my aunt believes I
am already an abbé?"

"Well, then, she will know that you are not fit to be
made even a sacristan."

"But Monsieur Fortier——"

"I tell you to depart—*limine linguæ.*"

"Well, then," cried Pitou, as a man who makes up his
mind to a painful resolution, but who, in fact, does make
it, "will you allow me to take my desk?" said he to the
abbé, hoping that during the time he would be perform-
ing this operation a respite would be given him, and the
abbé's heart would become impressed with more merciful
feelings.

"Most assuredly," said the latter, "your desk, with all
that it contains."

Pitou sorrowfully reascended the staircase, for the school-room was on the first floor. On returning to the room—in which, assembled around a large table, and pretending to be hard at work, were seated some fourteen boys—and carefully raising the flap of his desk to ascertain whether all the animals and insects which belonged to him were safely stowed in it, and lifting it so gently that it proved the great care he took of his favorites, he walked with slow and measured steps along the corridor.

At the top of the stairs was the Abbé Fortier, with out-stretched arm, pointing to the staircase with the end of his cat-o'-nine-tails.

It was necessary to pass beneath this terrible instru-ment of justice. Ange Pitou made himself as humble and as small as he possibly could, but this did not prevent him from receiving, as he passed by, a last thwack from the instrument to which Abbé Fortier owed his best pupils, and the employment of which, although more frequent and more prolonged on the back of Ange Pitou, had pro-duced the sorrowful results just witnessed.

While Ange Pitou, wiping away a last tear, was bend-ing his steps, his desk upon his head, toward the pious quarter of the town in which his aunt resided, let us say a few words as to his physical appearance and his antecedents.

CHAPTER II.

Louis Ange Pitou, as he himself said, in his dialogue with the Abbé Fortier, was, at the period when this his-tory commences, seventeen and a half years old. He was a tall, slender youth, with yellow hair, red cheeks, and blue eyes. The bloom of youth, fresh and innocent, was expanded over his wide mouth, the thick lips of which discovered when extended by a hearty laugh, two per-fectly complete rows of formidable teeth—particularly formidable to those of whose dinner he was about to par-take. At the end of his long bony arms were solidly at-tached hands as large as beetles, legs rather inclined to be bowed, knees as big as a child's head, which regularly made their way through his tight black breeches, and im-mense feet, which, notwithstanding, were at their ease in calf-skin shoes reddened by constant use ; such, with a sort of cassock, a garment something between a frock-coat and a blouse, is an exact and impartial description of the ex-disciple of the Abbé Fortier.

We must now sketch his moral character.

Ange Pitou had been left an orphan when only twelve years old, the time at which he had the misfortune to lose his mother, of whom he was the only child. That is to say, that since the death of his father, which event had occurred before he had attained the years of recollection, Ange Pitou, adored by his poor mother, had been allowed to do whatever he thought fit, which had greatly developed his physical education, but had altogether retarded the advancement of his moral faculties. Born in a charming village called Haramont, situated at the distance of a league from the town, and in the center of a wood, his first walks had been to explore the depths of his native forest, and the first application of his intelligence was that of making war upon the animals by which it was inhabited. The result of this application, thus directed toward one sole object, was, that at ten years old Pitou was a very distinguished poacher, and a bird-catcher of the first order ; and that almost without any labor, and above all, without receiving lessons from any one, but by the sole power of that instinct given by nature to man when born in the midst of woods, and which would seem to be a portion of that same instinct with which he has endowed the animal kingdom. And, therefore, every run of hare or rabbit within the circle of three leagues was known to him, and not a marshy pool, where birds were wont to drink, had escaped his investigation. In every direction were to be seen the marks made by his pruning-knife on trees that were adapted to catching birds by imitating their calls. From these different exercises it resulted that in some of them Pitou had attained the most extraordinary skill.

Thanks to his long arms and his prominent knees, which enabled him to climb the largest standard trees, he would ascend to their very summits, to take the highest nests, with an agility and a certainty which attracted the admiration of his companions, and which, in a latitude near to the equator, would have excited the esteem even of monkeys. In that sport, so attractive even to grown people, in which the bird-catcher inveigles the birds to light upon a tree set with limed twigs, by imitating the cry of the jay or the owlet—birds which, among the plumed tribe, enjoy the bitter hatred of the whole species, and to such an extent that every sparrow, every finch or tomtit, hastens at the call in the hope of plucking out a single feather from the common enemy, and, for the most part, leave all their own—Pitou's companions either made use of a natural owlet or a natural jay, or with some particular plant formed a pipe, by aid of which they managed to imitate the cry of either the one or the other of these birds. But Pitou disdained all such preparations, despised such petty subterfuges. It was upon his own resources that he relied, it was with his own natural means that he drew them into the snare. It was, in short, his own lips that modulated the shrieking and discordant cries, which brought around him not only other birds, but birds of the same species, who allowed themselves to be enticed, we will not say by this note, but by this cry, so admirably did he imitate it. As to the sport in the marshy pools, it was to Pitou the easiest thing in the world, and he would certainly have despised it as a pursuit of art, had it been less productive as an object of profit. But notwithstanding the contempt with which he regarded this sport, there was not one of the most expert in the art who could have vied with Pitou in covering with fern a pool that was too extensive to be completely laid—that is the technical term ; none of them knew so well as he how to give the proper inclination to his limed twigs, so that the most cunning birds could not drink either over or under them ; and, finally, none of them had that steadiness of hand and that clear-sightedness which must insure the due mixture, though in scientifically unequal quantities, of the rosin, oil, and glue, in order that the glue should not become either too fluid or too brittle.

Now, as the estimation of the qualities of a man changes according to the theater on which these qualities are produced, and according to the spectators before whom they are exhibited, Pitou, in his own native village, Haramont, amid his country neighbors—that is to say, men accustomed to demand of nature at least half their resources, and, like all peasants, possessing an instinctive hatred of civilization, Pitou enjoyed such distinguished consideration that his poor mother could not for a moment entertain the idea that he was pursuing a wrong path, and although the most perfect education that can be given, and at great expense, to a man, was not precisely that which her son, a privileged person in this respect, had given, gratis, to himself.

But when the good woman fell sick, when she felt that death was approaching, when she understood that she was about to leave her child alone and isolated in the world, she began to entertain doubts and looked around her for some one who would be the stay and the support of the future orphan. She then remembered that ten years before a young man had knocked at her door in the middle of the night, bringing with him a newly born child, to take charge of which he had not only given her a tolerably good round sum, but had deposited a still larger sum for the benefit of the child with a notary at Villers-Cotterets. All that she had then known of this mysterious young man was that his name was Gilbert; but about three years previous to her falling ill he had reappeared. He was then a man about twenty-seven years of age, somewhat stiff in his demeanor, dogmatical in his conversation, and cold in his manner; but this first layer of ice melted at once when his child was brought to him, on finding that he was hale, hearty, and smiling, and brought up in the way in which he had directed—that is to say, as a child of nature. He then pressed the hand of the good woman, and merely said to her:

" In the hour of need calculate upon me."

Then he had taken the child, had inquired the way to Ermenonville, and with his son performed the pilgrimage to the tomb of Rousseau, after which he returned to Villers-Cotterets. Then, seduced, no doubt, by the wholesome air he breathed there, by the favorable manner in which the notary had spoken of the school under the charge of the Abbé Fortier, he had left little Gilbert with the worthy man, whose philosophic appearance had struck him at first sight; for at that period philosophy held such great sway that it had insinuated itself even among churchmen.

After this he had set out again for Paris, leaving his address with the Abbé Fortier.

Pitou's mother was aware of all these circumstances. When at the point of death, those words, " In the hour of need calculate upon me," returned to her recollection. This was at once a ray of light to her; doubtless, Providence had regulated all this in such a manner that poor Pitou might find even more than he was about to lose. She sent for the curate of the parish; as she had never learned to write, the curate wrote, and the same day the letter was taken to the Abbé Fortier, who immediately added Gilbert's address, and took it to the post-office.

It was high time, for the poor woman died two days afterward. Pitou was too young to feel the full extent of the loss he had suffered. He wept for his mother, not from comprehending the eternal separation of the grave, but because he saw his mother cold, pale, disfigured. Then the poor lad felt instinctively that the guardian angel of their hearth had flown from it; that the house, deprived of his mother, had become deserted and uninhabitable. Not only could he not comprehend what was to be his future fate, but even how he was to exist the following day. Therefore, after following his mother's coffin to the churchyard, when the earth, thrown into the grave, resounded upon its lid, when the modest mound that covered it had been rounded off, he sat down upon it, and replied to every observation that was made to him as to his leaving it, by shaking his head and saying that he never left his mother, and that he would remain where she remained.

He stayed during the whole of that day and night, seated upon his mother's grave.

It was there that the worthy Dr. Gilbert—but have we already informed the reader that the future protector of Pitou was a physician?—it was there that the worthy doctor found him, when, feeling the full extent of the duty imposed upon him by the promise he had made, he had hastened to fulfil it, and this within forty-eight hours after the letter had been despatched.

Ange was very young when he had first seen the doctor, but it is well known that the impressions received in youth are so strong that they leave eternal reminiscences. Then the passage of the mysterious young man had left its trace in the house. He had there left the young child of whom we have spoken, and with him comparative ease and comfort; every time that Ange had heard his mother pronounce the name of Gilbert, it had been with a feeling that approached to adoration ; then again, when he had reappeared at the house a grown man, and with the title of doctor, when he had added to the benefits he had showered upon it the promise of future protection, Pitou had comprehended, from the fervent gratitude of his mother, that he himself ought also to be grateful, and the poor youth, without precisely understanding what he was saying, had stammered out the words of eternal remembrance and profound gratitude which had before been uttered by his mother.

Therefore, as soon as he saw the doctor appear at the grated gate of the cemetery, and saw him advancing toward him amid the mossy graves and broken cro   ', he recognized him, rose up, and went to meet him ; for he understood that to the person who had thus come, on being called for by his mother, he could not say no, as he had done to others ; he, therefore, made no further ·resistance than that of turning back to give a last look at the grave, when Gilbert took him by the hand and gently drew him away from the gloomy inclosure. An elegant cabriolet was standing at the gate ; he made the poor child get into it, and for the moment, leaving the house of Pitou's mother under the guardianship of public faith and the interest which misfortune always inspired, he drove his young protégé to the town and alighted with him at the best inn, which at that time was called The Dauphin. He was scarcely installed there when he sent for a tailor, who, having been forewarned, brought with him a quantity of ready-made clothes. He, with due precaution, selected for Pitou garments which were too long for him by two or three inches, a superfluity, which, from the rate at which our hero was growing, promised not to be of long duration. After this, he walked with him toward that quarter of the town which we have designated as the pious quarter.

The nearer Pitou approached this quarter, the slower did his steps become, for it was evident that he was about to be conducted to the house of his aunt Angelique ; and notwithstanding that he had but seldom seen his godmother —for it was Aunt Angelique who had bestowed on Pitou his poetical Christian name—he had retained a very formidable remembrance of his respectable relative.

And, in fact, there was nothing about Aunt Angelique

that could be in any way attractive to a child accustomed to all the tender cares of maternal solicitude. Aunt Angelique was at that time an old maid between fifty-five and fifty-eight years of age, stultified by the most minute practises of religious bigotry, and in whom an ill-understood piety had inverted every charitable, merciful, and humane feeling, to cultivate in their stead a natural dose of avaricious intelligence, which was increased day by day from her constant intercourse with the bigoted old gossips of the town. She did not precisely live on charity; but besides the sale of the thread she spun upon her wheel, and the letting out of chairs in the church, which office had been granted to her by the chapter, she from time to time received from pious souls, who allowed themselves to be deceived by her pretensions to religion, small sums which, from their original copper, she converted into silver, and then from silver into golden louis, which disappeared not only without any person seeing them disappear, but without any one ever suspecting their existence, and which were buried, one by one, in the cushion of the armchair upon which she sat to work, and when once in this hiding-place, they rejoined by degrees a certain number of their fellow-coins, which had been gathered one by one, and like them destined thenceforth to be sequestered from circulation, until the unknown day of the death of the old maid should place them in the hands of her heir.

It was, then, toward the abode of this venerable relation that Dr. Gilbert was advancing, leading the great Pitou by the hand.

We say the great Pitou, because from three months after his birth Pitou had been too tall for his age.

Mlle. Rose Angelique Pitou, at the moment when her door opened to give ingress to her nephew and the doctor, was in a perfect transport of joyous humor. While they were singing mass for the dead over the dead body of her sister-in-law in the church at Haramont, there was a wedding and several baptisms in the church of Villers-Cotterets, so that her chair-letting had, in a single day, amounted to six livres. Mlle. Angelique had, therefore, converted her pence into a silver crown, which, in its turn added to three others which had been put by at different periods, had given her a golden louis. This louis had, at this precise moment, been sent to join the others in the chair cushion, and these days of reunion were naturally days of high festivity to Mlle. Angelique.

It was at this moment, and after having opened her door, which had been closed during the important operation, and Aunt Angelique had taken a last walk round her armchair to assure herself that no external demonstration could reveal the existence of the treasure concealed within, that the doctor and Pitou entered.

The scene might have been particularly affecting ; but in the eyes of a man who was so perspicacious an observer as Dr. Gilbert, it was merely grotesque. On perceiving her nephew, the old bigot uttered a few words about her poor, dear sister, whom she had loved so much ; and then she appeared to wipe away a tear. On his side, the doctor, who wished to examine the deepest recesses of the old maid's heart before coming to any determination with respect to her, took upon himself to utter a sort of sermon on the duties of aunts toward their nephews. But by degrees, as the sermon was progressing and the unctuous words fell from the doctor's lips, the arid eyes of the old maid drank up the imperceptible tear which had moistened them ; all her features resumed the dryness of parchment, with which they appeared to be covered ; she raised her left hand to the height of her pointed chin, and with the right hand she began to calculate on her skinny fingers the quantity of pence which her letting of chairs produced for her per annum. So that chance having so directed it that her calculation had terminated at the same time with the doctor's sermon, she could reply at the very moment that whatever might have been the love she entertained for her poor sister, and the degree of interest she might feel for her dear nephew, the mediocrity of her receipts did not permit her, notwithstanding her double title of aunt and godmother, to incur any increased expense.

The doctor, however, was prepared for this refusal. It did not, therefore, in any way surprise him. He was a great advocate for new ideas ; and as the first volume of Lavater had just then appeared, he had already applied the physiognomic doctrines of the Zuric philosopher to the yellow and skinny features of Mlle. Angelique.

The result of this examination was, that the doctor felt assured, from the small sharp eyes of the old maid, her long and pinched up nose and thin lips, that she united in her single person the three sins of avarice, selfishness, and hypocrisy.

Her answer, as we have said, did not cause any species of astonishment. However, he wished to convince himself in his quality of observer of human nature, how far the devotee would carry the development of these three defects.

"But, mademoiselle," said he, " Ange Pitou is a poor orphan child, the son of your own brother, and in the name of humanity you cannot abandon your brother's son to be dependent on public charity."

"Well, now, listen to me, Monsieur Gilbert," said the old maid ; " it would be an increase of expense of at least six sous a day, and that at the lowest calculation ; for that great fellow would eat at least a pound of bread a day."

Pitou made a wry face ; he was in the habit of eating a pound and a half at his breakfast alone.

"And without calculating the soap for his washing," added Mlle. Angelique ; " and I recollect that he is a sad one for dirtying clothes."

In fact, Pitou did sadly dirty his clothes, and that is very conceivable when we remember the life he had led, climbing trees and lying down in marshes ; but we must render him this justice, that he tore his clothes even more than he soiled them.

"Oh, fy, mademoiselle !" cried the doctor, "fy, Mademoiselle Angelique ! Can you, who so well practise Christian charity, enter into such minute calculations with regard to your own nephew ? "

"And without calculating the cost of his clothes," cried the old devotee, most energetically, who suddenly remembered having seen her sister Madeleine busily employed in sewing patches on her nephew's jacket and knee-caps on his small clothes.

"Then," said the doctor, "am I to understand that you refuse to take charge of your nephew ? The orphan who has been repulsed from his aunt's threshold will be compelled to beg for alms at the threshold of strangers."

Mlle. Angelique, notwithstanding her avarice, was alive to the odium which would naturally attach to her, if from her refusal to receive her nephew he should be compelled to have recourse to such an extremity.

"No," said she ; "I will take charge of him."

"Ah !" exclaimed the doctor, happy to find a single

good feeling in a heart which he had thought completely withered.

"Yes," continued the devotee, "I will recommend him to the Augustin Friars at Bourg Fontaine, and he shall enter their monastery as a lay servant."

We have already said that the doctor was a philosopher. We know what was the meaning of the word philosopher in those days.

He, therefore, instantly resolved to snatch a neophyte from the Augustin brotherhood, and that with as much zealous fervor as the Augustins, on their side, could have displayed in carrying off an adept from the philosopher.

"Well, then," he rejoined, plunging his hand into his deep pocket, "since you are in such a position of pecuniary difficulty, my dear Mademoiselle Angelique, as to be compelled, from your deficiency in personal resources, to recommend your nephew to the charity of others, I will seek elsewhere for some one who can more efficaciously than yourself apply to the maintenance of your nephew the sum which I had designed for him. I am obliged to return to America. I will, before I set out, apprentice your nephew Pitou to some joiner or smith. He shall, however, himself choose the trade for which he feels a vocation. During my absence he will grow bigger, and on my return he will already have become acquainted with his business, and then—why, I shall see what can be made of him. Come, my child, kiss your aunt," continued the doctor, "and let us be off at once."

The doctor had not concluded the sentence, when Pitou rushed toward the antiquated spinster; his long arms were extended, and he was, in fact, most eager to embrace his aunt, on the condition that this kiss was to be the signal, between him and her, of an eternal separation.

But at the words "The Sum," the gesture with which the doctor had accompanied it, the thrusting his hand into his pocket, the silvery sound which that hand had incontinently given to a heap of crown-pieces, the amount of which might have been estimated by the tension of the pocket, the old maid had felt the fire of cupidity mount even to her heart.

"Oh!" cried she, "my dear Monsieur Gilbert, you must be well aware of one thing."

"And what is that?" asked the doctor.

"Why, good Heaven! that no one in the world can love this poor child half so much as I do."

And intwining her scraggy arms round Pitou's neck, she imprinted a sour kiss on each of his cheeks, which made him shudder from the tips of his toes to the roots of his hair.

"Oh, certainly," replied the doctor; "I know that well, and I so little doubted your affection for him that I brought him at once to you as his natural support. But that which you have just said to me, dear mademoiselle, has convinced me at the same time of your good-will and of your ability, and I see clearly that you are too poor to aid those who are poorer than yourself."

"Why, my good Monsieur Gilbert," rejoined the old devotee, "there is a merciful God in heaven, and from heaven does He not feed all His creatures?"

"That is true," replied Gilbert; "but although He gives food to the ravens, He does not put out orphans as apprentices. Now, this is what must be done for Ange Pitou, and this, with your small means, would doubtless cost you too much."

"But yet, if you were to give that sum, good Monsieur Gilbert—"

"What sum?"

"The sum of which you spoke, the sum which is there in your pocket," added the devotee, stretching her crooked finger toward the doctor's coat.

"I will assuredly give it, dear Mademoiselle Angelique," said the doctor; "but I forewarn you it will be on one condition."

"And what is that?"

"That the boy shall have a profession."

"He shall have one, and that I promise you on the faith of Angelique Pitou, most worthy doctor," cried the devotee, her eyes riveted on the pocket which was swaying to and fro.

"You promise it?"

"I promise you it shall be so."

"Seriously, is it not?"

"On the truth of the living God, my dear Monsieur Gilbert, I swear to do it."

And Mlle. Angelique horizontally extended her emaciated hand.

"Well, then, be it so," said the doctor, drawing from his pocket a well-rounded bag ; "I am ready to give the money, as you see.   On your side, are you ready to make yourself responsible to me for the child ?"

"Upon the true cross, Monsieur Gilbert."

"Do not let us swear so much, dear mademoiselle, but let us sign a little more."

"I will sign, Monsieur Gilbert, I will sign."

"Before a notary ?"

"Before a notary."

"Well, then, let us go at once to Papa Niguet."

Papa Niguet, to whom, thanks to his long acquaintance with him, the doctor applied this friendly title, was, as those know who are familiar with our work entitled "Joseph Balsamo," the notary of greatest reputation in the town.

Mlle. Angelique, of whom Master Niguet was also the notary, had no objection to offer to the choice made by the doctor.   She followed him, therefore, to the notary's office.   There the scrivener registered the promise made by Mlle. Rose Angelique Pitou, to take charge of and to place in the exercise of an honorable profession, Louis Ange Pitou, her nephew, and for so doing should annually receive the sum of two hundred livres.   The contract was made for five years ; the doctor deposited eight hundred livres in the hands of the notary, the other two hundred were to be paid to Mlle. Angelique in advance.

The following day the doctor left Villers-Cotterets, after having settled some accounts with one of his farmers, with regard to whom we shall speak hereafter.   And Mlle. Pitou, pouncing like a vulture upon the aforesaid two hundred livres payable in advance, deposited eight golden louis in the cushion of her armchair.

As to the eight livres which remained, they waited, in a small delf saucer which had, during the last thirty or forty years, been the receptacle of clouds of coins of every description, until the harvest of the following two or three Sundays had made up the sum of twenty-four livres, on attaining which, as we have already stated, the above-named sum underwent the golden metamorphosis, and passed from the saucer into the armchair.

CHAPTER III.

WE have observed the very slight degree of inclination which Ange Pitou felt toward a long-continued sojourn with his aunt Angelique; the poor child, endowed with instinct equal to, and perhaps superior to, that of the animals against whom he continually made war, had divined at once, we will not say all the disappointments—we have seen that he did not for a single moment delude himself upon the subject—but all the vexations, tribulations, and nnoyances to which he awould be exposed.

In the first place—but we must admit that this was by no means the reason which most influenced Pitou to dislike his aunt—Dr. Gilbert, having left Villers-Cotterets, there never was a word said about placing the child as an apprentice. The good notary had indeed given her a hint or two with regard to her formal obligations; but Mlle. Angelique had replied that her nephew was very young, and, above all, that his health was too delicate to be subjected to labor which would probably be beyond his strength. The notary, on hearing this observation, had in good faith admired the kindness of heart of Mlle. Pitou, and had deferred taking any steps as to the apprenticeship until the following year. There was no time lost, the child being then only in his twelfth year.

Once installed at his aunt's, and while the latter was ruminating as to the mode she should adopt whereby to make the most of her dear nephew, Pitou, who once more found himself in his forest, or very near to it, had already made his topographical observations in order to lead the same life at Villers-Cotterets as at Haramont.

In fact, he had made a circuit of the neighborhood, in which he had convinced himself that the best pools were those on the road to Damploux, that to Campeigne and that to Vivieres, and that the best district for game was that of the Bruyere-aux-Loups.

Pitou, having made this survey, took all the necessary measures for pursuing his juvenile sport.

The thing the most easy to be procured, as it did not

require any outlay of capital, was bird-lime ; the bark of the holly, brayed in a mortar and steeped in water, gave the lime ; and as to the twigs to be limed, they were to be found by thousands on every birch-tree in the neighborhood. Pitou, therefore, manufactured, without saying a word to any one on the subject, a thousand of limed twigs and a pot of glue of the first quality, and one fine morning, after having the previous evening taken, on his aunt's account at the baker's, a four-pound loaf, he set off at daybreak, remained out the whole day, and returned home when the evening had closed in.

Pitou had not formed such a resolution without duly calculating the effect it would produce. He had foreseen a tempest. Without possessing the wisdom of Socrates, he knew the temper of his aunt Angelique as well as the illustrious tutor of Alcibiades knew that of his wife Xantippe.

Pitou had not deceived himself in his foresight, but he thought he would be able to brave the storm by presenting to the old devotee the produce of his day's sport ; only he had not been able to foretell from what spot the thunder would be hurled at him.

The thunderbolt struck him immediately on entering the house.

Mlle. Angelique had ensconced herself behind the door, that she might not miss her nephew as he entered, so that at the very moment he ventured to put his foot into the room, he received a cuff upon the occiput, and in which, without further information, he at once recognized the withered hand of the old devotee.

Fortunately, Pitou's head was a tolerably hard one, and, although the blow had scarcely staggered him, he made believe, in order to mollify his aunt, whose anger had increased from having hurt her fingers in striking with such violence, to fall, stumbling as he went, at the opposite end of the room ; there, seated on the floor, and seeing that his aunt was returning to the assault, her distaff in one hand, he hastened to draw from his pocket the talisman on which he had relied to allay the storm, and obtain pardon for his flight. And this was two dozen of birds, among which were a dozen redbreasts and half a dozen thrushes.

Mlle. Angelique, perfectly astounded, opened her eyes widely, continuing to scold for form's sake ; but although still scolding, she took possession of her nephew's sport, retreating three paces toward the lamp.

"What is this?" she asked.

"You must see clearly enough, my dear little aunt Angelique," replied Pitou, "that they are birds."

"Good to eat?" eagerly inquired the old maid, who, in her quality of devotee, was naturally a great eater.

"Good to eat!" reiterated Pitou; "well, that is singular. Redbreasts and thrushes good to eat! I believe they are, indeed!"

"And where did you steal these birds, you little wretch?"

"I did not steal them; I caught them."

"Caught them—how?"

"By lime-twigging them."

"Lime-twigging—what do you mean by that?"

Pitou looked at his aunt with an air of astonishment; he could not comprehend that the education of any person in existence could have been so neglected as not to know the meaning of lime-twigging.

"Lime-twigging?" said he; "why, zounds! 'tis lime-twigging."

"Yes; but, saucy fellow, I do not understand what you mean by lime-twigging."

"Well, you see, aunt, in the forest here there are at least thirty small pools; you place the lime twigs around them, and when the birds go to drink there, as they do not, silly things, know anything about them, they run their heads into them and are caught."

"By what?"

"By the bird-lime."

"Ah! ah!" exclaimed Aunt Angelique; "I understand. But who gave you the money?"

"Money!" exclaimed Pitou, astonished that any one could have believed that he had ever possessed a penny; "money, Aunt Angelique?"

"Yes."

"No one."

"But where did you buy the bird-lime, then?"

"I made it myself."

"And the lime-twigs?"

"I made them also, to be sure."

"Therefore, these birds——"

"Well, aunt?"

"Cost you nothing?"

"The trouble of stooping to pick them up."

"And can you go often to these pools?"

"One might go every day."

"Good!"

"Only, it would not do."

"What would not do?"

"To go there every day."

"And for what reason?"

"Why, because it would ruin it."

"Ruin what?"

"The lime-twigging. You understand, Aunt Angelique, that the birds which are caught——"

"Well?"

"Well, they can't return to the pool."

"That is true," said the aunt.

This was the first time, since Pitou had lived with her, that Aunt Angelique had allowed her nephew was in the right, and this unaccustomed approbation perfectly delighted him.

"But," said he, "the days that one does not go to the pools one goes somewhere else. The days we do not catch birds, we catch something else."

"And what do you catch?"

"Why, we catch rabbits."

"Rabbits?"

"Yes; we eat the rabbits and sell their skins. A rabbit skin is worth two sous."

Aunt Angelique gazed at her nephew with astonished eyes; she had never considered him so great an economist. Pitou had suddenly revealed himself.

"But will it not be my business to sell the skins?"

"Undoubtedly," replied Pitou; "as Mamma Madeline used to do."

It had never entered the mind of the boy that he could claim any part of the produce of his sport, except that which he consumed.

"And when will you go out to catch rabbits?"

"Ah! that's another matter—when I can get the wires," replied Pitou.

"Well, then, make the wires."

Pitou shook his head.

" Why, you made the bird-lime and the twigs."

" Oh ! yes, I can make bird-lime, and I can set the twigs, but I cannot make brass wire; that is bought ready made at the grocer's."

" And how much does it cost ? "

" Oh ! for four sous," replied Pitou, calculating upon his fingers, " I could make at least two dozen."

" And with two dozen how many rabbits could you catch ? "

" That is as it may happen—four, five, six, perhaps— and they can be used over and over again if the game-keeper does not find them."

" See, now, here are four sous," said Aunt Angelique ; " go and buy some brass wire at Monsieur Dambrun's, and go to-morrow and catch rabbits."

" I will lay them to-morrow," said Pitou ; " but it will only be the next morning that I shall know whether I have caught any."

" Well, be it so ; but go and buy the wire."

Brass wire was cheaper at Villers-Cotterets than in the country, seeing that the grocers at Haramont purchased their supplies in the town ; Pitou, therefore, bought wire enough for twenty-four snares for three sous. He took the remaining penny back to his aunt.

This unexpected probity in her nephew almost touched the heart of the old maid. For a moment, she had the idea, the intention, of bestowing upon her nephew the penny which he had not expended ; unfortunately for Pitou, it was one that had been beaten out with a hammer, and which, in the dusk, might be passed for a two-sous piece. Mlle. Angelique thought it would never do to dis-possess herself of a coin by which she could make cent per cent., and she let it drop again into her pocket.

Pitou had remarked this hesitation, but had not analyzed it ; he never could have imagined that his aunt would give him a penny.

He at once set to work to make his wires.

The next day he asked his aunt for a bag.

" What for ? " inquired Mlle. Angelique.

" Because I want it," replied Pitou. Pitou was full of mystery.

Mlle. Angelique gave him the required bag, put into it the provision of bread and cheese which was to serve for breakfast and dinner to her nephew, who set out very early from the Bruyere-aux-Loups.

As to Aunt Angelique, she set to work to pick the twelve redbreasts which she had destined for her own breakfast and dinner. She carried two thrushes to the Abbé Fortier, and sold the remaining four to the host of the Golden Ball, who paid her three sous apiece for them, promising her to take as many as she would bring him at the same price.

Aunt Angelique returned home transported with joy. The blessing of Heaven had entered beneath her roof with Ange Pitou.

"Ah!" cried she, while eating her robin-redbreasts, which were as fat as ortolans and as delicate as beccaficos, "people are right in saying that a good deed never goes unrewarded."

In the evening Ange returned; his bag, which was magnificently rounded, he carried on his shoulders. On this occasion Aunt Angelique did not waylay him behind the door, but waited for him on the threshold, and instead of giving him a box on the ear, she received the lad with a grimace which very much resembled a smile.

"Here I am!" cried Pitou, on entering the room with all that firmness which denotes a conviction of having well employed one's time.

"You and your bag," said Aunt Angelique.

"I and my bag," said Pitou.

"And what have you in your bag?" inquired Aunt Angelique, stretching forth her hand with curiosity.

"Beech-mast," said Pitou.*

"Beech-mast!"

"Undoubtedly. You must understand, Aunt Angelique, that if old Father La Jeunesse, the gamekeeper at the Bruyere-aux-Loups, had seen me prowling over his grounds without my bag, he would have said to me, 'What do you come here after, you little vagabond?'

---

* Beech-mast, we must inform our readers who are less acquainted with forest terms than we are, is the fruit of the beech-tree. This fruit, of which a very good sort of oil is made, is, to the poor, a species of manna, which during the two months of the year, falls for them from heaven.

[Dumas should also have told his readers that beech-mast is excellent for pigs, and that pheasants, and indeed most kinds of game, are very fond of it.—TRANSLATOR.]

And this without calculating that he might have suspected something; while having my bag, were he to ask me what I was doing there, I should say to him, ' Why, I am come to gather mast—is it forbidden to gather mast?' ' No.' ' Well, then, if it is not forbidden, you have nothing to say.' And, indeed, should he say anything, Father La Jeunesse would be in the wrong."

"Then, you have spent your whole day in gathering mast instead of laying your wires, you idle fellow!" exclaimed Aunt Angelique, angrily, who, amid all the cunning of her nephew, thought that the rabbits were escaping her.

"On the contrary, I laid my snares while gathering the mast, so that he saw me at work at it."

"And did he say nothing to you?"

"Oh, yes, he said to me, ' You will present my compliments to your aunt Pitou.' Hey! Is not Father La Jeunesse a kind, good man?"

"But the rabbits?" again repeated the old devotee, whom nothing could divert from her fixed idea.

"The rabbits? Why, the moon will rise at midnight, and at one o'clock I will go and see if there are any caught."

"Where?"

"In the woods."

"How! would you go into the woods at one o'clock in the morning?"

"To be sure."

"And without being afraid?"

"Afraid—of what?"

Angelique was as much astounded at Pitou's courage as she had been astonished at his calculations.

The fact is, that Pitou, as simple as a child of nature, knew nothing of those fictitious dangers which terrify children born in cities.

Therefore, at midnight he went his way, walking along the churchyard wall without once looking back. The innocent youth who had never offended, at least according to his ideas of independence, either God or man, feared not the dead more than he did the living.

There was only one person of whom he felt any sort of apprehension, and this was Father La Jeunesse; and, therefore, did he take the precaution to go somewhat out of his way to pass by his house. As the doors and shutters were all closed, and there was no light to be perceived, Pitou, in order to assure himself that the keeper was really at home, and not upon the watch, began to imitate the barking of a dog, and so perfectly that Ronflot, the keeper's terrier, was deceived by it, and answered it by giving tongue with all his might, and by sniffing the air under the floor.

From that moment Pitou was perfectly reassured ; as Ronflot was at home, Father La Jeunesse must be there also. Ronflot and Father La Jeunesse were inseparable ; and at the moment the one was seen, it was certain that the other would soon make his appearance.

Pitou, being perfectly satisfied of this fact, went on the Bruyere-aux-Loups. The snares had done their work ; two rabbits had been caught and strangled.

Pitou put them into the capacious pocket of that coat, which, then too long for him, was destined within a year to become too short, and then returned to his aunt's house.

The old maid had gone to bed ; but her cupidity had kept her awake ; like Perrette, she had been calculating what her rabbit-skins might produce, and this calculation had led her on so far, that she had not been able to close her eyes ' and, therefore, was it with nervous tremulation that she asked the boy what success he had had.

"A couple," said he. "Ah, the deuce ! Aunt Angelique, it is not my fault that I have not brought more, but it appears that Father La Jeunesse's rabbits are of a cunning sort."

The hopes of Aunt Angelique were fulfilled, and even more. She seized, trembling with joy, the two unlucky quadrupeds and examined their skins, which had remained intact, and locked them up in her meat-safe, which never had seen such provisions as those it had contained since Pitou had hit upon the idea of supplying it.

Then, in a very honeyed tone, she advised Pitou to go to bed, which the lad, who was much fatigued, did instantly, and that without even asking for his supper, which raised him greatly in the opinion of his aunt.

Two days after this Pitou renewed his attempts, and on this occasion was more fortunate than the first. He brought home three rabbits. Two of them took the road to the Golden Ball, and the third that of the presbytery. Aunt Angelique was very attentive to the Abbé Fortier, who, on his side, strongly recommended her to the pious souls of the parish.

Things went on in this manner during three or four months. Aunt Angelique was enchanted, and Pitou found his position somewhat supportable. In fact, with the exception of the tender cares of his mother, Pitou led nearly the same life at Villers-Cotterets which he had done at Haramont. But an unexpected circumstance, which, however, might have been foreseen, at once dashed to the ground the milk-pitcher of the aunt, and put a stop to the excursions of the nephew.

A letter had been received from Dr. Gilbert, dated from New York. On placing his foot on the soil of the United States, the philosophic traveler had not forgotten his protégé. He had written to Master Niguet, the notary, to inquire whether his instructions had been carried into effect, and to claim the execution of the agreement if they had not been, or to cancel it altogether if the old aunt would not abide by her engagements.

The case was a serious one; the responsibility of the public officer was at stake; he presented himself at the house of Aunt Pitou, and with the doctor's letter in his hand, called upon her to perform the promise she had made.

There was no backing out; all allegations as to ill-health were at once belied by the physical appearance of Pitou. Pitou was tall and thin. Every standel of the forest was also thin and tall, but this did not prevent them from being in a perfectly healthy and thriving condition.

Mlle. Angelique asked for a delay of eight days, in order to make up her mind as to the trade or occupation in which she should place her nephew.

Pitou was quite as sorrowful as his aunt. The mode of life he led appeared to him a very excellent one, and he did not desire any other.

During these eight days there was no thought of going bird-catching or poaching; moreover, the winter had arrived, and in winter the birds find water everywhere; but some snow had fallen, and while that was on the ground Pitou did not dare go out to lay his snares. Snow retains the impression of footsteps, and Pitou possessed a pair of feet so huge that they gave Father La Jeunesse the greatest possible chance of ascertaining in four-and-twenty hours who was the skilful poacher who had depopulated his rabbit warren.

During these eight days the claws of the old maid again showed themselves. Pitou had once more found the aunt of former days, she who had caused him so much terror— and whom self-interest, the *primum mobile* of her whole life, had for awhile rendered as smooth as velvet.

As the day for the important decision approached, the temper of the old maid became more and more crabbed, and to such a degree that, about the fifth day, Pitou sincerely desired that his aunt would immediately decide upon some trade, be it what it might, provided it should no longer be that of the scolded drudge which he had been filling in the old maid's house.

Suddenly a sublime idea struck the mind of the old woman who had been so cruelly agitated. This idea restored her equanimity, which for six days had altogether abandoned her.

This idea consisted in entreating the Abbé Fortier to receive into his school, and this without any remuneration whatever, poor Pitou and enable him to obtain the purse for entering the seminary, founded by His Highness the Duke of Orleans. This was an apprenticeship which would cost nothing to Aunt Angelique, and M. Fortier, without taking into calculation the thrushes, blackbirds, and rabbits with which the old devotee had so abundantly supplied him for the last month, was bound to do something, more than for any other, for the nephew of the chair-letter of his own church. Thus kept as under a glass frame, Ange would continue to be profitable to her at the present time, and promise to be much more so in the future.

Consequently, Ange was received into the Abbé Fortier's school, without any charge for his education. This abbé was a worthy man, and not in any way interested ; giving his knowledge to the poor in mind, and his money to the poor in body. He was, however, intractable on one single point ; solecisms rendered him altogether furious ; barbarisms would send him almost out of his mind ; on these occasions he considered neither friends nor foes, neither poor nor rich, nor paying pupils, nor gratuitous scholars ; he struck all with agrarian impartiality and with Lacedemonian stoicism, and as his arm was strong, he struck severely.

This was well known to the parents, and it was for them to decide whether they would or would not send their sons to the Abbé Fortier's school, or if they did send them there, they knew they must abandon them entirely to his mercy, for when any maternal complaint was made to him, the abbé always replied to it by this device, which he had engraved on the handle of his cane, and on that of his cat-o'-nine-tails, " Who loves well chastises well."

Upon the recommendation of his aunt, Ange Pitou was, therefore, received by the Abbé Fortier. The old devotee, quite proud of this reception, which was much less agreeable to Pitou, whose wandering and independent mode of life it altogether destroyed, presented herself to Master Niguet, and told him that she had not only conformed to her agreement with Dr. Gilbert, but had even gone beyond it. In fact, Dr. Gilbert had demanded for Ange Pitou an honorable means of living, and she gave him much more than this, since she gave him an excellent education. And where was it that she gave him this education ? Why, in the very academy in which Sebastian Gilbert received his, and for which Master Niguet, by the doctor's orders, paid fifty livres per month.

It was indeed true that Ange Pitou received his education gratis ; but there was no necessity whatever for letting Dr. Gilbert into this secret. The impartiality and the disinterestedness of the Abbé Fortier were well known ; as His sublime master, he stretched out his arms, saying, " Suffer little children to come unto me ; " only the two hands affixed to these two paternal arms were armed, the one with a rudiment, and the other with a large birch rod ; so that in the greater number of instances, instead of receiving the children weeping and sending them away consoled, the-Abbé Fortier saw the children approach him with terror in their countenances and sent them away weeping.

The new scholar made his entrance into the schoolroom, with an old trunk under his arm, a horn inkstand in his hand, and two or three stumps of pens stuck behind his ears. The old trunk was intended to supply, as it best might, the absence of a regular desk. The inkstand was a gift from the grocer, and Mlle. Angelique had picked up the stumps of pens at M. Niguet, the notary's, when she had paid him a visit the evening before.

Ange Pitou was welcomed with that fraternal gentleness which is born in children and perpetuated in grown men, that is to say, with hootings. The whole time devoted to the morning class was passed in making game of him. Two of the scholars were kept for laughing at his yellow hair, and two others for ridiculing his marvelous knees, of which we have already slightly made mention. The latter had said that Pitou's legs looked like a well-rope in which a knot had been tied. This jest was attended with great success, had gone round the room, and excited general hilarity, and consequently the susceptibility of the Abbé Fortier.

Therefore, the account being made up at noon when about to leave the school, that is to say, after having remained four hours in class, Pitou, without having addressed a single word to any one, without having done anything but gape behind his trunk, Pitou had made six enemies in the school ; six enemies, so much the more inveterate that he had not inflicted any wrong upon them, and, therefore, did they over the fire-stove, which in the schoolroom represented the altar of their country, swear a solemn oath, some to tear out his yellow hair, others to punch out his earthenware blue eyes, and the remainder to straighten his crooked knees.

Pitou was altogether ignorant of these hostile intentions. As he was going out he asked a boy near him why six of their comrades remained in school, when all the rest were leaving it.

The boy looked askance at Pitou, called him a shabby tale-bearer, and went away, unwilling to enter into conversation with him.

Pitou asked himself how it could have happened that he, not having uttered a single word during the whole time, could be called a shabby tale-bearer. But while the class had lasted he had heard so many things said, either by the pupils or by the Abbé Fortier, which he could in no way comprehend, that he classed this accusation of his schoolfellow with those things which were too elevated for him to understand.

On seeing Pitou return at noon, Aunt Angelique, with great ardor for the success of an education for which it was generally understood she made great sacrifices, inquired of him what he had learned.

Pitou replied that he had learned to remain silent. The answer was worthy of a Pythagorean ; only a Pythagorean would have made it by a sign.

The new scholar returned to school at one o'clock, without too much repugnance. The hours of study in the morning had been passed by the pupils in examining the physical appearance of Pitou ; those of the afternoon were employed by the professor in examining his moral capabilities. This examination being made, the Abbé Fortier remained convinced that Pitou had every possible disposition to become a Robinson Crusoe, but very little chance of ever becoming a Fontenelle or a Bossuet.

During the whole time that the class lasted, and which was much more fatiguing to the future seminarist than that of the morning, the scholars who had been punished on account of him repeatedly held up their fists to him. In all countries, whether blessed with civilization or not, this demonstration is considered as a sign of threat. Pitou, therefore, determined to be on his guard.

Our hero was not mistaken ; on leaving, or, rather, when he had left, and got clear away from all the dependencies of the collegiate house, it was notified to Pitou by the six scholars, who had been kept in the morning, that he would have to pay for the two hours of arbitrary detention, with damages, interest and capital.

Pitou at once understood that he would have to fight a pugilistic duel. Although he was far from having studied the sixth book of the Æneid, in which young Dares and the old Entellus give proofs of their great skill in this manly exercise before the loudly applauding Trojan fugitives, he knew something of this species of recreation, to which the country people in his village were not altogether strangers. He, therefore, declared that he was ready to enter the lists with either of his adversaries who might wish to begin, and to combat, successively, with all his six enemies. This demonstration began to raise the last comer in the consideration of his schoolfellows.

The conditions were agreed on as Pitou had proposed. A circle was soon formed round the place of combat, and the champions, the one having thrown off his jacket, the other his coat, advanced toward each other.

We have already spoken of Pitou's hands. These hands, which were by no means agreeable to look at, were still less agreeable to feel. Pitou at the end of each arm whirled round a fist equal in size to a child's head, and although boxing had not at that time been introduced in France, and consequently Pitou had not studied the elementary principles of the science, he managed to apply to one of the eyes of his adversary a blow so hermetically directed, that the eye he struck was instantly surrounded by a dark, bistre-colored circle, so geometrically drawn that the most skilful mathematician could not have formed it more correctly with his compasses.

The second then presented himself. If Pitou had against him the fatigue occasioned by his first combat, on the other side, his adversary was visibly less powerful than his former antagonist. The battle did not last long. Pitou gave a straightforward blow at his enemy's nose, and his formidable fist fell with such weight, that instantly his two nostrils gave evidence of the validity of the blow by spouting forth a double stream of blood.

The third got off with merely a broken tooth ; he received much less damage than the two former. The other three declared that they were satisfied.

Pitou then pressed through the crowd, which drew back as he approached with the respect due to a conqueror, and he withdrew, safe and sound, to his own fireside, or, rather, to that of his aunt.

The next morning, when the three pupils reached the school, the one with his eye poached, the second with a fearfully lacerated nose, and the third with his lips swelled, the Abbé Fortier instituted an inquiry. But young collegians have their good points, too. Not one of the wounded whispered a word against Pitou, and it was only through an indirect channel, that is to say, from a person who had been a witness of the fight, but who was altogether unconnected with the school, that the Abbé Fortier learned, the following day, that it was Pitou who had done the damage to the faces of his pupils, which had caused him so much uneasiness the day before.

And, in fact, the Abbé Fortier was responsible to the parents, not only for the morals, but for the physical state of his pupils. Fortier had received complaints from the three families. A reparation was absolutely necessary.

Pitou was kept in school three days ; one day for the eye, one day for the bloody nose, and one day for the tooth.

This three days' detention suggested an ingenious idea to Mlle. Angelique. It was to deprive Pitou of his dinner every time that the Abbé Fortier kept him in school. This determination must necessarily have an advantageous effect on Pitou's education, since it would naturally induce him to think twice before committing a fault which would subject him to this double punishment.

Only, Pitou could never rightly comprehend why it was that he had been called a tale-bearer, when he had not opened his lips, and why it was he had been punished for beating those who had wished to beat him ; but if people were to comprehend everything that happens in this world, they would lose one of the principal charms of life—that of mystery and the unforeseen.

Pitou was, therefore, detained three days in school, and during those three days, he contented himself with his breakfast and supper.

Contented himself is not the word, for Pitou was by no means content ; but our language is so poor, and the academy so severe, that we must *content* ourselves with what we have.

Only that this punishment submitted to by Pitou, without saying a word of the aggression to which he had been subjected, and to which he had only properly replied, won him the esteem of the whole school. It is true that the three majestic blows he had been seen to deliver might also have had some little influence on his schoolfellows.

From that forward the life of Pitou was pretty nearly that of most scholars, with this sole difference, that from his compositions being more defective than those of any of the rest, he was kept twice as often as any of his co-disciples.

But, it must be said, there was one thing in Pitou's nature which arose from the primary education he received, or, rather, from that which he did not receive, a thing which is necessary to consider as contributing at least a third to the numerous keepings he underwent, and this was his natural inclination for animals.

The famous trunk which his aunt Angelique had dignified with the name of desk had become, thanks to its vastness, and the numerous compartments, with which Pitou had decorated its interior, a sort of Noah's ark, containing a couple of every species of climbing, crawling, or flying reptiles. There were lizards, adders, ant-eaters, beetles, and frogs, which reptiles became so much dearer to Pitou from their being the cause of his being subjected to punishment more or less severe.

It was in his walks during the week that Pitou made collections for his menagerie. He had wished for salamanders, which were very popular at Villers-Cotterets, being the crest of Francois I., and who had had them sculptured on every chimney-piece in the château. He had succeeded in obtaining them ; only one thing had strongly preoccupied his mind, and he ended by placing this thing among the number of those which were beyond his intelligence : it was that he had constantly found in the water these reptiles which poets have pretended exist only in fire. This circumstance had given to Pitou, who was a lad of precise mind, a profound contempt for poets.

Pitou being the proprietor of two salamanders, set to work to find a chameleon ; but this time his search was altogether vain, and success did not attend his labors. Pitou at last concluded, from these unfruitful researches, that the chameleon did not exist, or, at all events, that it existed in some other latitude.

This point being settled, Pitou did not obstinately continue his search for the chameleon.

The two other thirds of Pitou's keepings-in were occasioned by those accursed solecisms, and those confounded barbarisms, which sprung up in the themes written by Pitou, as tares do in a field of wheat.

As to Sundays and Thursdays, days when there was no attendance at school, he had continued to employ them in laying his lime-twigs or in poaching ; only, as Pitou was still growing taller, as he was already five feet six, and sixteen years of age, a circumstance occurred which somewhat withdrew Pitou's attention from his favorite occupations.

Upon the road to the Wolf's Heath is situated a small village, the same, perhaps, which gave a name to the beautiful Anne d'Heilly, the mistress of Francois I.

Near this village stood the farmhouse of Father Billot, as he was called throughout the neighborhood, and at the door of this farm house was standing, no doubt by chance, but almost every time when Pitou passed and repassed, a pretty girl from seventeen to eighteen years of age, fresh-colored, lively, jovial, and who was called by her baptismal name, Catherine, but still more frequently after her father's name, La Billote.

Pitou began by bowing to La Billote ; afterward, he, by degrees, became emboldened, and smiled while he was bowing ; then at last, one fine day, after having bowed, after having smiled, he stopped and although blushing deeply, ventured to stammer out the following words, which he considered as a great audacity on his part :

" Good-day, Mademoiselle Catherine."

Catherine was a good, kind-hearted girl, and she welcomed Pitou as an old acquaintance. He was, in point of fact, an old acquaintance, for during two or three years she had seen him passing and repassing before the farm gate at least once a week. Only that Catherine saw Pitou, and Pitou did not see Catherine. The reason was that at first, when Pitou used to pass by the farm in this manner, Catherine was sixteen years old, and Pitou but fourteen. We have just seen what happened when Pitou, in his turn, had attained his sixteenth year.

By degrees Catherine had learned to appreciate the talents of Pitou, for Pitou had given her evidence of his talents by offering to her his finest birds and his fattest rabbits. The result of this was that Catherine complimented him upon these talents, and that Pitou, who was the more sensible to compliments from his being so little habituated to receiving them, allowed the charm of novelty to influence him, and instead of going on straightforward, as heretofore, to the Wolf's Heath, he would stop half-way, and instead of employing the whole of his day in picking up beech-mast and in laying his wires, he would lose his time in prowling round Father Billot's farm, in the hope of seeing Catherine, were it only for a moment.

The result of this was a very sensible diminution in the produce of rabbit-skins, and a complete scarcity of robin-redbreasts and thrushes.

Aunt Angelique complained of this. Pitou represented to her that the rabbits had become mistrustful, and that the birds, who had found out the secret of his lime-twigs, now drank out of hollows of trees, or out of leaves that retained the water.

There was one consideration which consoled Aunt
Angelique for this increase in the intelligence of the rabbits and the cunning of the birds, which she attributed to
the progress of philosophy, and this was that her nephew
would obtain the purse, enter the seminary, pass three
years there, and on leaving it would be an abbé. Now,
being housekeeper to an abbé had been the constant aim
of Mlle. Angelique's ambition.

This ambition could not fail of being gratified, for Ange
Pitou, having once become an abbé, could not do otherwise than take his aunt for housekeeper, and, above all,
after what his aunt had done for him.

The only thing which disturbed the golden dreams of
the old maid was, when speaking of this hope to the Abbé
Fortier, the latter replied, shaking his head :

" My dear Demoiselle Pitou, in order to become an abbé
your nephew should give himself up less to the study of
natural history, and much more to ' De virus illustribus,'
or to the ' Selectæ e profanis scriptoribus.' "

" And which means ? " said Mlle. Angelique, inquiringly.

" That he makes too many barbarisms, and infinitely
too many solecisms," replied the Abbé Fortier.

An answer which left Mlle. Angelique in the most
afflicting state of vagueness and uncertainty.

CHAPTER IV.

THESE details were indispensable to the reader, whatever be the degree of intelligence we suppose him to possess, in order that he might comprehend the whole horror
of the position in which Pitou found himself on being
finally expelled from the school.

With one arm hanging down, the other maintaining the
equilibrium of the trunk upon his head, his ears still ringing with the furious vituperations of the Abbé Fortier, he
slowly directed his steps towards the Pleux, in a state of
meditation which was nothing more than stupor carried to
the highest possible degree.

At last an idea presented itself to his imagination, and
four words, which composed his whole thought, escaped
his lips :

"Oh, Lord, my aunt !"

And indeed what would Mlle. Angelique Pitou say to this complete overthrow of all her hopes ?

However, Ange Pitou knew nothing of the projects of the old maid, excepting as a faithful dog surmises the intentions of his master—that is to say, by an inspection of his physiognomy. Instinct is a most valuable guide, it seldom deceives ; while reason, on the contrary, may be led astray by the imagination.

The result of these reflections on the part of Ange Pitou, and which had given birth to the doleful exclamation we have given above, was the apprehension of the violent outbreak of discontent the old maid would give way to on receiving the fatal news. Now, he knew from sad experience the result of discontent in Mlle. Angelique. Only, upon this occasion the cause of discontent, arising from an incalculably important event, the result would attain a degree altogether incalculable.

It was under these terrific impressions that Pitou entered the Pleux. He had taken a quarter of an hour to traverse the distance between the great gate at the Abbé Fortier's and the entrance to this street, and yet it was scarcely three hundred yards.

At that moment the church clock struck twelve ; he then perceived that his final conversation with the Abbé Fortier and the slowness with which he had walked, had delayed him in all sixty minutes, and that, consequently, he was half an hour later than the time at which no more dinner was to be had in Aunt Angelique's abode.

We have already said that such was the salutary restraint which Aunt Angelique had added to his being kept in school, and on the wild ramblings of her nephew ; it was thus that in the course of a year she managed to economize some sixty dinners at the expense of her poor nephew's stomach.

But this time that which rendered more uneasy the retarded schoolboy was not the loss of his aunt's meager dinner, although his breakfast had been meager enough, for his heart was too full to allow him to perceive the emptiness of his stomach.

There is a frightful torment, well known to a student, however perverse he may be, and this is the illegitimate hiding in some retired corner, after being expelled from college ; it is the definitive and compelled holiday which he is constrained to take advantage of, while his fellow-students pass by him with their books and writings under their arm, proceeding to their daily task.   That college, formerly so hated, then assumes a most desirable form ; the scholar occupies his mind with the great affairs of themes and exercises to which he before so little directed his attention, and which are being proceeded with in his absence.   There is a strong similiarity between a pupil so expelled by his professor and a man who has been excom-municated by the church for his impiety, and who no longer has a right to enter one, although burning with desire to hear a mass.

And this was why the nearer he approached his aunt's house, his residence in that house appeared the more frightful to poor Pitou.   And this was why, for the first time in his life, his imagination pictured to him the school as a terrestrial paradise, from which the Abbé Fortier, as the exterminating angel, had driven him forth, with his cat-o'-nine-tails wielded as a flaming sword.

But yet, slowly as he walked, and although he halted at every ten steps he took—halts which became still longer as he approached nearer—he could not avoid at last reach-ing the threshold of that most formidable house.   Pitou then reached the threshold with shuffling feet, and me-chanically rubbing his hand on the seam of his nether garment.

"Ah ! Aunt Angelique, I am really very sick," said he, in order to stop her raillery or her reproaches,and perhaps also to induce her to pity him, poor boy !

"Good !" said Angelique.   "I well know what your sickness is ; and it would be cured at once by putting back the hands of the clock an hour and a half."

"Oh ! good heavens, no !" cried Pitou ; "for I am not hungry."

Aunt Angelique was surprised and almost anxious. Sickness equally alarms affectionate mothers and crabbed stepmothers—affectionate mothers, from the dangers caused by sickness ; and stepmothers from the heavy pulls it makes upon their purse.

"Well, what is the matter ?   Come, now, speak out at once," said the old maid.

On hearing these words, which were, however, pronounced without any very tender sympathy, Ange Pitou burst into tears ; and it must be acknowledged that the wry faces he made when proceeding from complaints to tears were the most terrifically ugly wry faces that could be seen.

"Oh ! my good aunt," cried he, sobbing, " a great misfortune has happened to me."

"And what is it ? " asked the old maid.

"The Abbé Fortier has sent me away," replied Ange, sobbing so violently that he was scarcely intelligible.

"Sent you away ? " repeated Mlle. Angelique, as if she had not perfectly comprehended what he said.

"Yes, aunt."

"And from where has he sent you ? "

"From the school."

And Pitou's sobs redoubled.

"From the school ? "

"Yes, aunt."

"What ! altogether ? "

"Yes, aunt."

"So there is no longer any examination, no competition, no purse, no seminary ? "

Pitou's sobs were changed into perfect howlings.

Mlle. Angelique looked at him, as if she would read the very heart of her nephew, to ascertain the cause of his dismissal.

"I will wager that you have again been among the bushes, instead of going to school. I would wager that you have again been prowling about Father Billot's farm. Oh, fy ! and a future abbé !"

Ange shook his head.

"You are lying !" cried the old maid, whose anger augmented in proportion as she acquired the certainty that the state of matters was very serious. "You are lying. Only last Sunday you were seen again in the Hall of Sighs, with La Billote."

It was Mlle. Angelique who was lying. But devotees have, in all ages, considered themselves authorized to lie, in virtue of that Jesuitical axiom, "It is permitted to assert that which is false, in order to discover that which is true."

"No one could have seen me in the Hall of Sighs," replied Pitou ; "that is impossible, for we were walking near the orangery."

"Ah, wretch! you see that you were with her."

"But, aunt," rejoined Pitou, blushing, "Mademoiselle Billot has nothing to do with this question."

"Yes, call her mademoiselle, in order to conceal your impure conduct. But I will let this minx's confessor know all about it."

"But, aunt, I swear to you that Mademoiselle Billot is not a minx."

"Ah! you defend her, when it is you that stand in need of being excused. Oh, yes; you understand each other better and better. What are we coming to, good Heaven! and children only sixteen years old!"

"Aunt, so far from there being any understanding between me and Catherine, it is Catherine who always drives me away from her."

"Ah! you see you are cutting your own throat; for now you call her Catherine right out. Yes, she drives you away from her, hypocrite, when people are looking at you."

"Ho! ho!" said Pitou to himself, illuminated by this idea. "Well, that is true. I had never thought of that."

"Ah, there again!" said the old maid, taking advantage of the ingenuous exclamation of her nephew, to prove his connivance with La Billote; "but let me manage it. I I will soon put all this to rights again. Monsieur Fortier is her confessor. I will beg him to have you shut up in prison, and order you to live on bread and water for a fortnight; and, as to Mademoiselle Catherine, if she requires a convent to moderate her passion for you, well, she shall have a taste of it. We will send her to St. Remy."

The old maid uttered these last words with such authority and with such conviction of her power that they made Pitou tremble.

"My good aunt," cried he, clasping his hands, "you are mistaken, I swear to you, if you believe that Mademoiselle Billot has anything to do with the misfortune that has befallen me."

"Impurity is the mother of all vices," sententiously rejoined Mlle. Angelique.

"Aunt, I again tell you that the Abbé Fortier did not send me away because I was impure; but he has dismissed me because I make too many barbarisms, mingled with solecisms, which every now and then escape me, and which deprive me, as he says, of all chance of obtaining the purse for the seminary."

"All chance, say you? Then you will not have that purse; then you will not be abbé; then I shall not be your housekeeper!"

"Ah, good Heaven, no, dear aunt!"

"And what is to become of you, then?" cried the old maid, in a savage tone.

"I know not!" cried Pitou, piteously, raising his eyes to heaven. "Whatever it my please Providence to order," he added.

"Ah! Providence, you say! I see how it is," exclaimed Mlle. Angelique. "Some one has been exciting his brain; some one has been talking to him of these new ideas; some one has been endeavoring to fill him with these principles of philosophy."

"It cannot be that, aunt; because no one gets into philosophy before having gone through his rhetoric; and I have never yet been able to get even so far as that."

"Oh, yes—jest!—jest! It is not of that philosophy that I am speaking. I speak of the philosophy of the philosophers, you wretch! I speak of the philosophy of Monsieur Arouet; I speak of the philosophy of Monsieur Jean Jacques; of the philosophy of Monsieur Diderot, who wrote 'La Religieuse.'"

Mlle. Angelique crossed herself.

"'La Religieuse!'" cried Pitou; "what is that, aunt?"

"You have read it, wretch!"

"I swear to you, aunt, that I have not."

"And this is the reason why you will not go into the church."

"Aunt, aunt, you are mistaken. It is the church that will not admit me."

"Why, decidedly, this child is a perfect serpent. .He even dares to reply."

"No, aunt; I answer, and that is all."

"Oh! he is lost!" exclaimed Mlle. Angelique, with all the signs of the most profound discouragement, and falling into her favorite armchair.

In fact, "He is lost!" merely signified, "I am lost!"

The danger was imminent; Aunt Angelique formed an

xtreme resolve. She rose as if some secret spring had
forced her to her feet, and ran off to the Abbé Fortier, to
ask him for an explanation, and above all to make a last
effort to get him to change his determination.

Pitou followed his aunt with his eyes, till she had
reached the door ; and when she had disappeared, he went
to the threshold and watched her walking with extraordinary rapidity toward the Rue de Soissons. He was surprised at the quickness of her movements ; but he had no
longer any doubt as to the intentions of Mlle. Angelique,
but was convinced that she was going to his professor's
house.

He could, therefore, calculate on at least a quarter of an
hour's tranquillity. Pitou thought of making a good use
of this quarter of an hour which Providence had granted
him. He snatched up the remainder of his aunt's dinner
to feed his lizards, caught two or three flies for his ants
and frogs ; then, opening successively a hutch and a cupboard, he set about feeding himself, for with solitude his
appetite had returned to him.

Having arranged all these matters, he returned to watch
at the door, that he might not be surprised by the return
of his second mother.

While he was watching, a handsome young girl passed
at the end of the Pleux, going along a narrow lane which
led from the end of the Rue de Soissons to that of the Rue
de l'Ormet. She was seated on a pillion on the back of a
horse loaded with two paniers ; the one full of fowls, the
other of pigeons. It was Catherine. On perceiving Pitou
standing at his door, she stopped.

Pitou, according to custom, blushed, then remained
with his mouth wide open, looking at, that is to say, admiring, for Mlle. Billot was in his eyes the most heavenly
sample of human beauty.

The young girl darted a glance into the street, saluted
Pitou with a little graceful nod, and continued on her
way.

Pitou replied to it, trembling with satisfaction.

This little scene lasted just time enough to occupy the
tall scholar's attention, who was quite lost in his contemplation, and continued eagerly gazing at the spot where
Mlle. Catherine had appeared, so as to prevent him from
perceiving his aunt when she returned from the Abbé

Fortier, who suddenly seized his hand, turning pale with anger.

Ange, being thus startlingly awakened from his sweet dream by that electrical shock which the touch of Mlle. Angelique always communicated to him, turned round, and seeing that the enraged looks of his aunt were fixed upon his hand, cast his own eyes down upon it, and saw with horror that it was holding the half of a large round of bread upon which he had apparently spread a too generous layer of butter, with a corresponding slice of cheese, and which the sudden appearance of Mlle. Catherine had made him entirely forget.

Mlle. Angelique uttered a cry of terror, and Pitou a groan of alarm ; Angelique raised her bony hand, Pitou bobbed down his head ; Angelique seized a broom-handle which unluckily was but too near her, Pitou let fall his slice of bread and butter, and took to his heels without further explanation.

These two hearts had understood each other, and had felt that henceforth there could be no communion between them.

Mlle. Angelique went into her house and double-locked the door. Pitou, whom the grating noise alarmed as a continuation of the storm, ran on still faster.

From this scene resulted an effect which Mlle. Angelique was very far from foreseeing, and which certainly Pitou in no way expected.

CHAPTER V.

PITOU ran as if all the demons of the infernal regions were at his heels, and in a few seconds he was outside the town.

On turning round the corner of the cemetery he very nearly ran his head against the hind part of a horse.

" Why, good Lord ! " cried a sweet voice, well known to Pitou, " where are you running to at this rate, Monsieur Ange ? You have very nearly made Cadet run away with me, you frightened us so much."

" Ah ! Mademoiselle Catherine," cried Pitou, replying rather to his own thoughts than to the question of the young girl. "Ah! Mademoiselle Catherine, what a misfortune! Great God! what a misfortune!"

"Oh! you quite terrify me!" said the young girl, pulling up her horse in the middle of the road. "What, then, has happened, Monsieur Ange?"

"What has happened?" said Pitou, and then lowering his voice, as if about to reveal some mysterious iniquity, "why it is that I am not to be an abbé, mademoiselle."

But instead of receiving the fatal intelligence with all those signs of commiseration which Pitou had expected, Mlle. Billot gave way to a long burst of laughter.

"You are not to be an abbé?" asked Catherine.

"No," replied Pitou, in perfect consternation, "it appears that it is impossible."

"Well, then, you can be a soldier," said Catherine.

"A soldier?"

"Undoubtedly. You should not be in such despair for such a trifle. Good Lord! I had first thought you had come to announce to me the death of your aunt."

"Oh!" said Pitou, feelingly, "it is precisely the same thing to me as if she were dead indeed, since she has driven me out of her house."

"I beg your pardon," said Catherine, laughing; "you have not now the satisfaction of weeping for her."

And Catherine began to laugh more heartily than before, which scandalized poor Pitou more than ever.

"But did you not hear that I was turned out-of-doors?" rejoined the student, in despair.

"Well, so much the better," she replied.

"You are very happy in being able to laugh in that manner, Mademoiselle Billot, and it proves that you have a most agreeable disposition, since the sorrows of others make so little impression upon you."

"And who has told you, then, that should a real misfortune happen to you, that I would not pity you, Monsieur Ange?"

"You would pity me if a real misfortune should befall me. But do you not, then, know that I have no other resource?"

"So much the better again!" cried Catherine.

"But one must eat," said he; "one cannot live without eating, and I, above all, for I am always hungry."

"You do not wish to work, then, Monsieur Pitou?"

"Work, and at what ? Monsieur Fortier and my Aunt Angelique have told me more than a hundred times that I was fit for nothing. Ah ! if they had only apprenticed me to a carpenter or a blacksmith, instead of wanting to make an abbé of me. Decidedly now, Mademoiselle Catherine," said Pitou, with a gesture of despair ; "decidedly there is a curse upon me."

"Alas !" said the young girl, compassionately, for she knew, as did all the neighborhood, Pitou's lamentable story. "There is some truth in what you have just now said, my dear Monsieur Ange ; but why do you not do one thing ?"

"What is it ?" cried Pitou, eagerly clinging to the proposal which Mlle. Billot was about to make, as a drowning man clings to a willow branch. "What is it, tell me ?"

"You had a protector ; at least, I think I have heard so."

"Doctor Gilbert."

"You were the schoolfellow of his son, since he was educated, as you have been, by the Abbé Fortier."

"I believe I was, indeed, and I have more than once saved him from being thrashed."

"Well, then, why do you not write to his father ? He will not abandon you."

"Why, I would certainly do so, did I know what had become of him : but your father, perhaps, knows this, Mademoiselle Billot, since Doctor Gilbert is his landlord."

"I know that he sends part of the produce of the farm to him in America, and pays the remainder to a notary at Paris."

"Ah !" said Pitou, sighing, "in America ; that is very far."

"You would go to America ? You ?" cried the young girl, terrified at Pitou's resolution.

"Who, I, Mademoiselle Catherine? Never, never ! If I knew where to go, and how to procure food, I should be very happy in France."

"Very happy," repeated Mlle. Billot.

Pitou cast down his eyes. The young girl remained silent. The silence lasted some time. Pitou was plunged in meditations which would have greatly surprised the Abbé Fortier, with all his logic.

These meditations, though rising from an obscure point, had become lucid; then they again became confused, though brilliant, like the lightning, whose origin is concealed, whose source is lost.

During this time, Cadet had again moved on, though at a walk, and Pitou walked at Cadet's side, with one hand leaning on one of the paniers. As to Mlle. Catherine, who had also become full of thought, she allowed her reins to fall upon her courser's neck, without fearing that he would run away with her. Moreover, there were no monsters on the road, and Cadet was of a race which had no sort of relation to the steeds of Hippolytus.

Pitou stopped mechanically when the horse stopped. They had arrived at the farm.

"Well, now, is it you, Pitou?" cried a broad-shouldered man, standing somewhat proudly by the side of a pond, to which he had led his horse to drink.

"Eh! good Lord! Yes, Monsieur Billot, it is myself."

"Another misfortune has befallen this poor Pitou," said the young girl, jumping off her horse, without feeling at all uneasy as to whether her petticoat hitched or not, to show the color of her garters; "his aunt has turned him out-of-doors."

"And what has he done to the old bigot?" said the farmer.

"It appears that I am not strong enough in Greek."

He was boasting, the puppy; he ought to have said in Latin.

"Not strong enough in Greek?" exclaimed the broad-shouldered man; "and why should you wish to be strong in Greek?"

"To construe Theocritus, and read the 'Iliad.'"

"And of what use would it be to you to construe Theocritus, and read the 'Iliad?'"

"It would be of use in making me an abbé."

"Bah!" ejaculated M. Billot, "and do 1 know the Greek? do I know Latin? do I know even French? do I know how to read? do I know how to write? That does not hinder me from sowing, from reaping, and getting my harvest into the granary."

"Yes, but you, Monsieur Billot, you are not an abbé, you are a cultivator of the earth, *agricola*, as Virgil says, *O fortunatos nimium——*"

" Well, and do you then believe that a cultivator is not equal to a black-cap ? Say, then, you shabby chorister you, is he not so, particularly when this cultivator has sixty acres of good land in the sunshine and a thousand louis in the shade."

" I had been always told that to be an abbé was the best thing in the world. It is true," added Pitou, smiling with his most agreeable smile, " that I did not always listen to what was told me."

" And I give you joy, my boy. You see that I can rhyme like any one else when I set to work. It appears to me that there is stuff in you to make something better than an abbé, and that it is a lucky thing for you not to take that trade, particularly as times now go. Do you see now, as a farmer I know something of the weather, and the weather just now is bad for abbés ? "

" Bah !" exclaimed Pitou.

" Yes, we shall have a storm," rejoined the farmer, " and not long first, believe me. You are honest, you are learned——"

Pitou bowed, much honored at being called learned, for the first time in his life.

" You can, therefore, gain a livelihood without that."

Mlle. Billot, while taking the fowls and pigeons out of the paniers, was listening with much interest to the dialogue between Pitou and her father.

" Gain a livelihood," rejoined Pitou ; " that appears a difficult matter to me."

" What can you do ?"

" Do ! why, I can lay lime-twigs and can set wires for rabbits. I can imitate, and tolerably well, the notes of birds, can I not, Mademoiselle Catherine ?"

" Oh, that is true enough," she replied ; " he can whistle like a blackbird."

" Yes ; but all this is not a trade, a profession," observed Father Billot.

" And that is what I say, by Heaven !"

" You swear ; that is already something."

" How, did I swear ?" said Pitou ; " I beg your pardon for having done so, Monsieur Billot."

" Oh ! there is no occasion, none at all," said the farmer ; " it happens also to me sometimes. Eh ! thunder of heaven !" cried he, turning to his horse, " will you be

quiet, hey? these devils of Perch horses, they must be always neighing and fidgeting about. But now, tell me,"
said he, again addressing Pitou, "are you lazy?"

"I do not know; I have never done anything but Latin
and Greek, and——"

"And what?"

"And I must admit that I did not take to them very
readily."

"So much the better," cried Billot; "that proves you
are not so stupid as I thought you."

Pitou opened his eyes to an almost terrific width; it was
the first time he had ever heard such an order of things
advocated, and which was completely subversive of all the
theories which up to that time he had been taught.

"I ask you," said Billot, "if you are so lazy as to be
afraid of fatigue."

"Oh! with regard to fatigue, that is quite another
thing," replied Pitou; "no, no, no; I could go ten
leagues without being fatigued."

"Good! that's something, at all events," rejoined Billot.
"By getting a few pounds of flesh more off your bones,
you could set up for a runner."

"A few pounds more!" cried Pitou, looking at his own
lanky form, his long arms and his legs, which had much
the appearance of stilts; "it seems to me, Monsieur Billot,
that I am thin enough as it is."

"Upon my word, my friend," cried Billot, laughing
very heartily, "you are a perfect treasure."

It was the first time that Pitou had been estimated at so
high a price, and therefore was he advancing from surprise
to surprise.

"Listen to me," said the farmer; "I ask you whether
you are lazy in respect to work?"

"What sort of work?"

"Why, work in general."

"I do not know, not I; for I have never worked."

Catherine also began to laugh, but this time Père Billot
took the matter in a serious point of view.

"Those rascally priests!" said he, holding his clinched
fists toward the town, "and this is the way they bring up
lads, in idleness and uselessness. In what way, I ask you,
can this great stripling here be of service to his brethren?"

"Ah! not of much use, certainly; that I know full

well," replied Pitou. "Fortunately, I have no brothers."

"By brethren I mean all men in general," observed Billot. "Would you, perchance, insist that all men are not brothers?"

"Oh, that I acknowledge; moreover, it is so said in the Gospel."

"And equals," continued the farmer.

"Ah! as to that," said Pitou, "that is quite another affair. If I had been the equal of Monsieur Fortier, he would not so often have thrashed me with his cat-o'-nine-tails and his cane; and if I had been the equal of my aunt, she would not have turned me out-of-doors."

"I tell you that all men are equal," rejoined the farmer, "and we will very soon prove it to the tyrants."

"*Tyrannis,*" added Pitou.

"And the proof of this is, that I will take you into my house."

"You will take me into your house, my dear Monsieur Billot!" cried Pitou, amazed. "Is it not to make game of me that you say this?"

"No. Come now, tell me, what would you require to live?"

"Bread."

"And with your bread?"

"A little butter or cheese."

"Well, well," said the farmer, "I see it will not be very expensive to keep you in food. My lad, you shall be fed."

"Monsieur Pitou," said Catherine, "had you not something to ask my father?"

"Who? I, mademoiselle? Oh, good Lord, no!"

"And why was it that you came here, then?"

"Because you were coming here."

"Ah!" cried Catherine, "that is really very gallant; but I accept compliments only at their true value. You came, Monsieur Pitou, to ask my father if he had any news of your protector."

"Ah, that is true!" replied Pitou. "Well, now, how very droll! I had forgotten that altogether."

"You are speaking of our worthy Monsieur Gilbert?" said the farmer, in a tone which evinced the very high consideration he felt for his landlord.

"Precisely," said Pitou. "But I have no longer any

need of him ; and since Monsieur Billot takes me into his
house, I can tranquilly wait till we hear from him."

"In that case, my friend, you will not have to wait
long, for he has returned."

"Really !" cried Pitou ; "and when did he arrive ?"

"I do not know exactly ; but what I know is, that he
was at Havre a week ago ; for I have in my holsters a
packet which comes from him, and which he sent to me
as soon as he arrived, and which was delivered to me this
very morning at Villers-Cotterets, and in proof of that,
here it is."

"Who was it told you that it was from him, father ?"
said Catherine.

"Why, zounds ! since there is a letter in the packet——"

"Excuse me, father," said Catherine, smiling, "but I
thought that you could not read. I only say this, father,
because you make a boast of not knowing how to read."

"Yes, I do boast of it. I wish that people should say,
'Father Billot owes nothing to any man—not even to a
schoolmaster. Father Billot made his fortune himself.'
That is what I wish people to say. It was not, therefore,
I who read the letter. It was the quartermaster of the
gendarmerie whom I happened to meet."

"And what did this letter tell you, father ? He is always well satisfied with us, is he not ?"

"Judge for yourself."

"And the farmer drew from his pocket a letter, which
he handed to his daughter,

Catherine read as follows :

"MY DEAR MONSIEUR BILLOT,—I arrive from America,
where I found a people richer, greater, and happier than
the people of our country. This arises from their being
free, which we are not. But we are also advancing toward a new era. Every one should labor to hasten the
day when the light shall shine. I know your principles,
Monsieur Billot. I know your influence over your brother
farmers, and over the whole of that worthy population of
workmen and laborers whom you order, not as a king, but
as a father. Inculcate in them principles of self-devoted-
ness and fraternity, which I have observed that you possess. Philosophy is universal ; all men ought to read their
duties by the light of its torch. I send you a small book,

in which all these duties and all these rights are set forth. This little book was written by me, although my name does not appear upon the title-page. Propagate the principles it contains, which are those of universal equality. Let it be read loud in the long winter evenings. Reading is the pasture of the mind, as the bread is the food of the body.

"One of these days I shall go to see you, and propose to you a new system of farm-letting, which is much in use in America. It consists in dividing the produce of the land between the farmer and the landlord. This appears to me more in conformity with the laws of primitive society ; and, above all, more in accordance with the goodness of God.

"Health and fraternity,
"HONORE GILBERT,
"Citizen of Philadelphia."

"Oh! oh!" cried Pitou, "this is a well-written letter."

"Is it not?" said Billot, delighted.

"Yes, my dear father," observed Catherine ; "but I doubt whether the quartermaster of the gendarmerie is of your opinion."

"And why do you think so?"

"Because it appears to me that this letter may not only bring the doctor into trouble, but you also, my dear father."

"Pshaw!" said Billot ; "you are always afraid. But that matters not. Here is the pamphlet ; and here is employment ready found for you, Pitou. In the evenings you shall read it."

"And in the daytime?"

"In the daytime you will take care of the sheep and cows. In the meantime, there is your pamphlet."

And the farmer took from one of his holsters one of those small pamphlets with a red cover, of which so great a number were published in those days, either with or without permission of the authorities.

Only in the latter case the author ran the risk of being sent to the galleys.

"Read me the title of that book, Pitou, that I may always speak of the title until I shall be able to speak of the work itself. You shall read the remainder to me another time."

Pitou read on the first page these words, which habit has since rendered very vague and very insignificant, but which at that period struck to the very fibers of all hearts :

"'Of the Independence of Man, and the Liberty of Nations.'"

"What do you say to that, Pitou ?" inquired the farmer.

"I say that it appears to me, Monsieur Billot, that independence and liberty are the same thing. My protector would be turned out of Monsieur Fortier's class for being guilty of a pleonasm."

"Pleonasm or not," cried the farmer, "the book is the book of a man."

"That matters not, father," said Catherine, with a woman's admirable instinct. "Hide it, I entreat you. It will bring you into trouble. As to myself, I know that I am trembling even at the sight of it."

"And why would you have it injure me, since it has not injured its author ?"

"And how can you tell that, father ? It is eight days since that letter was written ; and it could not have taken eight days for the parcel to have come from Havre. I also have received a letter this morning."

"And from whom ?"

"From Sebastian Gilbert, who has written to make inquiries. He desires me, even, to remember him to his foster-brother, Pitou. I had forgotten to deliver his message."

"Well !"

"Well, he says that his father had been expected to arrive in Paris, and that he had not arrived."

"Mademoiselle is right," said Pitou. "It seems to me that this non-arrival is disquieting."

"Hold your tongue, you timid fellow, and read the doctor's treaty," said the farmer ; "then you will become not only learned, but a man."

It was thus people spoke in those days ; for they were at the preface of that great Grecian and Roman history which the French nation imitated, during ten years, in all its phases, devotedness, proscriptions, victories, and slavery.

Pitou put the book under his arm with so solemn a gesture, that he completely gained the farmer's heart.

" And now," said Billot, " have you dined ? "

" No, sir," replied Pitou, maintaining the same religious, semi-heroic attitude he had assumed since the book had been intrusted to his care.

" He was just going to get his dinner, when he was driven out-of-doors," said the young girl.

" Well, then," said Billot, " go in and ask my wife for the usual farm fare, and to-morrow you shall enter on your functions."

Pitou, with an eloquent look, thanked M. Billot, and, led by Catherine, entered the farm kitchen, a domain placed under the absolute direction of Mme. Billot.

CHAPTER VI.

MME. BILLOT was a stout, buxom mamma, between thirty-five and thirty-six years old, round as a ball, fresh-colored, smooth-skinned, and cordial in her manners. She trotted continually from the fowl-house to the dove-cote, from the sheep-pens to the cow-stable. She inspected the simmering of her soup, the stoves on which her fricassees and ragouts were cooking, and the spit on which the joint was roasting, as does a general when surveying his cantonments, judging by a mere glance whether everything was in its right place, and by their very odor, whether the thyme and laurel leaves were distributed in due proportions in the stew-pans. She scolded from habit, but without the slightest intention that her scolding should be disagreeable ; and her husband, whom she honored as she would the greatest potentate of the earth, did not escape. Her daughter also got her share, though she loved her more that Mme. de Sevigne loved Mme. de Grignan ; and neither were her work-people overlooked, though she fed them better than any farmer in a circuit of ten leagues fed his. Therefore was it that when a vacancy occurred in her household there was great competition to obtain the place. But, as in heaven, unfortunately, there were many applicants, and comparatively but few chosen.

We have seen that Pitou, without having been an ap-
plicant, had been elected.   This was a happiness which he
appreciated at its just value, especially when he saw the
gold-colored manchet which was placed at his left hand,
the pot of cider which was on his right, and the piece of
pickled pork on a plate before him.   Since the moment
that he lost his poor mother, and that was about five years,
Pitou had not, even on great festival days, partaken of
such fare.

Therefore, Pitou, full of gratitude, felt, as by degrees
he bolted the bread which he devoured, and as he washed
down the pork with large draughts of the cider—therefore,
Pitou felt a vast augmentation of respect for the farmer,
of admiration for his wife, and of love for his daughter.
There was only one thing which disquieted him, and that
was the humiliating functions he would have to fulfil
during the day, of driving out the sheep and cows, a
function so little in harmony with that which awaited him
each evening, and the object of which was to instruct
humanity in the most elevated principles of sociality and
philosophy.

It was on this subject that Pitou was meditating immediately after his dinner.   But even in this reverie, the
influence of that excellent dinner was sensibly manifested.
He began to consider things in a very different point of
view to that which he had taken of them when fasting.
The functions of a shepherd and a cow-driver, which he
considered as so far beneath him, had been fulfilled by
gods and demi-gods.

Apollo, in a situation very similar to his own, that is to
say, driven from Olympus by Jupiter, as he, Pitou, had
been driven from Pleux by his aunt, had become a shepherd, and tended the flocks of Admettus.   It is true that
Admettus was a shepherd king ; but, then, Apollo was a
god !

Hercules had been a cow-keeper, or something very like
it ; since—as we are told by mythology—he seized the cows
of Geryon by the tail ; for, whether a man leads a cow by
the tail or by the head, depends entirely on the difference
of custom of those who take care of them, and that is all ;
and this would not in any way change the fact itself that
he was a cow-leader, that is to say, a cow-keeper.

And, moreover, Tityrus, reclining at the foot of an elmtree, of whom Virgil speaks, and who congratulates himself in such beautiful verses on the repose which Augustus has granted to him, he also was a shepherd.

And, finally, Melibæus was a shepherd, who so poetically bewails his having left his domestic hearth.

Certainly, all these persons spoke Latin well enough to have been abbés, and yet they preferred seeing their goats browse on the bitter cytisus to saying mass or to chanting vespers. Therefore, taking everything into consideration, the calling of a shepherd had its charms. Moreover, what was to prevent Pitou from restoring to it the poetry and the dignity it had lost? Who could prevent Pitou from proposing trials of skill in singing to the Menalcas and the Palemons of the neighboring villages? No one, undoubtedly. Pitou had more than once sung in the choir; and but for his having once been caught drinking the wine out of the Abbé Fortier's cruet, who, with his usual rigor, had on the instant dismissed the singing boy, this talent might have become transcendent. He could not play upon the pipe, 'tis true; but he could imitate the note of every bird, which is very nearly the same thing. He could not make himself a lute with pipes of unequal thickness, as did the lover of Syrinx; but from the linden-tree or the chestnut he could cut whistles, whose perfection had more than once produced the enthusiastic applause of his companions. Pitou, therefore, could become a shepherd without great derogation of his dignity. He did not lower himself to this profession, so ill appreciated in modern days. He elevated the profession to his own standard.

Besides which, the sheep-folds were placed under the special direction of Mlle. Billot; and receiving orders from her lips was not receiving orders.

But, on her part, Catherine watched over the dignity of Pitou.

The same evening, when the young man approached her, and asked her at what hour he ought to go out to rejoin the shepherds, she said, smiling:

"You will not go out at all."

"And why so?" said Pitou, with astonishment.

"I have made my father comprehend that the education you have received places you above the functions which he had allotted to you. You will remain at the farm."

"Ah! so much the better," said Pitou. "In this way I shall not leave you."

The exclamation had escaped the ingenuous Pitou. But he had no sooner uttered it than he blushed to his very ears; while Catherine, on her part, held down her head and smiled.

"Ah! forgive me, mademoiselle. It came from my heart in spite of me. You must not be angry with me on that account," said Pitou.

"Neither am I angry with you, Monsieur Pitou," said Catherine; "and it is no fault of yours if you feel pleasure in remaining with me."

There was a silence of some moments. This was not at all astonishing; the poor children had said so much to each other in so few words.

"But," said Pitou, "I cannot remain at the farm doing nothing. What am I to do at the farm?"

"You will do what I used to do. You will keep the books, the accounts with the work-people, and of our receipts and expenses. You know how to reckon, do you not?"

"I know my four rules," proudly replied Pitou.

"That is one more than ever I knew," said Catherine. "I never was able to get further than the third. You see, therefore, that my father will be a gainer by having you for his accountant; and, as I also shall gain, and you yourself will gain by it, everybody will be a gainer."

"And in what way will you gain by it, mademoiselle?" inquired Pitou.

"I shall gain time by it; and in that time I will make myself caps, that I may look prettier."

"Ah!" cried Pitou, "I think you quite pretty enough without caps."

"That is possible; but it is only your own individual taste," said the young girl, laughing. "Moreover, I cannot go and dance on a Sunday at Villers-Cotterets, without having some sort of a cap upon my head. That is all very well for your great ladies, who have the right of wearing powder and going bareheaded."

"I think your hair more beautiful as it is than if it were powdered," said Pitou.

"Come, come, now; I see you are bent on paying me compliments."

" No, mademoiselle, I do not know how to make them. We did not learn that at the Abbé Fortier's."

" And did you learn to dance there ? "

" To dance ? " inquired Pitou, greatly astonished.

" Yes, to dance."

" To dance, and at the Abbé Fortier's ? Good Lord, mademoiselle !—oh ! learn to dance, indeed ! "

" Then, you do not know how to dance ? "

" No," said Pitou.

" Well, then, you shall go with me to the ball on Sunday, and you will look at Monsieur de Charny while he is dancing. He is the best dancer of all the young men in the neighborhood."

" And who is this Monsieur de Charny ?" demanded Pitou.

" He is the proprietor of the Château de Boursonne."

" And he will dance on Sunday ? "

" Undoubtedly."

" And with whom ? "

" With me."

Pitou's heart sunk within him without his being able to ascertain a reason for it.

" Then," said he, " it is in order to dance with him that you wish to dress yourself so finely."

" To dance with him—with others—with everybody."

" Excepting with me."

" And why not with you ? "

" Because I do not know how to dance."

" You will learn."

" Ah ! if you would but teach me ; you, Mademoiselle Catherine. I should learn much better than by seeing Monsieur de Charny, I can assure you."

" We shall see that," said Catherine. " In the meantime, it is nine o'clock, and we must go to bed. Good night, Piton."

" Good night, Mademoiselle Catherine."

There was something both agreeable and disagreeable in what Mlle. Catherine had said to Pitou. The agreeable was, that he had been promoted from the rank of a cowkeeper and shepherd to that of a bookkeeper. The disagreeable was, that he did not know how to dance, and that M. de Charny did know. According to what Catherine had said, he was the best dancer in the whole neighborhood.

Pitou was dreaming all night that he saw M. de Charny dancing, and that he danced very badly.

The next day, Pitou entered upon his new office, under the direction of Catherine. Then, one thing struck him, and it was that, under some masters, study is altogether delightful. In the space of about two hours he completely understood the duties he had to perform.

"Ah, mademoiselle," exclaimed he, "if you had but taught me Latin, instead of that Abbé Fortier, I believe I never should have committed any barbarisms."

"And you would have become an abbé ?"

"And I should have been an abbé," replied Pittou.

"So then, you would have shut yourself up in a seminary, in which no woman would have entered."

"Well, now," cried Pitou, I really had never thought of that, Mademoiselle Catherine. I would much rather, then, not be an abbé."

The good man Billot returned home at nine o'clock. He had gone out before Pitou was up. Every morning the farmer rose at three o'clock, to see to the sending out of his horses and his wagoners. Then he went over his fields until nine o'clock, to see that every one was at his post, and that all his laborers were doing their duty. At nine o'clock he returned to the house to breakfast, and went out again at ten. One o'clock was the dinner hour ; and the afternoon was, like the morning, spent in looking after the workmen. Thus the affairs of worthy Billot were prospering marvellously. As he had said, he possessed sixty acres in the sunshine, and a thousand louis in the shade ; and it was even probable that, had the calculation been correctly made—had Pitou made up the account, and had not been too much agitated by the presence or remembrance of Mlle. Catherine, some few acres of land and some few hundred louis more would have been found than the worthy farmer had himself admitted.

At breakfast, Billot informed Pitou that the first reading of Dr. Gilbert's new book was to take place in the barn, two days after, at ten in the morning.

Pitou then timidly observed that ten o'clock was the hour for attending mass. But the farmer said that he had especially selected that hour to try his workmen.

We have already said that Father Billot was a philosopher.

He detested the priests, whom he considered as the apostles of tyranny; and finding an opportunity for raising an altar against an altar, he eagerly took advantage of it.

Mme. Billot and Catherine ventured to offer some observations; but the farmer replied that the women might, if they chose, go to mass, seeing that religion had been made expressly for women; but as to the men, they should attend the reading of the doctor's work, or they should leave his service.

Billot, the philosopher, was very despotic in his own house. Catherine alone had the privilege of raising her voice against his decrees. But if these decrees were so tenaciously determined upon that he knitted his brows when replying to her, Catherine became as silent as the rest.

Catherine, however, thought of taking advantage of the circumstance to benefit Pitou. On rising from table, she observed to her father that, in order to read all the magnificent phrases he would have to read on Sunday morning, Pitou was but miserably clad. That he was about to play the part of a master, since he was to instruct others, and that the master ought not to be placed in a position to blush in the presence of his disciples.

Billot authorized his daughter to make an arrangement with Dulauroy, the tailor at Villers-Cotterets, for a new suit of clothes for Pitou.

Catherine was right, for new garments were not merely a matter of taste with regard to Pitou. The breeches which he wore were the same which Dr. Gilbert had, five years before, ordered for him. At that time they were too long, but since then had become much too short. We are compelled to acknowledge, however, that, through the care of Mlle. Angelique, they had been elongated at least two inches every year. As to the coat and waistcoat, they had both disappeared for upward of two years, and had been replaced by the serge gown in which our hero first presented himself to the observation of our readers.

Pitou had never paid any attention to his toilet. A looking-glass was an unknown piece of furniture in the abode of Mlle. Angelique; and not having, like the handsome Narcissus, any violent tendency to fall in love with himself, Pitou had never thought of looking at himself

in the transparent rivulets near which he set his bird-
snares.

But, from the moment that Mlle. Catherine had spoken
to him of accompanying her to the ball ; from the moment the elegant cavalier, M. de Charny's, name had been
mentioned ; since the conversation about caps, on which
the young girl calculated to increase her attractions, Pitou
had looked at himself in a mirror ; and, being rendered
melancholy by the very dilapidated condition of his garments, had asked himself in what way he also could make
any addition to his natural advantages.

Unfortunately, Pitou was not able to find any solution
to this question.   The dilapidation of his clothes was positive.   Now, in order to have new clothes made, it was
necessary to have ready cash ; and during the whole
course of his existence, Pitou had never possessed a single
penny.

Pitou had undoubtedly read that when shepherds were
contending for the prize in music or in poetry, they decorated themselves with roses.   But he thought, and with
great reason, that, although such a wreath might well
assort with his expressive features, it would only place in
stronger relief the miserable state of his habiliments.

Pitou was, therefore, most agreeably surprised when,
on the Sunday morning, at eight o'clock, and at the moment he was racking his brains for some means of embel-
lishing his person, M. Dulauroy entered his room and
placed upon a chair a coat and breeches of sky-blue cloth
and a large white waistcoat with red stripes.

At the same instant a seamstress came in, and laid upon
another chair, opposite to the above-mentioned one, a
new shirt and a cravat.   If the shirt fitted well, she had
orders to complete the half dozen.

It was a moment teeming with surprise.   Behind the
seamstress appeared the hat-maker.   He had brought with
him a small cocked hat, of the very latest fashion, and of
most elegant shape, and which had been fabricated by M.
Cornu, the first hat-maker in Villers-Cotterets.

A shoemaker had also been ordered to bring shoes for
Pitou ; and he had with him a pair with handsome silver
buckles, made expressly for him.

Pitou could not recover his amazement ; he could not in
any way comprehend that all these riches were for him.

In his most exaggerated dreams he could not even have dared to wish for so sumptuous a wardrobe. Tears of gratitude gushed from his eyelids, and he could only murmur out these words :

"Oh ! Mademoiselle Catherine, Mademoiselle Catherine —never will I forget what you have done for me !"

Everything fitted remarkably well, and as if Pitou had been actually measured for them, with the sole exception of the shoes, which were too small by half. M. Laudreau the shoemaker, had taken measure by his son's foot who was four years Pitou's senior.

This superiority over young Laudreau gave a momentary feeling of pride to our hero ; but this feeling of pride was soon checked by the reflection that he would either be obliged to go to the dance in his old shoes or in no shoes at all, which would not be in accordance with the remainder of his costume. But this uneasiness was not of long duration. A pair of shoes which had been sent home at the same time to Farmer Billot fitted him exactly. It fortunately happened that Billot's feet and Pitou's were of the same dimensions, which was carefully concealed from Billot, for fear that so alarming a fact might annoy him.

While Pitou was busied in arraying himself in these sumptuous habiliments, the hair-dresser came in and divided Pitou's hair into three compartments. One, and the most voluminous, was destined to fall over the collar of his coat, in the form of a tail ; the two others destined to ornament the temples, by the strange and unpoetical name of dog's-ears—ridiculous enough, but that was the name given to them in those days.

And now there is one thing we must acknowledge—and this is that when Pitou, thus combed and frizzled, dressed in his sky-blue coat and breeches, with his rose-striped waistcoat and his frilled shirt, with his dog-ear curls, looked at himself in the glass, he found great difficulty in recognizing himself, and twisted himself about to see whether Adonis in person had not redescended on the earth.

He was alone ; he smiled graciously at himself ; and with head erect, his thumbs thrust into his waistcoat-pockets, he said, raising himself upon his toes :

"We shall see this Monsieur de Charny !"

It is true that Ange Pitou, in his new costume, resembled, as one pea does another, not one of Virgil's shepherds, but one of those so admirably painted by Watteau.

Consequently, the first step which Pitou made on entering the farm kitchen was a perfect triumph.

"Oh! mamma, only see," cried Catherine; "how well Pitou looks now!"

"The fact is, that one would hardly know him again," replied Mme. Billot.

Unfortunately, after the first general survey which had so much struck the young girl, she entered into a more minute examination of the details, and Pitou was less good-looking in the detailed than in the general view.

"Oh, how singular!" cried Catherine, "what great hands you have!"

"Yes," said Pitou, proudly, "I have famous hands, have I not?"

"And what thick knees!"

"That is a proof that I shall grow taller."

"Why, it appears to me that you are tall enough already, Monsieur Pitou," observed Catherine.

"That does not matter; I shall grow taller still," said Pitou. "I am only seventeen and a half years old."

"And no calves!"

"Ah! yes, that is true—none at all; but they will grow soon."

"That is to be hoped," said Catherine; "but no matter, you are very well as you are."

Pitou made a bow.

"Oh! oh!" exclaimed Billot, coming in at that moment, and also struck with Pitou's appearance. "How fine you are, my lad! How I wish your aunt Angelique could see you now!"

"And so do I," said Pitou.

"I wonder what she would say?"

"She would not say a word; she would be in a perfect fury."

"But, father," said Catherine, with a certain degree of uneasiness, "would she not have the right to take him back again?"

"Why, she turned him out-of-doors."

"And besides which," said Pitou, "the five years have gone by."

"What five years?" inquired Catherine.

"The five years for which Doctor Gilbert left a thousand livres."

"He had, then, left a thousand livres with your aunt?"

"Yes, yes, yes; to get me into a good apprenticeship."

"That *is* a man!" exclaimed the farmer. "When one thinks that I hear something of the same kind related of him every day. Therefore—for him," he added, stretching out his hand with a gesture of admiration, "will I be devoted in life and death."

"He wished that I should learn some trade," said Pitou.

"And he was right. And this is the way in which good intentions are thwarted. A man leaves a thousand francs that a child may be taught a trade, and instead of having him taught a trade, he is placed under the tuition of a bigoted priest. And how much did she pay to your Abbé Fortier?"

"Who?"

"Your aunt."

"She never paid him anything."

"What! Did she pocket the two hundred livres a year which that good Monsieur Gilbert paid?"

"Probably."

"Listen to me, for I have a bit of advice to give you, Pitou; whenever your bigoted old aunt shall walk off, take care to examine minutely every cupboard, every mattress, every pickle jar——"

"And for what?" asked Pitou.

"Because, do you see, you will find some hidden treasure, some good old louis, in some old stocking-foot. Why, it must undoubtedly be so, for she could never have found a purse large enough to contain all her savings."

"Do you think so?"

"Most assuredly. But we will speak of this at a more proper time and place. To-day we must take a little walk. Have you Doctor Gilbert's book?"

"I have it here, in my pocket."

"Father," said Catherine, "have you well reflected upon this?"

"There is no need for reflection," replied the farmer, "when one is about to do a good thing, my child. The doctor told me to have the book read, and to propagate the principles which it contains ; the book shall therefore be read, and the principles shall be propagated."

"And," said Catherine, timidly, "may my mother and I, then, go to attend mass ?"

"Go to mass, my child ; go with your mother," replied Billot. "You are women ; we who are men have other things to think of. Come, Pitou, we must be off, for we are waited for."

Pitou bowed majestically to Mme. Billot and Mlle. Catherine ; then, with head erect, he followed the worthy farmer, proud of having been thus, for the first time, called a man.

CHAPTER VII.

THERE was a numerous assemblage in the barn. Billot, as we have said, was much respected by his laborers, inasmuch as, though he scolded them unscrupulously, he fed and paid them well.

Consequently, every one of them had hastened eagerly to accept his invitation.

Moreover, at this period the people had been seized with that extraordinary fever which pervades nations when nations are about to set themselves to work to produce some great change. Strange, new words, which until then had scarcely ever been uttered, issued from mouths which had never before pronounced them. They were the words—Liberty, Independence, Emancipation— and, strange to say, it was not only among the people that these words were heard ; no, these words had been pronounced in the first place by the nobility, and the voice which responded to them was but an echo.

It was in the west that had first shone forth this light, which was destined to illuminate until it seared. It was in America that arose this sun, which, in accomplishing its course, was to make France one vast and burning mass, by the light of which the affrighted nations were to read the word Republic traced in vivid characters of blood.

But notwithstanding this, meetings in which political affairs were discussed were less frequent than might have been imagined. Men who had sprung up no one knew from where, apostles of an invisible and almost unknown deity, and traversed towns and country villages, strewing in their road words in praise of liberty. The government, blinded heretofore, began at length to open its eyes. Those who were at the head of the immense machine denominated the public chariot, felt that some of its wheels were paralyzed, without being able to comprehend whence the obstacle proceeded. The opposition existed in all minds, if it had not yet instilled itself into all hands and arms ; invisible, though present, though sensible, though threatening, and still more threatening from being, like ghosts, intangible, and from being divined, although it could not be clutched.

Twenty or twenty-five husbandmen, all in the employment of Billot, had assembled in the barn.

Billot entered it, followed by Pitou. All heads were instantly uncovered, and they waved their hats to welcome their loved master. It was plainly visible that all these men were ready to meet death should he but give the signal.

The farmer explained to the country people that the pamphlet which Pitou was about to read to them was the work of Dr. Gilbert. The doctor was well known throughout the whole district, in which he was the proprietor of several farms, the one rented by Billot being the most considerable.

A cask had been prepared for the reader. Pitou ascended this extempore forum and at once began.

It is to be remarked that people of the lower class, and I might almost venture to say, men in general, listen with most attention to that which they understand the least. It was evident that the general sense of the pamphlet escaped the perceptions of most of the enlightened among this rustic auditory, and even of Billot himself. But in the midst of that obscure phraseology from time to time flashed, like the lightnings in a dark sky charged with electricity, the luminous words of Independence, Liberty, Equality. Nothing more was necessary ; shouts of applause burst forth ; cries of "Long live Doctor Gilbert !" resounded on every side. Not more than one third of the pamphlet had been read ; it was decided that the remainder should be delivered on the two following Sundays.

The auditors were, therefore, invited for the next Sunday, and every one of them promised to attend.

Pitou had well performed his part ; he had read energet-

ically and well.   Nothing succeeds so well as success.   The
reader had taken his share of the plaudits which had been
addressed to the work, and, submitting to the influence
of this relative science, Billot himself felt growing within
him a certain degree of consideration for the pupil of the
Abbé Fortier.   Pitou, already a giant in his physical proportions, had morally grown ten inches in the opinion of
Billot.

But there was one thing wanting to Pitou's happiness :
Mlle. Catherine had not been present at his triumph.

But Father Billot, enchanted with the effect produced
by the doctor's pamphlet, hastened to communicate its
success to his wife and daughter.   Mme. Billot   e no
reply ; she was a short-sighted woman.

Mlle. Catherine smiled sorrowfully.

"Well, what is the matter with you now ?" said the
farmer.

"Father ! my dear father !" cried Catherine, "I fear
that you are running into danger."

"There, now, are you going to play the bird of ill-omen?
You are well aware that I like the lark better than the
owl."

"Father, I have already been told to warn you that eyes
are watching you."

"And who was it that told you this, if you please ?"

"A friend."

"A friend ? All advice is deserving of thanks. You
must tell the name of this friend. Who is he ? Come,
now, let us hear."

"A man who ought to be well informed on such
matters."

"But who is it ?"

"Monsieur Isidor de Charny."

"What business has that fop to meddle in such matters?
Does he pretend to give me advice upon my way of thinking ? Do I give him advice upon his mode of dressing ?
It appears to me that as much might be said on the one
subject as the other."

"My dear father, I do not tell you this to vex you.
The advice he gave me was well intended."

"Well, then, in return, I will give him my counsel, and
which you can on my behalf transmit to him."

"And what is that ?"

"It is that he and his fellows take good care what they are about. They shake these noble gentlemen about very nicely in the National Assembly; and more than once a great deal has been said of court favorites, male and female. Let him forewarn his brother, Monsieur Oliver Charny, who is out yonder, to look to himself, for it is said he is not on bad terms with the Austrian woman."

"Father," said Catherine, "you have more experience than we have ; act according to your pleasure."

"Yes, indeed," murmured Pitou, whose success had given him great confidence, "what business has your Monsieur Isidor to make and meddle ?"

Catherine either did not hear him, or pretended not to hear him, and there the conversation dropped.

The dinner was got through as usual. Never did dinner appear so long to Pitou. He was feverishly anxious to show himself abroad with Mlle. Catherine leaning on his arm. The Sunday was a monstrously great day to him, and he promised himself that the date, the 12th of July, should ever remain engraved upon his memory.

They left the farm at last at about three o'clock. Catherine was positively charming. She was a pretty, fair-haired girl with black eyes, slight and flexible as the willows that shaded the small spring from which the farm was supplied with water. She was, moreover, dressed with that natural coquetry which enhances the advantages of every woman, and her pretty little fantastic cap, made with her own hands, as she had told Pitou, became her admirably.

The ball did not, in general, commence till six o'clock. Four village minstrels, mounted upon a small stage formed of planks did the honors of this ball-room in the open air, on receiving a contribution of six shillings for every country dance.

While waiting for the opening of the dance, the company walked in the celebrated Hall of Sighs, of which Aunt Angelique had spoken, to see the young gentlemen of the town and the neighborhood play at tennis, under the direction of Master Farollet, tennis-master-in-chief to His Highness the Duke of Orleans. Master Farollet was considered a perfect oracle, and his decision in matters of *chasse* and *passe* and service was as irrevocable as were the laws of the Medes and Persians.

Pitou, without knowing why, would have very much desired to remain in the Hall of Sighs, but it was not for the purpose of remaining concealed beneath the shade of this double row of beech-trees that Catherine had attired herself in the becoming dress which had so much astonished Pitou.

Women are like the flowers which chance hath brought forth in the shade, their tendency is always toward the light : and one way or the other they must expand their fresh and perfumed petals in the sunshine, though it withers and destroys them.

The violet alone, as is asserted by the poets, has the modesty to remain concealed, but then it is arrayed in mourning, as if deploring her useless, because unnoticed, charms.

Catherine, therefore, dragged away at Pitou's arm, and so successfully, that they took the path to the tennis-court. We must, however, hasten to acknowledge that Pitou did not go very unwillingly. He also was as anxious to display his sky-blue suit and his cocked hat as Catherine was to show her Galatea cap and her shining short silk bodice.

One thing above all flattered our hero, and gave him a momentary advantage over Catherine. As no one recognized him, Pitou never having been seen in such sumptuous habiliments, they took him for some young stranger arrived in the town, some nephew or cousin of the Billot family ; some even asserted that he was Catherine's intended. But Pitou felt too great an interest in proving his own identity to allow the error to be of long continuance.

He gave so many nods to his friends, he so frequently took off his hat to his acquaintances, that at last the unworthy pupil of the Abbé Fortier was recognized in the spruce young countryman.

A sort of buzzing murmur quickly ran through the throng, and many of his former companions exclaimed, "Why, really, it is Pitou !" "Only look at Pitou !" "Did you see Ange Pitou ?"

This clamor at length reached the ears of Mlle. Angelique : but as this clamor informed her that the good-looking youth pointed out by it was her nephew, walking with his toes turned out and his elbows gracefully curved, the old maid, who had always seen Pitou walk with his toes turned in and his elbows stuck to his ribs, shook her head incredulously, and merely said :

"You are mistaken ; that is not my pitiful nephew."

The two young people reached the tennis-court. On that day there happened to be a match between the players of Soissons and those of Villers-Cotterets ; so that the game was very animated. Catherine and Pitou placed themselves close to the rope stretched to prevent the crowd from interfering with the players ; it was Catherine who had selected this place as being the best.

In about a minute the voice of Master Farollet was heard, calling out : "Two in—go over."

The players effectually changed places ; that is to say, that they each went to defend their quarters and attack those of their adversaries. One of the players, on passing by, bowed to Catherine with a smile ; Catherine replied by a courtesy, and blushed. At the same moment Pitou felt a nervous trembling shoot through Catherine's arm, which was leaning on his.

An unknown anguish shot through Pitou's heart.

"That is Monsieur de Charny," said he, looking at his companion.

"Yes," replied Catherine. "Ah ! you know him then ?"

"I do not know him," replied Pitou, "but I guessed that it was he."

And, in fact, Pitou had readily conceived this young man to be M. de Charny, from what Catherine had said to him the previous evening.

The person who had bowed to the young girl was an elegant gentleman, who might be twenty-three or twenty-four years of age ; he was handsome, of good stature, well formed, and graceful in his movements, as are all who have had an aristocratic education from their very cradle. All those manly exercises in which perfection can only be attained, but on the condition of their being studied from childhood, M. Isidore de Charny executed with remarkable perfection ; besides which, he was one of those whose costumes always harmonized with the pursuit he was engaged in. His hunting-dresses were quoted for their perfect taste ; his attire in the fencing-room might have served as a pattern to St. George himself ; and his riding coats were, or, rather, appeared to be, thanks to his manner of wearing them, of a particularly elegant shape.

On the day we are speaking of, M. de Charny, a younger brother of our old acquaintance, the Count de Charny, was attired in tight-fitting pantaloons of a light color, which set off to great advantage the shape of his finely formed and muscular limbs ; his hair was negligently dressed as for the morning, elegant tennis sandals for the moment were substituted for the red-heeled shoe or the top-boots ; his waistcoat was of white marsella, fitting as closely to his waist as if he had worn stays ; and, to sum up all, his servant was waiting upon the slope with a green coat embroidered with gold lace for his master to put on when the match was ended.

The animation of the game communicated to his features all the charm and freshness of youth, notwithstanding his twenty-three years, the nightly excesses he had committed, and the gambling parties he had attended, which frequently the rising sun had illuminated with its rays ; all this had made sad havoc in his constitution.

None of these personal advantages, which doubtless the young girl had remarked, had escaped the jealous eyes of Pitou. On observing the small hands and feet of M. de Charny, he began to feel less proud of that prodigality of nature which had given him the victory over the shoemaker's son, and he reflected that nature might have distributed in a more skilful manner over every part of his frame the elements of which it was composed.

In fact, with what there was too much in the hands, the feet, and the knees of Pitou, nature might have furnished him with a handsome, well-formed leg. Only, things were not in their right place : where there required a certain elegance of proportion, there was an unnatural thickness ; where a certain sleekness and rotundity would have been advantageous, there was an utter void.

Pitou looked at his legs with the same expression as the stag did of whom we have read in the fable.

"What is the matter with you, Monsieur Pitou ?" said Catherine, who had observed his discontented looks.

Pitou did not reply ; he could not have explained his feelings ; he, therefore, only sighed.

The game had terminated. The Viscount de Charny took advantage of the interval between the game just finished and the one about to commence, to come over to speak to Catherine. As he approached them nearer and nearer, Pitou observed the color heightening in the young girl's cheeks, and felt her arm become more and more trembling.

The viscount gave a nod to Pitou, and then, with that familiar politeness which the nobility of that period knew how to adopt with the citizens' daughters and grisettes, he inquired of Catherine as to the state of her health, and asked her to be his partner in the first dance. Catherine accepted. A smile conveyed the thanks of the young nobleman. The game was about to begin, and he was called for. He bowed to Catherine, and then left her with the same elegant ease with which he had approached her.

Pitou felt all the superiority which the man possessed over him, who could speak, smile, approach, and take leave in such a manner.

A month's study, employed in endeavoring to imitate the simple, though elegant, movements of M. de Charny, would only have produced a ridiculous parody, and this Pitou himself acknowledged.

If Pitou had been capable of entertaining a feeling of hatred, he would from that moment have detested the Viscount de Charny.

Catherine remained looking at the tennis-players until the moment when they called their servants to bring their coats to them. She then directed her steps toward the place set apart for dancing, to Pitou's great despair, who on that day appeared to be destined to go everywhere but where he wished.

M. de Charny did not allow Catherine to wait long for him. A slight change in his dress had converted him from a tennis-player into an elegant dancer.

The violins gave the signal, and he at once presented his hand to Catherine, reminding her of the promise she had made to dance with him.

That which Pitou experienced when he felt Catherine withdrawing her arm from within his, and saw the young girl blushing deeply as she advanced with her cavalier into the circle, was one of the most disagreeable sensations of his whole life. A cold perspiration stood upon his brow; a cloud passed over his eyes; he stretched out his hand and caught hold of the balustrade for support, for he felt that his knees, strongly constituted as they were, were giving way.

As to Catherine, she did not appear to have, and very probably even had not, any idea of what was passing in poor Pitou's heart. She was at once happy and proud— happy at being about to dance, and proud of dancing with the handsomest cavalier of the whole neighborhood.

If Pitou had been constrained to admire M. de Charny as a tennis-player, he was compelled to do him justice as a dancer. In those days the fashion had not yet sprung up of walking instead of dancing. Dancing was an art which formed a necessary part of the education of every one. Without citing the case of M. de Lauzun, who had owed his fortune to the manner in which he had danced his first steps in the king's quadrille, more than one noble- man owed the favor he had enjoyed at court to the manner in which he had extended his legs or pointed the extremity of his toe. In this respect the viscount was a model of grace and perfection, and he might, like Louis XIV., have danced in a theater with the chance of being ap- plauded, although he was neither a king nor an actor.

For the second time, Pitou looked at his own legs, and was obliged to acknowledge that unless some great meta- morphosis should take place in that portion of his in- dividuality, he must altogether renounce any attempt to succeed in vying with M. de Charny in the particular art which he was displaying at that moment.

The country dance having ended—for Catherine it had scarcely lasted a few seconds, but to Pitou it had ap- peared a century—she returned to resume the arm of her cavalier, and could not avoid observing the change which had taken place in his countenance. He was pale; the perspiration was streaming from his forehead, and a tear, half dried up by jealousy, was standing in his humid eye.

"Ah! good Heaven!" she exclaimed, "what is the matter with you, Pitou?"

"The matter is," replied the poor youth, "that I shall never dare to dance with you, after having seen you dance with Monsieur de Charny."

"Pshaw!" said Catherine, "you must not allow your- self to be cast down in this way; you will dance as well as you are able, and I shall not feel the less pleasure in danc- ing with you."

"Ah!" cried Pitou, "you say that, mademoiselle, to console me; but I know myself, and I feel assured that you will always feel more pleasure in dancing with the young nobleman than with me."

Catherine made no reply, for she would not utter a falsehood, only, as she was an excellent creature, and had begun to perceive that something extraordinary was passing in the heart of the poor youth, she treated him very kindly; but this kindness could not restore to him his lost joy and peace of mind. Father Billot had spoken truly; Pitou was beginning to be a man—he was suffering.

Catherine danced five or six country dances after this, one of which was with M. de Charny. This time, without suffering less in reality than before, Pitou was, in appearance, much more calm. He followed each movement which Catherine and her cavalier made with eager eyes. He endeavored from the motion of their lips to divine what they were saying to each other, and when during the figures of the dance, their hands were joined, he tried to discern whether their hands merely touched or pressed each other when they came in contact.

Doubtless, it was this second dance with De Charny that Catherine had been awaiting, for it was scarcely ended when the young girl proposed to Pitou to return to the farm. Never was proposal acceded to with more alacrity; but the blow was struck, and Pitou, while taking long strides which Catherine, from time to time was obliged to restrain, remained perfectly silent.

"What is the matter with you?" at length said Catherine to him, "and why is it that you do not speak to me?"

"I do not speak to you, mademoiselle," said Pitou, "because I do not know how to speak as Monsieur de Charny does. What would you have me say to you, after all the fine things which he whispered to you while dancing with you."

"Only see how unjust you are, Monsieur Ange; why, we were speaking of you."

"Of me, mademoiselle, and how so?"

"Why, Monsieur Pitou, if your protector should not return, you must have another found to supply his place."

"I am, then, no longer capable of keeping the farm accounts?" inquired Pitou, with a sigh.

"On the contrary, Monsieur Ange, it is the farm

accounts which are no longer worthy of being kept by you. With the education that you have received, you can find some more fitting occupation."

"I do not know what I may be fit for, but this I know, that I will not accept anything better if I am to obtain it through the Viscount de Charny."

"And why should you refuse his protection? His brother, the Count de Charny, is, it would appear, in high favor at court, and has married an intimate friend of the queen. He told me that, if it would be agreeable to you, he could obtain for you a place in the custom-house."

"Much obliged, mademoiselle; but I have already told you that I am well satisfied to remain as I am, and unless, indeed, your father wishes to send me away, I will remain at the farm."

"And why, in the devil's name, should I send you away?" cried a gruff voice, which Catherine tremblingly recognized to be that of her father.

"My dear Pitou," said Catherine, in a whisper, "do not say a word of Monsieur Isidor, I beg of you."

"Well, why don't you answer?"

"Why, really, I don't know," said Pitou, much confused; "perhaps you do not think me sufficiently well informed to be useful to you."

"Not sufficiently well informed, when you calculate as well as Bareine, and that you read well enough to teach our schoolmaster, who, notwithstanding, thinks himself a great scholar. No, Pitou; it is God who brings to my house the people who enter it, and when once they are in it they shall remain there as long as God pleases."

Pitou returned to the farm on this assurance; but although this was something, it was not enough. A great change had been operated in his mind between the time of his going out and returning; he had lost a thing which, once lost, is never recovered; this was confidence in himself, and, therefore, Pitou, contrary to his usual custom, slept very badly. In his waking moments he recalled to mind Dr. Gilbert's book. This book was written principally against the nobility, against the abuses committed by the privileged classes, against the cowardice of those who submitted to them. It appeared to Pitou that he only then began to comprehend all the fine things which he had read that morning, and he promised himself, as soon as it should be daylight, to read for his own satisfaction, and to himself, the masterpiece which he had read aloud and to everybody.

But as Pitou had slept badly he awoke late. He did not, however, the less determine on carrying into effect his project of reading the book. It was seven o'clock ; the farmer would not return until nine ; besides, were he to return earlier, he could not but approve an occupation which he had himself recommended.

He descended by a small staircase, and seated himself on a low bench which happened to be under Catherine's window. Was it accident that had led Pitou to seat himself precisely in that spot, or did he know the relative positions of that window and that bench ?

Be that as it may, Pitou was attired in his old everyday clothes, which there had not yet been time to get replaced, and which were composed of his black breeches, his green cassock, and his rusty-looking shoes. He drew the pamphlet from his pocket and began to read.

We would not venture to say that on beginning to read the eyes of Pitou were not, from time to time, turned from his book to the window ; but as the window did not exhibit the fair face of the young girl in its frame-work of nasturtiums and convolvuli, Pitou's eyes at length fixed themselves intently on his book.

It is true that as his hand neglected to turn over the leaves, and that the more fixed his attention appeared to be, the less did his hand move, it might be believed that his mind was fixed upon some other object, and that he was meditating instead of reading.

Suddenly it appeared to Pitou that a shade was thrown over the pages of the pamphlet, until then illuminated by the morning sun. This shadow, too dense to be that of a cloud, could, therefore, only be produced by some opaque body. Now, there are opaque bodies which are so delightful to look upon, that Pitou quickly turned round to ascertain what it was that thus intercepted his sunshine.

Pitou's hopes were, however, delusive. There was, in fact, an opaque body which robbed him of the daylight and heat which Diogenes desired Alexander not to deprive him of. But this opaque body, instead of being delightful, presented to his view a sufficiently disagreeable appearance.

It was that of a man about forty-five years old, who was taller and thinner than Pitou himself, dressed in a coat almost as threadbare as his own, and who was leaning his head over his shoulder, and appeared to be reading the pamphlet with a curiosity equal to Pitou's absence of mind.

Pitou was very much astonished, a gracious smile was playing round the lips of the dark-looking gentleman, exhibiting a mouth which had only retained four teeth, two in the upper and two in the lower jaw, crossing and sharpening themselves against one another, like the tusks of the wild boar.

"An American edition," said the man, with a strong nasal twang; "an octavo: 'On the Liberty of Man and the Independence of Nations, Boston, 1788.'"

While the man was reading, Pitou opened his eyes with progressively increasing astonishment, so that when the black man ceased speaking, Pitou's eyes had attained the greatest possible development of which they were capable. "Boston, 1788. That is right, sir," replied Pitou.

"It is the treatise of Doctor Gilbert," said the gentleman in black.

"Yes, sir," politely replied Pitou, rising from his seat, for he had been told that it was uncivil to remain sitting when speaking to a superior; and in the still ingenuous mind of Pitou this man had the right to claim superiority over him.

But on getting up, Pitou observed something of a rosy color moving toward the window, and which gave him a significant glance. This rosy something was Mlle. Catherine. The young girl looked at him with an extraordinary expression, and made strange signs to him.

"Sir, if it is not being indiscreet," said the gentleman in black, who, having his back turned toward the window, was altogether ignorant of what was passing, "may I ask to whom this book belongs?"

And he pointed with his finger to the pamphlet which Pitou held in his hand.

Pitou was about to say that the book belonged to M. Billot, when he heard the following words uttered in an almost supplicating tone:

"Say that it is your own."

The gentleman in black, who was at that moment all eyes, did not hear these words.

"Sir," said Pitou, majestically, "this book belongs to me."

The gentleman in black raised his head, for he began to remark that the amazed looks of Pitou were from time to time diverted from him, to fix themselves on one particular spot. He saw the window, but Catherine had divined the movement of the gentleman in black, and, rapid as a bird, she had disappeared.

"What are you looking at, up yonder?" inquired the gentleman in black.

"Well, now," replied Pitou smiling, "permit me to observe to you that you are very inquisitive—*curiosus*, or, rather, *avidus cognoscendi* as the Abbé Fortier, my preceptor, used to say."

"You say, then," rejoined the interrogator, without appearing in the slightest degree intimidated by the proof of learning which Pitou had just given, with the intention of affording the gentleman in black a higher idea of his acquirements than he had before entertained, "you say, then, that this book is yours?"

Pitou gave his eyes a furtive glance, so that the window came within the scope of his visual organs. Catherine's head again appeared at it, and made him an affirmative sign.

"Yes, sir," replied Pitou. "You are, perhaps, anxious to read it—*Avidus legendi libri*, or *legenda historia.*"

"Sir," said the gentleman in black, "you appear to be much above the position which your attire would indicate. *Non dives vestitu sed ingenio.* Consequently, I arrest you."

"How, you arrest me!" cried Pitou, completely astounded.

"Yes, sir; follow me, I beg of you."

Pitou no longer looked up in the air, but around him, and perceived two police sergeants who were awaiting the orders of the gentleman in black. The two sergeants seemed to him to have sprung from beneath the ground.

"Let us draw up our report, gentlemen," said the gentleman in black.

The sergeants tied Pitou's hands together with a rope, and between his hands remained Dr. Gilbert's book.

Then they fastened Pitou himself to a ring which was in the wall under the window.

Pitou was about to exclaim against this treatment, but he heard the voice which had so much influence over him, saying, "Let them do what they please."

Pitou, therefore, allowed them to do as they pleased, with a docility which perfectly enchanted the sergeants, and, above all, the gentleman in black. So that without the slightest mistrust they entered the farmhouse, the two sergeants to fetch a table, the gentleman in black to —but this we shall learn by and by.

The sergeants and the gentleman in black had scarcely entered the house when the soft voice was again heard.

"Hold up your hands," said the voice.

Pitou not only held up his hands, but his head, and he perceived the pale and terrified face of Catherine; she had a knife in her hand.

"Higher! higher!" said she.

Pitou raised himself on tiptoe.

Catherine leaned out of the window, the knife touched the rope, and Pitou recovered the liberty of his hands.

"Take the knife," said Catherine; "and in your turn cut the rope which fastens you to the ring."

It was not necessary to repeat this twice to Pitou. He cut the cord, and was then completely free.

"And now," said Catherine, "there is a double-louis. You have good legs; make your escape. Go to Paris, and acquaint the doctor——"

She could not complete the sentence. The two sergeants reappeared, and the double-louis fell at Pitou's feet.

Pitou quickly snatched it up. The sergeants were on the threshold of the door, where they remained for a moment or two, astonished at seeing the man at liberty who so short a time before they had so securely tied up. On seeing them, Pitou's hair stood on end, and he confusedly remembered the *in crinibus agues* of Euminedes.

The sergeants and Pitou remained for a short time in the position of two pointer dogs and a hare—motionless, and looking at one another. But as, at the slightest movement of the dogs, the hare springs off, at the first movement of the sergeants Pitou gave a prodigious bound and leaped over a high hedge.

The sergeants uttered a cry which made the exempt rush out of the house, who had a small casket under his arm. The exempt did not lose any time in parleying, but instantly ran after Pitou ; the two sergeants imitated his example ; but they were not active enough to jump, as he had done, over a hedge four feet and a half in height. They were, therefore, compelled to go round to a gate.

But when they reached the corner of the hedge, they perceived Pitou five hundred yards off in the plain, and hastening toward the forest, from which he was distant scarcely a quarter of a league, and which he would doubtless reach in some six or seven minutes.

At that moment Pitou turned round ; and, on perceiving the sergeants, who were pursuing him rather from a desire to perform their duty than with the hope of catching him, he redoubled his speed and soon disappeared in the skirts of the wood.

Pitou ran on at this rate for another quarter of an hour. He could have run two hours had it been necessary, for he had the wind of a stag, as well as its velocity.

But at the end of a quarter of an hour he felt instinctively that he must be out of danger. He stopped, drew breath, and listened ; and having assured himself that he had completely distanced his pursuers, he said to himself :

" It is incredible that so many events can have been crowded into three days ; " and he looked alternately at his double-louis and his knife.

" Oh ! " said he, " I wish I had only time to change my double-louis, and give two sous to Mademoiselle Catherine ; for I am much afraid that this knife will cut our friendship. No matter," added he "since she has desired me to go to Paris, let us go there."

And Pitou, having looked about him to ascertain what part of the country he had reached, and finding that he was between Bouronne and Yvors, took a narrow path which would lead him straight to Gondreville, which path was crossed by the road which led direct to Paris.

CHAPTER VIII.

But now let us return to the farm and relate the catastrophe of which Pitou's episode was the winding-up.

At about six o'clock in the morning an agent of the Paris police, accompanied by two sergeants, arrived at

Villers-Cotterets, had presented themselves to the commissary of police, and had requested that the residence of Farmer Billot might be pointed out to them.

When they came within about five hundred feet of the farm, the exempt perceived a laborer working in a field. He went to him and asked him whether he should find M. Billot at home. The laborer replied that M. Billot never returned home until nine o'clock—that is to say, before the breakfast hour. But at that very moment, as chance would have it, the laborer raised his eyes, and pointed to a man on horseback who was talking with a shepherd at the distance of a quarter of a league from the farm.

"And yonder," said he, "is the person you are inquiring for."

"Monsieur Billot?"

"Yes."

"That horseman?"

"Yes, that is Monsieur Billot."

"Well, then, my friend," rejoined the exempt, "do you wish to afford great pleasure to your master?"

"I should like it vastly."

"Go and tell him that a gentleman from Paris is waiting for him at the farm."

"Oh!" cried the laborer, "can it be Doctor Gilbert?"

"Tell him what I say—that is all."

The countryman did not wait to have the order repeated, but ran as hard as he could across the fields, while the police officer and the two sergeants went and concealed themselves behind a half-ruined wall which stood facing the gate of the farmyard.

In a very few minutes the galloping of a horse was heard. It was Billot who had hastened back.

He went into the farmyard, jumped from his horse, threw the bridle to one of the stable-boys, and rushed into the kitchen, being convinced that the first person he should see there would be Dr. Gilbert, standing beneath the immense mantelpiece; but he only saw Mme. Billot seated in the middle of the room, plucking the feathers from a duck with all the minute care which this difficult operation demands.

Catherine was in her own room, employed in making a cap for the following Sunday. As it appears, Catherine was determined to be prepared in good time; but if the women have one pleasure greater than that of being well dressed, it is that of preparing the articles with which they are to adorn themselves.

Billot paused on the threshold of the kitchen, and looked around inquiringly.

" Who, then, was it sent for me ? " said he.

" It was I," replied a flute-like voice behind him.

Billot turned round, and perceived the gentleman in black and the two sergeants.

" Heyday ! " cried he, retreating three paces from them, " and what do you want with me ? "

" Oh ! good heavens ! almost nothing, my dear Monsieur Billot," said the man with the flute-like voice ; " only to make a perquisition in your farm, that is all."

" A perquisition ? " exclaimed the astonished Billot.

" A perquisition," repeated the exempt.

Billot cast a glance at his fowling-piece, which was hanging over the chimney.

"Since we have a National Assembly," said he, " I thought that citizens were no longer exposed to such vexations, which belong to another age, and which appertain to a by-gone state of things. What do you want with me ? I am a peaceable and loyal man."

The agents of every police in the world have one habit which is common to them all—that of replying to the questions of their victims only while they are searching their pockets. While they are arresting them or tying their hands behind, some appear to be moved by pity. These tender-hearted ones are the most dangerous, inasmuch as they appear to be the most kind-hearted.

The one who was exercising his functions in the house of Farmer Billot was of the true Tapin and Desgre's school, made up of sweets, having always a tear for those whom they are persecuting, but who nevertheless do not use their hands to wipe their eyes.

The one in question, although heaving a deep sigh, made a sign with his hand to the two sergeants, who approached Billot. The worthy farmer sprung forward, and stretched out his hand to seize his gun, but it was diverted from the weapon—a doubly dangerous act at such a moment, as it might not only have killed the person about to use it, but the one against whom it was to be pointed. His hand was seized and imprisoned between two little hands, rendered strong by terror and powerful by supplication.

It was Catherine, who had run down-stairs on hearing the noise, and had arrived in time to save her father from committing the crime of rebelling against the constituted authorities.

The first moment of anger having passed by, Billot no longer offered any resistance. The exempt ordered that he should be confined in a room on the ground floor, and Catherine in a room on the first story. As to Mme. Billot, she was considered so inoffensive that no attention was paid to her, and she was allowed to remain in the kitchen. After this, finding himself master of the place, the exempt began to search the secretary, wardrobes, and chests of drawers.

Billot, on finding himself alone, wished to make his escape. But, like most of the rooms on the ground floor of the farm house, the windows of the one he was imprisoned in were secured by iron bars. The gentleman in black had, with a glance, observed these bars, while Billot, who had had them placed there, had forgotten them.

Then, peeping through the keyhole, he perceived the exempt and his two acolytes, who were ransacking everything throughout the house.

"Halloo!" cried he, "what is the meaning of all this? What are you doing there?"

"You can very plainly see that, my dear Monsieur Billot," said the exempt, "we are seeking for something which we have not yet found."

"But perhaps you are banditti, villains, regular thieves. Who knows?"

"Oh, sir!" replied the exempt, through the door, "you do us wrong. We are honest people as you are; only that we are in the pay of his majesty, and, consequently, compelled to obey his orders."

"His majesty's orders!" exclaimed Billot. "The king, Louis XVI., has ordered you to search my secretary, to turn everything topsy-turvy in my closets and my wardrobes?"

"Yes."

"His majesty," rejoined Billot, "who last year, when there was such a frightful famine that we were thinking of eating our horses—his majesty, who two years ago, when the hail-storm on the 13th of July destroyed our whole harvest, and did not then deign to feel any anxiety about us—what has he now to do with my farm, which he never saw, or with me, whom he does not know ?"

"You will pardon me, sir," said the exempt, opening the door a little, but with great precaution, and exhibiting his order, signed by the lieutenant of police, and which, according to the usual mode, was headed with these words, "In the king's name"—"his majesty has heard you spoken of, although he may not be personally acquainted with you; therefore, do not refuse the honor which he does you, and receive in a fitting manner those who present themselves to you in his name."

And the exempt, with a polite bow, and a friendly wink of the eye, closed the door again; after which the examination was resumed.

Billot said not a word more, but crossed his arms and paced up and down the room, like a lion in a cage. He felt that he was caught, and in the power of this man.

The investigation was silently continued. These men appeared to have dropped from the clouds. No one had seen them but the laborer who had been sent to fetch Billot. The dogs even in the yards had not barked on their approach. Assuredly the chief of this expedition must have been considered a skilful man, even by his own fraternity. It was evidently not his first enterprise of this nature.

Billot heard the moanings of his daughter, shut up in the room above his own, and he remembered her prophetic words; for there could not be a doubt that the persecution the farmer had been subjected to had for its cause the doctor's book.

At length the clock struck nine, and Billot, through his grated windows, could count his laborers, as they returned to the farmhouse to get their breakfast. On seeing this, he reflected, that, in case of any conflict, might, if not right, was on his side. This conviction made the blood boil in his veins. He had no longer the fortitude to restrain his feelings; and, seizing the door with both hands, he shook it so violently that, with two or three efforts of the same nature, he would have burst off the lock.

The police agents immediately opened the door, and

they saw the farmer standing close by it, with threatening looks. All was confusion in the house.

"But, finally," cried Billot, "what is it you are seeking for in my house? Tell me, or zounds! I will make you tell me."

The successive return of the laborers had not escaped the experienced eye of such a man as the exempt. He had counted the farm-servants, and had admitted to himself that in case of any combat, he would not be able to retain possession of the field of battle. He therefore approached Billot with a demeanor more honeyed even than before, and bowing almost to the ground, said:

"I will tell you what it is, dear Monsieur Billot, although it is against our custom. What we are seeking for in your house is a subversive book, an incendiary pamphlet, placed under ban by our royal censors."

"A book—and in the house of a farmer who cannot read?"

"What is there astonishing in that, if you are a friend to the author, and he has sent it to you?"

"I am not the friend of Doctor Gilbert; I am merely his humble servant. The friend of the doctor, indeed! that would be too great an honor for a poor farmer like me."

This inconsiderate outbreak, in which Billot betrayed himself by acknowledging that he not only knew the author, which was natural enough, he being his landlord, but he knew the book, insured the agent's victory. The latter drew himself up, assumed his most amiable air, and touching Billot's arm, said, with a smile which appeared to distend transversely over one half of his face:

"''Tis thou hast named him.' Do you know that verse, my dear Monsieur Billot?"

"I know no verses."

"It is by Racine, a very great poet."

"Well, what is the meaning of that line?" cried Billot.

"It means that you have betrayed yourself."

"Who, I?"

"Yourself."

"And how so?"

"By being the first to mention Monsieur Gilbert, whom we had the discretion not to name."

"That is true." said Billot.

" You acknowledge it, then ? "

" I will do more than that."

" My dear Monsieur Billot, you overwhelm us with kindness ; what is it you will do ? "

" If it is that book you are hunting after, and I tell you where that book is," rejoined the farmer, with an uneasiness which he could not altogether control, "you will leave off turning everything topsy-turvy here, will you not ? "

The exempt made a sign to his two assistants.

" Most assuredly," replied the exempt, " since it is that book which is the object of our perquisition. " Only," continued he, with his smiling grimace, "you may perhaps acknowledge one copy of it, when you may have ten in your possession."

" I have only one, and that I swear to you."

" But it is this, we are obliged to ascertain by a most careful search, dear Monsieur Billot," rejoined the exempt. " Have patience, therefore; in five minutes it will be concluded. We are only poor sergeants obeying the orders of the authorities, and you would not surely prevent men of honor—there are men of honor in every station of life, dear Monsieur Billot—you would not throw any impediment in the way of men of honor, when they are doing their duty."

The gentleman in black had adopted the right mode ; this was the proper course for persuading Billot.

" Well, do it, then," replied the farmer, " but do it quickly."

And he turned his back upon them.

The exempt then very gently again closed the door, and more gently still turned the key in the lock, at which Billot shrugged his shoulders in disdain, being certain of pulling open the door whenever he might please.

On his side, the gentleman in black made a sign to the sergeants, who resumed their investigation, and they set to work much more actively than before. Books, papers, linen, were all opened, examined, unfolded.

Suddenly, at the bottom of a wardrobe which had been completely emptied. they perceived a small oaken casket bound with iron. The exempt darted upon it as a vulture on his prey. At the mere sight, the scent, the handling of this object, he undoubtedly at once recognized that

which he was in search of, for he quickly concealed the
casket beneath his threadbare coat, and made a sign to the
two sergeants that his mission was affected.

Billot was again becoming impatient ; he stopped before
the locked door.

" Why, I tell you again that you will not find it, unless
I tell you where it is," he cried.   " It is not worth the
while to tumble and destroy all my things for nothing.   I
am not a conspirator.   In the devil's name, listen to me !
Do you not hear what I am saying ?   Answer me, or I will
set off for Paris, and will complain to the king, to the
National Assembly, to everybody."

In those days the king was always mentioned before the
people.

" Yes, my dear Monsieur Billot, we hear you, and we
are quite ready to do justice to your excellent reasoning.
Come, now, tell us where is this book ? And as we are
now convinced that you have only that single copy, we will
take it, and then we will withdraw and all will be over."

" Well," replied Billot, " the book is in the possession
of an honest lad to whom I have given it, with the charge
of carrying it to a friend."

" And what is the name of this honest lad ? " asked the
gentleman in black, in an insinuating tone."

" Ange Pitou ; he is a poor orphan whom I have taken
into my house from charity, and who does not even know
the subject of this book."

" Thanks, dear Monsieur Billot," said the exempt.

They threw the linen back again into the wardrobe, and
locked it up again, but the casket was not there.

" And where is this amiable youth to be found ? "

" I think I saw him as I returned, somewhere near the
bed of scarlet runners, close to the tunnel.   Go, take the
book from him ; but take care not to do him any injury."

" Injury !   Oh, my dear Monsieur Billot, how little you
know us.   We would not harm even a fly."

And he went toward the indicated spot.   When he got
near the scarlet runners he perceived Pitou, whose tall
stature made him appear more formidable than he was in
reality.   Thinking that the two sergeants would stand in
need of his assistance to master the young giant, the exempt had taken off his cloak, had rolled the casket in it,

and had hidden the whole in a secret corner, but where he could easily regain possession of it.

But Catherine, who had been listening with her ear glued, as it were, to the door, had vaguely heard the words "book, doctor, and Pitou." Therefore, finding the storm she had predicted had burst upon them, she had formed the idea of attenuating its effects. It was then that she prompted Pitou to say that he was the owner of the book.

We have related what then passed regarding it; how Pitou, bound and handcuffed by the exempt and his acolytes, had been restored to liberty by Catherine, who had taken advantage of the moment when the two sergeants went into the house to fetch a table to write upon, and the gentleman in black to take his cloak and casket.

We have stated how Pitou made his escape by jumping over a hedge, but that which we did not state is, that, like a man of talent, the exempt had taken advantage of this flight.

And, in fact, the twofold mission intrusted to the exempt having been accomplished, the flight of Pitou afforded an excellent opportunity to the exempt and his two men to make their escape also.

The gentleman in black, although he knew he had not the slightest chance of catching the fugitive, excited the two sergeants by his vociferations and his example to such a degree, that on seeing them racing through the clover, the wheat, and Spanish trefoil fields, one would have imagined that they were the most inveterate enemies of Pitou, whose long legs they were most cordially blessing in their hearts.

But Pitou had scarcely gained the cover of the wood, or had even passed the skirts of it, when the confederates halted behind a bush. During their race they had been joined by two other sergeants who had kept themselves concealed in the neighborhood of the farm, and who had been instructed not to show themselves, unless summoned by their chief.

"Upon my word," said the exempt, "it is very well that our gallant young fellow had not the casket instead of the book, for we should have been obliged to hire post-horses to catch him. By Jupiter! those legs of his are not men's legs, but those of a stag."

"Yes," replied one of the sergeants, "but he has not

got it, has he, Monsieur Wolfsfoot ; for, on the contrary, 'tis you who have it."

"Undoubtedly, my friend, and here it is," replied the exempt, whose name we have now given for the first time, or we should rather say the nickname which had been given to him on account of the lightness of his step and the stealthiness of his walk.

"Then we are entitled to the reward which was promised us," observed one of the sergeants.

"Here it is," said the exempt, taking from his pocket four golden louis, which he divided among his four sergeants, without any distinction as to those who had been actively engaged in the perquisition or those who had merely remained concealed.

"Long live the lieutenant of police !" cried the sergeant.

"There is no harm in crying, 'Long live the lieutenant !'" said Wolfsfoot, "but every time you utter such exclamations you should do it with discernment. It is not the lieutenant who pays."

"Who is it, then ?"

"Some gentleman or lady friend of his, I know not which, but who desires that his or her name may not be mentioned in the business."

"I would wager that it is the person who wishes for the casket," said one of the sergeants.

"Hear now, Rigold, my friend," said the gentleman in black ; "I have always affirmed that you are a lad replete with perspicacity, but until the day when the perspicacity shall produce its fruits by being amply recompensed, I advise you to be silent. What we have now to do is to make the best of our way on foot out of this neighborhood. That damned farmer has not the appearance of being very conciliatory, and as soon as he discovers that the casket is missing, he will despatch all his farm-laborers in pursuit of us, and they are fellows who can aim a gun as truly as any of his majesty's Swiss Guards."

This opinion was doubtless that of the majority of the party, for they all five set off at once, and, continuing to remain within the border of the forest, which concealed them from all eyes, they rapidly pursued their way, until, after walking three quarters of a league, they came out upon the public road.

This precaution was not a useless one, for Catherine had scarcely seen the gentleman in black and his two attendants disappear in pursuit of Pitou, than, full of confidence in him whom they pursued, who, unless some accident should happen to him, would lead them a long dance, she called her husbandmen, who were well aware that something strange was going on, although they were ignorant of the positive facts, to tell them to open her door for her.

The laborers instantly obeyed her, and Catherine, again free, hastened to set her father at liberty.

Billot appeared to be in a dream. Instead of at once rushing out of the room, he seemed to walk mistrustfully, and returned from the door into the middle of the apartment. It might have been imagined that he did not dare to remain in the same spot, and yet, that he was afraid of casting his eyes upon the articles of furniture which had been broken open and emptied by the sergeants.

"But," cried he, on seeing his daughter, "tell me, did they take the book from him?"

"I believe so, father," she replied; "but they did not take him."

"Whom do you mean?"

"Pitou; he escaped from them, and they are still running after him; they must already have got to Cayolles or Vauciennes."

"So much the better! Poor fellow! It is I who have brought this upon him."

"Oh, father, do not feel at all uneasy about him, but think only of what we have to do. Pitou, you may rest assured, will get out of this scrape; but what disorder—good Heaven! only look, mother!"

"Oh! my linen wardrobe!" cried Mme. Billot; "they have not even respected my linen wardrobe—what villains they must be!"

"They have searched the wardrobe where the linen was kept!" exclaimed Billot.

And he rushed toward the wardrobe, which the exempt, as we have before stated, had carefully closed again, and plunged his hands into piles of towels and table napkins, all confusedly huddled together.

"Oh!" cried he, "it cannot be possible!"

"What are you looking for, father?" inquired Catherine.

Billot gazed around him as if completely bewildered.

"Search! search if you can see it anywhere! But no; not in that chest of drawers—not in that secretary! Besides, it was there—there—it was myself who put it there. I saw it there only yesterday. It was not the book they were seeking for, the wretches! but the casket."

"What casket?" asked Catherine.

"Why, you know well enough."

"What—Doctor Gilbert's casket?" inquired Mme. Billot, who always, in matters of transcendent importance, allowed others to speak and act.

"Yes, Doctor Gilbert's casket," cried Billot, plunging his fingers into his thick hair; "that casket which was so precious to him!"

"You terrify me, my dear father," said Catherine.

"Unfortunate man that I am!" cried Billot, with furious anger; "and I, who had not in the slightest imagined such a thing—I, who did not even for a moment think of that casket! Oh, what will the doctor say? What will he think of me? That I am a traitor, a coward, a miserable wretch!"

"But, good Heaven! what did this casket contain, father?"

"I do not know; but this I know, that I had engaged, even at the hazard of my life, to keep it safe; and I ought to have allowed myself to be killed in order to defend it."

And Billot made a gesture of such despair that his wife and daughter started back with terror.

"Oh, God! oh, God! are you losing your reason, my poor father?" said Catherine.

And she burst into tears.

"Answer me, then," she cried; "for the love of Heaven, answer me."

"Pierre, my friend," said Mme. Billot, "answer your daughter—answer your wife."

"My horse! my horse!" cried the farmer; "bring out my horse!"

"Where are you going, father?"

"To let the doctor know—the doctor must be informed of this."

"But where will you find him?"

"At Paris. Did you not read in the letter he wrote to us that he was going to Paris? My horse! my horse!"

"And you will leave us thus, my dear father ! You will leave us in such a moment as this ? You will leave us full of anxiety and anguish ?"

"It must be so, my child ; it must be so," said the farmer, taking his daughter's face between his hands and convulsively fixing his lips upon it. " ' If ever you should lose this casket,' said the doctor to me, ' or, rather, should it ever be surreptitiously taken from you, the instant you discover the robbery, set off at once, Billot, and inform me of it, wherever I may be. Let nothing stop you, not even the life of a man.' "

" Good Lord ! what can this casket contain ? "

" Of that I know nothing ; all that I know is, that it was placed under my care, and that I have allowed it to be taken from me. Ah ! here is my horse. From the son, who is at college, I shall learn where to find the father."

And kissing his wife and daughter for the last time, the farmer jumped into his saddle and galloped across the country, in the direction of the high-road to Paris.

CHAPTER IX.

LET us return to Pitou.

Pitou was urged onward by the two most powerful stimulants known in this great world—Fear and Love.

Fear whispered to him in direct terms :

" You may be either arrested or beaten. Take care of yourself, Pitou."

And that sufficed to make him run as swiftly as a roe-buck.

Love had said to him, in the voice of Catherine :

" Escape quickly, my dear Pitou."

And Pitou had escaped.

These two stimulants combined, as we have said, had such an effect upon him that Pitou did not merely run, Pitou absolutely flew.

How useful did Pitou's long legs, which appeared to be knotted to him, and his enormous knees, which looked so ungainly in a ballroom, prove to him in the open country, when his heart, enlarged with terror, beat three pulsations in a second !

M. de Charny, with his small feet, his elegantly formed knees, and his symmetrically shaped calves, could not have run at such a rate as that.

Pitou recalled to his mind that pretty table, in which a stag is represented weeping over his slim shanks, reflected in a fountain ; and although he did not bear on his forehead the ornament which the quadruped deemed some compensation for his slender legs, he reproached himself for having so much despised his stilts.

For such was the appellation which Mme. Billot gave to Pitou's legs, when Pitou looked at them, standing before a looking-glass.

Pitou, therefore, continued making his way through the wood, leaving Poyolles on his right and Yvors on his left, turning round at every corner of a bush, to see, or, rather, to listen, for it was long since he had seen anything of his persecutors, who had been distanced at the outset by the brilliant proof of swiftness Pitou had given in placing a space of at least a thousand yards between them and himself, a distance which he was increasing every moment.

Why was Atalanta married ? Pitou would have entered the lists with her ; and to have excelled Hippomenes he would not assuredly have needed to employ, as she did, the subterfuge of the three golden apples.

It is true, as we have already said, that M. Wolfsfoot's agents, delighted at having possession of their booty, cared not a fig as to what became of Pitou ; but Pitou knew not this.

Ceasing to be pursued by the reality, he continued to be pursued by the shadows.

As to the black-clothed gentlemen, they had that confidence in themselves which renders human beings lazy.

"Run, run !" cried they, thrusting their hands into their pockets, and making the reward which M. Wolfsfoot had given them jingle in them, "run, good fellow, run ; we can always find you again should we want you."

Which, we may say in passing, far from being a vain boast, was the precise truth.

And Pitou continued to run as if he had heard the aside of M. Wolfsfoot's agents.

When he had, by scientifically altering his course, and turning and twisting as do the wild denizens of the forest, to throw the hounds off the scent, when he had doubled and turned so as to form such a maze that Nimrod himself would not have been able to unravel it, he at once made up his mind as to his route, and taking a sharp turn to the right, went in a direct line to the high-road which leads from Villers-Cotterets to Paris, near the heath of Gondreville.

Having formed this resolution, he bounded through the thicket, and after running for a little more than a quarter of an hour, he perceived the road inclosed by its yellow sand, and bordered with its green trees.

An hour after his departure from the farm he was on the king's highway.

He had run about four leagues and a half during that hour, as much as any rider could expect from an active horse going a good round trot.

He cast a glance behind him. There was nothing on the road.

He cast a glance before him. There were two women upon asses. Pitou had got hold of a small work on mythology, with engravings, belonging to young Gilbert; mythology was much studied in those days.

The history of the gods and goddesses of the Grecian Olympus formed part of the education of young persons. By dint of looking at the engravings, Pitou had become acquainted with mythology. He had seen Jupiter metamorphose himself into a bull, to carry off Europa into a swan, that he might approach and make love to the daughter of King Tyndarus. He had, in short, seen other gods transforming themselves into forms more or less picturesque; but that one of his majesty's police officers had transformed himself into an ass, had never come within the scope of his erudition. King Midas himself had never had anything of the animal but the ears—and he was a king—he made gold at will—he had, therefore, money enough to purchase the whole skin of the quadruped.

Somewhat reassured by what he saw, or, rather, by what he did not see, Pitou threw himself down on the grassy bank of the roadside, wiped with his sleeve his broad red face, and thus luxuriously reclining, he yielded himself up to the voluptuousness of perspiring in tranquillity.

But the sweet emanations from the clover and marjoram would not make Pitou forget the pickled pork made by

Mme. Billot, and the quarter of a six-pound loaf which Catherine allotted to him at every meal—that is to say, three times a day.

This bread, which at that time cost four sous and a half a pound—a most exorbitant price, equivalent at least to nine sous in our day—this bread, which was so scarce throughout France, and which, when it was eatable, passed for the fabulous *brioche* * which the Duchess of Polignac advised the Parisians to feed upon when flour should altogether fail them.

Pitou, therefore, said to himself, philosophically, that Mlle. Catherine was the most generous princess in the world, and that Father Billot's farm was the most sumptuous palace in the universe.

Then, as the Israelites on the banks of the Jordan, he turned a dying eye toward the East—that is to say, in the direction of that thrice-happy farm, and sighed heavily.

But sighing is not so disagreeable an operation to a man who stands in need of taking breath, after a violent race.

Pitou breathed more freely when sighing, and he felt his ideas, which for a time had been much confused and agitated, return to him gradually with his breath.

"Why is it," reasoned he with himself, "that so many extraordinary events have happened to me in so short a space of time ? Why should I have met with more accidents within the last three days than during the whole course of my previous life ?

"It is because I dreamed of a cat that wanted to fly at me," continued Pitou.

And he made a gesture signifying that the source of all his misfortunes had been thus already pointed out to him.

"Yes," added he, after a moment's reflection, " but this is not the logic of my venerable friend the Abbé Fortier. It is not because I dreamed of an irritated cat that all these adventures have happened to me. Dreams are only given to a man as a sort of warning, and this is why an author said, 'Thou hast been dreaming—beware ! *Cave somniasti !* '

"*Somniasti*," said Pitou, doubtingly, and with somewhat of alarm, " am I, then, again committing a barbar-

---

* A sort of dry cake made of flour, eggs, and saffron, which the Parisians eat with their coffee and milk.—TRANSLATOR.

ism ? Oh, no ; I am only making an elision ; it was *somniavisti* which I should have said, in grammatical language.

"It is astonishing," cried Pitou, considering himself admiringly, "how well I understand Latin since I no longer study it."

And after this glorification of himself, Pitou resumed his journey.

Pitou walked on very quickly, though he was much tranquilized. His pace was somewhat about two leagues an hour.

The result of this was that two hours after he had recommenced his walk, Pitou had got beyond Nanteuil, and was getting on toward Dammartin.

Suddenly the ears of Pitou, as acute as those of an Osage Indian, were struck with the distant sound of a horse's foot upon the paved road.

"Oh !" cried Pitou, scanning the celebrated verse of Virgil :

" ' Quadru pedante putrem soni tu quatit ungula campum.' "

And he looked behind him.

But he saw nothing.

Could it be the asses which he had passed at Levignon, and which had now come on at a gallop ? No ; for the iron hoof, as the poet calls it, rang out upon the paved road ; and Pitou, whether at Haramont or at Villers-Cotterets, had never known an ass, excepting that of Mother Sabot, that was shod, and even this was because Mother Sabot performed the duty of letter-carrier between Villers-Cotterets and Crespy.

He, therefore, momentarily forgot the noise he had heard, to return to his reflections.

Who could these men in black be who had questioned him about Dr. Gilbert, who had tied his hands, who had pursued him, and whom he had at length so completely distanced.

Where could these men have sprung from, for they were altogether unknown in the district ?

What could they have in particular to do with Pitou ? He who had never seen them, and who, consequently, did not know them.

How then, was it, as he did not know them, that they had known him? Why had Mlle. Catherine told him to set off for Paris? and why, in order to facilitate his journey, had she given him a louis of forty-eight francs? That is to say, two hundred and forty pounds of bread, at four sous a pound. Why, it was enough to supply him with food for eighty days, or three months, if he would stint his rations somewhat.

Could Mlle. Catherine suppose that Pitou was to remain eighty days absent from the farm?

Pitou suddenly started.

"Oh! oh!" he exclaimed, "again that horse's hoofs. This time," said Pitou, "I am not mistaken. The noise I hear is positively that of a horse galloping. I shall see it when he gets to the top of yon hill."

Pitou had scarcely spoken, when a horse appeared at the top of a hill he had just left behind him, that is to say, at the distance of about four hundred yards from the spot on which he stood.

Pitou, who would not allow that a police agent could have transmogrified himself into an ass, admitted at once that he might have got on horseback to regain the prey that had escaped him.

Terror, from which he had been for some time relieved, again seized on Pitou, and immediately his legs became even longer and more intrepid than when he had made such marvelous good use of them some two hours previously.

Therefore, without reflecting, without looking behind, without endeavoring to conceal his flight, calculating on the excellence of his steel-like sinews, Pitou, with a tremendous leap, sprung across the ditch which ran by the roadside, and began a rapid course in the direction of Ermenonville. Pitou did not know anything of Ermenonville, he only saw upon the horizon the summits of some tall trees, and he said to himself:

"If I reach those trees, which are undoubtedly on the border of some forest, I am saved."

And he ran toward Ermenonville.

On this occasion, he had to outvie a horse in running. Pitou had no longer legs but wings.

And his rapidity was increased after having run some hundred yards, for Pitou had cast a glance behind him, and had seen the horseman oblige his horse to take the same immense leap which he had taken over the ditch on the roadside.

From that moment there could be no longer a doubt in the mind of the fugitive that the horseman was, in reality, in pursuit of him, and, consequently, the fugitive had increased his speed, never again turning his head for fear of losing time. What most urged him on at that moment was not the clattering on the paved road—that noi was deadened by the clover and the fallow fields ; what nost urged him on was a sort of cry which pursued him, the last syllable of his name pronounced by the horseman, a sort of hou ! hou ! which appeared to be uttered angrily, and which reached him on the wings of the wind, which he was endeavoring to outstrip.

But after having maintained this sharp race during ten minutes, Pitou began to feel that his chest became oppressed—the blood rushing to his head—his eyes began to wander. It seemed to him that his knees became more and more developed—that his loins were filling with small pebbles. From time to time he stumbled over the furrows ; he who usually raised his feet so high when running, that every nail in the soles of his shoes were visible.

At last the horse, created superior to man in the art of running, gained on the biped Pitou, who, at the same time, heard the voice of the horseman, who no longer cried, "Hou ! hou !" but clearly and distinctly, "Pitou ! Pitou !"

All was over. All was lost.

However, Pitou endeavored to continue the race. It had become a sort of mechanical movement. Suddenly, his knees failed him ; he staggered and fell at full length with his face to the ground.

But at the same time that he thus fell he fully resolved not to get up again—at all events of his own free will; and he received a lash from a horsewhip, which wound round his loins.

With a tremendous oath, which was not unfamiliar to his ears, a well-known voice cried out to him :

"How now, you stupid fellow ! how now, you simpleton ! have you sworn to founder Cadet ?"

The name of Cadet at once dispelled all Pitou's suspense

"Ah !" cried he, turning himself round, so that instead of lying upon his face he lay upon his back—" ah ! I hear the voice of Monsieur Billot."

It was in fact, Goodman Billot. When Pitou was well assured of his identity, he assumed a sitting posture.

The farmer, on his side, had pulled up Cadet, covered with flakes of foam.

"Ah! dear Monsieur Billot," exclaimed Pitou, "how kind it is of you to ride in this way after me. I swear to you I should have returned to the farm after having expended the double-louis Mademoiselle Catherine gave me. But since you are here, take back your double-louis—for of course it must be yours—and let us return to the farm."

"A thousand devils !" exclaimed Billot. "Who was thinking of the farm ? Where are the *mouchards* ? "

"The *mouchards*?" inquired Pitou, who did not comprehend the meaning of this word, which had only just been admitted into the vocabulary of our language.

"Yes, the *mouchards*,"* rejoined Billot—"the men in black. Do you not understand me ?"

"Ah ! the men in black. You will readily understand, my dear Monsieur Billot, that I did not amuse myself by waiting for them."

"Bravo ! You have left them behind, then ?"

"Why, I flatter myself, after the race I have run, it was to be expected, as it appears to me."

"Then, if you were so sure of your affair, what the devil made you run at such a rate ?"

"Because I thought it was their chief who, not to be outwitted, was pursuing me on horseback. Well, well ! You are not quite so simple as I thought you. Then, as the road is clear, up, up, and away for Dammartin !"

"What do you mean by ' up, up ?' "

"Yes, get up and come with me."

"We are going, then, to Dammartin ?"

"Yes. I will borrow a horse there of old Lefranc. I will leave Cadet with him, for he can go no further, and to-night we will push on to Paris."

"Be it so, Monsieur Billot—be it so."

"Well, then, up—up ! "

Pitou made an effort to obey him.

---

* Spies—common informers—men who live by betraying others.—TRANSLATOR.

"I should much wish to do as you desire," said he; "but, my dear Monsieur Billot, I cannot."

"How—you cannot get up?"

"No."

"But just now you could manage to turn round."

"Oh, just now! that was by no means astonishing. I heard your voice, and at the same moment I received a swinging cut across the back. But such things can only succeed once. At present I am accustomed to your voice; and as to your whip, I feel well assured that you can only apply it to managing our poor Cadet, who is almost as heated as I am."

Pitou's logic, which, after all, was nothing more than the Abbé Fortier's, persuaded, and even affected, the farmer.

"I have not time to sympathize in your fate," said he to Pitou; "but, come now, make an effort and get up behind me."

"Why," said Pitou, "that would be, indeed, the way to founder Cadet at once, poor beast!"

"Pooh! in half an hour we shall be at old Lefranc's."

"But, it appears to me, dear Monsieur Billot," said Pitou, "that it would be altogether useless for me to go with you to old Lefranc's."

"And why so?"

"Because, although you have business at Dammartin, I have no business there—not I."

"Yes; but I want you to come to Paris with me. In Paris you will be of use to me. You have good stout fists, and I am certain it will not be long before hard knocks will be given there."

"Ah! ah!" cried Pitou, not much delighted with this prospect; "do you believe that?"

And he managed to get on Cadet's back; Billot dragged him up as he would a sack of flour.

The good farmer soon got on the high-road again, and so well managed his bridle, whip and spurs, that in less than half an hour, as he had said, they reached Dammartin.

Billot had entered the town by a narrow lane, which was well known to him. He soon arrived at Father Lefranc's farmhouse; and leaving Pitou and Cadet in the middle of the farmyard, he ran straight to the kitchen, where Father Lefranc, who was setting out to take a turn round his fields, was buttoning his gaiters.

"Quick—quick, my friend!" cried Billot, before Lefranc had recovered from the astonishment which his arrival had produced, "the strongest horse you have!"

"That is Margot," replied Lefranc; "and, fortunately, she is already saddled; I was going out."

"Well, Margot be it, then; only, it is possible I may founder her, and of that I forewarn you."

"What, founder Margot! and why so, I ask?"

"Because it is necessary that I should be in Paris this very night."

And he made a masonic sign to Lefranc, which was most significant.

"Well, founder Margot if you will," said old Lefranc; "you shall give me Cadet if you do."

"Agreed."

"A glass of wine?"

"Two."

"But it seemed to me that you were not alone?"

"No; I have a worthy lad there whom I am taking with me, and who is so fatigued that he had not the strength to come in here. Send out something to him."

"Immediately, immediately," said the farmer.

In ten minutes the two old comrades had each managed to soak in a bottle of good wine, and Pitou had bolted a two-pound loaf with half a pound of bacon. While he was eating, one of the farm-servants, a good fellow, rubbed him down with a handful of clean straw, to take the mud from his clothes, and with as much care as if he had been cleaning a favorite horse.

Thus freshened up and invigorated, Pitou had also some wine given to him, taken from a third bottle, which was the sooner emptied from Pitou's having his share from it; after which Billot mounted Margot, and Pitou, stiff as a pair of compasses, was lifted on behind him.

The poor beast, being thereunto urged by whip and spur, immediately trotted off bravely, under this double load, on the road to Paris, and without ceasing, whisked away the flies with its formidable tail, the thick hair of which threw the dust of the road on Pitou's back, and every now and then lashed his calfless legs, which were exposed to view, his stockings having fallen down to his ankles.

CHAPTER X.

It is eight leagues from Dammartin to Paris. The first four leagues were tolerably well got over ; but after they reached Bourget, poor Margot's legs at length began to grow somewhat stiff. Night was closing in.

On arriving at La Villette, Billot thought he perceived a great light extending over Paris.

He made Pitou observe the red light, which rose above the horizon.

" You do not see, then," said Pitou to him, " that there are troops bivouacking, and that they have lighted their fires."

" What mean you by troops ? " cried Billot.

" There are troops here," said Pitou ; " why should there not be some further on ? "

And, in fact, on examining attentively, Father Billot saw, on looking to the right, that the plain of St. Denis was dotted over with black-looking detachments of infantry and cavalry, which were marching silently in the darkness.

Their arms glistened occasionally with the pale reflection of the stars.

Pitou, whose nocturnal excursions in the woods had accustomed him to see clearly in the dark—Pitou pointed out to his master pieces of artillery, which had sunk up to the axles in the middle of the muddy plain.

" Oh ! oh !" cried Billot, " there is something new up yonder, then. Let us make haste ! Let us make haste !"

" Yes, yes ; there is a fire out yonder," said Pitou, who had raised himself on Margot's back. " Look ! look ! Do you not see the sparks ?"

Margot stopped. Billot jumped off her back, and approaching a group of soldiers in blue-and-yellow uniform, who were bivouacking under the trees by the roadside :

" Comrades," said he to them, " can you tell me what there is going on at Paris ? "

But the soldiers merely replied to him by oaths, which they uttered in the German language.

"What the devil is it they say?" inquired Billot, addressing Pitou.

"It is not Latin, dear Monsieur Billot," replied Pitou, trembling; "and that is all I can affirm to you."

Billot reflected, and looked again.

"Simpleton that I was," said he, "to attempt to question these *Kainserliks*."

And in his curiosity he remained motionless in the middle of the road.

An officer went up to him.

"Bass on your roat," said he; "bass on quickly."

"Your pardon, captain," replied Billot; "but I am going to Paris."

"Vell, mien Gott; vot den?"

"And as I see that you are drawn up across the road, I fear that we cannot get through the barriers."

"You can get drough."

And Billot remounted his mare, and went on.

But it was only to fall in the midst of the Bercheur Hussars, who encumbered the street of La Villette.

This time he had to deal with his own countrymen. He questioned them with more success.

"Sir," said he, "what has there happened at Paris, if you please?"

"That your headstrong Parisians," replied the hussar, "will have their Necker; and they are firing musket-shots at us, as if we had anything to do with the matter."

"Have Necker!" exclaimed Billot. "They had lost him, then?"

"Assuredly, since the king had dismissed him."

"The king had dismissed him!" exclaimed Billot, with the stupefaction of a devotee calling out against a sacrilege; "the king has dismissed that great man?"

"Oh! in good faith he has, my worthy sir; and, more than that, this great man is now on his road to Brussels."

"Well, then, in that case we shall see some fun," cried Billot, in a tremendous voice, without caring for the danger he was incurring by thus preaching insurrection in the midst of twelve or fifteen hundred royalist sabers.

And he again mounted Margot, spurring her on with cruel violence, until he reached the barrier.

As he advanced he perceived that the fire was increasing

and becoming redder. A long column of flame ascended from the barrier toward the sky.

It was the barrier itself that was burning.

A howling, furious mob, in which there were many women, and who, as usual, threatened and vociferated more loudly than the men, were feeding the fire with pieces of wainscoting, and chairs and tables, and other articles of furniture belonging to the clerks employed to collect the city dues.*

Upon the road were Hungarian and German regiments, who, leaning upon their grounded arms, were looking on with vacant eyes at this scene of devastation.

Billot did not allow this rampart of flames to arrest his progress. He spurred on Margot through the fire. Margot rushed through the flaming ruins; but when she had reached the inner side of the barrier she was obliged to stop, being met by a crowd of people coming from the center of the city, toward the suburbs. Some of them were singing, others shouting, "To arms !"

Billot had the appearance of being what he really was, a good farmer coming to Paris on his own affairs. Perhaps he cried out rather too loudly, "Make room ! make room !" but Pitou repeated the words so politely, "Room, if you please; let us pass !" that the one was a corrective of the other. No one had any interest in preventing Billot from going to his affairs, and he was allowed to pass.

Margot, during all this, had recovered her wind and strength; the fire had singed her coat. All these unaccustomed shouts appeared greatly to amaze her, and Billot was obliged to restrain the efforts she now made to advance, for fear of trampling under foot some of the numerous spectators whom curiosity had drawn together before their doors to see the gate on fire, and as many curious people who were running from their doors toward the burning toll-house.

Billot went on pushing through the crowd, pulling Margot first to the right, and then to the left, twisting and turning in every direction, until they reached the boulevard; but having got thus far, he was obliged to stop.

* The city of Paris is encircled by a wall, and at every entrance to it is a custom-house, where people coming from the country are obliged to give an account of the produce—poultry, meal, butter, eggs, etc.—and pay the city dues upon them.—TRANSLATOR.

A procession was then passing, coming from the Bastile, and going toward the place called the Garde Meuble, those two masses of stone which in those days formed a girdle which attached the center of the city to its out-works.

This procession, which obstructed the whole of the boulevard, was following a bier, on this bier were borne two busts; the one veiled with black crape, the other crowned with flowers.

The bust covered with crape was that of Necker, a minister who had not been disgraced, but dismissed. The one crowned with flowers was that of the Duke of Orleans, who had openly espoused at court the party of the Genevese economists.

Billot immediately inquired what was the meaning of this procession. He was informed that it was a popular homage paid to M. Necker and to his defender, the Duke of Orleans.

Billot had been born in a part of the country where the name of a Duke of Orleans had been venerated for a century and a half. Billot belonged to the new sect of philosophers, and considered Necker not only as a great minister, but as an apostle of humanity.

This was more than sufficient to excite Billot. He jumped off his horse, without being exactly aware of what he was about to do, shouting, "Long live the Duke of Orleans ! Long live Necker !" and he then mingled with the crowd. Having once got back into the thick of the throng, all personal liberty was at an end at once ; as every one knows, the use of our free will at once ceases. We wish what the crowd wishes, we do what it does. Billot, moreover, allowed himself the more easily to be drawn into this movement, from being near the head of the procession.

The mob kept on vociferating most strenuously, "Long live Necker ! no more foreign troops ! Down with foreign troops !"

Billot mingled his stentorian voice with all these voices.

A superiority, be it of whatever nature it may, is always appreciated by the people. The Parisian of the suburbs, with his faint, hoarse voice, enfeebled by inanition or worn out by drinking, duly appreciated the full, rich, and sonorous voice of Billot, and readily made way for him, so that without being too much elbowed, too much pushed about, too much pressed by the crowd, Billot at length managed to get up close to the bier.

About ten minutes after this, one of the bearers, whose enthusiasm had been greater than his strength, yielded his place to Billot.

As has been seen, the honest farmer had rapidly obtained promotion.

The day before he had been merely the propagator of the principles contained in Dr. Gilbert's pamphlet, and now he had become one of the instruments of the great triumph of Necker and the Duke of Orleans.

But he had scarcely attained this post when an idea crossed his mind.

"What had become of Pitou—what had become of Margot?"

Though carefully bearing his portion of the bier, he gave a glance behind him, and by the light of the torches which accompanied the procession, by the light of the lamps which illuminated every window, he perceived in the midst of the procession a sort of ambulating eminence, formed of five or six men, who were gesticulating and shouting.

Amid these gesticulations and shouts it was easy to distinguish the voice and recognize the long arms of his follower, Pitou.

Pitou was doing all he could to protect Margot; but despite all his efforts, Margot had been invaded. Margot no longer bore Billot and Pitou, a very honorable and sufficient burden for the poor animal.

Margot was bearing as many people as could manage to get upon her back, her croup, her neck; Margot looked in the obscurity of the night, which always magnifies the appearance of objects, like an elephant loaded with hunters going to attack a tiger.

Five or six furious fellows had taken possession of Margot's broad back, vociferating, "Long live Necker!" "Long live the Duke of Orleans!" "Down with the foreigners!" to which Pitou replied:

"You will break Margot's back!"

The enthusiasm was general.

Billot for a moment entertained the idea of rushing to the aid of Pitou and poor Margot; but he reflected that if he should only for a moment resign the honor of carrying

one of the corners of the bier, he would not be able to
regain his triumphal post. Then, he reflected that by the
barter he had agreed to with old Lefranc, that of giving
him Cadet for Margot, Margot belonged to him, and that
should any accident happen to Margot, it was, after all,
but an affair of some three or four hundred livres, and that
he, Billot, was undoubtedly rich enough to make the sacrifice of three or four hundred livres to his country.

During this time the procession kept on advancing; it
had moved obliquely to the left and had gone down the
Rue Montmartre to the Place des Victoires. When it
reached the Palais Royal some great impediment prevented
its passing on. A troop of men with green leaves in their
hats were shouting, "To arms!"

It was necessary to reconnoiter. Were these men who
blocked up the Rue Vivienne friends or enemies? Green
was the color of the Count d'Artois. Why, then these
green cockades?

After a minute's conference, all was explained.

On learning the dismissal of Necker, a young man had
issued from the Café Foy, had jumped upon a table in the
garden of the Palais Royal, and taking a pistol from his
breast, had cried, "To arms!"

On hearing this cry, all the persons who were walking
there had assembled round him and had shouted, "To
arms!"

We have already said that all the foreign regiments had
been collected around Paris. One might have imagined
that it was an invasion by the Austrians. The names of
those regiments alarmed the ears of all Frenchmen; they
were Reynac, Salis, Samade, Diesbach, Esterhazy, Roe-
mer; the very naming of them was sufficient to make the
crowd understand that they were the names of enemies.
The young man named them; he announced that the Swiss
were encamped in the Champs Elysées with four pieces of
artillery, and that they were to enter Paris that same
night, preceded by the dragoons, commanded by Prince
Lambesq. He proposed a new cockade which was not
theirs, snatched a leaf from a chestnut tree, and placed
it in the band of his hat. Upon the instant every one
present followed his example. Three thousand persons
had, in ten minutes, unleaved the trees of the Palais
Royal.

That morning no one knew the name of that young man ; in the evening it was in every mouth.

That young man's name was Camille Desmoulins.

The two crowds recognized each other as friends ; they fraternized, they embraced each other, and then the procession continued on its way.

During the momentary halt we have just described, the curiosity of those who had not been able to discover, even by standing on tiptoe, what was going on, had overloaded Margot with an increasing burden. Every inch on which a foot could be placed had been invaded, so that when the crowd again moved on, the poor beast was literally crushed by the enormous weight which overwhelmed her.

At the corner of the Rue Richelieu Billot cast a look behind him ; Margot had disappeared.

He heaved a deep sigh, addressed to the memory of the unfortunate animal, then, soon recovering from his grief, and calling up the whole power of his voice, he three times called Pitou, as did the Romans of ancient times, when attending the funeral of a relative. He imagined that he heard issuing from the center of the crowd a voice which replied to his own, but that voice was lost among the confused clamors which ascended toward heaven, half threatening, half with applauding acclamations.

The procession still moved on.

All the shops were closed ; but all the windows were open, and from every window issued cries of encouragement which fell like blessings on the heads of those who formed this great ovation.

In this way they reached the Place Vendôme.

But on arriving there the procession was obstructed by an unforeseen obstacle.

Like to those trunks of trees rooted up by a river that has overflown its banks, and which, on encountering the piers of a bridge, recoil upon the wreck of matter which is following them, the popular army found a detachment of the Royal Germans on the Place Vendôme.

These foreign soldiers were dragoons, who, seeing an inundation streaming from the Rue St. Honoré, and which began to overflow the Place Vendôme, loosened their horses' reins, who, impatient at having been stationed there during five hours, at once galloped furiously forward, charging upon the people.

The bearers of the bier received the first shock, and
were thrown down beneath their burden. A Savoyard,
who was walking before Billot, was the first to spring to
his feet again, raised the effigy of the Duke of Orleans, and,
placing it on the end of a stick, held it above his head,
crying :

"Long live the Duke of Orleans !" whom he had never
seen ; and "Long live Necker!" whom he did not
know.

Billot was about to do as much for the bust of Necker,
but found himself forestalled. A young man, about
twenty-four or twenty-five years old, and sufficiently well
dressed to deserve the title of a beau, had followed it with
his eyes, and which he could do more easily than Billot,
who was carrying it ; and as soon as the bust had fallen to
the ground, he had rushed toward it and seized upon it.

The good farmer, therefore, vainly endeavored to find it
on the ground ; the bust of Necker was already on the
point of a sort of pike, and side by side with that of the
Duke of Orleans, rallied around them a good portion of
the procession.

Suddenly a great light illuminates the square ; at the
same moment a violent explosion is heard ; the balls whiz
through the air ; something heavy strikes Billot on the
forehead; he falls. At first Billot imagined himself killed.

But as his sensations had not abandoned him ; as, excepting a violent pain in the head, he felt no other injury,
Billot comprehended that he was, even at the worst, but
wounded. He presses his hand to his forehead, to ascertain the extent of damage he had received, and perceived
at one and the same time that he had only a contusion on
the head, and that his hand was streaming with blood.

The elegantly dressed young man who had supplanted
Billot had received a ball full in his breast. It was he who
had died. The blood on Billot's hand was his. The blow
which Billot had experienced was from the bust of Necker,
which, losing its supporter, had fallen upon his head.

Billot uttered a cry, partly of anger, partly of terror.

He draws back from the young man, who was convulsed
in the agonies of death. Those who surrounded him also
drew back ; and the shout he had uttered, repeated by the
crowd, is prolonged like a funeral echo by the groups assembled in the Rue St. Honoré.

This shout was a second rebellion.

A second detonation was heard, and immediately deep vacancies hollowed in the mass attested the passage of the murderous projectiles.

To pick up the bust, the whole face of which was stained with blood ; to raise it above his head, and protest against this outrage in his sonorous voice, at the risk of being shot down, as had been the handsome young man whose body was then lying at his feet, was what Billot's indignation prompted him to effect, and which he did in the first moment of his enthusiasm.

But at the same instant a large and powerful hand was placed upon the farmer's shoulder, and with so much vigor that he was compelled to bend down beneath its weight. The farmer wishes to relieve himself from this pressure ; another hand, no less heavy than the first, falls on his other shoulder. He turned round, reddening with anger, to ascertain what sort of antagonist he had to contend with.

"Pitou !" he exclaimed.

"Yes, yes," replied Pitou. "Down ! down ! and you will soon see."

And redoubling his efforts, he managed to drag with him to the ground the opposing farmer.

No sooner had he forced Billot to lie down flat upon the pavement than another discharge was heard. The Savoyard who was carrying the bust of the Duke of Orleans, fell in his turn.

Then was heard the crushing of the pavement beneath the horses' hoofs ; then the dragoons charged a second time ; a horse, with streaming mane and furious as that of the Apocalypse, bounds over the unfortunate Savoyard, who feels the coldness of a lance penetrate his breast. He falls on Billot and Pitou.

The tempest rushed onward toward the end of the street, spreading, as it past, terror and death ! Dead bodies alone remained on the pavement of the square. All those who had formed the procession fled through the adjacent streets. The windows are instantly closed—a gloomy silence succeeds to the shouts of enthusiasam and the cries of anger.

Billot waited a moment, still restrained by the prudent Pitou : then, feeling that the danger was becoming more distant with the noise, while Piton, like a hare in its form, was beginning to raise, not his head, but his ears.

"Well, Monsieur Billot," said Pitou, "I think that you spoke truly, and that we have arrived here in the nick of time."

"Come, now, help me!"

"And what to do—to run away?"

"No. The young dandy is dead as a door-nail; but the poor Savoyard, in my opinion, has only fainted. Help me to put him on my back. We cannot leave him here, to be finished by those damned Germans."

Billot spoke a language which went straight to Pitou's heart. He had no answer to make but to obey. He took up the fainting and bleeding body of the poor Savoyard, and threw him, as he would have done a sack, across the shoulders of the robust farmer; who, seeing that the Rue St. Honoré was free, and in all appearance deserted, advanced with Pitou toward the Palais Royal.

CHAPTER XI.

THE street had, in the first place, appeared empty and deserted to Billot and Pitou, because the dragoons, being engaged in the pursuit of the great body of the fugitives, had turned into the market of St. Honoré, and had followed them up the Rue Louis le Grand and the Rue Gaillon. But as Billot advanced toward the Palais Royal, roaring instinctively, but in a subdued voice, the word "Vengeance," men made their appearance at the corners of the streets, at the end of alleys, and from under the carriage gateways, who, at first mute and terrified, looked around them; but, being at length assured of the absence of the dragoons, brought up the rear of this funereal march, repeating, first in hollow whispers, but soon aloud, and finally with shouts, the word "Vengeance! vengeance!"

Pitou walked behind the farmer, carrying the Savoyard's black cap in his hand.

They arrived thus, in gloomy and fearful procession, upon the square before the Palais Royal, where a whole people, drunk with rage, was holding council, and soliciting the support of French soldiers against the foreigners.

"Who are these men in uniform?" inquired Billot, on arriving in front of a company who were standing with grounded arms, stopping his passage across the square, from the gate of the palace to the Rue de Chartres.

"They are the French Guards!" cried several voices.

"Ah!" exclaimed Billot, approaching them, and showing them the body of the Savoyard, which was now a lifeless corpse—"ah! you are Frenchmen, and you allow us to be murdered by these Germans?"

The French Guards drew back with horror.

"Dead!" murmured a voice from within their ranks.

"Yes, dead! dead! assassinated! he, and many more besides."

"And by whom?"

"By the Royal German Dragoons. Did you not hear the cries, the firing, the galloping of their horses?"

"Yes, yes, we did!" cried two or three hundred voices; "they were butchering the people on the Place Vendôme!"

"And you are a part of the people. By heaven, you are!" cried Billot, addressing the soldiers. "It is, therefore, cowardly in you to allow your brothers to be butchered."

"Cowardly!" exclaimed several threatening voices in the ranks.

"Yes, cowardly. I have said it, and I repeat the word. Come, now," continued Billot, advancing three steps toward the spot from whence these murmurs had proceeded. "Well, now, will you not kill me, in order to prove that you are not cowards?"

"Good! that is all well, very well," said one of the soldiers. "You are a brave fellow, my friend, but you are a citizen, and can do what you will; but a military man is a soldier, do you see, and he must obey orders."

"So that," replied Billot, "if you had received orders to fire upon us—that is to say, upon unarmed men—you would fire; you who have succeeded the men of Fontenoy —you who gave the advantage to the English by telling them to fire first!"

"As to me, I know that I would not fire, for one," said a voice from the ranks.

"Nor I!—nor I!" repeated a hundred voices.

"The dragoons!—the dragoons!" cried several voices, at the same time that the crowd driven backward, began to throng the square, flying by the Rue de Richelieu.

And there was heard the distant sound of the galloping

of heavy cavalry upon the pavement, but which became louder at every moment.

"To arms !—to arms !" cried the fugitives.

"A thousand gods !" cried Billot, throwing the dead body of the Savoyard upon the ground, which he had till then held in his arms. "Give us your muskets, at least, if you will not yourselves make use of them."

"Well, then, yes ; by a thousand thunders, we will make use of them !" said the soldier to whom Billot had addressed himself, snatching out of his hand his musket, which the other had already seized. Come, come ; let us bite our cartridges, and if the Austrians have anything to say to these brave fellows, we shall see."

"Yes, yes, we'll see !" cried the soldiers, putting their hands into their cartouche boxes, and biting off the ends of their cartridges.

"Oh, thunder !" cried Billot, stamping his feet ; "and to think that I have not brought my fowling-piece ! But perhaps one of those rascally Austrians will be killed, and then I will take his carbine."

"In the meantime," said a voice, "take this carbine, it is ready loaded."

And at the same time an unknown man slipped a richly mounted carbine into Billot's hands.

At that instant the dragoons galloped into the square, riding down and sabering all that were in their way.

The officer who commanded the French Guards advanced four steps.

"Halloo ! there, gentlemen dragoons !" cried he. "Halt there, if you please !"

Whether the dragoons did not hear, or whether they did not chose to hear, or whether they could not at once arrest the violent course of their horses, they rode across the square, making a half-wheel to the right, and ran over a woman and an old man, who disapppared beneath their horses' heels.

"Fire, then—fre !" cried Billot.

Billot was standing close to the officer. It might have been thought that it was the latter who had given the word.

The French Guards presented their guns, and fired a volley, which at once brought the dragoons to a stand.

"Why, gentlemen of the guards," said a German officer,

advancing in front of his disordered squadron, "do you know that you are firing upon us?"

"Do we not know it?" cried Billot; and he fired at the officer, who fell from his horse.

Then the French Guards fired a second volley; and the Germans, seeing that they had on this occasion to deal, not with plain citizens, who would fly at the first saber cut, but with soldiers, who firmly waited their attack, turned to the right about, and galloped back to the Place Vendôme, amid so formidable an explosion of bravos and shouts of triumph, that several of their horses, terrified at the noise, ran off with their riders, and knocked their heads against the closed shutters of the shops.

"Long live the French Guards!" cried the people.

"Long live the soldiers of the country!" cried Billot.

"Thanks," replied the latter. "We have smelled gunpowder, and we are now baptized."

"And I, too," said Pitou. "I have smelled gunpowder."

"And what do you think of it?" inquired Billot.

"Why, really, I do not find it so disagreeable as I had expected," replied Pitou.

"But now," said Billot, who had had time to examine the carbine, and had ascertained that it was a weapon of some value, "but now, to whom belongs this gun?"

"To my master," said the voice which had already spoken behind him. "But my master thinks that you make too good a use of it to take it back again."

Billot turned round, and perceived a huntsman in the livery of the Duke of Orleans.

"And where is your master?" said he.

The huntsman pointed to a half-open Venetian blind, behind which the prince had been watching all that had passed.

"Your master is, then, on our side?" asked Billot.

"With the people, heart and soul," replied the huntsman.

"In that case, once more, 'Long live the Duke of Orleans!'" cried Billot. "My friends. the Duke of Orleans is with us. Long live the Duke of Orleans!"

And he pointed to the blind behind which the prince stood.

Then the blind was thrown completely open, and the Duke of Orleans bowed three times.

After which the blind was again closed.

Although of such short duration, his appearance had wound up the enthusiasm of the people to its acme.

"Long live the Duke of Orleans!" vociferated two or three thousand voices.

"Let us break open the armorers' shops!" cried a voice in the crowd.

"Let us run to the Invalides!" cried some old soldiers. "Sombreuil has twenty thousand muskets."

"To the Invalides!"

"To the Town Hall!" exclaimed several voices. "Flesselles, the provost of the merchants, has the key of the dépôt, in which the arms of the guards are kept. He will give them to us."

"To the Hôtel de Ville!" cried a fraction of the crowd.

And the whole crowd dispersed, taking the three directions which had been pointed out.

During this time, the dragoons had rallied round the Baron de Bezenval and the Prince de Lambesq, on the Place Louis XV.

Of this Billot and Pitou were ignorant. They had not followed either of the troops of the citizens, and they found themselves almost alone in the square before the Palais Royal.

"Well, dear Monsieur Billot, where are we to go next, if you please?" said Pitou.

"Why," replied Billot, "I should have desired to follow those worthy people; not to the gunmakers' shop, since I have such a beautiful carbine, but to the Hôtel de Ville, or the Invalides. However, not having come to Paris to fight, but to find out the address of Doctor Gilbert, it appears to me that I ought to go to the College of Louis le Grand, where his son now is; and then, after having seen the doctor, why, we can throw ourselves again into this fighting business." And the eyes of the farmer flashed lightnings.

"To go, in the first place, to the College Louis le Grand appears to me quite logical," sententiously observed Pitou, "since it was for that purpose that we came to Paris."

"Go, get a musket, a saber, a weapon of some kind or other, from some one or other of those idle fellows who are lying on the pavement yonder," said Billot, pointing to one out of five or six dragoons, who were stretched upon the ground, "and let us at once go to the college."

"But these arms," said Pitou, hesitating, "they are not mine."

"Whom, then, do they belong to?" asked Billot.

"To the king."

"They belong to the people," rejoined Billot.

And Pitou, strong in the opinion of the farmer, who knew that he was a man who would not rob a neighbor of a grain of millet, Pitou, with every necessary precaution, approached the dragoon who happened to be the nearest to him, and after having assured himself that he was really dead, took from him his saber, his musketoon, and his cartouche-box.

Pitou had a great desire to take his helmet also, only he was not quite certain that what Father Billot had said with regard to offensive weapons extended to defensive accouterments.

But while thus arming himself, Pitou directed his ears toward the Place Vendôme.

"Ho! ho!" said he, "it appears to me that the Royal Germans are coming this way again."

And, in fact, the noise of a troop of horsemen returning at a foot-pace could be heard. Pitou peeped from behind the corner of the coffee-house called La Regence, and perceived, at about the distance of the market of St. Honoré, a patrol of dragoons advancing, with their musketoons in hand.

"Oh, quick, quick!" cried Pitou, "here they are, coming back again."

Billot cast his eyes around him, to see if there was any means of offering resistance. There was scarcely a person in the square.

"Let us go, then," said he, "to the College Louis le Grand."

And he went up the Rue de Chartres, followed by Pitou; who, not knowing the use of the hook upon his belt, was dragging his long saber after him.

"A thousand thunders!" exclaimed Billot; "why, you look like a dealer in old iron. Fasten me up that lath there."

"But how?" asked Pitou.

"Why, so, by Heaven!—there!" said Billot.

And he hooked Pitou's long saber up to his belt, which enabled the latter to walk with more celerity than he could have done but for this expedient.

They pursued their way without meeting with any impediment, till they reached the Place Louis XV.; but there Billot and Pitou fell in with the column which had left them to proceed to the Invalides, and which had been stopped short in its progress.

"Well," cried Billot, "what is the matter?"

"The matter is, that we cannot go across the Bridge Louis XV."

"But you can go along the quays."

"All passage is stopped that way, too."

"And across the Champs Elysées?"

"Also."

"Then let us retrace our steps, and go over the bridge at the Tuileries."

The proposal was a perfectly natural one; and the crowd, by following Billot, showed that they were eager to accede to it. But they saw sabers gleaming half-way between them and the Tuileries Gardens. The quay was occupied by a squadron of dragoons.

"Why, these cursed dragoons are, then, everywhere!" murmured the farmer.

"I say, my dear Monsieur Billot," said Pitou, "I believe that we are caught."

"Pshaw! they cannot catch five or six thousand men; and we are five or six thousand men, at least."

The dragoons on the quay were advancing slowly, it is true, at a very gentle walk; but they were visibly advancing.

"The Rue Royale still remains open to us. Come this way; come, Pitou."

Pitou followed the farmer, as if he had been his shadow.

But a line of soldiers was drawn across the street, near the St. Honoré Gate.

"Ah! ah!" muttered Billot; "you may be in the right, friend Pitou."

"Hum!" was Pitou's sole reply.

But this word expressed, by the tone in which it had been pronounced, all the regret which Pitou felt at not having been mistaken.

The crowd, by its agitation and its clamors, proved that it was not less sensible than Pitou of the position in which it was then placed.

And, in fact, by a skilful maneuver, the Prince de Lambesq had surrounded, not only the rebels, but also those who had been drawn there from mere curiosity, and, by preventing all egress by the bridges, the quays, the Champs Elysées, and the Rue Royale and Les Gueillants, he had inclosed them in a bow of iron, the string of which was represented by the walls of the Tuileries Gardens, which it would be very difficult to escalade, and the iron gate of the Bont Tournant, which it was almost impossible to force.

Billot reflected on their position ; it certainly was not a favorable one ; however, as he was a man of calm, cool mind, full of resources when in danger, he cast his eyes around him, and perceiving a pile of timber lying beside the river.

" I have an idea," said he to Pitou ; " come this way."

Pitou followed him, without asking him what the idea was.

Billot advanced toward the timber, and seizing the end of a large block, said to Pitou, " Help me to carry this."

Pitou, for his part, without questioning him as to his intentions, caught hold of the other end of the piece of timber. He had such implicit confidence in the farmer that he would have gone down to the infernal regions with him, without even making any observation as to the length of the descent.

They were soon upon the quay again, bearing a load which five or six men of ordinary strength would have found difficult to raise.

Strength is always a subject of admiration to the mob, and although so compactly huddled together, they made room for Billot and Pitou to pass through them.

Then, as they felt convinced that the maneuver which was being accomplished was a maneuver of general interest, some men walked before Billot, crying, " Make room ! make room ! "

" Tell me now, Father Billot," inquired Pitou, after having carried the timber some thirty yards, " are we going far in this way ! "

" We are going as far as the gate of the Tuileries."

"Ho ! ho !" cried the crowd, who at once divined his intention.

And it made way for them more eagerly even than before.

Pitou looked about him, and saw that the gate was not more than thirty paces distant from them.

"I can reach it," said he, with the brevity of a Pythagorean.

The labor was so much the easier to Pitou, from five or six of the strongest of the crowd taking their share in the burden.

The result of this was a very notable acceleration in their progress.

In five minutes they had reached the iron gate.

"Come, now," said Billot, "clap your shoulders to it and all push together !"

"Good !" said Pitou. "I understand it now. We have just made a warlike engine ; the Romans use to call it a ram."

"Now, my boys," cried Billot, "once, twice, thrice !" And the joist, directed with a furious impetus, struck the lock of the gate with resounding violence.

The soldiers who were on guard in the interior of the garden hastened to resist this invasion. But at the third stroke the gate gave way, turning violently on its hinges, and through that gaping and gloomy mouth the crowd rushed impetuously.

From the movement that was then made the Prince de Lambesq perceived at once that an opening had been effected which allowed the escape of those whom he had considered as his prisoners. He was furious with disappointment. He urged his horse forward in order the better to judge of the position of affairs. The dragoons who were drawn up behind him imagined that the order had been given to charge, and they followed him. The horses, going off at full speed, could not be suddenly pulled up. The men, who wished to be revenged for the check they had received on the square before the Palace Royal, scarcely endeavored to restrain them.

The prince saw that it would be impossible to moderate their advance, and allowed himself to be borne away by it. A sudden shriek, uttered by the women and children, ascended to heaven, crying for vengeance against the brutal soldiers.

"HE RAN AND THREW HIS ARMS ROUND HIS FATHER'S NECK, UTTERING
A CRY OF JOY"

Dumas, Vol. Nine

A frightful scene then occurred, rendered still more terrific by the darkness. Those who were charged upon became mad with pain; those who charged them were mad with anger.

Then a species of defense was organized from the top of a terrace. The chairs were hurled down on the dragoons. The Prince of Lambesq, who had been struck on the head, replied by giving a saber cut to the person nearest him, without considering that he was punishing an innocent man instead of a guilty one, and an old man more than seventy years of age fell beneath his sword.

Billot saw this man fall, and uttered a loud cry. In a moment his carbine was at his shoulder. A furrow of light for a moment illuminated the darkness, and the prince had then died, had not his horse, by chance, reared at the same instant.

The horse received the ball in his neck, and fell.

It was thought that the prince was killed; the dragoons then rushed into the Tuileries, pursuing the fugitives, and firing their pistols at them.

But the fugitives, having now a greater space, dispersed among the trees.

Billot reloaded his carbine.

"In good faith, Pitou," said he, "I think that you were right. We really have arrived just in the nick of time."

"If I should become a bold, daring fellow," said Pitou, discharging his musketoon at the thickest group of dragoons. "It seems to me not so difficult as I had thought."

"Yes," replied Billot; "but useless courage is not real courage. Come this way, Pitou, and take care that your sword does not get between your legs."

"Wait a moment for me, dear Monsieur Billot; if I should lose you, I should not know which way to go. I do not know Paris as you do; I was never here before."

"Come along, come along," said Billot; and he went by the terrace by the water-side until he had got ahead of the line of troops which was advancing along the quay; but this time as rapidly as they could, to give their aid to the Lambesq dragoons, should such aid be necessary.

When they reached the end of the terrace, Billot seated himself on the parapet and jumped on to the quay.

Pitou followed his example.

CHAPTER XII.

ONCE upon the quay, the two countrymen saw glittering on the bridge near the Tuileries the arms of another body of men, which, in all probability, was not a body of friends; they silently glided to the end of the quay and descended the bank which leads along the Seine.

The clock of the Tuileries was just then striking eleven.

When they had got beneath the trees which line the banks of the river, fine aspen trees and poplars which bathe their feet in its current; when they were lost to the sight of their pursuers, hid by their friendly foliage, the farmer and Pitou threw themselves upon the grass and opened a council of war.

The question was to know, and this was suggested by the farmer, whether they should remain where they were; that is to say, in safety, or comparatively so, or whether they should again throw themselves into the tumult and take their share of the struggle which was going on, and which appeared likely to be continued the greater part of the night.

The question being mooted, Billot awaited the reply of Pitou.

Pitou had risen very greatly in the opinion of the farmer. In the first place, by the knowledge of which he had given proofs the day before, and afterward by the courage of which he had given such proofs during the evening.

Pitou instinctively felt this, but instead of being prouder from it, he was only the more grateful toward the good farmer. Pitou was naturally very humble.

"Monsieur Billot," said he, "it is evident that you are more brave, and I less a poltroon than I imagined. Horace, who, however, was a very different man to us, with regard to poetry, at least, threw away his arms and ran off at the very first blow. As to me I have still my musketoon, my cartridge-box, and my saber, which proves that I am braver than Horace."

"Well, what are you driving at?"

"What I mean is this, dear Monsieur Billot : that the bravest man in the world may be killed by a ball."

"And what then?" inquired the farmer.

"And then, my dear sir, thus it is : as you stated, on leaving your farm, that you were coming to Paris for an important object——"

"Oh, confound it! that is true, for the casket."

"Well, then, did you come about this casket—yes or no?"

"I came about the casket, by a thousand thunders! and for nothing else."

"If you should allow yourself to be killed by a ball, the affair for which you came cannot be accomplished."

"In truth, you are ten times right, Pitou."

"Do you hear that crashing noise—those cries?" continued Pitou, encouraged by the farmer's approbation; "wood is being torn like paper, iron is being twisted as if it were but hemp."

"It is because the people are angry, Pitou."

"But, it appears to me," Pitou ventured to say, "that the king is tolerably angry, too."

"How say you, the king?"

"Undoubtedly; the Austrians, the Germans, the Kainserliks, as you call them, are the king's soldiers. Well, if they charge the people—it is the king who orders them to charge—and for him to give such an order, he must be angry too."

"You are both right and wrong, Pitou."

"That does not appear possible to me, Monsieur Billot, and I dare not say to you that had you studied logic, you would not venture on such a paradox."

"You are right and you are wrong, Pitou, and I will presently make you comprehend how this can be."

"I do not ask anything better, but I doubt it."

"See you, now, Pitou, there are two parties at court : that of the king, who loves the people, and that of the queen, who loves the Austrians."

"That is because the king is a Frenchman, and the queen an Austrian," philosophically replied Pitou.

"Wait a moment. On the king's side are Monsieur Turgot and Monsieur Necker; on the queen's Monsieur de Breteuil and the Polignacs. The king is not the master, since he has been obliged to send away Monsieur

Turgot and Monsieur Necker. It is, therefore, the queen who is the mistress, the Breteuils and the Polignacs; therefore, all goes badly.

"Do you see, Pitou, the evil proceeds from Madame Deficit, and Madame Deficit is in a rage, and it is in her name that the troops charge; the Austrians defend the Austrian women—that is natural enough."

"Your pardon, Monsieur Billot," said Pitou, interrupting him, "but *deficit* is a Latin word which means to say a want of something. What is it that is wanting?"

"Zounds! why, money, to be sure; and it is because money is wanting, it is because the queen's favorites have devoured this money which is wanting, that the queen is called Madame Deficit. It is not, therefore, the king who is angry, but the queen. The king is only vexed—vexed that everything goes so badly."

"I comprehend," said Pitou; "but the casket?"

"That is true—that is true, Pitou; these devilish politics always drag me on further than I would go—yes, the casket before everything. You are right, Pitou; when I shall have seen Doctor Gilbert, why, then we can return to politics—it is a sacred duty."

"There is nothing more sacred than sacred duties," said Pitou.

"Well, then, let us go to the College Louis le Grand, where Sebastian Gilbert now is," said Billot.

"Let us go," said Pitou, sighing; for he would be compelled to leave a bed of moss-like grass, to which he had accustomed himself. Besides which, notwithstanding the over-excitement of the evening, sleep, the assiduous host of pure consciences and tired limbs, had descended with all its poppies to welcome the virtuous and heartily tired Pitou.

Billot was already on his feet, and Pitou was about to rise when the half hour struck.

"But," said Billot, "at half-past eleven o'clock, the College of Louis le Grand must, it would appear to me, be closed."

"Oh, most assuredly!" said Pitou.

"And then, in the dark," continued Billot, "we might fall into some ambuscade; it seems to me that I see the fires of a bivouac in the direction of the Palace of Justice. I may be arrested, or I may be killed; you are right, Pitou, I must not be arrested—I must not be killed."

It was the third time since that morning that Pitou's ears had been saluted with those words so flattering human pride :

"You are right."

Pitou thought he could not do better than to repeat the words of Billot.

"You are right," he repeated, lying down again upon the grass, "you must not allow yourself to be killed, dear Monsieur Billot."

And the conclusion of this phrase died away in Pitou's throat. *Vox faucibus hæsit*, he might have added, had he been awake ; but he was fast asleep.

Billot did not perceive it.

"An idea !" said he.

"Ah !" snored Pitou.

"Listen to me, I have an idea. Notwithstanding all the precautions I am taking, I may be killed. I may be cut down by a saber, or killed from a distance by a ball—killed suddenly upon the spot ; if that should happen, you ought to know what you will have to say to Doctor Gilbert in my stead ; but you must be mute, Pitou."

Pitou heard not a word of this, and consequently made no reply.

"Should I be wounded mortally, and not be able to fulfil my mission, you will, in my place, seek out Doctor Gilbert, and you will say to him—do you understand me, Pitou ?" added the farmer, stooping toward his companion, "and you will say to him—why, confound him, he is positively snoring, the sad fellow !"

All the excitement of Billot was at once damped on ascertaining that Pitou was asleep.

"Well, let us sleep, then," said he ; and he laid himself down by Pitou's side, without grumbling very seriously. For, however accustomed to fatigue, the ride of the previous day, and the events of the evening, did not fail to have a soporific effect on the good farmer.

And the day broke about three hours after they had gone to sleep, or, rather, we should say, after their senses were benumbed.

When they again opened their eyes, Paris had lost nothing of that savage countenance which they had observed the night before.

Only there were no soldiers to be seen, the people were everywhere.

The people arming themselves with pikes, hastily manufactured, with muskets, which the majority of them knew not how to handle, with magnificent weapons made centuries before, and of which the bearers admired the ornments, some being inlaid with gold or ivory, or mother-of-pearl, without comprehending the use or the mechanism of them.

Immediately after the retreat of the soldiers, the populace had pillaged the palace called the Garde Meuble.

And the people dragged toward the Hôtel de Ville two small pieces of artillery.

The alarm-bell was rung from the towers of Notre Dame, at the Hôtel de Ville, and in all the parish churches. There were seen issuing—and from where no one could tell—but as from beneath the pavement, legions of men and women, squalid, emaciated, in filthy rags, half naked, who, but the evening before, cried, "Give us bread!" but now vociferated, "Give us arms!"

Nothing could be more terrifying than these bands of specters, who, during the last three months, had poured into the capital from the country, passing through the city gates silently, and installing themselves in Paris, where famine reigned, like Arabian ghouls in a cemetery.

On that day, the whole of France, represented in Paris by the starving people from each province, cried to its king, "Give us liberty!" and to its God. "Give us food!"

Billot, who was first to wake, roused up Pitou, and they both set off to the College Louis le Grand, looking around them, shuddering and terrified at the miserable creatures they saw on every side.

By degrees, as they advanced toward that part of the town which we now call the Latin Quarter, as they ascended the Rue de la Harpe, as they approached the Rue St. Jacques, they saw, as during the times of La Fronde, barricades being raised in every street. Women and children were carrying to the tops of the houses ponderous folio volumes, heavy pieces of furniture, and precious marble ornaments, destined to crush the foreign soldiers, in case of their venturing into the narrow and tortuous streets of old Paris.

From time to time, Billot observed one or two of the

French Guards, forming the center of some meeting which they were organizing, and which, with marvelous rapidity, they were teaching the handling of a musket, exercises which women and children were curiously observing, and almost with a desire of learning them themselves.

Billot and Pitou found the college of Louis le Grand in flagrant insurrection ; the pupils had risen against their teachers, and had driven them from the building. At the moment when the farmer and his companion reached the grated gate, the scholars were attacking this gate, uttering loud threats, to which the affrighted principal replied with tears.

The farmer, for a moment, gazed on this intestine revolt, when suddenly, in a stentorian voice, he cried out :

" Which of you here is called Sebastian Gilbert ? "

" 'Tis I," replied a young lad, about fifteen years of age, of almost feminine beauty, and who, with the assistance of four or five of his comrades, was carrying a ladder wherewith to escalade the walls, seeing that they could not force open the gate.

" Come nearer to me, my child."

" What is it that you want with me ? " said young Sebastian to Billot.

" Do you wish to take him away ? " cried the principal, terrified at the aspect of two armed men, one of whom, the one who had spoken to young Gilbert, was covered with blood.

The boy, on his side, looked with astonishment at these two men, and was endeavoring, but uselessly, to recognize his foster-brother, Pitou, who had grown so immeasurably tall since he last saw him, and who was altogether metamorphosed by the warlike accouterments he had put on.

" Take him away ! " exclaimed Billot, " take away Monsieur Gilbert's son, and lead him into all this turmoil —expose him to receiving some unhappy blow ? Oh, no, indeed ! "

" Do you see, Sebastian," said the principal, " do you see, you furious fellow, that even your friends will have nothing to do with you ? For, in short, these gentlemen appear to be your friends. Come, gentlemen, come, my young pupils, come, my children," cried the poor principal, " obey me—obey me, I command you—obey me, I entreat you ! "

" *Oro obtestorque,*" said Piton.

" Sir," said young Gilbert, with a firmness that was extraordinary in a youth of his age, " return my comrades,
if such be your pleasure, but as to me, do you understand
me, I will go out."

He made a movement toward the gate; the professor
caught him by the arm.

But he, shaking his fine auburn curls upon his pallid
forehead :

" Sir," said he, " beware of what you are doing. I am
not in the same position as your other pupils—my father
has been arrested, imprisoned—my father is in the power
of the tyrants."

" In the power of the tyrants!" exclaimed the Billot.
" Speak, my child ; what is it that you mean ? "

" Yes, yes," cried several of the scholars, " Sebastian is
right ; his father has been arrested ; and, since the people
have opened the prisons, he wishes they should open his
father's prison, too."

" Oh ! oh !" said the farmer, shaking the bars of the
gate with his herculean arms, " they have arrested Doctor
Gilbert, have they ? By Heaven ! my little Catherine,
then, was right."

" Yes, sir," continued young Gilbert ; " they have arrested my father, and that is why I wish to get out, why
I wish to take a musket, why I wish to fight, until I have
liberated my dear father."

And these words were accompanied and encouraged by
a hundred furious voices, crying, in every key :

" Arms ! arms ! Let us have arms ! "

On hearing these cries, the crowd, which had collected
in the street, animated in its turn by a heroic ardor, rushed
toward the gate to give liberty to the collegians.

The principal threw himself upon his knees between his
scholars and the invaders, and held out his arms with a
supplicating gesture.

" Oh, my friends, my friends," cried he, " respect my
children."

" Do we not respect them ? " said a French Guard ;
" I believe we do, indeed. They are fine boys, and they
will do their exercise admirably."

" My friends, my friends, these children are a sacred
deposit which their parents have confided to me ; I am

responsible for them ; their parents calculate upon me ; for them I would sacrifice my life ; but, in the name of Heaven, do not take away these children !"

Hooting, proceeding from the street—that is to say, from the hindmost ranks of the crowd, replied to these piteous supplications.

Billot rushed forward, opposing the French Guards, the crowd, the scholars themselves.

"He is right, it is a sacred trust. Let them fight, let men get themselves killed, but let children live—they are seed for the future."

A disapproving murmur followed these words.

"Who is it that murmurs ?" cried Billot ; "assuredly, it cannot be a father. I, who am now speaking to you, had two men killed in my arms ; their blood is upon my shirt. See this !"

And he showed his shirt and waistcoat, all begrimed with blood, and with a dignified movement which electrified the crowd.

"Yesterday," continued Billot, "I fought at the Palais Royal, and at the Tuileries ; and this lad also fought there, but this lad has neither father nor mother ; moreover, he is almost a man."

And he pointed to Pitou, who looked proudly around him.

"To-day," continued Billot, "I shall fight again ; but let no one say to me—the Parisians were not strong enough to contend against the foreign soldiers, and they called children to their aid."

"Yes, yes," resounded on every side, proceeding from women in the crowd, and several of the soldiers ; "he is right, children ; go into the college ; go into the college."

"Oh, thanks, thanks, sir !" murmured the principal of the college, endeavoring to catch hold of Billot's hand through the bars of the gate.

"And, above all, take especial care of Sebastian ; keep him safe," said the latter.

"Keep me ! I say, on the contrary, that I will not be kept here !" cried the boy, livid with anger, and struggling with the college servants, who were dragging him away.

"Let me in," said Billot. "I will engage to quiet him."

The crowd made way for him to pass ; the farmer

dragged Pitou after him, and entered the courtyard of the college.

Already three or four of the French Gua~ ̇ ̇ ̇ ̇ ̇ about ten men placed themselves as sentinels at the gate, and prevented the egress of the young insurgents.

Billot went straight up to young Sebastian, and taking between his huge and horny palms the small white hands of the child :

"Sebastian," he said, "do you not recognize me ?"

"No."

"I am old Billot, your father's farmer."

"I know you now, sir."

"And this lad," rejoined Billot, pointing to his companion, "do you know him ?"

"Ange Pitou," said the boy.

"Yes, Sebastian, it is me—it is me."

And Pitou, weeping with joy, threw his arms round the neck of his foster-brother and former schoolfellow.

"Well," said the boy, whose brow still remained scowling, "what is now to be done ?"

"What ?" cried Billot. "Why, if they have taken your father from you, I will restore him to you. Do you understand ?"

"You ?"

"Yes, I—I, and all those who are out yonder with me. What the devil ! Yesterday we had to deal with the Austrians, and we saw their cartridge-boxes."

"In proof of which, I have one of them," said Pitou.

"Shall we not release his father ?" cried Billot, addressing the crowd.

"Yes ! yes !" roared the crowd. "We will release him !"

Sebastian shook his head.

"My father is in the Bastile," said he, in a despairing tone.

"And what then ?" cried Billot.

"The Bastile cannot be taken," replied the child.

"Then, what was it you wished to do, if such is your conviction ?"

"I wished to go to the open space before the castle. There will be fighting there, and my father might have seen me through the bars of the window."

"Impossible !"

"Impossible ? And why should I not do so ? One day, when I was walking out with all the boys here, I saw the head of a prisoner. If I could have seen my father as I saw that prisoner, I should have recognized him, and said : 'Do not be unhappy, father, I love you !'"

"And if the soldiers of the Bastile should have killed you ? "

"Well, then, they would have killed me under the eyes of my father."

"The death of all the devils ! " exclaimed Billot. "You are a wicked lad, to think of getting yourself killed in your father's sight, and make him die of grief in a cage—he who has only you in the world, he who loves you so tenderly ! Decidedly, you have a bad heart, Gilbert."

And the farmer pushed the boy from him.

"Yes, yes ; a wicked heart," howled Pitou, bursting into tears.

Sebastian did not reply.

And while he was meditating in gloomy silence, Billot was admiring his beautifully pale face, his flashing eyes, his ironical expressive mouth, his well-shaped nose, and his strongly developed chin—all of which gave testimony at once of his nobility of soul and nobility of race.

"You say that your father is in the Bastile," said the farmer, at length breaking the silence.

"Yes."

"And for what ? "

"Because my father is the friend of Lafayette and Washington ; because my father has fought with his sword for the independence of America, and with his pen for the liberty of France ; because my father is well known in both worlds as the detestor of tyranny ; because he has called down curses on the Bastile, in which so many have suffered ; and, therefore, have they sent him there ! "

"And when was this ? "

"Six days ago."

"And where did they arrest him ? "

"At Havre, where he had just landed."

"How do you know all this ? "

"I have received a letter from him."

"Dated from Havre ? "

"Yes."

"And it was at Havre itself that he was arrested ? "

"It was at Lillebonne."

"Come, now, child, do not feel angry with me, but give me all the particulars that you know. I swear to you that I will either leave my bones on the Place de la Bastile, or you shall see your father again."

Sebastian looked at the farmer, and seeing that he spoke from his heart, his angry feelings subsided.

"Well, then," said he, "at Lillebonne he had time to write in a book, with a pencil, these words :

"'Sebastian, I have been arrested, and they are taking me to the Bastile. Be patient, and study diligently. Lillebonne, 7th July, 1789.

"'P. S.—I am arrested in the cause of Liberty. I have a son in the College Louis le Grand, at Paris. The person who shall find this book is entreated, in the name of humanity, to get it conveyed to my son. His name is Sebastian Gilbert.'"

"And this book ?" inquired Billot, palpitating with emotion.

"He put a piece of gold into this book, tied a cord round it, and threw it out of the window."

"And—— ?"

"The curate of the place found it, and chose from among his parishioners a robust young man, to whom he said :

"'Leave twelve francs with your family, who are without bread, and with the other twelve go to Paris, carry this book to a poor boy whose father has just been arrested because he has too great a love for the people."

"The young man arrived here yesterday afternoon, and delivered to me my father's book. And this is the way I learned how my father had been arrested."

"Come, come," cried Billot, "this reconciles me somewhat with the priests. Unfortunately, they are not all like this one. And this worthy young man, what has become of him ?"

"He set off to return home last night. He hoped to carry back with him to his family five francs out of the twelve he had brought with him."

"Admirable ! admirable !" exclaimed Pitou, weeping for joy.

"Oh ! the people have good feelings ! Go on, Gilbert."

"Why, now, you know all."

"Yes."

"You promised me, if I would tell you all, that you would bring back my father to me. I have told you all; now, remember your promise."

"I told you that I would save him, or I would be killed in the attempt. That is true."

"And now, show me the book," said Billot.

"Here it is," said the boy, taking from his pocket a volume of the "Contrat Sociale."

"And where is your father's handwriting?"

"Here," replied the boy, pointing to what the doctor had written.

The farmer kissed the written characters.

"And now," said he, "tranquilize yourself. I am going to seek your father in the Bastile."

"Unhappy man!" cried the principal of the college, seizing Billot's hands. "How can you obtain access to a prisoner of state?"

"Zounds! by taking the Bastile."

Some of the French Guards began to laugh. In a few moments the laugh had become general.

"Why," said Billot, casting around him a glance flashing with anger, "what, then, is the Bastile, if you please?"

"Stone," said a soldier.

"Iron," said another.

"And fire," said a third. "Take care, my worthy man, you may burn your fingers."

"Yes, yes; you may burn yourself," reiterated the crowd, with horror.

"Ah, Parisians," exclaimed the farmer, "you have pick-axes, and you are afraid of stone! Ah! you have lead, and you fear iron. You have gunpowder, and you are afraid of fire. Parisians!—cowards!—Parisians!—poltroons! Parisians—machines for slavery! A thousand demons! where is the man of heart who will go with me and Pitou to take the king's Bastile? My name is Billot, a farmer of the Ile de France. Forward!"

Billot had raised himself to the very climax of audacity.

The crowd, rendered enthusiastic by his address, and, trembling with excitement, pressed around him, crying, "To the Bastile!"

Sebastian endeavored to cling to Billot, and the latter gently pushed him back.

"Child," said he, "what is the last word your father wrote to you?"

"Work," replied Sebastian.

"Well, then, work here. We are going to *work* down yonder; only our work is called destroying and killing."

The young man did not utter a word in reply. He hid his face with both hands, without even pressing the hand of Pitou, who embraced him; and he fell into such violent convulsions that he was immediately carried into the infirmary attached to the college.

"To the Bastile!" cried Billot.

"To the Bastile!" cried Pitou.

"To the Bastile!" shouted the crowd.

And they immediately commenced their march toward the Bastile.

CHAPTER XIII.

AND now we request our readers to allow us to give them an insight into the principal political events that had occurred since the period at which we abandoned the court of France.

Those who know the history of that period, or those whom dry, plain history may alarm, can skip over this chapter, and pass on to the next one, which completely dovetails in with Chapter XII.—the one we are now writing being intended for those very precise and exacting spirits who are determined to be informed on every point.

During the last year or two, something unheard of, unknown, something emanating from the past, and looking toward the future, was threatening and growling in the air.

It was the Revolution.

Voltaire had raised himself for a moment, while in his last agony, and, leaning upon his elbow in his death-bed, he had seen shining, even amid the darkness in which he was about to sleep forever, the brilliant lightnings of the dawn.

When Anne of Austria assumed the regency of France, says Cardinal de Retz, there was but one saying in every mouth, "The queen is so good!"

One day Mme. de Pompadour's physician, Quesnoy, who

had an apartment in her house, saw Louis XV. coming in. A feeling altogether unconnected with respect agitated him so much that he trembled and turned pale.

"What is the matter with you ?" said Mme. de Hausset to him.

"The matter is," replied Quesnoy, "that every time I see the king I say to myself, 'There is a man who, if he should feel so inclined, can have my head cut off.'"

"Oh, there's no danger of that !" rejoined Mme. de Hausset. "The king is so good !"

It is with these two phrases : "The king is so good !" "The queen is so good !" that the French Revolution was effected.

When Louis XV. died, France breathed again. The country was delivered at the same moment from the king, the Pompadours, the Dubarrys, and the *Parc aux Cerfs*.

The pleasures of Louis XV. had cost the nation very dear. On them alone were expended three millions of livres a year.

Fortunately, after him came a king who was young, moral, philanthropic, almost philosophical.

A king who, like the Emile of Jean Jacques Rousseau, had studied a trade, or, rather, we should say three trades.

He was a locksmith, a watchmaker, and a mechanician.

Being alarmed at the abyss over which he was suspended, the king began by refusing all favors that were asked of him. The courtiers trembled. Fortunately, there was one circumstance which reassured them—it was not the king who refused, but Turgot—it was, that the queen was not yet in reality a queen ; and, consequently, could not have that influence to-day which she might acquire to-morrow.

At last, toward the year 1777, she acquired that influence which had so long been desired. The queen became a mother. The king, who was already so good a king, so good a husband, could now also prove himself a good father.

How could anything be now refused to her who had given an heir to the crown ?

And besides, that was not all ; the king was also a good brother. The anecdote is well known of Beaumarchais being sacrificed to the Count de Provence, and yet the king did not like the Count de Provence, who was a pedant.

But, to make up for this, he was very fond of his younger brother, the Count d'Artois, the type of French wit, elegance, and nobleness.

He loved him so much that if he sometimes refused the queen any favor she might have asked of him, the Count d'Artois had only to add his solicitations to those of the queen, and the king had no longer the firmness to refuse.

It was, in fact, the reign of amiable men. M. de Calonne, one of the most amiable men in the world, was controller-general. It was Calonne who said to the queen:

"Madame, if it is possible, it is done; and if it is impossible, it shall be done."

From the very day on which this charming reply was circulated in all the drawing-rooms of Paris and Versailles, the red book, which every one had thought closed forever, was reopened.

The queen buys St. Cloud.

The king buys Rambouillet.

It is no longer the king who has lady favorites, it is the queen. Mmes. Diana and Jules de Polignac cost as much to France as La Pompadour and La Dubarry.

The queen is so good!

A reduction is proposed in the salaries of the high officers of the court. Some of them make up their minds to it. But one of the most habitual frequenters of the palace obstinately refuses to submit to this reduction; it is M. de Coigny. He meets the king in one of the corridors; a terrible scene occurs, the king runs away, and in the evening says, laughingly:

"Upon my word, I believe if I had not yielded, Coigny would have beaten me."

The king is so good!

And then the fate of a kingdom sometimes depends upon a very trivial circumstance; the spur of a page, for instance.

Louis XV. dies. Who is to succeed M. d'Aiguillon?

The king, Louis XVI., is for Marchant. Marchant is one of the ministers who had sustained the already tottering throne. Mesdames—that is to say, the king's aunts—are for M. de Maurepas, who is so amusing, and who writes such pretty songs. He wrote three volumes of them at Pontchartrain, which he calls his memoirs.

All this is a steeple-chase affair. The question was as

to who should arrive first. The king and queen at Arnouville or Mmes. de Pontchartrain.

The king has the power in his own hands ; the chances
are, therefore, in his favor.

He hastens to write :

" Set out the very moment you receive this for Paris.
I am waiting for you."

He slips his despatch into an envelope, and on the envelope he writes ·

" Monsieur le Comte de Marchant, at Arnouville."

A page of the king's stables is sent for ; the royal missive
is put into his hands, and he is ordered to mount a horse
and to go to Arnouville full speed.

And now that the page is despatched, the king can receive mesdames.

Mesdames—the same whom the king, their father, as
has been seen in " Balsamo," called Locque, Chiffe, and
Graille, three names eminently aristocratic—mesdames are
waiting at a door opposite to that by which the page goes
out, until he shall have left the room.

The page once gone out, mesdames may go in.

They go in, entreat the king in favor of M. Maurepas—
all this is a mere question of time—the king does not like
to refuse mesdames anything—the king is so good !

He will accede to their request when the page shall have
got so far on his journey that no one can come up with
him.

He contested the point with mesdames, his eyes fixed on
the time-piece. Half an hour will be sufficient for him.
The time-piece will not deceive him. It is the time-piece
which he himself regulates.

Twenty minutes have elapsed, and he yields.

" Let the page be overtaken," said he, " and all shall be
as you please."

Mesdames rush out of the room ; they will dispatch a
man on horseback ; he shall kill a horse, two horses, six
horses, but the page must be overtaken.

All these determinations are unnecessary ; not a single
horse will be killed.

In going down the staircase one of the page's spurs
struck against one of the stone steps and broke short off.
How could any one go at full speed with only one spur ?

Besides, the Chevalier d'Abrac is the chief of the great
stable, and he would not allow a courier to mount his
horse—he whose duty it was to inspect the couriers—if
the courier was about to set out in a manner that would
not do honor to the royal stables.

The page, therefore, could not set out without having
both his spurs.

The result of all this was, that instead of overtaking the
page on the road to Arnouville—galloping at full speed—
he was overtaken before he had left the courtyard of the
palace.

He was already in the saddle and was about to depart in
the most irreproachable good order.

The despatch is taken from him, the text of the missive
is left unchanged, for it was as good for the one as the
other.   Only, instead of writing the address, "To Monsieur de Marchant, at Arnouville," mesdames wrote, "To
Monsieur le Comte de Maurepas, at Pontchartrain."

The honor of the royal stable is saved, but the monarchy
is lost.

With Maurepas and Calonne, everything goes on marvelously well ; the one sings, the other plays ; but besides
the courtiers, there are the receivers-general, who also
have their functions to perform.

Louis XIV. began his reign by ordering two receivers-
general to be hanged, and with the advice of Colbert ;
after which he took Lavallière for his mistress and built
Versailles.   Lavallière cost him nothing.

But Versailles, in which he wished to lodge her, cost
him a round sum.

Then, in 1685, under the pretext that they were Pro-
testants, he drove a million of industrious men from
France.

And thus, in 1707, still under the *great* king, Boisguil-
bert said, speaking of 1698 :

"Things still went on well in those days : there was yet
some oil in the lamp.   But now all has come to an end
for want of aliment."

What could be said eighty years afterward, when the
Dubarrys, the Polignacs, had taken their fill ?   After

having made the people sweat water, they would make them sweat blood. That was all.

And all this in so delightful and polite a manner.

In former days the contractors of the public revenue were harsh, brutal, and cold, as the prison gates into which they cast their victims.

But in these days they are philanthropists; with one hand they despoil the people, that is true; but with the other they build hospitals for them.

One of my friends, a great financier, has assured me that out of one hundred and twenty millions, which the town dues bring in, the contractors managed to keep seventy millions for themselves.

It happened that at a meeting where the state of expenses was demanded, a counselor playing upon the word, said:

"It is not any particular state that we require; what we want are the states-general."

The sparks fell upon gunpowder, the powder ignited and caused a general conflagration.

Every one repeated the saying of the counselor, and the states-general were loudly called for.

The court fixed the opening of the states-general for the 1st of March, 1798.

On the 24th of August, 1788, M. de Brienne withdrew from public affairs. He was another who had managed the financial affairs with tolerable recklessness.

But on withdrawing he, at least, gave good counsel; he advised that Necker should be recalled.

Necker resumed the administration of affairs, and all again breathed confidence.

Notwithstanding this, the great question of the three orders were discussed throughout France.

Sieyes published his famous pamphlets upon the Tiers Etat.*

Dauphiny, the states of which province still met in spite of all the court could do, decided that the representations of the Tiers-Etat should be on an equality with that of the nobility and the clergy.

The assembly of the notables was reconstructed.

This assembly lasted thirty-six days; that is to say, from the 6th of November to the 8th of December, 1788.

* The Third Order, or Third Estate.

On this occasion the elements performed their part.
When the whip of kings does not suffice, the whip of the
Creator whistles in the air and compels the people to move
onward.

Winter came, accompanied by famine. Hunger and
cold opened the gates of 1789.

Paris was filled with troops ; its streets with patrols.

Two or three times the muskets of the soldiers were
loaded in the presence of the people who were dying with
hunger.

And then, the muskets being loaded, and the moment
having arrived for using them, they did not use them
at all.

One morning, the 28th of April, five days before the
opening of the states-general, a name was circulated among
the crowd.

This name was accompanied by maledictions, and the
most vituperative because this name was that of a workman who had become rich.

Reveillon, as was then asserted, Reveillon, the director
of the celebrated paper manufactory of the Faubourg St.
Antoine, Reveillon had said that the wages of workmen
ought to be reduced to fifteen sous a day.

And this was true.

It was also said that the court was about to decorate
him with the Black Ribbon—that is to say, with the Order
of St. Michael.

But this was an absurdity.

There is always some absurd rumor in popular commotions. And it is remarkable that it is also by this
rumor that they increase their numbers, that they recruit,
and at last become a revolution.

The crowd makes an effigy, baptizes it with the name of
Reveillon, decorates it with the Black Ribbon, sets fire to
it before Reveillon's own door, and then proceeds to the
square before the Hôtel de Ville, where it completes the
burning of the effigy before the eyes of the municipal
authorities, who see it burning.

Impunity emboldens the crowd, who give notice that
after having done justice on the effigy they will the following day do justice on the real person of the offender.

This was a challenge in due form addressed to the
public authorities.

The authorities sent thirty of the French Guards; and even then it was not the authorities who sent them, but their colonel, M. de Biron.

These thirty French Guards were merely witnesses of this great duel which they could not prevent. They looked on while the mob was pillaging the manufactory, throwing the furniture out of the windows, breaking everything, burning everything. Amid this hubbub, five hundred louis in gold was stolen.

They drank the wine in the cellars, and when there was no more wine, they drank the colors of the manufactory, which they took for wine.

The whole of the day of the 27th was employed in effecting this villainous spoliation.

A reinforcement was sent to the thirty men; it consisted of several companies of the French Guards, who, in the first place, fired blank cartridges, then balls. Toward evening there came to the support of the guards part of the Swiss regiment of M. de Bezenval.

The Swiss never make a jest of matters connected with revolution.

The Swiss forgot to take the balls out of their cartridges, and as the Swiss are naturally sportsmen and good marksmen, too, about twenty of the pillagers remained upon the pavement.

Some of them had about them a portion of the five hundred louis which we have mentioned, and which, from the secretary of Reveillon, had passed into the pockets of the pillagers, and from the pockets of the pillagers into those of the Swiss Guards.

Bezenval had done all this; he had done it out of his own head, as the vulgar saying has it.

The king did not thank him for what he had done, nor did he blame him for it.

Now, when the king does not thank, the king blames.

The parliament opened an inquiry.

The king closed it.

The king was so good!

Who it was that had stirred on the people to do this, no one could tell.

Has it not been often seen, during the great heats of summer, that conflagrations have taken place without any apparent cause?

The Duke of Orleans was accused of having excited this disturbance.

The accusation was absurd, and it fell to the ground.

On the 29th Paris was perfectly tranquil, or, at least, appeared to be so.

The 4th of May arrived. The king and the queen went in procession with the whole court to the Cathedral of Notre Dame to hear the "Veni Creator."

There were great shouts of "Long live the king!" and, above all, of "Long live the queen!"

The queen was so good!

This was the last day of peace.

The next day the shouts of "Long live the queen!" were not so frequent, but the mob cried more frequently, "Long live the Duke of Orleans!"

These cries wounded her feelings much, poor woman! She who detested the duke to such a degree that she said he was a coward.

As if there had ever been a coward in the Orleans family! from Monsieur, who gained the battle of Cassel, down to the Duke of Chartres who contributed to the gaining of those at Jemappes and Valmy.

It went so far that the poor woman was near fainting; she was supported, her head leaning on her shoulder.

Mme. Campan relates this incident in her memoirs.

But this reclining head raised itself up, haughty and disdainful. Those who saw the expression of those features were at once cured, and forever, of using the expression:

The queen is so good!

There exists three portraits of the queen: one painted in 1776, another in 1784, and a third in 1788.

I have seen all three of them. See them in your turn. If ever these three portraits are placed in the same gallery, the history of Marie Antoinette can be read in those three portraits.*

The meeting of the three orders, which was to have produced a general pacification, proved a declaration of war.

" Three orders," said Sieyes; "no, three nations."

On the 3d of May, the eve of the mass of the Holy Ghost, the king received the deputies at Versailles.

Some persons counseled him to substitute cordiality for etiquette.

* The three portraits are at Versailles.

The king would not listen to anything.

He, in the first place, received the clergy.

After them the nobility.

At last the Tiers Etat.

The Third had been waiting a long time.

The Third murmured.

In the assemblies of former times, the Tiers Etat pronounced their discourses on their knees.

There was no possibility of inducing the president of the Tiers Etat to go down on his knees.

It was decided that the Tiers Etat should not pronounce an oration.

In the sittings of the 5th the king put on his hat.

The nobility put on their hats.

The Tiers Etat were about to put on their hats also, but the king then took off his. He preferred holding it in his hand to seeing the Tiers Etat covered in his presence.

On Wednesday, the 10th of June, Sieyès entered the assembly; he found it almost entirely composed of the Tiers Etat.

The clergy and the nobility were assembled elsewhere.

"Let us cut the cable," said Sieyès, "it is now time."

And Sieyès proposed that the clergy and the nobility should be summoned to attend within an hour from that time at the latest.

In case of non-appearance, default should be pronounced against the absent

A German and Swiss army surrounded Versailles. A battery of artillery was pointed against the assembly.

Sieyès saw nothing of all this; he saw the people who were starving; but the Third, Sieyès was told, could not, of itself, form the states-general.

"So much the better," replied Sieyès; "it will form the National Assembly."

The absent did not present themselves; the proposal of Sieyès was adopted; the Tiers Etat called itself the National Assembly by a majority of four hundred votes.

On the 19th of June, the king orders the building in which the National Assembly held their meetings to be closed.

But the king, in order to accomplish such a *coup d'état*, needed some pretext.

The hall is closed for the purpose of making prepara-

tions for a royal sitting, which was to take place on the
following Monday.

On the 20th of June, at seven in the morning, the President of the National Assembly is informed that there will
be no meeting on that day.

At eight o'clock he presents himself at the door of the
hall, with a great number of the deputies.

The doors are closed, and sentinels are guarding the
doors.

The rain is falling.

They wish to break open the doors.

The sentinels had received their orders, and they present
their bayonets.

One of the deputies proposes that they should meet at
the Place d'Armes.

Another that it should be at Marly.

Guillotin proposes the Jeu de Paume.*

Guillotin!

What a strange thing that it should be Guillotin, whose
name, by adding an *e* to it, should become so celebrated
four years afterward,—how strange that it should be Guillotin who proposed the Jeu de Paume!

The Jeu de Paume, unfurnished, dilapidated, open to
the four winds of heaven.

To this great demonstration the king replies by the
royal word, "Veto!"

M. de Breze is sent to the rebels, to order them to
disperse.

"We are here by the will of the people," said Mirabeau,
"and we will not leave this place but with bayonets pointed
at our breasts!"

And not as it has been asserted, that he said, "By the
force of bayonets." Why is it that there is always behind
great men some paltry rhetorician who spoils his sayings,
under pretext of arranging them?

Why was there such a rhetorician behind Mirabeau at
the Jeu de Paume?

And behind Cambronne at Waterloo?

The reply was at once reported to the king.

He walked about for some time with the air of a man
who was suffering from ennui.

"They will not go away?" said he.

* The tennis-court.

" No, sire."

" Well, then, leave them where they are."

As is here shown, royalty was already bending beneath the hand of the people, and bending very low.

From the 21st of June to the 12th of July, all appeared tolerably calm, but it was that species of calm which so frequently precedes the tempest.

It was like the uneasy dream of an uneasy slumber.

On the 11th the king formed the resolution, urged to it by the queen, the Count d'Artois, the Polignacs—in fact, the whole of the Camarilla of Versailles; in short, he dismissed Necker.

On the 12th this intelligence reached Paris.

The effect which it produced has been already seen. On the evening of the 13th Billot arrived just in time to see the barriers burning.

On the 13th, in the evening, Paris was defending itself.

On the 14th, in the morning, Paris was ready to attack.

On the morning of the 14th Billot cried, " To the Bastile !" and three thousand men, imitating Billot, reiterated the same cry, which was about to become that of the whole population of Paris.

The reason was that there had existed during five centuries a monument which weighed heavily upon the breast of France, like the infernal rock upon the shoulders of Sisyphus.

" Only that, less confiding than the Titan in his strength, France had never attempted to throw it off.

This monument, the seal of feudality, imprinted on the forehead of Paris, was the Bastile.

The king was too good, as Mme. de Hausset had said, to have a head cut off.

But the king sent people to the Bastile.

When once a man became acquainted with the Bastile, by order of the king, that man was forgotten, sequestrated interred, annihilated.

He remained there until the king remembered him ; and kings have so many new things occurring around them every day, and of which they are obliged to think, that they often forget to think of old matters.

Moreover, in France there was not only one Bastile, there were twenty other Bastiles, which were called Fort l'Evêque St. Lazare the Châtelet, the Conciergerie, Vincennes, the

Castle of La Roche, the Castle of If, the Isles of St. Marguerite, Pignerolles, etc.

Only the fortress at the Gate St. Antoine was called the Bastile, as Rome was called *the* city.

It was the Bastile, *par excellence,* alone; it was of more importance than all the others.

During nearly a whole century, the governorship of the Bastile had continued in one and the same family.

The grandfather of this elect race was M. de Châteauneuf; his son Lavrillière succeeded him, who, in turn, was succeeded by his grandson, St. Florentin. The dynasty became extinct in 1777.

During this triple reign, the greater part of which passed during the reign of Louis XV., it would be impossible to state the number of *lettres de cachet.** St. Florentin alone received more than fifty thousand.

The *lettres de cachet* were a great source of revenue.

They were sold to fathers who wished to get rid of their sons.

They were sold to women who wished to get rid of their husbands.

The prettier the wives were, the less did the *lettre de cachet* cost them.

It then became, between them and the minister, an exchange of polite attentions, and that was all.

Since the end of the reign of Louis XIV., all the state prisons, and particularly the Bastile, were in the hands of the Jesuits.

Among the prisoners, it will be recollected, the following were of the greatest note.

The Iron Mask, Lauzun, Latude.

The Jesuits were connoisseurs; for greater security they confessed the prisoners.

For greater security still, the prisoners were buried under supposititious names.

The Iron Mask, it will be remembered, was buried under the name of Marchiali. He had remained forty-five years in prison.

Lauzun remained there fourteen years.

Latude, thirty years.

But, at all events, the Iron Mask and Lauzun had committed heinous crimes.

* Secret orders of imprisonment.

The Iron Mask, whether brother or not of Louis XIV., it is asserted, resembled King Louis XIV. so strongly that it was almost impossible to distinguish the one from the other.

It is exceedingly imprudent to dare to resemble a king.

Lauzun had been very near marrying, or did actually marry, the Grand Mademoiselle.

It is exceedingly imprudent to dare to marry the niece of King Louis XIII., the granddaughter of Henry IV.

But Latude, poor devil, what had he done ?

He had dared to fall in love with Mlle. Poisson, Dame de Pompadour, the king's mistress.

He had written a note to her.

This note, which a respectable woman would have sent back to the man who wrote it, was handed by Mme. de Pompadour to M. de Sartines, the lieutenant-general of police.

And Latude, arrested, fugitive, taken and retaken, remained thirty years locked up in the Bastile, the Castle of Vincennes and Bicêtre.

It was not, therefore, without reason that the Bastile was abhorred.

The people hated it as if it were a living thing ; they had formed of it a gigantic chimera, one of those monsters like those of Gevaudan, who pitilessly devour the human species.

The grief of poor Sebastian Gilbert will, therefore, be fully comprehended when he was informed that his father was in the Bastile.

Billot's conviction will be also understood : that the doctor would never be released from his prison unless he was released by force.

The frantic impulse of the people will be also understood when Billot vociferated, " To the Bastile ! "

Only that it was a senseless idea, as the soldiers had remarked, that the Bastile could be taken.

The Bastile had provisions, a garrison, artillery.

The Bastile had walls which were fifteen feet thick at their summit and forty at their base.

The Bastile had a governor, whose name was De Launay who had stored thirty thousand pounds of gunpowder in his cellars, and who had sworn, in case of being surprised by a *coup de main*, to blow up the Bastile, and with it half the Faubourg St. Antoine.

CHAPTER XIV.

BILLOT still walked on, but it was no longer he who shouted. The crowd, delighted with his martial air, recognized in this man one of their own class ; commenting on his words and action, they followed him, still increasing like the waves of the incoming tide.

Behind Billot, when he issued from the narrow streets and came upon the Quay St. Michael, marched more than three thousand men, armed with cutlasses, or pikes, or guns.

They all cried, "To the Bastile ! to the Bastile !"

Billot counseled with his own thoughts. The reflections which we have made at the close of the last chapter presented themselves to his mind, and by degrees all the fumes of his feverish excitement evaporated.

Then he saw clearly into his own mind.

The enterprise was sublime, but insensate. This was easily to be understood, from the affrighted and ironical countenances on which were reflected the impression produced by the cry of "To the Bastile !"

But, nevertheless, he was only the more strengthened in his resolution.

He could not, however, but comprehend that he was responsible to mothers, wives, and children for the lives of the men who were following him, and he felt bound to use every possible precaution.

Billot, therefore, began by leading his little army on to the square in the front of the Hôtel de Ville.*

There he appointed his lieutenant and other officers— watch-dogs—to restrain the flock.

"Let us see," thought Billot, "there is a power in France—there are even two—there are even three. Let us consult."

He entered the Hôtel de Ville, asking who was the chief of the municipality.

He was told it was the provost of the merchants, the Mayor of Paris, M. de Flesselles.

* Town House or City Hall.

"Ah! ah!" cried he, with a dissatisfied air, "Monsieur *de* Flesselles, a noble—that is to say, an enemy of the people."

"Why, no," they replied to him; "he is a man of talent."

Billot ascended the staircase of the Hôtel de Ville.

In the ante-chamber he met an usher.

"I wish to speak with Monsieur Flesselles," said he, perceiving that the usher was approaching him to ask him what he wanted.

"Impossible!" replied the usher; "he is now occupied in drawing up the lists of a militia force which the city is about to organize."

"That falls out marvelously well," observed Billot; "for I also am organizing a militia, and as I have already three thousand men enlisted, I am as good as Monsieur de Flesselles, who has not a single soldier yet afoot. Enable me, therefore, to speak with Monsieur de Flesselles, and that instantly. Oh! look out of the window, if you will."

The usher had, in fact, cast a rapid glance upon the quays, and had perceived Billot's men. He, therefore, hastened to inform the mayor, to whom he showed the three thousand men in question, as a postscript to his message.

This inspired the provost with a sort of respect for the person who wished to see him; he left the council-room and went into the ante-chamber, looking about for his visitor.

He perceived Billot, guessed that he was the person, and smiled.

"It was you who were asking for me, was it not?" said he.

"You are Monsieur de Flesselles, Provost of the Merchants, I believe?" replied Billot.

"Yes, sir. In what way can I be of service to you? Only speak quickly, for my mind is much occupied."

"Good Monsieur Provost," continued Billot, "how many powers are there in France?"

"Why, that is as people may choose to understand it, my dear sir," replied Flesselles.

"Say it, then, as you yourself understand it."

"Were you to consult Monsieur Bailly, he would tell you there is but one, the National Assembly; if you consult Monsieur de Dreux Breze, he would also tell you there is but one—the king."

"And you, Monsieur Provost—of these two opinions which is yours?"

"My own opinion, and above all, at the present moment is, that there is but one."

"The assembly or the king?" demanded Billot.

"Neither the one nor the other—it is the nation," replied Flesselles, playing with the frill of his shirt.

"Ah! ah! the nation?" cried the farmer.

"Yes; that is to say, those gentlemen who are waiting down yonder on the quay with knives and roasting-spits. The nation—by that I mean everybody."

"You may, perhaps, be right, Monsieur de Flesselles," replied Billot; "and they were not wrong in telling me that you are a man of talent."

De Flesselles bowed.

"To which of these three powers do you think of appealing, sir?" asked Flesselles.

"Upon my faith," said Billot, "I believe that when one has anything very important to ask, a man had better address himself at once to God and not to His saints."

"Which means to say that you are about to address yourself to the king?"

"I am inclined to do so."

"Would it be indiscreet to inquire what it is you think of asking of the king?"

"The liberation of Doctor Gilbert, who is in the Bastile."

"Doctor Gilbert?" solemnly asked M. de Flesselles; "he is a writer of pamphlets, is he not?"

"Say a philosopher, sir."

"That is one and the same thing, my dear Monsieur Billot. I think you stand but a poor chance of obtaining what you desire from the king."

"And why so?"

"In the first place, because, if the king sent Doctor Gilbert to the Bastile, he must have had reason for so doing."

"'Tis well," replied Billot; "he shall give me his reasons on the subject, and I will give him mine."

"My dear Monsieur Billot, the king is just now very busy, and he would not even receive you."

"Oh! if he does not receive me, I shall find some means of getting in without his permission."

"Yes; and when you have once got in, you will find there Monsieur Dreux Breze, who wil. have you shoved out-of-doors."

"Who will have me shoved out-of-doors?"

"Yes; he wished to do that to the National Assembly altogether. It is true that he did not succeed; but that is a stronger reason for his being in a furious rage, and taking his revenge on you."

"Very well; then I will apply to the assembly."

"The road to Versailles is intercepted."

"I will go there with my three thousand men."

"Take care, my dear sir. You would find on your road some four or five thousand Swiss soldiers and two or three thousand Austrians, who would make only a mouthful of you and your three thousand men. In the twinkling of an eye you would be swallowed."

"Ah, the devil! What ought I to do, then?"

"Do what you please; but do me the service to take away your three thousand men who are beating the pavement yonder with their pikes, and who are smoking. There are seven or eight thousand pounds of powder in our cellars here. A single spark might blow us all up."

"In that case, I think, I will neither address myself to the king nor to the National Assembly. I will address myself to the nation, and we will take the Bastile."

"And with what?"

"With the eight thousand pounds of powder that you are going to give me, Monsieur Provost."

"Ah, really" said Flesselles, in a jeering tone.

"It is precisely as I say, sir. The keys of the cellars, if you please."

"Hey! you are jesting, sure," cried the provost.

"No, sir, I am not jesting," said Billot.

And seizing Flesselles by the collar of his coat with both hands, "The keys," cried he, "or I call up my men."

Flesselles turned as pale as death. His lips and his teeth were closed convulsively; but when he spoke his voice was in no way agitated, and he did not even change the ironical tone he had assumed.

"In fact, sir," said he, "you are doing me a great service by relieving me from the charge of this powder. I will, therefore, order the keys to be delivered to you, as you desire. Only please not to forget that I am your first magistrate, and that if you have the misfortune to conduct yourself toward me before others in the way you have done when alone with me, an hour afterward you wou ld be hanged by the town guards. You insist on having this powder ?"

"I insist," replied Billot.

"And you will distribute it yourself ? "

"Myself."

"And when ? "

"This very moment."

"Your pardon. Let us understand each other. I have business which will detain me here about a quarter of an hour, and should rather like, if it is the same to you, that the distribution should not be commenced until I have left the place. It has been predicted to me that I shall die a violent death ; but I acknowledge that I have a very decided repugnance to being blown into the air."

"Be it so. In a quarter of an hour, then. But now, in my turn, I have a request to make."

"What is it ? "

"Let us both go close up to that window."

"For what purpose ? "

"I wish to make you popular."

"I am greatly obliged ; but in what manner ?"

"You shall see."

Billot took the provost to the window, which was open, and called out to his friends in the square below :

"My friends," said he, "you still wish to take the Bastile, do you not ?"

"Yes—yes—yes !" shouted three or four thousand voices.

"But you want gunpowder, do you not ?"

"Yes—gunpowder ! gunpowder !"

"Well, then, here is his honor, the provost, who is willing to give you all he has in the cellars of the Hôtel de Ville. Thank him for it, my friends."

"Long live the Provost of the Merchants ! Long live Monsieur de Flesselles !" shouted the whole crowd.

"Thanks, my friends ; thanks for myself—thanks for him !" cried Billot.

Then, turning toward the provost :

" And now, sir," said Billot, " it is no longer necessary that I should take you by the collar, while here alone with you, or before all the world ; for if you do not give me the gunpowder, the nation, as you call it, the nation will tear you to pieces."

" Here are the keys, sir," said the provost. " You have so persuasive a mode of asking, that it does not even admit of a refusal."

" What you say really encourages me," said Billot, who appeared to be meditating some other project.

" Ah, the deuce ! Can you have anything else to ask of me ? "

" Yes. You are acquainted with the governor of the Bastile ? "

" Monsieur de Launay ? "

" I do not know what his name is."

" His name is De Launay."

" Be it so. Well, do you know Monsieur de Launey ? "

" He is a friend of mine."

" In that case you must desire that no misfortune should happen to him."

" In fact, I should desire it."

" Well, then, the way to prevent any misfortune happening to him is, that he should surrender the Bastile to me, or, at all events, liberate the doctor."

" You do not imagine, surely, that I should have influence enough with him to induce him to surrender to you either his prisoner or his fortress, do you ? "

" That is my affair. All that I ask is, that you will give me an introduction to him."

" My dear Monsieur Billot, I forewarn you that if you go into the Bastile, you will go into it alone."

" Very well."

" I forewarn you, moreover, that if you enter it alone, you will, perhaps, not get out again."

" Marvelously well."

" Then I will give you your permission to go into the Bastile."

" I will wait for it."

" But it will be on still another condition."

" What is that ? "

" It is that you will not come to me again to-morrow and

ask me for a passport to the moon. I forewarn you that
I am not acquainted with any one in those regions."

"Flesselles! Flesselles!" said a hollow and threatening
voice from behind the provost of the merchants, "if you
continue to wear two faces—the one which laughs with the
aristocrats, the other which smiles upon the people, you
will perhaps receive, between this and to-morrow morning,
a passport for a world from which no one returns."

The provost turned round, shuddering.

"Who is this that speaks thus?" said he.

"'Tis I—Marat."

"Marat, the philosopher! Marat, the physician!" exclaimed Billot.

"Yes," replied the same voice.

"Yes—Marat, the philosopher; Marat, the physician,"
repeated Flesselles, "who, in this last capacity, ought to
attend to curing coughs, which would have been a sure
means of now having a goodly number of patients."

"Monsieur de Flesselles," replied the lugubrious inter-
locutor, "this worthy citizen has asked you for a passport
which will facilitate his seeing Monsieur de Launay. I
would observe to you that not only is he waiting for you,
but that three thousand men are waiting for him."

"'Tis well, sir; he shall soon have it."

Flesselles went to a table, passed one hand over his brow,
and with the other seizing a pen, he rapidly wrote several
lines.

"Here is your safe-conduct," said he, delivering the
paper to Billot.

"Read it," said Marat.

"I cannot read," said Billot.

"Well, then, give it to me. I can read."

Billot handed the paper to Marat.

This passport was conceived in the following terms:

"Monsieur Governor,—We, Provost of the Merchants of the city of Paris, send to you Monsieur Billot,
in order to concert with you as to the interests of the said
city.

"14th July, 1789.   De Flesselles."

"Good!" said Billot; "give it to me."

"You find this passport good as it is?" said Marat.

"Undoubtedly."

"Stop a minute. The provost is going to add a post-script to it, which will make it better."

And he went up to Flesselles, who had remained standing, his hand on the table, and who looked with a disdainful air at the two men with whom he was so particularly engaged, and a third one, half naked, who had just presented himself at the door, leaning upon a musketoon.

It was Pitou, who had followed Billot, and who held himself ready to obey the farmer's orders, be they what they might.

"Sir," said Marat to Flesselles, "the postscript which you are about to add, and which will render the passport so much better, is the following."

"Say on, Monsieur Marat."

Marat placed the paper on the table, and pointing with his finger to the place on which the provost was to write the required postscript:

"The Citizen Billot," said he, "having the character of bearer of a flag of truce, I confide his care to your honor."

Flesselles looked at Marat, as if he would rather have smashed his flat face with his fist than do that which he had requested.

"Would you resist, sir?" demanded Marat.

"No," replied Flesselles; "for, after all, you only ask me what is strictly right."

And he wrote the postscript demanded of him.

"However, gentlemen, you will be pleased to well observe this, that I do not answer for the safety of Monsieur Billot."

"And I—I will be answerable for it," said Marat, jerking the paper out of his hands; "for your liberty is the guarantee of his liberty—your head for the safety of his head. Here, worthy Billot," continued Marat, "here is your passport."

"Labrie!" cried M. de Flesselles—"Labrie!"

A lackey in grand livery entered the room.

"My carriage," said the provost.

"It is waiting for you, sir, in the courtyard."

"Let us go, then, said the provost. "There is nothing else which you desire, gentlemen?"

"No," simultaneously replied Billot and Marat.

"Am I to let them pass?" inquired Pitou.

"My friend," said Flesselles to him, "I would observe to you that you are rather too indecently attired to mount guard at my door. If you insist upon remaining here, turn your cartouche-box round in front, and set your back against the wall."

"Am I to let them pass?" Pitou repeated, with an air which indicated that he did not greatly relish the jest of which he had been the subject.

"Yes," said Billot.

Pitou made way for the provost to pass by him.

"Perhaps you were wrong in allowing that man to go," said Marat. "He would have been a good hostage to have kept. But, in any case, let him go where he will, you may feel perfectly assured that I will find him again."

"Labrie," said the provost of the merchants, as he was getting into his carriage, "they are going to distribute powder here. Should the Hôtel de Ville perchance blow up, I should like to be out of the way of the splinters. Let us get out of gunshot, Labrie, out of gunshot."

The carriage rattled through the gateway, and appeared upon the square, on which were growling some four or five thousand persons.

Flesselles was afraid that they might misinterpret his departure, which might be considered as a flight.

He leaned half-way out of the door.

"To the National Assembly!" cried he, in a loud voice to the coachman.

This drew upon him from the crowd a loud and continued outburst of applause.

Marat and Billot were on the balcony, and had heard the last words of Flesselles.

"My head against his," said Marat, "that he is not going to the National Assembly, but to the king."

"Would it not be well to have him stopped?" said Billot.

"No," replied Marat, with his hideous smile; "make yourself easy; however quickly he may go, we shall go still quicker than he. But now for the gunpowder."

"Yes, to the gunpowder," said Billot.

And they both went down the great staircase, followed by Pitou.

CHAPTER XV.

As M. de Flesselles had said, there were eight thousand pounds of gunpowder in the cellars of the Hôtel de Ville.

Marat and Billot went into the first cellar with a lantern, which they suspended to a hook in the ceiling.

Pitou mounted guard at the door.

The powder was in small kegs, containing each about twenty pounds. Men were stationed upon the stairs, forming a chain which reached the square, and they at once began to send up the kegs.

There was at first a momentary confusion. It was not known whether there would be powder enough for everybody, and they all rushed forward to secure their share. But the chain formed by Billot at length succeeded in making the people wait patiently for their turn, and the distribution was effected with something like an approach to order.

Every citizen received half a pound of powder—about thirty or forty shots.

But when every one had received the powder, it was perceived that muskets were sadly deficient ; there were scarcely five hundred among the whole crowd.

While the distribution was going on, a portion of this furious population who were crying out for arms went up to the rooms where the electors held their sittings. They were occupied in forming the National Guard, of which the usher had spoken to Billot.

They had just decreed that this civic militia should be composed of forty-eight thousand men. This militia but yet existed in the decree, and they were disputing as to the general who should command it.

It was in the midst of this discussion that the people invaded the Hôtel de Ville. They had organized themselves. They only asked to march—all they required was arms.

At that moment the noise of a carriage coming into the courtyard was heard. It was the provost of the merchants, who had not been allowed to proceed upon his journey, although he had exhibited a mandate from the king, ordering him to proceed to Versailles, and he was brought back by force to the Hôtel de Ville.

"Give us arms! give us arms!" cried the crowd, as soon as they perceived him at a distance.

"Arms!" cried he. "I have no arms; but there must be some at the arsenal."

"To the arsenal! to the arsenal!" cried the crowd.

And five or six thousand men rushed on to the Quay de la Grève.

The arsenal was empty.

They returned, with bitter lamentations, to the Hôtel de Ville.

The provost had no arms, or, rather, would not give them. Pressed by the people, he had the idea of sending them to the Chartreux.

The Chartreux opened its gates; they searched it in every direction, but did not find even a pocket-pistol.

During this time, Flesselles, having been informed that Billot and Marat were still in the cellars of the Hôtel de Ville, completing the distribution of the gunpowder, proposed to send a deputation to De Launay, to propose to him that he should withdraw the cannon from his ramparts, so as to be out of sight.

That which the evening before had made the crowd hoot most obstreperously was these guns, which, stretching forth their long necks, were seen beyond the turreted parapets. Flesselles hoped that, by causing them to disappear, the people would be contented by the concession, and would withdraw satisfied.

The deputation had just set forth, when the people returned in great fury.

On hearing the cries they uttered, Billot and Marat ran upstairs into the courtyard.

Flesselles, from an interior balcony, endeavored to calm the people. He proposed a decree which should authorrize the districts to manufacture fifty thousand pikes.

The people were about to accept this proposal.

"Decidedly this man is betraying us," said Marat.

Then, turning to Billot:

"Go to the Bastile," said he, "and do what you proposed to do. In an hour I will send you there twenty thousand men, and each man with a musket on his shoulder."

Billot, at first sight, had felt great confidence in this man, whose name had become so popular that it had reached even him. He did not even ask him how he calculated on procuring them. An abbé was there, imbued with the general enthusiasm of the moment, and crying, like all the rest, "To the Bastile!" Billot did not like abbés; but this one pleased him. He gave him the charge of continuing the distribution, which the worthy abbé accepted.

Then Marat mounted upon a post. There was at that moment the most frightful noise and tumult.

"Silence!" cried he. "I am Marat, and I wish to speak."

They were at once quieted, as if by magic, and every eye was directed toward the orator.

"You wish for arms?" he said.

"Yes, yes!" replied thousands of voices.

"To take the Bastile?"

"Yes, yes, yes!"

"Well, then, come with me, and you shall have them."

"And where?"

"To the Invalides, where there are twenty-five thousand muskets."

"To the Invalides! to the Invalides!" cried every voice.

"And now," said Marat to Billot, who had just called Pitou, "you will go to the Bastile?"

"Yes."

"Stay. It might happen that before my men arrive you may stand in need of assistance."

"In fact," said Billot, "that is possible."

Marat tore out a leaf from a small memorandum-book, and wrote four words upon it with a pencil.

"This comes from Marat."

Then he drew a sign upon the paper.

"Well!" cried Billot, "what would you have me do with this note, since you do not tell me the name or the address of the person to whom I am to deliver it?"

"As to the address, the man to whom I recommend you has none; as to his name, it is well known. Ask the first workman you may meet for Gonchon, the Mirabeau of the people."

"Gonchon—you will remember that name, Pitou."

"Gonchon or Gonchonius," said Pitou ; "I shall not forget it."

"To the Invalides ! to the Invalides !" howled the mob, with increasing ferocity.

"Well, then, go !" said Marat to Billot, "and may the genius of Liberty march before thee ! "

"To the Invalides ! " he then cried, in his turn.

And he went down the Quay de la Grève, followed by more than twenty thousand men.

Billot, on his side, took with him some five or six thousand. These were all armed in one way or another.

At the moment when they were about to proceed along the bank of the river, and the remainder were going toward the boulevard, the provost of the merchants called to them from a window.

"My friends," said he, "why is it that I see a green cockade in your hats ?"

They were the leaves of the linden-trees of Camille Desmoulins, which many had adopted merely from seeing others wear them, but without even knowing their signification.

"Hope ! hope ! " cried several voices.

"Yes; but the color that denotes hope is, at the same time, that of the Count d'Artois. Would you have the air of wearing the livery of a prince ? "

"No, no !" cried all the crowd, in chorus, and Billot louder than the rest.

"Well, then, you ought to change that cockade ; and, if you will wear a livery, let it, at least, be that of the city of Paris, the mother of us all—blue and red, my friends, blue and red." *

"Yes, yes ! " cried every tongue ; " blue and red."

Upon these words, every one trampled under foot his green cockade, every one called for ribbons ; as if by enchantment, the windows round the square were opened, and blue and red ribbons rained down in floods.

But all the ribbons that fell scarcely sufficed for a thousand men.

---

* Some time afterward, M. de Lafayette also made the observation that blue and red were likewise the colors of the House of Orleans, and added to them a third color, white, saying to those who received it from him, "I give you a cockade that will make the tour of the whole world."

Instantly, aprons, silk gowns, scarfs, curtains were torn, stripped, and cut in fragments ; these fragments were formed into bows, rosettes, and scarfs. Every one took his share.

After which Billot's small army again moved forward.

It kept on recruiting as it advanced ; all the arteries of the Faubourg St. Antoine sent to it as it passed the most ardent and the most active of their population.

They reached, in tolerably good order, the end of the Rue Lesdiguières, where already a mass of curious lookers-on—some timid, others calm, and others insolent—were gazing at the towers of the Bastile, exposed to an ardent sun.

The arrival of about a hundred of the French Guards from the boulevards.

The arrival of the popular drums by the Faubourg St. Antoine.

The arrival of Billot and his troop at once changed the character and the aspect of the assembled crowd ; the timid became emboldened, the calm became excited, and the insolent began to threaten.

"Down with the cannon! down with the cannon !" cried twenty thousand voices, threatening with their clinched fists the heavy guns which stretched forth their brazen necks from the embrasures of the platforms.

Just at that moment, as if the governer of the Bastile had heard these cries and was obeying these injunctions of the crowd, some artillerymen approached the guns, which they drew in, and at last they disappeared entirely.

The crowd clapped their hands ; they had then become a power, since the governor had yielded to their threats.

Notwithstanding this, the sentinels continued pacing backward and forward on the platforms. At every post was an Invalide and a Swiss.

After having cried, "Down with the cannon !" the crowd shouted "Down with the Swiss !" It was a continuation of the cry of the night before, "Down with the Germans !"

But the Swiss did not the less continue their guard, crossing the Invalides in their measured pacings up and down.

One of those who cried, "Down with the Swiss,"

became impatient ; he had a gun in his hand ; he pointed the muzzle of his gun at the sentinel and fired.

The ball struck the gray wall of the Bastile one foot below the coping stone of the tower, and immediately in front of the spot where the Swiss had passed. At the spot where the shot had struck, it left a white mark, but the sentinel did not stop, and did not even turn his head.

A loud rumor soon arose around the man who had fired, and thus was given the signal of attack as unheard of as it was senseless. There was more of terror than of anger in this rumor. Many persons conceived it was a crime punishable with death to have thus fired a musket-shot at the Bastile.

Billot gazed upon the dark-green mass like to those fabulous monsters which in ancient legends are represented to us as covered with scales. He counted the embrasures at which the cannon might at any given moment be rolled back to their places. He counted the number of muskets, the muzzles of which might be directed through the loopholes at the assembled crowd.

And Billot shook his head, recalling to mind the words uttered by Flesselles.

"We shall never be able to get in there," said he.

"And why shall we never be able to get in ?" said a voice close beside him.

Billot turned round and saw a man with a savage countenance, dressed in rags, and whose eyes sparkled like two stars.

"Because it appears to me impossible to take such a mass as that by force."

"The taking of the Bastile," said the man, "is not a deed of war, but an act of faith. Believe, and thou shalt succeed."

"Patience," said Billot, feeling in his pocket for his passport. The man was deceived as to his meaning.

"Patience," cried he ; "oh, yes, I understand you— you are fat—you—you look like a farmer."

"And I am one, in fact," said Billot.

"Then I can well understand why you say patience. You have been always well fed ; but look behind you for a moment and see those specters who are now surrounding us—see their dried-up veins, count their bones through the rents in their garments, and then ask them whether they understand the word patience."

"This is one who speaks well," said Pitou ; "but he terrifies me."

"He does not terrify me," said Billot ; and turning again toward the man :

"Yes, patience," he said, "but only for another quarter of an hour, that's all."

"Ah ! ah !" cried the man, smiling ; "a quarter of an hour ; that, indeed, is not too much. And what will you do between this and a quarter of an hour ?"

"During that time I shall have visited the Bastile, I shall know the number of its garrison, I shall know the intentions of its governor, I shall know, in fine, the way into it."

"Yes, if after that you could only find the way out of it."

"Well, supposing that I do not get out of it ; there is a man who will come and show me the way."

"And who is this man ?"

"Gonchon, the Mirabeau of the people."

The man gave a start. His eyes emitted flashes of fire.

"Do you know him ?" inquired he.

"No."

"Well, what mean you, then ?"

"Why, I'm going to know him ; for I was told that the first to whom I might speak on the square before the Bastile would lead me to him. You are on the square of the Bastile, take me to him."

"What do you want with him ?"

"To deliver to him this paper."

"From whom is it ?"

"From Marat, the physician."

"From Marat ! You know Marat ?" exclaimed the man.

"I have just left him."

"Where ?"

"At the Hôtel de Ville."

"What is he doing ?"

"He is going to arm twenty thousand men at the Invalides."

"In that case, give me that paper. I am Gonchon."

Billot drew back a step.

" You are Gonchon ?" cried he.

" My friends," said the man in rags, "here is one who does not know me, and who is asking whether it is true that I am Gonchon."

The crowd burst into a loud laugh. It appeared to all these men that it was impossible that any one could be so ignorant as not to know their favorite orator.

" Long live Gonchon !" cried two or three thousand voices.

" Take it," said Billot, handing the paper to him.

" Friends," cried Gonchon, after having read it, and laying his hand on Billot's shoulder, " this is a brother. Marat recommends him ; we can, therefore, rely upon him. What is your name ?" said he to the farmer.

" My name is Billot."

" And mine," rejoined Gonchon, " is Hache ; and between us both I trust we shall be able to do something." *

The crowd smiled at this sanguinary jest.

" Yes, yes, we shall soon do something !" cried they.

" Well, what are we going to do ?" asked several voices.

" Why, zounds !" cried Gonchon, "we are going to take the Bastile."

" This is as it should be," cried Billot ; " that is what I call speaking. Listen to me, brave Gonchon. How many men have you to back you ?"

" Thirty thousand, or somewhere near that."

" Thirty thousand men you have at your disposal ; twenty thousand who will soon be here from the Invalides, and ten thousand who are already here—why, 'tis more than enough to insure our success, or we shall never succeed at all."

" We shall succeed," replied Gonchon.

" I believe so. Well, then, call together your thirty thousand men. I, in the meantime, will go to the governor, and summon him to surrender. If he surrenders, so much the better ; we shall avoid much bloodshed. If he will not surrender, the blood that will be spilled will fall upon his head ; and in these days blood that is spilled in an unjust cause brings down misfortunes with it. Ask the Germans if it be not so."

* Billot, in French, means block—the block on which criminals' heads are struck off. Hache means ax.—TRANSLATOR.

"How long do you expect to remain with the governor?" asked Gonchon.

"As long as I possibly can; until the Bastile is completely invested, if it be possible. When I come out again the attack will begin."

"'Tis understood."

"You do not mistrust me?" said Billot to Gonchon, holding out his hand to him.

"Who—I?" replied Gonchon, with a smile of disdain, at the same time pressing the hand of the stout farmer, and with a strength that could not have been expected from his emaciated appearance; "I mistrust you? And for what reason, pray? It it were my will, upon a word, a sign given by me, I could have you pounded like glass, even were you sheltered by those formidable towers which to-morrow will no longer exist—were you protected by these soldiers who this evening will have espoused our party or will have ceased to exist. Go, then, and rely on Gonchon as he relies on Billot."

Billot was convinced, and walked toward the entrance of the Bastile, while the strange person with whom he had been conversing darted down the faubourg amid shouts, repeated a thousand times, of:

"Long live Gonchon! long live the Mirabeau of the people!"

"I do not know what the Mirabeau of the nobles may be," said Pitou to Billot, "but I think our Mirabeau a hideously ugly personage."

CHAPTER XVI.

WE will not describe the Bastile—it would be useless.

It lives as an eternal image, both in the memory of the old and in the imagination of the young.

We shall content ourselves with merely stating that, seen from the boulevard, it presented, in front of the square then called the Place de la Bastile, two twin towers, while its two fronts ran parallel with the banks of the canal which now exists.

The entrance to the Bastile was defended, in the first

place, by a guard-house, then by two lines of sentinels, and besides these by two drawbridges.

After having passed through these several obstacles, you came to the courtyard of the government house—that is to say, the residence of the governor.

From this courtyard a gallery led to the ditches of the Bastile.

At this other entrance, which opened upon the ditches, was a drawbridge, a guard-house, and an iron gate.

At the first entrance they wished to stop Billot; but Billot shows the passport he received from Flesselles, and they allow him to pass on.

Billot then perceives that Pitou is following him. Pitou had no permission; but he would have followed the farmer's steps down to the infernal regions, or would have ascended to the moon.

"Remain outside," said Billot. "Should I not come out again, it would be well there should be some one to remind the people that I have come in."

"That is perfectly right," said Pitou. "How long am I to wait before I remind them of it?"

"One hour."

"And the casket?" inquired Pitou.

"Ah! you remind me. Well, then, should I not get out again, should Gonchon not take the Bastile, or, in short, if, after having taken it, I should not be found, you must tell Doctor Gilbert, whom they will find, perhaps, that men who came from Paris took from me the casket which he confided to my care five years ago; that I, on the instant, started off to inform him of what had happened; that on arriving at Paris I was informed that he was in the Bastile; that I attempted to take the Bastile, and that in the attempt I left my skin there, which was altogether at his service."

"'Tis well, Father Billot," said Pitou; "only 'tis rather a long story, and I am afraid I may forget it."

"Forget what I have said to you?"

"Yes."

"I will repeat it to you, then."

"No," said a voice close to Billot's ear; "it would be better to write it."

"I do not know how to write," said Billot.

"I do. I am an usher."

" Ah ! you are an usher, are you ? " inquired Billot.

" Stanislaus Millard, usher in the court of the Châtelet."

And he drew from his pocket a long ink-horn, in which there were pens, paper, and ink—in fine, all that was necessary for writing.

He was a man about forty-five years old, tall, thin, and grave-looking, dressed entirely in black, as became his profession.

" Here is one who looks confoundedly like an undertaker," muttered Pitou.

" You say," inquired the usher, with great calmness, " that men who came from Paris carried off a casket which Dr. Gilbert confided to you ? "

" Yes."

" That is a punishable crime."

" These men belong to the police of Paris."

" Infamous robbers ! " murmured Millard.

Then, handing the paper to Pitou :

" Here, take this, young man," said he ; " it is the memorandum you require, and should he be killed "—he pointed to Billot—" should you be killed, it is to be hoped that I shall not be killed, too."

" And should you not be killed, what would you do ? " asked Pitou.

" I would do that which you were to have done," replied Millard.

" Thanks," said Billot.

And he held out his hand to the usher.

The usher grasped it with a vigor which could not have been anticipated from his lank, meager body.

" Then I may fully depend upon you ? " said Billot.

" As on Marat—as on Gonchon."

" Good," said Pitou ; " they form a trinity which, I am sure, I shall not find in Paradise."

Then, going up to Billot :

" Tell me, Father Billot, you will be prudent, will you not ? "

" Pitou," replied the farmer, with an eloquence which sometimes astonished people, when proceeding from one who had always led a country life, " forget not what I now say to you, that the most prudent line of conduct now in France is to be courageous."

And he passed the first line of sentinels, while Pitou returned toward the square.

At the drawbridge he was again obliged to parley.

Billot showed his passport; the drawbridge was let down, the iron-grated gate was opened.

Close beside the gate stood the governor.

This interior court, in which the governer was waiting for Billot, was the courtyard which served as a promenade for the prisoners. It was guarded by eight towers—that is to say, by eight giants. No window opened into it. Never did the sunshine on its pavement, which was damp and almost muddy. It might have been thought the bottom of an immense well.

In this courtyard was a clock, supported by figures representing enchained captives, which measured the hours, from which fell the regular and slow sounds of the minutes as they passed by, as in a dungeon the droppings from the ceiling eat into the pavement slabs on which they fall.

At the bottom of this well the prisoner, lost amid the abyss of stone, for a moment contemplated its cold nakedness, and soon asked to be allowed to return to his room.

Close beside the grated gate which opened on this courtyard, stood, as we have said, M. de Launay.

M. de Launay was a man from forty-five to fifty years of age. On that day he was dressed in a gray coat; he wore the red ribbon of the Order of St. Louis, and in his hand he carried a sword-cane.

This M. de Launay was a man of wicked disposition; the memoirs of Linguit had just bestowed upon him a sorrowful celebrity; he was almost as much detested as the prison itself.

In fact the De Launays, like the Châteauneufs, the Levrillières, and the St. Florentins, who held the *lettres de cachet* from father to son, the De Launays also from father to son transmitted the Bastile to one another.

For, as it is well known, it was not the minister who appointed the officers of this jail. At the Bastile all the places were sold to the highest bidder, from that of the governor himself down to that of the scullion. The governor of the Bastile was a jailer on a grand scale, an eating-house keeper wearing epaulets, who added to his salary of sixty thousand livres sixty thousand more, which he extorted and plundered.

It was highly necessary that he should recover the capital and interest of the money he had invested.

M. de Launay, in point of avarice, far surpassed his predecessors. This might, perhaps, have arisen from his having paid more for the place, and having foreseen that he would not remain in it so long as they did.

He fed his whole house at the expense of his prisoners. He had reduced the quantity of firing, and doubled the hire of furniture in each room.

He had the right of bringing yearly into Paris a hundred pipes of wine, free of duty. He sold his right to a tavern-keeper, who brought in wines of excellent quality. Then, with a tenth part of this duty, he purchased the vinegar with which he supplied his prisoners.

The unhappy prisoners in the Bastile had only one consolation—this was a small garden, which had been formed on one of the bastions. There they could walk—there for a few moments they could inhale pure air, the perfume of the flowers, and enjoy the light.

He rented this little garden to a gardener, and for the fifty livres a year which he received from him he had deprived the prisoners of this last enjoyment.

It is true that to rich prisoners his compliance was extreme. He conducted one of them to the house of his own mistress, who had thus her apartments furnished, and was kept in luxury, without its costing a stiver to him, De Launay.

See the work entitled "The Bastile Unveiled," and you will find in it this fact, and many others besides.

And, notwithstanding, this man was courageous.

From the previous evening the storm had been threatening around him. Since the previous evening, he perceived the waves of this great commotion, which, still ascending, beat against his walls.

And yet he was calm, though pale.

It is true that he had to support four pieces of artillery, ready prepared to fire ; around him, a garrison of Swiss and Invalides ; before him only an unarmed man.

For, on entering the Bastile, Billot had given Pitou his carbine to take care of.

He had understood that within the iron grating which he saw before him, a weapon would be more dangerous than useful to him.

Billot, with a single glance, observed all ; the calm and almost threatening attitude of the governor ; the Swiss and Invalides in the several guard-houses and on the platforms ; and the silent agitation of the artillerymen, who were stowing into the magazines of their ammunition wagons their cartridges.

The sentinels held their muskets at the make-ready ; the officers had their swords drawn.

The governor remained motionless ; Billot was obliged to advance toward him ; the iron-grated gate closed behind the bearer of the people's flag of truce with a sinister noise of grating iron, which, brave as he was, made the marrow of his bones chill within him.

" What want you with me again ? " said De Launay to him.

" Again ? " reiterated Billot ; " it appears to me, however, that this is the first time I have seen you, and, consequently, that you have yet no right to be wearied of seeing me."

" It is because I have been told that you come from the Hôtel de Ville."

" That is true.   I came from there."

" Well, then, only just now I received a deputation from the municipality."

" And for what purpose did it come ? "

" It came to obtain a promise from me that I would not be the first to fire.

" And you promised that you would not ? "

" Yes."

" And was this all ? "

" It also came to request that I would draw in my guns."

" And you did have them drawn in ; I know that, for I was on the square of the Bastile when this maneuver was executed."

" And you doubtless thought that I was yielding to the threats of the people ? "

" Why, zounds ! it did look very like it."

" Did I not tell you so, gentlemen ? " exclaimed De Launay, turning toward his officers ; " did I not tell you that we should be thought capable of such cowardice ? "

Then, turning to Billot :

" And you—from whom do you come ? "

" I come on behalf of the people," proudly replied Billot.

" 'Tis well," said De Launay, smiling ; " but you have some other recommendation, I suppose, for with that which you set forth, you would not have been allowed to pass the first line of my sentries."

" Yes—I have a safe-conduct from Monsieur de Flesselles, your friend."

" Flesselles ! You say that he is my friend," rejoined De Launay, looking intently at Billot, as if he would have read the inmost recesses of his heart. " From whom do you know that Monsieur de Flesselles is my friend ! "

" Why, I supposed him to be so."

" Supposed ?—oh, that is all ! 'Tis well. Let us see your safe-conduct."

Billot presented the paper to him.

De Launay read it once, then a second time, and turned and twisted it about to discover whether it did not contain some postscript between its pages ; held it up to the light, to see whether there were not some lines written between the lines of the missive.

" And this is all he has to say to me ? "

" All."

" You are sure ? "

" Perfectly sure."

" Nothing verbal ?"

" Nothing."

" 'Tis very strange ! " exclaimed De Launay, darting through one of the loopholes a glance at the crowd assembled in the square before the Bastile.

" But what would you have had him send to tell you ? " said Billot.

De Launay made an impatient gesture.

" Oh, nothing, nothing ! Come, now, tell me what you want ; but speak quickly, for I am pressed for time."

" Well, then, what I want is, that you should surrender the Bastile to us."

" What said you ? " cried De Launay, quickly turning round as if he thought he had misunderstood the farmer's meaning. " You say——"

" I say that I have come in the name of the people to demand that you surrender the Bastile."

De Launay shrugged up his shoulders.

" The people are, in truth, very strange animals," said he.

" Hey ! " cried Billot.

"And what do they want to do with the Bastile ?"

"They want to demolish it."

"And what the devil has the Bastile to do with the people ? Was ever a man of the people put into the Bastile ? The people, on the contrary, ought to bless every stone of which the Bastile is formed. Who are they who are put into the Bastile ? Philosophers, men of science, aristocrats, ministers, princes—that is to say, enemies of the people."

"Well, that proves that the people are not egotists," retorted Billot.

"My friend," said De Launay, with a shade of commiseration in his tone, "it is easy to perceive that you are not a soldier."

"You are quite right. I am a farmer.

"That you do not inhabit Paris."

"In fact, I am from the country."

"That you do not thoroughly know what the Bastile is."

"That is true. I only know what I have seen of it—that is to say, the exterior walls."

"Well, then, come along with me, and I will show you what the Bastile is."

"Ho! ho!" muttered Billot to himself, "he is going to lead me over some villainous trap-door, which will suddenly open under my feet, and then, good night, Father Billot."

But the intrepid farmer did not even blink, and showed himself ready to follow the governor of the Bastile.

"In the first place," said De Launay, "you must know that I have powder enough in my cellars to blow up, not only the Bastile itself, but with it at least half of the Faubourg St. Antoine."

"I know that," tranquilly replied Billot.

"Very well ; but now look at those four pieces of artillery."

"I see them."

"They enfilade the whole of this gallery, as you can also see ; and this gallery is defended, first by a guard-house ; secondly, by two ditches, which only can be crossed with the assistance of two drawbridges ; and lastly, by a grated iron gate."

"Oh! I do not say that the Bastile is badly defended,"

calmly observed Billot , " all that I say is, that it will be well attacked."

" Let us go on," said De Launay.

Billot gave an assenting nod.

" Here is a postern which opens on the ditches," said the governor ; "look at the thickness of the walls."

" Somewhere about forty feet."

" Yes, forty at the bottom and fifteen at the top. You see that although the people may have good nails, they would break them against the stones."

' I did not say," rejoined Billot, " that the people would demolish the Bastile before taking it. What I said was, that they would demolish it after having taken it."

" Let us go upstairs," said De Launay. Let us go up."

They went up some thirty steps.

The governor stopped.

" See," said he, " here is another embrasure, which opens on the passage by which you wish to enter ; this is only defended by a rampart gun ; but it has already acquired a certain reputation. You know the song ·

> " ' Oh, my tender Musette—
> Musette, my only love.' "

" Certainly," said Billot ; " I do know it ; but I do not think that this is the time to sing it."

" Wait a moment. Well, Marshal Saxe called this small cannon his Musette, because it sung correctly the air he best liked. That is a historical detail."

" Oh !" ejaculated Billot.

" Let us go up higher "—and they continued to climb up the stairs.

They soon reached a platform on the tower called La Compte.

" Ah ! ah !" ejaculated Billot.

" What is it ?" inquired De Launay,

" You have not had the cannon dismounted."

" I have had them drawn in—that's all."

" You know that I shall tell the people that cannon are still here."

" Tell them so."

" You will not have them dismounted, then ? "

" No."

" Decidedly ? "

"The king's cannon are here by the king's order, sir; they can only be dismounted by an order from the king."

"Monsieur de Launay," said Billot, feeling the importance of the moment, and raising his mind to the full height of it, with dignified eloquence, "Monsieur de Launay, the real king, whom I counsel you to obey, is yonder."

And he showed to the governor the gray crowd, some of whom were still covered with blood from the combat of the preceding evening, and whose undulating movements before the ditches made their arms gleam in the sunshine.

"Sir," said De Launay, in his turn, throwing his head back with a haughty air, "you may perhaps acknowledge two kings, but I, the governor of the Bastile, I know but one, and he is Louis, the sixteenth of that name, who has affixed his name to a commission by virtue of which I command here both men and things."

"You are not then a citizen?" cried Billot, in anger.

"I am a French gentleman," said the governor.

"Ah! that is true—you are a soldier, and you speak as a soldier."

"You have said the word, sir," replied De Launay, bowing. "I am a soldier, and I execute the orders I receive."

"And I, sir," said Billot, "I am a citizen, and my duty as a citizen being in opposition with your orders as a soldier, one of us two will die—whether it be the one who obeys his orders, or the one who fulfils his duty."

"It is probable, sir."

"Then you are determined to fire upon the people?"

"By no means—so long as they do not fire upon me. I have pledged my word to the envoys of Monsieur de Flesselles. You see that the guns have been drawn in, but at the first shot from the square upon my castle——"

"Well, at the first shot?"

"I will run to one of these guns—this one, for instance —I will myself wheel it to the embrasure, I will point it with my own hands, and I will fire it with the match you see standing here."

"You?"

"Yes, I."

"Oh! if I believed that," said Billot, "before allowing you to commit such a crime——"

"I have told you that I am a soldier, sir, and that I know nothing but my orders."

"Well, then, look!" said Billot, drawing De Launay toward an embrasure, and pointing out to him alternately two different points, the Faubourg St. Antoine and the boulevard; "yonder are those from whom in future you will receive your orders."

And he showed De Launay two dark, dense, and howling masses, who, compelled to take the form of the boulevards, undulated like an immense serpent, of which the head and the body could be seen, but the last rings of which were lost to sight, from the unevenness of the ground on which it crawled.

And all that could be seen of the gigantic reptile was refulgent with luminous scales.

It was the double troop, to which Billot had given rendezvous on the square of the Bastile—the one led by Marat, and the other by Gonchon.

On both sides they advanced, brandishing their arms and uttering the most terrific cries.

De Launay turned pale at the sight, and raising his cane:

"To your guns!" cried he.

Then, advancing toward Billot, with a threatening gesture:

"And you, wretch!" he exclaimed, "you who have come here under the pretext of parleying with me while the others are advancing to the attack, do you know that you deserve to die?"

And he half drew his sword from the cane which concealed it.

Billot saw the movement, and, rapid as the lightning, seizing De Launay by the collar and the waistband:

"And you," said he, as he raised him from the ground, "you deserve that I should hurl you over the ramparts, to break your bones against the sides of the ditch! But, God be thanked! I shall fight you in another manner!"

At that moment an immense and universal clamor, proceeding from below, and rushing through the air like the wild howlings of the hurricane, reached their ears, and M. de Losme, the major of the Bastile, appeared on the platform.

"Sir," cried he, addressing himself to Billot, "sir, be pleased to show yourself; all those people yonder believe that some misfortune has befallen you, and they are calling for you."

And in fact the name of Billot, which had been spread among the crowd by Pitou, was heard amid the clamor.

Billot had loosed his hold, and M. de Launay sheathed his sword.

Then there was a momentary hesitation between these three men ; cries calling for vengeance, and threatening shouts were heard.

"Show yourself then, sir," said De Launay ; "not that these clamors intimidate me, but that it may be known that I am a man who loyally keeps his word."

Then Billot put his head between the battlements, making a sign with his hand.

On seeing this, loud shouts of applause rose from the populace. It was, in a manner, the Revolution rising from the forehead of the Bastile in the person of this man of the people, who had been the first to trample on its platform as a conqueror.

"'Tis well, sir," then said De Launay ; "all is now terminated between us ; you have nothing further to do here. You are called for yonder ; go down."

Billot was sensible of this moderation in a man who had him completely in his power ; he went down the same staircase by which he had ascended the ramparts, the governor following him.

As to the major, he had remained there ; the governor had given him some orders in a whisper.

It was evident that M. de Launay had but one desire, and this was that the bearer of the flag of truce should become his enemy, and that as quickly as possible.

Billot walked across the courtyard without uttering a word. He saw the artillerymen standing by their guns. The match was smoking at the end of a lance.

Billot stepped before them.

"My friends," said he, "remember that I came to request your chief to prevent the spilling of blood, and that he has refused."

"In the name of the king, sir !" cried De Launay, stamping his foot, "leave this place !"

"Beware !" said Billot ; "for if you order me out in the name of the king, I shall come in again in the name of the people."

Then, turning toward the guard-house, before which the Swiss were standing :

"Come, now," said he, "tell me for which side are you ?"

The Swiss soldiers remained silent.

De Launay pointed with his finger to the iron gate.

Billot wished to essay a last effort.

"Sir," said he, "in the name of the nation, in the name of your brothers."

"Of my brothers ? You call my brothers those men who are howling 'Down with the Bastile !' 'Death to its governor !' They may be your brothers, sir, but most assuredly they are not mine."

"In the name of humanity, then."

"In the name of humanity which urges you on to come here with a hundred thousand men to cut the throats of a hundred unfortunate soldiers shut up in these walls."

"And by surrendering the Bastile you would be doing precisely that which would save their lives."

"And sacrifice my honor."

Billot said no more to him ; this logic of the soldier completely overcame him ; but turning to the Swiss and the Invalides :

"Surrender, my friends," cried he ; "it is still time. In ten minutes it will be too late."

"If you do not instantly withdraw, sir," in his turn cried De Launay, "on the word of a gentleman, I will order you to be shot."

Billot paused a moment, crossed his arms over his chest in token of defiance, exchanged a last threatening glance with De Launay, and passed through the gate.

CHAPTER XVII.

THE crowd was waiting ; scorched by the burning July sun, they were trembling, mad with excitement. Gonchon's men had just joined those of Marat. The Faubourg St. Antoine had recognized and saluted its brother the Faubourg St. Marceau.

Gonchon was at the head of his patriots. As to Marat, he had disappeared.

The aspect of the square was frightful.

On Billot's appearance the shouts redoubled.

" Well ? " said Gonchon, going up to him.

" Well, this man is a man of courage," said Billot.

" What mean you by saying ' This man is a man of courage ? ' " inquired Gonchon.

" I mean to say that he is obstinate."

" He will not surrender the Bastile ? "

" No."

" He will obstinately sustain the siege ? "

" Yes."

" And you believe that he will sustain it long ? "

" To the very death."

" Be it so !   Death he shall have ! "

" But what numbers of men we are about to expose to death ! " exclaimed Billot, doubting assuredly that God had given him the right which generals arrogate to themselves—as do kings and emperors—men who have received commissions to shed blood.

" Pooh ! " said Gonchon, " there are too many in this world, since there is not bread enough for half the population.   Is it not so, friends ? "

" Yes, yes ! " cried the crowd, with a sublime self-abnegation.

" But the ditch ! " observed Billot, inquiringly

" It is only necessary that it should be filled up at one particular spot," replied Gonchon, " and I have calculated that with half of the bodies we have here we could fill it up completely ; is it not so, friends ? "

" Yes, yes ! " repeated the crowd, with no less enthusiasm than before.

" Well, then, be it so," said Billot, though completely overcome.

At that moment De Launay appeared upon the terrace followed by Major de Losme and two or three officers.

" Begin ! " cried Gonchon to the governor.

The latter turned his back without replying.

Gonchon, who would perhaps have endured a threat, could not endure disdain ; he quickly raised his carbine to his shoulder, and a man in the governor's suite fell to the ground.

A hundred shots, a thousand musket shots, were fired at the same moment, as if they had only waited for the signal, and marbled with white the gray towers of the Bastile.

A silence of some seconds succeeded this discharge, as if the crowd itself had been alarmed at that which it had done.

Then a flash of fire, lost in a cloud of smoke, crowned the summit of a tower; a detonation resounded; cries of pain were heard issuing from the closely pressed crowd; the first cannon shot had been fired from the Bastile; the first blood had been spilled; the battle had commenced.

What the crowd experienced, which just before had been so threatening, very much resembled terror. That Bastile, defending itself by this sole act, appeared in all its formidable impregnability. The people had doubtless hoped that in those days, when so many concessions had been made to them, the surrender of the Bastile would be accomplished without effusion of blood.

The people were mistaken. The cannon shot which had been fired upon them gave them the measure of the Titanic work which they had undertaken.

A volley of musketry, well directed, and coming from the platform of the Bastile, followed closely on the cannon shot.

Then all was again silent for awhile, a silence which was interrupted only by a few cries, a few groans, a few complainings uttered here and there.

A shuddering, anxious movement could then be perceived among the crowd; it was the people who were picking up their killed and wounded.

But the people thought not of flying, or if they did think of it they were ashamed of the feeling when they considered their great numbers.

In fact, the boulevards, the Rue St. Antoine, the Faubourg St. Antoine, formed but one vast human sea; every wave had a head, every head two flashing eyes, a threatening mouth.

In an instant all the windows of the neighborhood were filled with sharpshooters, even those which were out of gunshot.

Whenever a Swiss soldier or an Invalide appeared upon the terraces or in one of the embrasures, a hundred muskets were at once aimed at him, and a shower of balls splintered the corners of the stones behind which the soldier was sheltered.

But they soon got tired of firing at insensible walls. It

was against human flesh that their balls were directed. It was blood that they wished to see spout forth, wherever the balls struck, and not dust.

Numerous opinions were emitted from amid the crowd.

A circle would then be formed around the orator, and when the people thought the proposal was devoid of sense, they at once left him.

A blacksmith proposed to form a catapult, upon the model of the ancient Roman machines and with it to make a breach in the walls of the Bastile.

A brewer, who commanded the Faubourg St. Antoine, and whose name has since acquired a fatal celebrity proposed to set fire to the fortress, by throwing into it a quantity of oil, which had been seized the night before, and which they were to ignite with phosphorus.

The firemen proposed to inundate with their fire-engines the priming of the cannon and the matches of the artillerymen, without reflecting that the most powerful of their engines could not throw water even to two thirds the height of the walls of the Bastile.

Billot listened to all these mad-brained proposals one after the other. On hearing the last, he seized a hatchet from the hands of a carpenter, and advancing amid a storm of bullets, which struck down all around him numbers of men, huddled together as thickly as ears of corn in a field, he reached a small guard-house near to the first drawbridge, and although the grape-shot was whizzing and cracking against the roof, he ascended it, and by his powerful and well-directed blows, succeeded in breaking the chains, and the drawbridge fell with a tremendous crash.

During the quarter of an hour which this seemingly insensate enterprise had occupied, the crowd was palpitating with excitement. At every report they expected to see the daring workman fall from the roof. The people forgot the danger to which they were exposed, and thought only of the danger which this brave man was incurring. When the bridge fell they uttered a loud, joyful cry and rushed into the first courtyard.

The movement was so rapid, so impetuous, so irresistible, that the garrison did not even attempt to prevent it.

Shouts of frantic joy announced this first advantage to M. de Launay.

No one even observed that a man had been crushed to atoms beneath the mass of woodwork. Then the four pieces of artillery which the governor had shown to Billot were simultaneously discharged with a frightful explosion and swept the first courtyard of the fortress.

The iron hurricane traced through the crowd a long furrow of blood. Ten men shot dead, fifteen or twenty wounded, were the consequences of this discharge.

Billot slid down from the roof of the guard-house to the ground, on reaching which he found Pitou, who had come there he knew not how. Pitou's eyes were quick, as are those of all poachers. He had seen the artillerymen preparing to put their matches to the touchholes of their guns, and seizing Billot by the skirts of his jacket jerked him violently toward him, and thus they were both protected by the angle of a wall from the effects of their first discharge.

From that moment the affair became really serious. The tumult was actually frightful—the combat a mortal one. Ten thousand muskets were at once fired round the Bastile, more dangerous in their effect to the besiegers than to the besieged.

At length a cannon served by the French Guards had mixed its thunder with the musketry.

The noise was frightful, but the crowd appeared to be more and more intoxicated by it; and this noise began to terrify even the besieged, who, calculating their own small number, felt they could never equal the noise which was then deafening them.

The officers of the Bastile felt instinctively that their soldiers were becoming disheartened. They snatched their muskets from them, and themselves fired at the crowd.

At this moment, and amid the noise of artillery and musketry, amid the howlings of the crowd, as some of them were rushing to pick up the dead bodies of their companions to form of them a new incitement—for their gaping wounds would cry aloud for vengeance against the besieged —there appeared at the entrance of the first courtyard a small group of unarmed, quiet citizens. They made their way through the crowd, and advanced, ready to sacrifice their lives, protected only by a white flag which preceded them, and which intimated that they were the bearers of a message to the governor.

It was a deputation from the Hôtel de Ville. The electors knew that hostilities had commenced, and, anxious to prevent the effusion of blood, had compelled Flesselles to send new proposals to the governor.

The deputies come, therefore, in the name of the city to summon M. de Launay to order the firing to cease, and to guarantee at once the lives of the citizens, his own, and those of the garrison ; to propose that he should receive one hundred men of the civic guard into the interior of the fortress.

This was the rumor, which was spread as the deputies advanced. The people, terrified at the enterprise they had undertaken ; the people who saw the dead bodies of their companions carried out on litters, were quite ready to support this proposal. Let De Launay accept a half defeat, and satisfy himself with half a victory.

At their approach, the fire of the second courtyard ceased. A sign was made to them that they might approach ; and they accordingly advanced, slipping on the insanguined pavement, striding over carcasses, and holding out their hands to the wounded.

Under this protection, the people form themselves into groups. The dead bodies and the wounded are carried out of the fortress ; the blood alone remains, marbling with large purple spots the pavement of the courtyard.

The fire from the fortress had ceased. Billot was leaving it, in order to stop that of the besiegers. At the door he meets Gonchon—Gonchon, altogether unarmed, exposing himself like one inspired, calm, as if he were invulnerable.

"Well," inquired he of Billot, "what has become of the deputation ? "

"It has gone into the fortress," replied Billot ; "order our men to cease firing."

"It will be useless," said Gonchon ; "they will not consent."

"That matters not," rejoined Billot ; "it is our duty to make the attempt. Let us respect the usages of war, since we have become soldiers."

"Be it so," said Gonchon.

Then, addressing himself to two men in the crowd, who appeared to command under him the whole of the assembled mass :

"Go, Elie—go, Hullin," said he, "and see that not a musket shot be fired."

The two aides-de-camp, rushed out, and obeying the orders of their chief, pressed through the crowded masses, and soon the firing of musketry diminished, and then ceased altogether.

A momentary quiet was established. Advantage was taken of it to attend to the wounded, the number of whom had already amounted to thirty-five or forty.

During this respite, the prison clock struck two. The attack had begun at noon, the combat had already lasted two hours.

Billot had returned to his post, and it was Gonchon in his turn who followed him.

His eyes were turned anxiously toward the gate. His impatience was visible.

"What is the matter with you?" inquired Billot.

"The matter is," replied Gonchon, "that if the Bastile is not taken within two hours from this time, all is lost."

"And why so?"

"Because the court will be informed of the work we are about, and will despatch the Swiss to us, under Bezenval, and Lambesq's dragoons; so that we shall then be caught between three fires."

Billott was compelled to acknowledge that there was some truth in what Gonchon was saying.

At length the deputies reappeared. From their countenances it was evident they had obtained no concession.

"Well," cried Gonchon, whose eyes sparkled with delight, "what did I tell you? Things that are predicted must happen. The accursed fortress is condemned!"

Then, without waiting even to put a question to the deputation, he sprung out of the first courtyard, crying:

"To arms, my children! to arms! The commandant refuses."

And, in fact, the governor had scarcely read the letter from Flesselles, when his countenance brightened; and, instead of acceding to the proposals which had been made to him, he exclaimed:

"Gentlemen Parisians, you have insisted on a battle; and now it is too late to speak of treating,"

The bearers of the flag of truce persisted in urging their suit; they represented to De Launay all the evils which his defending the castle might entail ; but he would not listen to them ; and he concluded by saying to the depu tation what he had said two hours before to Billot :

" Leave the fortress, or I will have you shot."

And the bearers of the flag of truce were compelled to leave the governor.

On this occasion it was De Launay who resumed the offensive. He appeared burning with impatience.

Before the deputies had reached the gate of the court-yard, the Musette of Marshal Saxe played a tune, and three persons fell, one of them dead, two others wounded.

One of the wounded was a French Guard, the other one of the deputies.

On seeing a man whose office should have rendered him sacred, carried forth covered with blood, the crowd became more enraged than ever.

Gonchon's two aides-de-camp had returned to their places at his side ; but each of them had had time to go home to change his dress.

It is true that one of them lived near the arsenal, the other in the Rue de Charonne.

Hullin, who had in the first place been a watchmaker at Geneva, then *chasseur* to the Marquis de Conflans, returned in his brilliant livery, which gave him the appearance of a Hungarian officer.

Elie, formerly an officer in the queen's regiment, had put on his uniform, which inspired the people with greater confidence, as it made them believe that the army was for them and with them.

The firing recommenced with greater fury than ever. And at that moment, the major of the Bastile. M. de Losme, approached the governor.

He was a brave and faithful soldier ; but there were some remains of the citizen in him ; and he saw with much regret what had taken place, and, above all, what was likely to ensue.

" Sir," said he to De Launay, " we have no provisions, and of this you must be aware."

" I know it," replied the governor.

" You also know that we have no orders."

" I beg your pardon, Monsieur de Losme ; my orders are to keep the gates of the Bastile closed, and it is for that purpose that the keys are intrusted to me."

" Sir, the keys are used as well to open the gates as to close them. Beware that you do not cause the massacre of the whole of the garrison, without saving the castle, two triumphs on the same day. Look at those men whom we are killing ; they appear to spring up from beneath the pavement. This morning there were at first only five hundred of them ; three hours ago there were ten thousand. They are more than sixty thousand now ; to-morrow they will be a hundred thousand. When our guns shall be silenced, and it must at last end in that, they will be strong enough to take the Bastile with their hands."

" You speak not like a soldier, Monsieur de Losme."

" I speak like a Frenchman, sir. I say, that his majesty, not having given us any orders—I say that the provost of the merchants having made us a proposal which was a very acceptable one, which was that of admitting a hundred men of the civic guard into the castle, you might, to avoid the evils which I foresee, accede to the proposal of Monsieur de Flesselles."

" In your opinion, then, Monsieur de Losme, the power which represents the city of Paris is a power which we ought to obey ? "

" In the absence of the direct authority of his majesty, yes, sir, it is my opinion."

" Well, then," said De Launay, leading the major into a corner of the courtyard, " read that, Monsieur de Losme."

And he handed him a small square piece of paper.

The major read it.

" Hold firm ! I amuse the Parisians with cockades and promises. Before the close of the day, Monsieur de Bezenval will send you a reinforcement. DE FLESSELLES."

" How, then, did this note reach you, sir ? " inquired the major.

" In the letter which the gentlemen of the deputation brought me. They thought that they were delivering to me a request to surrender the Bastile, while they were delivering to me an order to defend it."

The major bowed his head.

" Go to your post, Monsieur de Losme, and do not leave it until I send for you."

M. de Losme obeyed.

De Launay very quietly refolded the letter, and put it into his pocket. He then returned to his artillerymen, and recommended them to fire low, and to take good aim.

The artillerymen obeyed, as M de Losme had obeyed.

But the fate of the fortress was predestined. No human power could delay its fulfilment.

To every cannon shot the people replied by shouting : " We will have the Bastile ! "

And while mouths were shouting, arms were vigorously acting.

Among the voices which shouted most energetically, among the arms which were acting the most efficaciously, were the voices and arms of Pitou and Billot.

Only each of them proceeded according to his different nature.

Billot, courageous and confident, as in the bull-dog, had from the first rushed forward, defying ball and grape-shot.

Pitou, prudent and circumspect, like the fox, Pitou, endowed to a supreme degree with the instinct of self-preservation, made use of all his faculties to watch the danger and avoid it.

His eyes knew the embrasures which sent forth the most deadly fire ; they distinguished the almost imperceptible movement of the brazen mouth which was about to be fired. He had at last studied the thing so minutely, that he could divine the precise moment when the battery gun was about to be fired across the drawbridge.

Then his eyes having performed their office, it was the turn of his limbs to work for their proprietor.

His shoulders were drawn in, his chest contracted, his whole body did not seem to offer a larger surface than a plank when seen edgeways.

In these movements of Pitou, of the chubby Pitou—for Pitou was thin only in the legs—there remained only a geometrical line, which had neither breadth nor thickness.

He had selected for his post a corner in the passage from the first drawbridge to the second, a sort of vertical parapet formed by jutting stones. His head was protected by one of these stones, his body by another, his knees by a third, and Pitou congratulated himself that nature and the art of fortification were thus so agreeably combined that a stone was given him to protect each of the parts where a wound might have proved mortal.

From his corner, in which he was covered like a hare in its form, he now and then fired a shot; but merely for form sake, for he had before him only walls and pieces of timber; but this evidently pleased Billot, who from time to time called out:

"Fire, you lazy fellow, fire!"

And he, in his turn, would cry to Billot, but in order to calm his exuberant ardor instead of exciting it:

"But do not expose yourself so much, Father Billot."

Or else:

"Take care of yourself, Monsieur Billot; there is a cannon pointed at you. There, I have just heard them cocking the Musette!"

And scarcely had Pitou uttered these words, so full of foresight, than the cannon belched forth its grape-shot, sweeping the passage between the bridges.

Notwithstanding all these injunctions, Billot performed prodigies of strength and activity, but of perfect inutility. Not being able to shed his blood—and assuredly it was not his fault—he shed large and abundant drops of perspiration.

Ten times did Pitou seize him by the skirts of his jacket, and pulled him to the ground in spite of his great strength, at a moment when a discharge would have assuredly swept him off.

But each time Billot jumped up again, not only like Antæus, with renewed strength, but with some new idea.

At one time this idea consisted in venturing upon the platform of the bridge to hack at the beams which the chains upheld, as he had before done.

Then Pitou uttered the fearful howls to restrain the farmer, and finding that his howling was of no avail, he would rush from his place of safety to him, crying:

"Monsieur Billot, my dear Monsieur Billot, why, Madame Billot will be a widow, if you go on in this way."

And the Swiss soldiers could be seen placing their muskets obliquely through the embrasure of the Musette, to aim at the audacious man who was endeavoring to reduce their bridge to chips.

At another time he called upon his men to bring up a cannon to destroy the head-work of the bridge; but then the Musette was fired, the gunners retreated, and Billot

remained alone to load the gun and fire it, which again
brought out Pitou from his retreat.

"Monsieur Billot," cried he, "Monsieur Billot, in the
name of Mademoiselle Catherine, I conjure you, reflect a
moment! Should you get yourself killed, Mademoiselle
Catherine will be an orphan."

And Billot yielded to this reason, which appeared to
have much more influence on his mind than the first.

At length the fruitful imagination of the farmer gave
birth to another idea.

He ran toward the square, crying :

"A cart! bring a cart here !"

Pitou considered that that which was good would be
rendered excellent by being doubled. He followed Billot,
vociferating :

"Two carts! two carts!" and immediately ten carts
were brought.

"Some straw and some dry hay !" cried Billot.

"Some straw and some dry hay !" reiterated Pitou.

And almost instantly two hundred men came forward,
each carrying a truss of straw or hay.

They were obliged to call that they had ten times more
than they wanted. In an hour there was a heap of forage
which would have equaled the height of the Bastile.

Billot placed himself between the shafts of a cart loaded
with straw, and instead of dragging it he pushed it on
before him.

Pitou did the same without knowing what it could be
for, but thinking he could not do better than to imitate
the farmer.

Elie and Hullin divined Billot's intention ; they each
seized a cart and pushed it before them into the courtyard.

They had scarcely entered when they were assailed by a
discharge of grape-shot; they heard the balls strike with
a whizzing sound among the straw or hay, or against the
woodwork of the carts. But neither of the assailants
received a wound.

As soon as this discharge was over, two or three hundred men with muskets rushed on behind those who were
pushing forward the carts, and, sheltered by these moving
ramparts, they lodged themselves beneath the apron of the
bridge itself.

Then Billot drew from his pocket a flint, a steel, and some tinder, formed a match by rubbing gunpowder on paper, and set fire to it.

The powder ignited the paper, and the paper ignited the straw and hay.

Each formed a torch for himself, and the four carts were simultaneously set fire to.

The flames reached the apron, caught the timbers with its acerated teeth, and ran along the woodwork of the bridge.

A shout of joy then, uttered from the courtyard, was taken up by the crowd in the Square St. Antoine and reiterated with deafening clamor. They saw the smoke rising above the walls, and they hence imagined that something fatal to the besiegers was occurring.

In fact, the reddened chains detached themselves from the beams. The bridge fell, half broken and destroyed by fire, smoking and cracking. The firemen rushed forward with their engines, and soon extinguished the flames upon the bridge.

The governor ordered the Invalides to fire upon the people, but they refused.

The Swiss alone obeyed, but they were not artillerymen; they were therefore obliged to abandon the guns.

The French Guards, on the contrary, seeing that the enemy's fire was discontinued, brought up their gun and planted it before the gate; their third shot shivered it to pieces.

The governor had gone up to the platform of the castle to see whether the promised reinforcements were approaching, when he found himself suddenly enveloped in smoke. It was then that he precipitately descended and ordered the artillerymen to fire.

The refusal of the Invalides exasperated him. The breaking down of the gate made him at once comprehend that all was lost.

M. de Launay knew that he was hated. He felt that there was no salvation for him. During the whole time that the combat had lasted, he had matured the idea of burying himself beneath the ruins of the Bastile.

At the moment he felt assured that all further defense was hopeless, he snatched a match from the hand of one of the artillerymen, and sprung toward the cellar which served as a powder magazine.

"The gunpowder! the gunpowder!" cried twenty terrified voices, "the powder, the powder!"

They saw the burning match in the governor's hand. They guessed his purpose. Two soldiers rushed forward and crossed their bayonets before his breast just at the moment when he had opened the door.

"You may kill me," said De Launay, "but you cannot kill me quick enough to prevent me letting this match fall among the powder-casks; and then besieged and besiegers will all be blown to atoms."

The two soldiers stopped. Their bayonets remained crossed and pointed at De Launay's breast, but De Launay was still their commander, for all felt that he had the lives of the whole of them in his power. His actions had nailed every one to the spot on which he stood. The assailants perceived that something extraordinary was happening. They looked anxiously into the courtyard and saw the governor threatened and threatening in his turn.

"Hear me," cried De Launay to the besiegers; "as surely as I hold this match in my hand, with which I could exterminate you all, should any one of you make a single step to enter this courtyard, so surely will I set fire to the powder!"

Those who heard these words imagined that they already felt the ground trembling beneath their feet.

"What is your wish? what do you demand?" cried several voices, with an accent of terror.

"I wish for a capitulation," replied De Launay, "an honorable capitulation."

The assailants pay but little attention to what the governor says, they cannot credit such an act of despair; they wish to enter the courtyard. Billot is at their head. Suddenly Billot trembles and turns pale; he had just remembered Dr. Gilbert.

As long as Billot had thought only of himself, it was a matter of little importance to him whether the Bastile was blown up, and he blown up with it, but Gilbert's life must be saved at any cost.

"Stop!" exclaimed Billot, throwing himself before Elie and Hullin; "stop in the name of the prisoners!"

And these men, who feared not to encounter death themselves, retreated, pale and trembling, in their turn.

"What do you demand?" they cried, renewing the

question they had previously put to the governor by his own men.

"I demand that you should all withdraw," replied De Launay, fiercely. "I will not accept any proposal so long as there remains a single stranger in the Bastile."

"But," said Billot, "will you not take advantage of our absence to place yourself again in a state of defense?"

"If the capitulation is refused, you shall find everything in the state it now is, you at that gate, I where I am now standing."

"You pledge your word for that?"

"On the honor of a gentleman."

Some of them shook their heads.

"On the honor of a gentleman," reiterated De Launay. "Is there any one here who can still doubt, when a gentleman has pledged his honor?"

"No, no! no one!" repeated five hundred voices.

"Let paper, pen, and ink be brought here to me."

The orders of the governor were instantly obeyed.

"'Tis well," said De Launay.

Then turning toward the assailants:

"And now, you must retire."

Billot, Hullin, and Elie set the example, and were the first to withdraw.

All the others followed them.

De Launay placed the match by his side, and began writing the capitulation on his knee.

The Invalides and the Swiss soldiers, who felt that their existence depended on the result, gazed at him while he was writing with a sort of respectful terror.

De Launay looked round before allowing his pen to touch the paper. He saw that the courtyard was free of all intruders.

In an instant the people outside were informed of all that had happened within the fortress.

As M. de Losme had said, the population seemed to spring up from beneath the pavement. One hundred thousand men surrounded the Bastile.

They were no longer merely laborers and artisans, but citizens of every class had joined them. They were not merely men in the prime of life, but children and old men had rushed forward to the fight.

And all of them had arms of some description ; all of them shouted vehemently.

Here and there among the groups was to be seen a woman in despair, with hair disheveled, wringing her hands and uttering maledictions against the granite giant.

She is some mother whose son the Bastile has just annihilated, some daughter whose father the Bastile has just leveled with the ground, some wife whose husband the Bastile has just exterminated.

But during some moments no sounds had issued from the Bastile, no flames, no smoke. The Bastile had become as silent as the tomb.

It would have been useless to have endeavored to count the spots made by the balls which had marbled its surface. Every one had wished to fire a shot at the stone monster, the visible symbol of tyranny.

Therefore, when it was rumored in the crowd that the Bastile was about to capitulate, that its governor had promised to surrender, they could scarcely credit the report.

Amid this general doubt, as they did not yet dare to congratulate themselves, as they were silently awaiting the result, they saw a letter pushed forth through a loophole on the point of a sword.

Only between this letter and the besiegers there was the ditch of the Bastile, wide, deep, and full of water.

Billot calls for a plank ; three are brought and are pushed across the ditch, but being too short, did not reach the opposite side. A fourth is brought, which lodges on either edge of the ditch.

Billot had them lashed together as he best could, and then ventured unhesitatingly upon the trembling bridge.

The whole crowd remained breathlessly silent ; all eyes are fixed upon the man who appears suspended above the ditch, whose stagnant waters resemble those of the river Cocytus.

Pitou tremblingly seated himself on the edge of the slope, and hid his head between his knees.

His heart failed him, and he wept.

When Billot had got about two-thirds of the way over the plank, it twisted beneath his feet. Billot extends his arms, falls, and disappears in the ditch.

Pitou utters a fearful groan and throws himself into the

ditch, like a Newfoundland dog anxious to save his master.

A man then approached the plank from which Billot had just before been precipitated.

Without hesitation he walked across the temporary bridge. This man is Stanislaus Maillard, the usher of the Châtelet.

When he had reached the spot below which Pitou and Billot were struggling in the muddy ditch, he, for a moment, cast a glance upon them, and seeing that there was no doubt they would regain the shore in safety, he continued to walk on.

Half a minute afterward he had reached the opposite side of the ditch, and had taken the letter which was held out to him on the point of a sword.

Then, with the same tranquillity, the same firmness of step, he recrossed the ditch.

But at the moment when the crowd was pressing round him to hear the letter read, a storm of musket balls rained down upon them from the battlements, and a frightful detonation was heard.

One only cry, but one of those cries which announce the vengeance of a whole people, issues from every mouth.

"Trust then in tyrants!" exclaimed Gonchon.

And then, without thinking any more of the capitulation, without thinking any more of the powder magazine, without thinking of themselves or of the prisoners, without desiring, without demanding anything but vengeance, the people rushed into the courtyard, no longer by hundreds of men, but by thousands.

That which prevents the crowd from entering is no longer the musketry, but the gates, which are too narrow to admit them.

On hearing the detonation we have spoken of, the two soldiers who were still watching M. de Launay threw themselves upon him, a third snatched upon the match and extinguished it by placing his heel upon it.

De Launay drew the sword, which was concealed in his cane, and would have turned it against his own breast, but the soldiers seized it and snapped it in two.

He then felt that all he could do was to resign himself to the result; he therefore tranquilly awaited it.

The people rush forward; the garrison open their arms

to them ; and the Bastile is taken by assault—by main force, without a capitulation.

The reason for this was, that for more than a hundred years the royal fortress had not merely imprisoned inert matter within its walls—it had imprisoned thought also. Thought had thrown down the walls of the Bastile, and the people entered by the breach.

As to the discharge of musketry, which had taken place amid the general silence, during the suspension of hostilities ; as to this unforeseen aggression, as impolitic as it was murderous, it was never known who had ordered it, who had excited it, how it was accomplished.

There are moments when the destiny of a whole nation is being weighed in the scales of Fate. One of them weighs down the other. Every one already thinks he has attained the proposed end. Suddenly some invisible hand lets fall into the other scale the blade of a poniard or a pistol-ball.

Then all changes, and one only cry is heard, " Woe to the vanquished ! "

CHAPTER XVIII.

WHILE the people were thus rushing into the fortress, howling at once with joy and rage, two men were struggling in the muddy waters of the ditch.

These men were Pitou and Billot.

Pitou was supporting Billot. No shot had struck him ; he had not been wounded in any way ; but his fall had somewhat confused the worthy farmer.

Ropes were thrown to them—poles were held out to them.

Pitou caught hold of a pole, Billot a rope.

Five minutes afterward, they were carried in triumph by the people, and eagerly embraced, notwithstanding their muddy state.

One man gives Billot a glass of brandy, another stuffs Pitou's mouth full of sausages, and gives him wine to wash them down.

A third rubs them down with straw, and wishes to place them in the sun to dry their clothes.

Suddenly, an idea, or, rather, a recollection, shot

through the mind of Billot; he tears himself away from their kind cares and rushes into the Bastile.

" To the prisoners!" cried he—" to the prisoners!"

" Yes, to the prisoners!" cried Pitou, in his turn, bounding after the farmer.

The crowd, which until then had only thought of the executioners, shuddered when thinking of their victims.

They with one shout repeated : "Yes, yes, yes—to the prisoners!"

And a new flood of assailants rush through the barriers, seeming to widen the sides of the fortress by their numbers, and bearing liberty with them to the captives.

A dreadful spectacle then offered itself to the eyes of Billot and Pitou. The excited, enraged, maddened throng had precipitated themselves into the courtyard. The first soldier they had met was at once hacked to pieces.

Gonchon had quietly looked on. Doubtless he had thought that the anger of the people, like the currents of great rivers, does more harm when any impediment is thrown in its way to arrest it, than if allowed to tranquilly flow on.

Elie and Hullin, on the contrary, had thrown themselves before the infuriated sacrifices ; they prayed, they supplicated, uttering the sublime lie that they had promised life and safety to the whole garrison.

The arrival of Billot and Pitou was a reinforcement to them.

Billot, whom they were avenging, Billot was living, Billot was not even wounded. The plank had turned under his feet, and that was all ; he had taken a mud-bath, and nothing more.

It was, above all, against the Swiss that the people were particularly enraged, but the Swiss were nowhere to be found. They had had time to put on gray frocks, and they were taken for either servants or for prisoners.

The mob hurled large stones at the dial of the clock, and destroyed the figures of the two captives which supported it. They rushed to the ramparts to mutilate the cannon which had vomited forth death upon them. They even wreaked their vengeance on the stone walls, tearing their hands in endeavoring to displace them. When the first of the conquerors was seen upon the platform, all those who had remained without the fortress, that is to

say, a hundred thousand men, shout with clamorous joy;
"The Bastile is taken!"

This cry resounded through Paris, and spread itself
over the whole of France as if borne with the rapidity of
of eagles' wings.

On hearing this cry all hearts were softened, all eyes shed
tears, all arms were extended; there were no longer any
contending parties; there were no longer any inimical
castes; all Parisians felt that they were brothers, all men
felt that they were free.

A million of men pressed one another in a mutual embrace.

Billot and Pitou had entered the Bastile, following
some and followed by others; what they wished for was not
to claim their share in the triumph; it was the liberty of
the prisoners.

When crossing the courtyard of the government house,
they passed near a man in a gray coat who was standing
calmly, his hand resting on a gold-headed cane.

This man was the governor. He was quietly waiting
either that his friends should come to save him, or that
his enemies should come to strike him down.

Billot, on perceiving him, recognized him, uttered
a light exclamation of surprise, and went straight to
him.

De Launay also recognized Billot. He crossed his arms
and waited, looking at the farmer with an expression that
implied:

"Let me see; is it you that will give me the first
blow?"

Billot at once divined the meaning of his look, and
stopped.

"If I speak to him," said he to himself, "I shall cause
him to be recognized, and should he be recognized, his
death is certain."

And yet, how was he to find Dr. Gilbert amid this chaos
of confusion? How could he drag from the Bastile the
secret which its walls inclosed?

All this hesitation, these heroic scruples, were understood by De Launay.

"What is it that you wish?" asked De Launay, in an
undertone.

"Nothing," replied Billot, pointing with his finger to

the gate, indicating to him that escape was yet possible; "nothing. I shall be able readily to find Doctor Gilbert."

"Third Bertaudière," replied De Launay, in a gentle and almost affectionate tone of voice.

But he stirred not from the place on which he stood.

Suddenly a voice from behind Billot pronounced these words:

"Ah! there is the governor."

This voice was so calm, so hollow, that it appeared not to be of this world, and yet, each word it had uttered was a sharp poniard turned against the breast of De Launay.

He who had spoken was Gonchon.

These words, like the first sounds of an alarm-bell, excited a fearful commotion; all these men, drunk with revengeful feelings, started on hearing them; they looked around with flaming eyes, perceived De Launay, and at once darted upon and seized him."

"Save him," said Billot, as he passed near Elie and Hullin, "or they will murder him."

"Assist us to do so," said the two men.

"I am obliged to remain here," replied Billot, "for I also have some one to save."

In an instant De Launay had been surrounded by a thousand men, who dragged him along, lifted him up, and were bearing him away.

Elie and Hullin bounded after him, crying:

"Stop! stop! we promised him that his life should be saved!"

This was not true; but the thought of uttering this magnanimous falsehood had risen to the minds of these two generous men at the same moment.

In a second, De Launay, followed by Elie and Hullin, disappeared under the vaulted passage which led from the Bastile, amid loud voices of "To the Hôtel de Ville! to the Hôtel de Ville!"

It was a singular spectacle, to see this mournful and silent monument, which for centuries had been tenanted only by prisoners, their guards, and a gloomy governor, now become the prey of the people, who ran through the courtyards, ascended and descended the staircases, buzzing like a swarm of flies, and filling this granite hive with noise and movement.

De Launay, a living prey, was to some of the victors of as great value as the dead prey, the captured Bastile.

Billot, for a moment or two, followed De Launay with his eyes, who was carried rather than led, and appeared to soar above the crowd.

But, as we have said, he soon disappeared. Billot heaved a sigh, looked around him, perceived Pitou, and rushed toward a tower, crying :

"Third Bertaudière."

"A trembling jailer met him on his way.

"Third Bertaudière," said Billot.

"This way, sir," replied the jailer ; "but I have not the keys."

"Where are they ?"

"They took them from me."

"Citizen, lend me your hatchet," said Billot, to one of the men from the faubourg.

"I give it to you," replied the latter ; "I do not want it any more, since the Bastile is taken."

Billot snatched the hatchet, and ran up a staircase, conducted by the jailer.

The jailer stopped before a door.

"Third Bertaudière ?" said the man, inquiringly.

"Yes."

"This is it."

"The prisoner confined in this room is Doctor Gilbert, is it not ?"

"I do not know."

"He was brought here only five or six days ago ?"

"I do not know."

"Well, then," said Billot, "I shall soon know."

And he began chopping at the door with his hatchet.

The door was of oak, but it soon flew into splinters beneath the vigorous blows of the robust farmer.

In a few moments he had cut a hole through it, and could look into the room.

Billot placed his eye at the opening. Through it he could see the interior of the cell.

In the line of sunshine which penetrated into the dungeon through its grated window, a man was standing, his head thrown rather backward, holding in his hand one of the posts of his bedstead, and in an attitude of defense.

This man had evidently prepared himself to knock down the first person who should enter his room.

Notwithstanding his long beard, notwithstanding his pallid countenance, notwithstanding his short-cut hair, Billot recognized him. It was Dr. Gilbert.

"Doctor! doctor!" cried Billot to him, "is it you?"

"Who is it that is calling me?" inquired the prisoner.

"'Twas I—I, Billot, your friend."

"You, Billot?"

"Yes! yes!—he! he!—we! we!" cried the voices of twenty men, who had run into the passage on hearing the vigorous blows struck by Billot.

"But who are you?"

"We?—why, the conquerors of the Bastile. The Bastile is taken—you are free!"

"The Bastile is taken—I am free!" exclaimed the doctor.

And passing both his hands through the opening, he shook the door so violently that the hinges and the lock appeared nearly yielding to his powerful pressure, and part of a panel, already loosened by Billot, broke off, and remained in the prisoner's hands.

"Wait, wait," said Billot, who was afraid that a second effort of so violent a nature would exhaust his strength, which had been overtaxed—"wait."

And he redoubled his blows.

And, indeed, through the opening, which was every moment becoming wider, he could see the prisoner, who had seated himself upon his bench, pale as a specter, and incapable of raising the bedpost which was lying near him, and who but a few moments before another Samson, seemed strong enough to shake down the walls of the Bastile.

"Billot! Billot!" murmured he.

"Yes, yes! and I also, my good doctor—I, Pitou—you must remember poor Pitou, whom you placed at board with his aunt Angelique—Pitou who has come to liberate you."

"But I can get through that hole," cried the doctor.

"No, no!" cried all the voices; "wait."

All those present uniting their strength in one simultaneous effort, some slipping a crowbar between the door and the frame-work, others using a lever between the lock and doorpost, and the remainder pushing with all the might of their shoulders or their hands, the oak gave a last cracking sound, the wall gave way, and they all of them stumbled, one over the other, into the room.

In a moment Gilbert found himself in the arms of Pitou and Gilbert.

Gilbert, the little country lad of the Château de Taverney; Gilbert, whom we left bathed in his blood in a cavern of the Azores, was now a man from thirty-four to thirty-five years old, of pale complexion, though he was not sickly, with black hair, eyes penetrating and fixed. Never did his gaze lose itself in vacuity; never did it wander; when it was not fixed on some exterior object worthy to attract, it was fixed on his own thought, and became only more profound and more gloomy; his nose was straight, being attached to his forehead in a direct line; it rose above a lip of rather scornful expression, which, in the slight space between it and the nether lip, allowed one to perceive the dazzling enamel of his teeth. In ordinary times his dress was simple and grave, like that of a Quaker; but this simplicity was closely allied to elegance from its extreme neatness. His height was somewhat above the medium stature, and he was well formed; as to his strength, we have just seen the feats it could perform when in a state of over-excitement, whether caused by anger or enthusiastic feeling.

Although in prison for five or six days, the doctor had paid the same attention to his person; his beard, which had grown some few lines, caused the paleness of his complexion to contrast favorably with its darkness, and indicated only a negligence which certainly was not the prisoner's but his jailer's who had refused to give him a razor or to allow him to be shaved.

When he had pressed Billot and Pitou in his arms, he turned toward the crowd who had filled his dungeon. Then, as if a moment had sufficed to restore all his self-possession:

"The day which I had foreseen has then arrived," said he. "Thanks to you, my friends—thanks to the eternal genius which watches over the liberty of nations!"

And he held out both his hands to the men who had assisted Billot to break down the door, and who, recognizing in him, from the dignity of his demeanor, and his proud look, a man of superior genius, hardly dared to touch them.

On leaving the dungeon, he walked before all these men, leaning on Billot's shoulder, and followed by Pitou and his liberators.

The first moment had been devoted by Gilbert to friendship and to gratitude, the second had reestablished the distance which existed between the learned doctor and the ignorant farmer, the warm-hearted Pitou and the whole throng which had liberated him.

When he reached the door at the foot of the staircase, Gilbert stopped, on perceiving the broad sunshine which beamed full upon him. He paused, crossing his arms over his breast, and raising his eyes to heaven. "Hail to thee, lovely Liberty!" he exclaimed, "I saw thee spring to life in another world, and we are old friends. Hail to thee, lovely Liberty!"

And the smile of the doctor clearly said, that the cries he then heard of a whole people, inebriated with independence, was no new thing to him.

Then meditating for a few seconds :

"Billot," said he, "the people, then, have vanquished despotism?"

"Yes, sir."

"And you came here to fight?"

"I came to liberate you."

"You knew, then, of my arrest?"

"Your son informed me of it this morning."

"Poor Sebastian—have you seen him?"

"I have seen him."

"And he remained quietly at his school?"

"I left him struggling with four of the attendants of the infirmary."

"Is he ill—has he been delirious?"

"He wanted to come with us to fight."

"Ah!" ejaculated the doctor, and a smile of triumph passed over his features. His son had proved himself to be what he had hoped.

"And what did you say to him?" inquired the doctor.

"I said, since Doctor Gilbert is in the Bastile, let us take the Bastile ; and now the Bastile is taken. But that is not all."

"What is there then besides?" asked the doctor.

"The casket has been stolen."

"The casket which I had confided to your care?"

"Yes."

"Stolen! and by whom?"

"By some men dressed in black, who came into my house under the pretext of seizing your pamphlets; they arrested me, locked me up in a room, they searched the house all over, found the casket, and carried it off."

"When did this happen?"

"Yesterday."

"Ho! ho! there is an evident connection between my arrest and this robbery. The person who caused my arrest at the same time had the casket stolen. Let me but know the person who originated my arrest, and I shall know who it was contrived the robbery. Where are the archives of the fortress?" continued the doctor, turning to the jailer.

"In the courtyard of the government house, sir," replied the jailer.

"Then to the archives, my friends—to the archives!" cried the doctor.

"Sir," said the jailer, stopping him, "let me go with you, or speak a word in my favor to these worthy people, that no harm may happen to me."

"Be it so," said Gilbert.

Then addressing the crowd who surrounded him, and gazing at him with curiosity mingled with respect:

"My friends," said he, "I recommend this worthy man to you; he only fulfilled his office in opening and shutting the prison doors; but he was kind toward the prisoner; let no injury happen to him."

"No, no!" cried the crowd, with one accord, "no!—he need not fear; no harm shall be done to him. Let him come with us."

"I thank you, sir," said the jailer to the doctor; "but if you wish for anything in the archives, I advise you to move quickly, for I believe they are burning the papers."

"Oh! then, there is not an instant to be lost," cried Gilbert. "To the archives!"

And he hastened toward the courtyard of the government house followed by the crowd, at the head of which were still Billet and Pitou.

CHAPTER XIX.

ON reaching the door of the office in which the archives were kept, Gilbert perceived that a large heap of old papers was being burned.

Unhappily, it is a general consequence that after having obtained a victory, the first desire the people have to gratify is that of destruction.

The archives of the Bastile had been invaded.

This office was a vast hall, heaped up with registry books and plans ; the documents relating to all the prisoners who had been confined in the Bastile during the last hundred years were confusedly inclosed in it.

The people tore these papers to pieces with senseless rage ; it doubtless appeared to them that by destroying these registrations of imprisonment they were legally bestowing freedom on the prisoners.

Gilbert went into the hall, seconded by Pitou; he began to examine the register books which were still standing on the shelves ; that of the running year was not to be found.

The doctor, a man who was always so cool and calm, turned pale, and stamped with impatience.

At that moment Pitou caught sight of one of those heroic urchins who are always to be found in popular triumphs, who was carrying off on his head and running off with it toward the fire a volume similar in shape and binding to that which Dr. Gilbert had been examining.

He ran after him, and, with his long legs, speedily overtook him.

It was the register of the year 1789.

The negotiation did not occupy much time. Pitou was considered as one of the leaders of the conquerors, and explained to the boy that a prisoner had occasion to use that register, and the urchin yielded up his prey to him, consoling himself with the observation :

" It is all the same to me ; I can burn another."

Pitou opened the book, turned over the leaves, hunted through it, and on the last page found the words :

" This day, the 9th of July, 1789, came in the Sieur G.,

a philosopher and political writer, a very dangerous person ; to be kept in close and secret confinement."

He carried the book to the doctor.

" Here, Monsieur Gilbert," said he to him, " is not this what you are seeking for ? "

" Oh ! " cried the doctor, joyfully, and seizing hold of the book ; " yes, that is it."

And he read the words we have given above.

" And now," said he, " let us see from whom the order emanated."

And he examined the margin.

" Necker ! " he exclaimed ; " the order for my arrest signed by Necker, my friend Necker ! Oh ! most assuredly there must have been some foul plot ! "

" Necker is your friend ? " cried the crowd with respect, for it will be remembered that this name had great influence with the people.

" Yes, yes, my friends," said the doctor, " I am convinced that Monsieur Necker did not know that I was in prison. But I will at once go to him."

" Go to him—and where ? " inquired Billot.

" To Versailles, to be sure."

" Monsieur Necker is not at Versailles ; Monsieur Necker is exiled."

" And where ? "

" At Brussels."

" But his daughter ? "

" Ah ! I know nothing of her," replied Billot.

" His daughter is at his country house, at St. Quen," said a voice from the crowd.

" I am obliged to you," replied Gilbert, not knowing even to whom his thanks were addressed.

Then, turning toward those who were occupied in burning the papers :

" My friends," he said, " in the name of history, which in these archives would find matter for the condemnation of tyrants, let me conjure you not to pursue this work for destruction, demolish the Bastile, stone by stone, that not a vestige, not a trace of it remain, but respect the papers, respect the registers ; the enlightenment of the future is contained in them.

The crowd had scarcely heard these words, than, with its usual admirable intelligence, it duly weighed this reasoning.

"The doctor is right!" cried a hundred voices; "no more devastation of these papers! Let us remove all these papers to the Hôtel de Ville!"

A fireman who, with a number of his companions, had dragged an engine into the courtyard, on hearing the report that the governor was about to blow up the fortress, directed the pipe of his hose upon the burning pile, which, like to that of Alexandria, was about to destroy the archives of a world; in a few minutes it was extinguished.

"And at whose request were you arrested?" said Billot to Gilbert.

"Ah! that is precisely what I am endeavoring to discover and cannot ascertain—the name is left in blank."

Then, after a moment's reflection:

"But I will find it out," said he.

And tearing out the leaf on which the entry was made regarding him, he folded it up, and put it into his pocket. Then addressing himself to Billot and Pitou:

"My friends," said he, "let us leave this place; we have nothing further to do here."

"Well, let us go," replied Billot; "only it is a thing more easily talked about than done."

And, in fact, the crowd, urged into the interior courtyards by curiosity, were so closely packed, that egress was almost impossible. And, to add to the difficulty, the other liberated prisoners were standing close to the principal gate.

Eight prisoners, including Gilbert, had been liberated that morning.

Their names were: Jean Bechade, Bernard Laroche, Antoine Pujade, De White, Le Comte de Solage, and Tavernier.

The four first inspired but little interest. They were accused of having forged a bill of exchange, without any proof whatsoever being brought against them, and which led to the supposition that the charge against them was false; they had been only two years in the Bastile.

The Count de Solage was a man about thirty years of age, of joyous and expansive temperament; he embraced his liberators, congratulated them upon their victory, which he loudly extolled, and related to them the history of his captivity. He had been arrested in 1782, and imprisoned at Vincennes, his father having obtained a *lettre*

de cachet against him, and was removed from that castle
to the Bastile, where he had remained five years without
ever having seen a judge or having been examined even
once ; his father had been dead two years, and no one had
ever thought of him. If the Bastile had not been taken,
it is probable that no one would have ever remembered
that he was there.

De White was a man advanced in years, somewhere
about sixty ; he uttered strangely incoherent words, and
with a foreign accent. To the questions which poured in
upon him from all sides, he replied that he did not know
how long he had been incarcerated, or what had been the
cause of his arrest. He remembered that he was the cousin of M. de Sartines, and that was all. One of the turn-
keys, whose name was Guyon, said that he had seen M. de
Sartines, on one occasion, go into White's cell, where he
made him sign a power of attorney. But the prisoner had
completely forgotten the circumstance.

Tavernier was the oldest of them all. He had been shut
up for ten years in the Iles Sainte Marguerite ; thirty years
had he been immured in the Bastile. He was upward of
ninety years old, with white hair and long white beard ;
his eyes had become dimmed by remaining so long in a
dark cell, and he saw everything as through a cloud. When
the crowd broke open his door, he could not comprehend
what they wanted with him ; when they spoke to him of
liberty he shook his head ; then, afterward, when they
told him that the Bastile was taken :

"Ho ! ho !" cried he, "what will Louis XV., Madame
de Pompadour, and the Duke de la Vrillière say to all
this ?"

Tavernier was not even mad ; like De White, he had
become an idiot.

The joy of these men was frightful to behold, for it cried
aloud for vengeance, so much did it resemble terror. Two
or three of them seemed almost expiring in the midst of
the clamor raised by a hundred thousand voices. Poor
men ! they who during the whole time of their confinement in the Bastile had never heard two human voices
speaking at the same moment ; they who were no longer
accustomed to any noises but the low and mysterious one
of wood, when warping with the damp, that of the spider,
when, unperceived, he weaves his net with a ticking simi-

lar to that of an invisible pendulum, or of the affrighted
rat, which gnaws and flies at the least stir.

At the moment that Gilbert made his appearance, the
most enthusiastic among the crowd proposed that the prisoner should be carried in triumph—a proposal which was
unanimously adopted.

Gilbert would have much desired to avoid this species
of ovation; but there were no means of escaping it;
he had been at once recognized, as well as Billot and
Pitou.

Cries of "To the Hôtel de Ville! To the Hôtel de
Ville!" resounded on all sides, and Gilbert was raised in
an instant on the shoulders of twenty persons.

In vain did the doctor resist, in vain did Billot and Pitou
distribute among their victorious brethren the most vigorous fisticuffs; joy and enthusiasm had hardened the skins
of the populace. These, and even blows given with pike-
handles and the butt-ends of muskets, appeared only gentle
caresses to the conquerors, and only served to redouble
their delight.

Gilbert was therefore compelled to mount the triumphal
car.

This car was formed of a square table, in the middle of
which was stuck a lance, to serve as a support to the victor,
and enable him to preserve his balance.

The doctor, therefore, was raised above this sea of heads,
which undulated from the Bastile to the Arcade St. Jean,
a tempestuous sea, whose waves were bearing, in the midst
of pikes and bayonets, and arms of every description, of
every form, and of every age, the triumphant prisoners.

But at the same time, this terrible and irresistible ocean
was rolling on another group, so compact and closely
formed that it appeared an island. This group was the
one which was leading away De Launay as a prisoner.

Around this group rose cries not less tumultuous nor
less enthusiastic than those which accompanied the prisoners; but they were not shouts of triumph, they were
threats of death.

Gilbert, from his elevated position, did not lose a single
detail of this frightful spectacle.

He was the only one among all the prisoners who had
been restored to liberty who was in the enjoyment of all
his faculties. Five days of captivity were merely a dark

spot in his life.   His eyes had not been weakened or rendered dim by his short sojourn in the Bastile.

A combat, generally, does not have the effect of render-
ing the combatants pitiless, excepting during the time
that it continues.   Men, generally, when issuing from a
struggle in which they have risked their lives, without receiving injury, are full of kindly feelings toward their
enemies.

But in the great popular commotions, such as those of
which France had seen so many from the times of the Jac-
querie down to our own days, the masses whom fear has
withheld from aiding in the fight, whom noise has irritated, the masses at once ferocious and cowardly, endeavor,
after the victory has been gained, to claim their share of
the triumph which they had not dared to accelerate.
They take their share in the vengeance.

From the moment of his leaving the Bastile, the procession was the commencement of the governor's execution.

Elie, who had taken the governor's life under his own
responsibility, marched at the head of the group, protected
by his uniform and by the admiration of the people, who
had seen him one of the first to advance amid the enemy's
fire.   He carried his sword above his head, on the point
of which was the note which M. de Launay had caused to
be handed to the people through one of the loopholes of
the Bastile.

After him came the guard of the royal taxes, holding in
his hand the key of the fortress ; then Maillard, bearing
the standard ; and after him a young man carrying the regulations of the Bastile on his bayonet; an odious rescript,
by means of which so many bitter tears had flowed.

The governor walked next, protected by Hullin and two
or three others, but who disappeared amid the throng of
threatening fists, of waving sabers, and of quivering
lances.

By the side of this group, and rolling onward in an almost parallel line with it in the great artery of the Rue St.
Antoine, which leads from the boulevard to the river, another could be distinguished, not less threatening, not less
terrible than the first ; it was that which was dragging
forward Major de Losme, whom we have seen for a moment combating the will of the governor, and who at
length had been compelled to bow down his head before

the determination which De Launay had taken to defend himself.

Major de Losme was a worthy, brave, and excellent young man. Since he had been in the Bastile he had alleviated the sorrows of many of the prisoners by his kind treatment of them. But the people were ignorant of this. The people, from his brillant uniform, imagined that he was the governor. Whereas the governor, thanks to his gray coat, on which there was no embroidery whatsoever, and from which he had torn the ribbon of the Order of St. Louis, was surrounded, as it were, by a protecting doubt which could be dispelled by those only who were acquainted with his person.

Such was the spectacle which offered itself to the grieved eyes of Dr. Gilbert. His look, even in the midst of dangers, was always calm and observing, qualities which were inherent in his powerful organization.

Hullin, on leaving the Bastile, had called around him his most trusty and devoted friends, the most valiant of the popular soldiers of that day, and four or five had responded to his call, and endeavored to second him in his generous design of protecting the governor. Among them are three men of whom impartial history has consecrated the memory ; their names were Arne, Chollat, and De Lepine.

These men, preceded, as we have said, by Hullin and Maillard, were therefore endeavoring to defend the life of one whose death a hundred thousand men were clamorously calling for.

Around them had ranged themselves some grenadiers of the French Guard, whose uniform having become popular during the last two days, was an object of veneration to the people.

M. de Launay had escaped receiving any blow as long as the arms of his generous defenders were able to ward them off ; but he had not escaped insulting language and threats.

At the corner of the Rue de Jouy, of the five grenadiers of the French Guards who had joined the procession on leaving the Bastile, not one remained. They had one after the other been carried off on the way, by the enthusiasm of the crowd, and perhaps also by the calculation of assassins, and Gilbert had seen them disappear one after the other, like beads from a rosary from which the cord has been broken.

From that moment he had foreseen that the victory which had been gained was about to be tarnished by a sanguinary sacrifice; he had attempted to jump from the table which served him as a triumphal car, but arms of iron had riveted him to it. In his powerless position he had directed Billot and Pitou to rush forward to defend the governor, and both of them, obedient to his voice, had made every effort to cleave through the human waves and and get near to M. de Launay.

And, in fact, the little group of his defenders stood in great need of a reinforcement. Chollat, who had not tasted food since the previous evening, had felt his strength giving way, and at length had fainted; it was with great difficulty that he had been raised and saved from being trampled under foot.

But this was a breach made in the wall, a falling in of the dike,

A man rushed through this breach, and whirling the butt of his gun over his head, aimed a deadly blow at the uncovered head of the governor.

But De Lepine, who saw the terrific blow descending, had time enough to throw himself, with outstretched arms, between the governor and his assailant, and received on his forehead the blow intended for the governor.

Stunned by the shock, blinded with his own blood, which streamed into his eyes, he staggered, and covered his face with his hands, and, when he could again see, the governor was twenty paces from him.

It was at this moment that Billot, dragging Pitou after him through the crowd, came up to him.

He perceived that what exposed M. de Launay, above all, to observation, was his being the only man in the crowd who was bareheaded.

Billot took his hat, stretched out his arm, and placed it on the governor's head.

De Launay turned round and recognized Billot.

"I thank you," he said; "but whatever you may do, you will not save me."

"Let us only reach the Hôtel de Ville," said Hullin, "and I will answer for your safety."

"Yes," replied De Launay, "but shall we reach it?"

" With the help of God we will attempt it," rejoined Hullin.

And, in fact, there was some hope of succeeding, for they were just entering the square before the Hôtel de Ville ; but this square was thronged with men with naked arms, brandishing pikes and sabers. The report, which had flown from street to street, had announced to them that the governor and the major of the Bastile were being brought to them ; and like a pack of hungry hounds eager to be loosed upon their prey, they awaited, grinding their teeth and impatient for their approach.

As soon as they saw the procession approach they rushed toward the governor.

Hullin saw that this was the moment of extreme danger, of the last struggle ; if he could only get the governor to the front steps, and get him to rush up the staircase, De Launay was saved.

" To me, Elie !—to me, Maillard !—to me all men with hearts," cried he ; " our honor is at stake."

Elie and Maillard heard the appeal ; they made a rush into the center of the mob, and the people seconded them but too well ; they made way for them to pass, but closed in behind them.

In this manner Elie and Maillard were separated from the principal group, and were prevented returning to it.

The crowd saw the advantage it had gained, and made a furious effort. Like an enormous boa, it intwined its gigantic folds around the group. Billot was lifted off his feet and dragged away ; Pitou, who thought only of Billot, allowed himself to be forced away in the same throng. Hullin, being hurried on by the crowd, stumbled against the first step of the Hôtel de Ville, and fell. He got up, but it was to fall again almost immediately, and this time De Launay fell with him.

The governor was constant to the last ; up to the final moment he uttered not a single complaint : he did not ask for mercy, but he cried out in a loud, shrill tone :

" Tigers, that you are, at all events do not allow me to remain thus in suspense ; kill me at once ! "

Never was order more promptly executed than this reproachful request of the poor governor. In an instant around the fallen De Launay every head was bowed down toward him. For a moment nothing could be seen but upraised and threatening hands, grasping poniards which as suddenly disappeared; then was seen a head severed from the body, and which was raised, still streaming with blood, upon the end of a pike; the features had retained their livid and contemptuous smile.

This was the first.

Gilbert, from his elevated position, could see all that was passing; Gilbert had once more attempted to spring to the assistance of the governor, but two hundred arms prevented him.

He turned his head from the disgusting spectacle and sighed.

This head, with its staring eyes, was raised immediately in front, as if to salute him with a last look, of the window in which De Flesselles was standing surrounded and protected by the electors.

It would have been difficult to decide whether the face of the living or that of the dead man was the most pale and livid.

Suddenly an immense uproar arose from the spot on which was lying the mutilated body of De Launay. His pockets had been searched by his assassins, and in his breast-pocket had been found the note which the provost of the merchants had addressed to him, and which he had shown to De Losme.

This note, our readers may remember, was couched in the following terms:

"Hold firm! I amuse the Parisians with cockades and promises. Before the close of the day Monsieur de Bezenval will send you a reinforcement.

"DE FLESSELLES."

The most blasphemous imprecations rose from the pavement of the square to the window of the Hôtel de Ville in which De Flesselles was standing.

Without guessing the cause of this new tumult, he fully comprehended the threat, and hastily drew back from the window; but he had been seen, every one knew that he was there; the crowd rushed up the staircase, and this time the movement was so universal that the men who had been carrying Dr. Gilbert abandoned him to follow the living tide which was overflowing the great staircase.

Gilbert would also have ·gone into the Hôtel de Ville, not to threaten, but to protect Flesselles. He had already ascended three or four of the front steps, when he felt himself violently pulled back. He turned round to disengaged himself from this new obstruction, but he recognized Billot and Pitou.

"Oh!" exclaimed Gilbert, who from his commanding position could glance over the whole square, "what can they be doing yonder?"

And he pointed with his convulsively clinched hand to the corner of the Rue de la Tixeranderie.

"Come with us, doctor, come!" simultaneously cried Billot and Pitou.

"Oh, the assassins!" cried the doctor, "the assassins!"

And indeed at that moment Major de Losme fell, killed by a desperate blow from a hatchet—the people confounding in their rage the egotistical and barbarous governor, who had been the persecutor of his prisoners, with the generous man who had been their friend and reliever.

"Oh! yes, yes," said he; "let us be gone, for I begin to be ashamed of having been liberated by such men."

"Doctor," said Billot, "be not uneasy on that score. The men who fought down yonder are not the same men who are committing these horrid massacres."

But at the moment when the doctor was about to descend the steps which he had gone up, to hasten to the assistance of Flesselles, the flood which had poured into the building was again vomited forth. Amid the torrent of men was one who was struggling furiously as they dragged him forward.

"To the Palais Royal! to the Palais Royal!" cried the crowd.

"Yes, my friends—yes, my good friends—to the Palais Royal!" repeated the man.

And they went toward the river, as if this human inundation had wished, not to bear him toward the Palais Royal, but to drag him toward the Seine.

"Oh!" cried Gilbert, "here is another they are about to murder; let us endeavor to save him at least." But scarcely had he pronounced these words, when a pistol shot was heard, and De Flesselles disappeared amid the smoke.

Gilbert covered his eyes with both his hands, with a

gesture of excessive anger ; he cursed the people who, after having shown themselves so great, had not the firmness to remain pure, and had sullied the victory they had gained by a triple assassination.

Then, when he removed his hands from his eyes, he saw three heads raised above the crowd on three pikes.

The first was that of De Flesselles, the second that of De Losme, the third that of De Launay.

The one rose above the front steps of the Hôtel de Ville, the other from the middle of the Rue de la Tixeranderie, the third on the Quay Pelletier.

From their relative positions they assumed the form of a triangle.

"Oh, Balsamo ! Balsamo !" murmured the doctor, with a sigh ; "it is then such a triangle as this that is to be symbolical of liberty !"

And he ran along the Rue de la Vannerie, Billot and Pitou accompanying him.

CHAPTER XX.

AT the corner of the Rue Planche Mibray the doctor met a hackney-coach, made a sign to the coachman to stop, and hastily got into it.

Billot and Pitou quickly followed him.

"To the College of Louis le Grand !" cried Gilbert, and threw himself into one corner of the vehicle, where he fell into a profound reverie, which was respected by Billot and Pitou.

They went over the Pont au Change by the Rue de le Cité, the Rue St. Jacques, and at length reached the College Louis le Grand.

All Paris was trembling with emotion. The news had spread rapidly throughout the city ; rumors of the assassinations on the Place de la Grève were mingled with the glorious recital of the taking of the Bastile. On every face could be seen depicted the various emotions to which the news gave rise, according to the varied feelings they excited—the lightnings of the soul which thus betrayed themselves.

Gilbert had not once looked out of the coach window— Gilbert had not uttered a single word. There is always a ridiculous side in popular ovations, and Gilbert contemplated his ovation in that point of view.

And besides, it also appeared to him that notwithstanding all he had done to prevent it, some drops of the blood which had been shed would fall upon his head.

The doctor alighted from the hackney-coach at the college gate, and made a sign to Billot to follow him.

As to Pitou, he discreetly remained in the coach.

Sebastian was still in the infirmary. The principal, in person, on Dr. Gilbert's being announced, conducted him thither.

Billot, who although not a very acute observer, well knew the character of both father and son—Billot attentively examined the scene which was passing before his eyes.

Weak, irritable, and nervous as the boy had shown himself in the moment of despair, he evinced an equal degree of tranquillity and reserve in the moment of joy.

On perceiving his father he turned pale, and words failed him. A slight trembling shook his legs, and then he ran and threw his arms around his father's neck, uttering a cry of joy, which resembled a cry of grief, and then held him silently clasped within his arms.

The doctor responded as silently to this mute pressure; only after having embraced his son he looked at him with an expression that was more sorrowful than joyous.

A more skilful observer than Billot would have said that some misfortune or some crime existed in the relations between that youth and that man.

The youth was less reserved in his conduct toward Billot. When he could observe any one excepting his father, who had in the first moment engrossed all his attention, he ran to the good farmer, and threw his arms round his neck, saying:

"You are a worthy man, Monsieur Billot; you have kept your promise to me, and I thank you for it."

"Yes, yes," replied Billot; "and it was not without some trouble, I can assure you, Monsieur Sebastian. Your father was very nicely and safely locked up, and it was necessary to do a tolerable deal of damage before we could get him out."

"Sebastian," inquired the doctor, with some anxiety, "you are in good health?"

"Yes, father," replied the young man, "although you find me here in the infirmary."

Gilbert smiled.

"I know why it was you were brought here," said he.

The boy smiled in his turn.

"Have you everything you require here?" continued the doctor.

"Everything—thanks to you."

"I shall then, my dear boy, still recommend to you the same, the only line of conduct—study assiduously."

"Yes, father."

"I know that to you the word study is not a vain and monotonous word; if I believed it to be so, I would no longer say it."

"Father, it is not for me to reply to you on that head; it is the province of Monsieur Berardier, our excellent principal."

The doctor turned toward M. Berardier, who made a sign that he had something to say to him.

"I will speak to you again in a moment, Sebastian," said the doctor.

And he went over to the principal.

"Sir," said Sebastian, with anxious feeling, to Billot, "can anything unfortunate have happened to Pitou? The poor lad is not with you."

"He is at the door, in a hackney-coach," replied Billot.

"Father," said Sebastian, "will you allow Monsieur Billot to fetch Pitou to me? I should be very glad to see him."

Gilbert gave an affirmative nod; Billot left the room.

"What is it you would say to me?" inquired Gilbert of the Abbé Berardier.

"I wished to tell you, sir, that it is not study that you should recommend to the young lad, but, on the contrary, to amuse himself."

"And on what account, good abbé?"

"Yes, he is an excellent young man, whom everybody here loves as a son or as a brother, but——"

The abbé paused.

"But what?" cried Gilbert, with anxiety.

"But if great care be not taken, Monsieur Gilbert, there is something that will kill him."

"And what is that?" said Gilbert.

" The study which you so strongly recommend to him."

"Study ?"

" Yes, sir, study. If you could but see him seated at his desk, his arms crossed, poring over his dictionary, with eyes fixed——"

"Studying or dreaming ? " asked Gilbert.

" Studying, sir ; endeavoring to find a good expression —the antique style, the Greek or Latin form—seeking for it for hours together ; and see ! even at this very moment —look at him !"

And indeed the young man, although it was not five minutes since his father had been speaking to him, although Billot had scarcely shut the door after him, Sebastian had fallen into a reverie which seemed closely allied to ecstasy.

" Is he often thus ? " anxiously inquired Gilbert.

" Sir, I could almost say that this is his habitual state ; only see how deeply he is meditating."

"You are right, sir ; and when you observe him in this state, you should endeavor to divert his thoughts."

' " And yet it would be a pity, for the results of these meditations are compositions which will one day do great honor to the College Louis le Grand. I predict that in three years from this time that youth yonder will bear off all the prizes of our examination."

"Take care ! " replied the doctor ; "this species of absorption of thought, in which you see Sebastian now plunged, is rather a proof of weakness than of strength, a symptom rather of malady than of health. You are right, Monsieur Principal ; it will not do to recommend assiduous application to that child ; or, at least, we must know how to distinguish study from such a state of reverie."

" Sir, I can assure you that he is studying."

" What, as we see him now ? "

" Yes ; and the proof is, that his task is always finished before that of the other scholars. Do you see how his lips move ? He is repeating his lessons."

'· Well, then, whenever he is repeating his lessons in this manner, Monsieur Berardier, divert his attention from them. He will not know his lessons the worse for it, and his health will be the better for it."

"Do you think so ? "

" I am sure of it."

" Well," cried the good abbé, "you ought to understand these matters, you, whom Messieurs de Condorcet and Cabanis proclaim to be one of the most learned men now existing in the world."

"Only," rejoined Gilbert, "when you wish to draw him out of such reveries, you must do it with much precaution ; speak to him very softly in the first instance, and then louder."

"And why so ?"

"To bring him gradually back to this world, which his mind has left."

The abbé looked at the doctor with astonishment ; it would not have required much to make him believe that he was mad.

"Observe," continued the doctor ; "you shall see the proof of what I am saying to you."

Billot and Pitou entered the room at this moment ; in three strides Pitou was at the side of the dreaming youth.

"You asked for me, Sebastian," said Pitou to him ; "that was very kind of you."

And he placed his large head close to the pale face of the young lad.

"Look !" said Gilbert, seizing the abbé's arm.

And indeed, Sebastian thus abruptly aroused from his reverie by the cordial affection of Pitou, staggered, his face became more lividly pale, his head fell on one side, as if his neck had not sufficient strength to support it, a painful sigh escaped his breast, and then the blood again rushed to his face.

He shook his head and smiled.

"Ah, it is you, Pitou ; yes, that is true—I asked for you."

And then, looking at him :

"You have been fighting, then ?'

"Yes, and like a brave lad, too," said Billot.

"Why did you not take me with you ?" said the child, in a reproachful tone. "I would have fought also, and then I should at least have done something for my father."

"Sebastian," said Gilbert, going to his son, and pressing his head to his breast, "you can do much more for your father than to fight for him ; you can listen to his

advice, and follow it—become a distinguished and celebrated man."

" As you are ? " said the boy, with proud emotion.
" Oh ! it is that which I aspire to."

"Sebastian," said the doctor, " now that you have embraced both Billot and Pitou, our good friends, will you
come into the garden with me for a few minutes, that we
may have a little talk together ? "

" With great delight, father. Only two or three times
in my whole life have I been alone with you, and those
moments, with all their details, are always present in my
memory."

" You will allow us, good Monsieur Principal ? " said
Gilbert.

" How can you doubt it ? "

" Billot and Pitou, you must, my friends, stand in need
of some refreshment ? "

" Upon my word, I do," said Billot ; " I have eaten
nothing since the morning, and I believe that Pitou has
fasted as long as I have."

" I beg your pardon," replied Pitou, " I ate a crumb of
bread and two or three sausages just the moment before I
dragged you out of the water ; but a bath always makes
one hungry."

" Well, then, come to the refectory," said the Abbé
Berardier, " and you shall have some dinner."

" Ho ! ho !" cried Pitou.

" You are afraid of our college fare !" cried the abbé ;
" but do not alarm yourselves ; you shall be treated as invited guests. Moreover, it appears to me," continued
the abbé, " that it is not alone your stomach that is in a
dilapitated state, my dear Monsieur Pitou."

Pitou cast a look replete with modesty on his own
person.

" And that if you were offered a pair of breeches as well
as a dinner——"

" The fact is, I would accept them, good Monsieur
Berardier," replied Pitou.

" Well, then, come with me ; both the breeches and the
dinner are at your service."

And he led off Billot and Pitou by one door, while Gilbert and his son, waving their hands to them, went out at
another.

The latter crossed a yard which served as a play-ground to the young collegians, and went into a small garden reserved for the professors, a cool and shady retreat, in which the venerable Abbé Berardier was wont to read his Tacitus and his Juvenal.

Gilbert seated himself upon a bench, overshadowed by an alcove of clematis and virgin vines; then, drawing Sebastian close to him, and parting the long hair which fell upon his forehead:

"Well, my child," said he, "we are then once more united."

Sebastian raised his eyes to heaven.

"Yes, father, and by a miracle performed by God."

Gilbert smiled.

"If there be any miracle," said Gilbert, "it was the brave people of Paris who have accomplished it."

"My father," said the boy, "set not God aside in all that has just occurred; for I, when I saw you come in, instinctively offered my thanks to God for your deliverance."

"And Billot?"

"Billot I thanked after thanking God."

Gilbert reflected.

"You are right, child," said he; "God is everything. But now let us speak of you, and let us have some little conversation before we again separate."

"Are we then to be again separated, father?"

"Not for a long time, I presume. But a casket, containing some very precious documents, has disappeared from Billot's house, at the same time that I was arrested and sent to the Bastile. I must, therefore, endeavor to discover who it was that caused my imprisonment—who has carried off the casket."

"It is well, father; I will wait to see you again—till your inquiries shall be completed."

And the boy sighed deeply.

"You are sorrowful, Sebastian?" said the doctor, inquiringly.

"Yes."

"And why are you sorrowful?"

"I do not know. It appears to me that life has not been shaped for me as it has been for other children."

"What are you saying there, Sebastian?"

" The truth."

" Explain yourself."

" They all have amusements, pleasures, while I have none."

" You have no amusements, no pleasures ? "

" I mean to say, father, that I take no pleasure in those games which form the amusement of boys of my own age."

" Take care, Sebastian ; I should much regret that you should be of such a disposition. Sebastian, minds that give promise of a glorious future are like good fruits during their growth ; they have their bitterness, their acidity, their greenness, before they can delight the palate by their matured full flavor. Believe me, my child, it is good to have been young."

" It is not my fault that I am so," replied the young man, with a melancholy smile.

Gilbert pressed both his son's hands within his own, and fixing his eyes intently upon Sebastian's, continued :

" Your age, my son, is that of the seed when germinating ; nothing should yet appear above the surface of all that study has sown in you. At the age of fourteen, Sebastian, gravity is either pride, or it proceeds from malady. I have asked you whether your health was good, and you replied affirmatively. I am going to ask you whether you are proud ; try to reply to me that you are not."

" Father," said the boy, " on that head you need not be alarmed. That which renders me so gloomy is neither sickness nor pride—no, it is a settled grief."

" A settled grief, poor child ! And what grief, good Heaven, can you have at your age ? Come, now, speak out."

" No, father, no ; some other time. You have told me that you were in a hurry. You have only a quarter of an hour to devote to me. Let us speak of other things than my follies."

" No, Sebastian ; I should be uneasy were I to leave you so. Tell me whence proceeds your grief."

" In truth, father, I do not dare."

" What do you fear ? "

" I fear that in your eyes I shall appear a visionary ; or perhaps that I may speak to you of things that will afflict you."

"You afflict me much more by withholding your secret from me."

"You know well that I have no secrets from you, father."

"Speak out, then."

"Really, I dare not."

"Sebastian, you, who have the pretension of being a man, to——"

"It is precisely for that reason."

"Come, now, take courage."

"Well, then, father, it is a dream."

"A dream which terrifies you?"

"Yes, and no; for when I am dreaming I am not terrified; but as if transported into another world."

"Explain yourself."

"When still quite a child I had these visions. You cannot but remember that two or three times I lost myself in those great woods which surround the village in which I was brought up."

"Yes, I remember being told of it."

"Well, then, at those times I was following a species of phantom."

"What say you?" cried Gilbert, looking at his son with an astonishment that seemed closely allied to terror.

"Well, then, father, I will tell you all. I used to play, as did the other children in the village. As long as there were children with me, or near me, I saw nothing; but if I separated from them, or went beyond the last village garden, I felt something near, like the rustling of a gown. I would stretch out my arms to catch it, and I embraced only the air; but as the rustling sound became lost in the distance, the phantom itself became visible. It was at first a vapor as transparent as a cloud; then the vapor became more condensed, and assumed a human form. The form was that of a woman gliding along the ground rather than walking, and becoming more and more visible as it plunged into the shady parts of the forest. Then an unknown, extraordinary, and almost irresistible power impelled me to pursue this form. I pursued her with outstretched arms, mute as herself; for often I attempted to call her, and never could my tongue articulate a sound. I pursued her thus, although she never stopped, although I never could come up with her, until the same prodigy which announced her presence to me warned me of her departure. This woman vanished gradually from my sight, matter became once more vapor, the vapor became volatilized, and all was ended, and I, exhausted with fatigue, would fall down on the spot where she had disappeared. It was there that Pitou would find me, sometimes the same day, but sometimes only the next morning."

Gilbert continued gazing at his son with increasing anxiety. He had placed his fingers on his pulse. Sebastian at once comprehended the feeling which agitated the doctor.

"Oh! do not be uneasy, father," said he. "*I* know that there was nothing real in all this. I know that it was a vision, and nothing more."

"And this woman?" inquired the doctor, "what was her appearance?"

"Oh! as majestic as a queen."

"And her face, did you sometimes see it, child?"

"Yes."

"And how long ago?" asked Gilbert, shuddering.

"Only since I have been here," replied the youth.

"But here in Paris you have not the forest of Villers-Cotterets, the tall trees forming a dark and mysterious arch of verdure. At Paris you have no longer that silence, that solitude, the natural element of phantoms.

"Yes, father, I have all these."

"Where, then?"

"Here, in this garden."

"What mean you by staying here? Is not this garden set apart for the professors?"

"It is so, my father; but two or three times it appeared to me that I saw this woman glide from the courtyard into the garden, and each time I would have followed her, but the closed doors always prevented me. Then one day the Abbé Berardier, being highly satisfied with my composition, asked me if there was anything I particularly desired; and I asked him to allow me sometimes to walk in the garden with him. He gave me the permission. I came, and here, father, the vision reappeared to me."

Gilbert trembled.

"Strange hallucination," said he; "but, nevertheless, very possible in a temperament so highly nervous as yours. And you have seen her face, then?"

"Yes, father."

"Do you remember it?"

The youth smiled.

"Did you ever attempt to go near her?"

"Yes."

"To hold out your hand to her?"

"It was then that she would disappear."

"And, in your opinion, Sebastian, who is this woman?"

"It appears to me that she is my mother."

"Your mother!" exclaimed Gilbert, turning pale.

And he pressed his hand against his heart, as if to stop the bleeding of a painful wound.

"But this is all a dream," cried he; "and really I am almost as mad as you are."

The youth remained silent, and looked at his father.

"Well?" said the latter, in the accent of inquiry.

"Well," replied Sebastian, "it is possible that it may be all a dream; but the reality of my dream is no less existing."

"What say you?"

"I say that at the last festival of Pentecost, when we were taken to walk in the wood of Satory, near Versailles, and that while there, as I was dreaming under a tree, and separated from my companions——"

"The same vision again appeared to you?"

"Yes; but this time in a carriage, drawn by four magnificent horses. But this time real, absolutely living. I very nearly fainted."

"And why so?"

"I do not know."

"And what impression remained upon your mind from this new vision?"

"That it was not my mother whom I had seen appearing to me in a dream, since this woman was the same I always saw in my vision, and my mother was dead."

Gilbert rose and pressed his hand to his forehead. A strange swimming of the head had just seized him.

The young lad remarked his agitation, and was alarmed at his sudden paleness.

"Ah!" said he, "you see now, father, how wrong I was to relate to you all my follies."

"No, my child, no. On the contrary," said the doctor,

"speak of them often to me ; speak of them to me every time you see me, and we will endeavor to cure you of them."

Sebastian shook his head.

" Cure me ! and for what ? " asked he. " I have been accustomed to this dream. It has become a portion of my existence. I love that vision, although it flies from me, and sometimes seems to repel me. Do not, therefore, cure me of it, father. You may again leave me, travel once more, perhaps go again to America. Having that vision, I am not completely alone in the world."

" In fine," murmured the doctor, and pressing Sebastian to his breast, " till we meet again, my child," said he, " and then I hope we shall no more leave each other ; for should I again leave France, I will at least endeavor to take you with me."

" Was my mother beautiful ? " asked the child.

" Oh, yes, very beautiful ! " replied the doctor, in a voice almost choked by emotion.

" And did she love you as much as I love you ? "

" Sebastian ! Sebastian ! never speak to me of your mother ! " cried the doctor.

And pressing his lips for the last time to the forehead of the youth, he rushed out of the garden.

Instead of following him, the child fell back, overcome by his feelings, on the bench,

In the courtyard, Gilbert found Billot and Pitou, completely invigorated by the good cheer they had partaken of. They were relating to the Abbé Berardier all the circumstances regarding the capture of the Bastile.

Gilbert again entered into the conversation with the Abbé Berardier, in which he pointed out to him the line of conduct he should observe with regard to Sebastian.

He then got into the hackney-coach with his two companions.

CHAPTER XXI.

WHEN Gilbert resumed his place in the hackney-coach by the side of Billot, and opposite to Pitou, he was pale, and the perspiration was standing in large drops on his forehead.

But it was not in the nature of this man to remain for any time overwhelmed by any emotion whatsoever. He threw himself back into the corner of the carriage, pressed both his hands to his forehead, as if he wished to repress the boiling thoughts which raged within it, and, after remaining a few moments motionless, he withdrew his hands, and, instead of an agitated countenance, he exhibited features which were particularly calm.

"You told me, I think, my dear Monsieur Billot, that the king had dismissed Monsieur de Necker?"

"Yes, indeed, Monsieur Gilbert."

"And that the commotions in Paris originated in some measure from the disgrace of the minister?"

"Very much."

"And you added that Monsieur de Necker had immediately left Versailles."

"He received the king's letter while at dinner. In an hour afterward he was on the road to Brussels."

"To Brussels?"

"Where he is now, or ought to be."

"Did you not hear it said that he had stopped somewhere on the road?"

"Oh, yes; he stopped at St. Ouen, in order to take leave of his daughter, the Baroness de Staël."

"Did Madame de Staël go with him?"

"I have been told that he and his wife only set out for Brussels."

"Coachman!" cried Gilbert, "stop at the first tailor's shop you see."

"You wish to change your coat?" said Billot.

"Yes. In good sooth, this one smells too much of its contact with the walls of the Bastile; and a man cannot in such a dress discreetly pay a visit to the daughter of an ex-minister in disgrace. Search your pockets, and see if you cannot find a few louis for me."

"Ho, ho!" cried the farmer; "it seems that you have left your purse in the Bastile."

"That is according to the regulations," said Gilbert, smiling. "All articles of value are deposited in the registry office."

"And they remain there," said the farmer.

And opening his huge fist, which contained about twenty louis:

"Take these, doctor," said he.

Gilbert took ten louis. Some minutes afterward the hackney-coach was stopped at the door of a ready-made clothes shop.

It was still the usage in those days.

Gilbert changed his coat, soiled by the walls of the Bastile, for a very decent black one, such as was worn by the gentlemen of the Tiers Etat in the National Assembly.

A hair-dresser in his shop, a Savoyard shoe-cleaner in his cellar, completed the doctor's toilet.

The doctor then ordered the coachman to drive him to St. Ouen by the exterior boulevards, which they reached by going behind the walls of the park at Monceaux.

Gilbert alighted at the gate of M. Necker's house, at the moment when the cathedral clock of Dagobert struck seven in the evening.

Around this house, which erewhile was so much sought, so much frequented, reigned the most profound silence, disturbed only by the arrival of Gilbert.

And yet there was none of that melancholy appearance which generally surrounds abandoned country houses—of that gloominess even generally visible in a mansion, the master of which had been disgraced.

The gates being closed, the garden walks deserted, merely announced that the master was absent, but there was no trace of misfortune or precipitation.

Besides this, one whole portion of the château. the east wing, had still its window-shutters open, and when Gilbert was advancing toward this side, a servant, wearing the livery of M. de Necker, approached the visitor.

The following dialogue then took place through the iron gratings of the gate.

"Monsieur de Necker is not at home, my friend," said Gilbert.

"No, the baron left St. Ouen last Saturday, for Brussels."

"And her ladyship, the baroness?"

"Went with monsieur."

"But Madame de Staël?"

"Madame de Staël has remained here; but I do not know whether madame will receive any one; it is her hour for walking."

"Please to point out to me where she is, and announce to her Doctor Gilbert."

"I will go and inquire whether madame is in the house or not. Doubtless she will receive you, sir ; but, should she be taking a walk, my orders are that she is not to be disturbed."

"Very well ; go quickly, I beg of you."

The servant opened the gate, and Gilbert entered the grounds.

While relocking the gate, the servant cast an inquisitorial glance on the vehicle which had brought the doctor, and on the extraordinary faces of his two traveling companions ; then he went off, shaking his head like a man who feels somewhat perplexed, but who defies any other intellect to see clear into a matter where his own had been altogether puzzled.

Gilbert remained alone, waiting his return.

In about five minutes the servant reappeared.

"The Baroness de Staël is taking a walk," said he, and he bowed in order to dismiss Gilbert.

But the doctor was not so easily to be got rid of.

"My friend," said he, "be pleased to make a slight infraction in your orders, and tell the baroness, when you announce me to her, that I am a friend of the Marquis de Lafayette."

A louis, slipped into the lackey's hands, completely removed the scruples he had entertained, but which the name of the marquis had nearly half dispelled.

"Come in, sir," said the servant.

Gilbert followed him ; but instead of taking him into the house he led him into the park.

"This is a favorite side of the baroness," said the lackey to Gilbert, pointing out to him the entrance to a species of labyrinth ; "will you remain here a moment ?"

Ten minutes afterward he heard a rustling among the leaves, and a woman between twenty-three and twenty-four years of age, and of a figure rather noble than graceful, appeared to the eyes of Gilbert.

She seemed surprised on finding a man who still appeared young, when she had doubtless expected to meet one advanced in years.

Gilbert was a man of sufficiently remarkable appearance to strike at first sight so able an observer as Mme. de Staël.

The features of few men were formed with such pure lines, and these lines had assumed, by the exercise of an all-powerful will, a character of extraordinary inflexibility. His fine black eyes, which were always so expressive, had become somewhat veiled by his literary labors and the sufferings he had undergone, and had lost a portion of that mobility which is one of the charms of youth.

A wrinkle, which was at once deep and graceful, hollowed out at the corner of his thin lips, that mysterious cavity in which physiognomists place the seat of circumspection. It appeared that time alone, and a precocious old age, had given to Gilbert that quality with which nature had neglected to endow him.

A wide and well-rounded forehead, slightly receding toward the roots of his fine black hair, which for years powder had no longer whitened, gave evidence at once of knowledge and of thought, of study and imagination. With Gilbert, as with his master, Rousseau, his prominent eyebrows threw a deep shade over his eyes, and from this shade glanced forth the luminous point which revealed life.

Gilbert, notwithstanding his unassuming dress, presented himself before the future authoress of " Corinne " with a remarkably dignified and distinguished air ; an air, of which his well-shaped, tapering white hands, his small feet, and his finely formed and muscular legs, completed the noble appearance.

Mme. de Stael devoted some moments to examining Gilbert.

During this, Gilbert, on his side, had given a stiff sort of bow, and which slightly recalled the modest civility of the American Quakers, who grant to woman only the fraternity which protects instead of the respect which smiles.

Then with a rapid glance, he, in his turn, analyzed the person of the already celebrated young woman, and whose intelligent and expressive features were altogether devoid of beauty ; it was the head of an insignificant and frivolous youth, rather than that of a woman, but which surmounted a form of voluptuous luxuriance.

She held in her hand a twig from a pomegranate-tree, from which, from absence of mind, she was biting off the blossoms.

" Is it you, sir," inquired the baroness, " who are Doctor Gilbert ? "

"Yes, madame, my name is Gilbert."

"You are very young to have acquired so great a reputation—or, rather, does not that reputation appertain to your father, or to some relation older than yourself?"

"I do not know any one of the name of Gilbert but myself, madame. And if indeed there is, as you say, some slight degree of reputation attached to the name, I have a fair right to claim it."

"You made use of the name of the Marquis de Lafayette in order to obtain this interview with me, sir; and, in fact, the marquis has spoken to us of you—of your inexhaustible knowledge."

Gilbert bowed.

"A knowledge which is so much the more remarkable, and so much the more replete with interest," continued the baroness, "since it appears that you are not a mere ordinary chemist—a practitioner, like so many others, but that you have sounded all the mysteries of the science of life."

"I clearly perceive, madame, that the Marquis de Lafayette must have told you that I am somewhat of a sorcerer," replied Gilbert, smiling; "and if he has told you so, I know that he has talent enough to prove it to you, had he wished to do so."

"In fact, sir, he has spoken to us of the marvelous cures you often performed, whether on the field of battle or in the American hospitals, upon patients whose lives were altogether despaired of; you plunged them, the general told us, into a factitious death, which so much resembled death itself that it was difficult to believe it was not real."

"That factitious death, madame, is the result of a science almost still unknown, now confided only to the hands of some few adepts, but which soon will become common."

"It is mesmerism you are speaking of, is it not?" asked Mme. de Staël, with a smile.

"Of mesmerism—yes, that is it."

"Did you take lessons of the master himself?"

"Alas! madame, Mesmer himself was only a scholar. Mesmerism, or, rather, magnetism, was an ancient science known to the Egyptians and the Greeks. It was lost in the ocean of the Middle Ages. Shakespeare divined it in Macbeth. Urbain Grandier found it once more, and died for having found it. But the great master—my master—was the Count de Cagliostro?"

"That mountebank!" cried Mme. de Staël.

"Madame, madame, beware of judging as do contemporaries, and not as posterity will judge. To that mountebank I owe my knowledge, and perhaps the world will be indebted to him for its liberty."

"Be it so," replied Mme, de Staël, again smiling; "I speak without knowing—you speak with full knowledge of the subject. It is probable that you are right and I am wrong. But let us return to you. Why is it that you have so long kept yourself at so great a distance from France? Why have you not returned to take your place, your proper station, among the great men of the age such as Lavoisier, Cabanis, Condorcet, Bailly and Louis?"

At this last name Gilbert blushed, though almost imperceptibly.

"I have yet too much to study, madame, to rank myself all at once among these great masters."

"But you have come at last, though at an unpropitious moment for us; my father, who would, I feel assured, have been happy to be of service to you, has been disgraced, and left this three days ago."

Gilbert smiled.

"Baroness," said he, bowing slightly, "it is now only six days ago that I was imprisoned in the Bastile, pursuant to an order from Baron Necker."

Mme. de Staël blushed in her turn.

"Really, sir, you have just told me something that greatly surprises me. You in the Bastile?"

"Myself, madame."

"What had you done to occasion your imprisonment?"

"Those alone who threw me into prison can tell that."

"But you are no longer in prison?"

"No, madame, because the Bastile no longer exists."

"How can that be? Does the Bastile no longer exist?" cried Mme. de Staël, feigning astonishment.

"Did you not hear the firing of cannon?"

"Yes; but cannons are only cannons, that is all."

"Oh! permit me to tell you, madame, that it is impossible that Madame de Staël, the daughter of Monsieur de Necker, should not know, at this present time, that the Bastile has been taken by the people."

"I assure you, sir," replied the baroness, somewhat confused, "that being unacquainted with any of the events which have taken place since the departure of my father, I no longer occupy my time but in deploring his absence."

"Madame! madame!" said Gilbert, shaking his head, "the state messengers are so familiar with the road that leads to the château of St. Ouen, that at least one bearer of despatches must have arrived during the four hours that have elapsed since the capitulation of the Bastile."

The baroness saw that it was impossible for her to deny it without positively lying. She abhorred a falsehood; she therefore changed the subject of the conversation.

"And to what lucky event do I owe your visit, sir?" asked she.

"I wished to have the honor of speaking to Monsieur de Necker, madame."

"But do you know that he is no longer in France?"

"Madame, it appeared to me so extraordinary that Monsieur de Necker should be absent, so impolitic that he should not have watched the course of events——"

"That——"

"That I relied upon you, I must confess, madame, to tell me where I could find him."

"You will find him at Brussels, sir."

Gilbert fixed a scrutinizing gaze upon the baroness.

"Thank you, madame," said he, bowing; "I shall then set out for Brussels, as I have matters of the highest importance to communicate to him."

Mme. de Staël appeared to hesitate, then she rejoined:

"Fortunately I know you, sir," said she, "and that I know you to be a man of serious character. 'Tis true, important things might lose a great deal of their value by passing through other lips. But what can there be of importance to my father after his disgrace—after what has taken place?"

"There is the future, madame. And perhaps I shall not be altogether without influence over the future. But all these reflections are to no purpose. The most important thing for me and for him is that I should see Monsieur de Necker. Thus, madame, you say that he is at Brussels?"

"Yes, sir."

"It will take me twenty hours to go there. Do you know what twenty hours are during a revolution, and how many important events may take place during twenty hours? Oh! how imprudent it was for Monsieur de Necker, madame, to place twenty hours between himself and any event which might take place—between the hand and the object it desired to reach."

"In truth, sir, you frighten me," said Mme. de Staël, "and I begin to think that my father has really been imprudent."

"But what would you have, madame? Things are thus, are they not? I have, therefore, merely to make you a most humble apology for the trouble that I have given you. Adieu, madame."

But the baroness stopped him.

"I tell you, sir, that you alarm me," she rejoined; "you owe me an explanation of all this; you must tell me something that will reassure me."

"Alas! madame," replied Gilbert, "I have so many private interests to watch over at this moment that it is impossible for me to think of those of others; my life and honor are at stake, as would be the life and honor of Monsieur de Necker, if he could take advantage of the words which I shall tell him in the course of twenty hours."

"Sir, allow me to remember something that I have too long forgotten; it is that grave subjects ought not to be discussed in the open air, in a park, within reach of every ear."

"Madame," said Gilbert, "I am now at your house, and permit me to observe, that, consequently, it is you who have chosen the place where we now are. What do you wish? I am entirely at your command."

"I wish you to do me the favor to finish this conversation in my cabinet."

"Ah! ah!" said Gilbert to himself, "if I did not fear to confuse her, I would ask her whether her cabinet is at Brussels."

But without asking anything more, he contented himself with following the baroness, who began to walk quickly toward the château.

The same servant who had admitted Gilbert was found standing in front of the house. Mme. de Staël made a sign to him, and opening the doors herself, she led Gilbert

into her cabinet, a charming retreat, more masculine, it
is true, than feminine, of which the second door and the
two windows opened into a small garden, which was not
only inaccessible to others, but also beyond the reach of
all strange eyes.

When they had gone in, Mme. de Staël closed the door,
and turning toward Gilbert:

"Sir, in the name of humanity, I call upon you to tell
me the secret which is so important to my father, and
which has brought you to St. Ouen."

"Madame," said Gilbert, "if your father could now
hear me, if he could but know that I am the man who
sent the king the secret memoirs entitled 'Of the State of
Ideas and of Progress,' I am sure the Baron de Necker
would immediately appear, and say to me, 'Doctor Gilbert, what do you desire of me?—speak, I am listening.'"

Gilbert had hardly pronounced these words when a
secret door, which was concealed by a panel painted by
Vanloo, was noiselessly slid aside, and the Baron de Necker,
with a smiling countenance, suddenly appeared, standing
at the foot of a small winding staircase, at the top of
which could be perceived the dim rays of a lamp.

Then the Baroness de Staël courtesied to Gilbert, and,
kissing her father's forehead, left the room by the same
staircase which her father had just descended, and having
closed the panel, she disappeared.

Necker advanced toward Gilbert and gave him his
hand, saying:

"Here I am, Monsieur Gilbert; what do you desire of
me? speak, I am listening."

They both seated themselves.

"Monsieur le Baron," said Gilbert, "you have just
heard a secret which has revealed all my ideas to you. It
was I who, four years ago, sent an essay to the king on
the general state of Europe; it is I who, since then, have
sent him from the United States the various works he
has received on all the questions of conciliation and internal administration which have been discussed in France."

"Works of which his majesty," replied M. de Necker
bowing, "has never spoken to me without expressing a
deep admiration of them, though at the same time a profound terror at their contents."

" Yes, because they told the truth. Was it not because the truth was then terrible to hear, and having now become a fact, it is still more terrible to witness ? "

" That is unquestionably true, sir," said Necker.

" Did the king send these essays to you for perusal ? " asked Gilbert.

" Not all of them, sir ; only two ; one on the subject of the finances—and you were of my opinion with a very few exceptions ; but I nevertheless felt myself much honored by it."

"But that is not all ; there was one in which I predicted all the important events which have taken place."

" Ah ! "

" Yes."

" And which of them, sir, I pray ? "

" There were two in particular ; one was that the king would find himself some day compelled to dismiss you, in consequence of some engagements he had previously entered into."

" Did you predict my disgrace to him ? "

" Perfectly."

" That was the first event ; what was the second ? "

" The taking of the Bastile."

" Did you predict the taking of the Bastile ? "

" Monsieur le Baron, the Bastile was more than a royal prison, it was the symbol of tyranny. Liberty has commenced its career by destroying the symbol ; the revolution will do the rest."

" Have you duly considered the serious nature of the words you have just uttered, sir ? "

" Undoubtedly I have."

" And you are not afraid to express such a theory openly ? "

" Afraid of what ? "

" Afraid lest some misfortune should befall you."

" Monsieur de Necker," said Gilbert, smiling, " after once having got out of the Bastile, a man has nothing to fear."

" Have you then come out of the Bastile ? "

" I ought to ask you that question."

" Ask me ? "

" You, undoubtedly."

" And why should you ask me ? "

"Because it was you who caused my imprisonment there."

"I had you thrown into the Bastile?"

"Six days ago; the date, as you see, is not so very remote that you should not be able to recollect it."

"It is impossible."

"Do you recognize your own signature?"

And Gilbert showed the ex-minister a leaf of the jail-book to the Bastile and the *lettre de cachet* which was annexed to it.

"Yes," said Necker, "that is doubtless the *lettre de cachet*. You know that I signed as few as possible, and that the smallest number possible was still four thousand annually; besides which, at the moment of my departure, they made me sign several in blank. Your warrant of imprisonment, sir, must have been one of the latter."

"Do you mean to imply by this, that I must in no way attribute my imprisonment to you?"

"No, of course not."

"But, still, Monsieur le Baron," said Gilbert, smiling, "you understand my motives for being so curious; it is absolutely necessary that I should know to whom I am indebted for my captivity. Be good enough, therefore, to tell me."

"Oh! there is nothing easier. I have never left my letters at the ministry, and every evening I brought them back here. Those of this month are in the drawer B of this chiffonnier; let us look for the letter G in the bundle."

Necker opened the drawer, and looked over an enormous file, which might have contained some five or six hundred letters.

"I only keep those letters," said the ex-minister, "which are of such a nature as to cover my responsibility. Every arrest that I order insures me another enemy. I must therefore have guarded myself against such a contingency. The contrary would surprise me greatly. Let us see—G—G—, that is the one. Yes, Gilbert—your arrest was brought about by some one in the queen's household, my dear sir. Ah—ah!—in the queen's household—yes, here is a request for a warrant against a man named Gilbert. Profession not mentioned; black eyes, black hair. The description of your person follows. Traveling from

Havre to Paris.   That is all.   Then the Gilbert mentioned in the warrant must have been you."

"It was myself.   Can you trust me with that letter?"

"No; but I can tell you by whom it was signed."

"Please to do so."

"By the Countess de Charny."

"The Countess de Charny," repeated Gilbert.   "I do
not know her.   I have done nothing to displease her."

And he raised his head gently, as if endeavoring to
recall to mind the name of the person in question.

"There is, moreover, a small postscript," continued
Necker, "without any signature, but written in a hand I
know."

Gilbert stooped down and read in the margin of the
letter :

"Do what the Countess de Charny demands immediately."

"It is strange," said Gilbert.   "I can readily conceive
why the queen should have signed it, for I mentioned both
her and the Polignacs in my essays.   But Madame de
Charny——"

"Do you not know her?"

"It must be an assumed name.   Besides, it is not at all
to be wondered at that the nobilities of Versailles should
be unknown to me.   I have been absent from France for
fifteen years, during which time I only came back twice;
and I returned after my second visit to it, some four years
ago.   Who is this Countess de Charny?"

"The friend, the bosom companion of the queen; the
much beloved wife of the Count de Charny, a woman who
is both beautiful and virtuous—a prodigy, in short."

"Well, then, I do not know this prodigy."

"If such be the case, doctor, be persuaded of this, that
you are the victim of some political intrigue.   Have you
never spoken of Count Cagliostro?"

"Yes."

"Were you acquainted with him?"

"He was my friend.   He was even more than my friend
—he was my master, my saviour."

"Well, then, either Austria or the Holy See must have
demanded your incarceration.   You have published some
pamphlets, have you not?"

"Alas! yes."

"That is it precisely. All their petty revenges point toward the queen, like the magnetic needle which points toward the pole—the iron toward the loadstone. They have been conspiring against you—they have had you followed. The queen has ordered Madame de Charny to sign the letter, in order to prevent any suspicion ; and now all the mystery is cleared up."

Gilbert reflected for a moment. This moment of reflection reminded him of the box which had been stolen from Billot's house ; and with which neither the queen, nor Austria, nor the Holy See had any connection. This recollection led his mind to consider the matter in its right point of view.

"No," said he, "it is not that ; it cannot be that. But it matters not. Let us talk of something else."

"Of what ?"

"Of you."

"Of me ? What can you have to say of me ?"

"Only what you know, as well as any one else. It is that, before three days have elapsed, you will be reinstated in your ministerial capacity ; and then you may govern France as despotically as you please."

"Do you think so ?" said Necker, smiling.

"And you think so, too, since you are not at Brussels."

"Well, then," exclaimed Necker, "what will be the result ?—for it is the result I wish to come to."

"Here it is. You are beloved by the French. You will be soon adored by them. The queen was already tired of seeing you beloved. The king will grow tired of seeing you adored. They will acquire popularity at your expense, and you will not suffer it. Then you will become unpopular in your turn. The people, my dear Monsieur de Necker, is like a starving lion, which licks only the hand that supplies it with food, be it whose hand it may."

"After that ?"

"After that you will again be lost in oblivion."

"I—fall into oblivion ?"

"Alas! yes."

"And what will cause me to be forgotten ?"

"The events of the times."

"My word of honor for it you speak like a prophet."

"It is my misfortune to be one to a certain extent."

"Let us hear now what will happen ?"

"Oh, it is not difficult to predict what will happen, for that which is to happen is already in embryo in the Assembly. A party will arise that is slumbering at this moment. I am mistaken; it is not slumbering, but it hides itself. This party has for its chief a principle, and its weapon is an idea."

"I understand you—you mean the Orleanist party ?"

"No. I should have said of that one that its chief was a man and its weapon popularity. I speak to you of a party whose name has not even yet been pronounced. Of the republican party."

"Of the republican party ? Ah! that is too ridiculous."

"Do you not believe in its existence ?"

"A chimera."

"Yes, a chimera, with a mouth of fire that will devour you all."

"Well, then, I shall become a republican. I am one already."

"A republican from Geneva, certainly."

"But it seems to me that a republican is a republican."

"There is your mistake, my good baron. Our republicans do not resemble the republicans of other countries. Our republicans will first have to devour all privileges, then the nobility, and after that the monarchy. You may start with our republicans, but they will reach the goal without you, for you will not desire to follow them so far. No, Monsieur de Necker, you are mistaken, you are not a republican."

"Oh, if you understand it in that sense—no ; I love the king."

"And I, too," said Gilbert; "and everybody at this moment loves him as we do. If I were to say this to a mind of less caliber than yours, I should be hooted and laughed at; but believe what I tell you, Monsieur de Necker."

"I would readily do so, indeed, if there were any probability of such an event; but——"

"Do you know any of the secret societies ?"

"I have heard them much spoken of."

"Do you believe in their existence ?"

"I believe in their existence, but I do not believe they are very extensively disseminated."

"Are you affiliated to any one of them?"

"No."

"Do you belong even to a masonic lodge?"

"No."

"Well, then, Monsieur de Necker, I am a member of them all."

"Are you affiliated to some of these societies?"

"Yes, to all of them. Beware, Monsieur de Necker; they form an immense net that surrounds every throne. It is an invisible dagger that threatens every monarchy. We form a brotherhood of about three millions of men, disseminated throughout all classes of society. We have friends among the people, among the citizens, among the nobility, among princes, among sovereigns themselves. Take care, Monsieur de Necker; the prince with whom you might be irritated is perhaps an affiliated member. The valet who humbles himself in your presence may be an affiliated member. Your life is not yours—your fortune is not your own—your honor even is not yours. All this is directed by an invisible power, which you cannot combat, for you do not know it, and which may crush you, because it knows you. Well, these three millions of men, do you see, who have already made the American republic, these three millions of men will try to form a French republic; then they will try to make a European republic."

"But," said Necker, "their republic of the United States does not alarm me much, and I willingly accept such a form of government."

"Yes, but between America and ourselves there is a deep gulf. America is a new country, without prejudices, without aristocratic privileges, without monarchy. It has a fertile soil, productive land, and virgin forests. America, which is situated between a sea which serves as an outlet for its commerce, and an immense solitude which is a source of wealth to its population, while France!— just consider how much it would be necessary to destroy in France before France can resemble America."

"But, in fine, what do you intend to prove by this?"

"I mean to point out to you the path into which we are inevitably forced. But I would endeavor to advance into it without causing any shock, by placing the king at the head of the movement."

" As a standard ? "

" No, but as a shield."

" A shield ! " observed Necker, smiling. " You know but little of the king if you wish to make him play such a part."

" Pardon me—I know him well. Oh ! gracious Heaven ! I know full well he is a man similar to a thousand others whom I have seen at the head of small districts in America ; he is a good man without majesty, incapable of resistance, without originality of mind. But what would you have ? Were it only for his sacred title, he would still be a rampart against those men of whom I was speaking to you a short time ago ; and however weak the rampart may be, we like it better than no defense at all."

" I remember in our wars with the savage tribes of North America," continued Gilbert, " I remember having passed whole nights behind a clump of bulrushes, while the enemy was on the opposite bank of the river, and was firing upon us.

" A bulrush is certainly no great defense. Still, I must frankly acknowledge to you, Monsieur de Necker, that my heart beat more freely behind those large green tubes, which were cut through by the bullets as if they were thread-papers, than it did in the open field. Well, then, the king is my rush. It allows me to see the enemy, and it prevents the enemy from seeing me. That is the reason why I am a republican at New York or at Philadelphia, but a royalist in France. There our dictator was named Washington. Here, God knows what he will be named ; either dagger or scaffold."

" You seem to view things in colors of blood, doctor."

" You would have seen them in the same light as myself, if you had been, as I was, on the Place de Grève to-day."

" Yes, that is true ; I was told that a massacre had taken place there."

" There is something magnificent, do you see, in the people—but it is when well disposed. Oh, human tempests ! " exclaimed Gilbert, " how much do you surpass in fury all the tempests of the skies."

Necker became thoughtful.

" Why can I not have you near me, doctor ? " said he ; " you would be a useful counselor in time of need."

"Near you, Monsieur de Necker? I should not be so useful to you, and so useful to France, as where I wish to go?"

"And where do you wish to go?"

"Listen to me, sir. Near the throne itself there is a great enemy of the throne; near the king there is a great enemy of the king; it is the queen. Poor woman! who forgets that she is the daughter of Maria Theresa, or, rather, who only remembers it in a vainglorious point of view; she thinks to save the king, and ruins more than the king, for she destroys the monarchy. Well, it is necessary that we who love the king, we who love France, should unite together to neutralize her power and to annihilate her influence."

"Well, then, do as I said, sir: remain with me, assist me."

"If I were to remain near you, we should have but one sphere for action; you would be me, and I should be you. We must separate our forces, sir, and then they will acquire a double weight."

"And, with all that, what can we accomplish?"

"We may retard the catastrophe, perhaps, but certainly we cannot prevent it, although I can answer for the assistance of a powerful auxiliary, the Marquis de Lafayette."

"Is not Lafayette a republican?"

"As far as a Lafayette can be a republican. If we are absolutely to submit to the level of equality, believe me, we had better choose the level of nobility. I like equality that elevates, and not that which lowers, mankind."

"And you can answer for Lafayette?"

"Yes, so long as we shall require nothing of him but honor, courage, and devotedness."

"Well, then, speak; tell me what is it you desire?"

"A letter of introduction to His Majesty Louis XVI."

"A man of your worth does not need a letter of introduction; he may present himself without it."

"No; it suits me that I should be your creature; it is part of my project to be presented by you."

"And what is your ambition?"

"To become one of the king's physicians-in-ordinary."

"Oh, there is nothing more easy. But the queen?"

"When I have once seen the king, that will be my own affair."

"But if she should persecute you?"

"Then I will make the king assert his will."

"The king assert his will? You will be more than a man if you accomplish that."

"He who can control the physical part of a man must be a great simpleton indeed, if he does not some day succeed in controlling the mind."

"But do you not think that having been imprisoned in the Bastile is but a sorry recommendation for you, who wish to become the king's physician?"

"On the contrary, it is the very best. Have I not been, according to you, persecuted for the crime of philosophy?"

"I fear such is the case."

"Then the king will vindicate his reputation—the king will become popular by taking as his physician a pupil of Rousseau—a partisan of the new doctrines—a prisoner who has left the Bastile, in short. The first time you see him, make him duly weigh the advantage of such a course."

"You are always in the right; but when once you are employed by the king, can I rely upon you?"

"Entirely, so long as you shall follow the line of politics which we shall adopt?"

"What will you promise me?"

"To warn you of the precise moment when you must retreat."

Necker looked at Gilbert for a moment; then, in a more thoughtful tone:

"Indeed; that is the greatest service which a devoted friend can render to a minister, for it is the last one.

And he seated himself at his table to write to the king.

While he was thus occupied, Gilbert was again examining the letter demanding his arrest; he several times repeated:

"The Countess de Charny? who can she be?"

"Here, sir," said Necker, a few moments after, while he presented Gilbert with the letter he had just written.

Gilbert took the letter and read it.

It contained the following lines:

"SIRE,—Your majesty needs the services of a trustworthy person, with whom he may converse upon his affairs.

My last gift, my last service in leaving the king, is the present I make him of Doctor Gilbert.

"It will be sufficient for me to tell your majesty that Doctor Gilbert is not only one of the most skilful physicians living, but also the author of the works entitled 'Administrations and Politics,' which made so lively an impression upon the mind of your majesty.

"At your majesty's feet,
"BARON DE NECKER."

Necker did not date the letter, and gave it to Dr. Gilbert, closed only with an ordinary seal.

"And now," added he, " I am again at Brussels, am I not ?"

"Yes, certainly, and more so than ever. To-morrow morning, at all events, you shall hear from me."

The baron struck against the panel in a peculiar manner. Mme. de Staël again appeared ; only this time, in addition to her branch of pomegranate, she held one of Dr. Gilbert's pamphlets in her hands.

She showed him the title of it with a sort of flattering coquetry.

Gilbert took leave of M. de Necker, and kissed the hand of the baroness, who accompanied him to the door of the cabinet.

And he returned to his coach, where he found Pitou and Billot sleeping upon the front seat, the coachman sleeping on his box, and the horses sleeping upon their exhausted limbs.

CHAPTER XXII.

THE interview between Gilbert, Mme. de Staël, and M. de Necker had lasted about an hour and a half. Gilbert re-entered Paris at a quarter past nine o'clock, drove straight to the post-house, ordered horses and a post-chaise, and while Billot and Pitou were gone to rest themselves, after their fatigue, in a small hotel in the Rue Thiroux, where Billot generally put up when he came to Paris, Gilbert set off at a gallop on the road to Versailles.

It was late, but that mattered little to Gilbert. To men of his nature, activity is a necessity. Perhaps his journey might be a fruitless one. But he even preferred a useless journey to remaining motionless. For nervous temperaments, uncertainty is a greater torment than the most frightful reality.

He arrived at Versailles at half past ten; in ordinary times, every one would have been in bed and wrapped in the profoundest slumber. But that night no eye was closed at Versailles. They had felt the counter-shock of the terrible concussion with which Paris was still trembling.

The French Guards, the body-guards, the Swiss drawn up in platoons, and grouped near the openings of all the principal streets, were conversing among themselves or with those of the citizens whose fidelity to the monarchy inspired them with confidence.

For Versailles has, at all times, been a royalist city. Religious respect for the monarchy, if not for the monarch, is ingrafted in the hearts of its inhabitants, as if it were a quality of its soil. Having always lived near kings, and fostered by their bounty, beneath the shade of their wonders—having always inhaled the intoxicating perfume of the fleur-de-lis, and seen the brilliant gold of their garments, and the smiles upon their august lips, the inhabitants of Versailles, for whom kings have built a city of marble and porphyry, feel almost kings themselves; and even at the present day, even now, when moss is growing round the marble, and grass is springing up between the slabs of the pavement, now that gold has almost disappeared from the wainscoting, and that the shady walks of the parks are more solitary than a graveyard, Versailles must either belie its origin, or must consider itself as a fragment of the fallen monarchy, and no longer feeling the pride of power and wealth, must at least retain the poetical associations of regret, and the sovereign charms of melancholy. Thus, as we have already stated, all Versailles, in the night between the 14th and 15th July, 1789, was confusedly agitated, anxious to ascertain how the King of France would reply to the insult offered to his throne, and the deadly wound inflicted on his power.

By his answer to M. de Dreux Breze, Mirabeau had struck the very face of royalty.

By the taking of the Bastile, the people had struck it to the heart.

Still to narrow-minded and short-sighted persons, the

question seemed easy of solution. In the eyes of military
men, in particular, who were accustomed to see nothing
more than the triumph or defeat of brute force in the result of events, it was merely necessary to march upon
Paris. Thirty thousand men and twenty pieces of cannon
would soon reduce to a nonentity the conceit and the
victorious fury of the Parisians.

Never had monarchy so great a number of advisers, for
everybody uttered his opinions loudly and publicly.

The most moderate said :

" It is a very simple matter."

This form of language, it will be observed, is nearly
always applied, with us, to the most difficult circumstances.

" It is a very simple matter," said they. " Let them
begin by obtaining from the National Assembly a sanction
which it will not refuse. Its attitude has, for some time,
been reassuring to every one ; it will not countenance violence committed by the lower classes, any more than abuses
perpetrated by the upper.

" The Assembly will plainly declare that insurrection
is a crime ; that citizens who have representatives to explain their griefs to the king, and a king to do them justice, are wrong to have recourse to arms and to shed
blood.

" Being once armed with this declaration, which could
certainly be obtained from the Assembly, the king could
not avoid chastising Paris, like a good parent, that is to
say, severely.

" And then the tempest would be allayed, and the
monarchy would regain the first of its rights. The people
would return to their duty, which is obedience, and things
would go on in the usual way."

It was thus that the people in general were settling this
great question, upon the squares and boulevards.

But before the Place d'Armes, and in the vicinity of
the barracks, they treated the subject very differently.

There could be seen men altogether unknown in the
neighborhood, men with intelligent countenances and
sinister looks, disseminating mysterious advice to all around
them, exaggerating the news which was already sufficiently
serious, and propagating, almost publicly, the seditious
ideas which during two months had agitated Paris and
excited the suburbs.

Round these men groups were forming, some gloomy and hostile, some excited, composed of people whom these orators were reminding of their misery, their sufferings, the brutal disdain of the monarchy for the privations of the people. An orator said to them :

"During eight centuries that the people have struggled, what have they obtained ? Nothing. No social rights, no political rights. What is their fate ? That of the farmer's cow, from whom its calf is taken to be led to the shambles, its milk to be sold at the market, its meat to be taken to the slaughter-house, its skin to be dried at the tannery. In short, pressed by want, the monarchy has yielded, it has made an appeal to the states ; but now that the states are assembled, what does the monarchy ? Since the day of their convocation, it weighs heavily upon them. If the National Assembly is formed, it is against the will of the monarchy. Well, then, since our brethren of Paris have just given us such vigorous assistance, let us urge the National Assembly onward. Each step which it takes in the political arena is a victory for us ; it is the extension of our field, it is the increase of our fortune, it is the consecration of our rights. Forward ! forward ! citizens ! The Bastile is but the outwork of tyranny. The Bastile is taken—the citadel is before us ! "

In remote corners other meetings were formed, and other words pronounced. Those who pronounced them were men evidently belonging to a superior class, who had sought in the costume of the vulgar a disguise with which their white hands and distinguished accent contrasted strangely.

"People," exclaimed these men, "in truth you are deceived on both sides ; some ask you to retrace your steps, while others urge you onward. Some speak to you of political rights, of social rights ; but are you happier for having been permitted to vote through the medium of your delegates ? Are you any the richer since you have been represented ? Have you been less hungry, now that the National Assembly makes decrees ? No. Leave politics, then, to those who can read. It is not a written phrase or maxim that you need. It is bread, and again, bread ; it is the well-being of your children, the tranquillity and security of your wives. Who will give you all that? A king, firm in character, young in mind, and of a gen-

erous heart. That king is not Louis XVI.—Louis XVI.,
who is ruled by his wife, the iron-hearted Austrian. It is
—search carefully round the throne ; search there for him
who can render France happy, and whom the queen naturally detests, and that because he throws a shadow over
the picture, because he loves the French, and is beloved
by them."

Thus did public opinion manifest itself at Versailles ;
thus was civil war fomented everywhere.

Gilbert observed several of these groups, and then, having perceived the state of the public mind, he walked
straight to the palace, which was guarded by numerous
military posts, to protect it against whom no one knew.

Notwithstanding all these precautions, Gilbert, without
the slightest difficulty, crossed the first courtyard, and
reached the vestibule without having been asked by any
one where he was going.

When he had arrived at the Hall of the Œil de Bœuf,
he was stopped by one of the body-guards. Gilbert drew
from his pocket the letter of M. de Necker, whose signature he showed.

The guard cast his eye over it. The instructions he had
received were very strict ; and as the strictest instructions
are precisely those which most need to be interpreted, the
guard said to Gilbert :

" The order, sir, to allow no one to visit the king is
positive ; but as the case of a person sent by Monsieur de
Necker was evidently not foreseen, and as, according to all
probability, you are the bearer of important information
to his majesty, go in. I will take the responsibility upon
myself."

Gilbert entered.

The king was not in his apartments, but in the council-
room. He was just receiving a deputation from the National Guard of Paris, which had come to request the dismissal of the troops, the formation of a guard of citizens,
and his presence in the capital.

Louis had listened coldly ; then he had replied that the
situation of affairs required investigation ; and that, moreover, he was about to deliberate on the subject with his
council.

And, accordingly, he deliberated.

During this time the deputies were waiting in the gallery; and through the ground-glass windows of the doors they could observe the shadows of the royal councilors and the threatening attitude which they assumed.

By the study of this species of phantasmagoria, they could foresee that the answer would be unfavorable.

In fact, the king contented himself with saying that he would appoint some officers for the national militia, and would order the troops at the Champs de Mars to fall back.

As to his presence in Paris, he would only show this favor when the rebellious city had completely submitted.

The deputation begged, insisted, and conjured. The king replied that his heart was grieved, but that he could do nothing more.

And satisfied with this momentary triumph and this manifestation of a power which he no longer possessed, the king returned to his apartment.

He there found Gilbert. The guard was standing near him.

"What is wanted of me?" asked the king.

The body-guard approached him, and while he was apologizing to the king for having disobeyed his orders, Gilbert, who for many years had not seen the king, was silently examining the man whom God had given to France as her pilot during the most violent tempest the country had ever experienced.

That stout, short body, in which there was neither elasticity nor majesty; that inexpressive and low-formed brow; that pallid youthfulness contending against premature old age; the unequal struggle between a powerful physical organization and a mediocre intelligence, to which the haughtiness of rank alone gave a fitting importance—all this, to the physiognomist who had studied Lavater, to the magnetizer who had read the future with Balsamo, to the philosopher who had dreamed with Jean Jacques, to the traveler, in short, who had passed all the human races in review—all these implied degeneracy, dwindling, impotence, and ruin.

Gilbert was, therefore, struck dumb, not from a feeling of respect, but from grief, while contemplating this mournful spectacle.

The king advanced toward him.

"It is you," said he, "who bring me a letter from Monsieur de Necker."

"Yes, sire."

"Ah!" cried he, as if he had doubted it, "give it to me quickly."

And he pronounced these words in the tone of a drowning man, who cries out, "a rope!"

Gilbert presented the letter to the king.

Louis immediately grasped it, read it hurriedly, then, with a sign which was not altogether wanting in a sort of nobleness of manner:

"Leave us, Monsieur de Varicourt," said he to the body-guard.

Gilbert remained alone with the king. The room was lighted by a single lamp. It might have been thought the king had diminished the quantity of light, in order that no one should perceive on his wearied rather than careworn brow the anxious thoughts which crowded there.

"Sir," said he, fastening upon Gilbert a clearer and more penetrating gaze than the latter would have thought him capable of, "sir, is it true that you are the author of the memoirs which have so much struck me?"

"Yes, sire."

"What is your age?"

"Thirty-two years, sire; but study and misfortunes double age. Treat me as if I were an old man."

"Why did you omit so long to present yourself to me?"

"Because, sire, I did not wish to tell your majesty aloud what *I* could write to him more freely and more easily."

Louis XVI. reflected.

"Had you no other reason?" said he, suspiciously.

"No, sire."

"But still, either I am mistaken, or there were some peculiar circumstances which ought to have convinced you of my kindly feeling toward you."

"Your majesty intends to speak of that sort of rendez-vous which I had the temerity to give the king, when, after my first memoir, I begged him, five years ago, to place a light near his window, at eight o'clock in the evening, to indicate that he had read my work."

"And——?" said the king, with an air of satisfaction.

"And on the day and at the hour appointed the light was, in fact, placed where I had asked you to place it."

"And afterward?"

"Afterward, I saw it lifted up and set down again three times."

"And then?"

"After that I read the following words in the 'Gazette:'

"'He whom the light has called three times may present himself to him who has raised it three times, when he will be compensated.'"

"Those are, in fact, the very words of the advertisement," said the king.

"And there is the advertisement itself," said Gilbert, drawing from his pocket the number of the "Gazette" in which the advertisement he had just alluded to had been published five years previously.

"Well, very well," said the king; "I long expected you. You arrive at a moment I had quite ceased to expect you. You are welcome; for you come, like good soldiers, at the moment of the battle."

Then, looking once more attentively at Gilbert:

"Do you know, sir," said he to him, "that it is not an ordinary thing for a king to await the arrival of a person to whom he has said, 'Come to receive your reward,' and that that person should abstain from coming?"

Gilbert smiled.

"Come, now, tell me," said Louis XVI., "why did you not come?"

"Because I deserved no reward, sire."

"For what reason?"

"Born a Frenchman, loving my country, anxious for its prosperity, confounding my individuality with that of thirty millions of men, my fellow-citizens, I labored for myself while laboring for them. A man is not worthy of reward when he labors for his own interest."

"That is a paradox, sir; you had another reason."

Gilbert made no reply.

"Speak, sir, I desire it."

"Perhaps, sire, you have guessed rightly."

"Is not that it?" asked the king, in an anxious tone. "You found the position a very serious one, and you abstained."

"For fear of one still more serious. Yes, sire, your majesty has divined the truth."

"I like frankness," said the king, who could not conceal his agitation ; for he was of a timid nature, and blushed easily.

"Then," continued Louis XVI., "you predicted the king's fall to him, and you feared to be placed too near the ruins."

"No, sire, since it is just at the moment that danger is most imminent that I come to face the danger."

"Yes, yes, you have just left Necker, and you speak like him. The danger ! the danger ! Without doubt, it is dangerous at this moment to approach me. And where is Necker ?"

"Quite ready, I believe, to obey the orders of your majesty."

"So much the better ; I shall want him," said the king, with a sigh. "In politics we must not be headstrong. We think to do good and we do wrong. We even do good, and some capricious event mars our projects ; and though the plans laid were in reality good, we are accused of having been mistaken."

The king sighed again. Gilbert came to his assistance.

"Sire," said he, "your majesty reasons admirably ; but what is desirable at the present moment is to see into the future more clearly than has been done hitherto."

The king raised his head, and his inexpressive eyebrows slightly frowned.

"Sire, forgive me," said Gilbert, "I am a physician. When the danger is imminent, I speak briefly."

"Do you, then, attach much importance to the riot of to-day ?"

"Sire, it is not a riot—it is a revolution."

"And you wish me to make terms with rebels and assassins ? For, in fine, they have taken the Bastile by force ; it is an act of rebellion ; they have killed Monsieur de Launay, Monsieur de Losme, and Monsieur de Flesselles ; it is murder."

"I wish you to distinguish more correctly, sire. Those who took the Bastile are heroes ; those who assassinated Messieurs de Flesselles, De Losme, and De Launay are murderers."

The king colored slightly, and almost immediately this color disappeared, his lips become pale, and a few drops of perspiration trickled down his forehead.

"You are right, sire. You are a physician indeed, or a

surgeon, rather, for you cut to the quick. But let us return to the object of our interview. You are Doctor Gilbert, are you not? or, at least, it is with this name that your memoirs are signed."

"Sire, it does me great honor that your majesty has so good a memory, although, taking it all in all, I have no great reason to be proud of my name."

"How is that?"

"My name must, indeed, have been pronounced before your majesty, and that not long ago."

"I do not understand you."

"Six days ago I was arrested and thrown into the Bastile. Now, I have heard it said that no arrest of any importance was ever made without the king being aware of the fact."

"You in the Bastile!" said the king, opening his eyes widely.

"Here is the registration of my imprisonment, sire. Put in prison, as I have the honor to tell your majesty, six days ago, by order of the king, I came out of it at three o'clock to-day, by the grace of the people."

"To-day?"

"Yes, sire. Did your majesty hear the cannon?"

"Most undoubtedly."

"Well, then, the cannon opened the gates for me."

"Ah!" murmured the king, "I would willingly say that I am pleased at this event, had not the cannon of this morning been fired at the Bastile and at the monarchy at the same time."

"Oh, sire, do not make a prison the symbol of a principle; say, on the contrary, sire, that you rejoice that the Bastile is taken; for henceforward injustice will not be committed in the king's name without his cognizance—injustice similar to that of which I have just been the victim."

"But surely, sir, your arrest must have had a cause."

"None that I know of, sire; I was arrested on my return to France, and imprisoned, that is all."

"Really, sir," said Louis XVI., kindly, "is there not some egotism on your part, in speaking to me thus of yourself, when I so much need to have my own position spoken of?"

"Sire, all I require is, that your majesty will answer me one single question."

"What is it?"

"Was or was not your majesty concerned in my arrest?"

"I was not even aware of your return to France."

"I rejoice at this answer, sire; I shall then be enabled to declare openly that when your majesty is supposed to do wrong, you are nearly always calumniated; and to those who doubt it, I can cite myself as an example."

The king smiled.

"As a physician," said he, "you pour balm into the wound."

"Oh, sire, I shall pour in the balm abundantly; and, if you desire it, I will cure the wound, that I will answer for."

"I most assuredly desire it."

"You must desire it very firmly, sire."

"I do desire it firmly."

"Before going any further, sire," said Gilbert, "read that line written in the margin of my jail-book entry."

"What line?" asked the king, in an anxious tone.

Gilbert presented the page to the king. The king read: "By request of the queen."

The king frowned.

"Of the queen!" said he. "Can you have incurred her displeasure?"

"Sire, I am certain her majesty knows me still less than did your majesty."

"But still, you must have committed some fault; a man is not sent to the Bastile for nothing."

"It would seem so, since I have just come out of it."

"But Monsieur Necker has sent you to me, and the warrant of imprisonment was signed by him."

"It was so, undoubtedly."

"Then explain yourself more clearly. Review your past life. See if you do not find some circumstance in it which you had yourself forgotten."

"Review my past life! Yes, sire; I shall do it, and aloud; do not fear, it will not occupy much time. I have labored without intermission since I attained the age of sixteen; the pupil of Jean Jacques, the companion of Balsamo, the friend of Lafayette and of Washington, I have never had cause to reproach myself, since the day that I left France, for a single fault, nor even an error. When acquired science permitted me to attend the wounded or the sick, I always thought myself responsible to God for every one of my thoughts, and every action. Since God has given me the care of human beings as a surgeon, I have shed blood for the sake of humanity, while ready to give my own to soothe or to save my patient; as a physician, I have always been a consoler, and sometimes a benefactor. Fifteen years have thus passed away. God blessed my efforts; I saw return to life the greater part of the afflicted, who all kissed my hands. Those who died had been condemned by the will of God. No, I repeat it, sire, since the day when I left France, and that was fifteen years ago, I have done nothing with which I can reproach myself."

"You have associated with the innovators of America, and your writings have propagated their principles."

"Yes, sire; and I forgot this claim to the gratitude of kings and men."

The king was silent.

"Sire," continued Gilbert, "now my life is known to you; I have neither offended nor wounded any one—neither a beggar nor a queen—and I come to ask your majesty why I have been punished."

"I shall speak to the queen, Monsieur Gilbert; but do you think the *lettre de cachet* comes directly from the queen?"

"I do not say that, sire; I even think the queen merely recommended it."

"Ah! you see," cried Louis, quite joyfully.

"Yes; but you are aware, sire, that what a queen recommends, she commands."

"At whose request was the *lettre de cachet* granted?"

"Yes, sire," said Gilbert. "Look at it."

And he presented him the entry in the jail-book.

"The Countess de Charny!" exclaimed the king. "How, it is she who caused your arrest? But what can you have done to this poor Charny?"

"I did not even know that lady by name this morning, sire."

Louis passed his hand over his brow.

"Charny," murmured he, "Charny—sweetness, virtue, chastity itself!"

"You will see, sire," said Gilbert, laughing, "that I was imprisoned in the Bastile at the request of three theological virtues,"

"Oh ! I will clear this up at once," said the king.

And he went to the fireplace and pulled the bell.

An usher appeared.

"See if the Countess de Charny is with the queen," said Louis.

"Sire," said the usher, "the countess has just this instant crossed the gallery ; she is about stepping into her coach."

"Run after her," said Louis, eagerly, "and request her to come to my cabinet on an affair of importance."

Then turning toward Gilbert :

"Is that what you desire, sir ?" said he.

"Yes, sire," answered Gilbert ; "and I return a thousand thanks to your majesty."

CHAPTER XXIII.

GILBERT, on hearing the order to send for Mme. de Charny, had retired into the recess of a window.

As to the king, he was walking up and down in the room called the Œil de Bœuf, preoccupied at times with public affairs, at others with the pertinacity of this Gilbert, by whom, in spite of himself, he felt strangely influenced, and at a moment when nothing ought to have interested him but the affairs of Paris.

Suddenly the door of the cabinet was thrown open, the usher announced the Countess de Charny, and Gilbert, through the closed curtains, could perceive a woman whose flowing and silken robes grazed the half-opened door.

This lady was dressed, according to the fashion of the times, in a deshabille of gray silk, striped with a variety of colors, with a petticoat of the same stuff, and a sort of shawl, which, after being crossed over the chest, was fastened behind her waist, and showed to a great advantage the beauties of a full and well-developed bosom.   A small bonnet, coquettishly fixed on the summit of a high headdress, high-heeled shoes, which showed the exquisite shape of a beautiful instep, a small cane twirled by the gloved fingers of a slender and delicate hand, with tapering and perfectly aristocratic fingers, such was the person so anxiously expected by Gilbert.

The king stepped forward to meet her.

"You were just going out, countess, I was told."

"In truth, sire," replied the countess, "I was on the point of stepping into my carriage, when I received your majesty's order."

On hearing this firm-toned voice, the ears of Gilbert were suddenly assailed as with a rushing sound. The blood instantly suffused his cheeks, and a thousand shudders appeared to thrill through his whole system.

Despite himself, he made a step from the curtain, behind which he had secreted himself.

"She," stammered he—"she—Andrée——"

"Madame," continued the king, who, as well as the countess, had not observed the emotion of Gilbert, who was hidden in the shade, "I requested you to visit me for the purpose of obtaining some information from you."

"I am ready to comply with your majesty's wishes."

The king leaned in the direction of Gilbert, as if to warn him.

The latter, perceiving that the moment to show himself had not yet arrived, gradually withdrew himself again behind the curtain.

"Madame," said the king, "it is now eight or ten days since a warrant of imprisonment was requested of Monsieur de Necker——"

Gilbert, through the almost imperceptible opening between the curtains, fastened his gaze upon Andrée. The young woman was pale, feverish, and anxious, and appeared borne down by the weight of a secret prepossession, for which even she herself could not account.

"You hear me, do you not, countess?" asked Louis XVI., seeing that Mme. de Charny hesitated before answering.

"Yes, sire."

"Well, do you understand me, and can you answer my question?"

"I am endeavoring to remember," said Andrée.

"Permit me to assist your memory, countess. The warrant of imprisonment was demanded by you, and the demand was countersigned by the queen."

The countess, instead of answering, appeared to abandon herself more and more to that feverish abstraction which seemed to lead her beyond the limits of real life.

"But answer me, then, madame," said the king, who began to grow impatient.

"It is true," said she, trembling, "it is true. I wrote the letter, and her majesty the queen countersigned it."

"Then," asked Louis, "tell me the crime which had been committed by the person against whom such a document was required."

"Sire," said Andrée, "I cannot tell you what crime he had committed ; but what I can tell you is, that the crime was great."

"Oh ! can you not confide that even to me ?"

"No, sire."

"Not to the king ?"

"No. I hope your majesty will forgive me ; but I cannot."

"Then you shall tell it to him in person, madame," said the king ; "for what you have refused to King Louis XVI. you cannot refuse to Doctor Gilbert."

"To Doctor Gilbert !" exclaimed Andrée. "Great God ! where is he, then ?"

The king stepped aside to allow Gilbert to advance ; the curtains were thrown apart, and the doctor appeared, almost as pale as Andrée.

"Here he is, madame," said he.

At the sight of Gilbert the countess staggered. Her limbs shook beneath her. She fell backward, as does a person who is about to faint, and only maintained a standing position with the assistance of an armchair, on which she leaned in the sorrowful, motionless, and almost unconscious attitude of Eurydice at the moment when the serpent's venom reaches her heart.

"Madame," said Gilbert, bowing to her with mock politeness, "allow me to repeat the question which has just been put to you by his majesty."

The lips of Andrée could be seen to move, but no sound issued from them.

"What offense had I committed, madame, that an order from you should have caused me to be thrown into a loathsome dungeon ?"

On hearing this voice, Andrée bounded as if she had felt the tearing asunder of the fibers of her heart.

Then, on a sudden, casting upon Gilbert an icy look like that of a serpent :

"Me, sir," said she ; "I do not know you."

But while she pronounced these words, Gilbert, on his side, had looked at her with such intentness, he had loaded the brightness of his gaze with so much invincible audacity, that the countess cast down her eyes, completely overpowered.

"Countess," said the king, in a mild tone of reproach, "see where the abuse of a signature may lead you. Here is a gentleman whom you do not know, and you yourself confess it ; a man who is a great practitioner, a profound physician, a man who can be reproached for nothing."

Andrée raised her head, and almost petrified Gilbert by her contemptuous look.

He, however, remained calm and proud.

"I say, then," continued the king, "that having no cause for complaint against Monsieur Gilbert, that by thus persecuting him instead of another, it is on the head of an innocent man that punishment has fallen. Countess, this is wrong."

"Sire," said Andrée.

"Ah !" interrupted the king, who already trembled for fear of disobliging the favorite of his wife, "I know that you are kind-hearted, and that if you have punished some one through hatred, that person must have deserved it ; but you see that it will be necessary, in future, to avoid the recurrence of such mistakes."

Then turning toward Gilbert :

"You see, doctor, it is the fault of the times, rather than that of men. We are born in corruption, and we die in it ; but we will endeavor, at least, to ameliorate the condition of posterity, and you will, I trust, assist me in this work, Doctor Gilbert."

And Louis ceased speaking, thinking he had said enough to satisfy both parties.

Poor king ! had he pronounced those words before the National Assembly, not only would he have been applauded, but, moreover, he would have seen them reproduced in all the court journals.

But the two unrelenting enemies present at this interview appreciated but little his conciliating philosophy.

"With your majesty's permission," said Gilbert, "I will request the countess to repeat what she has already stated, namely, that she does not know me."

"Countess," said the king, "will you do what the doctor requests of you ?"

"I do not know Doctor Gilbert," repeated Andrée in a firm voice.

"But you know another Gilbert, my namesake; the Gilbert whose crime has been visited on me."

"Oh !" said Andrée, "I know that person, and I consider him an infamous wretch."

"Sire, it would not become me to interrogate the countess," said Gilbert ; "but deign to ask her of what that infamous man has been guilty."

"Countess, you cannot refuse acceding to so just a request."

"What he has done ?" said Andrée, "Doubtless the queen knew of what crime he had been guilty, since with her own hand she authorized the letter by means of which I applied for his arrest."

"But," said the king, "it is not quite sufficient that the queen should be convinced, it is necessary that I, too, should be convinced. The queen is the queen, but I am the king."

"Well, then, sire, the Gilbert mentioned in the warrant is a man who, sixteen years ago, committed a most fearful crime."

"Will your majesty ask the countess how old that man is at the present day ?"

The king repeated the question,

"From thirty to thirty-two," said Andrée.

"Sire," rejoined Gilbert, "if the crime was committed sixteen years ago, it was not committed by a man, but by a child, and if during these sixteen years, the man has deplored the crime committed by the child, does not that man deserve some little leniency ?"

"But, sir," asked the king, "you then know the Gilbert then in question ?"

"I know him, sire," said Gilbert.

"And has he committed no other fault except this one of his early youth ?"

"I do not know that since the day on which he committed—I will not say that fault, sire, for I am less indulgent than you, but that crime—I do not know that any one in this world has aught to reproach him with."

"No ; unless it is having dipped his pen in poison,

and having composed the most odious libels," cried
Andrée.

"Sire, please to ask the countess," said Gilbert, "if the
real object of the arrest of this Gilbert was not to afford
every facility to his enemies, or, rather, to his enemy, to
obtain possession of certain papers, which might have compromised a great lady, a lady of the court."

Andrée trembled from head to foot.

"Monsieur," faltered she.

"Countess, what is this casket?" asked the king, who
had perceived the trembling and the pallor of the countess.

"Ah! madame," cried Gilbert, feeling that he was
gaining the mastery, "no tergiversation—no subterfuge.
There have been misstatements enough on both sides. I
am the Gilbert who committed the crime—I am the Gilbert
of the libels—I am the Gilbert of the casket. You—you
are the great lady—the lady of the court. I call upon the
king to be our judge ; accept him, and we will tell to this
judge—to the king—to God—we will tell all that has occurred between us ; and the king shall decide while we
await the judgment of God."

"Say what you will, sir," rejoined the countess, "but
I can say nothing ; I do not know you."

"And you know nothing of this casket, neither?"

The countess convulsively closed her hands, and bit
her pale lips till they bled.

"No," said she ; "I know no more of it than I do of
you."

But the effort she made to pronounce these words was
such that her body trembled as does a statue on its pedestal during an earthquake.

"Madame, beware," said Gilbert. "I am, as you can
hardly have forgotten, the pupil of a man called Joseph
Balsamo. The power which he possessed over you he has
transmitted to me. For the last time, will you answer the
question I put to you : My casket?"

"No!" cried the countess, a prey to the most indescribable agitation, and making a movement to rush out of
the room.

"Well, then," said Gilbert, in his turn becoming pale,
and raising his threatening arm, "well, then, thou iron
nature, thou heart of adamant, bend, burst, and break

beneath the irresistible pressure of my will.   Wilt thou not speak, Andrée ?"

"No, no!" cried the countess.   "Help me, sire—help me!"

"Thou shalt speak!" cried Gilbert ; "and no one, were he the king, or even God himself, can withdraw thee from my power.   Thou shalt speak, then ; thou shalt reveal thy whole soul to the witness of this solemn scene ; and all that is contained in the recesses of thy conscience—all that which God alone can road in the depths of the deepest souls, you shall know, sire, from the lips of her who refuses to reveal them.   Sleep, Madame the Countess, sleep and speak.   I will it!"

Hardly were the words pronounced, when the countess stopped short in the midst of a suppressed cry, stretched forth her arms, and seeking support for her trembling limbs, fell, as if imploring a refuge, into the arms of the king, who, trembling himself, seated her upon an arm-chair.

"Oh!" said Louis XVI., "I have heard of things of this nature, but I never before witnessed anything to equal it.   Is it not to a magnetic sleep that she has just succumbed, sir ?"

"Yes, sire ; take the hand of the countess, and ask her why she caused me to be arrested," said Gilbert, as if the right to command belonged to him alone.

Louis XVI., quite thunder-struck by this marvelous scene, took two steps backward to convince himself that he was not himself asleep, and that what was taking place before him was not a dream ; then, like a mathematician who is interested in some new solution, he approached nearer to the countess, whose hand he took in his.

"Let us see, countess," said he ; "it was then you who caused the arrest of Doctor Gilbert ?"

Still, although asleep, the countess made one last effort, snatched her hand from that of the king, and gathering up all her strength :

"No," cried she ; "I will not speak!"

The king looked at Gilbert, as if to ask him which of the two would overcome the other—his will or that of Audrée.

Gilbert smiled.

"You will speak!" said he.

And, his eyes fixed upon the sleeping Andrée, he advanced a step toward the armchair.

Andrée shuddered.

"Will you not speak?" added he, taking a second step, which diminished the distance that separated him from the countess.

Every muscle of Andrée's frame became rigid in a supreme effort of reaction.

"Ah! you will not speak, then?" said he, taking a third stride which placed him at the side of Andrée, over whose head he placed his outstretched hand, "ah! you will not speak?"

Andrée was writhing in the most fearful convulsions.

"But take care, take care!" cried Louis XVI., you will kill her!"

"Fear nothing, sire; it is with the soul alone that I have to contend; the soul is struggling, but it will yield."

Then lowering his hand:

"Speak!" said he.

Andrée extended her arms, and made an effort to breathe, as if she had been under the pressure of a pneumatic machine.

"Speak!" repeated Gilbert, lowering his hand still more.

All the muscles of the young woman's body seemed about to burst. A fringe of froth appeared upon her lips, and a commencement of epilepsy convulsed her from head to foot.

Doctor! doctor!" said the king, "take care!"

But he, without noticing the king, lowered his hand a third time, and touching the top of the countess's head with the palm of that hand:

"Speak," said he; "it is my will."

Andrée, on feeling the touch of that hand, heaved a sigh—her arms fell motionless to her side—her head, which had been thrown backward, fell forward upon her breast —and a copious flood of tears oozed through her closed eyelids.

"My God! my God! my God!" faltered she.

"Invoke the Lord—be it so; he who operates in the name of God does not fear God."

"Oh!" said the countess, "how I hate you!"

"Abhor me, if you will, but speak."

"Sire, sire," exclaimed Andrée, "tell him that he consumes me, that he devours me, that he kills me!"

"Speak!" said Gilbert.

Then he made a sign to the king that he might interrogate her.

"So that, countess," said the king, again taking her hand, "he whom you wished to arrest, and whom you have caused to be arrested, was really the doctor himself?"

"Yes."

"And there was no mistake, no misunderstanding?"

"None."

"And the casket?" said the king.

"Well," articulated the countess, slowly, "could I allow that casket to remain in his possession?"

Gilbert and the king exchanged glances.

"And did you take it from him?" said Louis XVI.

"I had it taken from him."

"Oh! oh! tell me how that was managed, countess," said the king, forgetful of all ceremony, and kneeling down before Andrée. "You had it taken?"

"Yes."

"When, and by what means?"

"I ascertained that this Gilbert, who, during sixteen years, has already made two voyages to France, was about to make a third one, and this last time with the intention of remaining there."

"But the casket?" asked the king.

"I ascertained by means of the lieutenant of police, Monsieur de Crosne, that during one of his journeys he had bought some lands in the neighborhood of Villers-Cotterets—that the farmer who tenanted his lands enjoyed his whole confidence; I suspected that the casket might be left at his residence."

"What made you think so?"

"I went to see Mesmer. I made him put me to sleep, and I saw the casket while in that state."

"It was——"

"In a large clothes-press on the ground floor, hidden under some linen."

"This is wonderful!" said the king. "After that, tell me what took place."

"I returned to the house of Monsieur de Crosne, who,

having been recommended to do so by the queen, gave me one of his most skilful agents."

" What was the name of this agent ? " asked Gilbert.

Andrée shuddered as if a hot iron had touched her.

" I ask you his name ? " repeated Gilbert.

Andrée endeavored to resist.

" His name ? I will know it ! ' said the doctor.

" Wolfsfoot," she replied.

" After that ? " asked the king.

" Well, then, yesterday morning this man got possession of the casket. That is all."

" No, it is not all," said Gilbert. " You must now tell the king where the casket is at this moment."

" Oh ! " said Louis XVI., " you ask too much of her."

" No, sire."

" But by this Wolfsfoot, by means of Monsieur de Crosne, one might ascertain——"

" Oh, we shall know everything quicker, and much better, through the countess."

Andrée by a convulsive movement, the object of which was, doubtless, to prevent the words from escaping her lips, clinched her teeth with such violence as almost to break them.

The king pointed out this nervous convulsion to the doctor.

Gilbert smiled.

He touched with his thumb and forefinger the lower part of the face of Andrée, whose muscles were relaxed at the same moment.

" In the first place, countess, tell the king clearly that this casket belonged to Doctor Gilbert."

" Yes, yes, it belongs to him," said the sleeping woman, angrily.

" And where is it at this moment ? " asked Gilbert. " Make haste ! the king has not time to wait."

Andrée hesitated for a moment.

" At Wolfsfoot's house," said she.

Gilbert observed the hesitation, although it was scarcely perceptible.

" You are telling a falsehood ! " said he, " or, rather, you are endeavoring to tell one. Where is the casket ? I insist on knowing."

" At my house at Versailles," said Andrée, bursting into

tears, with a nervous trembling which shook her whole
frame, "at my house, where Wolfsfoot is waiting for me,
as we had previously agreed to meet at eleven o'clock to-
night."

Midnight was heard to strike.

"Is he still waiting there?"

"Yes."

"In which room is he?"

"They have just shown him into the drawing-room."

"What place does he occupy in the drawing-room?"

"He is standing, and leaning against the chimneypiece."

"And the casket?"

"It is on the table before him. Oh!"

"What is the matter?"

"Let us hasten to get him out of the house. Monsieur
de Charny, who was not to return till to-morrow, will
come back to-night, on account of the events that have
taken place. I see him; he is at Sèvres. Make him go
away, so that the count may not find him in the house."

"Your majesty hears that. In what part of Versailles
does Madame de Charny reside?"

"Where do you reside, countess?"

"On the Boulevard de la Reine, sire."

"Very well."

"Sire, your majesty has heard everything. That casket
belongs to me. Does the king order it to be returned to
me?"

"Immediately, sir."

And the king, having drawn a screen before Mme. de
Charny, which prevented her from being seen, called the
officer on duty, and gave him an order in a low voice.

CHAPTER XXIV.

A STRANGE preoccupation for a king whose subjects
were undermining his throne. The inquisitiveness of the
erudite man applied to a physical phenomenon, while the
most important political phenomenon was taking place
that France had ever known—that is to say, the transfor-
mation of a monarchy into a democracy. This sight, we
say, of a king forgetting himself during the most terrible
period of a tempest, would certainly have caused the great

minds of the time to smile, bent as they had been during three months on the solution of their problem.

While riot was raging in all its fury without, Louis, forgetting the terrible events of the day—the taking of the Bastile, the assassination of Flesselles, De Launay, and De Losme, the disposition of the National Assembly to revolt against the king—Louis was concentrating his mind on this examination of a theory; and the revelations of this strange scene absorbed him no less than the most vital interests of his government.

And thus, as soon as he had given the order which we have mentioned to the captain of his guards, he returned to Gilbert, who was removing from the countess the excess of fluid with which he had charged her, in order that her slumber might be more tranquil than under the effects of this convulsive somnambulism.

For an instant the respiration of the countess became calm and easy as that of a sleeping child. Then Gilbert, with a single motion of his hand, reopened her eyes, and put her into a state of ecstasy.

It was then that one could see the extraordinary beauty of Andrée, in all its splendor. Being completely freed from all earthly agitations, the blood, which had for an instant rushed to her face, and which momentarily had colored her cheeks, redescended to her heart, whose pulsations had recovered their natural state. Her face had again become pale, but of that beautiful pallor of the women of the East; her eyes, opened rather more than usual, were raised toward heaven, and left the pupils floating, as it were, in the pearl-like whiteness of their eyeballs; the nose, slightly expanded, appeared to inhale a purer atmosphere; and her lips, which had preserved all their vermilion, although her cheeks had lost a little of theirs, were slightly separated, and discovered a row of pearls of which the sweet moistness increased the brilliancy.

The head was gently thrown backward with an inexpressible grace almost angelic. It might have been said that this fixed look, increasing its scope of vision by its intensity, penetrated to the foot of the throne of God.

The king gazed at her as if dazzled. Gilbert turned away his head and sighed. He could not resist the desire to give Andrée this degree of superhuman beauty; and now, like Pygmalion—more unhappy even than Pygmalion, for he knew the insensibility of the beautiful statue—he trembled at the sight of his own production.

He made a sign without even turning his head toward Andrée, and her eyes closed instantly.

The king desired Gilbert to explain to him that marvelous state, in which the soul separates itself from the body, and soars, free, happy, and divine, above all terrestrial miseries.

Gilbert, like all men of truly superior genius, could pronounce the words so much dreaded by mediocrity, "I do not know." He confessed his ignorance to the king. He had produced a phenomenon which he could not explain. The fact itself existed, but the explanation of the fact could not be given.

"Doctor," said the king, on hearing this avowal of Gilbert, "this is another of those secrets which nature reserves for the learned men of another generation, and which will be studied thoroughly, like so many other mysteries which were thought insoluble. We call them mysteries : our fathers would have called them sorcery or witchcraft."

"Yes, sire," answered Gilbert, smiling ; "and I should have had the honor to be burned on the Place de Grève for the greater glory of a religion which was not understood by wise men without learning and priests devoid of faith."

"And under whom did you study this science ?" rejoined the king. "Was it with Mesmer ?"

"Oh, sire," said Gilbert, smiling, "I had seen the most astonishing phenomena of the science ten years before the name of Mesmer was pronounced in France."

"Tell me, now : this Mesmer, who has revolutionized all France, was he, in your opinion, a charlatan ? It seems to me that you operate much more simply than he. I have heard his experiments spoken of, and also those of Deslon and Puysegur. You know all that has been said on the subject, whether idle stories or positive truths."

"I have carefully observed all these discussions, sire."

"Well, then, what do you think of the famous vat or tub ?"

"I hope your majesty will excuse me if I answer doubtingly to all you ask me with regard to the magnetic art. Magnetism has not yet become an art."

" Ah ! "

" But it assuredly is a power, a terrific power, since it anniḃilates the will, since it isolates the soul from the body, and places the body of the somnambulist in the power of the magnetizer, while the former does not retain the power, nor even the desire, to defend itself. As for me, sire, I have seen strange phenomena produced, I have produced many myself. Well, I nevertheless still doubt."

" How ! you still doubt ? You perform miracles, and yet you are in doubt ? "

" No, I do not doubt—I do not doubt. At this moment even, I have a proof before my eyes of an extraordinary and incomprehensible power. But when that proof has disappeared, when I am at home alone in my library, face to face with all that human science has written during three thousand years, when science says no, when the mind says no, when reason says no, I doubt."

" And did your master also doubt, doctor ? "

" Perhaps he did, but he was less sincere than I. He did not express his doubt."

" Was it Deslon ? Was it Puysegur ? "

" No, sire, no. My master was a man far superior to all the men you have named. I have seen him perform the most marvelous things, especially with regard to wounds. No science was unknown to him. He had impregnated his mind with Egyptian theories. He had penetrated the arcana of ancient Assyrian civilization. He was a profound scholar, a formidable philosopher, having a great knowledge of human life, combined with a persevering will."

" Have I ever known him ? " asked the king.

Gilbert hesitated a moment.

" I ask you whether I ever knew him ? "

" Yes, sire. "

" And you call him——? "

" Sire," said Gilbert, " to pronounce that name before the king would, perhaps, render me liable to his displeasure. Now, especially at this moment, when the majority of Frenchmen are depreciating all royal authority, I would not throw a shade on the respect we all owe your majesty. "

" Name that man boldly, Doctor Gilbert, and be persuaded that I, too, have my philosophy—a philosophy of

sufficiently good material to enable me to smile at all the
insults of the present and all the threats of the future."
Gilbert still continued to hesitate.

The king approached him.

"Sir," said he to Gilbert, laughing, "call him Satan,
if you will, I shall find a shield to protect me from him—
the one which your dogmatizers do not possess—one that
they never will possess—one which I alone, perhaps, in
this century, possess, and bear without feeling shame—
religion."

"Your majesty believes as St. Louis did. It is true,"
said Gilbert.

"And in that lies all my strength, I confess, doctor. I
like science ; I adore the results of materialism ; I am a
mathematician, as you well know ; you know that the sum-
total of an addition or an algebraical formula fills my
heart with joy ; but when I meet people who carry algebra
to atheism, I have in reserve my profound, inexhaustible,
and eternal faith—a faith which places me a degree above
and a degree below them—above them in good, and beneath
them in evil. You see, then, doctor, that I am a man to
whom everything may be said, a king who can hear anything."

"Sire," said Gilbert, with a sort of admiration. "I
thank your majesty for what you have just said to me ; for
you have almost honored me with the confidence of a
friend."

"Oh ! I wish," the timid Louis hastened to exclaim, "I
wish all Europe could hear me speak thus. If Frenchmen
were to read in my heart all the energy of feeling, the
tenderness which it contains, I think they would oppose me
less."

The last portion of the king's sentence, which showed
that the king was irritated by the attack the royal prerogative had been subjected to, lowered Louis XVI. in the
estimation of Gilbert.

He hastened to say, without attempting to spare the
king's feelings :

"Sire, since you insist upon it, my master was the Count
de Cagliostro."

"Oh !" cried Louis, coloring, "that empiric !"

"That empiric !—yes, sire. Your majesty is doubtless
aware that the word you have just pronounced is one of the

noblest used in science. *Empiric* means ' the man who attempts'—the practitioner, the profound thinker, the man, in short, who is incessantly attempting after discoveries, does all that God permits men to do that is glorious and beautiful. Let but a man *attempt* during his whole life, and his life will be well occupied."

" Ah, sir, this Cagliostro whom you defend was a great enemy of kings."

Gilbert recollected the affair of the necklace.

" Is it not rather the enemy of queens your majesty intended to say ? "

Louis shuddered at this sharp home-thrust.

" Yes," said he, " he conducted himself in all the affairs of Prince Louis de Rohan in a manner which was more than equivocal."

" Sire, in that, as in other circumstances, Cagliostro carried out the human mission ; he sought his own ends. In science, in morals, in politics, there is neither good nor evil ; there are only stated phenomena or accomplished facts. Nevertheless, I will not defend him, sire. I repeat it, the man may often have merited blame ; perhaps some day this very blame may be considered as praise ; posterity reconsiders the judgments of men. But I did not study under the man, sire, but under the philosopher, under the great physician."

" Well, well," said the king, who still felt the double wound his pride and heart had received—" well ; but we are forgetting the Countess de Charny, and perhaps she is suffering."

" I will wake her up, sire, if your majesty desires it ; but I had wished that the casket might arrive here during her sleep."

" Why ? "

" To spare her a too harsh lesson."

" Here is somebody coming at this moment," said the king. " Wait."

In fact, the king's order had been punctually obeyed. The casket found at the hotel of the Countess de Charny, in the possession of the agent Wolfsfoot, was brought into the royal cabinet, under the very eyes of the countess, who did not see it.

The king made a sign of satisfaction to the officer who brought the casket. The officer then left the room.

" Well ! " said Louis XVI.

" Well, then, sire, that is, in fact, the very casket which had been taken away from me."

" Open it," said the king.

" Sire, I am willing to do so, if your majesty desire it ; but I have only to forewarn your majesty of one thing."

" What is that ? "

" Sire, as I told your majesty, this box contains only papers which are easily read, and might be taken, and on which depends the honor of a woman."

" And that woman is the countess ? "

" Yes, sire. That honor will not be endangered while this matter is confined to the knowledge of your majesty. Open it, sire," said Gilbert, approaching the casket, and presenting the key of it to the king.

" Sir," replied Louis XVI. coldly, " take away this box ; it belongs to you."

" Thank you, sire ; but what are we to do with the countess ? "

" Oh, do not, above all, wake her up here. I wish to avoid all recriminations and painful scenes."

" Sire," said Gilbert, " the countess will only awake in the place where you wish her to be carried."

" Well, let her be taken to the queen's apartment, then."

Louis rang the bell. An officer entered the room.

" Captain," said he, " the Countess de Charny has just fainted here, on hearing the news from Paris. Have her taken to the queen's room."

" How long will it take to carry her there ? " asked Gilbert of the king.

" About ten minutes," replied the latter.

Gilbert laid his hand on the countess.

" You will awake in three quarters of an hour," said he.

Two soldiers entered, the order having been given by the officer, who carried her away in an armchair.

" Now, Monsieur Gilbert, what more do you desire ? " asked the king.

" Sire, I desire a favor which would draw me nearer to your majesty, and procure me, at the same time, an opportunity to be useful to you."

The king endeavored to divine what he could mean.

"Explain yourself," said he.

"I should like to be one of the physicians-in-ordinary to the king," replied Gilbert; "I should be in the way of no one; it is a post of honor, but rather a confidential than a brilliant one."

"Granted," said the king. "Adieu, Monsieur Gilbert. Ah! by the by, a thousand compliments to Necker. Adieu."

Then, as he was leaving the room:

"My supper!" cried Louis, whom no event, however important, could induce to forget his supper.

CHAPTER XXV.

WHILE the king was learning to oppose the revolution philosophically, by going through a course of occult sciences, the queen, who was a much more substantial and profound philosopher, had gathered around her, in her large cabinet, all those who were called her faithful adherents, doubtless because there had been no opportunity afforded to any one of them either to prove or to try his fidelity.

In the queen's circle, also, the events of that terrible day had been related in all their details.

She had even been the first to be informed of them, for knowing her to be undaunted, they had not feared to inform her of the danger.

Around the queen were assembled generals, courtiers, priests, and ladies. Near the doors, and behind the tapestries which hung before them, might be seen groups of young officers, full of courage and ardor, who saw in all revolts a long-desired opportunity to evince their prowess in presence of the fair sex, as in a tournament.

All of these, whether intimately connected with the court, or devoted servants of the monarchy, had listened with attention to the news from Paris, which had been related by M. de Lambesq, who, having been present during those events, had hastened to Versailles with his regiment, still covered with the sand of the Tuileries, in order to state the real position of affairs to the affrighted courtiers, and thus afford them consolation ; for many of them, although the misfortune was sufficiently serious, had greatly exaggerated it in their apprehension.

The queen was seated at a table. It was no longer the gentle and lovely bride, the guardian angel of France whom we saw appear at the opening of this story, crossing the northern frontier, an olive-branch in her hand. It was no longer even that gracious and beautiful princess whom we saw one evening entering with the Princess de Lamballe into the mysterious dwelling of Mesmer, and seating herself, laughing and incredulous, near the symbolical vat, of which she had come to ask a revelation of the future.

No! It was the haughty and resolute queen, with frowning brow and scornful lip ; it was a woman whose heart had allowed a portion of its love to escape from it, to harbor, instead of that sweet and vivifying element, the first drops of gall, which, by constantly filtering into it, was finally to reach her blood.

It was, in short, the woman represented by the third portrait in the gallery of Versailles ; that is to say, no longer Marie Antoinette, no longer the Queen of France, but the woman who was now designated only by the name of the Austrian.

Behind her, in the shade, lay a motionless young woman, her head reclining on the cushion of a sofa, and her hand upon her forehead.

This was Mme. de Polignac.

Perceiving M. de Lambesq, the queen made one of those gestures indicative of unbounded joy, which mean :

" At last, we shall know all."

M. de Lambesq bowed, with a sign that asked pardon at the same time for his soiled boots, his dusty coat, and his sword, which, having been bent in his fall, could not be forced into its scabbard.

" Well, Monsieur de Lambesq," said the queen, " have you just arrived from Paris ? "

" Yes, your majesty."

" What are the people doing ? "

" They are killing and burning."

" Through maddening rage or hatred ? "

" No ; from sheer ferocity."

The queen reflected, as if she had felt disposed to be of

his opinion with regard to the people. Then, shaking her head :

"No, prince," said she, "the people are not ferocious; at least, not without a reason. Do not conceal anything from me. Is it madness? is it hatred?"

"Well, I think it is hatred carried to madness, madame."

"Hatred of whom? Ah! I see you are hesitating again, prince; take care, if you relate events in that manner, instead of applying to you as I do, I shall send one of my outriders to Paris; he will require one hour to go there, one to acquire information, one to return, and, in the course of three hours, this man will tell me everything that has happened, as accurately and as simply as one of Homer's heralds."

M. de Dreux Breze stepped forward with a smile upon his lips.

"But, madame," said he, "of what consequence to you is the hatred of the people? That can in no way concern you. The people may hate all, excepting you."

The queen did not even rebuke this piece of flattery.

"Come, come, prince," said she to M. de Lambesq, "speak out."

"Well, then, madame, it is true the people are acted upon by hatred."

"Hatred of me?"

"Of everything that rules."

"Well said! that is the truth. I feel it!" exclaimed the queen, resolutely.

"I am a soldier, your majesty," said the prince.

"Well, well, speak to us, then, as a soldier. Let us see what must be done."

"Nothing, madame."

"How—nothing!" cried the queen, taking advantage of the murmurs occasioned by these words among the wearers of embroidered coats and golden-sheathed swords of her company; "nothing! You, a prince of Lorraine, you can speak thus to the Queen of France at a moment when the people, according to your own confession, are killing and burning, and you can coolly say there is nothing to be done."

A second murmur, but this time of approbation, followed the words of Marie Antoinette.

She turned round, fixed her gaze on all the circle
which environed her, and among all those fiery eyes sought
those which darted forth the brightest flames, as if she
could read a greater proof of fidelity in them.

"Nothing!" continued the prince, "because, in allowing the Parisian to become calm—and he will become so—
for he is only warlike when he is exasperated. Why give
him the honors of a struggle, and risk the chances of a
battle? Let us keep quiet, and in three days there will no
longer be a question of a commotion in Paris."

"But the Bastile, sir?"

"The Bastile! Its doors will be closed, and those who
took it will be taken, that is all."

Some laughter was heard among the before silent group.
The queen continued:

"Take care, prince; you are now reassuring me too
much." And thoughtfully, her chin resting on the palm
of her hand, she advanced toward Mme de Polignac, who,
pale and sad, seemed absorbed in thought.

The countess had listened to all the news with visible
fear; she only smiled when the queen stopped opposite to
her and smiled; although this smile was pale and color-
less as a fading flower.

"Well, countess," asked the queen, "what do you say
to all this?"

"Alas! nothing," she replied.

"How, nothing?"

"No."

And she shook her head with an indescribable sigh of
despair.

"Come, come," said the queen, in a very low voice, and
stooping to the ear of the countess, "our friend Diana is
terrified."

Then she said, aloud:

"But where is Madame de Charny, the intrepid woman?
We need her assistance to reassure us, I think."

"The countess was about to go out, when she was summoned to the king's apartments."

"Ah! the king's," absently answered Marie Antoinette.

And only then did the queen perceive the strange silence
which pervaded all around her.

The truth was, these wonderful and incredible events,
accounts of which had successively reached Versailles like

repeated shocks, had prostrated the firmest hearts, perhaps more by astonishment than fear.

The queen understood that it was necessary to revive all these drooping spirits.

" Can no one advise me ? " said she. " Be it so ; I will advise myself."

They all drew near to Marie Antoinette.

" The people," said she, " are not bad at heart, they are only misled. They hate us because we are unknown to them ; let us become better friends."

" To punish them, then," said a voice ; " for they have doubted their masters, and that is a crime."

The queen looked in the direction from which the voice proceeded, and recognized M. de Bezenval.

" Oh, it is you, Monsieur le Baron," said she ; " do you come to give us your good counsel ? "

" The advice is already given," said Bezenval, bowing.

" Be it so," said the queen ; " the king will punish only as a tender father."

" ' Who loves well, chastises well,' " said the baron.

Then, turning toward M. de Lambesq :

" Are you not of my opinion, prince ? The people have committed several murders——"

" Which they unfortunately call retaliation," said a sweet voice, at the sound of which the queen turned in her seat.

" You are right, princess ; but it is precisely in that that their error consists, my dear Lamballe ; we shall be indulgent."

" But," replied the princess, in her mild manner, " before asking whether we must punish, I think we ought to ask whether we can conquer."

A general cry burst forth from those who were present, a cry of protestation against the truth which had just been spoken by those noble lips.

" Conquer ! and where are the Swiss ? " said one.

" And the Germans ? " said another.

" And the body-guards ? " cried a third.

" Can doubts be entertained about the army and the nobility ? " exclaimed a young man wearing the uniform of a lieutenant in the hussars of Berchiny. " Have we, then, deserved such a reproach ? Do but consider, madame, that no later than to-morrow, if he chose, the

king could assemble forty thousand men, throw these
forty thousand men into Paris, and destroy the city. Remember that forty thousand faithful troops are worth half
a million of revolted Parisians."

The young man who had just spoken these words had,
without doubt, a good many other similar reasons to
advance, but he stopped short on seeing the eyes of the
queen fixed upon him. He had spoken from the center of
a group of officers, and his zeal had carried him further
than was consistent with etiquette and his rank.

He checked himself accordingly, as we have already said,
feeling quite ashamed at the impression his words had
made.

But it was too late ; the queen had already been struck
with his enthusiastic manner.

"You understand the present condition of affairs, sir ?"
said she, kindly.

"Yes, your majesty," said the young man, blushing ;
"I was at the Champs Elysées."

"Then, do not fear to speak. Come nearer, sir."

The young man stepped forward, blushing, from the
group, which opened to let him pass, and advanced toward
the queen.

At the same moment the Prince de Lambesq and M. de
Bezenval retired a step or two, as if they considered it beneath their dignity to attend this sort of council.

The queen did not pay, or did not appear to pay, any
attention to this movement.

"You say, then, sir, that the king has forty thousand
men ?" asked she.

"Yes, your majesty."

"In the environs of Paris ?"

"At St. Denis, at St. Mande, and at Grenelle."

"Give me some details, sir—some details," exclaimed
the queen.

"Madame, the Prince de Lambesq and Monsieur de
Bezenval can give you them with infinitely more accuracy
than myself."

"Go on, sir. It pleases me to hear these details from
your lips. Under whose orders are those forty thousand
men ?"

"In the first place, under the orders of Monsieur de
Bezenval and Monsieur de Lambesq ; then under those of

the Prince de Condé, of Monsieur de Narbonne, Fritzlar, and Monsieur de Salkenaym."

"Is this true, prince?" asked the queen, turning toward M. de Lambesq.

"Yes, your majesty," answered the prince, bowing.

"On the heights of Montmartre," said the young man, "there is a complete park of artillery; in six hours the whole quarter of the town within the range of Montmartre could be laid in ashes. Let Montmartre give the signal to commence the fire; let it be answered by Vincennes; let ten thousand men debouch by the Champs Elysées, ten thousand more by the Barrière d'Enfer, ten thousand more by the Rue St. Martin, ten thousand more by the Bastile, make Paris hear our cannonading from the four cardinal points, and she cannot hold her ground for twenty-four hours."

"Ah! here is a man who, at all events, explains his views frankly; here is, at least, a clear and regular plan. What do you think of it, Monsieur de Lambesq?"

"I think," answered the prince, disdainfully, "that the lieutenant of hussars is a perfect general."

"He is, at least," said the queen, who saw the young officer turn pale with anger, "he is, at least, a soldier who does not despair."

"I thank you, madame," said the young man, bowing. I do not know what your majesty's decision will be, but I beg you to consider me among those who are ready to die for you; and, in so doing, I should only do that, I beg your majesty to believe, which forty thousand soldiers are ready to do, as well as all our chiefs."

And having said these words, the young man saluted the prince courteously who had almost insulted him.

This act of courtesy struck the queen still more than the protestations of fidelity which had preceded it.

"What is your name, sir?" asked she of the young officer.

"I am the Baron de Charny, madame," replied he, bowing,

"De Charny!" exclaimed Marie Antoinette, blushing in spite of herself; "are you, then, a relation of the Count de Charny?"

"I am his brother, madame."

And the young man bowed gracefully, even lower than he had done before.

"I ought," said the queen, recovering from her confusion, and casting a firm look around her, "I ought to have recognized you from hearing your first words, as one of my most faithful servants. Thank you, baron. How is it that I now see you at court for the first time ?"

"Madame, my elder brother, who is taking the place of my father, has ordered me to remain with the regiment, and during the seven years that I have had the honor of serving in the army of the king, I have only twice been at Versailles."

The queen looked for a considerable time at the young man's face.

"You resemble your brother," said she. "I shall reprimand him for having so long omitted to present you, and left you to present yourself at court."

And the queen turned in the direction of her friend the countess, who, during all this scene, had remained motionless and mute upon the sofa.

But it was not thus with the remainder of those present. The officers, electrified by the reception the queen had given to the young man, were exaggerating to the utmost among themselves the enthusiasm for the royal cause, and from every group expressions burst forth, evincing a heroism capable of subjugating the whole of France.

Marie Antoinette made the most of these manifestations, which evidently flattered her secret wishes.

She preferred to struggle rather than to suffer, to die rather than to yield. With this view, as soon as the first news had reached her from Paris, she had determined upon a stubborn resistance to the rebellious spirit which had threatened to swallow up all the prerogatives of the French monarchy.

If there is a blind and senseless degree of strength, it is that stimulated by figures and vain hopes.

A figure, followed by an agglomeration of zeros, will soon exceed all the resources of the universe.

The same may be said of the plans of a conspirator or a despot. On enthusiasm, which itself is based on imperceptible hope, gigantic conceptions are built, which evaporate before the first breath of wind, in less time than was required to condense them into a mist.

After hearing these few words pronounced by the Baron de Charny, after the enthusiastic hurrahs of the by-standers, Marie Antoinette could almost imagine herself at the head of a powerful army; she could hear the rolling of her harmless artillery, and she rejoiced at the fear which they would doubtless occasion among the Parisians, and had already gained a victory which she thought decisive.

Around her, men and women, beaming with youth, with confidence and love, were reckoning the number of those brilliant hussars, those heavy dragoons, those terrible Swiss, those well-equipped artillerymen, and laughed at the vulgar pikes and their coarse wooden handles, little thinking that on the points of these vile weapons were to be borne the noblest heads of France.

"As for me," murmured the Princess de Lamballe, "I am more afraid of a pike than of a gun."

"Because it is much uglier, my dear Thérèse," replied the queen, smiling. "But, at all events, compose yourself. Our Parisian pikemen are not a match for the famous Swiss pikemen of Morat; and the Swiss of the present day have something more than pikes; they have good muskets, with which they take good aim, thank Heaven!"

"Oh, as to that, I will answer for it," said M. de Bezenval.

The queen turned round once more toward Mme. de Polignac to see if all these assurances had restored her wonted tranquillity; but the countess appeared still paler and more trembling than before.

The queen, whose extreme tenderness of feeling often caused her to sacrifice her royal dignity for the sake of this friend, in vain seemed to solicit her to look more cheerful.

The young woman still continued gloomy, and appeared absorbed in the saddest thoughts. But this despondency only served to increase the queen's sorrow. The enthusiasm among the young officers maintained itself at the same pitch, and all of them, with the exception of the superior officers, were gathered round the Baron de Charny, and drawing up their plans for battle.

In the midst of this febrile excitement the king entered alone, unaccompanied by an usher, and with a smile upon his lips.

The queen, still greatly excited by the warlike emotions which she had aroused, rushed forward to meet him.

At the sight of the king all conversation had ceased, and

was followed by the most perfect silence; every one expected a kingly word—one of those words which electrify and subjugate.

When clouds are sufficiently loaded with electricity, the least shock, as is well known, is sufficient to produce a flash.

To the eyes of the courtiers, the king and queen advancing to meet each other, appeared like two electric bodies, from which the thunder must proceed.

They listened, and trembled, and eagerly awaited to catch the first words which were to proceed from royal lips.

"Madame," said Louis XVI., "amid all these events, they have forgotten to serve up my supper in my own apartment; be so kind as to have it brought here."

"Here?" exclaimed the queen, with an air of stupefaction.

"If you will permit it."

"But, sire——"

"You were conversing, it is true; but, while at supper, I shall converse also."

The mere word supper had chilled the enthusiasm of every one present. But on hearing the king's last words, "at supper I shall converse also," the young queen herself could hardly help thinking that so much calmness concealed some heroism.

The king doubtless thought by his tranquillity to overcome all the terror occasioned by the events that had taken place.

Undoubtedly the daughter of Marie Thrèèse could not conceive that at so critical a moment the son of St. Louis could still remain subject to the material wants of ordinary life.

Marie Antoinette was mistaken; the king was hungry, that was all.

——

CHAPTER XXVI.

On a word from Marie Antoinette, the king's supper was served on a small table in the queen's own cabinet.

But the contrary of what the princess had hoped soon happened. Louis XVI. ordered every one to be silent, but it was only that he might not be disturbed while at supper.

While Marie Antoinette was endeavoring to revive enthusiasm, the king was devouring a Perigord pie.

The officers did not think this gastronomical performance worthy of a descendant of St. Louis, and formed themselves into small groups, whose observations were not perhaps as respectful as circumstances ought to have demanded.

The queen blushed, and her impatience betrayed itself in all her movements. Her delicate, aristocratic, and nervous nature could not comprehend this domination of matter over mind.

She drew nearer to the king, with a view to bring those nearer to the table who had retired to a more distant part of the room.

" Sire," said she, " have you no orders to give ? "

" Ah ! ah ! " said the king, his mouth full, " what orders, madame ? Let us see ; will you be our Egeria in this difficult moment ? "

And while saying these words he bravely attacked a partridge stuffed with truffles.

" Sire," said the queen, " Numa was a pacific king. Now it is generally thought that what we need at present is a warlike king ; and if your majesty is to take antiquity for his model, as you cannot become a Tarquin, you must be a Romulus."

The king smiled with a tranquillity which almost seemed holy.

" Are these gentlemen warlike also ? " asked he.

And he turned toward the group of officers ; and his eyes, being animated by the cheering influence of his meal, appeared to all present to sparkle with courage.

" Yes, sire," they all cried, with one voice, " war ; we only ask for war."

" Gentlemen, gentlemen," said the king, " you do me, in truth, the greatest pleasure, by proving to me that when occasion may require it, I may rely upon you. But I have for the moment not only a council, but also a stomach ; the former will advise me what I ought to do, the second advises me to do what I am now doing."

And he laughed loudly, and handed his plate, full of fragments, to the officer who was in waiting, in exchange for a clean one.

A murmur of stupefaction and of rage passed like a shud

der through the group of gentlemen, who only required a
signal from the king to shed all their blood.

The queen turned round and stamped her foot.

The Prince de Lambesq immediately came to her.

"You see, madame," said he, "his majesty no doubt
thinks, as I do, that it is better to wait. It is prudence—
and although it is not one of mine, unfortunately, prudence is a necessary virtue in the times we live in."

"Yes, sir, yes ; it is a very necessary virtue," said the
queen, biting her lips till they bled.

With a deathlike sadness she reclined against the chimney-piece, her eye lost in darkness, and her soul overcome
by despair.

The singular contrast between the disposition of the
king and that of the queen struck every one with astonishment. The queen could hardly restrain her tears, while
the king continued his supper with the proverbial appetite of the Bourbon family.

The room gradually became empty, the various groups
melted away as does the snow in a garden before the rays
of the sun—the snow, beneath which the black and deso-
late earth soon makes its appearance here and there.

The queen, seeing this warlike group, upon which she
relied so much, gradually disappear, imagined that all her
power was vanishing, as in former times the breath of the
Lord had melted those vast armies of Assyrians and Amalekites, which one single mist sufficed to swallow up in its
darkness.

She was aroused from this species of torpor by the sweet
voice of the Countess Jules, who approached her with
Mme. Diana de Polignac, her sister in-law.

At the sound of this voice, the sweet future, with its
flowers and palm leaves, returned to the mind of this
haughty woman. A sincere and devoted friend was to
her of more value than ten kingdoms.

"Oh, thou, thou !" murmured she, clasping the Countess Jules in her arms. "I have, then, one friend left."

And the tears, which for so long a time had been restrained, burst forth from her eyelids, trickled down her
cheeks, and inundated her bosom, but instead of being
bitter, these tears were sweet, instead of oppressing her,
they disburdened her heart.

They both remained silent for a few moments, during

which the queen continued to hold the countess in her arms.

It was the duchess who first broke this silence, while still holding her sister-in-law by the hand.

"Madame," said she, with a voice so timid that she almost appeared ashamed, "I do not think your majesty will disapprove of the project which I am about to submit to your notice."

"What project?" asked the queen, attentively. "Speak, duchess, speak!"

And while preparing to listen to the Duchess Diana, the queen leaned upon the shoulder of her favorite, the countess.

"Madame," continued the duchess, "the opinion which I am about to pronounce comes from a person whose authority will not be doubted by your majesty; it comes from Her Royal Highness Madame Adelaide, the queen's aunt."

"What a singular preamble, dear duchess," said the queen, gaily. "Come, let us hear this opinion."

"Madame, circumstances are disheartening; the favors which our family enjoy from your majesty have been much exaggerated; calumny stains the august friendship which you deign to grant us in exchange for our respectful devotion."

"Well, then, duchess," said the queen, with a commencement of astonishment, "do you not think I have evinced sufficient courage? Have I not valiantly sustained my friends against public opinion, against the court, against the people, against the king himself?"

"Oh, madame, on the contrary; and your majesty has so nobly sustained her friends that she has opposed her breast to every blow, so that to-day the danger has become great, terrible even, the friends so nobly defended by your majesty would be both cowardly and unfaithful servants if they did not prove themselves deserving of your favor."

"Ah! this is well, this is beautiful," said Marie Antoinette, with enthusiasm, embracing the countess, whom she still pressed against her bosom while holding the hand of Mme. de Polignac in hers.

But both of them turned pale, instead of proudly raising their heads, after they had been thus caressed by their sovereign.

Mme. Jules de Polignac made a movement to disengage herself from the arms of the queen; but the latter still pressed her to her heart, despite her efforts to disengage herself.

"But," stammered Mme. Diana de Polignac, "your majesty does not, perhaps, well understand what we have the honor to make known to you, in order to enable you to ward off the blows which threaten your throne, your person, perhaps, on account of the very friendship with which you honor us. There is a painful mean, a bitter sacrifice to our hearts, but we must endure it; necessity commands it."

At these words it was the queen's turn to become pale, for she no longer perceived courageous and faithful friendship, but fear, beneath this exordium, and under the veil of this reserve.

"Let us see," said she; "speak, speak, duchess; what is this sacrifice?"

"Oh! the sacrifice is entirely on our side, madame," replied the latter. "We are, God knows for what reason, execrated in France; by disencumbering your throne, we shall restore all its splendor, all the warmth of the popular love, a love either extinguished or intercepted by our presence."

"You would leave me!" cried the queen, vehemently. "Who has said that? who has asked for that?"

And she cast a despairing look on the Countess Jules de Polignac, gently pushing her from her; the latter held down her head in great confusion.

"Not I," said the Countess Jules; "I, on the contrary, ask but to remain."

But these words were uttered in such a tone that they implied, "Order me to leave you, madame, and I will leave you."

Oh! holy friendship, thou sacred chain which can link together the hearts of even a sovereign and her subject in indissoluble bonds; oh! holy friendship, thou engenderest more heroism than even love or ambition, those two noble maladies of the human heart; but thou canst not brook deceit. The queen at once shattered to atoms the adored altar she had raised to thee in her heart; she required but a look, one only look, to reveal to her that which during ten years she had not perceived, she had not even surmised—coldness and interested calculation—excusable, justifiable, legitimate, perhaps ; but what can excuse, justify, or legitimize in the eyes of one who still fondly loves the abandonment of the one who has ceased to love ?

Marie Antoinette's only revenge for the pain which was thus inflicted on her was the ice-like coldness with which she gazed upon her friend.

"Ah ! Duchess Diana, this, then, is your opinion ?" cried she, compressing with her feverish hand the agitated pulsation of her heart.

"Alas ! madame," answered the latter, "it is not my choice, it is not my will which dictates to me what I am to do, it is the law of destiny."

"Yes, duchess," said Marie Antoinette. And, turning again toward the Countess Jules : "And you, countess, what say you to this ?"

The countess replied by a burning tear, as if from a remorseful pang ; but she had exhausted all her strength in the effort she had made.

"Well," said the queen, "well, it is gratifying to my feelings to see how much I am beloved. Thank you, my dear countess ; yes, you incur great danger here ; the anger of the people no longer knows any bounds ; yes, you are all in the right, and I alone was foolish. You ask to remain—that is pure devotedness ; but I cannot accept such a sacrifice."

The Countess Jules raised her beautiful eyes and looked at the queen. But the queen, instead of reading the devotedness of a friend in them, could only perceive the weakness of the woman.

"Thus, duchess," replied the queen, " *you* are resolved to leave me." And she emphasized the word "you."

"Yes, your majesty."

"Doubtless, for some one of your estates—a distant—a very distant one."

"Madame, in going away, in leaving you, it would be as painful to travel fifty leagues as one hundred and fifty."

"But do you, then, intend to go into some foreign country ?"

"Alas ! yes, madame."

A suppressed sigh tore the very depths of the queen's heart, but it did not escape her lips.

"And where are you going ?"

"To reside on the banks of the Rhine, madame."

"Well, you speak German, duchess," said the queen, with a look of indescribable sadness, "and it was I who taught it you. The friendship of your queen will, at least, have been useful to you to that extent, and I rejoice at it."

Then, turning to the Countess Jules :

"I do not wish to separate you, my dear countess," said she. "You desire to remain here, and I deeply appreciate that desire. But I—I, who fear for you—I insist on your departure—I order you to leave me."

And having said these words, she suddenly stopped, choked by emotions which, in spite of her heroism, she would, perhaps, not have had the power to control, had not she heard at that moment the voice of the king, who had taken no part whatever in what we have just been relating.

The king was at his dessert.

"Madame," said the king, "there is somebody in your apartment ; they are seeking you."

"But, sire," exclaimed the queen, throwing aside every other feeling but that of royal dignity, "in the first place, you have orders to give. Let us see, only three persons remain here ; but they are those with whom you have to deal ; Monsieur de Lambesq, Monsieur de Bezenval, and Monsieur de Broglie. Give your orders, sire ; give your orders."

The king raised his heavy eyes, and appeared to hesitate.

"What do you think of all this, Monsieur de Broglie ?" said he.

"Sire," replied the old marshal, "if you withdraw your army from the sight of the Parisians, it will be said that it was beaten by them. If you leave it in their presence, your army must beat them."

"Well said !" exclaimed the queen, grasping the marshal's hand.

"Well said !" cried M. de Bezenval.

The Prince de Lambesq was the only person present who shook his head.

"Well, and after that ?" said the king.

"Command : march !" cried the old marshal.

"Yes—march !" cried the queen.

"Well, then, since you all wish it, march !" said the king.

At that moment a note was handed to the queen; its contents were as follows:

"In the name of Heaven, madame, no rashness! I await an audience of your majesty."

"His writing!" murmured the queen.

Then, turning round, she said, in a low tone, to the woman who had brought the note:

"Is Monsieur de Charny in my room?"

"He has just arrived, completely covered with dust, and I even think with blood," answered the confidante.

"One moment, gentlemen," exclaimed the queen to M. de Bezenval and M. de Broglie; "wait for me here; I shall return."

And she passed into her own apartment in great haste.

The king did not even move his head.

CHAPTER XXVII.

On entering her dressing-room, the queen found the person there who had written the note brought by her waiting-woman.

He was a man thirty-five years of age, of lofty stature, with a countenance which indicated strength and resolution; his grayish-blue eye, sharp and piercing as that of the eagle, his straight nose, his prominent chin, gave a martial character to his physiognomy, which was enhanced by the elegance with which he wore the uniform of a lieutenant in the body-guards.

His hands were still trembling under his torn and ruffled cambric cuffs.

His sword had been bent, and could hardly be replaced in the scabbard.

On the arrival of the queen, he was pacing hurriedly up and down the dressing-room, absorbed by a thousand feverish and agitated thoughts.

Marie Antoinette walked straight to him.

"Monsieur de Charny!" she exclaimed, "Monsieur de Charny, you here?"

And seeing that the person whom she was addressing bowed respectfully, according to etiquette, she made a sign to her waiting-woman, who withdrew and closed the doors.

The queen scarcely waited for the door to be closed, when, seizing the hand of M. de Charny with vehemence :

"Count," cried she, "why are you here ?"

"Because I considered it my duty to come, madame," said the count.

"No ; your duty was to fly Versailles ; it was to do what we had agreed, to obey me ; it is, in fact, to do as all my friends are doing who fear to share my fate. Your duty is to sacrifice nothing to my destiny ; your duty is to separate yourself from me."

"To separate myself from you ?" said he.

"Yes ; to fly from me."

"And who, then, flies from you, madame ?"

"Those who are prudent."

"I think myself very prudent, madame, and that is why I now come to Versailles."

"And from where do you come ?"

"From Paris."

"From revolted Paris ?"

"From boiling, intoxicated, and insanguined Paris."

The queen covered her face with both her hands.

"Oh !" said she, "no one, not even you, will then come to bring me some good news."

"Madame, in the present circumstances, ask your messengers to tell you but one thing—the truth."

"And is it the truth you have just been telling me ?"

"As I do always, madame."

"You have an honest soul, sir, and a stout heart."

"I am a faithful subject, madame, that is all."

"Well, then, spare me for the moment, my friend ; do not tell me a single word. You have arrived at a moment when my heart was breaking. My friends, to-day, for the first time, overwhelm me with that truth which you have always told me. Oh, it was this truth, count ; it was impossible for them to withhold it from me any longer. It bursts forth everywhere : in the heavens, which are red ; in the air, which is filled with sinister noises : in the physiognomy of the courtiers, who are pale and serious. No, no, count ; for the first time in your life, tell me not the truth."

The count looked at the queen with amazement.

"Yes, yes," said she ; "you who know me to be courageous, you are astonished, are you not ?   Oh ! you are not yet at the end of your astonishment."

M. de Charny allowed an inquiring gesture to escape him.

" You will see by and by," said the queen, with a nervous laugh.

" Does your majesty suffer ? " asked the count.

" No, no, sir.   Come and sit down near me ; and not a word more about those dreadful politics.   Try to make me forget them."

The count obeyed with a sad smile.   Marie Antoinette placed her hand upon his forehead.

" Your forehead burns," said she.

" Yes, I have a volcano in my head."

" Your hand is icy cold."

And she pressed the count's hand between both hers.

" My heart is affected with a death-like coldness," said he.

" Poor Olivier ! I had told you so.   Let us forget it. I am no longer queen ; I am no longer threatened ; I am no longer hated.   No, I am no longer a queen.   I am a woman, that is all.   What is a whole universe to me ? One heart that loves me would suffice for me."

The count fell on his knees before the queen, and kissed her feet with the respect the Egyptians had for the goddess Isis.

" Oh, count, my only friend ! " said the queen, trying to raise him up, " do you know what the Duchess Diana is about to do ? "

" She is going to emigrate," answered Charny, without hesitating.

" He has guessed the truth," exclaimed Marie Antoinette.   " He has guessed it.   Alas ! was it, then, possible to guess it ? "

" Oh, certainly, madame," answered the count ; " one can imagine anything at such a moment as this."

" But you and your friends," exclaimed the queen, " why do you not emigrate, if you consider it so natural a step ? "

" In the first place, madame, I do not emigrate because I am profoundly devoted to your majesty, and because I have promised, not to you, but to myself, that I will not quit you for a single instant during the impending storm.

My brothers will not emigrate, because my conduct will be the model on which they will regulate theirs. In fine, Madame de Charny will not emigrate, because she loves your majesty sincerely, at least, so I believe."

"Yes, Andrée has a very noble heart," said the queen, with perceptible coldness.

"That is the reason why she will not leave Versailles," answered De Charny.

"Then I shall always have you near me," said the queen, in the same icy tone, which she varied, so as to express either her jealousy or her disdain.

"Your majesty has done me the honor to make me lieutenant of the guards," said the Count de Charny; "my post is at Versailles. I should not have left my post if your majesty had not intrusted me with the care of the Tuileries. 'It is a necessary exile,' said the queen to me, and I accepted that exile. Now, in all this, your majesty well knows the Countess de Charny has neither reproved the step, nor was she consulted with regard to it."

"It is true," replied the queen, in the same freezing tone.

"To-day," continued the count, with intrepidity, "I think my post is no longer at the Tuileries, but at Versailles. Well, may it not displease the queen, I have violated my orders, thus selecting the service I prefer; and here I am. Whether Madame de Charny be alarmed or not at the complexion of events—whether it be her desire to emigrate or not—I will remain near the queen, unless, indeed, the queen breaks my sword; in which case, having no longer the right to fight and to die for her on the floor of Versailles, I shall still have that of sacrificing it on its threshold, on the pavement."

The young man pronounced these simple words so valiantly and so loyally, they emanated so evidently from the depths of his heart, that the queen appeared suddenly to lose her haughtiness, a retreat behind which she had just concealed feelings more human than royal.

"Count," said she, "never pronounce that word again. Do not say that you will die for me, for, in truth, I know that you would do as you say."

"Oh, I shall always say it, on the contrary!" exclaimed M. de Charny. "I shall say it to everyone, and in every place. I shall say it and I shall do it, because the time has come, I fear, when all who have been attached to the kings of this earth must die."

"Count, count! what is it gives you this fatal fore-warning?"

"Alas! madame," replied De Charny, shaking his head, "and I, too, during that fatal American war, I, too, was affected like the rest with that fever of independence which pervaded all society. I, too, wished to take an active part in the emancipation of the slaves, as it was customary to say in those days, and I was initiated into the secrets of masonry. I became affiliated with a secret society, with the Lafayettes and the Lameths. Do you know what the object of this society was, madame? The destruction of thrones. Do you know what it had for its motto? Three letters—L. P. D."

"And what did these letters signify?"

"*Lilia pedibus destrue!* Trample the lilies under-foot!"

"Then what did you do?"

"I withdrew with honor. But for one who withdrew from the society, there were twenty who applied to be admitted into it. Well, then, what is happening to-day, madame, is the prologue to the grand drama which has been preparing in silence and in darkness for twenty years. At the head of the men who are stimulating Paris to resistance, who govern the Hôtel de Ville, who occupy the Palais Royal, and who took the Bastile, I recognized the countenances of my former affiliated brethren. Do not deceive yourself, madame; all the events which have just taken place are not the results of chance; they are outbreaks which had been planned for years."

"Oh, you think so! you think so, my friend!" exclaimed the queen, bursting into tears.

"Do not weep, madame, but endeavor to comprehend the present crisis," said the count.

"You wish me to comprehend it!" continued Marie Antoinette. "I, the queen—I, who was born the sovereign of twenty-five millions of men—you wish me to understand how these twenty-five millions of subjects, born to obey me, should revolt and murder my friends! No—that I shall never comprehend."

"And yet it is absolutely necessary for you to understand it, madame; for the moment this obedience becomes a burden to these subjects, to these men born to obey you, you become their enemy ; and until they have the strength to devour you, to do which they are sharpening their famished teeth, they will devour your friends, still more detested than you are."

"And, perhaps, you will next tell me that they are right, most sage philosopher," exclaimed the queen, imperiously, her eyes dilated, and her nostrils quivering with anger.

"Alas ! yes, madame, they are right," said the count, in his gentle and affectionate voice ; "for when I drive along the boulevards, with my beautiful English horses, my coat glittering with gold, and my attendants covered with more silver than would be necessary to feed three families, your people, that is to say, those twenty-five millions of starving men, ask themselves of what use I am to them—I, who am only a man like themselves."

"You serve them with this, marquis," exclaimed the queen, seizing the hilt of the count's sword ; "you serve them with the sword that your father wielded so heroically at Fontenoy, your grandfather at Steinkirk, your great-grandfather at Lens and at Rocroi, your ancestors at Ivry, at Marignan, and at Agincourt. The nobility serves the French nation by waging war. By war, the nobility has earned, at the price of its blood, the gold which decks its garments, the silver which covers its liveries. Do not, therefore, ask yourself, Olivier, how you serve the people, you who wield in your turn, and bravely, too, the sword which has descended to you from your forefathers."

"Madame ! madame !" said the count, shaking his head, "do not speak so much of the blood of the nobility ; the people, too, have blood in their veins ; go and see it running in streams on the Place de la Bastile ; go and count their dead, stretched out on the crimsoned pavement, and consider that their hearts, which now no longer beat, throbbed with as much feeling as that of a knight on the day when your cannon were thundering against them ; on the day when, seizing a new weapon in their unskilful hands, they sung in the midst of grape-shot—a thing which even our bravest grenadiers do not always. Ah ! madame—my sovereign, look not on me, I entreat you, with that frowning eye. What is a grenadier ? It is a gilt blue coat, covering the heart of which I was speaking to you a moment since. Of what importance is it to the bullet which pierces and kills, that the heart be covered with blue cloth or a linen rag ? Of what importance is it to the heart which is pierced through, whether the cuirass which protected it was cloth or canvas ? The time is come to think of all that, madame. You have no longer twenty-five millions of subjects, you have no longer twenty-five millions of men. You have twenty-five millions of soldiers."

" Who will fight against me, count ? "

" Yes, against you ; for they are fighting for liberty, and you stand between them and liberty."

A long silence followed the words of the count. The queen was the first to break it.

" In fine," said she, " you have told me this truth, which I had begged you not to tell me."

" Alas ! madame," replied Charny, " under whatever form my devotion may conceal it, under whatever veil my respect disguises it, in spite of me, in spite of yourself, examine it, listen to it, think of it. The truth is there, madame, is there forever, and you can no longer banish it from your mind, whatever may be your efforts to the contrary. Sleep ! sleep, to forget it, and it will haunt your pillow, will become the phantom of your dreams, a reality at your awakening !"

" Oh, count," said the queen, proudly, " I know a sleep which it cannot disturb."

" As for that sleep, madame, I do not fear it, more than does your majesty ; and perhaps I desire it quite as much."

" Oh !" exclaimed the queen, in despair, " according to you it is, then, our sole refuge ? "

" Yes ; but let us do nothing rashly, madame. Let us go no faster than our enemies, and we shall go straight to that sleep by the fatigues which we shall have to endure during so many stormy days."

And a new silence, still more gloomy than the first, appeared to weigh down the spirits of the two speakers.

They were seated, he near her, and she near him. They touched each other, and yet between them there was an immense abyss, for their minds viewed the future in a different light.

The queen was the first to return to the subject of their

conversation, but indirectly. She looked fixedly at the count. Then:

"Let us see, sir," said she. "One word as to ourselves, and you will tell me all—all—all. You understand me?"

"I am ready to answer you, madame."

"Can you swear to me that you came here only for my sake?"

"Oh! do you doubt it?"

"Will you swear to me that Madame de Charny had not written to you?"

"She?"

"Listen to me. I know that she is going out. I know that she has some plan in her mind. Swear to me, count, that it was not on her account that you returned."

At this moment a knock, or, rather, a scratch, at the door was heard.

"Come in," said the queen.

The waiting-woman again appeared.

"Madame," said she, "the king has just finished his supper."

The count looked at Marie Antoinette with astonishment.

"Well," said she, shrugging her shoulder, "what is there astonishing in that? Must the king not take his supper?"

Olivier frowned.

"Tell the king," replied the queen, without at all disturbing herself, "that I am just receiving news from Paris, and that I shall communicate it to him when I have received it."

Then, turning toward Charny:

"Go on," said she; "now that the king has supped, it is but natural that he should digest his food."

CHAPTER XXVIII.

THIS interruption had only caused a momentary suspension in the conversation, but had changed in nothing the twofold sentiment of jealousy which animated the queen at this moment—jealousy of love as a woman—jealousy of power as a queen.

Hence, it resulted that the conversation, which seemed exhausted during its first period, had, on the contrary, only been slightly glanced at, and was about to be revived more sharply than ever; as in a battle, where, after the cessation of the first fire, which had commenced the action on a few points, the fire which decides the victory soon becomes general all along the line.

The count, moreover, as things had arrived at this point, seemed as anxious as the queen to come to an explanation; for which reason, the door being closed again, he was the first to resume the conversation.

"You asked me if it was for Madame de Charny that I had come back," said he. "Has your majesty, then, forgotten that engagements were entered into between us, and that I am a man of honor?"

"Yes," said the queen, holding down her head, "yes, we have made engagements; yes, you are a man of honor; yes, you have sworn to sacrifice yourself to my happiness, and it is that oath which most tortures me, for in sacrificing yourself to my happiness, you immolate at the same time a beautiful woman and a noble character—another crime!"

"Oh, madame! now you are exaggerating the accusation. I only wish you to confess that I have kept my word as a gentleman."

"It is true; I am insensate—forgive me——"

"Do not call a crime that which originated in chance and necessity. We have both deplored this marriage, which alone could shield the honor of the queen. As for this marriage, there only remains for me to endure it, as I have done for many years."

"Yes," exclaimed the queen. "But do you think that I do not perceive your grief, that I do not understand your sorrow, which evince themselves in the shape of the highest respect? Do you think that I do not see all this?"

"Do me the favor, madame," said the count, bowing, "to communicate to me what you see, in order that if I have not suffered enough myself, and made others suffer enough, I may double the amount of suffering for myself, and for all those who surround me, as I feel certain of ever falling short of what I owe you."

The queen held out her hand to the count. The words

of the young man had an irresistible power, like everything that emanates from a sincere and impassioned heart.

"Command me then, madame," rejoined he ; "I entreat you, do not fear to lay your commands upon me."

"Oh ! yes, yes, I know it well. I am wrong ; yes, forgive me ; yes, it is true. But if you have anywhere some
hidden idol, to whom you offer up mysterious incense—if
for you there is some corner of the world an adored
woman—oh ! I no longer dare to pronounce that word—
it strikes me with terror ; and I fear that the syllables
which compose it should strike the air and vibrate in my
ear—well, then, if such a woman does exist, concealed
from every one, do not forget that you have publicly, in
the eyes of others as in your own, a young and beautiful
wife, whom you surround with care and attention, a wife
who leans upon your arm, and who, while leaning on your
arm, leans at the same time on your heart."

Olivier knit his brow, and the delicate lines of his face
assumed for a moment a severe aspect.

"What do you ask, madame ?" said he. "Do I separate myself from the Countess de Charny ? You remain
silent. Is that the reason, then ? Well, then, I am ready
to obey this order, even ; but you know that she is alone
in the world—she is an orphan. Her father, the Baron
de Taverney, died last year, like a worthy knight of the
olden time, who wishes not to see that which is about to
take place in ours. Her brother—you know that her
brother, Maison Rouge, makes his appearance once a year
at most—comes to embrace his sister, to pay his respects
to your majesty, and then goes away, without any one
knowing what becomes of him."

"Yes, I know all that."

"Consider, madame, that this Countess de Charny,
were God to remove me from this world, could resume her
maiden name, and the purest angel in heaven could not
detect in her dreams, in her thoughts, a single unholy
word or thought."

"Oh ! yes, yes," said the queen ; "I know that your
Andrée is an angel upon earth ; I know that she deserves
to be loved. That is the reason why I think she has a
brilliant future before her, while mine is hopeless. Oh !
no, no. Come, count, I beg of you, say not another word ;
I no longer speak to you as a queen. Forgive me, I forget

myself ; but what would you have ? There is in my soul
a voice which always sings happiness, joy, and love, although it is too often assailed by those sinister voices
which speak of nothing but misfortune, war, and death.
It is the voice of my youth, which I have survived.
Charny, forgive me, I shall no longer be young, I shall no
longer smile, I shall no longer love ! "

And the unhappy woman covered her burning eyes with
her thin and delicate hands, and the tear of a queen fil-
tered brilliant as a diamond between each one of her fingers.

The count once more fell on his knees before her.

"Madame, in the name of Heaven !" said he, "order
me to leave you, to fly from you, to die for you, but do
not let me see you weep."

And the count himself could hardly refrain from sobbing as he spoke.

"It is all over," said Marie Antoinette, raising her head
and speaking gently, with a smile replete with grace.

And with a beautiful movement, she threw back her
thick, powdered hair, which had fallen on her neck, white
as the driven snow.

"Yes, yes ; it is over," continued the queen. "I shall
not afflict you any more. Let us throw aside all these
follies. Great God ! it is strange that the woman should
be so weak, when the queen so much needs to be firm.
You come from Paris, do you not ? Let us converse
about it. You told me some things that I have forgotten : and yet they were very serious, were they not, Monsieur de Charny ?"

"Be it so, madame ; let us return to that fatal subject,
for, as you observe, what I have to tell you is very serious.
Yes, I have just arrived from Paris, and I was present at
the downfall of the monarchy."

"I was right to request you to return to *serious* matters,
and most assuredly, you make them more than sufficiently
gloomy. A successful insurrection, do you call that the
downfall of the monarchy ? What, is it because the Bastile has been taken, Monsieur de Charny, that you say the
monarchy is abolished ? Oh ! you do not reflect that the
Bastile was founded in France only in the fourteenth century, while monarchy has been taking root in the world
during the last six thousand years."

"I should be well pleased to deceive myself in this matter, madame," replied the count, "and then, instead of afflicting your majesty's mind, I should bring to you the most consoling news.   Unfortunately, the instrument will not produce any other sounds but those for which it was intended."

"Let us see, let us see ; I will sustain you, I who am but a woman ;   I will put you on the right path."

"Alas ! I ask for nothing better."

"The Parisians have revolted, have they not ? "

"Yes."

"In what proportion ?"

"In the proportion of twelve to fifteen."

"How do you arrive at this calculation ? "

"Oh ! very easily ; the people form twelve fifteenths of the body of the nation ; there remain two fifteenths for the nobility and one for the clergy."

"Your calculations are exact, count, and you have them at your fingers' ends.   Have you read the works of Monsieur and Madame de Necker ? "

"Those of Monsieur Necker ?   Yes, madame."

"Well, the proverb holds good," said the queen, gaily ; "we are never betrayed but by our own friends.   Well, then, here is my own calculation—will you listen to it ? "

"With all respect."

"Among these twelve fifteenths there are six of women, are there not ? "

"Yes, your majesty.   But——"

"Do not interrupt me.   We said there were six fifteenths of women, so let us say six ; two of indifferent or incapable old men—is that too much ? "

"No."

"There still remain four fifteenths, of which you will allow that at least two are cowards or lukewarm individuals —I flatter the French nation.   But finally, there remain two fifteenths ; I will grant you that they are furious, robust, brave, and warlike.   These two fifteenths, let us consider them as belonging to Paris only, for it is needless to speak of the provinces, is it not ?   It is only Paris that requires to be retaken ? "

"Yes, madame.   But——"

"Always but—wait a moment.   You can reply when I have concluded."

M. de Charny bowed.

"I therefore estimate," continued the queen, "the two fifteenths of Paris at one hundred thousand men—is that sufficient?"

This time the count did not answer. The queen rejoined:

"Well, then, to these hundred thousand men, badly armed, badly disciplined, and but little accustomed to battle, hesitating, because they know they are doing wrong, I can oppose fifty thousand men, known throughout Europe for their bravery, with officers like you, Monsieur de Charny; besides, that sacred cause which is denominated divine right, and in addition to all this, my own firm soul, which it is easy to move, but difficult to break."

The count still remained silent.

"Do you think," continued the queen, "that in a battle fought in such a cause, two men of the people are worth more than one of my soldiers?"

Charny said nothing.

"Speak—answer me! Do you think so?" exclaimed the queen, growing impatient.

"Madame," answered the count, at last, throwing aside, on this order from the queen, the respectful reserve which he had so long maintained, "on a field of battle, where these hundred thousand men would be isolated, undisciplined, and badly armed as they are, your fifty thousand soldiers would defeat them in half an hour."

"Ah!" said the queen, "I was then right."

"Wait a moment. But it is not as you imagine. And, in the first place, your hundred thousand insurgents in Paris are five hundred thousand."

"Five hundred thousand?"

"Quite as many. You had omitted the women and children in your calculation. Oh! Queen of France—oh! proud and courageous woman, consider them so many men, these women of Paris; the day will perhaps come when they will compel you to consider them as so many demons."

"What can you mean, count?"

"Madame, do you know what part a woman plays in a civil war? No, you do not. Well, I will tell you, and you will see that two soldiers against each woman would not be too many."

"Count, have you lost your senses ?".

Charny smiled sadly.

"Did you see them at the Bastile ?" asked he, "in the
midst of the fire, in the midst of the shot, crying to arms,
threatening with their fists your redoubtable Swiss soldiers,
fully armed and equipped, uttering maledictions over the
bodies of the slain, with that voice that excites the hearts
of the living. Have we not seen them boiling the pitch,
dragging cannon along the streets, giving cartridges to
those who were eager for the combat, and to the timid
combatants a cartridge and a kiss ? Do you know that as
many women as men trod the drawbridge of the Bastile,
and that at this moment, if the stones of the Bastile are
falling, it is by pick-axes wielded by women's hands ?
Ah ! madame, do not overlook the women of Paris, take
them into consideration ; think also of the children who
cast bullets, who sharpen swords, who throw paving-stones
from a sixth story ; think of them, for the bullet which
was cast by a child may kill your best general from afar
off, for the sword which it has sharpened will cut the ham-
strings of your war-horses, for the clouds of stones which
fall as from the skies will crush your dragoons and your
guards ; consider the old men, madame, for if they have
no longer the strength to raise a sword, they have still
enough to serve as shields. At the taking of the Bastile,
madame, there were old men. Do you know what they
did, those aged men whom you affect to despise ? They
placed themselves before the young men, who steadied
their muskets on their shoulders, that they might take
sure aim, so that the balls of your Swiss killed the helpless
aged man, whose body served as a rampart to the vigorous
youth. Include the aged men, for it is they, who, for the
last three hundred years, have related to succeeding generations the insults suffered by their mothers—the barren-
ness of their fields, caused by the devouring of their crops
by the noblemen's game—the odium attached to their
caste, crushed down by feudal privileges—and then the
sons seize a hatchet, a club, a gun—in short, any weapon
within their reach, and sally out to kill, fully charged
with the curses of the aged against all this tyranny, as the
cannon is loaded with powder and iron at Paris, this moment. Men, women, old men, and children, are all crying, ' Liberty ! deliverance !' Count everything that has

a voice, madame, and you may estimate the number of combatants of Paris at eight hundred thousand souls."

"Three hundred Spartans defeated the army of Xerxes, Monsieur de Charny."

"Yes ; but to-day your three hundred Spartans have increased to eight hundred thousand, and your fifty thousand soldiers compose the army of Xerxes."

The queen raised her head, her hands convulsively clinched, and her face burning with shame and anger.

"Oh ! let me fall from my throne," said she, "let me be torn to pieces by your five hundred thousand Parisians, but do not suffer me to hear a Charny, a man devoted to me, speak to me thus."

"If he speaks to you thus, madame, it is because it is necessary ; for this Charny has not in his veins a single drop of blood that is unworthy of his ancestors, or that is not all your own.

"Then let him march upon Paris with me, and there we will die together."

"Ignominiously," said the count, "without the possibility of a struggle. We shall not even fight ; we shall disappear like the Philistines or the Amalekites. March upon Paris !—but you seem to be ignorant of a very important thing—it is at the moment we shall enter Paris, the houses will fall upon us as did the waves of the Red Sea upon Pharaoh : and you will leave in France a name which will be accursed, and your children will be killed like the cubs of a wolf."

"How, then, should I fall, count ?" said the queen, with haughtiness. "Teach me, I entreat you."

"As a victim, madame," respectfully replied M. de Charny ; "as a queen, smiling and forgiving those who strike the fatal blow. Ah ! if you had five hundred thousand men like me, I should say : Let us set out on our march ! let us march to-night ! let us march this very instant ! And to-morrow you would reign at the Tuileries—to-morrow you would have reconquered your throne."

"Oh !" exclaimed the queen, "even you have given way to despair—you, in whom I had founded all my hopes."

"Yes, I have despaired, madame ; because all France thinks as Paris does ; because your army, if it were victorious in Paris, would be swallowed up by Lyons, Rouen,

Lisle, Strasburg, Nantes, and a hundred other devouring cities. Come, come, take courage, madame, return your sword into its scabbard."

"Ah! was it for this," cried the queen, "that I have gathered round me so many brave men? was it for this that I have inspired them with so much courage?"

"If that is not your opinion, madame, give your orders, and we will march upon Paris this very night. Say, what is your pleasure?"

There was so much devotion in this offer of the count, that it intimidated the queen more than a refusal would have done. She threw herself, in despair, on a sofa, where she struggled for a considerable time with her haughty soul.

At length, raising her head:

"Count," said she, "do you desire me to remain inactive?"

"I have the honor to advise your majesty to remain so."

"It shall be so—come back."

"Alas! madame, have I offended you?" said the count, looking at the queen with a sorrowful expression, but in which beamed indescribable love.

"No—your hand."

The count bowed gracefully, and gave his hand to the queen.

"I must scold you," said Marie Antoinette, endeavoring to smile.

"For what reason, madame?"

"How! you have a brother in the army, and I have only been accidentally informed of it."

"I do not comprehend——"

"This evening a young officer of the hussars of Berchigny——"

"Ah! my brother George!"

"Why have you never spoken to me of this young man? Why has he not a high rank in a regiment?"

"Because he is yet quite young and inexperienced; because he is not worthy of command as a chief officer; because, in fine, if your majesty has condescended to look so low as upon me, who am called Charny, to honor me with your friendship, it is not a reason that my relations should be advanced, to the prejudice of a crowd of brave noblemen, more deserving than my brothers."

"Have, you, then, still another brother ?"

"Yes, madame ; and one who is as ready to die for your majesty as the two others."

"Does he not need anything ?"

"Nothing, madame. We have the happiness to have not only our lives, but also a fortune, to lay at the feet of your majesty."

While he was pronouncing these last words, the queen, who was much moved by a trait of such delicate probity, and he himself palpitating with affection caused by the gracious kindness of her majesty, they were suddenly disturbed in their conversation by a groan from the adjoining room.

The queen rose from her seat, went to the door, and screamed aloud.

She had just perceived a woman who was writhing on the carpet and suffering the most horrible convulsions.

"Oh, the countess !" said she, in a whisper, to M. de Charny. "She has overheard our conversation."

"No, madame," answered he ; "otherwise she would have warned your majesty that we could be overheard."

And he sprung toward Andrée and raised her in his arms.

The queen remained standing at two steps from her, cold, pale, and trembling with anxiety.

CHAPTER XXIX.

ANDREE was gradually recovering her senses, without knowing from whom assistance came ; but she seemed instinctively to understand that some one had come to her assistance.

She raised her head, and her hands grasped the unhoped-for succor that was offered her.

But her mind did not recover as soon as her body ; it still remained vacillating, stupefied, somnolent, during a few minutes.

After having succeeded in recalling her to physical life, M. de Charny attempted to restore her moral senses. But he was struggling against a terrible and concentrated unconsciousness.

Finally, she fastened her open but haggard eyes upon

him, and with her still remaining delirium, without recognizing the person who was supporting her, she gave a loud shriek, and abruptly pushed him from her.

During all this time, the queen turned her eyes in another direction; she, a woman, she, whose mission it was to console, to strengthen this afflicted friend, she abandoned her.

Charny raised Andrée in his powerful arms, notwithstanding the resistance she attempted to make, and turning round to the queen, who was still standing pale and motionless:

"Pardon me, madame," said he, "something extraordinary must doubtless have happened. Madame de Charny is not subject to fainting, and this is the first time I have ever seen her in this state."

"She must, then, be suffering greatly," said the queen, who still reverted to the idea that Andrée had overheard their conversation.

"Yes, without doubt she is suffering," answered the count, "and it is for that reason that I shall ask your majesty the permission to have her carried to her own apartment. She needs the assistance of her attendants."

"Do so," said the queen, raising her hand to the bell.

But scarcely had Andrée heard the ringing of the bell, when she wrestled fearfully, and cried out in her delirium:

"Oh, Gilbert! that Gilbert!"

The queen trembled at the sound of this name, and the astonished count placed his wife upon a sofa.

At this moment a servant appeared to answer the bell.

"It is nothing," said the queen, making a sign to him with her hand to leave the room.

Then, being once more left to themselves, the count and the queen looked at each other. Andrée had again closed her eyes, and seemed to suffer from a second attack.

M. de Charny, who was kneeling near the sofa, prevented her from falling off of it.

"Gilbert!" repeated the queen. "What name is that?"

"We must inquire."

"I think I know it," said Marie Antoinette; "I think it is not the first time I have heard the countess pronounce that name."

But as if she had been threatened by this recollection of the queen, and that this threat had surprised her in the midst of her convulsions, Andrée opened her eyes, stretched out her arms to heaven, and, making a great effort, stood upright.

Her first look, an intelligent look, was this time directed at M. de Charny, whom she recognized, and greeted with caressing smiles.

Then, as if this involuntary manifestation of her thought had been unworthy of her Spartan soul, Andrée turned her eyes in another direction, and perceived the queen.

She immediately made a profound inclination.

"Ah! good Heaven, what, then, is the matter with you, madame?" said M. de Charny. "You have alarmed me—you, who are usually so strong and so courageous, to have suffered from a swoon?"

"Sir," said she, "such fearful events have taken place at Paris, that when men are trembling, it is by no means strange that women should faint. Have you then left Paris? Oh! you have done rightly."

"Good God! countess," said Charny, in a doubting tone, "was it, then, on my account that you underwent all this suffering?"

Andrée again looked at her husband and the queen, but did not answer.

"Why, certainly, that is the reason, count—why should you doubt it?" answered Marie Antoinette. "The Countess de Charny is not a queen: she has the right to be alarmed for her husband's safety."

Charny could detect jealousy in the queen's language.

"Oh, madame," said he, "I am quite certain that the countess fears still more for her sovereign's safety than for mine."

"But, in fine," asked Marie Antoinette, "why and how is it that we found you in a swoon in this room, countess?"

"Oh! it would be impossible for me to tell you that, madame; I cannot, myself, account for it; but in this life of fatigue, of terror, and painful emotions, which we have led for the last three days, nothing can be more natural, it seems to me, than the fainting of a woman."

"This is true," murmured the queen, who perceived that Andrée did not wish to be compelled to speak out.

"But," rejoined Andrée, in her turn, with that extraordinary degree of calmness which never abandoned her after she had once become the mistress of her will, and which was so much the more embarrassing in difficult circumstances, that it could easily be discerned to be mere affectation, and concealed feelings altogether human; "but even your majesty's eyes are at this moment humid."

And the count thought he could perceive in the words of his wife that ironical accent he had remarked but a few moments previously in the language of the queen.

"Madame," said he to Andrée, with a degree of severity to which his voice was evidently not accustomed, "it is not astonishing that the queen's eyes should be suffused with tears, for the queen loves her people, and the blood of the people has been shed."

"Fortunately, God has spared yours, sir," said Andrée, who was still no less cold and impenetrable.

"Yes; but it is not of her majesty that we are speaking, madame, but of you; let us, then, return to our subject; the queen permits us to do so."

Marie Antoinette made an affirmative gesture with her head.

"You were alarmed, then, were you not?"

"Who, I?"

"You have been suffering; do not deny it. Some accident has happened to you—what was it? I know not what it can have been, but you will tell us."

"You are mistaken, sir."

"Have you had any reason to complain of any one—of a man?"

Andrée turned pale.

"I have had no reason to complain of any one, sir; I have just come from the king's apartment."

"Did you come direct from there?"

"Yes, direct. Her majesty can easily ascertain that fact."

"If such be the case," said Marie Antoinette, "the countess must be right. The king loves her too well, and knows that my own affection for her is too strong for him to disoblige her in any way whatever."

"But you mentioned a name," said Charny, still persisting.

"A name?"

"Yes; when you were recovering your senses."

Andrée looked at the queen as if to ask her for assistance; but, either because the queen did not understand her, or did not wish to do so:

"Yes," said she, "you pronounced the name, Gilbert."

"Gilbert! Did I pronounce the name of Gilbert?" exclaimed Andrée, in a tone so full of terror that the count was more affected by this cry than he had been by her fainting.

"Yes!" exclaimed he, "you pronounced that name."

"Ah, indeed!" said Andrée, "that is singular."

And, by degrees, as the clouds close again, after having been rent asunder by the lightning, the countenance of the young woman, so violently agitated at the sound of that fatal name, recovered its serenity, and but a few muscles of her lovely face continued to tremble almost imperceptibly, like the last flashes of the tempest which vanish in the horizon.

"Gilbert," she repeated, "I do not know that name."

"Yes, Gilbert," repeated the queen. "Come, try to recollect, my dear Andrée."

"But, madame," said the count to Marie Antoinette, "perhaps it is mere chance, and this name may be unknown to the countess."

"No," said Andrée, "no; it is not unknown to me. It is that of a learned man, of a skilful physician who has just arrived from America, I believe, and who became intimate while there with Monsieur de Lafayette."

"Well, then?" asked the count.

"Well, then," repeated Andrée, with the greatest presence of mind, "I do not know him personally, but he is said to be a very honorable man."

"Then, why all this emotion, my dear countess?" observed the queen.

"This emotion? Have I, then, been excited?"

"Yes; one would have said that when you pronounced the name Gilbert, you felt as if undergoing a torture."

"It is possible; I will tell you how it happened. I met a person in the king's cabinet, who was dressed in black, a man of austere countenance, who spoke of gloomy and horrible subjects; he related, with the most frightful

reality, the assassination of Monsieur de Launay and
Monsieur de Flesselles. I became terrified on hearing this
intelligence, and I fell into the swoon in which you saw
me. It may be that I spoke at that time ; perhaps I then
pronounced the name of Monsieur Gilbert."

"It is possible," repeated M. de Charny, who was
evidently not disposed to push the questioning any
further. "But now you feel more reassured, do you not,
madame ?"

"Completely."

"I will then beg of you to do one thing, Monsieur de
Charny," said the queen.

"I am at the disposal of your majesty."

"Go and find out Messieurs de Bezenval, de Broglie,
and de Lambesq. Tell them to quarter their troops where
they now are. The king will decide to-morrow in council
what must then be done."

The count bowed ; but before leaving the room, he cast
a look at Andrée.

That look was full of affectionate anxiety.

It did not escape the queen.

"Countess," said she, "will you return to the king's
apartment with me ?"

"No, madame, no," replied Andrée, quickly.

"And why not ?"

"I ask your majesty's permission to withdraw to my
own apartment. The emotions I have undergone make
me feel the want of rest."

"Come, now, countess, speak frankly," said the queen.
"Have you had any disagreement with his majesty ?"

"Oh, by no means, madame—absolutely nothing."

"Oh, tell me if anything has happened ! The king
does not always spare my friends."

"The king is, as usual, full of kindness to me ; but——"

"But you have no great wish to see him. Is it not so ?
There must positively be something at the bottom of all
this, count," said the queen, with affected gaiety.

At this moment Andrée directed so expressive, so sup-
licating a look at the queen—a look so full of revelations,
that the latter understood it was time to put an end to
this minor war.

"In fact, countess," said she, "we will leave Monsieur
de Charny to execute the commission I intrusted to him,

and you can retire or remain here, according to your choice."

"Thank you, madame," said Andrée.

"Go then, Monsieur de Charny," continued Marie Antoinette, while she noticed the expression of gratitude which was visible on the features of Andrée.

Either the count did not perceive, or did not wish to perceive it. He took the hand of his wife, and complimented her on the return of her strength and color.

Then, making a most respectful bow to the queen, he left the room.

But while leaving the room, he exchanged a last look with Marie Antoinette.

The queen's look meant to say, "Return quickly." That of the count replied, "As soon as possible."

As to Andrée, she followed with her eyes every one of her husband's movements; her bosom palpitating, and almost breathless.

She seemed to accelerate with her wishes the slow and noble step with which he approached the door. She, as it were, pushed him out of the room with the whole power of her will.

Therefore was it that, as soon as he had disappeared, all the strength that Andrée had summoned to assist her in surmounting the difficulties of her position abandoned her; her face became pale, her limbs failed beneath her, and she fell into an armchair which was within her reach, while she endeavored to apologize to the queen for her involuntary breach of etiquette.

The queen ran to the chimney-piece, took a smelling-bottle of salts, and made Andrée inhale them, who was soon restored to her senses; but more by the power of her own will than by the efficacy of the attentions she received at the royal hands.

In fact, there was something strange in the conduct of these two women. The queen seemed to love Andrée; Andrée respected the queen greatly, and, nevertheless, at certain moments they did not appear to be, the one an affectionate queen, the other a devoted subject, but two determined enemies.

As we have already said, the potent will of Andrée soon restored her strength. She rose up, gently removed the queen's hand, and, courtesying to her:

"Your majesty," said she, "has given me permission to retire to my own room."

"Yes, undoubtedly; and you are always free, dear countess, and this you know full well. Etiquette is not intended for you. But before you retire, have you nothing to tell me?"

"I, madame?" asked Andrée.

"Yes, you, without doubt."

"No; what should I have to tell you?"

"In regard to this Monsieur Gilbert, the sight of whom has made so strong an impression upon you."

Andrée trembled, but she merely made a sign of denial.

"In that case, I will not detain you any longer, dear Andrée; you may go."

And the queen took a step toward the door of the dressing-room, which communicated with her bedroom.

Andrée, on her side, having made her obeisance to the queen, in the most irreproachable manner, was going toward the door.

But at the very moment she was about to open it, steps were heard in the corridor, and a hand was placed on the external handle of the door.

At the same time, the voice of Louis XVI. was heard, giving orders for the night to his valet.

"The king, madame!" said Andrée, retreating several steps, "the king!"

"And what of that? Yes, it is the king," said Marie Antoinette "Does he terrify you to such a degree as this?"

"Madame, in the name of Heaven," cried Andrée, "let me not see the king. Let me not meet the king face to face, at all events, this evening. I should die of shame."

"But, finally, you will tell me——"

"Everything—yes, everything—if your majesty requires it. But hide me!"

"Go into my boudoir," said Marie Antoinette. "You can leave it as soon as the king himself retires. Rest assured, your captivity will not be of long duration. The king never remains here long."

"Oh, thanks! thanks!" exclaimed the countess.

And rushing into the boudoir, she disappeared, at the very moment that the king, having opened the door, appeared upon the threshold of the chamber.

The king entered.

VOLUME II.

CHAPTER I.

How long the interview between Andrée and the queen lasted, it would be impossible for us to say; but it was certainly of considerable duration, for at about half-past twelve o'clock that night the door of the queen's boudoir was seen to open, and on the threshold, Andrée, almost on her knees, kissing the hand of Marie Antoinette.

After which, having raised herself up, the young woman dried her eyes, red with weeping, while the queen, on her side, re-entered her room.

Andrée, on the contrary, walked away rapidly, as if she desired to escape from her own thoughts.

After this, the queen was alone. When the lady of the bedchamber entered the room to assist her in undressing, she found her pacing the room with rapid strides, and her eyes flashing with excitement.

She made a quick movement with her hand, which meant to say, "leave me."

The lady of the bedchamber left the room without offering an observation.

The queen again found herself alone. She had given orders that no one should disturb her, unless it was to announce the arrival of important news from Paris.

Andrée did not appear again.

As for the king, after he had conversed with M. de la Rochefoucault, who endeavored to make him comprehend the difference there was between a riot and a revolution— he declared himself fatigued, went to bed, and slept as quietly as if he had returned from a hunt, and the stag (a well-trained courtier) had suffered himself to be taken in the grand basin of the fountain called the Swiss.

The queen, however, wrote several letters, went into an adjoining room, where her two children slept under the care of Mme. de Tourzel, and then went to bed, not for the sake of sleeping, like the king, but merely to meditate more at ease.

But soon after, when silence reigned around Versailles,

when the immense palace became plunged in darkness, when there could no longer be heard in the gardens aught but the tramp of the patrols upon the gravel walks, and in the long passages nothing but the ringing of muskets on the marble pavement, Marie Antoinette, tired of repose, felt the want of air, got out of bed, and putting on her velvet slippers and a long white dressing-gown, went to the window to inhale the ascending freshness of the cascades, and to seize in their flight those counsels which the night winds murmur to heated minds and oppressed hearts.

Then she reviewed in her mind all the astounding events which this strange day had produced.

The fall of the Bastile, that visible emblem of royal power; the uncertainties of Charny, her devoted friend; that impassioned captive who for so many years had been subjected to her yoke, and who, during all those years, had never breathed anything but love, now seemed, for the first time, to sigh from regret and feelings of remorse.

With that synthetic habit with which the knowledge of men and events endows great minds, Marie Antoinette immediately divided the agitation which oppressed her into two portions, the one being her political misfortunes, the other the sorrows of her heart.

The political misfortune was that great event, the news of which had left Paris at three o'clock in the afternoon, and was then spreading itself over the whole world, and weakening in every mind that sacred reverence which until then had always been accorded to kings, God's mandatories upon earth.

The sorrow of her heart was the gloomy resistance of Charny to the omnipotence of his well-beloved sovereign. It appeared to her like a presentiment, that without ceasing to be faithful and devoted, his love would cease to be blind, and might begin to argue with itself on its fidelity and its devotedness.

This thought grieved the queen's heart poignantly, and filled it with that bitter gall which is called jealousy, an acrid poison which ulcerates at the same instant a thousand little wounds in a wounded soul.

Nevertheless, grief in the presence of misfortune was logically an inferiority.

Thus, rather from reasoning than from conscientious motives, rather from necessity than from instinct, Marie Antoinette first allowed her mind to enter into the grave reflections connected with the dangerous state of political affairs.

In which direction could she turn? Before her lay hatred and ambition—weakness and indifference at her side.

For enemies, she had people who, having commenced with calumny, were now organizing a rebellion.

People whom, consequently, no consideration would induce to retreat.

For defenders—we speak of the greater portion at least of those men who, little by little, had accustomed themselves to endure everything, and who, in consequence, no longer felt the depth of their wounds—their degradation; people who would hesitate to defend themselves, for fear of attracting attention.

It was, therefore, necessary to bury everything in oblivion—to appear to forget, and yet to remember—to feign to forgive, and yet not pardon.

This would be conduct unworthy of a queen of France; it was especially unworthy of the daughter of Marie Theresa—that high-minded woman.

To resist! to resist!—that was what offended royal pride most strenuously counseled. But was it prudent to resist? Could hatred be calmed down by shedding blood? Was it not terrible to be surnamed "The Austrian?" Was it necessary, in order to consecrate that name, as Isabeau and Catherine de Medici had consecrated theirs, to give it the baptism of a universal massacre?

And then, if what Charny had said was true, success was doubtful.

To combat and to be defeated!

Such were the political sorrows of the queen, who, during certain phases of her meditation, felt a sensation like that which we experience on seeing a serpent glide from beneath the brambles, awakened by our advancing steps. She felt, on emerging from the depths of her sufferings as a queen, the despair of the woman who thinks herself but little loved, when in reality she had been loved too much.

Charny had said what we have already heard him say, not from conviction, but from lassitude. He had, like many others, drunk calumny from the same cup that she had. Charny, for the first time, had spoken in such affectionate terms of his wife, Andrée being until then almost forgotten by her husband. Had Charny then perceived that his young wife was still beautiful ? And at this single idea, which stung her like the envenomed bite of the asp, Marie Antoinette was astounded to find that misfortune was nothing in comparison with sorrow.

For what misfortune had failed to do, grief was gradually effecting within her soul. The woman sprung furiously from the chair in which the queen had calmly contemplated danger.

The whole destiny of this privileged child of suffering revealed itself in the condition of her mind during that night.

For, how was it possible to escape misfortune and grief at the same time ? she would ask herself, with constantly renewing anguish. Was it necessary to determine on abandoning a life of royalty, and could she live happily in a state of mediocrity ?—was it necessary to return to her own Trianon and to her Swiss cottage, to the quiet shores of the lake and the humble amusements of the dairy ?—was it necessary to allow the people to divide among them the shreds of monarchy, excepting some few fragments which the woman could appropriate to herself from the contested revenues of a few faithful servants, who would still persist in considering themselves her vassals ?

Alas ! it was now that the serpent of jealousy began to sting still deeper.

Happy ! Could she be happy with the humiliation of despised love ?

Happy ! Could she be happy by the side of the king— that vulgar husband, in whom everything was deficient to form the hero ?

Happy ! Could she be happy with M. de Charny, who might be so with some woman whom he loved—by the side of his own wife, perhaps ?

And this thought kindled in the poor queen's breast all those flaming torches which consumed Dido even more than her funeral pile.

But in the midst of this feverish torture she saw a ray of hope ; in the midst of this shuddering anguish she felt a sensation of joy. God, in His infinite mercy, has He not created evil to make us appreciate good?

Andrée had intrusted the queen with all her secrets; she had unveiled the one shame of her life to her rival. Andrée, her eyes full of tears, her head bowed down to the ground, had confessed to the queen that she was no longer worthy of the love and the respect of an honorable man; therefore, Charny could never love Andrée.

But Charny is ignorant of this. Charny will ever be ignorant of that catastrophe at Trianon, and its consequences. Therefore, to Charny it is as if the catastrophe had never taken place.

And while making these reflections, the queen examined her fading beauty in the mirror of her mind, and deplored the loss of her gayety, the freshness of her youth.

Then she thought of Andrée, of the strange and almost incredible adventures which she had just related to her.

She wondered at the magical working of blind fortune, which had brought to Trianon, from the shade of a hut and the muddy furrows of a farm, a little gardener's boy, to associate his destinies with those of a highly born young lady, who was herself associated with the destinies of a queen.

"Thus," said she to herself, "the atom which was thus lost in the lowest regions has come, by a freak of superior attraction, to unite itself, like a fragment of a diamond, with the heavenly light of the stars."

This gardener's boy, this Gilbert, was he not a living symbol of that which was occurring at that moment—a man of the people, rising from the lowness of his birth to busy himself with the politics of a great kingdom; a strange comedian, in whom were personified, by a privilege granted to him by the evil spirit who was then hovering over France, not only the insult offered to the nobility, but also the attack made upon the monarchy by a plebeian mob.

This Gilbert, now become a learned man—this Gilbert, dressed in the black coat of the Tiers Etat, the counselor of M. de Necker, the confidant of the King of France, would now find himself, thanks to the revolution, on an equal footing with the woman whose honor, like a thief, he had stolen in the night.

The queen had again become a woman, and, shuddering

in spite of herself at the sad story related by Andrée, she
was endeavoring to study the character of this Gilbert,
and to learn by herself to read in human features what
God had placed there to indicate so strange a character;
and, notwithstanding the pleasure she had experienced on
seeing the humiliation of her rival, she still felt a linger-
ing desire to attack the man who had caused a woman
such intensity of suffering.

Moreover, notwithstanding the terror generally inspired
by the sight of monsters, she felt a desire to look at, and
perhaps even to admire, this extraordinary man who by a
crime had infused his vile blood into the most aristocratic
veins in France; this man who appeared to have organized
the revolution, in order that it should open the gates of
the Bastile for him, in which, but for that revolution, he
would have remained immured forever, to teach him that
a plebeian must remember nothing.

In consequence of this connecting link in her ideas, the
queen reverted to her political vexations, and saw the
responsibility of all she had suffered accumulate upon one
single head.

Thus the author of the popular rebellion that had just
shaken the royal power by leveling the Bastile, was Gilbert; he whose principles had placed weapons in the
hands of the Billots, the Maillards, the Elies, and the
Hullins.

Gilbert was, therefore, both a venomous and a terrible
being—venomous, because he had caused the loss of Andrée
as a lover; terrible, because he had just assisted in over-
throwing the Bastile as an enemy.

It was, therefore, necessary to know, in order to avoid
him; or, rather, to know him, in order to make use of him.

It was necessary, at any cost, to converse with this man,
to examine him closely, and to judge him personally.

Two thirds of the night had already flown away, three
o'clock was striking, and the first rays of the rising sun
gilded the high tops of the trees in the park, and the
summits of the statues of Versailles.

The queen had passed the whole night without sleeping;
her dimmed vision lost itself in the shaded streaks of the
mild light.

A heavy and burning slumber gradually seized the unfortunate woman.

She fell back, with her neck overhanging the back of the armchair, near the open window.

She dreamed that she was walking in Trianon, and that there appeared to her eyes, at the extremity of a flower-bed, a grinning gnome, similar to those we read of in German ballads; that this sardonic monster was Gilbert, who extended his hooked fingers toward her.

She screamed aloud.

Another cry answered hers.

That cry roused her from her slumber.

It was Mme. de Tourzel who had uttered it. She had just entered the queen's apartment, and seeing her exhausted and gasping in an armchair, she could not avoid giving utterance to her grief and surprise.

"The queen is indisposed!" she exclaimed. "The queen is suffering. Shall I send for a physician?"

The queen opened her eyes. This question of Mme. de Tourzel coincided with the demands of her own curiosity.

"Yes, a physician!" she replied. "Doctor Gilbert!—send for Doctor Gilbert!"

"Who is Doctor Gilbert?" asked Mme. de Tourzel.

"A new physician, appointed by the king only yesterday, I believe, and just arrived from America."

"I know who her majesty means," said one of the queen's ladies-in-waiting, who had rushed into the room on hearing Mme. de Tourzel scream.

"Well?" said the queen inquiringly.

"Well, madame, the doctor is in the king's antechamber."

"Do you know him, then?"

"Yes, your majesty," stammered the woman.

"But how can you know him? He arrived here from America some eight or ten days ago, and only came out of the Bastile yesterday."

"I know him."

"Answer me distinctly. Where did you know him?" asked the queen, in an imperious tone.

The lady cast down her eyes.

"Come, will you make up your mind to tell me how it happens that you know this man?"

"Madame, I have read his works; and his works having given me a desire to see the author, I had him pointed out to me."

"Ah!" exclaimed the queen, with an indescribable look of haughtiness and reserve—"ah! it is well. Since you know him, go and tell him that I am suffering, and that I wish to see him."

While waiting for the doctor's arrival, the queen made her ladies in attendance enter the room; after which she put on a dressing-gown and adjusted her hair.

CHAPTER II.

A FEW moments after the queen had expressed the above desire, a desire which the person to whom it had been mentioned had complied with, Gilbert, who felt astonished, slightly anxious, and profoundly agitated, but still without showing any external marks of it, Gilbert presented himself to Marie Antoinette.

The firm and noble carriage, the delicate pallor of the man of science and of thought, to whom study had given a second nature—a pallor still more enhanced by the black dress which was not only worn by all the deputies of the Tiers Etat, but also by those who had adopted the principles of the revolution; the delicate white hand of the surgical operator, surrounded by a plain muslin wrist-band; his slender though well-formed limbs, which none of those at court could surpass in symmetry, even in the estimation of the connoisseurs of the Œil de Bœuf; combined with all these, there was a mixture of respectful timidity toward the woman, and of calm courage toward the patient, but no signs of servility toward her as a queen. Such were the plainly written signs that Marie Antoinette, with her aristocratic intelligence, could perceive in the countenance of Gilbert, at the moment when the door opened to admit him into her bed-chamber.

But the less Gilbert was provoking in his demeanor, the more did the queen feel her anger increase. She had figured him to herself as a type of an odious class of men; she had considered him instinctively, though almost involuntarily, as one of those impudent heroes of which she had so many around her. The author of the sufferings of Andrée, the bastard pupil of Rousseau, that miserable abortion who had grown up to manhood, that pruner of trees who had become a philosopher and a subduer of souls

—Marie Antoinette, in spite of herself, depicted him in her mind as having the features of Mirabeau—that is to say, of the man she most hated, after the Cardinal de Rohan and Lafayette.

It had seemed to her, before she saw Gilbert, that it required a gigantic physical development to contain so colossal a mind.

But when she saw a young, upright, and slender man, of elegant and graceful form, of sweet and amiable countenance, he appeared to her as having committed the new crime of belying himself by his exterior. Gilbert, a man of the people, of obscure and unknown birth! Gilbert, the peasant, the clown, and the serf !—Gilbert was guilty, in the eyes of the queen, of having usurped the external appearance of a gentleman and a man of honor. The proud Austrian, the sworn enemy of lying and deception in others, became indignant, and immediately conceived a violent hatred for the unfortunate atom whom so many different motives combined to induce her to abhor.

For those who were intimate with her nature, for those who were accustomed to read in her eyes either serenity of temper or indications of an approaching storm, it was easy to discern that a tempest, full of thunder-claps and flashes of lightning, was raging in the depths of her heart.

But how was it possible for a human being, even a woman, to follow, in the midst of this hurricane of passions and anger, the succession of strange and contrasting feelings which clashed together in the queen's brain and filled her breast with all the mortal poisons described by Homer ?

The queen, with a single look, dismissed all her attendants, even Mme. de Misery.

They immediately left the room.

The queen waited till the door had been closed on the last person. Then casting her eyes upon Gilbert, she perceived that he had not ceased to gaze at her.

So much audacity offended her. The doctor's look was apparently inoffensive ; but, as it was continual, and seemed full of design, it weighed heavily upon her.

Marie Antoinette felt compelled to repress its importunity.

"Well, then, sir," said she, with the abruptness of a

pistol-shot, "what are you doing there, standing before me and gazing at me, instead of telling me with what complaint I am suffering?"

This furious apostrophe, rendered more forcible by the flashing of her eyes, would have annihilated any of the queen's courtiers—it would even have compelled a marshal of France, a hero, or a demi-god, to fall on his knees before her.

But Gilbert tranquilly replied:

"It is by means of the eyes, madame, that the physician must first examine his patient. By looking at your majesty, who sent for me, I do not satisfy an idle curiosity —I exercise my profession—I obey your orders."

"Then you must have studied me sufficiently."

"As much as lay in my power, madame."

"Am I ill?"

"Not in the strict sense of the word. But your majesty is suffering from great over-excitement."

"Ah! ah!" said Marie Antoinette ironically, "why do you not say at once that I am in a passion?"

"Let your majesty allow me, since you have ordered the attendance of a physician, to express myself in medical terms."

"Be it so. But what is the cause of my over-excitement?"

"Your majesty has too much knowledge not to be aware that the physician discovers the sufferings of the body, thanks to his experience and the traditions of his studies; but he is not a sorcerer, who can discover at first sight the depths of the human soul."

"By this you mean to imply that the second or third time you could tell me not only from what I am suffering, but also what are my thoughts?"

"Perhaps so, madame," coldly replied Gilbert.

The queen appeared to tremble with anger; her words seemed to be hanging on her lips, ready to burst forth in burning torrents.

She, however, restrained herself.

"I must believe you," said she, "you who are a learned man."

And she emphasized these last words with so much contempt, that the eye of Gilbert appeared to kindle, in its turn, with the fire of anger.

But a struggle of a few seconds' duration sufficed to this man to give him a complete victory.

Accordingly, with a calm brow, and unembarrassed expression, he almost immediately rejoined :

"It is too kind of your majesty to give me the title of a learned man, without having received any proofs of my knowledge."

The queen bit her lip.

"You must understand that I do not know if you are a scientific man," she replied ; "but I have heard it said, and I repeat what everybody says."

"Well, then," said Gilbert, respectfully, and bowing still lower than he had done hitherto, "a superior mind like that of your majesty must not blindly repeat what is said by the vulgar."

"Do you mean the people ?" said the queen, insolently.

"The vulgar, madame," repeated Gilbert, with a firmness which made the blood thrill in the queen's veins, and gave rise to emotions which were as painful to her as they had hitherto been unknown.

"In fine," answered she, "let us not discuss that point. You are said to be learned, that is all that is essential. Where have you studied ?"

"Everywhere, madame."

"That is not an answer."

"Nowhere, then."

"I prefer that answer. Have you studied nowhere ?"

"As it may please you, madame," replied the doctor, bowing, "and yet it is less exact than to say everywhere."

"Come, answer me, then," exclaimed the queen, becoming exasperated ; "and, above all, for Heaven's sake, Monsieur Gilbert, spare me such phrases."

Then, as if speaking to herself :

"Everywhere ! everywhere ! what does that mean ? It is the language of a charlatan, a quack, of a physician who practises in the public squares ! Do you mean to overawe me by your sonorous syllables ?"

She stepped forward with ardent eyes and quivering lips.

"Everywhere ! Mention some place ; come, explain your meaning, Monsieur Gilbert."

"I said everywhere," answered Gilbert, coldly, "because, in fact, I have studied everywhere, madame ; in the

hut and in the palace, in cities and in the desert, upon our
own species and upon animals, upon myself and upon others,
in a manner suitable to one who loves knowledge and
studies it where it is to be found, that is to say, everywhere."

The queen, overcome, cast a terrible glance at Gilbert,
while he, on his part, was eying her with terrible perseve-
rance. She became convulsively agitated, and, turning
round, upset a small stand, upon which her chocolate had
been served up in a cup of Sèvres porcelain. Gilbert saw
the table fall, saw the broken cup, but did not move a
finger.

The color mounted to the cheeks of Marie Antoinette;
she raised her cold, moist hand to her burning temples,
but did not dare to raise her eyes again to look on Gilbert.

But her features assumed a more contemptuous, more
insolent expression than before.

"Then, under what great master did you study?" continued the queen, again taking up the conversation at the
point where she had left off.

"I hardly know how to answer your majesty, without
running the risk of again wounding your majesty."

The queen perceived the advantage that Gilbert had
given her, and threw herself upon it like a lioness upon
her prey.

"Wound me—you wound me—you!" exclaimed she.
"Oh, sir, what are you saying there?—you wound a
queen! You are mistaken, sir, I can affirm to you. Ah!
Doctor Gilbert, and you have not studied the French language in as good schools as you have studied medicine;
people of my station are not to be wounded, Doctor Gilbert;
you may weary them, that is all."

Gilbert bowed, and made a step toward the door; but it
was not possible for the queen to discover in his countenance
the least show of anger, the least sign of impatience.

The queen, on the contrary, was stamping her feet with
rage; she sprung toward Gilbert as if to prevent him from
leaving the room.

He understood her.

"Pardon me, madame," said he, "it is true, I committed the unpardonable error to forget that as a physician
I was called to see a patient. Forgive me, madame; hereafter I shall remember it." And he came back.

"Your majesty," continued he, "is rapidly approaching a nervous crisis. I will venture to ask you not to give way to it; for in a short time it would be beyond your power to control it. At this moment, your pulse must be imperceptible, the blood is rushing to the heart; your majesty is suffering, your majesty is almost suffocating, and perhaps it would be prudent for you to summon one of your ladies-in-waiting."

The queen took a turn round the round, and seating herself:

"Is your name Gilbert?" asked she.

"Yes, Gilbert, madame."

"Strange! I remember an incident of my youth, the strange nature of which would doubtless wound you much, were I to relate it to you. But it matters not; for if hurt, you will soon cure yourself—you who are no less a philosopher than a learned physician."

And the queen smiled ironically.

"Precisely so, madame," said Gilbert; "you may smile, and, little by little, subdue your nervousness by irony. It is one of the most beautiful prerogatives of the intelligent will, to be able thus to control itself. Subdue it, madame, subdue it; but, however, without making a too violent effort."

This prescription of the physician was given with so much suavity and such natural good-humor, that the queen, while feeling the bitter irony contained in his words, could not take offense at what Gilbert had said to her.

She merely returned to the charge, recommencing the attacks where she had discontinued them.

"This incident of which I spoke," continued she, "is the following."

Gilbert bowed, as a sign that he was listening.

The queen made an effort, and fixed her gaze upon him.

"I was the dauphiness at that time, and I inhabited Trianon. There was in the gardens a little, dark-looking, dirty boy, covered with mud, a crabbed boy, a sort of sour Jean Jacques, who weeded, dug, and picked off the caterpillars with his little crooked fingers. His name was Gilbert."

"It was myself, madame," said Gilbert phlegmatically.

"You!" said Marie Antoinette, with an expression of hatred. "I was, then, right; but you are, then, a learned man?"

"I think that, as your majesty's memory is so good, you

must also remember dates," rejoined Gilbert. "It was in 1772, if I am not mistaken, that the little gardener's boy of whom your majesty speaks weeded the flower-beds of Trianon to earn his bread. We are now in 1789. It is, therefore, seventeen years, madame, since the events to which you allude took place. It is more time than is necessary to metamorphose a savage into a learned man; the soul and the mind operate quickly in certain positions, like plants and flowers which grow rapidly in hothouses. Revolutions, madame, are the hotbeds of the mind. Your majesty looks at me, and notwithstanding the perspicacity of your scrutiny, you do not perceive that the boy of sixteen has become a man of thirty-three; you are, therefore, wrong to wonder that the ignorant, the ingenuous little Gilbert should, after having witnessed these revolutions, have become a learned man and a philosopher."

"Ignorant! be it so; but ingenuous—ingenuous, did you say?" furiously cried the queen, "I think you called that little Gilbert ingenuous."

"If I am mistaken, madame, or if I praised this little boy for a quality which he did not possess, I do not know how your majesty can have ascertained more correctly than myself that he had the opposite defect."

"Oh! that is quite another matter," said the queen, gloomily; "perhaps we shall speak of that some other time; but in the meantime let me speak of the learned man, of the man brought to perfection, of the perfect man I see before me."

Gilbert did not take up the word perfect. He understood but too well that it was a new insult.

Let us return to our subject, madame," replied Gilbert; "tell me for what purpose did your majesty order me to come to her apartment?"

"You propose to become the king's physician," said she. "Now you must understand, sir, that I attach too much importance to the health of my husband to trust it in the hands of a man whom I do not know perfectly."

"I offered myself to the king, madame," said Gilbert, "and I was accepted, without your majesty having any just cause to conceive the least suspicion as to my capacity or want of zeal. I am, above all, a political physician, madame, recommended by Monsieur Necker. As for the rest, if the king is ever in want of my science, I shall prove myself a good physical doctor, so far as human science can be of use to the Creator's works. But what I shall be to the king, more particularly, besides being a good adviser, and a good physician, is a good friend."

"A good friend!" exclaimed the queen, with a fresh outburst of contempt. "You, sir, a friend of the king!"

"Certainly," replied Gilbert, quietly; "why not, madame?"

"Oh, yes; all in virtue of your secret power, by the assistance of your occult science," murmured she, "who can tell? We have already seen the Jacques and the Maillotins; perhaps we shall go back to the dark ages. You have resuscitated philters and charms. You will soon govern France by magic, you will be a Faust or a Nicholas Flamel."

"I have no such pretensions, madame."

"And why have you not, sir? How many monsters more cruel than those of the gardens of Armida, more cruel than Cerberus himself, would you not put to sleep on the threshold of our hell?"

When she had pronounced the words, "would you not put to sleep," the queen cast a scrutinizing look on the doctor.

This time Gilbert blushed, in spite of himself.

It was a source of indescribable joy to Marie Antoinette; she felt that, this time, the blow she had struck had inflicted a real wound.

"For you have the power of causing sleep; you who have studied everything and everywhere, you doubtless have studied magnetic science with the magnetizers of our century, who make sleep a treacherous instrument, and who read their secrets in the sleep of others!"

"In fact, madame, I have often, and for a long time, studied under the learned Cagliostro."

"Yes; he who practised and made his followers practise that moral theft of which I was just speaking; the same who, by the aid of that magic sleep which I call infamous, robbed some of their souls and others of their bodies."

Gilbert again understood her meaning, but this time he turned pale, instead of reddening. The queen trembled with joy to the very depths of her heart.

"Ah! wretch!" murmured she to herself, "I have wounded you, and I can see the blood."

But the profoundest emotions were never visible for any length of time on the countenance of Gilbert. Approaching the queen, therefore, who, quite joyful on account of her victory, was imprudently looking at him :

"Madame," said he, "your majesty would be wrong to deny the learned men of whom you have been speaking the most beautiful appendage to their science, which is the power of throwing, not victims, but subjects, into a magnetic sleep ; you would be wrong, in particular, to contest the right they have to follow up, by all possible means, a discovery of which the laws, once recognized and regulated, are perhaps intended to revolutionize the world."

And while approaching the queen, Gilbert had looked at her, in his turn, with that power of will to which the nervous Andrée had succumbed.

The queen felt a chill run through her veins as he drew nearer to her.

"Infamy," said she, "be the reward of those men who make an abuse of certain dark and mysterious arts to ruin both the soul and body. May infamy rest upon the head of Cagliostro !"

"Ah !" replied Gilbert, with the accent of conviction, "beware, madame, of judging the faults committed by human beings with so much severity."

"Sir——"

"Every one is liable to err, madame ; all human beings commit injuries on their fellow-creatures, and were it not for individual egotism, which is the foundation of general safety, the world would become but one great battle-field. Those are the best who are good, that is all. Others will tell you that those are best who are the least faulty. Indulgence must be the greater, madame, in proportion to the elevated rank of the judge. Seated as you are on so exalted a throne, you have less right than any other person to be severe toward the faults of others. On your worldly throne, you should be supremely indulgent, like God, who, upon His heavenly throne, is supremely merciful."

"Sir," said the queen, "I view my rights in a different light from you, and especially my duties. I am on the throne to punish or reward."

"I do not think so, madame. In my opinion, on the

contrary, you are seated on the throne, you, a woman and a queen, to conciliate and to forgive."

"I suppose you are not moralizing, sir."

"You are right, madame, as I was only replying to your majesty. This Cagliostro, for instance, madame, of whom you were speaking a few moments since—and whose science you were contesting—I remember—and this is a remembrance of something anterior to your recollection of Trianon—I remember that in the gardens of the Château de Taverney he had occasion to give the Dauphiness of France a proof of his science—I know not what it was, madame—but you must recollect it well; for that proof made a profound impression upon her, even so much as to cause her to faint."

Gilbert was now striking blows in his turn; it is true that he was dealing them at random, but he was favored by chance, and they hit the mark so truly that the queen became pale.

"Yes," said she, in a hoarse voice, "yes, he made me see, as in a dream, a hideous machine; but I know not that, up to the present time, such a machine has ever really existed."

"I know not what he made you see, madame," rejoined Gilbert, who felt satisfied with the effect he had produced; "but I do know that it is impossible to dispute the appellation of learned to a man who wields such a power as that over his fellow-creatures."

"His fellow-creatures!" murmured the queen, disdainfully.

"Be it so; I am mistaken," replied Gilbert; "and his power is so much the more wonderful, that it reduces to a level with himself, under the yoke of fear, the heads of monarchs and princes of the earth."

"Infamy! infamy! I say again, upon those who take advantage of the weakness or the credulity of others."

"Infamous!—did you call infamous those who make use of science?"

"Their science is nothing but chimeras, lies, and cowardice!"

"What mean you by that, madame?" asked Gilbert, calmly.

"My meaning is that this Cagliostro is a cowardly

mountebank, and that his pretended magnetic sleep is a crime."

"A crime?"

"Yes, a crime," continued the queen; "for it is the result of some potion, some philter, some poison—and human justice, which I represent, will be able to discover the mystery and punish the inventor."

"Madame! madame!" rejoined Gilbert, with the same patience as before, "a little indulgence, I beg, for those who have erred."

"Ah! you confess their guilt, then?"

The queen was mistaken, and thought from the mild tone of Gilbert's voice that he was supplicating pardon for himself.

She was in error, and Gilbert did not allow the advantage she had thus given him to escape.

"What?" said he, dilating his flashing eyes, before the gaze of which Marie Antoinette was compelled to lower hers, as if suddenly dazzled by the rays of the sun.

The queen remained confounded for a moment, and then, making an effort to speak:

"A queen can no more be questioned than she can be wounded," said she; "learn to know that also, you who have but so newly arrived at court. But you were speaking, it seems to me, of those who have erred, and you asked me to be indulgent toward them."

"Alas! madame," said Gilbert, "where is the human creature who is not liable to reproach? Is it he who has ensconced himself so closely within the deep shell of his conscience that the look of others cannot penetrate it? Is it this which is so often denominated virtue? Be indulgent, madame."

"But according to this opinion, then," replied the queen imprudently, "there is no virtuous being in your estimation, sir; you, who are the pupil of those men whose prying eyes seek the truth, even in the deepest recesses of the human conscience."

"It is true, madame."

She laughed, and without seeking to conceal the contempt which her laughter expressed.

"Oh! pray, sir," exclaimed she, "do remember that you are not now speaking on a public square, to idiots, to peasants, or to patriots."

"I am aware to whom I am speaking, madame, of this you may be fully persuaded," replied Gilbert.

"Show more respect, then, sir, or more adroitness; consider your past life—search the depths of that conscience which men who have studied everywhere must possess in common with the rest of mankind, notwithstanding their genius and their wisdom—recall to your mind all that you may have conceived that was vile, hurtful, and criminal—all the cruelties, the deeds, the crimes even, you have committed. Do not interrupt me; and when you have summed up all your misdeeds, learned doctor, you will bow down your head, and become more humble. Do not approach the dwelling of kings with such insolent pride, who, until there is a new order of things, were established by Heaven to penetrate the souls of criminals, to examine the folds of the human conscience, and to inflict chastisement upon the guilty, without pity and without appeal.

"That, sir," continued the queen, "is what you ought to do. You will be thought the better of, on account of your repentance. Believe me, the best mode of healing a soul so diseased as yours would be to live in solitude, far from the grandeurs which give men false ideas of their own worth. I would advise you, therefore, not to approach the court, and to abandon the idea of attending the king during sickness. You have a cure to accomplish, for which God will esteem you more than for any other—the cure of yourself. Antiquity had a proverb which expressed the following maxim, sir, ' *Ipse cura medici.*'"

Gilbert, instead of being irritated at this proposal, which the queen considered as the most disagreeable of conclusions, replied, with gentleness:

"Madame, I have already done all that your majesty advises."

"And what have you done, sir?"

"I have meditated."

"Upon yourself?"

"Yes, upon myself, madame."

"And in regard to your conscience?"

"Especially on the subject of my conscience, madame."

"Do you think, then, I am sufficiently well informed of what you saw in it?"

"I do not know what your majesty means by those

words, but I think I can discover their meaning, which is, 'How many times a man of my age must have offended God.'"

"Really--you speak of God?"

"Yes."

"You!"

"Why not?"

"A philosopher? Do philosophers believe in the existence of a God?"

"I speak of God, and I believe in Him."

"And you are still determined not to withdraw from court?"

"No, madame; I remain."

And the queen's countenance assumed a threatening expression, which it would be impossible to describe.

"Oh! I have reflected much upon the subject, madame, and reflections have led me to know that I am not less worthy than another; every one has his faults. I learned this axiom, not by pondering over books, but by searching the consciences of others."

"You are universal and infallible, are you not?" said the queen, ironically.

"Alas! madame, if I am not universal, if I am not infallible, I am, nevertheless, very learned in human misery, well versed in the greatest sorrows of the mind. And this is so true, that I could tell, by merely seeing the livid circle round your wearied eyes, by merely seeing the line which extends from one eyebrow to the other, by merely seeing at the corners of your mouth a contraction which is called by the prosaic name of wrinkle—I can tell you, madame, how many severe trials you have undergone, how many times your heart has palpitated with anguish, to how many secret dreams of joy your heart has abandoned itself, to discover its error on awaking.

"I will tell you all that, madame, when you shall desire it; I will tell it you, for I am sure of not being contradicted. I will tell it you, by merely fastening upon you a gaze which can read and wishes to read your mind; and when you have felt the power of that gaze, when you have felt the weight of this curiosity sounding to your inmost soul, like the sea that feels the weight of the lead that plunges into its depths, then you will understand that I am able to do much, madame, and that if I pause awhile, you should be grateful to me for it, instead of provoking me on to war."

This language, supported by a terrible fixity of the will of provocation, exercised by man upon the woman—this contempt for all etiquette in presence of the queen, produced an unspeakable effect upon Marie Antoinette.

She felt as if a mist were overshadowing her brow, and sending an icy chill through her ideas ; she felt her hatred turning into fear ; and letting her hands fall heavily by her side, retreated a step to avoid the approach of the unknown danger.

" And now, madame," said Gilbert, who clearly perceived all that was passing in her mind, " do you understand that it would be very easy for me to discover that which you conceal from everybody, and that which you conceal even from yourself ; do you understand that it would be easy for me to stretch you on that chair, which your fingers are now instinctively seeking as a support ? "

" Ah ! " exclaimed the queen, who was terrified, for she felt an unknown chill invading even her heart.

" Were I but to utter to myself a word which I will not utter," continued Gilbert, " were I but to summon up my will, which I renounce, you would fall as if thunderstricken into my power. You doubt what I am telling you, madame. Oh ! do not doubt it ; you might perhaps tempt me once—and if once you tempted me. But no, you do not doubt it, do you ? "

The queen, almost on the point of falling, exhausted, oppressed, and completely lost, grasped the back of her armchair with all the energy of despair and the rage of useless resistance.

" Oh ! " continued Gilbert, " mark this well, madame ; it is, that if I were not the most respectful, the most devoted, the most humble of your subjects, I should convince you by a terrible experiment. Oh ! you need fear nothing. I prostrate myself humbly before the woman, rather than before the queen. I tremble at the idea of entertaining any project which might, even in the slightest way, inquire into your thoughts ; I would rather kill myself than disturb your soul."

" Sir ! sir ! " exclaimed the queen, striking the air with her arms, as if to repel Gilbert, who was standing more than three paces from her.

"And still," continued Gilbert, "you caused me to be thrown into the Bastile. You only regret that it is taken, because the people, by taking it, reopened its gates for me. There is hatred visible in your eyes, toward a man against whom personally you can have no cause of reproach. And see, now, I feel that since I have lessened the influence by means of which I have controlled you, you are perhaps resuming your doubts with your returning respiration."

In fact, since Gilbert had ceased to control her with his eyes and gestures, Marie Antoinette had reassumed her threatening attitude, like the bird, which, being freed from the suffocating influence of the air-pump, endeavors to regain its song and its power of wing.

"Ah! you still doubt; you are ironical; you despise my warnings. Well, then, do you wish me to tell you, madame, a terrible idea that has just crossed my mind? This is what I was on the point of doing. Madame, I was just about to compel you to reveal to me your most intimate troubles, your most hidden secrets. I thought of compelling you to write them down on the table which you touch at this moment, and afterward, when you had awakened and come to your senses again, I should have convinced you by your own writing of the existence of that power which you seen to contest; and also how real is the forbearance, and, shall I say it?—yes, I will say it—the generosity of the man whom you have just insulted, whom you have insulted for a whole hour, without his having for a single instant given you either a reason or a pretext for so doing."

"Compel me to sleep! compel me to speak in my sleep —me! me!" exclaimed the queen, turning quite pale. "Would you have dared to do it, sir? But do you know what that is? Do you know the grave nature of the threat you make? Why, it is the crime of high treason, sir. Consider it well. It is a crime which, after awakening from my sleep, I should have punished with death."

"Madame," said Gilbert, watching the feverish emotions of the queen, "be not so hasty in accusing, and especially in threatening. Certainly, I should have possessed myself of all your secrets; but be convinced that it would not have been on an occasion like this: it would not have been during an interview between the queen and her subject, between a woman and a stranger. No; I should have put the queen to sleep, it is true—and nothing would have been easier—but I should not have ventured to put her to sleep, I should not have allowed myself to speak to her, without having a witness."

"A witness?"

"Yes, madame, a witness, who would faithfully note all your words, all your gestures, all the details, in short, of the scene which I should have brought about, in order that, after its termination, you could not doubt for a single moment longer."

"A witness, sir!" repeated the queen, terrified; "and who would that witness have been? But consider it maturely, sir, your crime would then have been doubled, for in that case you would have had an accomplice."

"And if this accomplice, madame, had been none other than the king?" said Gilbert.

"The king!" exclaimed Marie Antoinette, with an expression of fear that betrayed the wife more energetically than the confession of the somnambulist could have done. "Oh, Monsieur Gilbert! Monsieur Gilbert!"

"The king," continued Gilbert, calmly, "the king is your husband, your supporter, your natural defender. The king would have related to you, when you were awakened from your slumber, how respectful and proud I was in being able to prove my science to the most revered of sovereigns."

And after having spoken these words, Gilbert allowed the queen sufficient time to meditate upon their importance.

The queen remained silent for several minutes, during which nothing was heard but the noise of her agitated breathing.

"Sir," replied she, after this pause, "from all that you have now told me, you must be a mortal enemy——"

"Or a devoted friend, madame."

"It is impossible, sir; friendship cannot exist in unison with fear or mistrust."

"The friendship, madame, that exists between a subject and a queen cannot subsist except by the confidence which the subject may inspire her with. You will already have said to yourself that he is not an enemy whom, after the

first word, we can deprive of the means of doing harm,
especially when he is the first to renounce the use of his
weapons."

"May I believe, sir, what you have been saying?" said
the queen, looking thoughtfully at Gilbert.

"Why should you not believe me, madame, when you
have every proof of my sincerity?"

"Men change, sir—men change."

"Madame, I have made the same vow that certain illustrious warriors made before starting on an expedition, as
to the use of certain weapons in which they were skilled.
I shall never make use of my advantages but to repel the
wrong that others may attempt to do me. Not for *offense*,
but for *defense*. That is my motto."

"Alas!" said the queen, feeling humbled.

"I understand you, madame. You suffer because you
see your soul in the hands of a physician—you who re-
belled at times against the idea of abandoning the care of
your body to him. Take courage; be confident. He
wishes to advise you well who has this day given you proof
of such forbearance as that you have received from me.
I desire to love you, madame; I desire that you should be
beloved by all. The ideas I have already submitted to the
king I will discuss with you."

"Doctor, take care!" exclaimed the queen, gravely.
"You caught me in your snare; after having terrified the
woman, you think to control the queen."

"No, madame," answered Gilbert; "I am not a con-
temptible speculator. I have ideas of my own; and I can
conceive that you have yours. I must, from this very
moment, repel this accusation—one that you would forever make against me—that I had intimidated you in order
to subjugate your reason. I will say more, that you are
the first woman in whom I have found united all the passions of a woman and all the commanding qualities of a
man. You may be at the same time a woman and a friend.
All humanity might be concentrated in you, were it necessary. I admire you, and I will serve you. I will serve
you without any remuneration from you, merely for the
sake of studying you, madame. I will do still more for
your service. In case I should seem to you to be a too
inconvenient piece of palace furniture, or if the impression
made by the scene of to-day should not be effaced from

your memory, I shall ask you, I shall pray you to dismiss me."

"Dismiss you!" exclaimed the queen, with a joyful air that did not escape Gilbert.

"Well, then, it is agreed, madame," replied he, with admirable presence of mind. "I shall not even tell the king what I had intended, and I shall depart. Must I go to a great distance to reassure you, madame?"

She looked at him, and appeared surprised at so much self-denial.

"I perceive," said he, "what your majesty thinks. Your majesty, who is better acquainted than is generally thought with the mysteries of the magnetic influence which so much alarmed you a few minutes since—your majesty says to herself that at a distance from her I shall be no less dangerous and troublesome."

"How is that?" exclaimed the queen.

"Yes, I repeat it, madame. He who would be hurtful to any one by the means you have reproached my masters and myself for employing, could practise his hurtful power equally well were the distance a hundred leagues, as at three paces. Fear nothing, madame. I shall not attempt it."

The queen remained thoughtful for a moment, not knowing how to answer this extraordinary man, who made her waver even after she had formed the firmest resolutions.

On a sudden, the noise of steps heard from the end of the gallery made Marie Antoinette raise her head.

"The king," said she, "the king is coming."

"In that case, madame, answer me, I pray you—shall I remain here, or shall I leave you?"

"But——"

"Make haste, madame. I can avoid seeing the king, if you desire it. Your majesty may show me a door by which I can withdraw."

"Remain!" said the queen to him.

Gilbert bowed courteously, while Marie Antoinette endeavored to read in his features to what extent triumph would reveal more than either anger or anxiety.

Gilbert remained perfectly impassible.

"At least," said the queen to herself, "he ought to have manifested some slight satisfaction."

CHAPTER III.

THE king entered the room quickly and heavily, as was his custom.

He had a busy, inquisitive air, that contrasted strangely with the icy rigidity of the queen's demeanor.

The fresh complexion of the king had not abandoned him. Having risen early, and feeling quite proud of the sound health he enjoyed by inhaling the morning air, he was breathing noisily and stepped out vigorously on the floor.

"The doctor," said he, "what has become of the doctor?"

"Good morning, sire. How do you do this morning? Do you feel much fatigued?"

"I have slept six hours; that is my allowance. I am very well. My mind is clear. You look rather pale, madame. I was told that you had sent for the doctor."

"Here is Doctor Gilbert," said the queen, stepping from before the recess of a window, in which the doctor had concealed himself till that moment.

The king's brow at once cleared up. Then:

"Ah! I forgot," said he. "You sent for the doctor. Have you been unwell?"

The queen blushed.

"You blush!" exclaimed Louis XVI.

She turned crimson.

"Another secret," said the king.

"What secret, sire?" exclaimed the queen, haughtily.

"You do not understand me. I tell you that you, who have your own favorite physicians, you would not have sent for Doctor Gilbert, unless you felt the desire, which I know——"

"What desire?"

"You always have to conceal your sufferings from me."

"Ah!" exclaimed the queen, regaining courage.

"Yes," continued Louis XVI.; "but take good care. Monsieur Gilbert is one of my confidential friends; and if you tell him anything, he will be sure to tell it me."

Gilbert smiled.

" As for that, no, sire," said he.

" Well, then, the queen is corrupting my people ! "

Marie Antoinette gave one of those little stifled laughs which imply merely a wish to interrupt a conversation, or that the conversation is very tedious.

Gilbert understood her, but the king did not.

" Let us see, doctor," said he, " as it seems to amuse the queen, tell me what she has been saying to you."

" I was asking the doctor," said Marie Antoinette, in her turn, " why you had sent for him so early. I must, indeed, confess that his presence at Versailles at so unusual an hour perplexes me and makes me uneasy."

" I was waiting for the doctor," replied the king, looking gloomy, " to speak on politics with him."

" Ah ! very well," said the queen.

And she seated herself as if to listen.

" Come, doctor," rejoined the king, taking a step toward the door.

Gilbert made a profound bow to the queen, and was about to follow Louis XVI.

" Where are you going ? " exclaimed the queen. " What ! are you going to leave me ? "

" We are not going to talk on gay subjects, madame. It would be as well for us to spare you so much care."

" Do you call my sorrow care ? " exclaimed the queen, majestically.

" A still better reason for doing so, my dear."

" Remain here ; I wish it," said she. " Monsieur Gilbert, I imagine you will not disobey me."

" Monsieur Gilbert—Monsieur Gilbert ! " exclaimed the king, much vexed.

" Well, then, what is the matter ? "

" Why, Monsieur Gilbert, who was to give me some advice, who was to talk freely to me, according to his conscience, Monsieur Gilbert will now no longer do so."

" And why not ? " exclaimed the queen.

" Because you will be present, madame."

Gilbert made a sort of gesture, to which the queen immediately attributed some important meaning.

" In what manner," said she, to second it, " will Monsieur Gilbert risk to displease me, if he speaks according to his conscience ? "

" It is easily understood, madame," said the king.

"You have a political system of your own. It is not always ours ; so that——"

"So that Monsieur Gilbert, you clearly say, differs essentially from me in my line of politics."

"That must be the case, madame," replied Gilbert, " judging from the ideas which your majesty knows me to entertain. Only your majesty may rest assured that I shall tell the truth as freely in your presence as to the king alone."

"Ah ! that is already something," exclaimed Marie Antoinette.

"The truth is not always agreeable," hastily murmured Louis XVI.

"But it is useful," observed Gilbert.

"Or even uttered with good intention," added the queen.

"In that view of the case, I agree with you," interposed Louis XVI. "But if you were wise, madame, you would leave the doctor entire freedom of speech, and which I need——"

"Sire," replied Gilbert, "since the queen herself calls for the truth, and as I know her majesty's mind is sufficiently noble and powerful not to fear it, I prefer to speak in presence of both my sovereigns."

"Sire," said the queen, "I request it."

"I have full faith in your majesty's good sense," said Gilbert, bowing to the queen. "The subject is the happiness and glory of his majesty the king."

"You are right to put faith in me," said the queen. "Begin, sir."

"All this is very well," continued the king, who was growing obstinate, according to his custom ; "but, in short, the question is a delicate one, and I know well that as to myself you will greatly embarrass me by being present."

The queen could not withhold a gesture of impatience. She rose, then seated herself again, and darted a penetrating and cold look at the doctor, as if to divine his thoughts.

Louis XVI., seeing that there was no longer any means of escaping the ordinary and extraordinary inquisitorial rack, seated himself in his armchair, opposite Gilbert, and heaved a deep sigh.

"What is the point in question?" asked the queen, as soon as this singular species of council had been thus constituted and installed.

Gilbert looked at the king once more, as if to ask him for his authority to speak openly.

"Speak! Good Heaven, go on, sir, since the queen desires it."

"Well, then, madame," said the doctor, "I will inform your majesty in a few words of the object of my early visit to Versailles. I came to advise his majesty to proceed to Paris."

Had a spark fallen among the eight thousand pounds of gunpowder at the Hôtel de Ville, it could not have produced the explosion which those words caused in the queen's heart.

"The king proceeds to Paris! The king! Ah!" and she uttered a cry of horror that made Louis XVI. tremble.

"There!" exclaimed the king, looking at Gilbert, "what did I tell you, doctor?"

"The king!" continued the queen, "the king in the midst of a revolted city! the king amid pitchforks and scythes! the king among the men who massacred the Swiss, and who assassinated Monsieur de Launay and Monsieur de Flesselles! the king crossing the square of the Hôtel de Ville, and treading in the blood of his defenders! You must be deprived of your senses, sir, to speak thus. Oh! I repeat it, you are mad!"

Gilbert lowered his eyes like a man who is restrained by feelings of respect; but he did not answer a single word.

The king, who felt agitated to the bottom of his soul, turned about in his seat like a man undergoing tortures on the gridiron of the Inquisition.

"Is it possible," continued the queen, "that such an idea should have found a place in an intelligent mind—in a French heart? What, sir, do you not then know that you are speaking to the successor of St. Louis—to the great-grandson of Louis XIV.?"

The king was beating the carpet with his feet.

"I do not suppose, however," continued the queen, "that you desire to deprive the king of the assistance of his guards and his army, or that you are seeking to draw him out of his palace, which is a fortress, to expose him,

alone and defenseless, to the blows of his infuriated enemies ; you do not wish to see the king assassinated, I suppose, Monsieur Gilbert ?"

"If I thought that your majesty for a single moment
entertained an idea that I am capable of such treachery,
I should not be merely a madman, but should look upon
myself as a wretch. But Heaven be thanked, madame!
you do not believe it any more than I do. No, I came to
give my king this counsel, because I think the counsel
good, and even superior to any other."

The queen clinched her hand upon her breast with so
much violence as to make the cambric crack beneath its
pressure.

The king shrugged up his shoulders, with a slight movement of impatience.

"But for Heaven's sake," cried he, "listen to him,
madame ; there will be time enough to say no when you
have heard him."

"The king is right, madame," said Gilbert, "for you
do not know what I have to tell your majesties. You
think yourself surrounded by an army which is firm,
devoted to your cause, and ready to die for you ; it is an
error. Of the French regiments, one half are conspiring
with the regenerators to carry out their revolutionary
ideas."

"Sir," exclaimed the queen, "beware ! You are insulting the army !"

"On the contrary, madame," said Gilbert, "I am its
greatest eulogist. We may respect our queen, and be devoted to the king, and still love our country, and devote
ourselves to liberty."

The queen cast a flaming look, like a flash of lightning,
at Gilbert.

"Sir," she said to him, "this language——"

"Yes, this language offends you, madame. I can
readily understand that ; for, according to all probability,
your majesty hears it now for the first time."

"We must, nevertheless, accustom ourselves to it,"
muttered Louis XVI., with the submissive good sense
that constituted his chief strength.

"Never !" exclaimed Marie Antoinette, "never !"

"Let us see. Listen, listen ! I think what the doctor
says is full of reason."

The queen sat down, trembling with rage.

Gilbert continued :

"I was going to say, madame, that I have seen Paris, ay, and that you have not even seen Versailles. Do you know what Paris wishes to do at this moment ?"

"No," said the king, anxiously.

"Perhaps it does not wish to take the Bastile a second time," said the queen, contemptuously.

"Assuredly not, madame," continued Gilbert; "but Paris knows that there is another fortress between the people and their sovereign. Paris proposes to assemble the deputies of the forty-eight districts of which it is composed, and send them to Versailles."

"Let them come ! let them come !" exclaimed the queen, in a tone of ferocious joy. "Oh ! they will be well received here ! "

"Wait, madame," replied Gilbert, "and beware. These deputies will not come alone."

"And with whom will they come ?"

"They will come supported by twenty thousand National Guards."

"National Guards !" said the queen. "What are they ?"

"Ah ! madame, do not speak lightly of that body; it will some day become a power—it will bind and loosen."

"Twenty thousand men ! " exclaimed the king.

"Well, sir," replied the queen, in her turn, "you have here ten thousand men that are worth a hundred thousand rebels ; call them, call them, I tell you ; the twenty thousand wretches will here find their punishment, and the example needed by all this revolutionary slime which I would sweep away, ay, in a week, were I but listened to for an hour."

Gilbert shook his head sorrowfully.

"Oh, madame," said he, "how you deceive yourself, or, rather, how you have been deceived ! Alas ! alas ! have you reflected on it ? A civil war, provoked by a queen ; one only has done this, and she carried with her to the tomb a terrible epithet ; she was called the Foreigner."

"Provoked by me, sir ! How do you understand that ? Was it I who fired upon the Bastile without provocation ? "

"Ah, madame, " cried the king, "instead of advocating violent measures, listen to reason."

" To weakness ! "

" Come now, Antoinette, listen to the doctor," said the
king, austerely. " The arrival of twenty thousand men
is not a trifling matter, particularly if we should have to
fire grape-shot upon them."

Then, turning toward Gilbert :

" Go on, sir," said he ; " go on."

" All these hatreds, which become more inveterate from
estrangement—all these boastings, which become courage
when opportunity is afforded for their realization—all the
confusion of a battle, of which the issue is uncertain—oh !
spare the king, spare yourself, madame, the grief of wit-
nessing them !" said the doctor. " You can, perhaps, by
gentleness disperse the crowd which is advancing. The
crowd wishes to come to the king—let us forestall it ; let
the king go to the crowd. Let him, though now surrounded by his army, give proof to-morrow of audacity
and political genius. Those twenty thousand men of
whom we are speaking might, perhaps, conquer the king
and his army. Let the king go alone and conquer these
twenty thousand men, madame ; they are the people."

The king could not refrain from giving a gesture of assent, which Marie Antoinette at once observed.

" Wretched man !" cried she to Gilbert, " but you do
not, then, perceive the effect which the king's presence in
Paris would produce, under the conditions you require ? "

" Speak, madame."

" It would be saying, ' I approve ;' it would be saying,
' You did right to kill my Swiss ;' it would be saying
' You have acted rightly in murdering my officers, in setting fire to and making my capital stream with blood ; you
have done right in dethroning me. I thank you, gentlemen, I thank you.'"

And a disdainful smile rose to the lips of Marie Antoinette.

" No, madame, your majesty is mistaken."

" Sir ! "

" It would be saying. There has been some justice in
the grief of the people. I am come to pardon. It is I
who am the chief of the nation, and the king. It is I who
am at the head of the French revolution, as in former
days Henry III. placed himself at the head of the League.
Your generals are my officers, your National Guards my

soldiers, your magistrates are my men of business. Instead of urging me onward, follow me, if you are able to do so. The greatness of my stride will prove to you once more that I am the King of France, the successor of Charlemagne.'"

"He is right," said the king, in a sorrowful tone.

"Oh!" exclaimed the queen, "for mercy's sake, listen not to this man—this man is your enemy."

"Madame," said Gilbert, "his majesty himself is about to tell you what he thinks of the words I have spoken."

"I think, sir, that you are the first who, up to this moment, has dared to speak the truth to me."

"The truth!" cried the queen. "Gracious Heaven! what is it you are saying?"

"Yes, madame," rejoined Gilbert, "and impress yourself fully with this fact, that truth is the only torch which can point out and save royalty from the dark abyss into which it is now being hurled."

And while uttering these words, Gilbert bowed humbly, as low as even to the knees of Marie Antoinette.

CHAPTER IV.

FOR the first time the queen appeared deeply moved. Was it from the reasoning, or from the humility, of the doctor?

Moreover, the king had risen from his seat with a determined air; he was thinking of the execution of Gilbert's project.

However, from the habit which he had acquired, of doing nothing without consulting the queen:

"Madame," said he to her, "do you approve it?"

"It appears it must be so," replied the queen.

"I do not ask you for any abnegation," said the king.

"What is it, then, you ask?"

"I ask you for the expression of a conviction which will strengthen mine."

"You ask of me a conviction?"

"Yes."

"Oh! if it be only that I am convinced, sir."

"Of what?"

"That the moment has arrived which will render monarchy the most deplorable and the most degrading position which exists in the whole world."

"Oh!" said the king, "you exaggerate; deplorable, I will admit, but degrading, that is impossible."

"Sir, the kings, your forefathers, have bequeathed to you a very mournful inheritance," said the queen, sorrowfully.

"Yes," said Louis XVI., "an inheritance which I have the grief to make you share, madame."

"Be pleased to allow me, sire," said Gilbert, who truly compassionated the great misfortunes of his fallen sovereigns; "I do not believe that there is any reason for your majesty to view the future in such terrific colors as you have depicted it. A despotic monarchy has ceased to exist, a constitutional empire commences."

"Ah, sir," said the king, "and am I a man capable of founding such an empire in France?"

"And why not, sire?" cried the queen, somewhat comforted by the last words of Gilbert.

"Madame," replied the king, "I am a man of good sense and a learned man. I see clearly, instead of endeavoring to see confusedly into things, and I know precisely all that is necessary for me to know, to administer the government of this country. From the day on which I shall be precipitated from the height of the inviolability of an absolute prince—from the day on which it shall be allowed to be discovered that I am a mere plain man—I lose all the factitious strength which alone was necessary to govern France, since, to speak truly, Louis XIII., Louis XIV., and Louis XV. sustained themselves completely, thanks to this factitious strength. What do the French now require? A master. I feel that I am only capable of being a father. What do the revolutionists require? A sword. I do not feel that I have strength enough to strike."

"You do not feel that you have strength to strike!" exclaimed the queen, "to strike people who are destroying the property of your children, and who would carry off, even from your own brow, one after the other, every gem that adorns the crown of France!"

"What answer can I make to this?" calmly said Louis XVI. "Would you have me reply, No? By so doing, I should raise up in your mind one of those storms which are the discomfort of my life. You know how to hate. Oh, so much the better for you. You know how to be unjust, and I do not reproach you with it. It is a great quality in those who have to govern."

"Do you, perchance, consider me unjust toward the revolution? Now, tell me that?"

"In good faith, yes."

"You say yes, sire? you say yes?"

"If you were the wife of a plain citizen, my dear Antoinette, you would not speak as you do."

"I am not one."

"And that is the reason for my excusing you; but that does not mean that I approve your course. No, madame, no, you must be resigned; we succeeded to the throne of France at a period of the storm and tempest. We ought to have strength enough to push on before us that car armed with scythes, and which is called Revolution, but our strength is insufficient."

"So much the worse," said Marie Antoinette, "for it is over our children that it will be driven."

"Alas! that I know; but at all events we shall not urge it forward."

"We will make it retrograde, sire?"

"Oh!" cried Gilbert, with a prophetic accent, "beware, madame; in retrograding it will crush you."

"Sir," said the queen, impatiently, "I observe that you carry the frankness of your counsels very far."

"I will be silent, madame."

"Oh! good heaven! let him speak on," said the king. "What he has now announced to you, if he has not read it in twenty newspapers during the last eight days, it is because he has not chosen to read them. You should, at least, be thankful to him that he does not convey the truths he utters in a bitter spirit."

Marie Antoinette remained silent for a moment; then, with a deep-drawn sigh:

"I will sum up," she said, "or, rather, I will repeat my arguments. By going to Paris voluntarily it will be sanctioning all that has been done there."

"Yes," replied the king, "I know that full we. "

"Yes, it would be humiliating—disowning your army, which is preparing to defend you."

"It is to spare the effusion of French blood," said the doctor.

"It is to declare that henceforward tumultuous risings and violence may oppose such a direction to the will of the king as may best suit the views of insurgents and traitors."

"Madame, I believe," said Gilbert, "that you had just now the goodness to acknowledge that I had had the good fortune to convince you."

"Yes, I just now did acknowledge it ; one corner of the veil had been raised up before me. But now, sir—oh, now that I am becoming blind, as you have termed it, and I prefer looking into my own mind to see reflected there those splendors to which education, tradition, and history have accustomed me, I prefer considering myself still a queen than to feel myself a bad mother to this people who insult and hate me."

"Antoinette ! Antoinette !" cried Louis XVI., terrified at the sudden paleness which pervaded the queen's face, and which was nothing more than the precursor of a terrible storm of anger.

"Oh ! no, no, sire, I will speak !" replied the queen.

"Beware, madame !" said he.

And with a glance, the king directed the attention of Marie Antoinette to the presence of the doctor.

"Oh ! this gentleman knows all that I was about to say ; he knows even everything I think, said the queen, with a bitter smile at the recollection of the scene which had just before occurred between her and the doctor. "And, therefore, why should I restrain myself ? This gentleman, moreover, has been taken by us for our confidant, and I know not why I should have any fear of speaking. I know that you are carried, dragged away, like the unhappy prince in my dear old German ballads. Whither are you going ? Of that I know nothing ; but you are going whence you will never return."

"Why, no, madame ; I am going simply and plainly to Paris," replied Louis XVI.

Marie Antoinette raised her shoulders.

"Do you believe me to be insane ?" said she, in a voice of deep irritation. "You are going to Paris ? 'Tis well. Who tells you that Paris is not an abyss which I see not, but which I can divine ? Who can say whether, in the tumultuous crowd by which you will necessarily be surrounded, you will not be killed ? Who knows from whence a chance shot may proceed ? Who knows, amid a hundred thousand upraised and threatening hands, which it is that has directed the murderous knife ? "

" Oh, on that head you need not have the slightest apprehension. They love me ! " exclaimed the king.

" Oh, say not that, sire, or you will make me pity you. They love you, and they kill, they assassinate, they massacre those who represent you on the earth ; you, a king—you, the image of God. Well, the governor of the Bastile was your representative ; he was the image of the king. Be well assured of this, and I shall not be accused of exaggeration when I say it : If they have killed De Launay, that brave and faithful servant, they would have killed you, sire, had you been in his place, and much more easily than they killed him, for they know you, and know that instead of defending yourself, you would have bared your breast to them."

" Conclude," said the king.

" But I had thought that I had concluded, sire."

" They will kill me ? "

" Yes, sire."

" Well ? "

" And my children ! " exclaimed the queen.

Gilbert thought it time that he should interfere.

" Madame," said he, " the king will be so much respected at Paris, and his presence will cause such transports, that if I have a fear, it is not for the king, but for those fanatics who will throw themselves to be crushed beneath his horses' feet, like the Indian fakirs beneath the car of their idol."

" Oh, sir, sir ! " cried Marie Antoinette.

" This march to Paris will be a triumph, madame."

" But, sire, you do not reply."

" It is because I agree somewhat with the doctor, madame."

" And you are impatient, are you not, to enjoy this great triumph ? "

" And the king, in this case, would be right," said Gilbert : " for this impatience would be a further proof of the profoundly just discrimination with which his majesty judges men and things. The more his majesty shall hasten to accomplish this, the greater will his triumph be."

"Yes, you believe that, sir?"

"I am positive it will be so. For the king, by delaying it, would lose all the advantage to be derived from its spontaneousness. But reflect, madame, reflect, that the initiative of this measure may proceed from another quarter, and such a request would change, in the eyes of the Parisians, the position of his majesty, and would give him, in some measure, the appearance of acceding to an order."

"There, hear you that?" exclaimed the queen. "The doctor acknowledges it—they would order you. Oh, sire, think of that."

"The doctor does not say that they have ordered, Madame."

"Patience—patience! only delay a little, sire, and the request, or, rather, the order, will arrive."

Gilbert slightly compressed his lips with a feeling of vexation, which the queen instantly caught, athough it was almost as evanescent as the lightning.

"What have I said!" murmured she. "Poor simpleton! I have been arguing against myself."

"In what, madame?" inquired the king.

"In this—that by a delay I should make you lose the advantage of your initiative; and, nevertheless, I have to ask for a delay."

"Ah, madame, ask everything, exact anything, excepting that."

"Antoinette," said the king, taking her hand, "you have sworn to ruin me."

"Oh, sire!" exclaimed the queen, in a tone of reproach, which revealed all the anguish of her heart. "And can you speak thus to me?"

"Why, then, do you attempt to delay this journey?" asked the king.

"Consider truly, madame, that under such circumstances, the fitting moment is everything—reflect on the importance of the hours which are flying past us at such a period, when an enraged and furious people are counting them anxiously as they strike."

"Not to-day, Monsieur Gilbert; to-morrow, sire, oh, to-morrow! grant me till to-morrow. and I swear to you I will no longer oppose this journey."

"A day lost," murmured the king.

"Twenty-four long hours," said Gilbert; reflect on that, Madame."

"Sire, it must be so," rejoined the queen, in a supplicating tone.

"A reason—a reason!" cried the king.

"None, but my despair, sire—none, but my tears—none, but my entreaties."

"But between this and to-morrow what may happen? Who can tell this?" said the king, completely overcome by seeing the queen's despair.

"And what is there that could happen?" said the queen, at the same time looking at Gilbert with an air of entreaty.

"Oh," said Gilbert, "out yonder—nothing yet. A hope, were it even as vague as a cloud, would suffice to make them wait patiently till to-morrow; but——"

"But it is here, is it not?" said the king.

"Yes, sire, it is here that we have to apprehend."

"It is the Assembly?"

Gilbert gave an affirmative nod.

"The Assembly," continued the king, "with such men as Monsieur Monnier, Monsieur Mirabeau, and Monsieur Sieyès, is capable of sending me some address which would deprive me of all the advantage of my good intentions."

"Well, then," exclaimed the queen, with gloomy fury, "so much the better, because you would then refuse—because then you would maintain your dignity as a king—because then you would not go to Paris, and if we must here sustain a war, well, here will we sustain it—because, if we must die, we will die here, but as illustrious and unshrinking monarchs—which we are—as kings, as masters, as Christians who put their trust in God, from whom we hold the crown."

On perceiving this feverish excitement of the queen, Louis XVI. saw that there was nothing to be done but to yield to it.

He made a sign to Gilbert, and advancing to Marie Antoinette, whose hand he took:

"Tranquilize yourself, madame," said he to her; "all

shall be done as you desire. You know, my dear wife, that I would not do anything which would be displeasing to you, for I have the most unbounded affection for a woman of your merit, and, above all, of your virtue."

And Louis XVI. accentuated these last words with inexpressible nobleness, thus exalting with all his power the so much calumniated queen, and that in the presence of a witness capable, should it be requisite, of properly reporting all he had heard and seen.

This delicacy profoundly moved Marie Antoinette, who, grasping with both hands the hand which the king held out to her:

"Well, then, only till to-morrow, sire—no later; that shall be the last day; but I ask you that as a favor on my knees. To-morrow, at the hour which may please you, I swear to you you shall set out for Paris."

"Take care, madame, the doctor is a witness," said the king, smiling.

"Sire, you have never known me to forfeit my word," replied the queen.

"No, but there is only one thing I acknowledge——"

"What is that?"

"It is, that I am anxious, resigned as you appear to be, to know why you have asked me for this delay of twenty-four hours. Do you expect some news from Paris?—some intelligence from Germany? Is there anything——"

"Do not question me, sire."

"The king was as inquisitive as Figaro was lazy; anything that excited his curiosity delighted him.

"Is there any question as to the arrival of troops—of a reinforcement—of any political combination?"

"Sire, sire!" murmured the queen, in a reproachful tone.

"It is a question of——"

"There is no question in the matter," replied the queen.

"Then it is a secret?"

"Well, then, yes; the secret of an anxious woman, that is all."

"A caprice, is it not?"

"Caprice, if you will."

"The supreme law."

"That is true! Why does it not exist in politics as in

philosophy ? Why are kings not permitted to make their political caprices supreme laws ? "

"It will come to that, you may rest assured. As to myself, it is already done," said the king, in a jocose tone. "Therefore, till to-morrow."

" Till to-morrow !" sorrowfully rejoined the queen.

" Do you keep the doctor with you ? " asked the king.

" Oh, no, no !" cried the queen, with a sort of eagerness, which made Gilbert smile.

"I will take him with me, then."

Gilbert bowed a third time to the Queen Marie Antoinette, who, this time, returned his salutation more as a woman than a queen.

Then, as the king was going toward the door, he followed the king.

"It appears to me," said the king, as they proceeded along the gallery, " that you are on good terms with the queen, Monsieur Gilbert."

" Sire," replied the doctor, " it is a favor for which I am indebted to your majesty."

" Long live the king !" cried the courtiers, who already thronged the antechambers.

" Long live the king ! " repeated a crowd of officers and foreign soldiers in the courtyard, who were eagerly hastening toward the palace doors.

These acclamations, which became louder as the crowd increased, gave greater delight to the heart of Louis XVI. than any he had before received, although he had so frequently been greeted in the same manner.

As to the queen, still seated where the king had left her, near the window, and where she had just passed such agonizing moments, when she heard the cries of devotedness and love which welcomed the king as he passed by, and which gradually died away in the distance, under the porticoes, or beneath the thickets of the park :

" Long live the king !" cried she ; "yes, long live the king ! The king will live, and that, in despite of thee, infamous Paris ! thou odious gulf, thou sanguinary abyss, thou shalt not swallow up this victim ! I will drag him from thee, and that with this little, this weak arm. It threatens thee at this moment—it devotes thee to the execration of the world, and to the vengeance of God !"

And pronouncing these words with a violence of hatred

which would have terrified the most furious friends of the
revolution, could they have seen and heard her, the queen
stretched forth toward Paris her weak arm, which shone
from beneath the lace which surrounded it like a sword
starting from its scabbard.

Then she called Mme. de Campan, the lady-in-waiting
in whom she placed the most confidence, and shutting
herself up with her in her cabinet, ordered that no one
should be admitted to her presence.

CHAPTER V.

THE following morning the sun rose brilliant and pure
as on the preceding day.   Its bright rays gilded the marble
and the gravel walks of Versailles.

The birds, grouped in thousands on the first trees of the
park, saluted, with their deafening songs, the new and
balmy day of joy thus promised to their love.

The queen had risen at five o'clock.   She had given
orders that the king should be requested to go to her
apartment as soon as he should wake.

Louis XVI., somewhat fatigued from having received a
deputation of the Assembly, which had come to the palace
the preceding evening, and to which he had been obliged
to reply—this was the commencement of speech-making—
Louis XVI. had slept somewhat later than usual to recover
from his fatigue, and that it might not be said that he was
not as vigorous as ever.

Therefore, he was scarcely dressed when the queen's
message was delivered to him ; he was at that moment
putting on his sword.   He slightly knit his brow.

"What !" said he, "is the queen already up ? "

"Oh, a long time ago, sire."

"Is she again ill ?"

"No, sire."

"And what can the queen want so early in the morning ? "

"Her majesty did not say."

The king took his first breakfast, which consisted in a
bowl of soup and a little wine, and then went to the queen's
apartment.

He found the queen full dressed as for a ceremonious

reception--beautiful, pale, imposing. She welcomed her husband with that cold smile which shone like a winter's sun upon the cheeks of the queen, as when in the grand receptions at court it was necessary she should cast some rays upon the crowd.

The king could not comprehend the sorrow which pervaded that smile and look. He was already preparing himself for one thing, that is to say, the resistance of Marie Antoinette to the project which had been proposed the day before.

"Again some new caprice," thought he.

And this was the reason for his frowning.

The queen did not fail, by the first words she uttered, to strengthen this opinion.

"Sire," said she, "since yesterday I have been reflecting much——"

"There, now—now it is coming!" cried the king.

"Dismiss, if you please, all who are not our intimate friends," said the queen.

The king, though much annoyed, ordered his officers to leave the room.

One only of the queen's women remained ; it was Mme. Campan.

Then the queen, laying both her beautiful hands on the king's arm, said to him :

"Why are you dressed already ? That was wrong."

"How wrong ? and why ?"

"Did I not send word to you not to dress yourself until you had been here ? I see you have already your coat on and your sword. I had hoped you would have come in your dressing-gown."

The king looked at her, much surprised.

This fantasy of the queen awakened in his mind a crowd of strange ideas, the novelty of which only rendered the improbability still stronger.

His first gesture was one of mistrust and uneasiness.

"What is it that you wish ?" said he. "Do you pretend to retard or prevent that which we had yesterday agreed upon ?"

"In no way, sire."

"Let me entreat you not to jest on a matter of so serious a nature. I ought and I will go to Paris. I can no longer avoid it. My household troops are prepared. The

persons who are to accompany me were summoned last night
to be ready."

"Sire, I have no pretensions of that nature, but——"

"Reflect," said the king, working himself up by degrees
to gain courage, "reflect that the intelligence of my intended journey must have already reached the Parisians—
that they have prepared themselves—that they are expect-
ing me—that the very favorable feelings, as were predicted
to us, that this journey has excited in the public mind, may
be changed into dangerous hostility. Reflect, in fine——"

"But, sire, I do not at all contest what you have done
me the honor to say to me. I resigned myself to it yesterday—this morning I am still resigned."

"Then, madame, why all this preamble?"

"I do not make any."

"Pardon me, pardon me; then, why all these questions
regarding my dress, my projects?"

"As to your dress that I admit," said the queen, endeavoring again to smile; but that smile, from so frequently fading away, became more and more funereal.

"What observations have you to make upon my dress?"

"I wish, sire, that you would take off your coat."

"Do you not think it becoming? It is a silk coat of a
violet color. The Parisians are accustomed to see me
dressed thus: they like to see me in this, with which,
moreover, the blue ribbon harmonizes well. You have
often told me so yourself."

"I have, sire, no objections to offer to the color of your
coat."

"Well, then?"

"But to the lining."

"In truth you puzzle me with that eternal smile. The
lining—what jest——"

"Alas! I no longer jest."

"There—now you are feeling my waistcoat; does that
displease you too? White taffeta and silver, the embroidery worked by your own hand—it is one of my favorite
waistcoats."

"I have nothing to say against the waistcoat, neither."

"How singular you are! Is it, then, the frill or the
embroidered cambric shirt that offends you? Why must
I not appear in full dress when I am going to visit my
good city of Paris?"

A bitter smile contracted the queen's lips; the nether lip particularly, that which the Austrian was so much reproached for; it became thicker, and advanced as if it were swelled by all the venom of hatred and of anger.

"No," said she, "I do not reproach you for being so well dressed, sire, but it is the lining—the lining, I say again and again."

"The lining of my embroidered coat! Ah, will you at least explain yourself?"

"Well, then, I will explain. The king, hated, considered an incumbrance, who is about to throw himself into the midst of seven hundred thousand Parisians, inebriated with their triumph and their revolutionary ideas, the king is not a prince of the Middle Ages, and yet he ought to make his entry this day into Paris in a good iron cuirass, in a helmet of good Milan steel; he should protect himself in such a way that no ball, no arrow, no stone, no knife, could reach his person."

"That is in fact true," said Louis XVI., pensively; but, my good friend, as I do not call myself nor Charles the Eighth, nor Francis the first, nor even Henry the fourth, as the monarchy of my day is one of velvet and of silk, I shall go naked under my silken coat, or to speak more correctly, I shall go with a good mark at which they may aim their balls, for I wear the jewel of my orders just over my heart."

The queen uttered a stifled groan.

"Sire," said she, "we begin to understand each other. You shall see, you shall see that your wife jests no longer."

She made a sign to Mme. Campan, who had remained at the further end of the room, and the latter took from a drawer of the queen's chiffonier a wide, oblong flat parcel wrapped up in a silken cover.

"Sire," said the queen, "the heart of the king belongs, in the first place, to France, that is true; but I fully believe that it belongs to his wife and children. For my part, I will not consent that this heart should be exposed to the balls of the enemy—I have adopted measures to save from every danger my husband, my king, the father of my children."

While saying this, she unfolded the silk which covered it, and displayed a waistcoat of fine steel mail, crossed with such marvelous art that it might have been thought an

Arabian watered stuff, so supple and elastic was its tissue,
so admirable the play of its whole surface.

"What is that?" said the king.

"Look at it, sire."

"A waistcoat, it appears to me."

"Why, yes, sire."

"A waistcoat that closes up to the neck."

"With a small collar, intended, as you see, to line the
collar of the waistcoat or the cravat."

The king took the waistcoat in his hands and examined
it very minutely.

The queen, on observing this eagerness, was perfectly
transported. The king, on his part, appeared delighted,
counting the rings of this fairy net which undulated beneath his fingers with all the malleability of knitted wool.

"Why," exclaimed he, "this is admirable steel!"

"Is it not, sire?"

"I really cannot imagine where you can have procured
this."

"I bought it last night, sire, of a man who long since
wished me to purchase it of him, in the event of your
going out on a campaign."

"It is admirable, admirable!" repeated the king, examining it as an artist.

"And it will fit you as well as a waistcoat made by your
tailor, sire."

"Oh! do you believe that?"

"Try it on."

The king said not a word, but took off his violet-colored
coat.

The queen trembled with joy; she assisted Louis XVI.
in taking off his orders, and Mme. Campan the rest.

The king, however, unbuckled his sword, and laid it on
the table.

If any one at that moment had contemplated the face
of the queen, they would have seen it lighted up by one
of those triumphant smiles which supreme felicity alone
bestows.

The king allowed her to divest him of his cravat, and
the delicate fingers of the queen placed the steel collar round
his neck.

Then Marie Antoinette herself fastened the hooks of his
corselet, which adapted itself beautifully to the shape of

the body, being lined throughout with a fine doe-skin for the purpose of preventing any uncomfortable pressure from the steel.

This waistcoat was longer than an ordinary cuirass ; it covered the whole body.

With the waistcoat and shirt over it, it did not increase the volume of the body even half a line. It did not, in the slightest degree, inconvenience any movement of the wearer.

"Is it very heavy ? " asked the queen.

" No."

"Only see, my king, it is a perfect wonder, is it not ? " said the queen, clapping her hands, and turning to Mme. de Campan, who was just buttoning the king's ruffles.

Mme. de Campan manifested her joy in as artless a manner as did the queen.

"I have saved my king !" cried Marie Antoinette. "Test this invisible cuirass, prove it, place it upon a table, try if you can make any impression upon it with a knife ; try if you can make a hole through it with a ball— try it—try it !"

"Oh !" exclaimed the king, with a doubting air.

" Only try it," repeated she, with enthusiasm.

"I would willingly do so from curiosity," replied the king.

"You need not do so ; it would be superfluous, sire."

"How, it would be superfluous that I should prove to you the excellence of your wonder ?"

"Ah! thus it was with all the men. Do you believe that I would have given faith to the judgment of another —of an indifferent person when the life of my husband, the welfare of France was in question ?"

"And yet, Antoinette, it seems to me that this is precisely what you have done—you have put faith in another."

She shook her head with a delightful playful obstinacy.

"Ask her," said she, pointing to the woman who was present, "ask our good Campan there what we have done this morning ?"

"What was it, then ? Good Heaven !" ejaculated the king, completely puzzled.

"This morning—what am I saying—last night, after dismissing all the attendants, we went, like two mad-brained women, and shut ourselves up in her room, which is at the far end of the wing occupied by the pages. Now the pages were sent off last night to prepare the apartments at Rambouillet, and we felt well assured that no one could interrupt us before we had executed our project."

"Good Heaven! you really alarm me! What were the designs then of these two Judiths?"

"Judith effected less, and certainly with less noise. But for that the comparison would be marvelously appropriate. Campan carried the bag which contained this breastplate; as for me, I carried a long hunting-knife which belonged to my father, that infallible blade which killed so many wild boars."

"Judith! still Judith!" cried the king, laughing.

"Oh! Judith had not the heavy pistol which I took from your armory, and which I made Weber load for me."

"A pistol!"

"Undoubtedly. You ought to have seen us running in the dark—startled, agitated at the slightest noise—avoiding everybody for fear of their being indiscreet, creeping like two little mice along the deserted corridors.

"Campan locked three doors and placed a mattress against the last, to prevent our being overheard; we put the cuirass on one of the figures which they use to stretch my gowns on, and placed it against a wall. And I, with a firm hand, too, I can assure you, struck the breastplate with the knife; the blade bent, flew out of my hand, and bounding back, stuck into the floor, to our great terror."

"The deuce!" exclaimed the king.

"Wait a little."

"Did it not make a hole?" asked Louis XVI.

"Wait a little, I tell you. Campan pulled the knife out of the board. 'You are not strong enough, madame,' she said, 'and perhaps your hand trembles. I am stronger, as you shall see.' She, therefore, raised the knife, and gave the figure so violent a blow, so well applied, that my poor German knife snapped off short against the steel mail.

"See, here are two pieces, sire. I will have a dagger made for you out of one of them."

"Oh! this is absolutely fabulous," cried the king, "and the mail was not injured?"

"A slight scratch on the exterior ring, and there are three, one over the other."

"I should like to see it."

"You shall see it."

And the queen began to undress the king again with wonderful celerity, in order that he might the sooner admire her idea and her high feats in arms.

"Here is a place that is somewhat damaged, it would appear to me," said the king, pointing to a slight depression over a space of about an inch in circumference.

"That was done by the pistol-ball, sire."

"How, you fired off a pistol loaded with ball—you?"

"Here is the ball, completely flattened, and still black. Here, take it, and now do you believe that your life is in safety?"

"You are my tutelar angel," said the king, who began slowly to unhook the mailed waistcoat, in order to examine more minutely the traces left by the knife and the pistol-shot.

"Judge of my terror, dear king," said Marie Antoinette, "when on the point of firing the pistol at the breastplate. Alas! the fear of the report, that horrible noise which you know has so frightful an effect upon me, was nothing; but, it appeared to me, that in firing at the waistcoat destined to protect you, I was firing at you, yourself; I was afraid of wounding you; I feared to see a hole in the mail, and then my efforts, my trouble, my hopes were forever lost."

"My dear wife," said Louis XVI., having completely unhooked the coat of mail and placed it on the table, "what gratitude do I not owe you!"

"Well, now, what is it you are doing?" asked the queen.

And she took the waistcoat and again presented it to the king.

But he, with a smile, replete with nobleness and kindness:

"No," said he, "I thank you."

"You refuse it?" said the queen.

"I refuse it."

"Oh! but reflect a moment, sire."

"Sire!" cried Mme. Campan, in a supplicating tone, "but 'tis your salvation—'tis your life!"

"That is possible," said the king.

"You refuse the succor which God himself has sent us?"

"Enough! enough!" said the king.

"Oh! you refuse! you refuse!"

"Yes; I refuse."

"But they will kill you."

"My dear Antoinette, when gentlemen in this eighteenth century are going out to battle, they wear a cloth coat, waistcoat, and shirt; this is all they have to defend them against musket-balls; when they go upon the field of honor to fight a duel, they throw off all but their shirt, that is for the sword. As for myself, I am the first gentleman of my kingdom; I will do neither more nor less than my friends; and there is more than this—while they wear cloth, I alone have the right to wear silk. Thanks, my good wife; thanks, my good queen—thanks."

"Ah!" exclaimed the queen, at once despairing and delighted, "why cannot his army hear him speak thus?"

As to the king, he quietly completed his toilet, without even appearing to understand the act of heroism he had just performed.

"Is the monarchy, then, lost?" murmured the queen, "when we can feel so proudly at such a moment?"

CHAPTER VI.

On leaving the queen's apartment, the king immediately found himself surrounded by all the officers and all the persons of his household who had been appointed by him to attend him on his journey to Paris.

The principal personages were MM. de Beauvau, de Villeroy, de Nesle, and d'Estaing.

Gilbert was waiting, in the middle of the crowd, till Louis XVI. should perceive him, were it only to cast a look upon him in passing.

It could be easily perceived that the whole of the throng there present were still in doubt, and that they could not credit that the king would persist in following up the resolution he had come to.

"After breakfast, gentlemen," said the king, "we will set out."

Then, perceiving Gilbert:

"Ah! you are there, doctor," he continued, "you know that I take you with me."

"At your orders, sire."

The king went into his cabinet, where he was engaged two hours.

He afterward attended mass with all his household; then, at about nine o'clock he sat down to breakfast.

The repast was taken with the usual ceremonies, excepting that the queen, who, after attending mass, was observed to be out of spirits, her eyes swelled and red, had insisted on being present at the king's repast, but without partaking of it in the slightest manner, that she might be with him to the last moment.

The queen had brought her two children with her, who already much agitated, doubtless by what the queen had said to them, were looking anxiously from time to time at their father's face, and then at the crowd of officers of the guards who were present.

The children, moreover, from time to time, by order of their mother, wiped away a tear, which every now and then would rise to their eyelids, and the sight of this excited the pity of some and the anger of others, and filled the whole assembly with profound grief.

The king ate on stoically. He spoke several times to Gilbert, without taking his eyes off his plate; he spoke frequently to the queen, and always with deep affection.

At last, he gave instructions to the commanders of his troops.

He was just finishing his breakfast, when an officer came in to announce to him that a compact body of men, on foot, coming from Paris, had just appeared at the end of the grand avenue leading to the Place d'Armes.

On hearing this, the officers and guards at once rushed out of the room. The king raised his head and looked at Gilbert, but seeing that Gilbert smiled, he tranquilly continued eating.

The queen turned pale, and leaned toward M. de Beauvau, to request him to obtain information.

M. de Beauvau ran out precipitately.

The queen then drew near to the window.

Five minutes afterward M. de Beauvau returned.

"Sire," said he, on entering the room, "they are National Guards, from Paris, who, hearing the rumor spread yesterday in the capital of your majesty's intention to visit the Parisians, assembled to the number of some ten thousand, for the purpose of coming out to meet you on the road, and not meeting you so soon as they expected, they have pushed on to Versailles."

"What appears to be their intentions?" asked the king.

"The best in the world," replied M. de Beauvau.

"That matters not," said the queen, "have the gates closed."

"Take good care not to do that," said the king; "it is quite enough that the palace doors remain closed."

The queen frowned, and darted a look at Gilbert.

The latter was awaiting this look from the queen for one half his prediction was already fulfilled. He had promised the arrival of twenty thousand men, and ten thousand had already come.

The king turned to M. de Beauvau.

"See that refreshments be given to these worthy people," said he.

M. de Beauvau went down a second time. He transmitted to the cellarman the order he had received from the king.

After doing this, he went up-stairs again.

"Well?" said the king, in a tone of inquiry.

"Well, sire, your Parisians are in high discussion with the gentlemen of the guards."

"How!" cried the king, "there is a discussion?"

"Oh! one of pure courteousness. As they have been informed that the king is to set out in two hours, they wish to await his departure, and march behind his majesty's carriage."

"But," inquired the queen in her turn, "they are on foot, I suppose?"

"Yes, madame."

"But the king has horses to his carriage and the king travels fast, very fast—you know, Monsieur de Beauvau, that the king is accustomed to traveling very rapidly."

These words, pronounced in the tone the queen pronounced them, implied:

"Put wings to his majesty's carriage."

The king made a sign with his hand to stop the colloquy.

"I will go at a walk."

The queen heaved a sigh which almost resembled a cry of anger.

"It would not be right," tranquilly added Louis XVI., "that I should make these worthy people run, who have taken the trouble to come so far to do me honor. My carriage shall be driven at a walk, and a slow walk, too, so that everybody may be able to follow me."

The whole of the company testified their admiration by a murmur of approbation; but at the same time, there was seen on the countenances of several persons, the reflection of the disapproval which was expressed by the features of the queen, at so much goodness of soul which she considered as mere madness.

A window was opened.

The queen turned round amazed. It was Gilbert, who, in his quality of physician, had only exercised the right which appertained to him of renewing the air of the dining-room, thickened by the odors of the viands and the breathing of two hundred persons.

"What is that?" asked the king.

"Sire," replied Gilbert, "the National Guards are down there on the pavement, exposed to the heat of the sun, and they must feel it very oppressive."

"Why not invite them up-stairs to breakfast with the king?" sarcastically said one of her favorite officers to the queen.

"They should be taken to some shady place—put them into the marble courtyard, into the vestibules, wherever it is cool," said the king.

"Ten thousand men in the vestibules!" exclaimed the queen.

"If they are scattered everywhere, there will be room enough for them," said the king.

"Scattered everywhere!" cried Marie Antoinette, "why, sir, you will teach them the way to your own bedchamber."

This was the prophecy of terror which was to be realized at Versailles before three months had elapsed.

"They have a great many children with them, madame," said Gilbert, in a gentle tone.

"Children!" exclaimed the queen.

"Yes, madame; a great many have brought their children with them, as if on a party of pleasure. The children are dressed as little National Guards, so great is the enthusiasm for this new institution."

The queen opened her lips as if about to speak ; but, almost instantly, she held down her head.

She had felt a desire to utter a kind word ; but pride and hatred had stopped it ere it had escaped her lips.

Gilbert looked at her attentively.

" Ah ! " cried the king, " those poor children. When people bring children with them, it is plain that they have no intention to do harm to the father of a family ; another reason for putting them in a cooler place, poor little things; let them in, let them in."

Gilbert, then gently shaking his head, appeared to say to the queen, who had remained silent :

" There, madame ; that is what *you* ought to have said. I had given you the opportunity ; your kind words would have been repeated, and you would have gained two years of popularity."

The queen comprehended Gilbert's mute language, and a blush suffused her face.

She felt the error she had committed, and immediately excused herself by a feeling of pride and resistance, which she expressed by a glance, as a reply to Gilbert.   During this time, M. de Beauvau was following the king's orders relating to the National Guards.

Then were heard shouts of joy and benediction from that armed crowd admitted by the king's order to the interior of the palace.

The acclamations, the fervent wishes, the loud hurrahs, ascended as a whirlwind to the hall in which the king and queen were seated, whom they reassured with regard to the disposition of the so much dreaded inhabitants of Paris.

" Sire," said M. de Beauvau, " in what order is it that your majesty determines the procession shall be conducted ? "

" And the discussion between the National Guards and my officers ? "

" Oh, sire, it has evaporated, vanished ; those worthy people are so happy that they now say, ' We will go wherever you may please to place us.   The king is our king as much as he is everybody else's king.   Wherever he may be, he is ours."

The king looked at Marie Antoinette, who curled, with an ironical smile, her disdainful lip.

"Tell the National Guards," said Louis XVI., "they may place themselves where they will."

"Your majesty," said the queen, "will not forget that your body-guards have the right of surrounding your carriage."

The officers, who perceived that the king was somewhat undecided, advanced to support the arguments of the queen.

"That is the case, undoubtedly," replied the king. "Well, we shall see."

M. de Beauvau and M. de Villeroy left the room, to take their stations and to give the necessary orders.

The clock of Versailles struck ten.

"Well, well," said the king, "I shall put off my usual labors till to-morrow ; these worthy people ought not to be kept waiting."

The king rose from the table.

Marie Antoinette went to the king, clasped him in her arms, and embraced him. The children clung weeping to their father's neck. Louis XVI., who was much moved, endeavored gently to release himself from them ; he wished to conceal the emotions which would soon have become overpowering.

The queen stopped all the officers as they passed by her, seizing the one by the arm, others by their swords.

"Gentlemen, gentlemen," said she, "I confide in you," And this eloquent exclamation recommended to them to be watchful for the safety of the king, who had just descended the staircase.

All of them placed their hands upon their hearts and upon their swords.

The queen smiled to thank them.

Gilbert remained in the room till almost the last.

"Sir," said the queen to him, "it was you who advised the king to take this step. It was you who induced the king to come to this resolution, in spite of my entreaties. Reflect, sir, that you have assumed a fearful responsibility as regards the wife, as regards the children."

"I am sensible of that," coldly replied Gilbert.

"And you will bring the king back to me safe and unhurt ?" she said, with a solemn gesture.

"Yes, madame."

"Reflect, that you will answer for his safety with your head."

Gilbert bowed.

"Reflect that your head is answerable," cried Marie Antoinette.

"Upon my head be the risk," said the doctor, again bowing. "Yes, madame; and this pledge I should consider as a hostage of but little value, if I considered the king's safety to be at all threatened. But I have said, madame, that it is to a triumph that I this day conduct his majesty."

"I must have news of him every hour," added the queen.

"You shall, madame; and this I swear to you."

"Go, sir—go at once. I hear the drums, the king is about to leave the palace."

Gilbert bowed, and descending the grand staircase, found himself face to face with one of the king's aides-de-camp, who was seeking him by order of his majesty.

They made him get into a carriage which belonged to M. de Beauvau, the grand master of the ceremonies not allowing, as he had not produced proofs of his nobility, that he should travel in one of the king's carriages.

Gilbert smiled, in finding himself alone in a carriage with arms upon its panels, M. de Beauvau being on horseback, curveting by the side of the royal carriage.

Then it struck him that it was ridiculous in him thus to be occupying a carriage on which was painted a princely coronet and armorial bearings.

This scruple was still annoying him, when, from the midst of a crowd of National Guards, who were following the carriage, he heard the following conversation, though carried on in a half whisper, by men who were curiously stretching out their necks to look at him.

"Oh! that one—that is the Prince de Beauvau."

"Why," cried a comrade, "you are mistaken."

"I tell you it must be so, since the carriage has the prince's arms upon it."

"The arms—the arms! I say that means nothing."

"Zounds!" said another, "what do the arms prove?"

"They prove that if the arms of Monsieur de Beauvau are upon the coach, it must be Monsieur de Beauvau who is inside of it."

"Monsieur de Beauvau—is he a patriot?" asked a woman.

"Pooh !" exclaimed the National Guard.

Gilbert again smiled.

"But I tell you," said the first contradictor, "that is not the prince—the prince is stout, and that one is thin ; the prince wears the uniform of a commandant of the guards, that one wears a black coat ; it is his intendant."

A murmur which was by no means favorable to Gilbert rose among the crowd, who had degraded him by giving him this title, which was not at all flattering.

"Why, no, by the devil's horns !" cried a loud voice, the sound of which made Gilbert start ; it was the voice of a man who, with his elbows and his fists, was clearing his way to get near the carriage. "No," said he, "it is neither Monsieur de Beauvau nor his intendant. It is the brave and famous patriot, and even the most famous of all the patriots. Why, Monsieur Gilbert, what the devil are you doing in the carriage of a prince ?"

"Ha ! it is you, Father Billot ?" exclaimed the doctor.

"By Heaven !" replied the farmer, "I took good care not to lose the opportunity."

"And Pitou ?" asked Gilbert.

"Oh ! he is not far off. Halloo ! Pitou, where are you ? Come this way—come quickly !"

And Pitou, on hearing this invitation, managed, by a dexterous use of his shoulders, to slip through the crowd till he reached Billot's side, and then, with admiration, bowed to Gilbert.

"Good-day, Monsieur Gilbert," said he.

"Good-day, Pitou, good-day, my friend."

"Gilbert, Gilbert, who is he ?" inquired the crowd of one another.

"Such is fame," thought the doctor, "well understood at Villers-Cotterets—yes : but at Paris, popularity is everything."

He alighted from the carriage, which continued its onward progress at a walk, while Gilbert moved on with the crowd, on foot, leaning on Billot's arm.

He, in a few words, related to the farmer his visit to Versailles, the good disposition of the king and the royal family ; he in a few minutes preached such a propaganda of royalism to the group by which he was surrounded, that, simple and delighted, these worthy people, who were yet easily induced to receive good impressions, ut-

tered loud and continued shouts of " Long live the king ! "
which, taken up by those who preceded them, soon
reached the head of the line, and deafened Louis XVI. in
his carriage.

" I will see the king ! " cried Billot, electrified.   " I
must get close to him, and see him well—I came all this
way on purpose.   I will judge him by his face—the eye of
an honest man can always speak for itself.   Let us get
nearer to his carriage—Monsieur Gilbert, shall we not ? "

" Wait a little, and it will be easy for us to do so," replied Gilbert, " for I see one of Monsieur de Beauvau's
aides-de-camp, who is seeking for some one, coming this
way."

And, in fact, a cavalier, who, managing his horse with
every sort of precaution, amid the groups of fatigued but
joyous pedestrians, was endeavoring to get near the carriage which Gilbert had just left.

Gilbert called to him.

" Are you not looking, sir, for Doctor Gilbert ? " he
inquired.

" Himself," replied the aide-de-camp.

" In that case, I am he."

" Monsieur de Beauvau sends for you, at the king's
request."

These high-sounding words made Billot's eyes open
widely, and on the crowd they had the effect of making
them open their ranks to allow Gilbert to pass.   Gilbert
glided through them, followed by Billot and Pitou, the
aide-de-camp going before them, who kept on repeating :

" Make room, gentlemen, make room ; let us pass, in
the king's name, let us pass."

Gilbert soon reached the door of the royal carriage,
which was moving onward as if drawn by Merovingian
oxen.

CHAPTER VII.

THUS pushing and thus pushed, but still following M.
de Beauvau's aide-de-camp, Gilbert, Billot, and Pitou at
length reached the carriage, in which the king, accompanied by MM. d'Estaing and de Villeroy, was slowly advancing amid the crowd which continually increased.

Extraordinary, unknown, unheard-of spectacle! for it was the first time that such a one had been seen. All those National Guards from the surrounding villages, impromptu soldiers suddenly sprung up, hastened with cries of joy to greet the king in his progress, saluting him with their benedictions endeavoring to gain a look from him, and then, instead of returning to their homes, taking place in the procession, and accompanying their march toward Paris.

And why? No one could have given a reason for it. Were they obeying an instinct? They had seen, but they wished again to see, this well-beloved king.

For it must be acknowledged that at this period Louis XVI. was an adored king, to whom the French would have raised altars, had it not been for the profound contempt with which Voltaire had inspired them for all altars.

Louis XVI., therefore, had no altars raised to him, but solely because the free-thinkers of that day had too high an esteem for him to inflict upon him such a humiliation.

Louis XVI. perceived Gilbert leaning upon the arm of Billot; behind them marched Pitou, still dragging after him his long saber.

"Ah, doctor!" cried the king, "what magnificent weather, and what a magnificent people!"

"You see, sire," replied Gilbert.

Then, turning toward the king:

"What did I promise your majesty?"

"Yes, sir, yes; and you have worthily fulfilled your promise."

The king raised his head, and with the intention of being heard:

"We move but slowly." said he, "and yet it appears to me that we advance but too rapidly for all that we have to see."

"Sire," said M. de Beauvau, "and yet at the pace your majesty is going you are traveling about one league in three hours. It would be difficult to go more slowly."

In fact, the horses were stopped every moment: harangues and replies were interchanged; the National Guards fraternized—the word was only then invented—with the body-guard of his majesty.

"Ah!" said Gilbert to himself, who contemplated this

singular spectacle as a philosopher, "if they fraternize with the body-guards, it was because before being friends they ha been enemies."

"I say, Monsieur Gilbert," said Billot, in a half whisper, "I have had a good look at the king, I have listened to him with all my ears. Well, my opinion is that the king is an honest man."

And the enthusiasm which animated Billot was so overpowering that he raised his voice in uttering these last words to such a pitch that the king and his staff heard him.

The officers laughed outright.

The king smiled, and then, nodding his head:

"That is praise which pleases me," said he.

These words were spoken loud enough for Billot to hear them.

"Oh, you are right, sire, for I do not give it to everybody," replied Billot, entering at once into conversation with his king, as Michaud, the miller, did with Henry IV.

"And that flatters me so much the more," rejoined the king, much embarrassed at not knowing how to maintain his dignity as a king and speak graciously as a good patriot.

Alas! the poor prince was not yet accustomed to call himself King of the French.

He thought that he was still called the King of France.

Billot, beside himself with joy, did not give himself the trouble to reflect whether Louis, in a philosophical point of view, had abdicated the title of a king to adopt the title of a man. Billot, who felt how much this language resembled rustic plainness, Billot applauded himself for having comprehended the king, and for having been comprehended by him.

Therefore, from that moment Billot became more and more enthusiastic. He drank from the king's looks, according to the Virgilian expression, deep draughts of love for constitutional royalty, and communicated it to Pitou, who, too full of his own love and the superfluity of Billot, it overflowed at first in stentorian shouts, then in more squeaking, and finally in less articulate ones of:

"Long live the king! Long live the father of the people!"

This modification in the voice of Pitou was produced by

degrees in proportion as he became more and more hoarse.

Pitou was as hoarse as a bull-frog when the procession reached the Point du Jour, where the Marquis de Lafayette, on his celebrated white charger, was keeping in order the undisciplined and agitated cohorts of the National Guard, who had from five o'clock that morning lined the road to receive the royal procession.

At this time it was nearly two o'clock.

The interview between the king and this new chief of armed France passed off in a manner that was satisfactory to all present.

The king, however, began to feel fatigued ; he no longer spoke, he contented himself with merely smiling.

The general-in-chief of the Parisian militia could no longer utter a command, he only gesticulated.

The king had the satisfaction to find that the crowd as frequently cried, "Long live the king !" as "Long live Lafayette !" Unfortunately, this was the last time he was destined to enjoy this gratification of his self-love.

During this, Gilbert remained constantly at the door of the king's carriage, Billot near Gilbert, Pitou near Billot.

Gilbert, faithful to his promise, had found means since his departure from Versailles to despatch four couriers to the queen.

These couriers had each been the bearer of good news, for at every step of his journey the king had seen caps thrown up in the air as he passed, only on each of these caps shone the colors of the nation—a species of reproach addressed to the white cockade which the king's guards and the king himself wore in their hats.

In the midst of his joy and his enthusiasm, this discrepancy in the cockades was the only thing which annoyed Billot.

Billot had on his cocked hat an enormous tri-colored cockade.

The king had a white cockade in his hat ; the taste of the subject and the king were not, therefore, absolutely similar.

This idea so much perplexed him that he could not refrain from unburdening his mind upon the subject to Gilbert at a moment when the latter was not conversing with the king.

"Monsieur Gilbert," said he to him, "how is it that his majesty does not wear the national cockade?"

"Because, my dear Billot, either the king does not know that there is a new cockade, or he considers that the cockade he wears ought to be the cockade of the nation."

"Oh, no! oh, no! since his cockade is a white one, and our cockade—ours—is a tri-colored one."

"One moment," said Gilbert, stopping Billot just as he was about to launch with heart and soul into the arguments advanced by the newspapers of the day, "the king's cockade is white, as the flag of France is white. The king is in no way to blame for this. Cockade and flag were white long before he came into the world. Moreover, my dear Billot, that flag has performed great feats, and so has the white cockade. There was a white cockade in the hat of Admiral de Suffren when he reestablished our flag in the East Indies. There was a white cockade in the hat of Assas, and it was by that the Germans recognized him in the night, when he allowed himself to be killed rather than that they should take his soldiers by surprise. There was a white cockade in the hat of Marshal Saxe when he defeated the English at Fontenoy. There was, in fine, a white cockade in the hat of the Prince de Condé, when he beat the Imperialists at Rocroi, at Fribourg, and at Lens. The white cockade has done all this, and a great many other things, my dear Billot, while the national cockade, which will perhaps make a tour round the world, as Lafayette has predicted, has not yet had time to accomplish anything, seeing that it exists only for the three last days. I do not say that it will rest idle, do you understand, but, in short, having as yet done nothing, it gives the king full right to wait till it has done something."

"How! the national cockade has as yet done nothing?" cried Billot; "has it not taken the Bastile?"

"It has," said Gilbert, sorrowfully; "you are right, Billot."

"And that is why," triumphantly rejoined the farmer, "that is why the king ought to adopt it."

Gilbert gave a furious nudge with his elbow into Billot's ribs, for he had perceived the king was listening, and then, in a low tone:

"Are you mad, Billot?" said he: "and against whom

was the Bastile taken, then ? Against royalty, it seems to me. And now you would make the king wear the trophies of your triumph, and the insignia of his own defeat. Madman ! the king is all heart, all goodness, all candor, and you would wish him to show himself a hypocrite ? "

" But," said Billot, more humbly, without, however, giving up the argument altogether, " it was not precisely against the king that the Bastile was taken, it was against despotism."

Gilbert shrugged up his shoulders, but with the delicacy of the superior man, who will not place his foot on his inferior, for fear that he should crush him.

" No," said Billot, again becoming animated, " it is not against our good king that we have fought, but against his satellites."

Now, in those days, they said, speaking politically, satellites instead of saying soldiers, as they said in the theaters, courser instead of horse.

" Moreover," continued Billot, and with some appearance of reason, " he disapproves them, since he comes thus in the midst of us ; and if he disapproves them, he must approve us. It is for our happiness and his honor that we have worked, we, the conquerors of the Bastile."

" Alas ! alas ! " murmured Gilbert, who did not know how to conciliate the appearance of the king's features with that which he knew must be passing in his heart.

As to the king, he began, amid the confused murmurs of the march, to understand some few words of the conversation entered into by his side.

Gilbert, who perceived the attention which the king was paying to the discussion, made every effort to lead Billot on to less slippery ground than that on which he had ventured.

Suddenly the procession stopped ; it had arrived at the Cours de la Reine, at the gate formerly called La Conference, in the Champs Elysées.

There a deputation of electors and aldermen, presided by the new mayor, Bailly, had drawn themselves up in fine array, with a guard of three hundred men, commanded by a colonel, besides at least three hundred members of the National Assembly, taken, as it will be readily imagined, from the ranks of the Tiers Etat.

Two of the electors united their strength and their address to hold in equilibrium a vast salver of gilt plate, upon which were lying two enormous keys, the keys of the city of Paris during the days of Henry IV.

This imposing spectacle at once put a stop to all individual conversation, and every one, whether in the crowd or in the ranks, immediately directed their attention to the speeches about to be pronounced on the occasion.

Bailly, the worthy man of science, the admirable astronomer, who had been made a deputy in defiance to his own will, a mayor in spite of his objections, an orator notwithstanding his unwillingness, had prepared a long speech. This speech had for its exordium, according to the strictest laws of rhetoric, a laudatory encomium on the king, from the coming into power of M. Turgot, down to the taking of the Bastile. Little was wanting, such privilege has eloquence, to attribute to the king the initiative in the acts of the people.

Bailly was delighted with the speech he had prepared, when an incident—it is Bailly himself who relates this incident, in his Memoirs—when an incident furnished him with a new exordium, very much more picturesque than the one he had prepared—the only one, moreover, which remained engraved on the minds of the people, always ready to seize upon good and, above all, fine-sounding phrases, when founded upon a material fact.

While walking toward the place of meeting, with the aldermen and the electors, Bailly was alarmed at the weight of the keys which he was about to present to the king.

"Do you believe," said he, laughingly, "that after having shown these to the king, that I will undergo the fatigue of carrying them back to Paris?"

"What will you do with them, then?" asked one of the electors.

"What will I do with them?" said Bailly; "why, I will give them to you, or I will throw them into some ditch at the foot of a tree."

"Take good care not to do that," cried the elector, completely horrified. "Do you know that these keys are the same which the city of Paris offered to Henry IV., after the siege?" They are very precious, they are inestimable antiquities."

"You are right," rejoined Bailly : " the keys offered to

Henry IV., the conqueror of Paris, and which are now to be offered to Louis XVI., hey? Why, I declare, now," said the worthy mayor to himself, "this would be a worthy antithesis in my speech."

And instantly he took a pencil and wrote above the speech he had prepared the following exordium:

"Sire, I present to your majesty the keys of the good city of Paris. They are the same which were offered to Henry IV. He had reconquered his people; to-day the people have reconquered their king."

The phrase was well turned, and it was also true. It implanted itself in the memories of the Parisians, and of all the speeches, all the works of Bailly, this only survived.

As to Louis XVI., he approved it by an affirmative nod, but coloring deeply at the same time; for he felt the epigrammatic irony which it conveyed, although concealed beneath a semblance of respect and oratorical flourishes.

"Oh! Marie Antoinette," murmured Louis XVI. to himself, "would not allow herself to be deceived by this pretended veneration of Monsieur Bailly, and would reply in a very different manner to that which I am about to do to the untoward astronomer."

And these reflections were the cause why Louis XVI., who had paid too much attention to the commencement of the speech, did not listen at all to the conclusion of it, nor to that of the president of the electors, M. Delavigne, of which he heard neither the beginning nor the end.

However, the addresses being concluded, the king, fearing not to appear sufficiently delighted with her efforts to say that which was agreeable to him, replied in a very noble tone, and without making any allusion to what the orators had said, that the homage of the city of Paris and of the electors was exceedingly gratifying to him.

After which he gave orders for the procession to move on toward the Hôtel de Ville.

But before it recommenced its march, he dismissed his body-guard, wishing to respond by a gracious confidence to the half politeness which had been evinced to him by the municipality through their organs, the president of electors and M. Bailly.

Being thus alone, amid the enormous mass of National Guards and spectators, the carriage advanced more rapidly.

Gilbert and his companion Billot still retained their posts on the right of the carriage.

At the moment when they were crossing the Place Louis XV., the report of a gun was heard, fired from the opposite side of the Seine, and a white smoke arose, like a veil of incense, toward the blue sky, where it suddenly vanished.

As if the report of this musket-shot had found an echo within his breast, Gilbert had felt himself struck, as by a violent blow. For a second his breath failed him, and he hastily pressed his hand to his heart, where he felt a sudden and severe pain.

At the same instant a cry of distress was heard around the royal carriage ; a woman had fallen to the ground, shot through the right shoulder.

One of the buttons of Gilbert's coat, a large steel button, cut diamond fashion, as they were worn at the period, had just been struck diagonally by that same ball.

It had performed the office of a breastplate, and the ball had glanced off from it ; this had caused the painful shock which Gilbert had experienced.

Part of his waistcoat and frill had been torn off by the ball.

This ball, on glancing from the button, had killed the unfortunate woman, who was instantly removed from the spot, bleeding profusely.

The king had heard the shot, but had seen nothing.

He leaned toward Gilbert, and, smiling, said :

"They are burning gunpowder yonder to do me honor."

" Yes, sire," replied Gilbert.

But he was careful not to mention to his majesty the nature of the ovation which they were offering to him.

In his own mind, however, he acknowledged that the queen had reason for the apprehensions she had expressed, since, but for him standing immediately before, and closing the carriage door, as it were, hermetically, that ball, which had glanced off from his steel button, would have gone straight to the king's breast.

And now from what hand had proceeded this so well-aimed shot ?

No one then wished to inquire, so that it will never now be known.

Billot, pale from what he had just seen, his eyes incessantly attracted to the rent made in Gilbert's coat, waistcoat, and frill, Billot excited Pitou to shout as loudly as he could, "Long live the Father of the French!"

The event of the day was so great that this episode was quickly forgotten.

At last Louis XVI. arrived in front of the Hôtel de Ville, after having been saluted on the Pont Neuf by a discharge of artillery, which, at all events, were not loaded with ball.

Upon the façade of the Hôtel de Ville was an inscription, in large letters, black in the daylight, but which, when it was dark, were to form a brilliant transparency. This inscription was the result of the generous lucubrations of the municipal authorities.

The inscription was as follows:

"To Louis XVI., Father of the French, and King of a Free People."

Another antithesis, much more important than the one contained in M. Bailly's speech, and which excited shouts of admiration from all the Parisians assembled in the square.

The inscription attracted the attention of Billot.

But as Billot could not read, he made Pitou read the inscription to him.

Billot made him read it a second time, as if he had not understood it perfectly at first.

Then, when Pitou had repeated the phrase, without varying in a single word:

"Is it that?" cried he, "is it that?"

"Undoubtedly," replied Pitou.

"The municipality has written that the king is a king of a free people?"

"Yes, Father Billot."

"Well, then," exclaimed Billot, "since the nation is free, it has the right to offer its cockade to the king."

And with one bound, rushing before the king, who was then alighting from his carriage at the front steps of the Hôtel de Ville:

"Sire," said he, "you saw on the Pont Neuf that the Henry IV., in bronze, wore the national cockade."

"Well!" cried the king.

" Well, sire, if Henry IV. wears the national cockade, you can wear it, too."

" Certainly," said Louis XVI., much embarrassed, " and if I had one——"

" Well," cried Billot, in a louder tone, and raising his hand, " in the name of the people I offer you this one in the place of yours ; accept it."

Bailly intervened.

The king was pale. He began to see the progressive encroachment. He looked at Bailly, as if to ask his opinion.

" Sire," said the latter, " it is the distinctive sign of every Frenchman."

" In that case, I accept it," said the king, taking the cockade from Billot's hands.

And putting aside his own white cockade, he placed the tri-colored one in his hat.

An immense triumphant hurrah was echoed from the great crowd in the square.

Gilbert turned away his head, much grieved.

He considered that the people were encroaching too rapidly, and that the king did not resist sufficiently.

" Long live the king ! " cried Billot, who thus gave the signal for a second round of applause.

" The king is dead," murmured Gilbert ; " there is no longer a king in France."

An arch of steel had been formed by a thousand swords held up, from the place at which the king had alighted from his carriage to the door of the hall in which the municipal authorities were waiting to receive him.

He passed beneath this arch and disappeared in the gloomy passages of the Hôtel de Ville.

" That is not a triumphal arch," said Gilbert ; " but the caudine forks."

Then, with a sigh :

" Ah ! what will the queen say to this ?"

CHAPTER VIII.

In the interior of the Hôtel de Ville the king received the most flattering welcome ; he was styled the Restorer of Liberty.

Being invited to speak—for the thirst for speeches became every day more intense—and the king wishing, in short, to ascertain the feelings of all present, he placed his hand upon his heart, and said :

" Gentlemen, you may always calculate on my affection."

While he was thus listening in the Hôtel de Ville to the communications from the government—for from that day a real government was constituted in France, besides that of the throne and the National Assembly—the people outside the building were admiring the beautiful horses, the gilt carriage, the lackeys, and the coachman of his majesty.

Pitou, since the entry of the king into the Hôtel de Ville, had, thanks to a louis given by Father Billot, amused himself in making a goodly quantity of cockades, of red and blue ribbons, which he had purchased with the louis, and with these, which were of all sizes, he had decorated the horses' ears, the harness, and the whole equipage.

On seeing this, the imitative people had literally metamorphosed the king's carriage into a cockade shop.

The coachman and the footmen were profusely ornamented with them.

They had, moreover, slipped some dozens of them into the carriage itself.

However, it must be said, that M. de Lafayette, who had remained on horseback, had endeavored to restrain these honest propagators of the national colors, but had not been able to succeed.

And, therefore, when the king came out :

" Oh, oh ! " cried he, on seeing this strange bedizenment of his equipage.

Then, with his hand, he made a sign to M. Lafayette, to approach him.

M. de Lafayette respectfully advanced, lowering his sword as he came near the king.

"Monsieur de Lafayette," said the king to him, "I was looking for you to say to you that I confirm your appointment to the command of the National Guards."

And he got into his carriage amid a universal acclamation.

As to Gilbert, tranquilized henceforward as to the personal safety of the king, he had remained in the hall with Bailly and the electors.

The speechifying had not yet terminated.

However, on hearing the loud hurrahs which saluted the departure of the king, he approached a window, to cast a last glance on the square, and to observe the conduct of his two country friends.

They were both, or, at least, they appeared to be, still on the best terms with the king.

Suddenly, Gilbert perceived a horseman advancing rapidly along the Quay Pelletier, covered with dust, and obliging the crowd, which was still docile and respectful, to open its ranks and let him pass.

The people, who were good and complaisant on this great day, smiled while repeating :

"One of the king's officers—one of the king's officers !"

And cries of "Long live the king !" saluted the officer as he passed on, and women patted his horse's neck, which was white with foam.

This officer at last managed to reach the king's carriage, and arrived there at the moment when a servant was closing the door of it.

"What ! is it you, Charny ?" cried Louis XVI.

And then, in a lower tone :

"How are they all out yonder ?" he inquired.

Then in a whisper :

"The queen ?"

"Very anxious, sire," replied the officer, who had thrust his head completely into the carriage window.

"Do you return to Versailles ?"

"Yes, sire."

"Well, then, tell our friends they have no cause for uneasiness. All has gone off marvelously well."

Charny bowed, raised his head, and perceived M. de Lafayette, who made a friendly sign to him.

Charny went to him, and Lafayette shook hands with

him ; and the crowd, seeing this, almost carried both officer and horse as far as the quay, where, thanks to the
vigilant orders given to the National Guards, a line was
formed to facilitate the king's departure.

The king ordered that the carriage should move out at a
walking pace till it reached the Place Louis XV.   There
he found his body-guards, who were awaiting the return
of the king, and not without impatience ; so that this impatience, in which every one participated, kept on increasing every moment, and the horses were driven on at a pace
which increased in rapidity as they advanced upon the
road to Versailles.

Gilbert, from the balcony of the window, had fully comprehended the meaning of the arrival of this horseman,
although he did not know his person. He readily imagined the anguish which the queen must have suffered,
and especially for the last three hours, for during that
time he had not been able to despatch a single courier to
Versailles, amid the throng by which he was surrounded,
without exciting suspicion or betraying weakness.

He had but a faint idea of all that had been occurring
at Versailles.

We shall now return there with our readers, for we do
not wish to make them read too long a course of history.

The king had received the last courier from the queen
at three o'clock.

Gilbert had found means to despatch a courier just at
the moment the king entered the Hôtel de Ville, under
the arch formed by the swords of the National Guards.

The Countess de Charny was with the queen. The
countess had only just left her bed, which from severe in-
disposition she had kept since the previous day.

She was still very pale. She had hardly strength to
raise her eyes, the heavy lids of which seemed to be constantly falling, weighed down either with grief or shame.

The queen, on perceiving her, smiled, but with that
habitual smile which appears to those familiar with the
court to be stereotyped upon the lips of princes and of
kings.

Then as if overjoyed that her husband was in safety :

"Good news again !" exclaimed the queen to those
who surrounded her ; " may the whole day pass off as
well ! "

Oh, madame," said a courtier, "your majesty alarms yourself too much. The Parisians know too well the responsibility which weighs upon them."

" But, madame," said another courtier, who was not so confiding, "is your majesty well assured as to the authenticity of this intelligence?"

"Oh, yes!" replied the queen. "The person who writes to me has engaged, at the hazard of his head, to be responsible for the safety of the king. Moreover, I believe him to be a friend."

"Oh! if he is a friend," rejoined the courtier, bowing, "that is quite another matter."

Mme. de Lamballe, who was standing at a little distance, approached.

"It is," said she, "the lately appointed physician, is it not?"

"Yes, Gilbert," unthinkingly replied the queen, without reflecting that she was striking a fearful blow at one who stood close beside her.

"Gilbert!" exclaimed Andrée, starting as if a viper had bit her to the heart, "Gilbert, your majesty's friend?"

Andrée had turned round with flashing eyes, her hands clinched with anger and shame, and seemed proudly to accuse the queen, both by her looks and attitude.

"But, however——" said the queen, hesitating.

"Oh, madame, madame!" murmured Andrée, in a tone of the bitterest reproach.

A mortal silence pervaded the whole room, after this mysterious incident.

In the midst of this silence, a light step was heard upon the tesselated floor of the adjoining room.

"Monsieur de Charny!" said the queen, in a half whisper, as if to warn Andrée to compose herself.

Charny had heard—he had seen all—only he could not comprehend it.

He remarked the pallid countenance of Andrée, and the embarrassed air of Marie Antoinette.

It would have been a breach of etiquette to question the queen; but Andrée was his wife, he had the right to question her.

He, therefore, went to her, and in the most friendly tone: "What is the matter, madame?" said he.

Andrée made an effort to recover her composure.

"Nothing, count," she replied.

Charny then turned toward the queen, who, notwith-standing her profound experience in equivocal positions, had ten times essayed to muster up a smile, but could not succeed.

"You appear to doubt the devotedness of this Monsieur Gilbert," said he to Andrée. "Have you any motive for suspecting his fidelity?"

Andrée was silent.

"Speak, madame, speak," said Charny, insistingly.

Then, as Andrée still remained mute:

"Oh, speak, madame!" cried he. "This delicacy now becomes condemnable. Reflect, that on it may depend the safety of our master."

"I do not know, sir, what can be your motive for saying that," replied Andrée.

"You said, and I heard you say it, madame—I appeal, moreover, to the princess"—and Charny bowed to the Princess de Lamballe—"you exclaimed, with an expression of great surprise, 'Gilbert, your majesty's friend.'"

"'Tis true, you did say that, my dear," said the Princess de Lamballe, with her habitual ingenuousness.

Then, going closer to Andrée:

"If you do know anything, Monsieur de Charny is right."

"For pity's sake, madame, for pity's sake!" said Andrée, in an imploring tone, but so low that it could not be heard by any one but the princess.

The princess retired a few steps.

"Oh, good Heaven! it was but a trifling matter," said the queen, feeling that should she any longer delay to interfere she would be failing in propriety. "The countess was expressing her apprehensions, which doubtless were but vague. She had said that it was difficult for a man who had taken part in the American revolution, one who is the friend of Monsieur Lafayette, to be our friend."

"Yes, vague," mechanically repeated Andrée—"very vague."

"A fear of a similar nature to one which had been expressed by one of these gentlemen before the countess had expressed it here," rejoined Marie Antoinette.

And with her eyes she pointed out the courtier whose doubts had given rise to this discussion.

But it required more than this to convince Charny. The great confusion which had appeared on his entering the room, persuaded him that there was some mystery in the affair.

He, therefore, persisted.

"It matters not, madame," said he.   "It seems to me that it is your duty not to express vain fears, but, on the contrary, to state precise facts."

"What, sir," said the queen, with some asperity, "you are returning to that subject."

"Madame!"

"Your pardon, but I find that you are still questioning the Countess de Charny."

"Excuse me, madame," said Charny; "it is from interest for——"

"For your self-love, is it not?   Ah! Monsieur de Charny," added the queen, with an ironical expression, of which the count felt the whole weight, "acknowledge the thing frankly.   You are jealous."

"Jealous! jealous!" cried De Charny, coloring—"but of what?   I ask this of your majesty."

"Of your wife, apparently," replied the queen, harshly.

"Madame!" stammered Charny, perfectly astounded at this unlooked-for attack.

"It is perfectly natural," drily rejoined Marie Antoinette;   "and the countess assuredly is worth the trouble."

Charny darted a look at the queen, to warn her that she was going too far.

But this was useless trouble, superfluous precaution. When this lioness was wounded, and felt the burning pain galling her heart, she no longer knew restraint.

"Yes, I can comprehend your being jealous, Monsieur de Charny; jealous and uneasy; it is the natural state of every soul that loves, and which, consequently, is on the watch."

"Madame!" repeated Charny.

"And, therefore, I," pursued the queen, "I experience precisely the same feelings which you do at this moment. I am at once a prey to jealousy and anxiety."   She emphasized the word jealousy.   "The king is at Paris, and I no longer live."

"But, madame," observed Charny, who could not at all

comprehend the meaning of this storm, the thunder of which appeared to growl more fiercely and the lightning to flash more vividly every moment, "you have just now received news of the king, the news was good, and you must feel more tranquil."

"And did you feel tranquilized when the countess and myself, a moment ago, endeavored to reassure you?"

Charny bit his lip.

Andrée began to raise her hand, at once surprised and alarmed—surprised at what she heard—alarmed at what she thought she understood.

The silence which had ensued after the first question which Charny had addressed to Andrée was now renewed, and the company seemed anxiously awaiting Charny's answer to the queen. Charny remained silent.

"In fact," resumed the queen, with still increasing anger, "it is the destiny of people who love to think only of the object of their affection. It would be happiness to those poor hearts to sacrifice pitilessly everything, yes, everything, to the feeling by which they are agitated. Good Heaven! how anxious am I with regard to the king!"

One of the courtiers ventured to remark that other couriers would arrive.

"Oh, why am I not at Paris, instead of being here? why am I not with the king?" said Marie Antoinette, who had seen that Charny had become agitated since she had been endeavoring to instill that jealousy into his mind which she so violently experienced.

Charny bowed.

"If it be only that, madame," said he, "I will go there; and if, as your majesty apprehends, the king is in any danger, if that valuable life be exposed, you may rely, madame, that it shall not be from not having exposed mine in his defense."

' That I know."

Charny bowed and moved toward the door.

"Sir, sir!" cried Andrée, rushing between Charny and the door, "be careful of yourself."

Nothing was wanting to the completion of this scene but this outburst of the fears of Andrée.

And, therefore, as soon as Andrée had been thus impelled, and in spite of herself, to cast aside her habitual coldness—no sooner had she uttered these imprudent words and evinced this unwonted solicitude, than the queen became frightfully pale.

"Why, madame," she cried to Andrée, "how is this, that you here usurp the part of the queen?"

"Who—I, madame?" stammered Andrée, comprehending that she had, for the first time, allowed to burst forth from her lips the fire which for so long a period had consumed her soul.

"What!" continued Marie Antoinette; "your husband is in the king's service. He is about to set out to seek the king. If he is exposing his life, it is for the king, and when the question is the service of the king, you advise Monsieur de Charny to be careful of himself."

On hearing these appalling words, Andrée was near fainting. She staggered, and would have fallen to the floor had not Charny rushed forward and caught her in his arms.

An indignant look, which Charny could not restrain, completed the despair of Marie Antoinette, who had considered herself an offended rival, but who, in fact, had been an unjust queen.

"The queen is right," at length said Charny, with some effort, "and your movement, madame, was inconsiderate. You have no husband, madame, when the interests of the king are in question; and I ought to be the first to request you to restrain your sensibility, if I presumed that you deigned to feel any alarm for me."

Then, turning toward Marie Antoinette:

"I am at the queen's orders," said he, coldly, "and I set out at once. It is I who will bring you news of the king—good news, madame, or I will not bring any."

Then, having spoken these words, he bowed almost to the ground, and left the room before the queen, moved at once by terror and by anger, had thought of detaining him.

A moment afterward was heard the noise of a horse's hoofs clattering over the pavement of the courtyard, and which was galloping at full speed.

The queen remained motionless, but a prey to internal agitation so much the more terrible from her making the most violent efforts to conceal it.

Some understood, while others could not comprehend

the cause of this agitation, but they all showed that they respected their sovereign's tranquillity.

Marie Antoinette was left to her own thoughts.

Andrée withdrew with the rest from the apartment, abandoning Marie Antoinette to the caresses of her two children, whom she had sent for, and who had been brought to her.

CHAPTER IX.

NIGHT had returned, bringing with it its train of fears and gloomy visions, when suddenly shouts were heard from the front of the palace.

The queen started and rose up. She was not far from a window, which she opened.

Almost at the same instant, servants, transported with joy, ran into the queen's room, crying:

" A courier, madame, a courier ! "

Three minutes afterward, a hussar rushed into the antechamber.

He was a lieutenant dispatched by M. de Charny. He had ridden at full speed from Sèvres.

" And the king ? " said Marie Antoinette.

" His majesty will be here in a quarter of an hour," replied the officer, who was so much out of breath that he could scarcely articulate.

" Safe and well ? " asked the queen.

" Safe, well, and smiling, madame," replied the officer.

" You have seen him, then ? "

" No, madame, but Monsieur de Charny told me so, when he sent me off."

The queen started once more at hearing this name, which chance had thus associated with that of the king.

" I thank you, sir ; you had better rest yourself," said the queen to the young gentleman.

The young officer made his obeisance and withdrew.

Marie Antoinette, taking her children by the hand, went toward the grand entrance of the palace, where were already assembled all the courtiers and the servants.

The penetrating eye of the queen perceived on the first step, a female form attired in white: her elbow leaning

upon the stone balustrade, and looking eagerly into the
darkness, that she might first discern the approach of the
king's carriage.

It was Andrée, whom even the presence of the queen
did not arouse from her fixed gaze.

She who generally was so eager to fly to the side of her
mistress evidently had not seen her, or disdained to appear
to have seen her.

She, then, bore her ill-will for the vivacity which she
had shown that afternoon, and from which cruel vivacity
she had so much suffered ?

Or else, carried away by a powerfully interesting sentiment, she was, with eager anxiety, looking for the return
of Charny, to whom she had manifested so much affectionate apprehension.

A twofold poniard stab to the queen, which deepened a
wound that was still bleeding.

She lent but an absent ear to the compliments and joyful congratulations of her other friends, and the courtiers
generally.

She even felt for a moment her mind abstracted from
the violet grief which had overwhelmed her all the evening.   There was even a respite to the anxiety excited in
her heart by the king's journey, threatened by so many
enemies.

But with her strong mind she soon chased all that was
not legitimate affection from her heart.   At the feet of
God she cast her jealousy.   She immolated her anger and
her secret feelings to the holiness of her conjugal vow.

It was doubtless God who thus endowed her, for her
quiet and support, with this faculty of loving the king,
her husband, beyond every being in the world.

At that moment, at least, she so felt, or thought she
felt it ; the pride of royalty raised the queen above all
terrestrial passions ; love of the king was her egotism.

She had, therefore, driven from her breast all the petty
vengeance of a woman, and the coquettish frivolity of the
lover, when the flambeaus of the escort appeared at the
end of the avenue.

These lights increased in volume every moment, from
the rapidity with which the escort advanced.

They could hear the neighing and the hard breathing
of the horses.   The ground trembled, amid the silence of

the night, beneath the weight of the squadrons which surrounded and followed the king's carriage.

The gates were thrown open, the guards rushed forth to receive the king with shouts of enthusiasm. The carriage rolled sonorously over the pavement of the great courtyard.

Dazzled, delighted, fascinated, strongly excited by the varied emotions she had experienced during the day, by those which she then felt, the queen flew down the stairs to receive the king.

Louis XVI., as soon as he had alighted from his carriage, ascended the staircase with all the rapidity which was possible, surrounded as he was by his officers, all agitated by the events of the day and their triumph ; while in the courtyard, the guards, mixing unceremoniously with the grooms and equerries, tore from the carriages and the harness all the cockades which the enthusiasm of the Parisians had attached to them.

The king and the queen met upon a marble landing. The queen, with a cry of joy and love, several times pressed the king to her heart.

She sobbed as if, on thus meeting him, she had believed she was never again to see him.

Yielding thus to the emotions of an overflowing heart, she did not observe the silent pressure of their hands which Charny and Andrée had just exchanged.

This pressure of the hand was nothing ; but Andrée was at the foot of the steps ; she was the first Charny had seen and touched.

The queen, after having presented her children to the king, made Louis XVI. kiss them, and then the dauphin, seeing in his father's hat the new cockade, on which the torches cast an ensanguined light, exclaimed, with childish astonishment :

" Why, papa, what have you on your cockade ? Is it blood ?"

It was the national red.

The queen uttered a cry, and examined it in her turn.

The king bent down his head, under the pretense of again kissing his little daughter, but in reality to conceal his shame.

Marie Antoinette, with profound disgust, tore the cockade from the hat, without seeing—the noble, furious

woman—that she was wounding to the heart a nation that
would one day know how to avenge itself.

"Throw it away, sir," said she, "throw it away!"

And she threw this cockade down the stairs, upon which
trampled the feet of the whole escort which accompanied
the king to his apartments.

This strange transition had extinguished all conjugal
enthusiasm in the queen's heart. She looked around, but
without apparent intention, for M. de Charny, who was
standing at his ordinary post near the king, with the stiff
formality of a soldier.

"I thank you, sir," she said to him, when their eyes
met, after several moments of hesitation on the part of
the count; "I thank you, sir. You have well fulfilled
your promise."

"To whom are you speaking?" inquired the king.

"To Monsieur de Charny," said she boldly.

"Yes, poor Charny; he had trouble enough to get near
me. And Gilbert—what has become of him? I do not
see him," added Louis.

The queen, who had become more cautious since the
lesson of the afternoon:

"Come in to supper," said she, in order to change the
conversation. "Monsieur de Charny," pursued she,
"find the Countess de Charny, and bring her with you.
We will have a family supper."

In this she acted as a queen. But she sighed on observing that Charny, who, till then, had appeared gloomy, at
once became smiling and joyful.

CHAPTER X.

BILLOT was in a state of perfect ecstasy.

He had taken the Bastile; he had restored Gilbert to
liberty; he had been noticed by Lafayette, who called him
by his name; and, finally, he had seen the burial of
Foulon.

Few men, in those days, were as much execrated as
Foulon. One only could, in this respect, have competed
with him, and this was his son-in-law. M. Berthier de
Savigny.

They had both of them been singularly lucky the day following the capture of the Bastile.

Foulon died on that day, and Berthier managed to escape from Paris.

That which had raised to its climax the unpopularity of Foulon was, that on the retirement of M. Necker he had accepted the place of the virtuous Genevese, as he was then called, and had been comptroller-general during three days.

And therefore, there was much singing and dancing at his burial.

The people had at one time thought of taking the body out of the coffin, and hanging it; but Billot had jumped upon a post, and had made a speech on the respect due to the dead, and the hearse was allowed to continue on its way.

As to Pitou, he had become a perfect hero.

Pitou had become the friend of M. Elie and M. Hullin, who deigned to employ him to execute their commissions.

He was, besides, the confidant of Billot—of Billot, who had been treated with distinction by M. de Lafayette as we have already said, and who sometimes employed him as a police guard about his person, on account of his brawny shoulders, his herculean fists, and his indomitable courage.

Since the journey of the king to Paris, Gilbert, who had been, through M. Necker, put in communication with the principal members of the National Assembly and the municipality, was incessantly occupied with the education of the republic, still in its infancy.

He, therefore, neglected Billot and Pitou, who, neglected by him, threw themselves ardently into the meetings of the citizens, in the midst of which political discussions of transcendent interest were constantly agitated.

At length, one day, after Billot had employed three hours in giving his opinion to the electors, as to the best mode of victualing Paris, and fatigued with his long speech, though proud of having played the orator, he was resting with delight, lulled by the monotonous voices of his successors, which he took good care to listen to, Pitou came in, greatly agitated, and gliding like an eel through the Sessions Hall of the electors in the Hôtel de Ville, and, in a palpitating tone, which contrasted greatly with the usual placidity of his enunciation :

"Oh, Monsieur Billot!" said he, "dear Monsieur Billot!"

"Well, what is it?"

"Great news!"

"Good news?"

"Glorious news!"

"What is it, then?"

"You know that I had gone to the club of the 'Virtues,' at the Fontainebleau barrier?"

"Yes, and what then?"

"Well, they spoke there of a most extraordinary event."

"What was it?"

"Do you know that that villain Foulon passed himself off for dead, and carried it so far as to allow himself to be buried?"

"How! passed himself for dead? How say you?— pretended to allow himself to be buried? Nonsense! He is dead enough; for was I not at his funeral?"

"Notwithstanding that, Monsieur Billot, he is still living."

"Living?"

"As much alive as you and I are."

"You are mad!"

"Dear Monsieur Billot, I am not mad. The traitor, Foulon, the enemy of the people, the leech of France, the peculator, is not dead."

"But since I tell you he was buried after an apoplectic fit; since I tell you that I saw the funeral go by, and even that I prevented the people from dragging him out of his coffin to hang him."

"And I have just seen him alive. Ah, what do you say to that?"

"You?"

"As plainly as I now see you, Monsieur Billot. It appears that it was one of his servants who died, and the villain gave him an aristocratic funeral. Oh, all is discovered. It was from fear of the vengeance of the people that he acted thus."

"Tell me all about it, Pitou."

"Come into the vestibule for a moment, then, Monsieur Billot. We shall be more at our ease there."

They left the hall, and went into the vestibule.

"First of all, we must know whether Monsieur Bailly is here."

"Go on with your story; he is here."

"Good! Well, I was at the club of the Virtues, listening to the speech of a patriot. Didn't he make grammatical faults! It was easily seen that he had not been educated by the Abbé Fortier."

"Go on, I tell you. A man may be a good patriot, and yet not be able to read or write."

"That is true," said Pitou. "Well, suddenly a man came in, completely out of breath. 'Victory!' cried he, 'victory! Foulon was not dead! Foulon is still alive! I have discovered him—I have found him!'"

"Everybody there was like you, Father Billot. No one would believe him. Some said, 'How! Foulon?' 'Yes.' Others said, 'Pshaw! impossible!' And others said, 'Well, while you were at it, you might as well have discovered his son-in-law, Berthier.'"

"Berthier!" cried Billot.

"Yes, Berthier de Savigny. Don't you recollect our intendant at Compiègne, the friend of Monsieur Isidore de Charny?"

"Undoubtedly; he who was always so proud with everybody, and so polite with Catherine?"

"Precisely," said Pitou; "one of those horrible contractors—a second leech to the French people—the execration of all human nature—the shame of the civilized world, as said the virtuous Laustalot."

"Well, go on, go on!" cried Billot.

"That is true," said Pitou—*ad eventum festina*—which means to say, Monsieur Billot, 'hasten to the winding up.' Wait a moment."

"I am waiting; but you make my blood boil."

"Ah, but listen. I am hot enough, too. I tell you that he had given it out that he was dead, and had one of his servants buried in his place. Fortunately, Providence was watching."

"Providence, indeed!" disdainfully exclaimed the Voltairian Billot.

"I intended to say, the nation," rejoined Pitou, with humility. "This good citizen, this patriot, out of breath, who announced the news to us, recognized him at Vitry, where he had concealed himself."

"Ah! ah!"

"Having recognized him, he denounced him, and the syndic, whose name is Monsieur Raepp, instantly arrested him."

"And what is the name of the brave patriot who had the courage to do all this?"

"Of informing against Foulon?"

"Yes."

"Well, his name is Monsieur St. Jean."

"St. Jean! Why, that is a lackey's name."

"And he was precisely the lackey of the villain Foulon. Aristocrat, you are rightly served. Why had you lackeys?"

"Pitou, you interest me," said Billot, going close to the narrator.

"You are very kind, Monsieur Billot. Well, then, here is Foulon denounced and arrested; they are bringing him to Paris. The informer had run on ahead to announce the news, and receive the reward for his denunciation; and, sure enough, in a few moments afterward Foulon arrived at the barrier."

"And it was there that you saw him?"

"Yes. He had a very queer look, I can tell you. They had twisted a bunch of stinging-nettles round his neck, by way of cravat."

"What say you? stinging-nettles? And what was that for?"

"Because it appears that he had said—rascal as he is! —that bread was for men, oats for horses, but that nettles were good enough for the people."

"Did he say that, the wretch?"

"Yes, by Heaven! he said so, Monsieur Billot."

"Good! there, now, you are swearing."

"Bah!" cried Pitou, with a swaggering air, "between military men! Well, they brought him along on foot, and the whole of the way they were giving him smashing blows on the back and on his head."

"Oh! oh!" cried Billot, somewhat less enthusiastic.

"It was very amusing," continued Pitou, "only that everybody could not get at him to give him a blow, seeing that there were ten thousand persons hooting after him."

"And after this?" asked Billot, who began to reflect.

"After that they took him to the president of the St. Marcel district—a good patriot, you know."

"Yes—Monsieur Acloque."

"Cloque—yes, that is it—who ordered him to be taken to the Hôtel de Ville, seeing that he did not know what to do with him; so that you will soon see him."

"But how happens it that it is you who have come to announce this, and not the famous St. Jean?"

"Why, because my legs are six inches longer than his. He had set off before me, but I soon came up with him and passed him. I wanted to inform you first, that you might inform Monsieur Bailly of it."

"What luck you have, Pitou!"

"I shall know much more than this to-morrow."

"And how can you tell that?"

"Because this same St. Jean, who denounced Monsieur Foulon, proposed a plan to catch Monsieur Berthier, who has run away."

"He knows, then, where he is?"

"Yes; it appears that he was their confidential man, this good Monsieur St. Jean; and that he received a great deal of money from Foulon and his son-in-law, who wished to bribe him."

"And he took the money?"

"Certainly; the money of an aristocrat is always good to take; but he said, 'A good patriot will not betray his nation for money.'"

"Yes," murmured Billot; "he betrays his masters, that is all. Do you know, Pitou, that your Monsieur St. Jean appears to me to be a worthless vagabond?"

"That is possible, but it matters not; they will take Monsieur Berthier as they have taken Master Foulon, and they will hang them nose to nose. What horrid, wry faces they will make, looking at each other—hey?"

"And why should they be hanged?"

"Why, because they are vile rascals, and I detest them."

"What! Monsieur Berthier who has been at the farm—Monsieur Berthier, who, during his tours into the Isle de France, has drunk our milk and eaten of our bread, and sent the gold buckles to Catherine from Paris? Oh, no, no; they shall not hang him!"

"Bah!" repeated Pitou, ferociously, "he is an aristocrat—a wheedling rascal!"

Billot looked at Pitou with stupefaction. Beneath the gaze of the farmer, Pitou blushed to the very whites of his eyes.

Suddenly, the worthy cultivator perceived M. Bailly, who was going from the hall into his own cabinet; he rushed after him to inform him of the news.

But it was now for Billot, in his turn, to be treated with incredulity.

"Foulon! Foulon!" cried the mayor, "what folly!"

"Well, Monsieur Bailly, all I can say is, here is Pitou, who saw him."

"I saw him, Monsieur Mayor," said Pitou, placing his hand on his heart, and bowing.

And he related to M. Bailly all he had before related to Billot.

They observed that poor Bailly turned very pale; he at once understood the extent of the catastrophe.

"And Monsieur Acloque sends him here?" murmured he.

"Yes, Monsieur Mayor."

"But how is he sending him?"

"Oh, there is no occasion to be uneasy," said Pitou, who misunderstood the anxiety of Bailly; "there are plenty of people to guard the prisoner. He will not be carried off."

"Would to God he might be carried off!" murmured Bailly.

Then, turning to Pitou:

"Plenty of people—what mean you by that, my friend?"

"I mean plenty of people."

"People!"

"More than twenty thousand men, without counting the women," said Pitou, triumphantly.

"Unhappy man!" exclaimed Bailly. "Gentlemen, gentlemen assessors!"

And he related to the electors all he had just heard.

While he was speaking, exclamations and cries of anguish burst forth from all present.

The silence of terror pervaded the hall, during which a confused, distant, indescribable noise assailed the ears of those assembled, like that produced by the rushing of blood to the head in attacks upon the brain.

"What is that?" inquired an elector.

"Why, the noise of the crowd, to be sure," replied another.

Suddenly a carriage was heard rolling rapidly across the square; it contained two armed men, who helped a third to alight from it, who was pale and trembling.

Foulon had at length become so exhausted by the ill-usage he had experienced, that he could no longer walk, and he had been lifted into a coach.

Behind the carriage, led on by St. Jean, who was more out of breath than ever, ran about a hundred young men, from sixteen to eighteen years of age, with haggard countenances and flaming eyes.

They cried, "Foulon! Foulon!" running almost as fast as the horses.

The two armed men were, however, some few steps in advance of them, which gave them the time to push Foulon into the Hôtel de Ville, and its doors were closed against the hoarse barkers from without.

"At last we have him here," said his guards to the electors, who were waiting at the top of the stairs. "By Heaven! it was not without trouble!"

"Gentlemen! gentlemen!" cried Foulon, trembling, "will you save me?"

"Ah, sir," replied Bailly, with a sigh, "you have been very culpable."

"And yet, sir," said Foulon, entreatingly, his agitation increasing, "there will, I hope, be justice to defend me."

At this moment the exterior tumult was redoubled.

"Hide him quickly!" cried Bailly to those around him, "or——"

He turned to Foulon.

"Listen to me," said he; "the situation is serious enough for you to be consulted. Will you—perhaps it is not yet too late—will you endeavor to escape from the back part of the Hôtel de Ville?"

"Oh! no," exclaimed Foulon; "I should be recognized—massacred!"

"Do you prefer to remain here in the midst of us? I will do, and these gentlemen will do, all that is humanly possible to defend you; will you not, gentlemen?"

"We promise it," cried all the electors, with one voice.

"Oh! I prefer remaining with you, gentlemen. Gentlemen, do not abandon me!"

"I have told you, sir," replied Bailly, with dignity, "that we will do all that may be humanly possible to save you."

At that moment a frightful clamor arose from the square, ascended into the air, and invaded the Hôtel de Ville through the open windows.

"Do you hear ? do you hear ?" murmured Foulon, perfectly livid with terror.

In fact, the mob had rushed, howling and frightful to behold, from all the streets leading to the Hôtel de Ville, and above all, from the Quay Lepelletier and the Rue de la Vannir.

Bailly went to a window.

Knives, pikes, scythes, and muskets glistened in the sunshine. In less than ten minutes the vast square was filled with people. It was the whole of Foulon's train, of which Pitou had spoken, and which had been increased by curious idlers, who, hearing a great noise, had run to the Place de Grève, as toward a common center.

All these voices, and there were more than twenty thousand, cried incessantly :

"Foulon ! Foulon !"

Then it was seen that the hundred young men who had been the precursors of this furious mob pointed out to this howling mass the gate by which Foulon had entered the building ; this gate was instantly threatened, and they began to beat it down with the butt-ends of their muskets and with crow-bars.

Suddenly it flew open.

The guards of the Hôtel de Ville appeared, and advanced upon the assailants, who, in their first terror, retreated and left a large open space in the front of the building.

This guard stationed itself upon the front steps, and presented a bold front to the crowd.

The officers, moreover, instead of threatening, harangued the crowd in friendly terms, and endeavored to calm it by their protestations.

Bailly had become quite confused. It was the first time that the poor astronomer had found himself in opposition to the popular tempest.

"What is to be done ?" demanded he of the electors ; "what is to be done ?"

"We must try him."

"No trial can take place when under the intimidation of the mob," said Bailly.

"Zounds!" exclaimed Billot, "have you not, then, men enough to defend you?"

"We have not two hundred men."

"You must have a reinforcement, then."

"Oh! if Monsieur Lafayette were but informed of this!"

"Well, send and inform him of it."

"And who would venture to attempt it? Who could make his way through such a multitude?"

"I would," replied Billot.

And he was about to leave the hall.

Bailly stopped him.

"Madman!" cried he, "look at that ocean. You would be swallowed up even by one of its waves. If you wish to get to Monsieur de Lafayette, and even then I would not answer for your safety, go out by one of the back doors. Go!"

"'Tis well!" tranquilly replied Billot.

And he darted out of the room with the swiftness of an arrow.

CHAPTER XI.

THE clamor, which kept on constantly increasing from the square, clearly proved that the exasperation of the mob was becoming greater. It was no longer hatred that they felt, it was abhorrence; they no longer merely threatened, they foamed.

The cries of "Down with Foulon! Death to Foulon!" crossed each other in the air, like projectiles in a bombardment. The crowd, which was still augmenting, pressed nearer to the entrance of the Hôtel de Ville, till they, as it may be said, almost suffocated the civic guards at their post.

And already there began to circulate among the crowd, and to increase in violence, those rumors which are the precursors of violence.

These rumors no longer threatened Foulon only, but the electors who protected him.

"They have let the prisoner escape!" said some.

"Let us go in! let us go in!" said others.

"Let us set fire to the Hôtel de Ville!"

"Forward! forward!"

Bailly felt that as M. de Lafayette did not arrive, there was only one resource left to them.

And this was, that the electors should themselves go down, mix in with the groups, and endeavor to pacify the most furious among them.

"Foulon! Foulon!"

Such was the incessant cry, the constant roaring of those furious waves.

A general assault was preparing; the walls could not have resisted it.

"Sir," said Bailly to Foulon, "if you do not show yourself to the crowd, they will believe that we have allowed you to escape; they will force the door, will come in here, and once here, should they find you, I can no longer be responsible for anything."

"Oh! I did not know that I was so much execrated!" exclaimed Foulon.

And, supported by Bailly, he dragged himself to the window.

A fearful cry resounded immediately on his presenting himself. The guards were driven back, the doors broken in, a torrent of men precipitated themselves up the staircase, into the corridors, into the rooms, which were invaded in an instant.

Bailly threw around the prisoner all the guards who were within call, and then he began to harangue the crowd.

He wished to make these men understand that to assassinate might sometimes be doing justice, but that it was never an act of justice.

He succeeded, after having made the most strenuous efforts, after having twenty times imperiled his own existence.

"Yes, yes!" cried the assailants, "let him be tried! let him be tried; but let him be hanged!"

They were at this point in the argument when General de Lafayette reached the Hôtel de Ville, conducted there by Billot.

The sight of his tricolored plume, one of the first which

had been worn, at once assuaged their anger, and the tumult ceased.

The commander-in-chief of the National Guard had the way cleared for him, and addressing the crowd, repeated, though in more energetic terms, every argument that Bailly had endeavored to enforce.

His speech produced a great effect on all those who were near enough to hear it, and the cause of Foulon was completely gained in the electors' hall.

But on the square were twenty thousand furious people, who had not heard M. de Lafayette, and who remained implacable in their frenzy.

"Come, now," said Lafayette, at the conclusion of his oration, very naturally imagining that the effect he had produced on those who surrounded him had extended to all outside, " come, now, this man must be tried."

" Yes," cried the mob.

" And consequently I order that he be taken to prison," added Lafayette.

" To prison ! to prison ! " howled the mob.

At the same time the general made a sign to the guards of the Hôtel de Ville, who led the prisoner forward.

The crowd outside understood nothing of all that was going on, excepting that their prey was about to appear. They had not even an idea that any one had the slightest hope of disputing it with them.

They scented, if we may be permitted the expression, the odor of the human flesh which was descending the staircase.

Billot had placed himself at the window with several electors, whom Bailly also joined, in order to follow the prisoner with their eyes, while he was crossing the square, escorted by the civic guards.

On the way, Foulon here and there addressed a few incoherent words to those around him, which, although they were protestations of confidence, clearly evinced the most profound and ill-disguised terror.

" Noble people," said he, while descending the staircase, " I fear nothing ; I am in the midst of my fellow-citizens."

And already bantering laughs and insults were being uttered around him, when suddenly he found himself outside of the gloomy archway, at the top of the stone steps which lead into the square.

Immediately one general cry, a cry of rage, a howling threat, a roar of hatred, burst from twenty thousand lungs. On this explosion of the public feeling, the guards conducting the prisoner are lifted from the ground, broken, dispersed; Foulon is seized by twenty powerful arms, raised above their shoulders, and carried into the fatal corner, under the lamp-post; ignoble and brutal executioner of the anger of the people, which they termed their justice.

Billot, from his window, saw all this, and cried out against it; the electors also did all they could to stimulate the guards, but they were powerless.

Lafayette, in despair, rushed out of the Hôtel de Ville, but he could not break through the first rank of that crowd, which spread out like an immense lake between him and the victim.

The mere spectators of this scene jumped upon posts, on window-sills, on every jutting part of a building, in order to gain a better view, and they encouraged by their savage shouts the frightful effervescence of the actors.

The latter were playing with their victim, as would a troop of tigers with an inoffensive prey.

They were disputing who should hang Foulon; at last they understood that if they wished to enjoy his agony, it was necessary that their several functions should be agreed upon.

But for that he would have been torn to pieces.

Some of them raised up Foulon, who had no longer strength enough to cry out.

Others, who had taken off his cravat and torn his coat, placed a rope round his neck.

And others, who had climbed up the lamp-post, had handed to their companions below the rope which they put round the neck of the ex-minister.

For a moment they raised Foulon above their heads and showed him thus to the crowd—a rope twined round his neck, and his hands tied behind him.

Then, when the crowd had had due time to contemplate the sufferer, when they had clapped their hands sufficiently, the signal was given, and Foulon, pale and bleeding, was hoisted up to a level with the lantern, amid a hooting more terrible even than death.

All those who, up to that time, had not been able to see

anything, then perceived the public enemy raised above the heads of the crowd.

New shouts were then heard ; but these were against the executioners. Were they about to kill Foulon so expeditiously ?

The executioners merely shrugged their shoulders, and pointed to the rope.

The rope was old ; it could be seen to give way, strand bv strand. The despairing movements which Foulon made in his agony at length broke the last strand ; and Foulon, only half strangled, fell heavily upon the pavement.

He was only at the preface of his torments, he had only penetrated into the vestibule of death.

They all rushed toward the sufferer ; they were perfectly secure wth regard to him ; there was no chance of his escaping them ; in falling, he had broken his leg a little below the knee.

And yet, some imprecations arose, imprecations which were unintelligible and calumniatory ; the executioners were accused ; they were considered as clumsy and unskilful. They, on the contrary, who had been so ingenious, they who had expressly chosen an old worn-out rope, in the hope that it would break.

A hope which the event, as has been related, had fully realized.

They made a knot in the rope, and again fixed it round the neck of the unhappy man, who, half dead, with haggard eyes, looked around, endeavoring to discover whether in that city which is called the center of the civilized universe, whether one of the bayonets of that king of whom he was the minister, and who had a hundred thousand, would not be raised in his defense amid that horde of cannibals.

But there was nothing there to meet his eyes but hatred, but insult, but death.

"At least, kill me at once, without making me endure these atrocious torments !" cried the despairing Foulon.

"Well, now," replied a jeering voice, "why should we abridge your torments ? you have made ours last long enough."

"And, besides," said another, "you have not yet had time enough to digest your nettles."

"Wait, wait a little," cried a third; "his son-in-law, Berthier, will be brought to him. There is room enough for him on the opposite lamp-post!"

"We shall see what wry faces the father and son-in-law will make at each other," added another.

"Finish me! finish me at once!" cried the wretched man.

During this time, Bailly and Lafayette were begging, supplicating, exclaiming, and endeavoring to get through the crowd; suddenly, Foulon was again hoisted by the rope, which again broke, and their prayers, their supplications, their agony, no less painful than that of the sufferer himself, were lost, confounded, and extinguished amid the universal laugh which accompanied this second fall.

Bailly and Lafayette, who, three days before, had been the sovereign arbiters of the will of six hundred thousand Parisians, a child now would not listen to them—the poeple even murmured at them—they were in their way—they were interrupting this great spectacle.

Billot had vainly given them all the aid of his uncommon strength; the powerful athlete had knocked down twenty men, but in order to reach Foulon it would be necessary to knock down fifty, a hundred, two hundred, and his strength is exhausted, and when he pauses to wipe from his brow the perspiration and the blood which is streaming from it, Foulon is raised a third time to the pulley of the lamp-post.

This time they had taken compassion upon him, the rope was a new one.

At last the condemned is dead, the victim no longer suffers.

Half a minute has sufficed to the crowd to assure itself that the vital spark was extinguished. And now that the tiger has killed, he may devour his prey.

The body, thrown from the top of the lamp-post, did not even fall to the ground. It was torn to pieces before it reached it.

The head was separated from the trunk in a second, and in another second raised on the end of a pike. It was very much in fashion in those days to carry the heads of one's enemies in that way.

At this sanguinary spectacle Bailly was horrified. That

head appeared to him to be the head of the Medusa of ancient days.

Lafayette, pale, his drawn sword in his hand, with disgust repulsed the guards who had surrounded him, to excuse themselves for not having been the strongest.

Billot, stamping his feet with rage, and kicking right and left, like one of his own fiery Perche horses, returned into the Hôtel de Ville, that he might see no more of what was passing on that ensanguined square.

As to Pitou, his fieriness of popular vengeance was changed into a convulsive movement, and he had fled to the river's bank, where he closed his eyes and stopped his ears, that he might neither see nor hear.

Consternation reigned in the Hôtel de Ville; the electors began to comprehend that they would never be able to direct the movements of the people, but in the manner which should suit the people.

All at once, while the furious mob were amusing themselves with dragging the mutilated remains of Foulon through the gutters, a new cry, a new shout, rolling like distant thunder, was heard, proceeding from the opposite side of the river.

A courier was seen galloping over the bridge. The news he was bringing was already known to the crowd. They had guessed it from the signs of their most skilful leaders, as a pack of hounds take up the scent from the inspiration of their finest nosed and best practised blood-hounds.

The crowd rushed to meet this courier, whom they surrounded, they scent that he has touched their new prey; they feel that he is going to speak of M. Berthier.

And it was true.

Interrogated by ten thousand voices, all howling at once, the courier is compelled to reply to them.

"Monsieur Berthier de Savigny has been arrested at Compiègne."

Then he proceeds into the Hôtel de Ville, where he announces the same tidings to Lafayette and to Bailly.

"Good—good! I knew it," said Lafayette.

"We knew it," said Bailly, "and orders have been given that he should be kept there."

"Kept there?" repeated the courier.

"Undoubtedly; I have sent two commissaries with an escort."

"An escort of two hundred men, was it not?" said an elector; "it is more than sufficient."

"Gentlemen," replied the courier, "this is precisely what I was sent to tell you. The escort has been dispersed, and the prisoner carried off by the multitude."

"Carried off!" exclaimed Lafayette. "Has the escort allowed the prisoner to be carried off?"

"Do not blame them, general; all that it was possible to do they did."

"But Monsieur Berthier?" anxiously inquired Bailly.

"They are bringing him to Paris, and he is at Bourget by this time."

"But should they bring him here," cried Bailly, "he is lost."

"Quick! quick!" cried Lafayette, "five hundred men to Bourget. Let the commissioners and Monsieur Berthier stop there—let them stop there. During the night we will consider what is to be done."

"But who would venture to undertake such a commission?" said the courier, who was looking with terror at that waving sea of heads, every wave of which sent forth its threatening roar.

"I will!" cried Billot; "at least I will save *him*."

"But you would perish in the attempt," cried the courier; "the road is black with people."

"I will go, nevertheless," said the farmer.

"It is useless now," murmured Bailly, who had been listening to the noises from without. "Hush! do you not hear that?"

They then heard, from the direction of the Porte St. Martin, a rushing noise, like that of the sea when beating over the shingles on a beach.

"It is too late," said Lafayette.

"They are coming! they are coming!" murmured the courier. "Do you not hear them?"

"A regiment! a regiment!" cried Lafayette, with that generous ebullition of humanity which was the most brilliant feature of his character.

"What! By God's death!" exclaimed Bailly, who swore perhaps for the first time in his life, "you seem to forget that our army—ours!—is precisely that crowd whom you wish to fight."

And he hid his face in his hands.

The shouts which had been heard in the distance were re-echoed by the people in the streets, and thus communicated to the crowd upon the square with the rapidity of a train of gunpowder.

Then those who were insulting the remains of Foulon left their sanguinary game, to rush forward in pursuit of a new vengeance.

The adjacent streets immediately disgorged a large proportion of that howling mob, who hurried from the square with upraised knives and menacing gestures toward the Rue St. Martin, to meet the new funeral procession.

CHAPTER XII.

THE junction having been accomplished, both parties were equally eager to return to the square.

A strange scene then ensued.

Some of those ingenious persons whom we have seen upon the Place de Grève presented to the son-in-law the head of Foulon on the end of a pike.

M. Berthier was coming along the Rue St. Martin. They were then just crossing the Rue St. Méry.

He was in his own cabriolet, a vehicle which at that period was considered as eminently aristocratic—a vehicle which more than any other excited popular animadversion; for the people had so often complained of the reckless rapidity with which they were driven, either by young fops or dancing girls who drove themselves, and which, drawn by a fiery horse, sometimes ran over, but always splashed the unfortunate, pedestrian.

Berthier, in the midst of all the shouts, the hootings, and the threats of the infuriated mob, was talking tranquilly with the elector Rivière, the commissary sent to Compiègne to save him, but who, being abandoned by his colleague, had with much difficulty saved himself.

The people had begun with the cabriolet; they had torn off the head of it, so that Berthier and his companion were completely exposed, not only to the view, but to the blows, of the populace.

As they moved onward, his misdeeds were related to him, commented upon, and exaggerated by the popular fury.

" He wished to starve Paris," cried one.

" He had the rye and wheat cut when it was green ; and then, a rise in the price of corn having taken place, he realized enormous sums."

"Not only did he do that," said they, "which was enough in itself, but he was conspiring."

In searching him they had found a pocket-book. In this pocket-book were incendiary letters, orders for massacre, proof that ten thousand cartridges had been distributed to his agents. So said the crowd.

These were all monstrous absurdities ; but, as is well known, the mob, when in a paroxysm of rage, gives out, as positive facts, the most absurd improbabilities.

The person whom they accused of all this was a man who was still young, not being more than from thirty to thirty-two years of age, elegantly dressed, almost smiling, though greeted every moment by injurious epithets and even blows. He looked with perfect indifference at the infamous placards which were held up to him, and without affectation continued his conversation with Rivière.

Two men, irritated at his assurance, had wished to terrify him, and to diminish this self-confidence. They had mounted on the steps on each side of the cabriolet, and each of them placed the point of his bayonet on Berthier's breast.

But Berthier, brave even to temerity, was not to be moved by such a trifle. He had continued to converse with the elector, as if those two muskets were but inoffensive accessories to the cabriolet.

The mob, profoundly exasperated by this disdain, which formed so complete a contrast to the terror of Foulon— the mob roared round the vehicle, and waited with impatience for the moment when, instead of a threat, they might inflict a wound.

It was then that Berthier had fixed his eyes on a misshapen and bloody object, which was held up and danced before him, and which he suddenly recognized as the head of his father-in-law, and which the ruffians who bore it held down close to his lips.

They wished to make him kiss it.

M. Rivière, indignant at this brutality, pushed the pike away with his hand.

Berthier thanked him by a gesture, and did not even

deign to turn round to follow this hideous trophy with his eyes. The executioners carried it behind the cabriolet, holding it over Berthier's head.

They thus arrived on the Place de Grève, and the prisoner, after unheard-of efforts by the civic guards, who had been reassembled in some order, was delivered into the hands of the electors of the Hôtel de Ville.

A dangerous charge, a fearful responsibility, which made Lafayette once more turn pale, and poor Bailly's heart swell almost to breaking.

The mob, after having hacked away for awhile at the cabriolet, which had been left at the foot of the front steps, again placed themselves in the most advantageous positions, kept guard on all the issues from the building, made all their preparations, and placed new ropes in the pulleys of the lanterns.

Billot, at the sight of Berthier, who was tranquilly ascending the great staircase of the Hôtel de Ville, tore his hair, and could not restrain himself from weeping bitterly.

Pitou, who had left the river's bank, and had come on the quay again when he thought that Foulon's execution had been accomplished—Pitou, terrified, notwithstanding his hatred for M. Berthier, guilty in his eyes not only of all the mob reproached him with, but also of having given gold buckles to Mlle. Catherine—Pitou crouched down sobbing behind a bench.

During this time, Berthier had entered the grand Hall of Council as coolly as if all the tumult had reference to some other person, and quietly conversed with the electors.

He knew the greater portion of them, and was even intimate with some of them.

The latter avoided him with the instinctive terror with which timid minds are inspired by the contact of an unpopular man.

Therefore, Berthier soon found himself almost alone with Bailly and Lafayette.

He made them relate to him all the particulars of Foulon's death. Then, shrugging up his shoulders:

"Yes," said he, "I can understand it. They hate us because we are the instruments with which royalty has tortured the people."

"Great crimes are laid at your door, sir," said Bailly, austerely.

"Sir," replied Berthier, "if I had committed all the crimes with which I am reproached, I should be less or more than a man—a wild beast or a demon. But I shall be tried, I presume, and then the truth will be ascertained."

"Undoubtedly," said Bailly.

"Well, then," rejoined Berthier, "that is all I desire. They have my correspondence, and it will be seen whose orders I have obeyed ; and the responsibility will fall on those to whom it rightly appertains."

The electors cast their eyes upon the square, from which arose the most frightful clamor.

Berthier understood this mute reply.

Then Billot, pushing through the throng which surrounded Bailly, went up to the intendant, and offering his huge honest hand :

"Good-day, Monsieur de Savigny," said he to him.

"How ! is that you, Billot ?" cried Berthier, laughing, and grasping firmly the hand which was held out to him. "What, have you come to Paris to join in these disturbances, you, my worthy farmer, who used to sell your wheat so well in the market at Villers-Cotterets, Cressy, and Soissons ?"

Billot, notwithstanding his democratic tenderness, could not but admire the tranquillity of this man, who could thus smile at a moment when his life was hanging by a thread.

"Install yourselves, gentlemen," said Bailly to the electors ; we must now proceed to the examination of the charges against the accused."

"Be it so," said Berthier ; "but I must warn you of one thing, gentlemen, and that is, that I am perfectly exhausted. For the last two days I have not slept. To-day, from Compiègne to Paris, I have been pushed about, beaten, dragged along. When I asked for something to eat, they offered me hay, which is not excessively refreshing. Therefore, give me some place where I can sleep, if it be only for an hour."

At that moment Lafayette left the room for a short time, to ascertain the state of matters outside. He returned more dispirited than ever.

"My dear Bailly," said he to the mayor, "exasperation is at its height; to keep Monsieur Berthier here would be exposing ourselves to a siege. To defend the Hôtel de Ville would be giving these furious madmen the pretext which they wish. Not to defend the Hôtel de Ville would be acquiring the habit of yielding every time we were attacked."

During this time, Berthier had sat down, and then stretched himself at full length upon a bench.

He was preparing himself to sleep.

The desperate howls from below were audible to him, for he was near an open window; but they did not disturb him. His countenance retained the serenity of a man who forgets all, to allow sleep to weigh down his eyelids.

Bailly was deliberating with the electors and Lafayette.

Billot had his eyes fixed upon Berthier.

Lafayette was rapidly taking the votes of the electors; after which, addressing the prisoner, who was beginning to slumber:

"Sir," said he, "be pleased to get ready."

Berthier heaved a sigh, then, raising himself on his elbow:

"Ready for what?" he inquired.

"These gentlemen have decided that you are to be transferred to the Abbaye."

"To the Abbaye? Well, be it so," said the intendant. "But," continued he, looking at the confused electors, and whose confusion he readily comprehended, "but, one way or the other, let us finish this."

And an explosion of anger and furious impatience long restrained burst forth from the square.

"No, gentlemen, no," exclaimed Lafayette, "we can not allow him to depart at this moment!"

Bailly's kind heart and undaunted courage impelled him to come to a sudden resolution. He went down into the square with two of the electors, and ordered silence.

The people knew as well as he did what he was about to say; but, as they were fully bent on committing another crime, they would not even listen to a reproach; and as Bailly was opening his lips to speak, a deafening clamor arose from the mob, drowning his voice before a single word could be heard.

Bailly, seeing that it would be impossible for him to

proffer even a syllable, returned into the Hôtel de Ville,
pursued by cries of "Berthier—Berthier!"

But other cries resounded in the midst of those, cries
similar to the shrill notes which suddenly are heard in
the choruses of demons by Weber or by Meyerbeer, and
these were, "To the lantern—to the lantern!"

On seeing Bailly come back pale and disheartened, Lafayette rushed out in his turn.   He is young, he is ardent,
he is beloved.   That which the old man could not effect,
his popularity being but of yesterday, he, Lafayette—he,
the friend of Washington and of Necker, would undoubtedly obtain at the first word.

But in vain was it that the people's general threw himself into the most furious groups.   In vain did he speak
in the name of justice and humanity.   In vain was it that,
recognizing, or feigning to recognize, certain leaders of
the people, did he supplicate them, grasping their hands,
and endeavoring to allay their fury.

Not one of his words was listened to; not one of his
gestures was understood; not one of the tears he shed
was seen.

Repulsed step by step, he threw himself upon his knees
on the *perron* of the Hôtel de Ville, conjuring these tigers,
whom he called his fellow-citizens, not to dishonor the
nation, not to dishonor themselves, not to elevate to the
rank of martyrs guilty men, to whom the law would award
a degrading death, which degradation was a portion of
their punishment.

As he persisted in his entreaties, he was at last personally threatened in his turn: but he defied all threats.
Some of these furious wretches drew their knives and
raised them as if to strike.

He bared his breast to their blows, and their weapons
were instantly lowered.

But if they thus threatened Lafayette, the threat was
still more serious to Berthier.

Lafayette, thus overcome, re-entered the Hôtel de Ville
as Bailly had done.

The electors had all seen Lafayette vainly contending
against the tempest.   Their last rampart was overthrown.

They decided that the guard of the Hôtel de Ville should
at once conduct Berthier to the Abbaye.

It was sending Berthier to certain death.

"Come, then," said Berthier, when this decision was announced. And eyeing all these men with withering contempt, he took his station in the center of the guards, after having thanked Bailly and Lafayette for their exertions and, in his turn, held out his hand to Billot.

Bailly turned away his face to conceal his tears—Lafayette, to conceal his indignation.

Berthier descended the staircase with the same firm step with which he had ascended it.

At the moment that he appeared on the *perron*, a furious howl assailed him, making even the stone step on which he had placed his foot tremble beneath him.

But he, disdainful and impassible, looked at all those flashing eyes calmly and unflinchingly, and, shrugging his shoulders, pronounced these words:

"What a fanatic people! What is there to make them howl thus?"

He had scarcely uttered these words, when he was seized upon by the foremost of the mob. They had rushed on to the *perron* itself, and clutched him, though surrounded by his guards. Their iron hands dragged him along. He lost his footing, and fell into the arms of his enemies, who in a second dispersed his escort.

Then an irresistible tide impelled the prisoner over the same path, stained with blood, which Foulon had been dragged over only two hours before.

A man was already seated astride the fatal lamp, holding a rope in his hand.

But another man had clung to Berthier, and this man was dealing out with fury and delirium, blows and imprecations on the brutal executioners.

He continually cried:

"You shall not have him! You shall not kill him!"

This man was Billot, whom despair had driven mad, and mad as twenty madmen.

To some he shrieked:

"I am one of the conquerors of the Bastile!"

And some of those who recognized him became less furious in their attack.

To others he said:

"Let him be fairly tried. I will be responsible for him. If he is allowed to escape, you shall hang me in his stead."

Poor Billot! poor worthy man! The whirlwind swept

him away, he and Berthier, as the water-spout carries away a feather or a straw in its vast spirals.

He moved on without perceiving anything. He had reached the fatal spot.

The thunderbolt is less swift.

Berthier, who had been dragged along backward—Berthier, whom they had raised up, seeing that they stopped, raised his eyes, and perceived the infamous, degrading halter swinging above his head.

By an effort as violent as it was unexpected, he tore himself from the grasp of those who held him, snatched a musket from the hands of a National Guard, and inflicted several wounds on his self-appointed executioners with his bayonet.

But in a second a thousand blows were aimed at him from behind. He fell, and a thousand other blows from the ruffians who encircled him rained down upon him.

Billot had disappeared beneath the feet of the assassins.

Berthier had not time to suffer. His life's blood and his soul rushed at once from his body through a thousand gaping wounds.

Then Billot was witness to a spectacle more hideous than he had yet seen. He saw a fiend plunge his hand into the open breast of the corpse, and tear out the still smoking heart.

Then, sticking this heart on the point of his saber, he held it above the heads of the shouting mob, which opened before him as he advanced, and he carried it into the Hôtel de Ville, and laid it on the table of the grand council, where the electors held their sessions.

Billot, that man of iron nerve, could not support this frightful sight ; he fell fainting against a post about ten paces from the fatal lantern.

Lafayette, on seeing this infamous insult offered to his authority—offered to the revolution which he directed, or, rather, which he had believed he should direct—Lafayette broke his sword, and threw it at the faces of the assassins.

Pitou ran to pick up the farmer, carried him off in his arms, whispering into his ear :

"Billot ! father Billot, take care ; if they see that you are fainting, they will take you for his accomplice, and will kill you, too. That would be a pity—so good a patriot ! "

And thereupon, he dragged him toward the river, concealing him as well as he was able from the inquisitive looks of some zealous patriots who were murmuring.

CHAPTER XIII.

BILLOT, who, conjointly with Pitou, had been engaged in all the glorious liberations, began to perceive that the cup was becoming bitter. When he had completely recovered his senses, from the refreshing breezes on the river's bank :

"Monsieur Billot," said Pitou to him, "I regret Villers-Cotterets—do not you ?"

These words, like the refreshing balm of calmness and virtue, aroused the farmer, whose vigor returned to him, and he pushed through the crowd, to get away at once from the scene of butchery.

"Come," said he to Pitou, "you are right."

And he at once determined on going to find Gilbert, who was residing at Versailles, but who, without having revisited the queen after the journey of the king to Paris, had become the right hand of Necker, who had been re-appointed minister, and was endeavoring to organize property by generalizing poverty.

Pitou had as usual followed Billot.

Both of them were admitted into the study in which the doctor was writing.

"Doctor," said Billot, "I am going to return to my farm."

"And why so ?" inquired Gilbert.

"Because I hate Paris."

"Ah, yes ! I understand," coldly observed Gilbert. "You are tired."

"Worn out."

"You no longer like the revolution ?"

"I should like to see it ended."

Gilbert smiled sorrowfully.

"It is only now beginning," he rejoined.

"Oh !" exclaimed Billot.

"That astonishes you, Billot ?" asked Gilbert.

"What astonishes me the most, is your perfect coolness."

"My friend," said Gilbert to him, "do you know whence my coolness proceeds?"

"It can only proceed from a firm conviction."

"Guess what that conviction is."

"That all will end well."

Gilbert smiled still more gloomily than the first time.

"No; on the contrary, from the conviction that all will end badly."

Billot cried out with astonishment.

As to Pitou, he opened his eyes to an enormous width. He thought the argument altogether illogical.

"Let us hear," said Billot—"let us hear; for it seems to me that I did not rightly understand you."

"Take a chair, Billot," said Gilbert, "and sit down close to me."

Billot did as he was ordered.

"Closer, closer still, that no one may hear but yourself."

"And I, Monsieur Gilbert?" said Pitou, timidly, making a move toward the door, as if he thought the doctor wished him to withdraw.

"Oh, no; stay here," replied the doctor. "You are young; listen."

Pitou opened his ears, as he had done his eyes, to their fullest extent, and seated himself on the ground, at Father Billot's feet.

This council was a singular spectacle, which was thus held in Gilbert's study, near a table heaped up with letters, documents, new pamphlets, and newspapers, and within four steps of a door, which was besieged by a swarm of petitioners, or people having some grievance to complain of. These people were all kept in order by an old clerk, who was almost blind and had lost an arm.

"I am all attention," said Billot. "Now explain yourself, my master, and tell us how it is that all will finish badly."

"I will tell you. Billot. Do you see what I am doing at this moment, my friend?"

"You are writing lines."

"But the meaning of those lines, Billot?"

"How would you have me guess that, when you know that I cannot even read them?"

Pitou timidly raised his head a little above the table,

and cast his eyes on the paper which was lying before the doctor.

" They are figures," said he.

" That is true ; they are figures, and which are at once the salvation and ruin of France."

" Well, now ! " exclaimed Billot.

" Well, now ! well, now ! " repeated Pitou.

" These figures, when they are presented to-morrow," continued the doctor, " will go to the king's palace, to the mansions of the nobility, and to the cottage of the poor man, to demand of all of them one quarter of their income."

" Hey ? " ejaculated Billot.

" Oh, my poor aunt Angelique ! " cried Pitou, " what a wry face she will make ! "

" What say you to this, my worthy friend ? " said Gilbert. " People make revolutions, do they not ? Well, they must pay for them."

" Perfectly just ! " heroically replied Billot. " Well, be it so—it will be paid."

" Oh, you are a man who is already convinced, and there is nothing to astonish me in your answers ; but those who are not convinced ? "

" Those who are not so ? "

" Yes ; what will they do ? "

" They will resist ! " replied Billot, and in a tone which signified that he would resist energetically if he were required to pay a quarter of his income to accomplish a work which was contrary to his convictions.

" Then there would be a conflict," said Gilbert.

" But the majority ? " said Billot.

" Conclude your sentence, my friend."

" The majority is there to make known its will."

" Then there would be aggression."

Billot looked at Gilbert, at first doubtingly, and then a ray of intelligence sparkled in his eye.

" Hold, Billot ! " said the doctor. " I know what you are about to say to me. The nobility and the clergy possess everything, do they not ? "

" That is undoubted," replied Billot, " and therefore the convents——"

" The convents ? "

" The convents overflow with riches."

"*Notum certumque*," grumbled Pitou.

"The nobles do not pay taxes in proportion to their income. Thus I, a farmer, pay more than twice the amount of taxes paid by my neighbors, the three brothers Charny, who have between them an income of two hundred thousand livres."

"But, let us see," continued Gilbert. "Do you believe that the nobles and the priests are less Frenchmen than you are?"

Pitou picked up his ears at this proposition, which sounded somewhat heretical at the time, when patriotism was calculated by the strength of elbows on the Place de Grève.

"You do not believe a word of it, do you, my friend? You cannot imagine that these nobles and priests, who absorb everything and give back nothing, are as good patriots as you are?"

"That is true."

"An error, my dear friend, an error. They are even better, and I will prove it to you."

"Oh! that, for example, I deny."

"On account of their privileges, is it not?"

"Zounds! yes."

"Wait a moment."

"Oh, I can wait."

"Well, then, I certify to you, Billot, that in three days from this time the person who will have the most privileges in France will be the man who possesses nothing."

"Then I shall be that person," said Pitou, gravely.

"Well, yes, it will be you."

"But how can that be?"

"Listen to me, Billot. These nobles, and these ecclesiastics, whom you accuse of egotism, are just beginning to be seized with that fever of patriotism which is about to make the tour of France. At this moment they are assembled like so many sheep on the edge of the ditch; they are deliberating; the boldest of them will be the first to leap over it, and this will happen to-morrow, perhaps to-night; and after him, the rest will jump it."

"What is the meaning of that, Monsieur Gilbert?"

"It means to say that, voluntarily abandoning their prerogatives, feudal lords will liberate their peasants, proprietors of estates their farms and the rents due to them, the dove-cote lords their pigeons."

"Oh, oh!" ejaculated Pitou, with amazement; "you think they will give up all that?"

"Oh!" cried Billot, suddenly catching the idea, "that will be splendid liberty, indeed."

"Well, then, and after that, when shall we all be free—what shall we do next?"

"The deuce!" cried Billot, somewhat embarrassed, "what shall be done next?" Why, we shall see."

"Ah! there is the great word," exclaimed Gilbert—"We shall see."

He rose from his chair with a gloomy brow, and walked up and down the room for a few minutes; then, returning to the farmer, whose hand he seized with a violence which seemed almost a threat:

"Yes," said he, "we shall see. We shall all see—you, as I shall; he, as you and I shall; and that is precisely what I was reflecting on just now, when you observed that composure which so much surprised you."

"You terrify me. The people united, embracing one another, forming themselves into one mass to insure their general prosperity—can that be a subject which renders you gloomy, Monsieur Gilbert?"

The latter shrugged up his shoulders.

"Then," said Billot, questioning in his turn, "what will you say of yourself if you now doubt, after having prepared everything in the old world, by giving liberty to the new?"

"Billot," rejoined Gilbert, "you have just, without at all suspecting it, uttered a word which is the solution of the enigma—a word which Lafayette has uttered, and which no one, beginning with himself, perhaps fully understands. Yes, we have given liberty to the new world."

"You!—and Frenchmen, too! That is magnificent."

"It is magnificent; but it will cost us dear," said Gilbert, sorrowfully.

"Pooh! the money is spent; the bill is paid," said Billot, joyously. "A little gold, a great deal of blood, and the debt is liquidated."

"Blind enthusiast!" said Gilbert, "who sees not in this dawning in the west the germ of ruin to us all? Alas! why do I accuse them, when I did not see more

clearly than they ? They having given liberty to the new
world, I fear, I fear greatly, was totally ruining the old
one."

" *Rerum novus nascitur ordo !* " exclaimed Pitou, with
great revolutionary self-possession.

"Silence, child," said Gilbert.

"Was it, then, more difficult to overcome the English
than it is now to quiet the French ?" asked Billot.

"A new world," repeated Gilbert—"that is to say, a
vast open space, a clear table to work upon ; no laws, but
no abuses ; no ideas, but no prejudices.   In France, thirty
thousand square leagues of territory for thirty millions of
people ; that is to say, that, should the space be equally
divided, scarcely room for a cradle or a grave for each.
Out yonder, in America, two hundred thousand square
leagues for three millions of persons ; frontiers which are
ideal, for they border on the desert, which is to say im-
mensity.   In those two hundred thousand leagues, navi-
gable rivers, having a course of a thousand leagues ; virgin
forests, of which God alone knows the limits ; that is to
say, all the elements of life, of civilization, and of a brilliant future.   Oh ! how easy it is, Billot, when a man is
called Lafayette, and is accustomed to wield a sword,
when a man is called Washington, and is accustomed to
reflect deeply—how easy it is to combat against walls of
wood, of earth, of stone, of human flesh.   But when, instead of founding, it is necessary to destroy ; when we
see in the old order of things that we are obliged to attack
walls of bygone crumbling ideas, and behind the ruins
even of these walls that crowds of people and of interests
still take refuge ; when, after having found the idea, we
find that, in order to make the people adopt it, it will be
necessary, perhaps, to decimate that people, from the old
who remember, down to the child who has still to learn,
from the monument which is the recollection down to the
instinct which is the germ of it—then, oh then, Billot !
it is a task which will make all those shudder who can see
behind the horizon.   I am far-sighted, Billot, and I
shudder."

"Pardon me, sir," said Billot, with his sound good
sense ; " you accused me, a short time since, of hating the
revolution, and now you are making it execrable to me."

"But have I told you that I renounce it ?"

"*Errare humanum est*," murmured Pitou, "*sed perseverare diabolicum.*"

And he drew his feet toward him with his hands.

"I shall, however, persevere," continued Gilbert; "for although I see the obstacles, I can perceive the end, and that end is splendid, Billot. It is not only the liberty of France that I am dreaming of, but it is equality before the laws—equality of rights; it is not the fraternity of our own citizens, but fraternity between all nations. I may be losing my own soul, my body may perhaps perish in the struggle," continued Gilbert, in a melancholy tone, "but it matters not; the soldier who is sent to the assault of a fortress, sees the cannon on its ramparts, sees the balls with which they are loaded, sees the match placed near the touch-hole; he sees even more than this, he sees the direction in which they are pointed, he feels that this piece of black iron may pass through his own breast; but he still rushes onward—the fortress must be taken. Well, we are soldiers, father Billot. Forward, then! and over the heaps of our dead bodies may one day march the generations of which this boy now present is the advance guard."

"I do not really know why you despair, Monsieur Gilbert. Is it because an unfortunate man was this day murdered on the Place de Grève?"

"And why were you, then, so much horrified? Go, then, Billot, and cut throats also."

"Oh! what are you now saying, Monsieur Gilbert?"

"Zounds! a man should be consistent. You came here, all pale, all trembling—you who are so brave, so strong—and you said to me, 'I am tired out.' I laughed in your face, Billot: and now that I explain to you why you were pale, why you were worn out, it is you who laugh at me in turn."

"Speak, speak; but first of all give me the hope that I shall return cured, consoled, to my fields."

"Your fields! Listen to me, Billot—all our hope is there. The country—a sleeping revolution, which wakes up once in a thousand years, and gives royalty the vertigo every time it awakens—the country will wake up in its turn, when the day shall come for purchasing or conquering those wrongly acquired territories of which you just now spoke, and with which the nobility and clergy are

gorged, even to choking.   But to urge on the country to
a harvest of ideas, it will be necessary to urge on the
countrymen to the conquest of the soil.   Man, by becoming a proprietor, becomes free ; and in becoming free, he
becomes a better man.   To us, then, privileged laborers,
to whom God has consented that the veil of the future
shall be raised, to us, then, the fearful work, which, after
giving liberty to the people, shall give them the property
of the soil.   Here, Billot, will be a good work, and a sorry
recompense, perhaps, but an active, powerful work, full of
joys and vexations, of glory and calumny.   The country
is still lulled in a dull, impotent slumber, but it awaits
only to be awakened by our summons, and that new dawn
shall be our work.   When once the country is awakened,
the sanguinary portion of our labors will be terminated,
and its peaceable labors, the labors of the country, will
commence."

"What, then, do you now advise that I should do, Monsieur Gilbert ?"

"If you wish to be useful to your country, to the nation, to your brother men, to the world, remain here, Billot ; take a hammer and work in this Vulcan's furnace,
which is forging thunders for the whole world."

"Remain here to see men butchered, and perhaps at
last learn to butcher them myself."

"How so ?" said Gilbert, with a faint smile.   "You,
Billot, become a murderer !   What is it you are saying ?"

"I say that should I remain here as you request me,"
cried Billot, trembling with agitation, "I say that the
first man whom I shall see attaching a rope to a lamp-post,
I will hang that man with these my hands."

Gilbert's smile became more positive.

"Well, now," said he, "I find you understand me, and
now you also are a murderer."

"Yes ; a murderer of vile wretches."

"Tell me, Billot, you have seen De Losme, De Launay,
De Flesselles, Foulon, and Berthier slaughtered ?"

"Yes."

"What epithet did those who slaughtered them apply
to them ?"

"They call them wretches."

"Oh ! that is true," said Pitou, "they did call them
wretches."

"Yes ; but it is I who am right, and not they," rejoined Billot.

"You will be in the right," said Gilbert, "if you hang them ; but in the wrong if they hang you."

Billot hung down his head under this heavy blow ; then suddenly raising it again with dignity :

"Will you venture to maintain," said he, "that those who assassinate defenseless men, and who are under the safeguard of public honor, will you maintain that they are as good Frenchmen as I am ?"

"Ah !" said Gilbert, "that is quite another question. Yes, in France we have several sorts of Frenchmen. First of all, we have the people, to which Pitou belongs, to which you belong, to which I belong ; then we have the French clergy, and then the French nobility. Three classes of Frenchmen in France, each French in his own point of view, that is to say, as regards their interests, and this without counting the King of France, who is also a Frenchman in his way. Ah ! Billot, here you see in these different modes of all these Frenchmen considering themselves French, here is the real secret of the revolution. You will be a Frenchman in your own way, the Abbé Maury will be a Frenchman in his way, Mirabeau will be a Frenchman in a mode that differs from that of the Abbé Maury, and the king will be a Frenchman in another way than that of Mirabeau. Well, Billot, my excellent friend, thou man of upright heart and sound judgment, you have just entered upon the second part of the question which I am now engaged upon. Do me the pleasure, Billot, to cast your eyes on this."

And Gilbert presented a printed paper to the farmer.

"What is this ?" asked Billot, taking the paper.

"Read."

"Why, you know full well that I cannot read."

"Tell Pitou to read it, then."

Pitou rose, and standing on tiptoes looking at the paper over the farmer's shoulders :

"This is not French," said he ; "it is not Latin, neither is it Greek."

"It is English," replied Gilbert.

"I do not know English," said Pitou, proudly.

"I do," said Gilbert, "and will translate the paper to you ; but, in the first place, read the signature."

" P I T T," spelled Pitou; "what does P 1 T T
mean ? "

" I will explain it to you," replied Gilbert.

CHAPTER XIV.

" PITT," rejoined Gilbert, " is the son of Pitt."

" Well, now ! " cried Pitou ; " that is just as we have it
in the Bible.   There is, then, Pitt the first and Pitt the
second ? "

" Yes, and Pitt the first, my friends—listen attentively
to what I am going to tell you——"

" We are listening," replied Billot and Pitou at the same
moment.

" This Pitt the first was, during thirty years, the sworn
enemy of France ; he combated in the retirement of his
cabinet, to which he was nailed by the gout, Montcalm
and Vaudreuil in America, Bailly de Suffren and D'Estaing
on the seas, Noailles and Broglie on the continent.   This
Pitt the first made it a principle with him that it was
necessary to destroy the influence which France had gained
over the whole of Europe ; during thirty years he reconquered from us, one by one, all our colonies—one by one,
all our factories, the whole of our possessions in the East
Indies, a hundred leagues of territory in Canada, and then,
when he saw that France was three quarters ruined, he
brings forward his son to ruin her altogether."

" Ah, ah ! " exclaimed Billot, evidently much interested,
"so that the Pitt we have now——"

" Precisely," replied Gilbert, " he is the son of the Pitt
whom we have had, and whom you already know, father
Billot, whom Pitou knows, whom all the universe knows,
and this Pitt junior was thirty years old this last May."

" Thirty years old ? "

" Yes ; you see that he has well employed his time, my
friends.   Notwithstanding his youth, he has now governed
England for seven years—seven years has he put in practise
the theory of his father."

" Well, then, we are likely to have him for a long time
yet," said Billot.

" And it is the more probable that the vital qualities

are very tenacious among the Pitts. Let me give you a proof of it."

Pitou and Billot indicated by a motion of their heads that they were listening with the greatest attention.

Gilbert continued :

"In 1778, the father of our enemy was dying; his physicians announced to him that his life was merely hanging by a thread, and that the slightest effort would break that thread. The English Parliament was then debating on the question of abandoning the American colonies and yielding to their desire for independence, in order to put a stop to the war which threatened, fomented as it was by the French, to swallow up the riches and all the soldiers of Great Britain. It was at the moment when Louis XVI., our good king, he on whom the whole nation has just conferred the title of 'Father of French Liberty,' had solemnly recognized the independence of America ; and on the fields of battle in that country, and in their councils, the swords and genius of the French had obtained the mastery. England had offered to Washington, that is to say, to the chief of the insurgents, the recognition of American nationality on condition that the new nation should ally itself with England against France."

"But," said Billot, "it appears to me this proposition was not a decent one, to be either offered or accepted."

"My dear Billot, this is what is called diplomacy, and in the political world, these sorts of ideals are much admired. Well, Billot, however immoral you may consider the matter, in spite of Washington, the most faithful of men, Americans would have been found to accede to this degrading concession on the part of England. But Lord Chatham, the father of Pitt, the man who had been given over by the physicians, this dying man, this phantom who was already standing knee-deep in the grave, this Chatham who, it might be thought, could have desired naught more on this earth but repose, before sleeping beneath his monument this feeble old man determined on appearing in the Parliament where the question was about to be discussed.

"On entering the House of Lords he was leaning on the one side on the arm of his son William Pitt, then only nineteen years of age, and on the other on that of his son-in-law, Lord Mahon. He was attired in his magnificent robes, which formed a derisive contrast to his own emaciated form. Pale as a specter, his eyes half extinguished beneath his languishing eyelids, he desired his friends to lead him to his usual seat on the bench appropriated to earls, while all the lords rose at his entrance, astounded at the unexpected apparition, and bowed to him in admiration as the Roman Senate might have done had Tiberius, dead and forgotten, returned among them. He listened in silence and with profound attention to the speech of the Duke of Richmond, the mover of the proposition, and when he had concluded, Lord Chatham rose to reply.

" Then this dying man summoned up strength enough to speak for three whole hours ; he found fire enough within his heart to lend lightnings to his eyes ; in his soul he found accents which stirred up the hearts of all who heard him.

" It is true that he was speaking against France, it is true that he was instilling into the minds of his countrymen the hatred which he felt, it is true that he had called up all his energies, all his fervent eloquence, to ruin and devour this country, the hated rival of his own. He forbid that America should be recognized as independent, he forbid all sort of compromise, he cried war ! war ! He spoke as Hannibal spoke against Rome, as Cato against Carthage ? He declared that the duty of every loyal Englishman was to perish ruined, rather than to suffer that a colony, even one single colony, should detach itself from the mother country. Having concluded his peroration, having hurled his last threat, he fell to the ground as if thunder-stricken.

" He had nothing more to do in this world—he was carried expiring from the house.

" Some few days afterward he was dead."

" Oh ! oh ! cried both Billot and Pitou, simultaneously, "what a man this Lord Chatham was ! "

" He was the father of the young man of thirty who is now occupying our attention," pursued Gilbert. " Lord Chatham died at the age of seventy. If the son lives to the same age, we shall have to endure William Pitt forty years longer. This is the man, father Billot, with whom we have to contend ; this is the man who now governs Great Britain, who well remembers the names of Lameth, of Rochambeau, and Lafayette. who at this moment knows the name of every man in the National Assembly ; he who has sworn a deadly hatred to Louis XVI., the author of the treaty of 1778 ; the man, in short, who will not breathe freely as long as there shall be a loaded musket in France and a full pocket. Do you begin to understand ? "

" I understand that he has a great detestation of France ; yes, that is true, but I do not altogether see your meaning."

" Nor I," said Pitou.

" Well, then, read these four words." And he presented a paper to Pitou.

" English again ! " cried Pitou.

" Yes ; these are the words—' Don't mind the money.' "

" I hear the words, but I do not understand them," rejoined Pitou.

Gilbert translated the words, and then :

" But more than this ; he further on reiterates the same advice for he says : ' Tell them not to be sparing of money, and they need not send me any accounts.' "

" Then they are arming," said Billot.

" No ; they are bribing."

" But to whom is this letter addressed ? "

" To everybody and to nobody. The money which is thus given, thus strewn abroad, thus lavished, is given to peasants, to artisans, to wretches, to men, in short, who will degrade our revolution."

Father Billot held down his head ; these words explained many things.

" Would you have knocked down De Launay with the butt-end of a musket, Billot ? "

" No."

" Would you have killed Flesselles by firing a pistol at him ? "

" No."

" Would you have carried the still bleeding heart of Berthier and placed it on the table of the electors ? "

" Infamy ! " exclaimed Billot. " On the contrary, however guilty this man may have been, I would have allowed myself to be torn to pieces could I have saved him by it ; and the proof of this is that I was wounded in defending him, and that but for Pitou, who dragged me to the river-side——"

" Oh ! that is true," cried Pitou, " but for me father Billot would have had but a bad time of it."

" Well, then, see you now, Billot, there are many men

who would act as you have done, when they feel that they have some one to assist them near them, and who, on the contrary, if abandoned to bad examples, become wicked, then ferocious—then, when the evil is done, why, 'tis done."

"But, in short," observed Billot, objectingly, "admitting that Mr. Pitt, or, rather, his money, had something to do with the death of Flesselle, of Foulon, and of Berthier, what would he gain by it ?"

Gilbert began to laugh with that inaudible laugh which astonishes the simple, but which makes the thinking shudder.

"What would he gain by it ?" he exclaimed, "can you ask that ?"

"Yes, I do ask it."

"I will tell you. It is this : you were much pleased with the revolution, were you not—you who walked in blood to take the Bastile ?"

"Yes, I was pleased with it."

"Well, you now like it less—well ! now you regret Villers-Cotterets, your farm, the quietude of your plain, the shades of your great forests."

"*Frigida tempe*," murmured Piton.

"Oh, yes, you are right," sighed Billot.

"Well, then, you, father Billot, you, a farmer, you, the proprietor of land, you, a child of the Isle of France, and consequently a Frenchman of the olden time, you represent the third order, you belong to that which is called the majority. Well, then, you are disgusted."

"I acknowledge it."

"Then the majority will become disgusted as you are."

"And what then ?"

"And you will one day open your arms to the soldiers of the Duke of Brunswick or of Mr. Pitt, who will come to you in the name of those two liberators of France to restore wholesome doctrine."

"Never !"

"Pshaw ! wait a little."

"Flesselles, Berthier, and Foulon were at bottom rascals," observed Piton.

"Assuredly, as Monsieur de Sartines and Monsieur de Maurepas were villains, as Monsieur d'Argenson and Monsieur de Philippeaux were before them, as Monsieur Law was, as the Le Blanc, the De Paris, the Duvernays were villains, as Foquet was, as Mazarin was also, as Lamblanq, as Enguerraud de Marigny were villains, as Monsieur de Brienne is toward Monsieur de Calonne, as Monsieur de Calonne is toward Monsieur de Necker, as Monsieur de Necker will be to the administration which we shall have in two years."

"Oh! oh! doctor," murmured Billot, "Monsieur Necker a villain—never!"

"As you will be, my good Billot, a villain in the eyes of little Pitou here, in case one of Mr. Pitt's agents should teach him certain theories, backed by the influence of a pint of brandy and ten livres per day for getting up disturbances. This word *villain*, do you see, Billot, is the word by which, in revolutions, we designate the man who thinks differently from us; we are all destined to bear that name more or less; some will bear it so far that their countrymen will inscribe it on their tombs, others so much further that posterity will ratify the epithet. This, my dear Billot, is what I see and which you do not see. Billot, Billot! people of real worth must therefore not withdraw."

"Bah!" cried Billot, "even were honest people to withdraw, the revolution would still run its course; it is in full motion."

Another smile rose to the lips of Gilbert.

"Great child!" cried he, "who would abandon the handle of the plow, unyoke the horses from it, and then say: 'Good! the plow has no need of me, the plow will trace its furrow by itself.' But, my friends, who was it undertook the revolution? Honest people, were they not?"

"France flatters herself that it is so. It appears to me that Lafayette is an honest man, it appears to me that Bailly is an honest man, it appears to me that Monsieur Necker is an honest man, it appears to me that Monsieur Elie, Monsieur Hullin, and Monsieur Maillard, who fought side by side with me, are honest people, it appears to me that you yourself——"

"Well, Billot, if honest people, if you, if I, if Maillard, if Hullin, if Elie, if Necker, if Bailly, if Lafayette should withdraw, who would carry on the work? Why, those wretches, those assassins, those villains whom I have pointed out to you—the agents, the agents of Mr. Pitt!"

"Try to answer that, father Billot," said Pitou, convinced of the justice of the doctor's argument.

"Well, then," replied Billot, "we will arm ourselves, and shoot these villains down as if they were dogs."

"Wait a moment. Who will arm themselves?"

"Everybody."

"Billot, Billot! remember one thing, my good friend, and it is this, that what we are doing at this moment is called—what do you call what we are now doing, Billot?"

"Talking politics, Monsieur Gilbert."

"Well, in politics there is no longer any absolute crime; one is a villain or an honest man, as we favor or thwart the interests of the man who judges us. Those whom you call villains will always give some specious reasons for their crimes; and to many honest people, who may have had a direct or an indirect interest in the commission of these crimes, these very villains will appear honest men also. From the moment that we reach that point, Billot, we must beware. There will then be men to hold the plow-handle. It will move onward, Billot—it will move onward, and without us."

"It is frightful," said the farmer, "but if it moves onward without us, where will it stop?"

"God only knows," exclaimed Gilbert; "as to myself, I know not."

"Well, then, if you do not know, you who are a learned man, Monsieur Gilbert, I, who am an ignoramus, cannot be expected to know anything of the matter. I augur from it——"

"Well, what do you augur from it? Let us hear."

"I augur from it that what we had better do—I mean Pitou and myself—is to return to the farm. We will again take to the plow—the real plow—that of iron and wood, with which we turn up the earth, and not the one of flesh and blood, called the French people, and which is as restive as a vicious horse. We will make our corn grow instead of shedding blood, and shall live free, joyous and happy as lords in our own domain. Come with us, come with us, Monsieur Gilbert. The deuce! I like to know where I am going."

"One moment, my stout-hearted friend," cried Gilbert.

"No, I know not whither I am going. I have told you so, and I repeat it to you; however, I still go on, and I will continue still to do so. My duty is traced out to me; my life belongs to God, but my works are the debt which I shall pay to my country. If my conscience says to me, 'Go on, Gilbert, you are in the right road—go on,' that is all that I require. If I am mistaken, men will punish me—but God will absolve me."

"But sometimes men punish those who are not mistaken. You said so yourself just now."

"And I say it again. It matters not, I persist, Billot; be it an error or not, I shall go on. To guarantee that the events will not prove my inability, God forbid that I should pretend to do so. But before all, Billot, the Lord has said, 'Peace be to the man of good intentions.' Therefore be one of those to whom God . has promised peace. Look at Monsieur de Lafayette, in America as well as France—this is the third white charger he has worn out, without counting those he will wear out in future. Look at Monsieur de Bailly, who wears out his lungs. Look at the king, who wears out his popularity. Come, come, Billot, let us not be egotistical. Let us also wear ourselves out a little. Remain with me, Billot."

"But to do what, if we do not prevent evil being done?"

"Billot, remember never to repeat those words; for I should esteem you less. You have been trampled under foot, you have received hard fisticuffs, hard knocks from the butt-ends of muskets, and even from bayonets when you wished to save Foulon and Berthier."

"Yes, and even a great many," replied the farmer, passing his hand over his still painful body.

"And as to me," said Pitou, "I had one eye almost put out."

"And all that for nothing," added Billot.

"Well, my children, if instead of their being only ten, fifteen, twenty of your courage, there had been a hundred, two hundred, three hundred, you would have saved the unhappy man from the frightful death which was inflicted on him; you would have spared the nation the blot which has sullied it. And that is the reason why, instead of returning to the country, which is tolerably tranquil—that is why, Billot, I exact as far as I can exact anything of

yon, my friend, that you should remain at Paris—that I
may have always near me a vigorous arm, an upright heart;
that I might test my mind and my works on the faithful
touch-stone of your good sense and your pure patriotism;
and, in fine, that we might strew around us, not gold—for
that we have not—but our love of country and of the
public welfare, in which you would be my agent with a
multitude of misled, unfortunate men—my staff, should
my feet slip—my staff, should I have occasion to strike
a blow."

"A blind man's dog," said Billot, with sublime simplicity.

"Precisely," said Gilbert, in the same tone.

"Well," said Billot, "I accept your proposal. I will be
whatever you may please to make me."

"I know that you are abandoning everything—fortune,
wife, child, and happiness, Billot. But you may be
tranquil; it will not be for long."

"And I," said Pitou, "what am I to do?"

"You?" said Gilbert, looking at the ingenuous and
hardy youth, who boasted not much of his intelligence;
"you, you will return to the farm, to console Billot's
family, and explain to them the holy mission he has
undertaken."

"Instantly!" cried Pitou, trembling with joy at the
idea of returning to Catherine.

"Billot," said Gilbert, "give him your instructions."

"They are as follows," said Billot.

"I am all attention."

"Catherine is appointed by me as mistress of the house.
Do you understand?"

"And Madame Billot?" exclaimed Pitou, somewhat
surprised at this slight offered to the mother, to the advancement of the daughter.

"Pitou,' said Gilbert, who had at once caught the idea
of Billot, from seeing a slight blush suffuse the face of
the honest farmer, "remember the Arabian proverb, 'to
hear is to obey.'"

Pitou blushed in his turn. He had almost understood
and felt the indiscretion of which he had been guilty.

"Catherine has all the judgment of the family," added
Billot, unaffectedly, in order to explain his idea.

Gilbert bowed in token of assent.

"Is that all?" inquired the youth.

"All that I have to say," replied Billot.

"But not as regards me," said Gilbert.

"I am listening," observed Pitou, well disposed to attend to the Arabian proverb cited by Gilbert.

"You will go with a letter I shall give you to the College Louis le Grand," added Gilbert. "You will deliver that letter to the Abbé Berardier; he will intrust Sebastian to you, and you will bring him here. After I have embraced him, you will take him to Villers-Cotterets, where you will place him in the hands of the Abbé Fortier, that he may not altogether lose his time. On Sundays and Thursdays he will go out with you. Make him walk in the meadows and in the woods. It will be more conducible to my tranquillity and his health that he should be in the country yonder than here."

"I have understood you perfectly," said Pitou, delighted to be thus restored to the friend of his childhood, and to the vague aspirations of a sentiment somewhat more adult, which had been awakened within him by the magic name of Catherine.

He rose and took leave of Gilbert, who smiled—and of Billot, who was dreaming.

Then he set off, running at full speed, to fetch Sebastian Gilbert, his foster-brother, from the college.

"And now we," said Gilbert to Billot, "we must set to work."

CHAPTER XV.

A DEGREE of calmness had succeeded at Versailles to the terrible moral and political agitations which we have placed before the eyes of our readers.

The king breathed again, and although he could not help reflecting on the suffering his Bourbon pride had endured during his journey to Paris, he consoled himself with the idea of his reconquered popularity.

During this time M. de Necker was organizing, and by degrees losing his.

As to the nobility, they were beginning to prepare their defection or their resistance.

The people were watching and waiting.

During this time the queen, thrown back, as it were,
on the resources of her own mind, assured that she was
the object of many hatreds, shut herself up closely, almost
concealed herself ; for she also knew that although the
object of hatred to many, she was at the same time the
object of many hopes.

Since the journey of the king to Paris, she had scarcely
caught a glimpse of Gilbert.

Once, however, he had presented himself to her in the
vestibule which led to the king's apartments.

And there, as he had bowed to her very humbly and respectfully, she was the first to begin a conversation with
him.

"Good-day, sir," said she to him ; "are you going to
the king ?"

And then she added, with a smile, in which there was a
slight tinge of irony :

"Is it as counselor, or as physician ?"

"It is as his physician, madame," replied Gilbert. "I
have to-day an appointed service."

She made a sign to Gilbert to follow her. The doctor
obeyed.

They both of them went into a small sitting-room, which
led to the king's bedroom.

"Well, sir," said she, "you see that you were deceiving
me when you assured me the other day, with regard to
the journey to Paris, that the king was incurring no
danger."

"Who, I, madame ?" cried Gilbert, astonished.

"Undoubtedly ; was not the king fired at ?"

"Who has said that, madame ?"

"Everybody, sir ; and, above all, those who saw the
poor woman fall almost beneath the wheels of the king's
carriage. Who says that ? Why, Monsieur de Beauvau
and Monsieur d'Estaing, who saw your coat torn and your
frill perforated by the ball."

"Madame !"

"The ball which thus grazed you, sir, that might have
killed the king, as it killed that unfortunate woman ! for,
in short, it was neither you nor that poor woman that the
murderers wished to kill."

"I do not believe in such a crime," replied the doctor,
hesitating.

"Be it so; but I believe in it, sir," rejoined the queen, fixing her eyes on Gilbert.

"At all events, if there was intentional crime, it ought not to be imputed to the people."

"Ah!" she exclaimed. "To whom, then, must it be attributed? Speak."

"Madame," continued Gilbert, shaking his head, "for some time past I have been watching and studying the people. Well, then, the people, when they assassinate in revolutionary times, the people kill with their hands; they are then like the furious tiger, the irritated lion. The tiger and the lion use no intermediary agent between their fury and their victim; they kill for killing's sake; they spill blood to spill it; they like to dye their teeth, to steep their claws in it."

"Witness Foulon and Berthier, you would say. But was not Flesselles killed by a shot from a pistol? I was so told, at least; but after all," continued the queen, in a tone of irony, "perhaps it was not true; we crowned heads are so surrounded by flatterers."

Gilbert, in his turn, looked intently at the queen.

"Oh! as to him," said he, "you do not believe more than I do, madame, that it was the people who killed him. There were people who were interested in bringing about his death."

The queen reflected.

"In fact," she replied, "that may be possible."

"Then," said Gilbert, bowing, as if to ask the queen if she had anything more to say to him.

"I understand, sir," said the queen, gently, stopping the doctor with an almost friendly gesture; "however that may be, let me tell you that you will never save the king's life so effectually by your medical skill, as you did three days ago with your own breast."

Gilbert bowed a second time.

But as he saw that the queen remained, he remained also.

"I ought to have seen you again, sir," said the queen, after a momentary repose.

"Your majesty had no further need of me," said Gilbert.

"You are modest."

"I wish I were not so. madame."

"And why?"

"Because, being less modest, I should be less timid, and consequently better able to serve my friends or to frustrate enemies."

"Why do you make that distinction? You say, *my* friends, but do not say *my* enemies."

"Because, madame, I have no enemies; or, rather, because I will not, for my part, at least, admit that I have any."

The queen looked at him with surprise.

"I mean to say," continued Gilbert, "that those only are my enemies who hate me, but that I, on my side, hate no one."

"Because?"

"Because I no longer love any one, madame."

"Are you ambitious, Monsieur Gilbert?"

"At one time I hoped to become so, madame."

"And——"

"And that passion proved abortive, as did every other."

"There is one, however, that still remains in it," said the queen, with a slight shade of artful irony.

"In my heart? And what passion is that, good Heaven?"

"Your—patriotism."

Gilbert bowed.

"Oh, that is true," said he. "I adore my country, and for it I would make every sacrifice."

"Alas!" said the queen, with undefinable melancholy, "there was a time when a good Frenchman would not have expressed that thought in the terms you now have used."

"What does the queen mean to say?" respectfully inquired Gilbert.

"I mean to say, sir, that in the times of which I speak it was impossible for a Frenchman to love his country, without, at the same time, loving his queen and king."

Gilbert blushed: he bowed, and felt within his heart one of those electric shocks which, in her seducing intimacies, the queen produced on those who approached her.

"You do not answer me, sir," she said.

"Madame!" cried Gilbert, "I may venture to boast that no one loves the monarchy more ardently than myself."

"Are we living in times, sir, when it is sufficient to say this ? and would it not be better to prove it by our acts ?"

"But, madame," said Gilbert, with surprise, "I beg your majesty to believe that all the king or queen might command——"

"You would do—is it not so ?"

"Assuredly, madame."

"In doing which, sir," said the queen, resuming, in spite of herself, a slight degree of her accustomed haughtiness, "you would only be fulfilling a duty."

"Madame——"

"God, who has given omnipotence to kings," continued Marie Antoinette, "has released them from the obligation of being grateful to those who merely fulfil a duty."

"Alas ! alas ! Madame," rejoined Gilbert, "the time is approaching when your servants will deserve more than your gratitude, if they will only fulfil their duty."

"What is it you say, sir ?"

"I mean to say, madame, that in these days of disorder and demolition, you will in vain seek for friends where you have been accustomed to find servants. Pray, pray to God, madame, to send you other servants, other supporters, other friends than those you have."

"Do you know any such ?"

"Yes, madame."

"Then point them out to me."

"See now, madame ; I, who now speak to you, I was your enemy but yesterday."

"My enemy ! and why were you so ?"

"Because you ordered that I should be imprisoned."

"And to-day ?"

"To-day, madame," replied Gilbert, bowing, "I am your servant."

"And your object ?"

"Madame——"

"The object for which you have become my servant ? It is not in your nature, sir, to change your opinion, your belief, your affections so suddenly. You are a man, Monsieur Gilbert, whose remembrances are deeply planted ; you know how to perpetuate your vengeance. Come, now, tell me what was the motive of this change ?"

"Madame, you reproached me but now with my loving my country too passionately."

"No one can ever love it too much, sir ; the only question is to know how we love it. For myself, I love my country." Gilbert smiled. "Oh ! no false interpretation, sir ; my country is France. A German by blood, I am a French woman in my heart. I love France; but it is through the king. I love France from the respect due to God, who has given us the throne. And now to you, sir."

"To me, madame ?"

"Yes, it is now for you to speak. I understand you, do I not ? To you it is quite another matter. You love France merely and simply for France herself."

"Madame," replied Gilbert, bowing, "I should fail in respect to your majesty, should I fail in frankness."

"Oh !" exclaimed the queen, "frightful, frightful period ! when all people who pretend to be people of worth isolate two things which have never been separated from each other ; two principles which have always gone hand in hand—France and her king. But have you not a tragedy of one of your poets, in which it is asked of a queen who has been abandoned by all, 'What now remains to you ?' and to which she replies, 'Myself !' Well, then, like Medea, I also will say, 'Myself !' and we shall see."

And she angrily left the room, leaving Gilbert in amazement.

She had just raised to his view, by the breath of her anger, one corner of the veil behind which she was combining the whole work of the counter-revolution.

"Come, come," said Gilbert to himself, as he went into the king's room, "the queen is meditating some project."

"Really," said the queen to herself, as she was returning to her apartment, "decidedly, there is nothing to be made of this man. He has energy, but he has no devotedness."

Poor princess ! with whom the word devotedness is synonymous with civility

CHAPTER XVI.

GILBERT returned to M. Necker after his professional visit to the king, whom he had found as tranquil as the queen was agitated.

The king was composing speeches, he was examining accounts, he was meditating reforms in the laws.

This well-intentioned man, whose look was so kind, whose soul was so upright, whose heart erred only from prejudices inherent to the royal condition, this man was absolutely bent on producing trivial reforms in exchange for the serious inroads made on his prerogative. He was obstinately bent on examining the distant horizon with his short-sighted eyes, when an abyss was yawning beneath his feet. This man inspired Gilbert with a feeling of profound pity. As to the queen, it was not thus, and in spite of his impassibility, Gilbert felt that she was one of those women whom it was necessary to love passionately, or to hate even to the death.

When she had returned to her own apartment, Marie Antoinette felt as if an immense burden were weighing on her heart.

And, in fact, whether as a woman or as a queen, she felt that there was nothing stable around her—nothing which could aid her in supporting even a portion of the burden which was crushing her.

On whichever side she turned her eyes, she saw only hesitation and doubt.

The courtiers anxious with regard to their fortunes, and realizing what they could.

Relations and friends thinking of emigrating.

The proudest woman of them all, Andrée, gradually becoming estranged from her in heart and mind.

The noblest and the most beloved of all the men who surrounded her, Charny, wounded by her caprice and a prey to doubt.

This position of affairs caused her great anxiety ; she, who was instinct and sagacity personified.

How could this man, who was purity itself, how could this heart, without alloy, have changed so suddenly ?

"No, he has not yet changed," said the queen to herself, sighing deeply, "but he is about to change."

He is about to change ! Frightful conviction to the woman who loves passionately, and insupportable to the woman who loves with pride.

Now, the queen loved Charny both passionately and proudly. The queen was suffering, therefore, from two wounds.

And yet, at that very time, at the time when she felt the consciousness of having acted wrongly, of the evil she had committed, she had still time to remedy it.

But the mind of that crowned woman was not a flexible mind. She could not descend to waver even though she knew she was acting unjustly; had it been toward an indifferent person, she might have, or would have, wished to have shown some greatness of soul, and then she might perhaps have asked for forgiveness.

But to the man whom she had honored with an affection at once so tender and so pure, to him whom she had deigned to admit to a participation in her most secret thoughts, the queen considered it would be degrading to make the slightest concession.

The misfortune of queens who condescend to love a subject is to love them always as queens, but never as women.

Marie Antoinette estimated herself at so high a price, that she thought there was nothing human which could compensate her love, not even blood, not even tears.

From the moment she felt that she was jealous of Andrée, she had begun to dwindle morally.

The consequence of this inferiority was her caprice.

The consequence of her caprice was anger.

The consequence of her anger was evil thoughts, which always bring in their train evil actions.

Charny did not enter into any of the considerations which we have just stated; but he was a man, and he had comprehended that Marie Antoinette was jealous of his wife.

Of his wife, toward whom he had never shown any affection.

There is nothing which so much revolts an upright heart, one altogether incapable of treachery, as to see that it is believed capable of treachery.

There is nothing which so much conduces to direct the attention toward a person as the jealousy with which that person is honored.

Above all, if that jealousy be really unjust.

Then the person who is suspected reflects.

He alternately considers the jealous heart and the person who has caused that jealousy.

The greater the soul of the jealous person, the greater is the danger into which it throws itself.

In fact, how is it possible to suppose that a person of expansive heart, of superior intelligence, of legitimate pride, could become agitated for a mere nothing, or for anything of trifling value. Why should a woman who is beautiful be jealous? Why should a woman of superior intellect be jealous? Why should a woman of the highest rank and power be jealous? How could it be supposed that, possessing all these advantages, a woman could be jealous for a mere nothing, or for anything of trifling value?

Charny knew that Mlle. Andrée de Taverney had been long a friend of the queen—that in former days she had been well treated, always preferred by her. How, then, was it that she no longer loved her? How was it that Marie Antoinette had all at once become jealous of her?

She must, therefore, have discerned some secret and mysterious beauty which M. de Charny had not discovered, and undoubtedly because he had not sought for it.

She had, therefore, felt that Charny might have perceived something in this woman, and that she, the queen, had lost in the comparison.

Or, again, she might have believed that she perceived that Charny loved her less, without there being any extraneous cause for this diminution of his passion.

There is nothing more fatal to the jealous than the knowledge which they thus give to others of the temperature of that heart which they wish to keep in the most fervid degree of heat.

How often does it happen that the loved object is informed of his coldness—of a coldness which he had begun to experience without being able to account for it.

And when he discovers that, when he feels the truth of the reproach, say, madame, how many times have you found that he has allowed your chains to be again thrown round him, that his languishing flame has been rekindled?

Oh! unskilfulness of lovers! It is, however, true that where much art or adroitness is exercised, there scarcely ever exists a great degree of love.

Marie Antoinette had, therefore, herself taught Charny to believe, by her own anger and injustice, that his heart was less full of love than formerly.

And as soon as he knew this, he endeavored to account for it. and, looking around him, very naturally discovered the cause of the queen's jealousy.

Andrée, the poor, abandoned Andrée, who had been a bride, but had never been a wife'

He pitied Andrée.

The scene of the return from Paris had unveiled the secret of this deep-rooted jealousy, so carefully concealed from all eyes.

The queen also clearly saw that all was discovered, and as she would not bend before Charny, she employed another method, which, in her opinion, would lead to the same end.

She began to treat Andrée with great kindness.

She admitted her to all her excursions, to all her evening parties; she overwhelmed her with caresses; she made her the envy of all the other ladies of the court.

And Andrée allowed her to do all this, with some astonishment, but without feeling grateful for it. She had for years said to herself that she belonged to the queen, that the queen could do as she pleased with her, and therefore was it that she submitted to it.

But, on the other side, as it was necessary that the irritation of the woman should be vented on some one, the queen began to severely ill-treat Charny. She no longer spoke to him; she was absolutely harsh to him; she affected to pass evenings, days, weeks, without observing that he was present.

Only, when he was absent, the heart of the poor woman swelled with anxiety; her eyes wandered around eagerly, seeking him, whom the moment they perceived, they were instantly averted from.

Did she need the support of an arm, had she an order to give, had she a smile to throw away, it was bestowed on the first comer.

But this first comer never failed to be a handsome and distinguished man.

The queen imagined she was curing her own wound by wounding Charny.

The latter suffered, but was silent. Not an angry or impatient gesture escaped him. He was a man possessing great self-command, and although suffering frightful torture, he remained, to appearance, perfectly impassible.

Then was seen a singular spectacle, a spectacle which women alone can furnish and fully comprehend.

Andrée felt all the sufferings of her husband, and as

she loved him with that angelic love which never had conceived a hope, she pitied him, and allowed him to perceive she did so.

The result of this compassion was a sweet and tacit reconciliation. She endeavored to console Charny without allowing him to perceive that she comprehended the need he had of consolation.

And all this was done with that delicacy which may be called essentially feminine, seeing that women alone are capable of it.

Marie Antoinette, who had sought to divide in order to reign, perceived that she had made a false move, and that she was only drawing together two souls by the very means which she had adopted to keep them separate.

Then the poor woman, during the silence and the solitude of night, endured the most frightful paroxysms of despair, such as would make us wonder that God had created beings of sufficient strength to support them.

And the queen would assuredly have succumbed to so many ills but for the constant occupation given to her mind by political events. No one complains of the hardness of a bed when his limbs are exhausted by fatigue.

Such were the circumstances under which the queen had been living since the return of the king to Versailles, up to the day when she thought seriously of resuming the absolute exercise of her power.

For in her pride she attributed to her decadency the species of depreciation to which for some time the woman had been subjected.

To her energetic mind, to think was to act. She, therefore, commenced her combinations without losing a moment.

Alas! these combinations which she was then meditating were those which wrought out her perdition.

CHAPTER XVII.

Unfortunately, in the queen's opinion, all the facts which had occurred were merely accidents, which a firm and active hand might remedy. It was only necessary to concentrate her power.

The queen, seeing that the Parisians had so suddenly

transformed themselves into soldiers, and appeared to wish for war, resolved on showing them what real war was.

"Up to this time, they have only had to deal with the Invalides, or with Swiss, but ill supported and wavering ; we will show them what it is to have opposed to them two or three well-disciplined and royalist regiments.

"Perhaps there may be a regiment of this description, which has already put to flight some of these rebellious rioters, and has shed blood in the convulsions of civil war. We will have the most celebrated of these regiments ordered here. The Parisians will then understand that their best policy will be to abstain from provocation."

This was after all the quarrels between the king and the National Assembly with regard to the veto. The king, during two months, had been struggling to recover some tattered shreds of sovereignty ; he had, conjointly with the administration and Mirabeau, endeavored to neutralize the Republican outburst which was endeavoring to efface royalty in France.

The queen had exhausted herself in this struggle, and was exhausted above all from having seen the king succumb.

The king, in this contention, had lost all his power and the remains of his popularity. The queen had gained an additional name—a nickname.

One of those words which were altogether foreign to the ears of the people, and from that reason more pleasing to the ears of the people ; a name which had not yet become an insult, but which was soon to become the most opprobrious of all ; a witty saying, which afterward was changed into a sanguinary rallying cry.

In short, she was called Mme. Veto.

This name was destined to be borne in revolutionary songs beyond the banks of the Rhine, to terrify in Germany the subjects and the friends of those who, having sent to France a German queen, had some right to be astonished that she was insulted by the name of the Autrichienne (the Austrian woman).

This name was destined in Paris to accompany, in the insensate dancing-rings, on days of massacre, the last cries, the hideous agonies of the victims.

Marie Antoinette was thenceforth called Mme. Veto, until the day when she was to be called the Widow Capet.

She had already changed her name three times. After having been called the Autrichienne, she was next called Mme. Deficit.

After the contests in which the queen had endeavored to interest her friends by the imminence of their own danger, she had remarked that sixty thousand passports had been applied for at the Hôtel de Ville.

Sixty thousand of the principal families of Paris and of France had gone off to rejoin in foreign countries the friends and relatives of the queen.

A very striking example, and one which had forcibly struck the queen.

And, therefore, from that moment she meditated a skilfully concerted flight; a flight supported by armed force should it be necessary; a flight which had for its object safety, after which the faithful who remained in France might carry on the civil war—that is to say, chastise the revolutionists.

The plan was not a bad one. It would assuredly have succeeded; but behind the queen the evil genius was also watching.

Strange destiny! that woman who inspired so many with enthusiastic devotedness, could nowhere find discretion.

It was known at Paris that she wished to fly before she had even persuaded herself to adopt the measure.

Marie Antoinette did not perceive that from the moment her intention had become known her plan had become impracticable.

However, a regiment, celebrated for its royalist sympathies, the Flanders regiment, arrived at Versailles by forced marches.

This regiment had been demanded by the municipal authorities at Versailles, who, tormented by the extraordinary guards, and by the strict watch it was necessarry to keep around the palace, incessantly threatened by fresh demands for distributions of provisions, and successive disturbances, stood in need of some other military force than the National Guards and the militia.

The palace had already quite enough to do to defend itself.

The Flanders regiment arrived, as we have said, and that it should at once assume the importance with which it was intended to be invested, it was necessary that a brilliant reception should be given to it, that it might at once attract the attention of the people.

The Count d'Estaing assembled all the officers of the National Guard and all those of the corps then present at Versailles, and went out to meet it.

The regiment made a solemn entry into Versailles, with its park of artillery and its ammunition wagons.

Around this group, which then became central, assembled a crowd of young gentlemen who did not belong to any regular corps.

They adopted a sort of uniform by which they could recognize one another, and were joined by all the officers unattached, all the chevaliers of the Order of St. Louis, whom danger or interest had brought to Versailles.

After this they made excursions to Paris, where were seen these new enemies, fresh, insolent, and puffed up with a secret which was sure to escape them as soon as an opportunity should present itself.

At that moment the king might have escaped. He would have been supported, protected on his journey, and Paris, perhaps, still ignorant and ill prepared, would have allowed his departure.

But the evil genius of the Autrichienne was still watching.

Liège revolted against the emperor, and the occupation which the revolt gave to Austria prevented her from thinking of the Queen of France.

The latter, on her side, thought that in delicacy she must abstain from asking any aid at such a moment.

Then events, to which impulsion had been given, continued to rush on with lightning-like rapidity.

After the ovation in honor of the Flanders regiment, the body-guard decided on giving a dinner to the officers of that regiment.

This banquet, this festival, was fixed for the first of October. Every important personage in the town was invited to it.

And what, then, was the object of this banquet? To fraternize with the Flanders soldiers. And why should not soldiers fraternize with one another, since the districts and provinces fraternized?

Was it forbidden by the constitution that gentlemen should fraternize?

The king was still the master of his regiments, and he alone commanded them ; the palace of Versailles was his own property ; he alone had a right to receive into it whomsoever he might please.

And why should he not receive brave soldiers and worthy gentlemen within it, men who had just come from Douai, where they had behaved well ?

Nothing could be more natural. No one thought of being astonished, and still less of being alarmed at it.

This repast, to be taken thus in union, was about to cement the affection which ought always to subsist between all the corps of the French army destined to defend both liberty and royalty.

Besides, did the king even know what had been agreed upon ?

Since the events of Paris, the king, free, thanks to his concessions, no longer occupied himself with public matters ; the burden of affairs had been taken from him. He desired to reign no longer, since others reigned for him, but he did not think that he ought to weary himself by doing nothing all day long.

The king, while the gentlemen of the National Assembly were fraudulently cutting and contriving—the king amused himself by hunting.

The king, while the nobility and the reverend bishops were abandoning, on the 4th of August, their dove-cots and their feudal rights, their pigeons and their parchments—the king, who was very willing, as all the world were doing it, to make some sacrifices, abolished all his hunting train, but he did not cease to hunt on that account.

Now, the king, who, while the officers of the Flanders regiment were to be dining with his body-guards—the king would be enjoying the pleasures of the chase, as he did every day ; the tables would be cleared away before his return.

This would even inconvenience him so little, and he would so little inconvenience the banquet in question, that it was resolved to ask the queen to allow the festival to be given within the walls of the palace itself.

The queen saw no reason for refusing this hospitality to the Flanders soldiers.

She gave them the theater for the banquet-room, in

which she allowed them for that day to construct a flooring even with the stage, that there might be ample space
for the guards and their guests.

When a queen wishes to be hospitable to French gentlemen, she is so to the full extent of her power. This was
their dining-room, but they also required a drawing-room;
the queen allowed them to use the Saloon of Hercules.

On a Thursday, the 1st of October, as we have already
said, this feast was given, and which was destined to fill
so fatal a page in the history of the blindness and improv-
idence of royalty.

The king had gone out hunting.

The queen was shut up in her own apartments, sorrowful and pensive, and determined not to hear either the
ringing of the glasses when the officers gave their toasts,
or the sound of their enthusiastic cheers.

Her son was in her arms; Andrée was with her; two
women were at work in one corner of the room; those
were the only persons with her.

The brilliantly attired officers, with their waving plumes
and bright gleaming arms, by degrees entered the palace;
their horses neighed before the grated gates of the royal
stables, their clarions sounded as they approached, and
the bands of the Flanders regiment and the guards filled
the air with harmonious sounds.

Outside the gilded railings of the courtyard of the
palace was a pale, inquisitive crowd, gloomily anxious,
watching, analyzing, and commenting on the joyous festival within, and the airs played by the military bands.

In gusts, like the squalls of a distant tempest, there ex-
haled from the open portals of the palace the sounds of
merriment with the odors of the savory viands.

It was very imprudent to allow this crowd of starving
people to inhale the odors of the good cheer and wine—to
allow these morose people to hear these sounds of jovial
festivity.

The festival was, however, continued without anything
disturbing its conviviality; for a time, all was conducted
with sobriety and order; the officers, full of respect for
the uniform they wore, at first conversed in an undertone,
and drank moderately; during the first half-hour, the
program which had been agreed upon was strictly adhered
to.

The second course was put on the table.

M. de Lusignan, the colonel of the Flanders regiment, rose and proposed four toasts. They were to the health of the king, the queen, the dauphin, and the royal family.

Four shouts of applause reechoed from the vaulted roofs, and struck the ears of the sorrowful spectators outside the palace.

An officer rose—perhaps he was a man of judgment and of courage—a man of sound good sense, who foresaw the issue of all this—a man sincerely attached to that royal family to whom he had just drunk so noisily.

This man comprehended that among these toasts there was one which was omitted, which probably might present itself to their attention.

He, therefore, proposed this toast, "The Nation."

A long murmur preceded a long shout.

"No, no," cried every person present, except the proposer of the toast.

And the toast to the nation was contemptuously rejected.

The festival had just assumed its real character, the torrent had formed its real course.

It has been said, and it is still repeated, that the person who proposed this toast was but an instigator of an opposing manifestation.

However this might be, his words produced an untoward effect. To forget the nation might have been but a trifle, but to insult it was too much. It avenged itself.

As from this moment the ice was broken, as to the reserved silence succeeded boisterous cries and excited conversation, discipline became but a chimerical modesty; the dragoons, the grenadiers, the "hundred Swiss" were sent for, and even all the private soldiers in the palace.

The wine was pushed round quickly; ten times were the glasses filled; when the dessert was brought in, it was absolutely pillaged. Intoxication became general, the soldiers forgot that they were drinking with their officers; it was, in reality, a fraternal festival.

From all parts were heard shouts of "Long live the king! long live the queen!" So many flowers, so many lights, illuminating the brilliantly gilded arches, so many loyal lightnings darting from the eyes of these brave men, was a spectacle which would have been grateful to the eyes of the queen and reassuring to those of the king.

This so unfortunate king, this so sorrowful queen, why were they not present at such a festival ?

"Some officious partisans withdrew from the dining-room, and ran to Marie Antoinette's apartments, and related, exaggerated, to her what they had seen.

Then the sorrowing eyes of the queen become reanimated, and she rises from her chair. There is, then, some loyalty left, some affection in French hearts !

There is, therefore, something still to hope.

At the doors were soon assembled a crowd of courtiers ; they entreat, they conjure the queen to pay a visit merely to show herself for a moment in the festive hall, where two thousand enthusiastic subjects are consecrating, by their hurrahs, the religion of monarchical principles.

"The king is absent," she sorrowfully replied. "I cannot go there alone."

"But with Monseigneur the Dauphin," said some imprudent persons who still insisted on her going.

"Madame! madame !" whispered a voice into her ear, "remain here, I conjure you to remain."

The queen turned round—it was the Count de Charny.

"What !" cried she, "are you not below with all those gentlemen ?"

"I was there, madame, but have returned. The excitement down yonder is so great that it may prejudice your majesty's interests more than may be imagined."

Marie Antoinette was in one of her sullen, her capricious days, with regard to Charny. It pleased her on that day to do precisely the contrary of everything that might have been agreeable to the count.

She darted at him a disdainful look, and was about to address some disobliging words to him, when, preventing her by a successful gesture :

"For mercy's sake, madame," added he, "at least, await the king's advice."

He thought by this to gain time.

"The king ! the king !" exclaimed several voices ; "the king has just returned from hunting."

And this was the fact.

Marie Antoinette rises and runs to meet the king, who, still booted and covered with dust, entered the room.

"Sire," cried she, "there is below a spectacle worthy of the King of France. Come with me—come with me !"

And she took the king's arm and dragged him away without looking at Charny, who dug his nails with anger into his breast.

Leading her son with her left hand, she descended the staircase. A whole flood of courtiers preceded or urged her on. She reaches the door of the theater at the moment when, for the twentieth time, the glasses were being emptied with shouts of "Long live the king! long live the queen!"

CHAPTER XVIII.

At the moment when the queen appeared with the king and their son on the stage of the opera, an immense acclamation, as sudden and as loud as the explosion of a mine, was heard from the banqueting-tables and boxes.

The inebriated soldiers, the officers, delirious with wine and enthusiasm, waving their hats and sabers above their heads, shouted, "Long live the king! long live the queen! long live the dauphin!"

The bands immediately played, "Oh, Richard! oh, my king!"

The illusion of this air had become so apparent, it so well expressed the thoughts of all present, it so faithfully translated the meaning of this banquet, that all, as soon as the air began, immediately sung the words.

The queen, in her enthusiasm, forgot that she was in the midst of inebriated men; the king, though surprised, felt with his accustomed sound sense that it was no place for him, and that it was going beyond his conscientious feelings; but weak and flattered at once more finding a popularity and zeal which he was no longer habituated to meet from his people, he by degrees allowed himself to be carried away by the general hilarity.

Charny, who, during the whole festival, had drunk nothing but water, followed the king and queen; he had hoped that all would have terminated without their being present, and then it would have been but of slight importance; they might have disavowed, have denied everything; but he turned pale at the thought that the presence of the king and queen would become a historical fact.

But his terror was increased greatly when he saw his

brother George approach the queen, and, encouraged by her smile, address some words to her.

He was not near enough to hear the words, but by his gestures he could comprehend that he was making some request.

To this request the queen made a sign of assent; and suddenly taking from her cap the cockade she wore upon it, gave it to the young man.

Charny shuddered, stretched forth his arms, and uttered a cry.

It was not even the white cockade, the French cockade, which the queen presented to her imprudent knight; it was the black cockade, the Austrian cockade, the cockade which was so hateful to French eyes.

What the queen then did was no longer a mere imprudence; it was an act of absolute treason.

And yet all these poor fanatics whom God had doomed to ruin were so insensate that when George Charny presented to them this black cockade, those who wore the white cockade threw it from them, those who had the tricolored one trampled it beneath their feet.

And then the excitement became so great, that unless they had wished to be stifled with their kisses, or to trample under foot those who threw themselves on their knee᳠ before them, the august hosts of the Flanders regimen felt obliged to retreat toward their apartments.

All this might have been considered as a sample of French folly, which the French are always ready enough to pardon, if these orgies had not gone beyond the point of enthusiasm; but they soon went much further.

Good royalists, when eulogizing the king, must necessarily somewhat ill-treat the nation.

That nation, in whose name so much vexation had been offered to the king, that the bands had undoubtedly the right to play; " Peut on affliger ce qu'on aime ? " ("Can we afflict those whom we love ?")

It was while this air was being played, that the king, the queen, and the dauphin withdrew.

They had scarcely left the theater when, exciting each other, the boon companions metamorphosed the banqueting-room into a town taken by assault.

Upon a signal given by M. Perseval, aid-de-camp to the Count d'Estaing, the trumpets sounded a charge.

A charge, and against whom? Against the absent enemy. Against the people.

A charge ! music so enchanting to French ears that it had the effect of transforming the stage of the opera-house at Versailles into a battle-field, and the lovely ladies who were gazing from the boxes at the brillant spectacle were the enemy.

The cry " To the assault ! " was uttered by a hundred voices, and the escalade of the boxes immediately commenced. It is true that the besiegers were in a humor which inspired so little terror that the besieged held out their hands to them.

The first who reached the balcony was a grenadier in the Flanders regiment ; M. de Perseval tore a cross from his own breast, and decorated the grenadier with it.

It is true that it was a Limbourg cross, one of those crosses which are scarcely considered crosses.

And all this was done under the Austrian colors, with loud vociferations against the national cockade.

Here and there some hollow and sinister sounds were uttered.

But, drowned by the howling of the singers, by the hurrahs of the besiegers, by the inspiring sounds of the trumpets, these noises were borne with threatening import to the ears of the people, who were, in the first place, astonished, and then became indignant.

It was soon known outside the palace, in the square, and afterward in the streets, that the black cockade had been substituted for the white one, and that the tricolored cockade had been trampled under foot. It was also known that a brave officer of the National Guard, who had, in spite of threats, retained his tricolored cockade, had been seriously wounded even in the king's apartments.

Then, it was vaguely rumored that one officer alone had remained motionless, sorrowful, and standing at the entrance of that immense banqueting-room converted into a circus, wherein all these madmen had been playing their insensate pranks, and had looked on, listened to, and had shown himself, loyal and intrepid soldier as he was, submissive to the all-powerful will of the majority, taking upon himself the faults of others, accepting the responsibility of all the excesses committed by the army, represented on that fatal day by the officers of the Flanders

regiment ; but the name of this man, wise alone amid so
many madmen, was not even pronounced ; and had it been,
it would never have been believed that the Count de Charny,
the queen's favorite, was the man who, although ready to
die for her, had suffered more painfully than any other
from the errors she had committed.

As to the queen, she had returned to her own apartments,
completely giddy from the magic of the scene.

She was soon assailed by a throng of courtiers and flatterers.

"See," said they to her, "what is the real feeling of
your troops ; judge from this whether the popular fury
for anarchical ideas, which has been so much spoken of,
could withstand the ferocious ardor of French soldiers for
monarchical ideas." And as all these words corresponded
with the secret desire of the queen, she allowing herself
to be led away by these chimeras, not perceiving that
Charny had remained at a distance from her.

By degrees, however, the noises ceased ; the slumber of
the mind extinguished all the ignes-fatui, the phantasmagoria of intoxication. The king, besides, paid a visit to
the queen at the moment she was about to retire, and let
fall these words, replete with profound wisdom :

"We shall see to-morrow."

The imprudent man, by this saying, which to any other
person but to the one to whom it was addressed, would
have been a warning and sage counsel, he had revivified
in the queen's mind feelings of provocation and resistance
which had almost subsided.

"In fact," murmured she, when the king had left her—
"this flame, which was confined to the palace this evening, will spread itself into Versailles during the night, and
to-morrow will produce a general conflagration throughout
France. All these soldiers, all these officers who have this
evening given me such fervent pledges of their devotedness,
will be called traitors, rebels to the nation, murderers of
their country. They will call the chiefs of these aristocrats, the subalterns of the stipendiaries of Pitt and Co-
burg, satellites of the barbarous powers, of the savages of
the north.

"Each of these heads which has worn the black cockade
will be doomed to be fixed to the lamp-post on the Place
de Grève.

"Each of those breasts from which so loyally escaped those shouts of 'Long live the queen!' will on the first popular commotion be pierced with ignoble knives and infamous pikes.

"And it is I, again—I, always I, who have been the cause of all this. I shall have condemned to death all these brave and faithful servants—I, the inviolable sovereign. They are hypocritically left unassailed when near me, but when away from me will be insulted from hatred.

"Oh! no; rather than be ungrateful to such a degree as that, toward my only, my last friends—rather than be so cowardly and so heartless, I will take the fault upon myself. It is for me that all this has been done; upon me let all their anger fall. We shall then see how far their anger will be carried—we shall see up to which step of my throne the impure tide will dare to ascend."

And to the queen, animated by these thoughts, which drove sleep from her pillow, and on which she meditated during the greater part of the night, the result of the events of the next day was no longer doubtful.

The next day came, clouded over with gloomy regrets, and ushered in by threatening murmurs.

On that day the National Guards, to whom the queen had presented their colors, came to the palace with heads cast down and averted eyes, to thank her majesty.

It was easy to divine, from the attitude of these men, that they did not approve what had occurred; but, on the contrary, that they would have loudly disapproved it had they dared.

They had formed part of the procession, and had gone out to welcome the Flanders regiment; they had received invitations to the banquet, and had accepted them. Only, being more citizens than soldiers, it was they who, during the debauch, had uttered those disapproving groans which had not been heeded.

These observations on the following day had become a reproach, a blame.

When they came to the palace to thank the queen, they were escorted by a great crowd.

And taking into consideration the serious nature of the circumstances, the ceremony became an imposing one.

The parties on both sides were about to discover with whom they would have to deal.

On their side, all those soldiers and officers who had so compromised themselves the evening before, were anxious to ascertain how far they would be supported by the queen in their imprudent demonstrations, and had placed themselves before that people whom they had scandalized and insulted, that they might hear the first official words which should be uttered from the palace.

The weight of the whole counter-revolution was then hanging suspended over the head of the queen.

It was, however, still within her power to have withdrawn from this responsibility.

But she, proud as the proudest of her race, with great firmness cast her clear and penetrating gaze all around her, whether friends or enemies, and addressing herself in a sonorous voice to the officers of the National Guards:

"Gentlemen," said she, "I am much pleased at having presented you with your colors. The nation and the army ought to love the king as we love the nation and the army. I was delighted with the events of yesterday."

Upon these words, which she emphasized in her firmest tone of voice, a murmur arose from the crowd, and loud applause reechoed from the military ranks.

"We are supported," said the latter.

"We are betrayed," said the former.

Thus, poor queen, that fatal evening of the 1st of October was not an accidental matter! thus, unfortunate woman, you do not regret the occurrences of yesterday—you do not repent!

And, so far from repenting, you are delighted with them!

Charny, who was in the center of a group, heard, with a sigh of extreme pain, this justification—nay, more than that, this glorification of the orgies of the king's guards.

The queen, on turning away her eyes from the crowd, met those of the count, and she fixed her looks on the countenance of her lover, in order to ascertain the impression her words had produced upon him.

"Am I not courageous?" was the import of this look.

"Alas! madame, you are far more mad than courageous," replied the gloomy countenance of the count.

CHAPTER XIX

At Versailles, the court was talking heroically against the people.

At Paris, they were becoming knight-errants against the court alone ; knight-errantry was running about the streets.

These knights of the people were wandering about in rags, their hands upon the hilt of a saber or the butt-end of a pistol, questioning their empty pockets or their hollow stomachs.

While at Versailles they drank too much, at Paris, alas! they did not eat enough.

There was too much wine on the tablecloths at Versailles ; not sufficient flour in the bakers' shops at Paris.

Strange circumstances ! a melancholy blindness, which, now that we are accustomed to the fall of thrones, will excite a smile of pity from political men.

To make a counter-revolution, and provoke to a combat people who are starving !

Alas ! will say History, compelled to become a materialist philosopher, no people ever fight so desperately as those who have not dined.

It would, however, have been very easy to have given bread to the people, and then, most assuredly, the bread of Versailles would have appeared less bitter.

But the flour of Corbeil ceased to arrive. Corbeil is so far from Versailles ; who, then, living with the king and queen, could have thought of Corbeil ?

Unhappily, from this forgetfulness of the court, Famine, that specter which sleeps with so much difficulty, but which so easily awakens—Famine had descended, pale and agitated, into the streets of Paris. She listens at all the corners of the streets ; she recruits her train of vagabonds and malefactors ; she glues her livid face against the windows of the rich and of the public functionaries.

The men remember those commotions which had cost so much blood ; they recall to mind the Bastile ; they recollect Foulon, Berthier, and Flesselles ; they fear to have the opprobrious name of assassins again attached to them, and they wait.

But the women, who have as yet done nothing but suffer! When women suffer, the suffering is triple—for the child, who cries and who is unjust, because it has not a consciousness of the cause—for the child who says to its mother: "Why do you not give me bread?"—for the husband, who, gloomy and taciturn, leaves the house in the morning to return to it in the evening still more gloomy and taciturn; and finally, for herself, the painful echo of conjugal and maternal sufferings. The women burn to do something in their turn; they wish to serve their country in their own way.

Besides, was it not a woman who had brought about the 1st of October at Versailles?

It was, therefore, for the women, in their turn, to bring about the 5th of October at Paris.

Gilbert and Billot were sitting in the Café de Foy,* in the Palais Royal. It was at the Café de Foy that motions were proposed. Suddenly the door of the coffee-house is thrown open, and a woman enters it, much agitated. She denounces the black and white cockades which from Versailles have invaded Paris; she proclaims the public danger.

It will be remembered that Charny had said to the queen:

"Madame, there will be really much to apprehend when the women begin to stir themselves."

This was also the opinion of Gilbert.

Therefore, on seeing that the women were actually bestirring themselves, he turned to Billot, uttering only these five words:

"To the Hôtel de Ville."

Since the conversation which had taken place between Billot, Gilbert, and Pitou—and in consequence of which Pitou had returned to Villers-Cotterets with young Sebastian Gilbert—Billot obeyed Gilbert upon a single word, a gesture, a sign, for he had fully comprehended that if he was strength, Gilbert was intelligence.

They both rushed out of the coffee-house, crossed the garden of the Palais Royal diagonally, and then through the Cour des Fontaines reached the Rue St. Honoré.

* A celebrated coffee-house.

When they were near the corn-market, they met a young girl coming out of the Rue Bourdenais, who was beating a drum.

Gilbert stopped, astonished.

"What can this mean?" said he.

"Zounds! doctor, don't you see," said Billot, "it is a pretty girl who is beating a drum—and really, not badly, on my faith!"

"She must have lost something," said a passer-by.

"She is very pale," rejoined Billot.

"Ask her what she wants," said Gilbert.

"Ho! my pretty girl!" cried Billot, "what are you oeating that drum for?"

"I am hungry," she replied, in a weak but shrill voice.

And she continued on her way, beating the drum.

Gilbert had waited.

"Oh! oh!" cried he, "this is becoming terrible."

And he looked more attentively at the women who were following the young girl with the drum.

They were haggard, staggering, despairing.

Among these women there were some who had not tasted food for thirty hours.

From among these women, every now and then, would break forth a cry which was threatening even from its very feebleness, for it could be divined that it issued from famished mouths.

"To Versailles!" they cried—"to Versailles!"

And on their way, they made signs to all the women whom they perceived in the houses, and they called to all the women who were at their windows.

A carriage drove by; two *ladies* were in that carriage; they put their heads out of the windows and began to laugh.

The escort of the drum-beater stopped. About twenty women seized the horses, and then, rushing to the coach doors, made the two ladies alight and join their group, in spite of their recriminations and a resistance which two or three hard knocks on the head soon terminated.

Behind these women, who proceeded but slowly, on account of their stopping to recruit as they went along, walked a man with his hands in his pockets.

This man, whose face was thin and pale, of tall, lank stature, was dressed in an iron-gray coat, black waistcoat

and small-clothes ; he wore a small, shabby, three-cornered
hat placed obliquely over his forehead.

A long sword beat against his thin but muscular legs.

He followed, looking, listening, devouring everything
with his piercing eyes, which rolled beneath his black
eyelids.

"Hey! why, yes," cried Billot, "I certainly know that
face ; I have seen it at every riot."

"It is Maillard, the usher," said Gilbert.

"Ah! yes, that's he—the man who walked over the
plank after me at the Bastile ; he was more skilful than I
was, for he did not fall into the ditch."

Maillard disappeared with the women at the corner of a
street.

Billot felt a great desire to do as Maillard had done, but
Gilbert dragged him on to the Hôtel de Ville.

It was very certain that the gathering would go there,
whether it was a gathering of men or of women. Instead
of following the course of the river, he went straight to
its mouth.

They knew at the Hôtel de Ville what was going on in
Paris ; but they scarcely noticed it.   Of what importance
was it, in fact, to the phlegmatic Bailly or to the aristocratic Lafayette that a woman had taken it into her head
to beat a drum ? It was anticipating the carnival, and
that was all.

But when, at the heels of this woman who was beating
the drum, they saw two or three thousand women—when,
at the sides of this crowd, which was increasing every
minute, they saw advancing a no less considerable troop
of men, smiling in a sinister manner, and carrying their
hideous weapons—when they understood that these men
were smiling at the anticipation of the evil which these
women were about to commit, an evil the more irremedi-
able from their knowing that the public forces would not
attempt to stop the evil before it was committed, and that
the legal powers would not punish afterward, they began
to comprehend the serious nature of the circumstances.

These men smiled because the ill they had not dared to
commit, they would gladly have seen committed by the
most inoffensive half of the human kind.

In about half an hour there were ten thousand women
assembled on the Place de Grève.

These ladies, seeing that their numbers were sufficient, began to deliberate with their arms akimbo.

The deliberation was by no means a calm one ; those who deliberated were, for the most part, porteresses, market-women, and prostitutes. Many of these women were royalists, and far from thinking of doing any harm to the king and queen, would have allowed themselves to be killed to serve them. The noise which was made by this strange discussion might have been heard across the river, and by the silent towers of Notre Dame, which, after seeing so many things, were preparing themselves to hear things still more curious.

The result of the deliberation was as follows :

" Let us just go and burn the Hôtel de Ville, where so many musty papers are made out to prevent our eating our daily food."

And in the Hôtel de Ville they were at that moment trying a baker who had sold bread to the poor under weight.

It will be easily comprehended that the dearer bread is, the better is every operation of this nature ; only the more lucrative it is, the more dangerous.

In consequence, the admirers of lamp justice were only waiting for the baker with a new rope.

The guards of the Hôtel de Ville wished to save the unhappy culprit, and used all their strength to effect it. But for some time past it has been seen that the result but ill accorded with these philanthropic intentions.

The women rushed on these guards, dispersed them, made a forcible entry into the Hôtel de Ville, and the sack began.

They wished to throw into the Seine all they could not carry away.

The men were, therefore, to be cast into the water— the building itself set fire to.

This was rather heavy work.

There was a little of everything in the Hôtel de Ville.

In the first place, there were three hundred electors.

There were also the assistants.

There were the mayors of the different districts.

" It would take a long time to throw all these men into the water," said a woman, who was in a hurry to conclude the affair.

"They deserve it richly, notwithstanding, observed another.

"Yes ; but we have no time to spare."

"Well, then," cried another, "the quickest way will be to burn them all, and everything with them."

They ran about looking for torches, and to get fagots to set fire to the municipality. While this was doing, in order not to lose time, they caught an abbé, the Abbé Lefevre Dormesson, and strung him up.

Fortunately for the abbé, the man in the gray coat was there ; he cut the rope, and the poor abbé fell from a height of seventeen feet, sprained one of his feet, and limped away amid shouts of laughter from these Megœras.

The reason for the abbé being allowed to get away was that the torches were lighted, and the incendiaries had already these torches in their hands, and they were about to set fire to the archives ; in two minutes the whole place would have been in a blaze.

Suddenly the man in the gray coat rushed forward and snatched torches and fagots out of the women's hands ; the women resisted—the man lay about him right and left with the lighted torches, setting fire to their petticoats, and while they were occupied in extinguishing it, he extinguished the papers which had already been ignited.

Who, then, is this man who thus opposes the frightful will of ten thousand furious creatures ?

Why, then, do they allow themselves to be governed by this man ? They had half hanged the Abbé Lefevre ; they could hang that man more effectually, seeing that he would be no longer there to prevent them from hanging whom they pleased.

Guided by this reasoning, a frantic chorus arose from them, threatening him with death, and to these threats deeds were added.

The women surrounded the man with the gray coat, and threw a rope round his neck.

But Billot hastened forward. Billot was determined to render the same service to Maillard, which Maillard had rendered the abbé.

He grasped the rope, which he cut into three pieces, with a well-tempered and sharp knife, which at that moment served its owner to cut a rope, but which, in an extremity, wielded as it was by a powerful arm, might serve him still more importantly.

And while cutting the rope and getting piece by piece of it as he could, Billot cried:

"Why, you unfortunate wretches, you do not then recognize Monsieur Maillard?"

At that well-known and redoubtable name all these women at once paused; they looked at one another, and wiped the perspiration from their brows.

The work had been a difficult one, and although they were in the month of October, they might well perspire in accomplishing it.

"A conqueror of the Bastile—and that conqueror Maillard? Maillard, the usher of the Châtelet! Long live Maillard!"

Threats were immediately turned into caresses; they embrace Maillard, and all cry, "Long live Maillard!"

Maillard exchanged a hearty shake of the hand and a look with Billot.

The shake of the hand implied, "We are friends!"

The look implied, "Should you ever stand in need of me, you may calculate upon me."

Maillard had resumed an influence over these women, which was so much the greater from their reflecting that they had committed some trifling wrong toward him, and which he had to pardon.

But Maillard was an old sailor on the sea of popular fury; he knew the ocean of the faubourgs, which is raised by a breath, and calmed again by a word.

He knew how to speak to these human waves, when they allow you time enough to speak.

Moreover, the moment was auspicious for being heard. They had all remained silent around Maillard.

Maillard would not allow that Parisian women should destroy the municipal authorities, the only power to protect them; he would not allow them to annihilate the civic registers, which proved that their children were not all bastards.

The harangue of Maillard was of so novel a nature, delivered in so loud and sarcastic a tone, that it produced a great effect.

No one should be killed—nothing should be burned.

But they insist on going to Versailles. It is there that

exists the evil. It is there that they pass their nights in orgies, while Paris is starving. It is Versailles that devours everything. Corn and flour are deficient in Paris, because, instead of coming to Paris, they are sent direct from Corbeil to Versailles.

It would not be thus, if the great baker, the baker's wife, and the baker's little boy were at Paris.

It was under these nicknames that they designated the king, the queen, and the dauphin—those natural distributors of the people's bread.

They would go to Versailles.

Since these women are organized into troops, since they have muskets, cannon, and gunpowder—and those who have not muskets nor gunpowder have pikes and pitchforks—they ought to have a general.

And why not? the National Guard has one.

Lafayette is the general of the men.

Maillard is the general of the women.

M. Lafayette commands his do-little grenadiers, which appear to be an army of reserve, for they do so little when there is so much to be done.

Maillard will command the active army.

Without a smile, without a wink, Maillard accepts his appointment.

Maillard is general commandant of the women of Paris.

The campaign will not be a long one, but it will be decisive.

CHAPTER XX.

It was really an army that Maillard commanded.

It had cannons—deprived of carriages and wheels, it is true; but they had been placed on carts. It had muskets —many of which were deficient in locks and triggers, it is true; but every one had a bayonet.

It had a quantity of other weapons—very awkward ones, it is true; but they were weapons.

It had gunpowder, which was carried in pocket-handkerchiefs, in caps, and in pockets; and in the midst of these living cartouch-boxes walked the artillerymen with their lighted matches.

That the whole army was not blown into the air during

this extraordinary journey, was certainly a perfect miracle.

Maillard at one glance appreciated the feelings of his army. He saw that it would be of no use to keep it on the square where it had assembled, nor to confine it within the walls of Paris, but to lead it on to Versailles, and, once arrived there, to prevent the harm which it might attempt to do.

This difficult, this heroic task, Maillard was determined to accomplish.

And, in consequence, Maillard descends the steps and takes the drum which was hanging from the shoulders of the young girl.

Dying with hunger, the poor young girl has no longer strength to carry it. She gives up the drum, glides along a wall, and falls with her head against a post.

A gloomy pillow—the pillow of hunger!

Maillard asks her name. She replies that it is Madeleine Chambry. Her occupation had been carving in wood for churches. But who now thinks of endowing churches with those beautiful ornaments in wood, those beautiful statues, those magnificent basse-relievos, the masterpieces of the fifteenth century.

Dying with hunger, she had become a flower-girl in the Palais Royal.

But who thinks of purchasing flowers when money is wanting to buy even bread? Flowers, those stars which shine in the heaven of peace and abundance—flowers are withered by storms of wind and revolutions.

Being no longer able to sculpture her fruits in oak— being no longer able to sell her roses, her jasmines and lilies, Madeleine Chambry took a drum, and beat the terrible reveille of hunger.

She also must go to Versailles—she who had assembled all this gloomy deputation; only, as she is too feeble to walk, she is to be carried there in a cart.

When they arrive at Versailles, they will ask that she may be admitted into the palace, with twelve other women; she is to be the famished orator, and she will there plead before the king the cause of all those that are starving.

This idea of Maillard's was much applauded.

And thus by a word Maillard had at once changed every hostile feeling.

They did not before this know why they were going th。 e ; they did not know what they were going to do there.

But now they know; they know that a deputation of twelve women, with Madeleine Chambry at their head, were going to supplicate the king, in the name of hunger, to take compassion on his people.

Somewhere about seven thousand women were there assembled. They commenced their march, going along the quays.

But on arriving at the Tuileries, loud shouts were heard.

Maillard jumped upon a post in order to be seen by the whole of his army.

" What is it that you want ? " he asked them.

" We wish to pass through the Tuileries."

" That is impossible," replied Maillard.

" And why is it impossible ? " cried seven thousand voices.

" Because the Tuileries is the king's house and the king's gardens ; because to pass through them without the king's permission would be to insult the king—and more than that, it would be attacking, in the king's person, the liberty of all."

" Well, then, be it so," say the women ; " ask permission of the Swiss." *

Maillard went to the Swiss, his cocked hat in his hand.

" My friend," said he, " will you allow these ladies to go through the Tuileries ? They will only go through the archway, and will not do any injury to the plants or trees."

The only answer the Swiss gave was to draw his long rapier, and to rush upon Maillard.

Maillard drew his sword, which was full a foot shorter, and their weapons crossed.

While they were tilting at each other, a woman went behind the Swiss and gave him a fearful blow upon the head with a broom-handle, and laid him at Maillard's feet. At the same time, another woman was about to run the Swiss through the body with a thrust of her bayonet.

Maillard sheaths his sword, takes that of the Swiss under one arm, the musket of the woman under the other,

* The porter, or gate-keeper.

picks up his hat, which had fallen to the ground during the struggle, puts it upon his head, and then leads his victorious troops through the Tuileries, where, in fulfilment of the promise he had made, no sort of damage was committed by them.

Let us, therefore, allow them to continue their way quietly through the Cours la Reme, and go on toward Sèvres, where they separated into two bands, and let us return to what is going on at Paris.

These seven thousand women had not failed in drowning the electors, in hanging the Abbé Lefevre and Maillard, and burning the Hôtel de Ville, without making a certain degree of noise.

On hearing this noise, which had been reechoed even in the most remote quarters of the capital, Lafayette had hastened toward the Hôtel de Ville.

He was passing a sort of review at the Champ de Mars. He had been on horseback from eight o'clock in the morning; he reached the square of the Hôtel de Ville just as the clock was striking twelve.

The caricatures of those days represented Lafayette as a centaur, the body of which was the famous white horse which had become proverbial. The head was that of the commandant of the National Guard.

From the commencement of the revolution, Lafayette spoke on horseback, Lafayette eat on horseback, Lafayette gave all his orders on horseback.

It often even happened that he slept on horseback.

And, therefore, when by chance he could sleep on his bed, Lafayette slept soundly.

When Lafayette reached the Quay Pelletier, he was stopped by a man who had been riding at full gallop on an admirably swift horse.

This man was Gilbert; he was going to Versailles—he was going to forewarn the king of the visit with which he was threatened, and to place himself at his orders.

In two words he related all that had happened to Lafayette.

After that he rode off again at full speed.

Lafayette went on toward the Hôtel de Ville.

Gilbert toward Versailles. Only, as the women were going on the right bank of the Seine, he took the left side of the river.

The square before the Hôtel de Ville, having been vacated by the women, was soon afterward filled with men.

These men were National Guards, receiving pay or not receiving it—old French Guards, above all, who, having gone over to the people, had lost their privileges of king's guards—privileges which had been inherited by the Swiss and the body-guards.

To the noise made by the women had succeeded the noise of the alarm-bell and the drums, calling the people to arms.

Lafayette made his way through all this crowd, alighted from his horse at the foot of the steps, and without paying any attention to the acclamations, mingled with threats, excited by his presence, he began to dictate a letter to the king upon the insurrection which had taken place that morning.

He had got to the sixth line of his letter, when the door of the secretary's office was violently thrown open.

Lafayette raised his eyes. A deputation of grenadiers demanded to be received by the general.

Lafayette made a sign to the deputation that they might come in.

They entered the room.

The grenadier who had been appointed spokesman of the deputation advanced to the table.

"General," said he, in a firm voice, "we are deputed by ten companies of grenadiers. We do not believe that you are a traitor ; but we are betrayed. It is time that all this should come to an end. We cannot turn our bayonets against women who are asking us for bread. The Provisioning Committee is either peculating, or it is incompetent ; in either the one or the other case, it is necessary that it should be changed. The people are unhappy, the source of their unhappiness is at Versailles. It is necessary to go there to fetch the king and bring him to Paris. The Flanders regiment must be exterminated, as well as the body-guards, who have dared to trample under foot the national cockade. If the king be too weak to wear the crown, let him abdicate ; we will crown his son. A Council of Regency will be nominated, and all will then go well."

Lafayette gazed at the speaker with astonishment. He had witnessed disturbances, he had wept over assassinations ; but this was the first time that the breath of revolution had in reality been personally addressed to him.

This possibility that the people saw of being able to do without the king, amazed him—it did more, it confounded him.

"How is this?" cried he. "Have you, then, formed the project of making war upon the king, and thus compel him to abandon us?"

"General," replied the spokesman, "we love and we respect the king; we should be much hurt should he leave us; for we owe him much. But, in short, should he leave us, we have the dauphin."

"Gentlemen! gentlemen!" cried Lafayette, "beware of what you are doing; you are attacking the crown, and it is my duty not to allow such a step."

"General," replied the National Guard, bowing, "we would for you shed the last drop of our blood. But the people are unhappy; the source of the evil is at Versailles. We must go to Versailles and bring the king to Paris. It is the people's will."

Lafayette saw that it was necessary to sacrifice his own feelings; and this was a necessity from which he never shrunk.

He descends into the center of the square, and wishes to harangue the people; but cries of "To Versailles! to Versailles!" drowned his voice.

Suddenly a great tumult was heard proceeding from the Rue de la Vannerie. It is Bailly, who, in his turn, is coming to the Hôtel de Ville.

At the sight of Bailly cries of "Bread! bread! To Versailles!" burst from every side.

Lafayette, on foot, lost amid the crowd, feels that the tide continues rising higher and higher, and will completely swallow him up.

He presses through the crowd in order to reach his horse, with the same ardor that a shipwrecked mariner swims to reach a rock.

At last he grasps his bridle, vaults on his charger's back, and urges him on toward the entrance of the Hôtel de Ville; but the way is completely closed to him; walls of men have grown up between him and it.

"Zounds, general!" cry the men, "you must remain with us."

At the same time, tremendous shouts are heard of "To Versailles! to Versailles!"

Lafayette wavers, hesitates.   Yes, undoubtedly, by going
to Versailles, he may be very useful to the king ; but will
he be able to master and restrain this crowd who are urging
him to Versailles ?

Suddenly a man descends the steps, pushes through the
crowd, a letter in his hand, and makes such good use of
his feet and elbows, particularly the latter, that he at
length reaches Lafayette.

This man was the ever indefatigable Billot.

" Here, general," said he, " this comes from the Three
Hundred."

It was thus the electors were called.

Lafayette broke the seal and began to read it to himself ;
but twenty thousand voices at once cried out :

" The letter ! the letter ! "

Lafayette was, therefore, compelled to read the letter
aloud.   He makes a sign to request they will be silent.
Instantaneously, and as by a miracle, silence succeeds to
the immense tumult, and Lafayette reads the following
letter, not one word of which was lost by the people :

" Seeing the state of circumstances and the desire of the
people, and on the representation of the commandant-
general that it was impossible to refuse, the electors assembled in council authorize the commandant-general, and
even order him, to repair to Versailles.

" Four commissaries of the district will accompany
him."

Poor Lafayette had absolutely represented nothing of
the electors, who were by no means disinclined to leave
some portion of the responsibility of the events which were
about to happen, on his shoulders.   But the people—they
believed that he had really made representations, and this
coincided so precisely with their views, that they made
the air ring with their shouts of " Long live Lafayette ! "

Lafayette turned pale, but in his turn repeated, "To
Versailles ! "

Fifteen thousand men followed him, with a more silent
enthusiasm, but which was at the same time more terrible,
than that of the women who had gone forward as the
advance guard.

All those people were to assemble again at Versailles to
ask the king for the crumbs which fell from the table of
the body-guards during the orgies of the 1st of October.

CHAPTER XXI.

As usual, they were completely ignorant at Versailles of what was going on at Paris.

After the scenes which we have described, and at the occurrence of which the queen had openly congratulated herself, the queen was reposing herself, after her fatigue.

She had an army, she had her devotees, she had counted her enemies, she wished to begin the contest.

Had she not the defeat of the 14th of July to avenge? Had she not the king's journey to Paris, a journey from which he had returned with the tricolored cockade in his hat, to forget, and to make her court forget also?

Poor woman! she but little expected the journey which she herself would be shortly compelled to take.

Since her altercation with Charny, she had scarcely spoken to him. She affected to treat Andrée with her former friendliness, which had for a time been deadened in her heart—but which was forever extinguished in that of her rival.

As to Charny, she never turned toward or looked at him, but when she was compelled to address herself to him upon matters regarding his service, or to give him an order.

It was not a family disgrace; for on the very morning on which the Parisians were to leave Paris to come to Versailles, the queen was seen talking affectionately with young George de Charny, the second of the three brothers, who, in contradiction to Olivier, had given such warlike counsels to the queen on the arrival of the news of the capture of the Bastile.

And, in fact, at nine in the morning, as the young officer was crossing the gallery, to announce to the huntsman that the king intended going out, when Marie Antoinette, returning from mass in the chapel saw him, she called him to her.

"Where are you running thus, sir?" said she to him.

"As soon as I perceived your majesty, I ran no longer," replied George; "on the contrary, I instantly stopped, and

I was waiting humbly for the honor you have done me in addressing me."

"That does not prevent you, sir, from replying to my question, and telling me whither you were going."

"Madame," replied George, "I am on duty to day, and form part of the escort. His majesty hunts to-day, and I am going to the huntsman to make arrangements for the meet."

"Ah! the king hunts again to-day," said the queen, looking at the big dark clouds which were rolling on from Paris toward Versailles. "He is wrong to do so. The weather appears to be threatening; does it not, Andrée?"

"Yes, madame," absently replied the Countess de Charny.

"Are you not of that opinion, sir?'

"I am so, madame; but such is the king's will.

"May the king's will be done in the woods and on the high-roads," replied the queen, with that gaiety of manner which was habitual with her, and which neither the sorrows of the heart nor political events could ever deprive her of.

Then, turning toward Andrée:

"It is but just that he should have this amusement," said the queen to her, in a whisper.

And then, aloud, to George:

"Can you tell me, sir, where the king intends hunting?"

"In the Meudon Wood, madame."

"Well, then, accompany him, and watch carefully over his safety."

At this moment the Count de Charny had entered the room. He smiled kindly at Andrée, and shaking his head, ventured to say to the queen:

"That is a recommendation which my brother will not fail to remember, madame; not in the midst of the king's pleasures, but in the midst of his dangers."

At the sound of the voice which had struck upon her ear before her eyes had warned her of the presence of Charny, Marie Antoinette started, and, turning round:

"I should have been much astonished," said she, with disdainful harshness, "if such a saying had not proceeded from the Count Olivier de Charny."

"And why so, madame?" respectfully inquired the count.

"Because it prophesies misfortune, sir."

Andrée turned pale on seeing that the color fled from her husband's cheeks.

He bowed without offering a reply.

Then, on a look from his wife, who appeared to be amazed at his being so patient:

"I am really extremely unfortunate," he said, "since I no longer know how to speak to the queen without offending her."

The *no longer* was emphasized in the same manner as a skilful actor would emphasize the more important syllables.

The ear of the queen was too well exercised not to perceive at once the stress which Charny had laid upon his words:

"*No longer!*" she exclaimed sharply, "*no longer;* what mean you by *no longer?*"

"I have again spoken unfortunately, it would appear," said De Charny, unaffectedly.

And he exchanged a look with Andrée, which the queen this time perceived.

She, in her turn, became pale, and then her teeth firmly set together with rage.

"The saying is bad," she exclaimed, "when the intention is bad."

"The ear is hostile," said Charny, "when the thought is hostile."

And after this retort, which was more just than respectful, he remained silent.

"I shall wait to reply," said the queen, "until the Count de Charny is more happy in his attacks."

"And I," said De Charny, "shall wait to attack until the queen shall be more fortunate than she has lately been in servants."

Andrée eagerly seized her husband's hand, and was preparing to leave the room with him.

A glance from the queen restrained her. She had observed this gesture.

"But, in fine, what has your husband to say to me?" asked the queen.

"He had intended telling your majesty that, having been sent to Paris yesterday by the king, he had found the city in a most extraordinary state of ferment."

"Again!" cried the queen; "and on what account?
The Parisians have taken the Bastile, and are now oc-
cupied in demolishing it—what can they require more?
Answer me, Monsieur de Charny."

"That is true, madame," replied the count; "but, as
they cannot eat the stones, they are calling out for bread
—they say that they are hungry."

"That they are hungry! that they are hungry!" exclaimed the queen; "and what would they have us do in
that respect?"

"There was a time," observed Charny, "when the queen
was the first to compassionate the sufferings of the people;
there was a time when she would ascend even to the garrets of the poor, and the prayers of the poor ascended
from the garrets to God with blessings on her head."

"Yes," bitterly replied the queen, "and I was well re-
warded, was I not, for the compassion which I felt for the
misery of others?   One of the greatest misfortunes which
ever befell me was in consequence of having ascended to
one of these garrets."

"Because your majesty was once deceived," said Charny,
"because she bestowed her favors and her grace upon a
miserable wretch, ought she to consider all human nature
upon a level with that infamous woman? Ah, madame!
madame! how at that time were you beloved!"

The queen darted a furious glance at Charny.

"But, finally," she said, "what did actually take place
in Paris yesterday? Tell me only things that you have
yourself seen, sir; I wish to be sure of the truth of your
words."

"What I saw, madame! I saw a portion of the populace crowded together on the quays, vainly awaiting the
arrival of flour. I saw others standing in long files at the
bakers' doors, uselessly waiting for bread. What I saw was
a starving people; husbands looking sorrowfully at their
wives, mothers looking sorrowfully at their children.
What I saw! I saw clinched and threatening hands held
up in the direction of Versailles. Ah! madame! madame!
the dangers of which I just now spoke to you are approaching—the opportunity of dying for your majesty—a
happiness which my brother and myself will be the first to
claim. I fear the day is not far distant when it will be
offered to us."

The queen turned her back to Charny with an impatient gesture, and went to her window and placed her pale though burning face against a pane of glass. This window looked into the marble courtyard.

She had scarcely done this when she was seen to start.

"Andrée!" cried she, "come here and see who is this horseman coming toward us; he appears to be the bearer of very urgent news."

Andrée went to the window, but almost immediately recoiled a step from it, turning very pale.

"Ah! madame," cried she, in a tone of reproach.

Charny hastened toward the window; he had minutely observed all that had passed.

"That horseman," said he, looking alternately at the queen and at Andrée, "is Doctor Gilbert."

"Ah! that is true," said the queen; and in a tone which rendered it impossible, even to Andrée, to judge whether the queen had drawn her to the window in one of her fits of feminine vengeance, to which poor Marie Antoinette sometimes gave way, or whether her eyes, weakened by watching and the tears she had shed, could no longer recognize, at a certain distance, even those whom it was her interest to recognize.

An ice-like silence immediately ensued, and the three principal characters in this scene interrogated and replied to one another merely by looks.

It was, in fact, Gilbert who was coming, bringing with him the untoward news which Charny had predicted.

Although he had hurriedly alighted from his horse, although he had rapidly ascended the staircase, although the three agitated faces of the queen, Andrée, and Charny were turned toward the door which led to this staircase, and by which the doctor ought to have entered the room, this door did not open.

There was, then, on the part of these three persons, an anxious suspense of some minutes.

Suddenly, a door on the opposite side of the room was opened, and an officer came in.

"Madame," said he, "Doctor Gilbert, who has come for the purpose of conversing with the king on important and urgent matters, demands to have the honor of being received by your majesty, the king having set out for Meudon an hour ago."

"Let him come in !" said the queen, fixing on the door a look which was firm even to harshness ; while Andrée, as if naturally she ought to find a supporter in her husband, drew back and supported herself on the count's arm.

Gilbert soon made his appearance on the threshold of the door.

CHAPTER XXII.

GILBERT cast a glance on the several personages whom we have placed on the stage, and advancing respectfully toward Marie Antoinette :

"Will the queen permit me," said he, "in the absence of her august husband, to communicate to her the news of which I am the bearer ?"

"Speak, sir," said Marie Antoinette. "On seeing you coming at so rapid a pace, I summoned up all my fortitude, for I felt well assured that you were bringing me some fearful news."

"Would the queen have preferred that I should have allowed her to be surprised ? Forewarned, the queen, with that sound judgment, that elevated mind by which she is characterized, the queen would advance to meet the danger ; and then, perhaps the danger might retreat before her."

"Let us see, sir—what is this danger ?"

"Madame, seven or eight thousand women have set out from Paris, and are coming armed to Versailles."

"Seven or eight thousand women !" cried the queen, with an air of contempt.

"Yes ; but they will, most likely, have stopped on the way ; and, perhaps, on arriving here, their numbers will amount to fifteen or twenty thousand."

"And for what purpose are they coming ?"

"They are hungry, madame, and they are coming to ask the king for bread."

The queen turned toward Charny.

"Alas ! madame," said the count, "that which I predicted has now happened."

"What is to be done ?" asked Marie Antoinette.

"The king should, in the first place, be informed of it," said Gilbert.

The queen turned quickly toward him.

"The king! Oh, no!" she cried, "what good purpose would it answer to expose him to such a meeting?"

This cry burst forth from the heart of Marie Antoinette almost involuntarily. It was a convincing manifestation of the intrepidity of the queen, of her consciousness of possessing a firmness which was altogether personal to her, and, at the same time, of her consciousness of her husband's weakness, which she ought not to have admitted even to herself, and should not, more particularly, have revealed to strangers.

But was Charny a stranger? and Gilbert, was he a stranger?

No; did not those two men, on the contrary, appear to be elected by Providence, the one to be the safeguard of the queen, the other to protect the king?

Charny replied at once to the queen and to Gilbert; he resumed all his empire, for he had made the sacrifice of his pride.

"Madame," said he, "Monsieur Gilbert is right; it is necessary that the king should be informed of this occurrence. The king is still beloved; the king will present himself to these women; he will harangue them, he will disarm them."

"But," observed the queen, "who will undertake to give this information to the king? The road between this and Meudon is no doubt already intercepted, and it would be a dangerous enterprise."

"The king is in the forest of Meudon?"

"Yes; and it is probable the roads——"

"Your majesty will deign to consider me as a military man," said Charny, unostentatiously; "a soldier, and one whose duty it is to expose his life——"

And, having said these words, he did not wait for a reply; he listened not to the sigh which escaped the queen, but ran rapidly down the staircase, jumped upon one of the guards' horses, and hastened toward Meudon, accompanied by two cavaliers.

He had scarcely disappeared, and had replied by a sign to a farewell gesture which Andrée addressed to him from the window, when a distant noise, which resembled the roaring of the waves in a storm, made the queen listen anxiously. This noise appeared to proceed from the furthest trees on the Paris road, which, from the apartment in which the queen was, could be seen towering above the fog at some distance from the last houses of Versailles.

The horizon soon became as threatening to the eye as it had been to the ear ; a hail shower began to checker the dark-gray haze.

And yet, notwithstanding this threatening state of the heavens, crowds of persons were entering Versailles.

Messengers arrived continually at the palace.

Every messenger brought intelligence of numerous columns being on their way from Paris, and every one thought of the joys and the easy triumphs of the preceding days, some of them feeling at heart a regret that was akin to remorse, others an instinctive terror.

The soldiers were anxious, and looking at one another, slowly took up their arms. Like drunken people, who endeavor to shake off the effects of wine, the officers, demoralized by the visible uneasiness of their soldiers and the murmurs of the crowd, with difficulty breathed in this atmosphere, impregnated as it was with misfortunes which were about to be attributed to them.

On their side, the body-guards—somewhere about three hundred men—coolly mounted their horses, and with that hesitation which seizes men of the sword when they feel they have to deal with enemies whose mode of attack is unknown to them.

What could they do against women who had set out threatening, and with arms, but who had arrived disarmed, and who could no longer raise even their hands, so enervated were they with fatigue, so emaciated were they by hunger ?

And yet, at all hazards, they formed themselves into line, drew their sabers, and waited.

At last, the women made their appearance ; they had come by two roads. Half-way between Paris and Versailles they had separated, one party coming by St. Cloud, the other by Sèvres.

Before they separated, eight loaves had been divided among them ; it was all that could be found at Sèvres.

Thirty-two pounds of bread for seven thousand persons !

On arriving at Versailles they could scarcely drag themselves along. More than three fourths of them had scattered their weapons along the road. Maillard had induced the remaining fourth to leave their arms in the first houses they came to in Versailles.

Then, on entering into the town :

"Come now," said he, "that they may not doubt that we are friends to royalty, let us sing, 'Vive Henri Quatre.'"

And in a dying tone, and with voices that had not strength enough to ask for bread, they chanted the royal national air.

The astonishment was, therefore, great at the palace when, instead of shouts and threats, they heard them singing the loyal air—when, above all, they saw the female choristers staggering—for hunger has somewhat the effect of drunkenness—and these wretched women, leaning their haggard, pale, and livid faces, begrimed with dirt, down which the rain and perspiration were streaming, against the gilded railings, and these faces appearing to be more than doubled by the number of hands which grasped those railings for support.

After a time would now and then escape from these horribly fantastic groups lugubrious howlings—in the midst of these agonized faces would appear eyes flashing lightnings.

Also, from time to time, all these hands, abandoning the railings which sustained them, were thrust through the space between them, and stretched forth toward the palace.

Some of them were open and trembling—these were soliciting.

Others were clinched and nervously agitated—these were threatening.

Oh ! the picture was a gloomy one.

The rain and mud—so much for the heavens and earth.

Hunger and threatening gestures—so much for the besiegers.

Pity and doubt—such were the feelings of the defenders.

While waiting the return of Louis XVI., agitated, but firmly resolved, the queen gave orders for the defense of the palace. By degrees, the courtiers, the officers, and the high dignitaries of the state grouped themselves around her.

In the midst of them she perceived M. de St. Priest, the minister for Paris.

" Go and inquire, sir," she said to him, " what it is these people want."

M. de St. Priest immediately went down the staircase, crossed the courtyard, and approached the railing.

" What is it that you demand ?" said he to the women.

" Bread ! bread ! bread !" simultaneously cried a thousand voices.

" Bread !" replied M. de St. Priest, impatiently ; "when you had but one master, you never were in want of bread. Now that you have twelve hundred, you see to what they have reduced you."

And M. de St. Priest withdrew amid the threatening shouts of the famished creatures, giving strict orders that the gates should be kept closed.

But a deputation advances, before which it is absolutely necessary that the gates should be thrown open.

Maillard had presented himself to the National Assembly in the name of the women ; he had succeeded in persuading them that the president, with a deputation of twelve women, should proceed to the palace to make a statement to the king of the position of affairs.

At the moment when the deputation, with Mounier at its head, left the assembly, the king returned to the palace at full gallop, entering it by the stable-yard.

Charny had found him in the forest at Meudon.

" Ah ! it is you, sir," cried the king, on perceiving him. "Is it me whom you are seeking ?"

" Yes, sire."

" What, then, has happened ? You seem to have ridden hard."

"Sire, there are at this moment ten thousand women at Versailles, who have come from Paris, and who are crying for bread."

The king shrugged up his shoulders, but it was more from a feeling of compassion than of disdain.

"Alas !" said he, " if I had bread for them, I should not have waited their coming from Paris to ask it of me."

But without making any further observation, he cast a mournful look toward the place where the hounds were continuing their chase of the stag which he was obliged to abandon.

" Well, then, sir, let us go to Versailles," said he.

And he rode off toward Versailles.

He had just arrived there, as we have said, when frightful cries were heard proceeding from the Place d'Armes.

" What is the meaning of that ?" inquired the king.

" Sire," cried Gilbert, entering the room, pale as death, " they are your guards, who, led on by Monsieur George de Charny, are charging upon the president of the National Assembly and a deputation which he is leading here."

" Impossible !" exclaimed the king.

" Listen to the cries of those whom they are assassinating. Look ! look at the people who are flying in terror."

" Let the gates be thrown open !" cried the king. " I will receive the deputation."

" But, sire !" exclaimed the queen.

" Let the gates be opened," said Louis XVI. ; " the palaces of kings ought to be considered as asylums."

" Alas ! excepting, perhaps, for kings themselves," said the queen.

CHAPTER XXIII.

CHARNY and Gilbert rushed down-stairs.

" In the name of the king !" cried the one.

" In the name of the queen !" cried the other.

And both of them added :

" Open the gates."

But this order was no sooner executed than the president of the National Assembly was thrown down in the courtyard and trampled under foot.

Two of the women forming the deputation were wounded close by his side.

Gilbert and Charny threw themselves into the crowd. These two men—the one proceeding from the highest class of society, the other from the lowest—met, working in the same cause.

The one wishes to save the queen, from his ardent love for the queen ; the other wishes to save the king, from his love for royalty.

On the gates being opened, the women rushed into the

courtyard, and had thrown themselves into the ranks of the body-guards and those of the Flanders regiment. They threaten, they entreat, they caress. Who could resist women when they implore those whom they address in the name of their sisters, their mothers?

"Room, gentlemen, room for the deputation!" cried Gilbert.

And all the ranks were immediately opened to allow Mounier to pass with the unhappy women he was about to present to the king.

The king having been informed by Charny, who had hastened to him, waited for the deputation in the room contiguous to the chapel.

It was Mounier who was to speak in the name of the Assembly.

It was Madeleine Chambry, the flower-girl, who had beaten the drum, who was to speak in the name of the women.

Mounier said a few words to the king, and presented to him the young flower-girl.

The latter stepped forward a pace or two and wished to speak, but could only utter these words:

"Sire—bread!"

And she fell fainting to the ground.

"Help! help!" cried the king.

Andrée hurried forward, and handed her smelling-bottle to the king.

"Ah, madame!" said Charny to the queen, in a reproachful tone.

The queen turned pale, and withdrew to her own apartment.

"Prepare the equipages," said she; "the king and I are going to Rambouillet."

During this time, poor Madeleine Chambry was recovering her senses, and finding herself in the king's arms, who was making her inhale the salts he held in his hand, she uttered a cry of shame, and wished to kiss his hand.

But the king prevented her.

"My lovely child," said he, "allow me to embrace you, you are well worth the trouble."

"Oh, sire! sire! since you are so kind," said the young girl, "give me an order——"

"What order?" inquired the king.

"An order to have wheat sent to Paris, so that famine may cease."

"My dear child," said the king, "I will willingly sign the order you request, but in truth I am afraid it will not be of much service to you."

The king seated himself at a table and began to write, when suddenly a single musket-shot was heard, followed by a tolerable quick fire of musketry.

"Ah! good God! good God!" exclaimed the king, "what can have happened? See what it is, Monsieur Gilbert."

A second charge upon another group of women had been made, and this charge had brought about the isolated musket-shot and the volley which had been heard.

The isolated musket-shot had been fired by a man in the crowd, and had broken the arm of M. de Savonnière, a l'eutenant in the guards, at the moment when that arm was raised to strike a young soldier, who was behind a entry-box, and who, with uplifted and unarmed hands, was protecting a woman who was on her knees behind him.

This musket-shot was replied to on the part of the guards by five or six shots from their carbines.

Two of the shots told. A woman fell dead.

Another was carried off, seriously wounded.

The people became irritated, and in their turn two of the body-guards fell from their horses.

At the same instant, cries of "Room! room!" are heard; they were the men from the Faubourg St. Antoine, who were arriving, dragging with them three pieces of artillery, with which they formed a battery opposite to the principal gate of the palace.

Fortunately, the rain was falling in torrents; the match is uselessly applied to the touch-holes of these guns; the priming, completely soddened by the rain, does not ignite.

At this moment a voice whispers into the ear of Gilbert:

"Monsieur de Lafayette is coming; he cannot be more than half a league from Versailles."

Gilbert in vain attempts to discover who has given him this information; but from whomsoever it might come, it was valuable.

He looks around him—sees a horse without a rider—it belonged to one of the two guards who had just been killed.

He leaps into the saddle, and sets off in a gallop on the road toward Paris.

The second horse without a rider follows him; but he had scarcely gone twenty paces over the square, when the horse is stopped by the bridle. Gilbert believes his intention has been divined, and that some one wishes to pursue him. He casts a look behind him as he rides off.

They were not thinking of him at all; but they were hungry. They think of nothing but obtaining food, and the poor horse is instantly butchered by a hundred knives.

In a moment it is cut into a hundred pieces.

During this time the king had been informed, as Gilbert had been, that General Lafayette was about to arrive.

He had signed, at the request of Mounier, his acceptance of the Rights of Man.

He had signed, at the request of Madeleine Chambry, the order for corn to be sent to Paris.

Furnished with this decree and this order which it was thought would have tranquilized all minds, Maillard, Madeleine Chambry, and a thousand of the women had set out on their return to Paris.

Just beyond the first houses of Versailles they met Lafayette, who, pressed by Gilbert, was riding at full speed, having ordered the National Guards to follow him as quickly as possible.

"Long live the king!" cried Maillard and the women, waving the decrees above their heads.

"What was it, then, you were saying to me of the dangers to which his majesty is exposed?" said Lafayette, with astonishment.

"Come on, general, come on!" cried Gilbert, continuing to urge him onward, "you shall yourself judge of them."

And Lafayette spurred on his horse.

The National Guards entered Versailles with drums beating and colors flying.

At the first sounds of the drum which penetrated the palace, the king felt that some one was respectfully touching his arm.

He turned round; it was Andrée.

"Ah! it is you, Madame de Charny," said he. "What is the queen doing?"

"Sire, the queen sends to entreat that you will leave Versailles, that you will not wait for the Parisians. At the head of your guards and the soldiers of the Flanders regiment, you can go anywhere."

"Are you of that opinion, Monsieur de Charny?" inquired the king.

"Yes, sire, if you at once determine on passing the frontier, but if not——"

"If not?"

"It would be better to remain here."

The king shook his head.

He remains, not because he has the courage to remain, but because he has not firmness enough to decide on going.

He murmured, in a low tone :

"A fugitive king! a fugitive king!"

Then, turning to Andrée :

"Go and tell the queen to set out alone."

Andrée left the room to execute her mission.

Ten minutes afterward the queen came in and seated herself by the king's side.

"For what purpose have you come here, madame?" asked Louis XVI.

"To die with you, sire," replied the queen.

"Ah!" murmured Charny, "it is now that she is truly beautiful."

The queen shuddered ; she had heard him.

"I believe, indeed, it would be better that I should die than live," said she, looking at him.

At that moment the march of the National Guards was heard under the windows of the palace.

Gilbert rapidly entered the room.

"Sire," said he to the king, "you have nothing further to apprehend ; Monsieur de Lafayette is below."

The king did not like M. de Lafayette, but he did not carry his feelings further than dislike.

With regard to the queen, it was a very different matter. She frankly hated him, and took no pains to conceal her hatred.

The result of this was that Gilbert received no reply, although he had believed that the intelligence he had communicated was the most favorable he could have brought at such a moment.

But Gilbert was not a man to allow himself to be intimidated by royal silence.

"Your majesty has heard?" cried he to the king, in a firm tone. "Monsieur de Lafayette is below, and places himself at your majesty's orders."

The queen continued silent.

The king made an effort to restrain his feelings.

"Let some one go and tell him that I thank him, and invite him, in my name, to come upstairs."

An officer bowed, and left the room.

The queen drew back a step or two.

But the king with a gesture that was almost imperative, made her resume her position.

The courtiers formed themselves into two groups.

Charny and Gilbert, with two or three others, remained near the king.

All the rest retreated behind the queen's chair, and arranged themselves in a half circle round her.

The footsteps of a man, ascending the staircase alone, were heard, and M. de Lafayette appeared in the doorway.

In the midst of the silence which his appearance produced, a voice issuing from the group surrounding the queen pronounced these words:

"There is Cromwell!"

Lafayette smiled.

"Cromwell would not have presented himself alone to Charles the First," said he.

Louis XVI. turned frowningly toward these terrible friends who wished to make an enemy of a man who had hastened to his assistance.

Then, addressing Charny:

"Count," said he, "I shall remain. Monsieur de Lafayette being here, I have nothing more to fear. Order the troops to withdraw to Rambouillet. The National Guards will be posted at the exterior ditches, the body-guards at those immediately near the palace."

Then, turning to Lafayette:

"Come with me, general, I have to speak with you."

And as Gilbert was taking a step toward the door:

"No, doctor," cried the king, "you will not be one too many. Come with us."

And showing the way to Lafayette and Gilbert, he went into a cabinet, into which they both followed him.

The queen followed them with her eyes, and when the door had closed behind them :

"Ah !" cried she, "it was to-day that we ought to have escaped from this. To-day there was still time. To-morrow, perhaps, it will be too late."

And she, in her turn, left the room, to withdraw to her own apartments.

A great light, similar to that of an extensive conflagration, illuminated the windows of the palace.

It was an immense bonfire, at which the Parisians were roasting the different joints of the horse they had killed.

The night was tolerably tranquil. The Assembly continued its sitting till three o'clock in the morning.

At three o'clock, and before the members separated, they sent two of their ushers, who took a round through Versailles, visited the environs of the palace, and then went round the park.

All was, or all appeared to be, quiet.

The queen had wished to leave the palace by the gate which communicated with Trianon, but the National Guards had refused to allow her to pass.

She had alleged her fears, and she had been answered that she was safer at Versailles than she could be elsewhere.

She had, in consequence, retired to her apartments ; and she, in fact, felt reassured when she saw that she was protected by the most faithful of her guards.

At her door she had found George de Charny. He was armed, and leaning upon the small musketoon used by the guards as well as the dragoons. This was unusual ; the guards in the interior of the palace stood sentry with their sabers only.

On perceiving him, the queen went up to him.

"Ah ! it is you, baron," she said.

"Yes, madame."

"Always faithful."

"Am I not at my post ?"

"Who placed you here ?"

"My brother, madame."

"And where is your brother ?"

"He is with the king."

"And why with the king ?"

"Because he is the head of the family," he said, "and

in that capacity has a right to die for the king, who is the head of the state."

"Yes," said Marie Antoinette, with a certain degree of bitterness, "while you have only the right of dying for the queen."

"That would be great happiness for me," said the young man, bowing, "should God ever permit me to fulfil that duty."

The queen made a step to withdraw, but a suspicion was gnawing at her heart.

She stopped, and, half turning her head :

"And—the countess," she inquired, "what has become of her ?"

"The countess, madame, came in about ten minutes since, and she has ordered a bed to be prepared for her in your majesty's antechamber."

The queen bit her lips.

Whenever she had occasion to make inquiry with regard to any of the De Charny family, she was always sure to find that they were rigidly attending to their duties, be they what they might.

"Thanks, sir," said the queen, with a charming gesture of the head and hands at the same time, "thanks for your watching so carefully over the queen. You will, in my name, thank your brother for watching over the king so carefully."

And after saying this she went to her own room. In the ante-chamber she found Andrée, not lying down, but still sitting up and respectfully awaiting her return.

She could not prevent herself from holding out her hand to her.

"I have just been thanking your brother-in-law, George, countess," she said, "and I told him to thank your husband, and I now thank you, in turn."

Andrée made a low courtesy, and stood aside to allow the queen to pass, who then went into her bedroom.

The queen did not tell her to follow her. This devotedness, from which she felt affection was withdrawn, and which, however icy cold it might be, she knew would exist till death, weighed heavily upon her feelings.

As we have before said, at three in the morning everything was quiet in the palace at Versailles.

Gilbert had left it with M. de Lafayette, who had been

on horseback for twelve hours, and who was so much fatigued that he could scarcely stand. On leaving the palace he met Billot, who had accompanied the National Guards. He had seen Gilbert set off ; he had thought that Gilbert might have occasion for him at Versailles, and he had, therefore, followed him like a dog who runs to rejoin his master who had left the house without him.

The Assembly, reassured by the report made to it by its ushers, had adjourned.

It was hoped that this tranquillity would not be disturbed during the night.

But they had calculated wrongly.

In almost all popular movements, by which great revolutions are prepared, there is a pausing time, during which people believe that all is terminated, and that they may sleep quietly.

They deceive themselves.

Behind the men who made the first commotion, there are others who are awaiting the completion of this first movement, calculating that the first, either from fatigue or being satisfied, do not desire to proceed further, and therefore repose.

It is then that in their turn these unknown men, the mysterious agents of fatal passions, glide darkly in the shade, take up the movement where it had been abandoned, and urge it onward to its utmost limits : and when they awake those who had opened out the way to them and had laid down half-way on the road, believing that their journey was performed, that the end was gained, they are terrified at the frightful progress which has been made.

There was a very different impulsion during this terrible night, and given by two troops which had arrived at Versailles—the one in the evening, the other during the night.

The first had come because it was hungry, and it asked for bread.

The second had come from hatred, and asked for vengeance.

We know who it was led on the first—Maillard and La-fayette.

But now. who was it that led on the second ? History mentions not their names ; but as history has failed in this, tradition names :

Marat.

We already know him ; we have seen him at the fêtes given at the time of the marriage of Marie Antoinette, cutting off legs and arms on the Place Louis XV.; we have seen him in the square before the Hôtel de Ville, urging on the citizens.

At length, we see him gliding along in the night, like those wolves who prowl along the sheep-folds, waiting until the shepherds shall be asleep, to venture on their sanguinary work.

Verrière.

As to this one, we have mentioned his name for the first time. He was a deformed dwarf, a hideous hunchback, but whose legs appeared immeasurably long in proportion to his body. At every storm which disturbed the depths of society, this sanguinary monster was seen to rise with scum and agitate himself upon its surface. Two or three times during the most terrible tumults he was seen passing through Paris huddled upon a black charger, and similar to one of the figures in the Apocalypse, or to one of those inconceivable demons to which the pencil of Callot has given birth in his picture of the temptations of St. Anthony.

One day at a club, and mounted on the table, he was attacking, threatening, and accusing Danton. It was at the period when the popularity of the man of the 2d of September was vacillating. Danton felt that this venomous attack of Verrière would altogether complete his ruin. He felt that he was lost—lost like the lion who perceives the hideous head of a serpent at two inches from his lips. He looked around him, seeking either a weapon or some one to back him. Fortunately, he caught sight of another little hunchback ; he immediately caught him under the arms, raised him and placed him upon the table immediately opposite his hump-backed brother.

" My friend," said he to him, " reply to that gentleman ; I yield the floor to you."

The whole assembly roared with laughter, and Danton was saved—for that time, at least.

There were then, according to tradition, Marat, Verrière, and besides them,

The Duke d'Aiguillon.

The Duke d'Aiguillon ; that is to say, one of the most inveterate enemies of the queen.

The Duke d'Aiguillon disguised as a woman.

And who was it said this ? Everybody.

The Abbé Delille and the Abbé Maury, these two abbés who so little resemble each other.

To the first was attributed the famous line :

" As a man, he's a coward ; as a woman, an assassin."

As to the Abbé Maury, that is another affair.

A fortnight after the occurrence of the events we are relating, the Duke d'Aiguillon met him on the terrace of the Feuillans and was about to accost him.

" Keep on your way, strumpet ! " said the Abbé Maury, and he majestically left the duke perfectly astounded.

It was, therefore, said that these three men, Marat, Verrière, and the Duke d'Aiguillon arrived at Versailles at about four o'clock in the morning.

They were leading the second troop of which we have spoken.

It was composed of men who follow in the wake of those who combat to conquer.

They, on the contrary, come to pillage and to assassinate.

They had undoubtedly assassinated a little at the Bastile, but they had not pillaged at all.

Versailles offered a delightful compensation.

About half-past five in the morning the palace was startled from its sleep.

A musket-shot had been fired in the marble courtyard.

Five or six hundred men had suddenly presented themselves at the gate, and exciting, animating, pushing on one another, some of them had climbed over the railings, while the others, by a united effort, at length forced open the gate.

It was then that a shot fired by the sentinel had given the alarm.

One of the assailants fell dead. His bleeding corpse was stretched upon the pavement.

This shot had divided this group of pillagers, whose aim was to obtain possession of the plate in the palace, and that of some of them, perhaps, to seize upon the king's crown.

Separated as by the blow of an immense hatchet, the crowd is divided into two groups.

One of the groups goes to attack the queen's apartments,

the other ascends toward the chapel—that is to say, toward the apartments of the king.

Let us first follow the one proceeding toward the king's apartments.

You have seen the waves rising when a high tide is setting in, have you not? Well, then, the popular wave is similar to it—with this sole difference, that it keeps on advancing without receding.

The whole of the king's guards at that moment consisted of a sentinel who was guarding the door, and an officer who rushed precipitately out of the ante-chamber, armed with a halberd which he had snatched from the hand of a terrified Swiss.

"Who goes there?" cried the sentinel, "who goes there?"

And as no answer was given, and as the flood of men still ascended:

"Who goes there?" he cried for the third time.

And he leveled his musket.

The officer feels at once what would be the result of a shot fired in the apartments, he strikes up the sentinel's gun, and rushing toward the assailants, he places his halberd across the top of the staircase, thus completely preventing any one from passing.

"Gentlemen, gentlemen!" cried he, "what do you want? What do you require?"

"Nothing—nothing," said several voices; "let us pass; we are good friends of his majesty."

"You are good friends of his majesty, and you make war on him?"

This time there was no answer—a laugh and nothing else.

A man seized the stock of the halberd that the officer would not leave go of. To make him quit his hold, the man struck his hand.

The officer snatched the halberd from the hands of his adversary, grasped the oaken stock with both of his, and dealing his adversary a blow on the head with all his strength, broke his skull.

The violence of the blow broke the halberd in two.

The officer, consequently, had two arms instead of one—a stick and a poniard.

He whirled the stick round—struck with the poniard,

During this time the sentry had opened the door of the ante-chamber, and called for assistance.

Five or six guards came out.

"Gentlemen! gentlemen!" said the sentinel, "assist Monsieur de Charny."

The sabers sprung from the scabbards, glittered for an instant in the light of the lamp which burned above the staircase, and to the right and left of Charny furiously attacked the assailants.

Cries of pain were heard, blood flowed, the wave of people retreated down the steps, and showed them covered with blood.

The door of the ante-chamber opened again, and the sentinel cried:

"Enter, gentlemen, the king orders it."

The guards profited by this moment of confusion among the crowd. They rushed toward the door. Charny entered last. The gate closes upon him, and the two large bolts shoot into their places.

A thousand blows are struck at once on the door. It would hold good, however, for ten minutes.

Ten minutes! during these ten minutes some assistance might arrive.

Let us see what the queen is doing.

The second group has darted toward the small apartments; but the staircase is narrow—scarce two people can pass at once.

George de Charny watches there.

At the third. Who goes there? no answer—he fires.

At the sound of the report the queen's door opens.

Andrée comes out, pale but calm.

"What is it?" asked she.

"Madame," cried George, "save her majesty; it is her life they want; I am opposed to a thousand, but I will hold out as long as possible. Quick! quick!" Then, as the assailants precipitated themselves on him, he shut the door, crying, "Draw the bolt! draw the bolt! I shall live long enough to allow the queen to fly." And turning, he pierced the two first he met in the corridor with his bayonet.

The queen had heard everything.

Two of her women, Mme. Hogue and Mme. Thibault, were dressing her. Then, half dressed, the two women conducted her through a corridor to the king; while calm and indifferent to her own danger, Andrée drew bolt after bolt, as she followed the steps of Marie Antoinette.

CHAPTER XXIV.

BETWIXT the two apartments a man waited for the queen. This man was Charny.

"The king!" cried Marie Antoinette, on seeing the blood on the dress of the young man. "The king! Monsieur, you promised to save the king!"

"The king is saved, madame," replied Charny.

And looking toward the doors which the queen had left open, in order to reach the Œil de Bœuf,* where at this time were assembled the queen, Mme. Royale,† the dauphin, and a few guards, Charny was about to ask what had become of Andrée, when his eyes met those of the queen.

This look stopped the question which was about to issue from his lips.

But the queen's look had dived into the recesses of Charny's heart.

There was no need for his speaking. Marie Antoinette had divined his thought.

"She is coming," said the queen, "you need not be uneasy."

And she ran to the dauphin, and clasped him in her ┐rms.

* The Œil de Bœuf, which has so very frequently been mentioned in this book, had a historical interest. It was an oval room in the great palace of Versailles, and its history, compiled recently by one of the most distinguished writers of France, comprises more pages than the annals of many a European kingdom. In the coterie of the Regent Duke of Orleans, of Louis XV., and of the early days of the reign of Louis XVI., flourished, and not until the days of the Emperor Napoleon did it lose its prestige. The scandal of this room was one of the great causes which made the whole of the bourgeoisie and middle classes of France so cordially detest the old monarchy, and induced them to throw the whole weight of their influence into the cause of the Revolution. Such scenes as were enacted there made Lafayette, Beauharnais, De Romoeub, and other nobles use all their influence to destroy a throne built up by crime, and with courtiers and courtesans as its supporters.

† The title given to the eldest daughters of the kings of France.

Andrée, immediately after this, closed the last door, and in her turn entered the room called the Œil de Bœuf.

Andrée and Charny did not exchange a word.

The smile of the one replied to the smile of the other, and that was all.

Strange to say, these two hearts, which had so long been severed, began to entertain feelings which responded to each other.

During this time the queen looked around her, and as if she felt delight in finding Charny in fault :

"The king," she inquired, "where is the king ?"

"The king is seeking for you, madame," tranquilly replied Charny; "he went to your apartment by one corridor, while you were coming here by another."

At the same instant loud cries were heard in the adjoining room.

They were the assassins, who were vociferating, "Down with the Austrian woman ! Down with the Messaline ! Down with the Veto ! She must be strangled ! She must be hanged !"

At the same time two pistol-shots were heard, and two balls pierced through the door at different heights.

One of these balls passed only a quarter of an inch above the head of the dauphin, and then buried itself in the opposite wainscoting.

"Oh ! my God ! my God !" cried the queen falling upon her knees.

The five or six guards, upon a sign made to them by Charny, then placed themselves before the queen and the two royal children, thus forming a rampart for them with their bodies.

At that moment the king appeared, his eyes full of tears, his face pale as death ; he was calling for the queen, as the queen had called for him.

He perceived her, and threw himself into her arms.

"Saved ! saved !" exclaimed the queen.

"By him, madame," cried the king, pointing to Charny, "and you are saved by him also, are you not ?"

"By his brother," replied the queen.

"Sir," said Louis XVI. to the count, "we owe so much to your family, so much that we shall never be able to repay the debt."

The queen's eyes met those of Andrée, and she turned away her head, blushing deeply.

The blows of the assailants were heard endeavoring to destroy the door.

"Come, gentlemen," said Charny, "we must defend our position here for another hour. There are seven of us, and it will take them full an hour to kill us if we defend ourselves resolutely. Before an hour elapses it will be impossible that a reinforcement should not arrive to the assistance of their majesties."

Saying these words, Charny seized a large press which was standing in one of the corners of the royal room.

His example was instantly followed, and a heap of furniture was piled up against the door, between which the guards took care to leave loopholes, through which they could fire on the assailants.

The queen took her two children in her arms, and raising her hands above their heads, she prayed.

The children restrained their cries and tears.

The king went into the cabinet contiguous to the Œil de Bœuf, in order to burn some valuable papers which he did not wish to fall into the hands of the assassins.

The latter were attacking the door more desperately than ever. At every instant, splinters were seen flying before the blows given by a sharp hatchet, or wrenched out by large pincers.

By the opening which had been thus made, pikes with reddened points, bayonets reeking with blood were forced through, attempting to hurl death on those within.

At the same time, the balls pierced the frame-work above the barricades, and left long traces on the gilded plaster of the ceiling.

At length a bench rolls from the top of the press; the press itself was partly damaged. One whole panel of the door, which formed the front of the press, gave way, and they could see, in the place of the bayonets and pikes, arms covered with blood pass through it and grasp the sides of the opening, which every moment became wider.

The guards had discharged their last cartridge, and this they had not done uselessly, for through this increasing opening could be seen the floor of the gallery covered with the wounded and dead bodies.

On hearing the shrieks of the women, who believed that

through this opening death was advancing upon them, the king returned.

"Sire," said Charny, "shut yourself up with the queen in the furthest room from this; close every door after you; place two of us behind the doors. I demand to be the last, and to guard the last door. I will answer for it that we hold out two hours; they have been more than forty minutes in breaking through this one."

The king hesitated; it appeared to him to be humiliating to fly thus from room to room, to entrench himself thus behind every cupboard.

If the queen had not been there, he would not have retreated a single step.

If the queen had not her children with her, she would have remained as firmly as the king.

But alas! poor human beings, kings or subjects, we have always in our hearts some secret opening by which courage escapes and terror enters.

The king was about to give the order to fly to the remotest room, when suddenly the arms were withdrawn, the pikes and bayonets disappeared, the shouts and threats at once ceased.

A general silence ensued, every one remaining with distended lips, eagerly listening ears, and suppressed respiration.

Then they heard the measured steps of regular troops advancing.

"They are the National Guards!" cried Charny.

"Monsieur de Charny!" cried a voice, and at the same time the well-known face of Billot appeared at the opening.

"Billot!" cried Charny, "is it you, my friend?"

"Yes, yes, 'tis I," replied the honest farmer, "and the king and queen, where are they?"

"They are here."

"Safe and sound?"

"Safe and sound."

"May God be praised! This way, Monsieur Gilbert, this way!" cried he, in his stentorian voice.

At the name of Gilbert, the hearts of two women bounded with very different feelings.

The heart of the queen and the heart of Andrée.

Charny turned round instinctively. He saw both Andrée and the queen turn pale at this name.

He shook his head, and sighed.

"Open the door, gentlemen," said the king.

The guards hastened to obey his orders, throwing aside the remains of the barricade.

During this time the voice of Lafayette was heard crying:

"Gentlemen of the National Guard of Paris, I last night pledged my word to the king that no injury should be done to any one belonging to his majesty. If you allow his guards to be massacred, you will make me forfeit my word of honor, and I shall no longer be worthy to be your chief."

When the door was opened, the two persons first perceived were General Lafayette and Gilbert; a little to their left stood Billot, perfectly delighted at the share he had taken in the king's deliverance.

It was Billot who had gone to awaken Lafayette.

Behind Lafayette, Gilbert, and Billot was Captain Goudran, commanding the company of the center St. Phillippe de Roule.

Mme. Adelaide was the first who rushed forward to greet Lafayette, and throwing her arms round his neck with all the gratitude of terror:

"Ah, sir!" she exclaimed, "it is you who have saved us."

Lafayette advanced respectfully, and was about crossing the threshold of the Œil de Bœuf, when an officer stopped his progress.

"Your pardon, sir," said he to him, "but have you right of admission?"

"If he have not," said the king, holding out his hand to Lafayette, "I give it to him."

"Long live the king! long live the queen!" cried Billot.

The king turned toward him.

"That is a voice I know," said he, smiling.

"You are very kind, sire," replied the worthy farmer. "Yes, yes; you heard that voice on the journey to Paris. Ah! had you but remained in Paris instead of returning here!"

The queen knit her brows.

"Yes," she said, "since you Parisians are so very amiable."

"Well, sir," said the king to M. de Lafayette, as if he had been asking him. "In your opinion, what ought now to be done?"

"Sire," respectfully replied M. de Lafayette, "I think it would be well that your majesty should show yourself on the balcony."

The king asked Gilbert for his opinion, but merely by a look.

Louis XVI. then went straight to the window, and without hesitation opened it himself and appeared upon the balcony.

A tremendous and unanimous shout burst from the people.

"Long live the king!"

Then a second cry followed the first.

"The king to Paris!"

Between these two cries, and sometimes overwhelming them, some formidable voices shouted:

"The queen! the queen!"

At this cry everybody shuddered; the king turned pale, Charny turned pale, even Gilbert himself turned pale.

The queen raised her head.

She was also pale, but with compressed lips and frowning brow; she was standing near the window. Mme. Royale was leaning against her. Before her was the dauphin, and on the fair head of the child reclined her convulsively clinched hand, white as the purest marble.

"The queen! the queen!" reiterated the voices, becoming more and more formidable.

"The people desire to see you, madame," said Lafayette.

"Oh! do not go, my mother!" said Mme. Royale, in great agony, and throwing her arms round the queen's neck.

The queen looked at Lafayette.

"Fear nothing, madam," said he to her.

"What!" she exclaimed, "and quite alone?"

Lafayette smiled, respectfully, and with the delightful manner which he retained even to his latest days, he took the two children from their mother and made them first ascend the balcony.

Then, offering his hand to the queen:

"If your majesty will deign to confide in me," said he, "I will be responsible for all."

And he conducted the queen on to the balcony.

It was a terrible spectacle, and one likely to cause the vertigo. For the marble courtyard was transformed into a human sea full of roaring waves.

"At the sight of the queen an immense cry was uttered by the whole of this crowd, and no one could have been positive whether it was a cry of menace or of joy.

Lafayette kissed the queen's hand, then loud applause burst forth.

In the noble French nation there is, even in the veins of the lowest born, chivalric blood.

The queen breathed more freely.

Then, suddenly shuddering :

"And my guards, sir," said she, "my guards, who have saved my life, can you do nothing for them ?"

"Let me have one of them, madame," said Lafayette.

"Monsieur de Charny ! Monsieur de Charny !" cried the queen.

But Charny withdrew a step or two ; he had understood what was required of him.

He did not wish to make an apology for the evening of the 1st of October.

Not having been guilty, he required no amnesty.

Andrée, on her side, was impressed with the same feeling. She had stretched out her hand to Charny for the purpose of preventing him.

Her hand met the hand of the count, and these two hands were pressed within each other.

The queen had observed this, notwithstanding she had so much to observe at that moment.

Her eyes flashed fire, and with a palpitating heart and broken accents :

"Sir," said she to another guard, "sir, come here, I command you."

The guard obeyed.

He had not, moreover, the same motives for hesitating as Charny had.

M. de Lafayette drew the guard on to the balcony, and taking his own tricolored cockade from his hat, placed it in that of the guard, after which he embraced him.

"Long live Lafayette ! long live the body-guard !" shouted fifty thousand voices.

Some few wished to utter some hollow growlings, the last threat of the disappearing tempest.

But they were overwhelmed by the universal acclamation.

"Come," said Lafayette, "all is ended, and fine weather has returned."

Then, stepping into the room :

"But that it should not again be overcast, sire, there still remains a sacrifice for you to make."

"Yes," said the king, pensively, "to leave Versailles, is it not ?"

"And come to Paris—yes, sire."

"Sir," said the king, "you may announce to the people that at one o'clock I, the queen, and my children, will set out for Paris."

Then, turning to the queen :

"Madame," said he, "you had better retire to your own apartment, and prepare yourself."

This order of the king appeared to remind Charny of an event of importance which he had forgotten.

He rushed from the room, preceding the queen.

"Why are you going to my apartment, sir ?" said the queen, harshly, to him ; "you have no need to go there."

"I earnestly trust it may be so, madame," replied Charny ; "but be not uneasy ; if really I am not needed there, I shall not remain long enough to cause my presence to be displeasing to your majesty."

The queen followed him ; traces of blood stained the floor, and the queen saw them. She closed her eyes, and seeking an arm to guide her, she took that of Charny, and walked some steps in this way as a blind person.

Suddenly she felt that every nerve in Charny's body shuddered.

"What is the matter, sir ?" she said, opening her eyes.

Then, suddenly :

"A dead body ! a dead body !" she exclaimed.

"Your majesty will excuse my withdrawing my arm," said he. "I have found that which I came to seek in your apartment—the dead body of my brother George."

It was, in fact, the dead body of the unfortunate young man, whom his brother had ordered to allow himself to be killed rather than that the queen should be approached.

He had punctually obeyed.

CHAPTER XXV.

THE circumstances we have just related have been re-
counted in a hundred different ways; for they were certainly the most interesting which occurred in the great
period between 1789 and 1795, and which is called the
French Revolution.

They will be related in a hundred various ways still;
but we can affirm beforehand, that no one will relate them
with more impartiality than we do.

But of what service will all these narratives be, however true they are? Did ever a political lesson prove
instructive to a political man?

No; queens have wept: no; kings have been murdered,
and yet their successors have never profited by the cruel
lesson which fate had given them.

Faithful subjects have been prodigal of their devotedness, without those whom fatality had destined to misfortune having derived any advantage from it.

Alas! we have seen the queen almost stumble over the
body of one of those men whom kings, when they depart,
leave bleeding upon the road which they have traversed
in their fall.

A few hours after the cry of terror which the queen
had uttered, and at the moment when, with the king and
her children, she was about to leave Versailles, where she
was never to return, the following scene took place in an
interior courtyard, damp from the rain, and which a
sharp autumnal wind had begun to dry.

A man dressed in black was leaning over a dead body.

A man dressed in the uniform of the Royal Guards was
kneeling on the opposite side of this body.

At three paces from them a third person was standing,
with clasped hands and fixed eyes, gazing intently at
them.

The dead body was that of a young man of from twenty-
two to twenty-three years of age, the whole of whose blood
appeared to have escaped through large wounds in his
head and chest.

His chest was scarred with frightful gashes, the skin

surrounding them was of a livid white; it appeared still to heave with the disdainful breathings of a hopeless defense.

His half-opened mouth, his head thrown back with an expression of pain and anger, recalled to the mind the beautiful statue of the dying gladiator.

"And life, with a long groan, fled to the abode of shadows."

The man dressed in black was Gilbert.

The officer on his knees was the Count de Charny.

The man standing near them was Billot.

The corpse was that of the Baron George de Charny.

Gilbert, leaning over the body, gazed at it with that sublime intentness which, with the dying, retains life when about to escape, and, with the dead, almost recalls the soul which has taken flight.

"Cold, stiff—he is dead—positively dead!" said he, at length.

The Count de Charny uttered a hoarse groan, and pressing in his arms the insensible body, burst into sobs so heartrending that the doctor shuddered and Billot ran to hide his head in a corner of the small courtyard.

Then, suddenly, the count raised the body, placed it against the wall, and slowly withdrew, still looking at it as if he expected that his dead brother would become reanimated and follow him.

Gilbert remained still kneeling on one knee, his head reclining on his hand, pensive and motionless.

Billot then left his dark corner and went up to Gilbert; he no longer heard the count's sobs, which had torn his heart.

"Alas! alas! Monsieur Gilbert," said he, "this, then, is really what we have to expect in civil war, and that which you predicted to me is now happening—only it is happening sooner than I expected, and even sooner than you yourself expected. I saw these villains murdering unworthy people; and now I see these villains murdering honest people. I saw them massacre Flesselles; I saw them massacre Monsieur de Launay; I saw Foulon massacred; I saw Berthier massacred. I then shuddered in every limb, and I felt a horror for all men."

"And yet the men they were then killing were miserable wretches."

"It was then, Monsieur Gilbert, that you predicted the time would come when they would kill honest people."

"They have killed the Baron de Charny. I no longer shudder—I weep; I have no longer a horror of others—I fear I may resemble them."

"Billot!" cried Gilbert.

But without listening, Billot continued:

"Here is a young man whom they have assassinated, Monsieur Gilbert. He was a mere boy, he was fairly combating, he was not assassinating, but he has been assassinated."

Billot heaved a sigh, which seemed to issue from the bottom of his heart.

"Ah! the unhappy youth," he cried. "I knew him when he was a child. I have seen him pass by when he was going from Boursonne to Villers-Cotterets on his little gray pony; he was carrying bread to the poor from his mother.

"He was a beautiful boy, with a fair, rosy complexion, and large blue eyes; he was always smiling. Well, it is very extraordinary, since I saw him stretched out there, bloody and disfigured, it is not a corpse that I behold in him, but always the smiling child of former days, carrying a basket in his left hand and a purse in his right.

"Ah! Monsieur Gilbert, in truth I believe I have now had enough of it, and do not desire to see anything more; for you predicted this to me. The time will come when I shall also see you die, and then——"

Gilbert gently shook his head.

"Billot," said he, "be calm; my hour has not yet come."

"Be it so; but mine has come, doctor. I have a harvest down yonder which has rotted, fields that are lying fallow, a family whom I love ten times more dearly on seeing this dead body, whose family are weeping for him."

"What do you mean to say, my dear Billot? Do you believe, perchance, that I am going to afflict myself about you?"

"Oh, no!" replied Billot, ingenuously; "but as I suffer, I complain; and as complaining leads to nothing, I calculate on alleviating my own sufferings in my own way."

"Which means to say that——"

"It means that I desire to return to my farm, Monsieur Gilbert."

" Again, Billot ?

" Ah ! Monsieur Gilbert, there is a voice down yonder which is calling for me."

" Take care, Billot ; that voice is advising you to desert."

" I am not a soldier, and therefore, there is no desertion, Monsieur Gilbert.

" What you are wishing to do would be a desertion far more culpable than that of a soldier."

" Explain that to me, doctor."

" How you have come to Paris to demolish ; and you would fly as soon as the building is falling."

" Yes, that I may not crush my friends."

" Or, rather, that you may not be crushed yourself."

" Why, why !" replied Billot, " it is not forbidden that a man should think a little of himself."

" Ah ! that is a magnificent calculation, indeed ; as if stones did not roll, as if in rolling they did not crush, and even at a distance, the timid men who would fly from them."

" Oh ! you are well aware that I am not a timid man, Monsieur Gilbert."

" Then you will remain, Billot ; I have occasion for you here."

" My family also stands in need of me down yonder."

Billot ! Billot ! I thought that you had agreed with me that a man who loves his country has no family."

" I should like to know whether you would use the same language, if Sebastian were there, there, lying as that young man does."

And he pointed to the dead body.

" Billot," replied Gilbert, in a hollow tone, " the day will arrive when my son shall see me as I now see that body."

" So much the worse for him, doctor, if on that day he should be as calm as you are now."

" I hope that he will be a better man than I am, Billot, and that he will be firmer still, and precisely because I shall have given him an example of firmness."

" Then you would have the child accustom himself to see blood flowing around him, that he should in his youthful years acquire the habit of great conflagrations, of gibbets and riots—attacks in the dark—that he should see kings threatened, queens insulted, and then, when he has become as hard as his sword-blade, and quite as cold, you would still expect that he should love, that he should respect you."

"No, I would not have him see all that, Billot; and that is the reason for my sending him back to Villers-Cotterets, and which I now almost regret."

"How! You now regret it?"

"Yes."

"And why do you now regret?"

"Because he would this day have seen exemplified the axiom of the lion and the rat, which to him is but a fable."

"What do you mean to say, Monsieur Gilbert?"

"I say that he would have seen a poor farmer, whom chance has brought to Paris, a brave and honest man, who can neither read nor write, who never could have believed that his life could have influenced, either for good or evil, the high destinies which he scarcely dared to raise his eyes to—I say, that he would have seen that man who had already, at one time, wished to leave Paris, as he again wishes it—I say that he would have seen this man contribute efficaciously to save the life of a king, a queen, and two royal children."

Billot stared at Gilbert with astonished eyes.

"And how so, Monsieur Gilbert?" says he.

"How so, you sublimely ignorant fellow. I will tell you how. By waking at the first noise that was made; by guessing that this noise was a tempest ready to burst upon Versailles; by running to wake up Monsieur Lafayette—for Monsieur Lafayette was asleep."

"Zounds! that was perfectly natural, for he had been twelve hours on horseback, and twenty-four hours that he had not been in bed."

"By leading him to the palace," continued Gilbert; "and by bringing him at once into the midst of the assassins and crying, 'Stop, wretches, here is the avenger!'"

"Well, now, that is really true—I did all that."

"Well, then, Billot, you see that this is a great compensation. If you did not prevent this young man being assassinated, you have perhaps prevented the assassination of the king, the queen, and the two children. Ungrateful man! and you ask to leave the service of the country at the very moment when the country recompenses you."

"But who will ever know what I have done, since I, myself, even had no idea of it ?"

"You and I, Billot—and is not that enough ?"

Billot reflected for a moment, then, holding out his rough hand to the doctor :

"I declare you are right, Monsieur Gilbert," said he ; "but you know that man is but a weak, egotistical, inconstant creature. There is but you, Monsieur Gilbert, who is firm, generous, and constant. What is it that has made you so ?"

"Misfortune," said Gilbert, with a smile, in which there was more sorrow than in a sob.

"That is singular," said Billot ; "I had thought that misfortune made men wicked."

"The weak—yes."

"And I should be unfortunate and become wicked."

"You may, perhaps, be unfortunate ; but you will never become wicked, Billot."

"Are you sure of that ?"

"I will answer for you."

"In that case——" said Billot, sighing.

"In that case——" repeated Gilbert.

"Why, I will remain with you ; but more than once I know I shall again be vacillating."

"And every time it happens, Billot, I shall be near you to sustain your firmness."

"Well, again I say, so be it," sighed the farmer.

Then, casting a last look on the body of the Baron George de Charny, which the servants were about to remove on a bier :

"It matters not," said Billot, "he was a handsome boy, that little George de Charny, on his little gray pony, with a basket on his left arm and his purse in the other."

CHAPTER XXVI.

WE have seen, under circumstances long anterior to those we have now related, the departure of Pitou and Sebastian Gilbert.

Our intention being, for the present, to abandon the principal personages of our history, to follow the two young travelers, we hope that our readers will allow us to enter into some details relating to their arrival at Villers-Cotterets.

Gilbert had commissioned Pitou to go to the College Louis le Grand and to bring Sebastian to him. For this purpose they put Pitou into a hackney-coach, and as they had confided Sebastian to Pitou, they confided Pitou to the care of the coachman.

In about an hour the coach brought back Pitou; Pitou brought back Sebastian.

Gilbert and Billot were waiting for them in an apartment which they had taken in the Rue St. Honoré, a little above the Church of the Assumption.

Gilbert explained to his son that he was to set out the same evening with Pitou, and asked him whether he would not be well pleased to return to the great woods he so much loved.

"Yes, father," replied the boy, "provided that you will come to see me at Villers-Cotterets, or that you allow me to come to see you at Paris."

"You may be easy on that score, my child," replied Gilbert, kissing his son's forehead; "you know that now I shall never be happy when away from you."

As to Pitou, he colored with delight at the idea of setting out the same evening.

He turned pale with happiness when Gilbert placed, within one of his, both Sebastian's hands, and in the other ten double louis, of the value of forty-eight livres each.

A long series of instructions, almost all regarding the health of his companion were given by the doctor to Pitou, to which he religiously listened.

Sebastian cast down his large eyes to conceal his tears.

Pitou was weighing and jingling his louis in his immense pocket.

Gilbert gave a letter to Pitou, who was thus installed in his functions, *pro tem.*, of tutor.

This letter was for the Abbé Fortier.

The doctor's harangue being terminated, Billot spoke in his turn.

"Monsieur Gilbert," said he, "has confided to you the health of Sebastian; I will confide to you his personal safety. You have a pair of stout fists; in a case of need, make good use of them."

"Yes," said Pitou ; "and, besides them, I have a saber."

"Do not make an abuse of that."

"I will be merciful," said Pitou ; " *clemens ero.*"

"A hero, if you will," repeated Billot, but not intending to say it jeeringly.

"And now," said Gilbert, " I will point out to you the way in which Sebastian should travel."

"Oh !" cried Pitou, " it is only eighteen leagues from Paris to Villers-Cotterets ; we will talk all the way, Sebastian and I."

Sebastian looked at his father as if to ask him whether it would be very amusing to talk during the journey of eighteen leagues with Pitou.

Pitou caught this glance.

"We will speak Latin," said he, "and we shall be taken for learned men."

This was the dream of his ambition, the innocent creature !

How many others, with ten double louis in their pockets, would have said :

" We will buy gingerbrea..."

Gilbert appeared for a moment to be in doubt.

He looked at Pitou, then at Billot.

"I understand you," said the latter ; "you are asking yourself whether Pitou is a proper guide, and you hesitate to confide your child to him."

"Oh !" said Gilbert, "it is not to him that I confide him."

"To whom, then ?"

Gilbert looked up to heaven ; he was still too much a Voltairean to dare to reply :

"To God !"

And the affair was settled. They resolved, in consequence, without making any change in Pitou's plan, which promised, without exposing him to too much fatigue, a journey replete with amusement to Sebastian ; but it was decided they should not commence it until the following morning.

Gilbert might have sent his son to Villers-Cotterets by one of the public conveyances, which at that period were running between Paris and the frontiers, or even in his own carriage ; but we know how much he feared the isolation of thought for young Sebastian, and nothing so much isolates dreaming people as the motion and rumbling noise of a carriage.

He, therefore, took the two young travelers as far as Bourget, and then showing them the open road, on which a brilliant sun was shining, and bordered by a double row of trees, he embraced his son again, and opening his arms, said :

" Now go !"

Pitou, therefore, set off, leading Sebastian, who several times turned round to blow kisses to his father, who was standing, his arms crossed, upon the spot where he had taken leave of his son, following him with his eyes, as if he were following a dream.

Pitou raised himself to the full height of his extraordinary stature. Pitou was very proud of the confidence reposed in him by a person of Mr. Gilbert's importance, one of the king's physicians-in-ordinary.

Pitou prepared himself scrupulously to fulfil the task intrusted to him, which combined the functions of a tutor and almost those of a governess.

Moreover, it was with full confidence in himself that he was conducting little Sebastian ; he traveled very quietly, passing through villages which were all in commotion and terror since the events at Paris, which had only just occurred ; for although we have brought up these events to the 5th and 6th of October, it must be remembered that it was toward the end of July or the beginning of August that Pitou and Sebastian left Paris.

Besides this, Pitou had retained his helmet for a head-dress, and his long saber as a defensive weapon.

These were all that he had gained by the events of the 13th and 14th of July, but this twofold trophy satisfied his ambition, and by giving him a formidable air, at the same time sufficed for his safety.

Moreover, this formidable air, to which indubitably the helmet and dragoon's saber greatly concurred, Pitou had acquired it independently of them. A man has not assisted in taking the Bastile, he has not even merely been present at it, without having retained something heroic in his deportment.

Pitou had, in addition to this, become somewhat of an advocate.

No one could have listened to the resolutions passed at the Hôtel de Ville, to the orations of M. Bailly, the harangues of M. de Lafayette, without becoming somewhat of an orator ; above all, if he has already studied the Latin *Conciones*, of which French eloquence at the close of the eighteenth century was rather a pale though a tolerably correct imitation.

Furnished with these two powerful modes of argument, to which two vigorous fists were no mean adjuncts, and, possessing a rare amenity of smile and a most interesting appetite, Pitou journeyed on agreeably toward Villers-Cotterets.

For the curious in politics he had news, besides which he could manufacture them in case of need, having resided in Paris, where, from that period, their fabrication has been always remarkable.

He related how M. Berthier had left immense buried treasures, which the government would some day manage to dig up. How M. de Lafayette, the paragon of all glory, the pride of provincial France, was no longer considered in Paris but as a half-used-up doll, whose white horse was a fertile subject for the concoction of jests and caricatures. How M. Bailly, whom M. de Lafayette honored with his most intimate friendship, as well as all the members of his family, was an aristocrat, and that scandalous people said even worse things of him.

When he related all this, Pitou raised tempests of anger against him, but he possessed the *quos ego* of all these storms. He would then relate unpublished anecdotes of the Austrian woman.

His inexhaustible fancy procured for him an uninterrupted succession of excellent repasts, until he arrived at Vauciennes, the last village on the road before reaching Villers-Cotterets.

As Sebastian, on the contrary, ate little or nothing—as he did not speak at all—as he was a pale and sickly looking youth, every one who felt interested for Sebastian admired the vigilant and paternal care of Pitou toward him, who caressed, cosseted, attended on the boy, and into the bargain, ate his part of the dinners, without seeming to have any other motive than that of being agreeable to him.

When they arrived at Vauciennes, Pitou appeared to

hesitate; he looked at Sebastian, Sebastian looked at Pitou.

Pitou scratched his head. This was his mode of expressing his embarrassment.

Sebastian knew enough of Pitou to be aware of this peculiarity.

"Well, what is the matter, Pitou?" asked Sebastian.

"The matter is, that if it were the same thing to you, and if you were not too tired, instead of continuing our way straight on, we would return to Villers-Cotterets through Haramont."

And Pitou, honest lad, blushed while expressing this wish, as Catherine would have blushed when expressing a less innocent desire.

Sebastian at once understood him.

"Ah, yes!" said he; "it was there our poor mother, Pitou, died."

"Come, my brother, come!"

Pitou pressed Sebastian to his heart with an energy that almost suffocated him, and taking the boy's hand, he began running down the cross-road, which leads along the valley of Wuala, and so rapidly, that, after going a hundred paces, poor Sebastian was completely out of breath and was obliged to say:

"Too fast, Pitou, too fast!"

Pitou stopped; he had not perceived that he was going too fast, it being his usual pace.

He saw that Sebastian was pale and out of breath.

He took him on his shoulders and carried him.

In this way Pitou might walk as fast as he pleased.

As it was not the first time that Pitou had carried Sebastian, Sebastian made no objection.

They thus reached Largny. There Sebastian, feeling that Pitou was panting, declared that he had rested long enough, and that he was ready to walk at any pace that might suit Pitou.

Pitou, being full of magnanimity, moderated his pace.

Half an hour after this, Pitou was at the entrance of Haramont, the pretty village where he first saw the light, as says the romance of a great poet—a romance, the music of which is of more value than the words.

When they reached it, the two boys cast a look around them to discover their old haunts.

The first thing which they perceived was the crucifix which popular piety habitually places at the entrance to all villages.

Alas! even at Haramont they felt the strange progression which Paris was making toward atheism. The nails which fastened the right arm and the feet of the figure of Christ had broken off from rust having eaten through them. The figure was hanging suspended only by the left arm, and no one had had the pious idea of replacing the symbol of that liberty, that equality, that fraternity which every one was in those days preaching.

Pitou was not devout, but he had the traditions of his childhood. That this holy symbol should have been thus neglected, wounded him to the heart. He searched the hedges for one of those creeping plants which are as thin and as tenacious as iron wire, laid his helmet and his saber on the grass, climbed up the cross, refastened the arm of the divine martyr to it, kissed the feet, and descended.

During this time Sebastian was praying on his knees at the foot of the cross. For whom was he praying? Who can tell?

Perhaps for that vision of his childhood which he fondly hoped once more to find beneath the great trees, for that unknown mother who is never unknown, for if she has not nourished us from her breast, yet is she still our mother.

His holy action being accomplished, Pitou replaced his helmet on his head and replaced his saber in his belt.

When Sebastian had concluded his prayer, he made the sign of the cross, and again took Pitou's hand.

Both of them, then, entered the village, and advanced toward the cottage in which Pitou had been born, in which Sebastian had been nursed.

Pitou knew every stone in Haramont, and yet he could not find the cottage. He was obliged to inquire what had become of it, and the person he applied to showed him a small house built of stone, with a slated roof.

The garden of this house was surrounded by a wall.

Aunt Angelique had sold her sister's house, and the new proprietor, having full right to do so, had pulled down everything—the old walls, which had again become dust —the old door, with a hole cut in it to allow ingress to the cat—the old windows, with their panes half glass, half paper, upon which had appeared in strokes the elementary lessons Pitou had received in writing—the thatched roof with its green moss, and the plants which had grown and blossomed on its summit. The new proprietor had pulled down all this—all had disappeared.

The gate was closed, and lying on the threshold was a big black dog, who showed his teeth to Pitou.

"Come," said Pitou, the tears starting from his eyes, "let us be gone, Sebastian. Let us go to a place where at least I am sure that nothing will have changed."

And Pitou dragged Sebastian to the cemetery where his mother had been buried.

He was right, the poor boy! There, nothing had been changed ; only the grass had grown ; it grows so rapidly in cemeteries that there was some chance even that he would not be able to recognize his mother's grave. For-tunately, at the same time that the grass had grown, a branch of a weeping-willow which Pitou had planted had, in three years, become a tree. He went straight to the tree and kissed the earth which it overshadowed, with the same instinctive piety with which he had kissed the feet of the figure of Christ.

When he rose from the ground, he felt the branches of the willow, agitated by the wind, waving around his head.

He then stretched out his arms, and clasping the branches, pressed them to his heart.

It was as if he was holding the hair of his mother, which he was embracing for the last time.

The two youths remained a considerable time by the side of this grave, and evening was approaching.

It was necessary that they should leave it, the only thing that appeared to have any remembrance of Pitou.

"When about to leave it, Pitou for a moment had the idea of breaking off a slip of the willow and placing it in his helmet ; but just when he was raising his hand to do so, he paused.

It appeared to him that it would be giving pain to his poor mother to tear off a branch from a tree, the roots of which, perhaps, were intwined round the decaying deal coffin in which her remains reposed.

He again kissed the ground, took Sebastian by the hand, and left the cemetery.

All the inhabitants of the village were either in the fields or in the woods; few persons, therefore, had seen Pitou; and, disguised as he was by his helmet and his long saber, among those persons no one had recognized him.

He, therefore, took the road to Villers-Cotterets, a delightful road, which runs through the forest for nearly three quarters of a league without any living or animated object thinking of diverting his grief.

Sebastian followed, mute and pensive as himself.

They arrived at Villers-Cotterets at about five in the afternoon.

CHAPTER XXVII.

PITOU arrived at Villers-Cotterets by that part of the park which is called the Pheasantry. He walked across the dancing-place, always abandoned during the week, and to which he had, three weeks previously, conducted Catherine.

What a number of things had happened to Pitou and to France during those three weeks!

Then, having followed the long avenue of chestnut-trees, he reached the square before the château, and knocked at the back door of the college presided over by the Abbé Fortier.

It was full three years since Pitou had left Haramont, while it was only three weeks since he had left Villers-Cotterets. It was, therefore, very natural that he should not have been recognized at Haramont, and that he should have been recognized at Villers-Cotterets.

In a moment a rumor ran through the town that Pitou had returned there with young Sebastian Gilbert; that both of them had gone into the house of the Abbé Fortier; that Sebastian looked much the same as when he had left them, but that Pitou had a helmet and a long sword.

The result of this was that a great crowd had assembled at the principal gate; for they calculated that if Pitou had gone into the château by the small private door, he would come out of it by the great gate in the Rue de Soissons.

This was his direct road for going to the Pleux.

In fact, Pitou remained at the Abbé Fortier's only long

enough to deliver into the hands of the abbé's sister the letter from the doctor, the young lad himself, and five double louis destined to pay his board.

The Abbé Fortier's sister was at first much terrified when she saw so formidable a soldier advancing through the garden ; but soon, beneath the dragoon's helmet, she recognized the placid and honest face of Pitou, which somewhat tranquilized her.

And, finally, the sight of the five double louis reassured her altogether.

This terror of the poor old maid can be the more readily explained by informing our readers that the Abbé Fortier had gone out with his pupils to give them a walk, and that she was quite alone in the house.

Pitou, after having delivered the letter and the five double louis, embraced Sebastian, and left the house, clapping his helmet on his head with due military bravado.

Sebastian had shed some tears on separating from Pitou, although the separation was not to be of long duration, and notwithstanding that his society was not exceedingly amusing ; but his hilarity, his mildness, his continued obligingness, had touched the heart of young Gilbert. Pitou had the disposition of those fine great Newfoundland dogs, who sometimes fatigue you very much, but who, in the end, disarm your anger by licking your hand.

There was one thing which diminished Sebastian's grief, which was that Pitou promised that he would often go to see him. One thing diminished Pitou's regret, and this was that Sebastian thanked him for his promise.

But now let us for awhile follow our hero from the house of the Abbé Fortier to that of his aunt Angelique, situated, as our readers already know, at the further end of the Pleux.

On leaving the Abbé Fortier's house, Pitou found some twenty persons who were waiting for him. His strange equipment, a description of which had been given throughout the town, was in part known to those assembled. On seeing him thus return from Paris, where so much fighting was going on, they presumed that Pitou had been fighting too, and they wished to hear the news.

This news Pitou communicated with his accustomed majesty. The taking of the Bastile, the exploits of M. Billot and of M. Maillard, of MM. Elie and Hullin ; how

Billot had fallen into the ditch of the fortress, and how he, Pitou, had dragged him out of it ; finally, how they had saved M. Gilbert, who, during six or seven days, had been one of the prisoners confined there.

The auditors already knew the most of these details that Pitou had related to them; but they had read all these details in the newspapers of the day, and, however faithful the editor of a newspaper may be in his writings, he always knows less than an ocular witness who relates the incidents—who may be interrupted, and who resumes—who may be questioned, and replies.

Now Pitou resumed, replied, gave all the details, showing, when interrupted, the greatest obligingness—in all his answers, the greatest possible amenity.

The result of all this was that in about an hour's conversation at the door of the Abbé Fortier, in which he gave a succinct narrative, the Rue de Soissons was crowded with auditors, when one of the persons present, observing some signs of anxiety in Pitou's countenance, took upon himself to say :

"But he is fatigued, poor Pitou, and we are keeping him here upon his legs, instead of allowing him to go to his aunt Angelique's house, poor, dear woman, who will be so delighted at seeing him again."

"It is not that I am fatigued," said Pitou, " but that I am hungry.   I have never been fatigued, but I am always hungry.

Then, and in consequence of this ingenuous declaration, the crowd, who highly respected the cravings of Pitou's stomach, respectfully made way for him to pass, and Pitou, followed by some persons more inveterately curious than the rest, was permitted to wend his way to the Pleux—that is to say, to the house of his aunt Angelique.

Aunt Angelique was not at home, and had gone doubtless to visit some neighbors, and the door was locked.

Several persons then invited Pitou to go to their houses and take the nourishment he stood in need of ; but Pitou proudly refused.

"But," said they to him, "you see, dear Pitou, that your aunt's door is locked."

"The door of an aunt cannot remain locked before an obedient and hungry nephew," said Pitou, majestically.

And drawing his long saber, the sight of which made

men and children start back with affright, he introduced
the point of it between the bolt and the staple of the lock,
gave a vigorous jerk, and the door flew open, to the great
admiration of all present, who no longer doubted the great
exploits of Pitou, since they saw him with so much audacity expose himself to the anger of the ill-tempered old
maid.

The interior of the house was in precisely the same state
as when Pitou had left it. The famous leather armchair
royally held its state in the center of the room ; two or
three other mutilated chairs and stools formed the lame
court of the great armchair ; at the end of the room was
the kneading-trough ; on the right, the cupboard and the
chimney.

Pitou entered the house with a bland smile. He had no
quarrel with all these poor articles of furniture ; on the
contrary, they were the friends of his youth. They were,
it is true, almost as hard in their nature as Aunt Angelique, but when they were opened, there was something
good to be found in them ; while, had Aunt Angelique
been opened, her inside would certainly have been found
dryer and worse than her exterior.

Pitou, upon the instant, gave a proof of what we have
advanced, to the persons who had followed him, and who,
seeing what was going on, were waiting outside the house,
curious to see what would be the result when Aunt Angelique should return home.

It was, moreover, very perceptible that all these persons
felt great sympathy for Pitou. We have said that Pitou
was hungry, so hungry that it had been perceived by the
change in his countenance.

Therefore, he lost no time ; he went straight to the
kneading-trough and cupboard.

In former times—we say former times, although scarcely
three weeks had elapsed since Pitou's departure ; for, in
our opinion, time is to be measured, not by its duration,
but by the events which have occurred—in former times,
Pitou, unless urged on by the evil spirit, or by irresistible
hunger, both of them infernal powers and which much
resemble each other—in former times, Pitou would have
seated himself upon the threshold of the closed door, and
humbly waited the return of Aunt Angelique ; when she
had returned, would have bowed to her with a soft smile :

then, standing aside, would have made room for her to pass, would have followed her into the house, would have gone for a loaf and knife, that she might measure out his portion to him ; then, his share being cut off, he would have cast a longing eye, a single look, tearful and magnetic—he thought it so, at least—magnetic to such a degree as to call forth the cheese or any other dainty from the shelf of the cupboard.

An electricity which rarely succeeded, but which, however, sometimes did succeed.

But now, Pitou having become a man, no longer acted thus ; he tranquilly raised the lid of the bread-trough, drew from his pocket his long clasp-knife, took the loaf and angularly cut off a slice which might have weighed a good kilogramme (two pounds), as is elegantly said since the adoption of the new-system weights.

Then he let fall the loaf into the trough again, and the cover on the loaf.

After which, without allowing his equanimity to be at all disturbed, he went to the cupboard.

It appeared to Pitou for an instant that he heard the growing voice of Aunt Angelique ; but the cupboard door creaked upon its hinges, and this noise, which had all the power of reality, drowned the other, which had only the influence of imagination.

At the time when Pitou was one of the household, the avaricious aunt would provide only viands of a coarse description, such as Marolles cheese, or thin slices of highly salted bacon, surrounded by the verdant leaves of an enormous cabbage ; but since this fabulous devourer had left the country, the aunt, in despite of her avarice, would cook up for herself dishes that would last her a whole week, but which were of a much more succulent description.

Sometimes it would be a good piece of beef à la mode, surrounded by carrots and onions, stewed in the gravy : sometimes a haricot of mutton with savory potatoes, big as a child's head, or long as cucumbers ; sometimes a calf's foot, flavored with some shallots in vinegar, to give it more piquancy ; sometimes it was a gigantic omelet made in the great frying-pan and variegated with a quantity of chives and parsley, or enameled with slices of bacon, one of which sufficed for the dinner of the old woman, even on the days when she had the greatest appetite.

During the whole week, Aunt Angelique would, with great discretion, enjoy the savory dish, making only such breaches in the precious morsel as the exigencies of the moment required.

Each day did she rejoice in being alone to consume such good things, and during the thrice happy week she thought of her nephew, Ange Pitou, as often as she placed her hand upon the dish or raised a mouthful to her lips.

Pitou was in great good luck.

He had fallen upon a day—it was Monday—when Aunt Angelique had cooked an old cock with rice, which had boiled so long surrounded with its bland covering of paste, that the bones had left the flesh and the flesh had become almost tender.

It was a formidable dish—it was served up in a deep, wide porringer, which, though black externally, was resplendent and attractive to the eye.

The meat was placed above the rice, looking like small islands on the bosom of a vast lake, and the cock's comb, rising above them all, looked like the crest of Ceuta in the Straits of Gibraltar.

Pitou had not even the courtesy to utter one word of admiration on seeing this great marvel.

Spoiled by good living, he forgot, the ungrateful fellow, that such magnificence had never until then inhabited the cupboard of Aunt Angelique.

He held his great hunch of bread in his right hand.

He seized the vast dish in his left, and held it in equilibrium by the pressure of his immense square thumb, buried as far as the first joint in the unctuous mess, the odor of which was grateful to his olfactory organs. At this moment it appeared to Pitou that a shadow interposed between the light of the doorway and himself.

He turned round smiling, for Pitou's was one of those artless dispositions whose faces always give evidence of the satisfaction of their hearts.

The shadow was the body of Aunt Angelique.

Of Aunt Angelique, more miserly, more crabbed, and more skin and bone than ever.

In former days—we are obliged incessantly to return to the same figure of speech—that is to say, to the comparative, as comparison alone can express our thought; in former times, at the sight of Aunt Angelique, Pitou

would have let fall the dish, and while Aunt Angelique
would have bent forward in despair to pick up the fragments of her fowl and the grains of rice, he would have
bounded over her head, and would have taken to his heels,
carrying off his bread under his arm.

But Pitou was no longer the same ; his helmet and his
saber had less changed him, physically speaking, than his
having associated with the great philosophers of the day
had changed him morally.

Instead of flying, terrified, from his aunt, he approached
her with a gracious smile, opened wide his arms—and although she endeavored to escape the pressure, embraced
her with all his might, squeezing the old maid so energetically to his breast, while his hands, the one loaded with
the dish containing the fowl and rice, and the other with
the bread and knife, were crossed behind her back.

When he had accomplished this most nephew-like act,
which he considered as a duty imposed upon him, and
which it was necessary to fulfil, he breathed with all the
power of his vast lungs, and said :

"Aunt Angelique, you may well be surprised, but it is
indeed your poor Pitou."

When he had clasped her so fervently in his arms, the
old maid imagined that, having been surprised in the very
act by her, Pitou had wished to suffocate her, as Hercules
in former days had strangled Antæus.

She, on her side, breathed more freely when she found
herself relieved from this dangerous embrace.

Only Aunt Angelique might have remarked that Pitou
had not even manifested his admiration of the dish he was
devouring.

Pitou was not only ungrateful, but he was also ill-
bred.

But there was one thing which disgusted Aunt Angelique more than the rest ; and this was, that while she
would be seated in state in her leather armchair, Pitou
would not even dare to sit down on one of the dilapidated
chairs or one of the lame stools which surrounded it ; but,
instead of this, after having so cordially embraced her,
Pitou had very coolly ensconced himself in her own armchair, had placed the dish between his knees, and was
leisurely devouring its contents.

In his powerful right hand he held the knife already

mentioned, the blade of which was wide and long, a perfect spatula, with which Polyphemus himself might have eaten his pottage.

In the other hand he held a bit of bread of three fingers wide and six inches long ; a perfect broom, with which he swept up the rice, while on its side the knife, in seeming gratitude, pushed the meat upon the bread.

A learned, though pitiless maneuver, the result of which, in a few minutes, was that it caused the blue and white of the interior of the dish to become visible, as during the ebbing tide we gradually perceive the rings and marks upon the quays of a seaport.

We must renounce attempting to describe the frightful perplexity and despair of Aunt Angelique.

At one moment she imagined that she could call out.

Pitou, however, smiled at her with such a fascinating air, that the words expired before Aunt Angelique could give them utterance.

Then she attempted to smile, in her turn, hoping to exorcise that ferocious animal, called hunger, and which had taken up his abode in the stomach of her nephew.

But the proverb is right ; the famished stomach of Pitou remained both deaf and dumb.

His aunt, instead of smiling, wept.

This somewhat incommoded Pitou, but it did not prevent his eating.

"Oh ! oh ! aunt, how good you are," said he, "to cry thus with joy on my arrival. Thanks, my good aunt, thanks !"

And he went on devouring.

Evidently the French revolution had completely denaturalized this man.

He bolted three quarters of the fowl and left a small quantity of the rice at the bottom of the dish, saying :

"You like the rice best, do you not, my dear aunt ? It is softer for your teeth. I leave you the rice."

This attention, which she no doubt imagined to be a sarcasm, almost suffocated Aunt Angelique. She resolutely advanced toward young Pitou, snatched the dish from his hands, uttering a blasphemous expression, which twenty years subsequently would have appeared admirably suitable to a grenadier of the old guard.

Pitou heaved a sigh.

"Oh, aunt," cried he, "you regret your fowl, do you not?"

"The villain!" cried Aunt Angelique, "I believe that he is jeering me."

Pitou rose from his chair.

"Aunt," said he, majestically, "it was not my intention to eat without paying for what I eat. I have money. I will, if you please, board regularly with you, only I shall reserve to myself the right of choosing my own dinner."

"Rascal!" exclaimed Aunt Angelique.

"Let us see—we will calculate each portion at four sous; I now owe you for one meal—four sous' worth of rice and two sous' of bread—six sous."

"Six sous!" cried the aunt; "six sous! Why, there is eight sous' worth of rice and six sous' of bread, without counting anything else."

"Oh! I know I have not allowed anything for the fowl, my good aunt, knowing that it came from your poultry-yard; he was an old acquaintance; I knew him at once by his comb."

"He was worth his price, however."

"He was five years old, at least. I stole him from under his mother's wing for you; he was then barely as big as my fist, and I recollect even that you beat me, because, when I brought him home to you, I did not bring you corn enough to feed him the next day. Mademoiselle Catherine gave me some barley; he was my property, and I ate my property; I had a good right to do so."

His aunt, mad with anger, pulverized the revolutionary hero with a look; she had no voice.

"Get out of this!" murmured she.

"What, at once, so soon after having dined, without even giving me time to digest my dinner. Ah! aunt, aunt, that is by no means polite."

"Out with you."

Pitou, who had again sat down, rose from the armchair; he found, and that with a most lively feeling of satisfaction, that his stomach could not have contained a single grain of rice more than he had swallowed.

"Aunt," said he, majestically, "you are an unfeeling relation. I will demonstrate to you that you are now acting as wrongly toward me as you have always done; that you are still as harsh, still as avaricious as ever. Well! I will not allow you to go about telling every one that I have devoured your property."

He placed himself on the threshold of the door, and in a stentorian voice, which might be heard not only by the inquisitive persons who had accompanied him and had been present during the whole of this scene, but also by every one who was passing at a distance of five hundred paces.

"I call these worthy people to witness that, having arrived from Paris, on foot, after having taken the Bastile—being tired and hungry, I seated myself in this house—that I ate my relation's provisions—that I was so harshly reproached for the food of which I partook—that I was so pitilessly driven from the house, that I feel myself compelled to go."

Pitou delivered this exordium in so pathetic a tone that the neighbors began to murmur against the old woman.

"A poor traveler," continued Pitou, "who has walked nine leagues—a worthy lad honored with the confidence of Monsieur Gilbert and Monsieur Billot, and who was charged by them to bring back Sebastian Gilbert to the Abbé Fortier—one of the conquerors of the Bastile—a friend of Monsieur Bailly and of General Lafayette—I call upon you all to witness that I have been turned out."

The murmurs went on increasing.

"And," pursued he, "as I am not a mendicant, as, when I am reproached for the bread I eat, I pay for it, here is half a crown which I lay down as payment for that which I have eaten in my aunt's house."

And saying this, Pitou proudly drew a half crown from his pocket, and threw it on the table, from which, in the sight of all, it rebounded, hopped into the dish, and half buried itself in the remaining rice.

The last trait completely confounded the old woman. She bent down beneath the universal reprobation to which she had exposed herself, and which was testified by a long, loud murmur. Twenty hands were held out to Pitou, who left the hut shaking the dust from his shoes on the threshold, and disappeared from his aunt's eyes, escorted by a crowd of persons offering him his meals and lodging, happy to be the host of a conqueror of the Bastile, a friend of M. Bailly and of General Lafayette.

Aunt Angelique picked the half crown out of the rice,

wiped it, and put it into a saucer, where it was to wait, with many others, its transmigration into an old louis.

But while putting by this half crown of which she had become possessed in so singular a manner, she sighed, reflecting that perhaps Pitou had had full right to eat the whole of the contents of the dish, since he had so amply paid for it.

CHAPTER XXVIII.

Pitou wished, after having fulfilled the first duties of obedience, to satisfy the first feelings of his heart.

It is a very delightful feeling to obey, when the orders of the master are in perfect unison with the secret sympathies of the person who obeys.

He, therefore, made the best use of his legs ; and going along the narrow alley which leads from the Pleux to the Rue Lonnet, which forms a sort of green girdle to that portion of the town, he went straight across the fields that he might the sooner arrive at Billot's farm.

But his rapid course was soon slackened ; every step he took brought back some recollection to his mind.

When any one returns to the town or to the village in which he was born, he walks upon his youth—he walks on his past days, which spread themselves, as the English poet says, like a carpet beneath the feet, to do honor to the traveler who returns.

He finds at each step a recollection in the beatings of his heart.

Here he has suffered—there he has been happy ; here he has sobbed with grief—there he has wept with joy.

Pitou, who was no analyzer, was compelled to be a man. He discovered traces of the past as he proceeded on his way, and he arrived with his soul replete with sensations at the farm of Dame Billot.

When he perceived, at a hundred paces before him, the long-slated roofs—when he measured with his eyes the old elm-trees bending down over the moss-grown chimneys—when he heard the distant sound of the cattle, the barking of the dogs, the carts lumbering along the road, he placed his helmet more proudly on his head, grasped

his dragoon's saber with more firmness, and endeavored
to give himself a martial appearance, such as was fitting
to a lover and a soldier.

At first, no one recognized him—a proof that his effort
was attended with tolerable success.

A stable-boy was standing by the pond watering his
horses, and, hearing a noise, turned round, and through
the tufted head of a withy tree he perceived Pitou, or,
rather, a helmet and a saber.

The stable-boy seemed struck with stupefaction.

Pitou, on passing him, called out :

"Hilloa ! Barnaut ! good day, Barnaut !"

The boy, astounded that the helmet and the saber knew
his name, took off his small hat, and let fall the halter by
which he held the horses.

Pitou passed on smiling.

But the boy was by no means reassured ; Pitou's benev-
olent smile had remained concealed beneath his helmet.

At the same moment Dame Billot perceived the approach
of this military man through the windows of the dining-
room.

She immediately jumped up.

In country places, everybody was then on the alert ; for
alarming rumors were spread abroad, of brigands who
were destroying the forest trees, and cutting down fields
of corn though still unripe.

What did the arrival of this soldier portend ? Was it
an attack, or was it assistance ?

Dame Billot had taken a general survey of Pitou as he
approached. She asked herself what could be the meaning of such country-looking garments with so brilliant a
helmet ; and, we must confess it, her suppositions tended
as much toward suspicion as toward hope.

The soldier, whoever he might be, went straight to the
kitchen.

Dame Billot advanced two steps toward the newcomer.
Pitou, on his side, that he might not be behindhand in
politeness, took off his helmet.

"Ange Pitou !" she exclaimed, " you here, Ange ?"

"Good day, Ma'am Billot," replied Pitou.

"Ange ! Oh, good Heaven ! who ever would have
guessed it ? Why, you have enlisted then ?"

"Oh, enlisted !" cried Pitou.

And he smiled somewhat disdainfully.

Then he looked around, seeking for one he did not find there.

Dame Billot smiled ; she guessed the meaning of Pitou's looks.

Then, with great simplicity .

" You are looking for Catherine ! " she said.

"To pay my respects to her," replied Pitou ; " yes, Madame Billot."

"She is attending to the drying of the linen. Come, now, sit down ; look at me—speak to me."

" Very willingly," said Pitou.   " Good day—good day —good day, Madame Billot."

And Pitou took a chair.

Around him were soon grouped, and at the doors and on the steps of the staircases, all the servant-maids and the farm-laborers, to whom the stable-boy had quickly communicated the arrival of the soldier.

And as each of them came in, they might be heard whispering :

" Why, it is Pitou ! "

" Yes, 'tis he, indeed ! "

" Really ! "

Pitou cast a benign glance on all his former comrades. His smile, to most of them, was a caress.

" And you have come from Paris, Ange ? " said the mistress of the house.

" Straight, Madame Billot."

" And how is your master ? "

"Very well, Madame Billot."

" And how are things going on in Paris ? "

" Very badly."

" Ah ! "

And the circle of auditors drew nearer.

" The king ? " inquired the farmer's wife.

Pitou shook his head, and gave a clacking sound with his tongue, which was very humiliating for the monarchy.

" The queen ? "

Pitou, to this question, made no reply at all.

" Oh ! " exclaimed Mme. Billot.

" Oh ! " repeated all present.

" Come, now, speak on, Pitou," said Mme. Billot.

" Well, ask me anything you please," replied Pitou, who

did not wish to communicate all the interesting news he brought, in the absence of Catherine.

"Why have you a helmet?" asked Mme. Billot.

"It is a trophy," said Pitou.

"And what is a trophy, my friend?" inquired the good woman.

"Ah! that is true, Mme. Billot," replied Pitou, with a protecting smile: "you cannot know what a trophy is. A trophy is when one has vanquished an enemy, Madame Billot."

"You have, then, vanquished an enemy, Pitou?"

"One!" replied Pitou, disdainfully. "Ah! my good Madame Billot, you do not know, then, that we two, Monsieur Billot and I, have taken the Bastile?"

This magic sentence electrified the audience. Pitou felt the breath of the astonished auditors upon his hair as they bent forward to gaze at him, and their hands on the back of his chair.

"Tell us—tell us a little of what our man has done," said Mme. Billot, with pride, but trembling with apprehension at the same time.

Pitou looked around to see if Catherine were coming; but she came not.

It appeared to him absolutely insulting, that to hear such recent news, and brought by such a courier, Mlle. Billot did not at once leave her linen.

Pitou shook his head; he was beginning to be out of humor.

"Why, you see, it would take a long time to tell it all," said he.

"And you are hungry?" inquired Mme. Billot.

"It may be so "

"Thirsty?"

"I will not say no."

Instantly farm-laborers and servants hastened to procure him refreshment, so that Pitou soon had within his reach a goblet, bread, meats, and fruits of every description before he had even reflected on the bearing of his answer.

Pitou had a warm liver, as they say in the country—that is to say, he digested quickly; but, however quick might be his digestion, it was still amply occupied with Aunt Angelique's fowl and rice; not more than half an hour having elapsed since he had absorbed the last mouthful.

What he had asked for, therefore, did not enable him to gain so much time as he had anticipated, so rapidly had he been served.

He saw that it was necessary for him to make a desperate effort, and he set himself to work to eat.

But whatever may have been his good-will, after a moment or two he was compelled to pause.

"What is the matter with you?" asked Mme. Billot.

"Why—really, I must say——"

"Bring Pitou something to drink."

"I have cider here, Ma'am Billot."

"But perhaps you like brandy better?"

"Brandy!"

"Yes; perhaps you are accustomed to drink it in Paris."

The worthy woman imagined that during twelve days' absence Pitou had had time enough to be corrupted.

Pitou indignantly repelled the supposition.

"Brandy!" cried he again, "and for me—oh, never!"

"Well, then, speak."

"But if I now tell you the whole story," said Pitou, "I shall have to begin it again for Mademoiselle Catherine, and it is a very long one."

Two or three persons rushed out toward the laundry, to fetch Mlle. Catherine.

But while they were all running about in search of her, Pitou mechanically turned his head toward the staircase which led up to the first story of the house, and being seated precisely opposite this staircase, he saw Mlle. Catherine, through an open door, looking out of a window.

Catherine was looking in the direction of the forest—that is to say, toward Boursonne.

Catherine was so much absorbed in contemplation that the unusual movement in the house had not struck her; nothing within it had attracted her attention, which seemed to be wholly engrossed by what was happening without.

"Ah! ah!" cried he, sighing, looking toward the forest, toward Boursonne, toward Monsieur Isidor de Charny. "Yes, that is it."

And he heaved a second sigh, more melancholy than the first.

And at this moment the messengers returned, not only from the laundry, but from every place in which it was probable Mlle. Catherine might be found.

"Well?" inquired Mme. Billot.

"We have not seen mademoiselle."

"Catherine! Catherine!" cried Mme. Billot.

The young girl did not hear her.

Pitou then ventured to speak.

"Madame Billot," said he, "I well know why they did not find Mademoiselle Catherine at the laundry."

"And why did they not find her?"

"Because she is not there."

"You know, then, where she is?"

"Yes."

"Where is she, then?"

"Yonder—upstairs."

And taking Dame Billot by the hand, he made her go up the three or four steps of the staircase, and showed her Catherine, who was sitting on the sill of the window.

"She is dressing her hair," said the good woman.

"Alas! no; her hair is already dressed," replied Pitou, in a melancholy tone.

The farmer's wife paid no attention to Pitou's melancholy, but, in a loud voice, she called:

"Catherine! Catherine!"

The young girl started with surprise, quickly closed her window, and said:

"What is the matter?

"Come down, then, Catherine!" cried Dame Billot, little doubting the joyful effect her words would produce upon her. "Come down here; here is Ange just arrived from Paris."

Pitou, with great anxiety, listened for the answer which Catherine would make.

"Ah!" coldly replied Catherine.

So coldly that poor Pitou's heart sunk within him.

And she descended the staircase with all the phlegmatic manner of the Flemish women we see in the paintings of Van Ostade and Brauer.

"Well," said she, when she reached the kitchen floor, "why, it is really Pitou!"

Pitou bowed, blushing deeply, and trembling in every nerve.

"He has a helmet," said a servant-maid, whispering into her mistress's ear.

Pitou overheard her, and watched the effect produced on Catherine's countenance.

A lovely countenance, perhaps somewhat paler, but still full and peach-like.

But Catherine did not evince any admiration for Pitou's helmet.

"Ah! he has a helmet," she said, "and for what purpose?"

This time indignation mastered every other feeling in the mind of the bold youth.

"I have a helmet and a saber," said he, proudly, "because I have fought and killed German dragoons and Swiss soldiers; and if you doubt it, Mademoiselle Catherine, ask your father, and he will tell you."

Catherine's mind was so preoccupied that she heard only the last words uttered by Pitou.

"And how is my father?" inquired she. "How happens it that he did not return with you? Is there bad news from Paris?"

"Very bad," replied Pitou.

"I thought that everything had been arranged," observed Catherine.

"Yes, that is true; but everything is disarranged again," rejoined Pitou.

"Was there not a reconciliation between the king and the people, and was not Monsieur Necker recalled?"

"But little is thought of Monsieur Necker," said Pitou.

"And yet that satisfied the people, did it not?"

"It so well satisfied them that the people are now about to do themselves justice, and to kill all their enemies."

"All their enemies!" exclaimed Catherine, with astonishment; "who, then, are the enemies of the people?"

"The aristocrats, to be sure," said Pitou.

Catherine turned pale.

"But who do they call aristocrats?" she asked.

"Why, those who have large estates—those who have fine country-seats—those who starve the nation—those who have all, while we have nothing."

"Go on, go on!" impatiently cried Catherine.

"Those who have beautiful horses and fine carriages, when we are obliged to go on foot."

"Great God!" exclaimed the young girl, becoming so pale as to be positively livid.

Pitou remarked this change in her countenance.

"I call aristocrats some persons of your acquaintance."

"Of my acquaintance?"

"Of our acquaintance?" said Dame Billot.

"But who is it, then?" said Catherine, persistingly.

"Monsieur Berthier de Savigny, for instance."

"Monsieur Berthier de Savigny?"

"Who gave you the gold buckles which you wore the day you danced with Monsieur Isidor."

"Well?"

"Well, I saw people eating his heart, I, who am now speaking to you."

A cry of terror was uttered by all present. Catherine threw herself back in the chair which she had taken.

"You saw that?" cried Mme. Billot, trembling with horror.

"And Monsieur Billot saw it, too."

"Oh, good God!"

"Yes, and by this time they must have killed or burned all the aristocrats of Paris and Versailles."

"It is frightful!" murmured Catherine.

"Frightful? and why so? You are not an aristocrat, you, Mademoiselle Billot?"

"Monsieur Pitou," said Catherine, with gloomy energy, "it appears to me that you were not so ferocious before you went to Paris."

"And I am not more so now, mademoiselle," said Pitou, somewhat staggered; "but——"

"But then do not boast of the crimes committed by the Parisians, since you are not a Parisian, and that you did not commit these crimes."

"I was so far from committing them," said Pitou, "that Monsieur Billot and myself narrowly escaped being murdered while defending Monsieur Berthier."

"Oh, my good father! my brave father! I recognize him there!" enthusiastically exclaimed Catherine.

"My good, my worthy man!" cried Mme. Billot, her eyes streaming with tears. "Tell me, what did he do?"

Pitou then related the whole of the dreadful scene which

had occurred on the Place de Grève, the despair of Billot, and his desire to return to Villers-Cotterets.

"Why did he not return, then?" cried Catherine, and in an accent that deeply moved Pitou's heart.

Dame Billot clasped her hands.

"Monsieur Gilbert would not allow it," replied Pitou.

"Does Monsieur Gilbert wish, then, that my husband should be killed?" said Mme. Billot, sobbing.

"Does he wish, then, that my father's house should be ruined?" added Catherine, in the same tone of gloomy melancholy.

"Oh, by no means!" cried Pitou. "Monsieur Billot and Monsieur Gilbert understand each other. Monsieur Billot will remain still some time at Paris, to finish the revolution."

"What! by themselves—all alone?" cried Dame Billot.

"No; with Monsieur Bailly and Monsieur de Lafayette."

"Ah!" cried the farmer's wife, with admiration, "if he indeed is with Monsieur de Lafayette and Monsieur Bailly——"

"When does he think of returning?" inquired Catherine.

"Oh, as to that, mademoiselle, I cannot tell."

"And you, Pitou, how happens it, then, that you have returned?"

"Who—I? Why, I brought back Sebastian Gilbert to the Abbé Fortier, and I have come here to bring you Monsieur Billot's instructions."

Pitou, while saying the words, rose, not without a certain degree of diplomatic dignity, which was understood, if not by the servants, at all events by their mistresses.

Dame Billot rose, and at once dismissed all the laborers and servants.

Catherine, who had remained seated, studied the thoughts of Pitou even in the depths of his soul before they issued from his lips.

"What can he have told him to say to me?" she asked herself.

CHAPTER XXIX.

THE two women summoned up all their attention to listen to the desires of this honored husband and father. Pitou was well aware that the task was a difficult one ; he had seen both Dame Billot and Catherine filling their several stations at the farm ; he knew the habit of command of the one, and the firm independence of the other.

Catherine, who was so gentle a daughter, so laborious, so good, had acquired, by virtue of these very qualities, a very great ascendency over every person connected with the farm ; and what is the spirit of domination, if it is not a firm will not to obey ?

Pitou knew, in explaining his mission, how much pleasure he was about to cause to the one, and how much grief he would inflict upon the other.

Reducing Mme. Billot to play a secondary part appeared to him unnatural, absurd. It gave Catherine more importance with regard to Pitou, and under actual circumstances Catherine by no means needed this.

But at the farm he represented one of Homer's heroes —a mouth—a memory, but not an intellectual person ; he expressed himself in the following terms :

"Madame Billot, Monsieur Billot's intention is that you should have the slightest possible annoyance."

"And how so ?" said the good woman, much surprised.

"What is the meaning of the word annoyance ?" said Catherine.

"I mean to say," replied Pitou, "that the management of a farm like yours is a species of government replete with cares and labor, that there are bargains to be made——"

"And what of that ?" said the worthy woman.

"Payments——"

"Well ?"

"Fields to plow——"

"Go on."

"Money to be collected——"

"Who says the contrary ?"

"No one, assuredly, Madame Billot ; but in order to make bargains, it is necessary to travel about."

"I have my horse."

"In paying, it is often necessary to dispute."

"Oh ! I have a good tongue."

"To cultivate the fields."

"Am I not accustomed to agriculture ?"

"And to get in the harvest. Ah ! that is quite another matter. Meals have to be cooked for the laborers, the wagoners must be assisted."

"For the welfare of my good man, to do all these would not frighten me," cried the worthy woman.

"But, Madame Billot—in short—so much work—and—getting rather aged——"

"Ah !" cried Dame Billot, looking askance at Pitou.

"Come to my assistance, Mademoiselle Catherine," said the poor lad, finding his energy diminishing by degrees as his position became more and more difficult.

"I do not know what I am to do to assist you," replied Catherine.

"Well, then, this is the plain fact," rejoined Pitou. "Monsieur Billot does not desire that Madame Billot should be subjected to so much trouble——"

"And who, then ?" cried she, interrupting him, trembling at once with admiration and respect.

"He has chosen some one who is stronger, and who is both himself and yourself. He has appointed Mademoiselle Catherine."

"My daughter Catherine to govern the house !" exclaimed the wounded mother, with an accent of mistrust and inexpressible jealousy.

"Under your direction, my dear mother," the young girl hastened to say, and blushing deeply.

"By no means—by no means !" cried Pitou, who, from the moment he had summoned up courage enough to speak out, was determined to go through with it ; "it is not so. I must execute my commission to the letter. Monsieur Billot delegates and authorizes Mademoiselle Catherine, in his stead and place, to attend to all the work and all the affairs of the house."

Every one of these words, which bore the accent of truth, penetrated the heart of the housekeeper ; and so excellent was her nature that, instead of allowing the jealousy she had at first naturally felt to become more bitter, or her anger to become more violent, the certainty of her diminution in importance appeared to make her more resigned, more obedient, and more convinced of the infallibility of her husband's judgment.

Was it possible that Billot could be mistaken? was it possible to disobey Billot?

These were the only two arguments which the worthy woman used to convince herself.

And her resistance at once ceased.

She looked at her daughter, in whose eyes she saw only modesty, confidence, the desire to succeed, unalterable tenderness, and respect. She yielded absolutely.

"Monsieur Billot is right," she said; "Catherine is young; she has a good head—she is even headstrong."

"'Oh! yes," said Piton, certain that he had flattered the self-love of Catherine at the same time that he indulged in an epigram at her expense.

"Catherine," continued Dame Billot, "will be more at her ease than I should be upon the road. She could better look after the laborers for whole days than I could. She would sell better; she would make purchases with greater sureness; she would know how to make herself obeyed."

Catherine smiled.

"Well, then," continued the good woman, without even being compelled to make an effort to restrain a sigh, "here is our Catherine, who is going to have all her own way; she will run about as she pleases—she will now have the command of the purse—now she will always be seen upon the roads—my daughter, in sort, transformed into a lad——"

"You need be under no apprehension for Mademoiselle Catherine," said Pitou, with a self-sufficient air; "I am here, and I will accompany her wherever she goes."

This gracious offer, on which Ange perhaps calculated to produce an effect, produced so strange a look on the part of Catherine that he was quite confused.

The young girl blushed—not as women do when anything agreeable has been said to them, but with a sort of double feeling of anger and impatience, evincing at once a desire to speak and the necessity of remaining silent.

Pitou was not a man of the world, and therefore could not appreciate these shades of feeling.

But having comprehended that Catherine's blushing was not a perfect acquiescence :

"What !" said he, with an agreeable smile, which displayed his powerful teeth under his thick lips, "what ! you say not a word, Mademoiselle Catherine ?"

"You are not aware, then, Monsieur Pitou, that you have uttered a stupidity ?"

"A stupidity !" exclaimed the lover.

"Assuredly !" cried Dame Billot, "to think of my daughter Catherine going about with a body-guard."

"But, in short, in the woods !" said Pitou, with an air so ingenuously conscientious that it would have been a crime to laugh at him.

"Is that also in the instructions of our good man ?" continued Dame Billot, who thus evinced a certain disposition for epigram.

"Oh !" added Catherine, "that would be too indolent a profession, which neither my father would have advised Monsieur Pitou to adopt, nor would Monsieur Pitou have accepted it."

Pitou rolled his large and terrified eyes from Catherine to Dame Billot ; the whole scaffolding of his building was giving way.

Catherine, as a true woman, at once comprehended the painful disappointment of Pitou.

"Monsieur Pitou," said she, "was it at Paris that you have seen young girls compromising their reputation in this way, by always dragging young men after them ?"

"But you are not a young girl, you," stammered Pitou, "since you are the mistress of the house."

"Come, come, we have talked enough for to-night," abruptly said Dame Billot. "The mistress of the house will have much to do to-morrow, when I shall give up the house to her, according to her father's orders. Come, Catherine, we must prepare for bed. Good night, Pitou."

Pitou bowed with great deference to the two ladies, which Catherine returned with a slight inclination of the head.

Poor Ange retired for the night to the small room he had formerly occupied at the farm, and although greatly disappointed at the coldness of Catherine's reception, he soon fell asleep, to which the fatigue of the day greatly induced.

The next morning he was up soon after day break, but saw nothing of Catherine until the whole family assembled at the breakfast-table.

After this substantial repast was concluded, a ceremony was commenced before the astounded eyes of Pitou, a ceremony that was not deficient in grandeur nor in poetry, from its rustic simplicity.

Dame Billot drew her keys from off the bunch, one by one, and delivered them to Catherine, giving her a list of the linen, of the furniture, the provisions, and the contents of the cellars. She conducted her daughter to the old secretary or bureau, made of mahogany, inlaid with ivory and ebony, somewhere about the year 1738 or 1740, in the secret drawer of which father Billot locked up his most valuable papers, his golden louis, and all the treasures and archives of the family.

Catherine gravely allowed herself to be invested with the supreme command over everything, and took due note of the secret drawers; she questioned her mother with much intelligence, reflected on each answer, and the information she required being obtained, appeared to store it up in the depths of her memory, as a weapon in reserve in case of any contest.

After the furniture and household articles had been examined, Dame Billot went on to the cattle, the lists of which were carefully made out.

Horses, oxen, and cows; sheep, whether in good order or sick; lambs, goats, fowls, and pigeons—all were counted and noted down.

But this was merely for the sake of regularity.

Of this branch of the farm business the young girl had for a long time past been the special administratrix.

There was scarcely a hen in the barn-yard of which she did not know the cackle; the lambs were familiar with her in a month; the pigeons knew her so well they would frequently completely surround her in their flight; often even they would perch upon her shoulders after having cooed at her feet.

The horses neighed when Catherine approached. She alone could make the most restive of them obey. One of them, a colt, bred upon the farm, was so vicious as to allow no one to approach him; but he would break his halter and knock down his stall to get to Catherine, putting his nose into her hand, or into her pocket, to get at the crust of bread he was always sure of finding there.

Nothing was so beautiful or so smile-inspiring as this lovely fair-haired girl, with her large blue eyes, her white neck, her round arms, her small fat hands, when she came out with her apron full of corn to a spot near the pond, where the ground had been beaten and saltpetered to harden it for a feeding-place, and on which she would throw the grain she brought by handfuls.

Then would be seen all the young chickens, all the pigeons, all the young lambs, hurrying and scrambling toward the pond; the beaks of the birds soon made the flooring appear speckled, the red tongues of the young goats licked the ground, or picked up crisp buckwheat. This area, darkened by the layers of corn, in five minutes became as white and clean as the delf plate of the laborer when he has finished his meal.

Certain human beings have in their eyes a fascination that subdues, or a fascination that terrifies; two sensations so powerful over the brute creation that they never think of resisting them.

Which of us has not seen a savage bull looking for several minutes, with melancholy expression, at a child who smiles at him without comprehending the danger he is running? He pities him.

Which of us has not seen the same bull fix a sinister and affrighted look on a robust farmer, who masters him by the steadiness of his gaze and by a mute threat? The animal lowers his head, he appears to be preparing for the combat; but his feet seem rooted in the ground—he shudders—he is terrified.

Catherine exercised one of these two influences on all that surrounded her; she was at once so calm and so firm, there was so much gentleness, and yet so much decided will, so little mistrust, so little fear, that the animal standing near her did not feel even the temptation of an evil thought.

And this extraordinary influence she, with greater reason, exercised over thinking beings. She possessed a charm that was irresistible; not a man in the whole district had ever smiled when speaking of Catherine; no young man entertained an evil thought toward her; those who loved her wished to have her for their wife: those who

did not love her would have desired that she were their
sister.

Pitou, with head cast down, his hands hanging listless
by his side, his ideas wandering, mechanically followed
the young girl and her mother while they were taking a
list of the farm stock.

They had not addressed a word to him. He was there
like a guard in a tragedy ; and his helmet did not a little
contribute to give that singular appearance.

After this they passed in review all the male and female
servants of the farm.

Dame Billot made them form a half circle, in the center
of which she placed herself.

" My children," said she, " our master is not yet coming back from Paris, but he has chosen a master for us in
his place. It is my daughter Catherine, who is here—she
is young and strong. As to myself, I am old, and my
head is weak. Our master has done rightly. Catherine
is now your mistress. She is to receive and give money.
As to her orders, I shall be the first to receive and execute
them : any of you who may be disobedient will have to
deal with her."

Catherine did not add a single word ; she tenderly embraced her mother.

The effect of this kiss was greater than that of any well-
rounded phrase. Dame Billot wept—Pitou was much
affected.

All the servants received the announcement of the new
reign with acclamations.

Catherine immediately entered on her new functions,
and allotted to all their several services. Each received
her mandate, and set out immediately to execute it, with
the good-will which every one demonstrates at the commencement of a reign.

Pitou was the only one remaining, and he at length, approaching Catherine, said to her :

" And I ?"

" Ah ! you," replied Catherine, " I have no orders to
give you."

" How ! I am, then, to remain without having anything
to do ?"

" What do you wish to do ?"

" Why, what I did before I went to Paris."

" Before going there, you were received into the house by my mother."

" But you are now the mistress ; therefore, point out the work I am to do."

" I have no work for you, Monsieur Ange."

" And why ? "

" Because you—you are a learned man, a Parisian gentleman, to whom such rustic labors would not be suitable."

" Can it be possible ! " exclaimed Pitou.

Catherine made a sign, which implied, " It is even so."

" I a learned man ! " repeated Pitou.

" Undoubtedly."

" But look at my arms, Mademoiselle Catherine."

" That matters not."

" But, in short, Mademoiselle Catherine," said the poor lad, in despair, " why is it that under the pretext of my being a learned man, you would force me to die of hunger ? You do not know, then, that the philosopher Epictetus became a menial servant that he might have bread to eat ?—that Æsop, the fable writer, earned his bread by the sweat of his brow ? They were, however, people much more learned than I am."

" What would you have ? As I have said before, it is even so."

" But Monsieur Billot accepted me as forming part of his household, and he has sent me back from Paris that I may still be so."

" That may be the case ; for my father might have compelled you to undertake things which I, his daughter, would not venture to impose upon you."

" Do not impose them upon me, Mademoiselle Catherine."

" But then you would remain in idleness, and that I could not at all allow. My father had the right to do so, he being the master, and which I could not do, being merely his agent. I have charge of his property, and I must take care that his property be productive."

" But once I am willing to work, I shall be productive ; you must see clearly, mademoiselle, that you keep swimming round in the same vicious circle."

" What say you ? " cried Catherine, who did not comprehend the grandiloquent phrases of Pitou ; " what mean you by a vicious circle ? "

"We call a bad argument a vicious circle, mademoiselle.
No; let me remain at the farm, and send me on your
messages if you will. You will then see whether I am a
learned man and an idle fellow. Besides which, you
have books to keep, accounts to put in order. Arithmetic is my particular forte."

"It is not, in my opinion, sufficient occupation for a
man," said Catherine.

"Why, then, it would seem I am fit for nothing," said
Pitou.

"Continue to live here," said Catherine, in a gentler
tone; "I will reflect upon it, and we will see."

"You require to reflect in order that you may know
whether you ought to keep me here. But what have I
done to you, then, Mademoiselle Catherine? Ah! you
were not thus formerly."

Catherine gave an almost imperceptible shrug of her
shoulders.

She had no good reasons to give to Pitou, and nevertheless it was evident that his pertinacity fatigued her.

Therefore, breaking off the conversation:

"Enough of this, Monsieur Pitou," said she; "I am
going to La Ferte-Milon."

"Then I will run and saddle your horse, Mademoiselle
Catherine."

"By no means. On the contrary, remain where you
are."

"You refuse, then, to allow me to accompany you?"

"Remain here," said Catherine, imperatively.

Pitou remained as if nailed to the spot, holding down
his head and restraining a tear, which seared his eyeballs
as if it had been molten lead.

Catherine left Pitou where he was, went out, and ordered
one of the farm servants to saddle her horse.

"Ah!" murmured Pitou, "you think me changed,
Mademoiselle Catherine, but it is you who are so, and
much more changed than I am."

CHAPTER XXX.

DAME BILLOT, resigned without affectation to under-take the functions of an upper servant, had, without ill-humor, and with good-will, resumed her occupations. Movement, which had for an instant been suspended throughout the agricultural hierarchy, soon returned, and the farm once more resembled the interior of a humming and industrious hive.

While they were getting her horse ready, Catherine reentered the house; she cast a glance at Pitou, whose body remained motionless, but whose head turned like a weather-cock, following each movement which the young girl made until she went up-stairs to her own room.

"What was it Catherine had gone to her room for?" said Pitou to himself.

Poor Pitou, what had she gone there for? She went there to dress her hair, to put on a clean cap and a pair of finer stockings.

Then when this supplementary toilet was completed, as she heard her horse pawing the ground beneath the window, she came down, kissed her mother, and set out.

Reduced to positive idleness, and feeling but ill-assured, from a slight glance, half indifferent, half compassionate, which Catherine had addressed to him as she left the door, Pitou could not endure to remain in such a state of anxious perplexity.

Since Pitou had once more seen Catherine, it appeared to him that the life of Catherine was absolutely necessary to him.

And, besides, in the depths of his heavy and dreaming mind, something like a suspicion came and went with the regularity of the pendulum of a clock.

It is the peculiar property of ingenuous minds to per-ceive everything in equal degree. These sluggish natures are not less sensible than others; they feel, but they do not analyze.

Analysis is the habit of enjoying and suffering; a man must have become, to a certain degree, habituated to sensation to see their ebullition in the depth of that abyss which is called the human heart.

There are no old men who are ingenuous.

When Pitou had heard the horse's footsteps at a certain distance from the house, he ran to the door. He then perceived Catherine, who was going along a narrow cross-road, which led from the farm to the high-road to La Ferte-Milon, and terminated at the foot of a hill, whose summit was covered by the forest.

From the threshold of the door he breathed forth an adieu to the young girl, which was replete with regret and kindly feeling.

But this adieu had scarcely been expressed by his hand and heart, when Pitou reflected on one circumstance.

Catherine might have forbidden him to accompany her, but she could not prevent him from following her.

Catherine could, if she pleased, say to Pitou, "I will not see you;" but she could not very well say to him, "I forbid your looking at me."

Pitou, therefore, reflected that, as he had nothing to do, there was nothing in the world to prevent him from gaining the wood and keeping along the road which Catherine was going; so that, without being seen, he would see her from a distance through the trees.

It was only a league and a half from the farm to La Ferte-Milon. A league and a half to go there, and a league and a half to return. What was that to Pitou?

Moreover, Catherine would get to the high-road by a line which formed an angle with the forest. By taking a straight direction, Pitou would gain a quarter of a league, so that the distance for him would be only two leagues and a half for the whole journey.

Two leagues and a half was a mere nothing of a walk for a man who appeared to have robbed Tom Thumb, or to have at least pilfered the seven-league boots which Tom had taken from the ogre.

Pitou had scarcely imagined this project before he put it into execution.

While Catherine was going toward the high-road, he, Pitou, stooping down behind the high, waving corn, stole across to the forest.

In an instant he had reached the border of the wood; and once there, he jumped across the wide ditch which bounded it, and rushed beneath the trees, less graceful but as rapid as a terrified deer.

He ran for a quarter of an hour in this way, and at the end of that time he perceived the wood becoming lighter, for he had nearly reached the opposite edge near the road.

There he stopped, leaning against an enormous oak, which completely concealed him behind its knotted trunk. He felt perfectly sure that he had got ahead of Catherine.

He waited ten minutes—even a quarter of an hour—but saw no one.

Had she forgotten something that she should have taken with her at the farm? This was possible.

With the greatest possible precaution Pitou crept near the road, stretched out his head from behind a great beech-tree, which grew upon the very edge of the ditch, belonging, as it were, half to the road, half to the forest. From this he had a good view of the plain, and could have perceived anything that was moving upon it; he, however, could discern nothing.

He felt assured, therefore, that Catherine must have returned to the farm.

Pitou retraced his steps. Either she had not yet reached the farm, and he would see her return to it, or she had reached it, and he would see her come out again.

Pitou extended the compass of his long legs, and began to remeasure the distance which separated him from the plain.

He ran along the sandy part of the road, which was softer to his feet, when he suddenly paused.

Pitou had raised his eyes, and at the opposite end of the road he saw at a great distance, blending as it were with the blue horizon of the forest, the white horse and the red jacket of Catherine.

The pace of Catherine's horse was an amble.

The horse, ambling along, had left the high-road, having turned into a bridle-path, at the entrance of which was a direction post, bearing the following inscription:

"Path leading from the road of La Ferté-Milon to Boursonne."

It was, as we have said, from a great distance that Pitou perceived this, but we know that distance was of no consequence to Pitou.

"Ah!" cried he, again darting into the forest, "it is

not, then, to La Ferte-Milon that she was going, but to Boursonne! And yet, I am not mistaken; she said La Ferte-Milon more than ten times; she had a commission given to her to make purchases at La Ferte-Milon. Dame Billot herself spoke of La Ferte-Milon."

And while saying these words, Pitou continued running. Pitou ran faster and faster still. Pitou ran like a madman.

For Pitou, urged on by doubt, the first symptom of jealousy—Pitou was no longer biped. Pitou appeared to be one of those winged machines, which Dædalus in particular, and the great mechanicians of antiquity in general, imagined so well, but, alas! executed so badly.

He greatly resembled, at that moment, those figures stuffed with straw, with long reed arms, placed over lay shops, and which the wind keeps turning in every direction.

Arms, legs, head, all are in motion, all are turning, all seem to be flying.

Pitou's immensely long legs measured paces of at least five feet, so widely could he distend them; his hands, like two broad bats at the end of two long sticks, struck upon the air like oars. His head—all mouth, all nostrils, and all eyes—absorbed the air, which they sent forth again in noisy breathings.

No horse could have been animated to so great a fury of speed.

No lion could have had a more ferocious desire of coming up with his prey.

Pitou had more than half a league to run, when he perceived Catherine; he did not give her time enough to go a quarter of a league, while he was running twice that distance.

His speed, was, therefore, double that of a horse that was trotting.

At length he came to a line with the object of his pursuit.

The extremity of the forest was then not more than five hundred paces from him. He could see the light more clearly through the trees, and just beyond them was the estate of Boursonne.

Catherine pulled up her horse. Pitou instantly stopped.

It was time, for the poor devil's breath was fast failing him.

It was no longer merely for the purpose of seeing Catherine that Pitou followed her—it was to watch her.

She had spoken that which was false. What could be her object?

That mattered not. In order to gain a certain degree of authority over her, it was necessary to surprise her, and prove that she had uttered a flagrant falsehood.

Pitou threw himself head foremost into the underwood and thorns, breaking through them with his helmet, and using his saber to clear the way when it was necessary.

However, as Catherine was now only moving on at a walk, from time to time the crackling noise of a branch being broken reached her ear, which made both the horse and the mistress prick up their ears.

Then Pitou, whose eyes never for a moment lost sight of Catherine, stopped, which was of some advantage to him, as it enabled him to recover his breath, and it destroyed, at the same time, any suspicion that Catherine might entertain.

This, however, could not last long, nor did it.

Pitou suddenly heard Catherine's horse neigh, and this neighing was replied to by the neighing of another horse. The latter could not yet be seen.

But however this might be, Catherine gave hers a smart cut with her holly switch; and the animal, which had blown for a few moments, set off again at a full trot.

In about five minutes—thanks to this increase of speed —she had come up with a horseman who had hastened toward her with as much eagerness as she had shown to reach him.

Catherine's movement had been so rapid and unexpected, that poor Pitou had remained motionless, standing in the same place, only raising himself on the tops of his toes that he might see as far as possible.

The distance was too great to enable him to see clearly.

But if he did not see, what Pitou felt, as if it had been an electric shock, was the delight and the blushing of the young girl. It was the sudden start which agitated her whole body. It was the sparkling of her eyes, usually so gentle, but which then became absolutely flashing.

Neither could he see who was the cavalier. He could not distinguish his features; but, recognizing by his air, by his green velvet hunting-coat, by his hat with its broad

loop, by the easy and graceful motion of his head, that he
must belong to the very highest class of society, his memory
at once reverted to the very handsome young man, the
elegant dancer of Villers-Cotterets—his heart, his mouth,
every fiber of his nerves, murmured the name of Isidor de
Charny.

And it was so, in fact.

Pitou heaved a sigh, which was very much like a roar;
and, rushing anew into the thicket, he advanced within
twenty paces of the two young people, then too much occupied with each other to remark whether the noise they
heard was caused by the rushing of a quadruped or of a
biped through the underwood.

The young man, however, turned his head toward Pitou,
raised himself up in his stirrups, and cast a vague look
around him.

But at the same moment, and in order to escape this
investigation, Pitou threw himself flat on his face.

Then, like a serpent, he glided along the ground about
ten paces more, and having then got within hearing distance, he listened.

"Good day, Monsieur Isidor," said Catherine.

"Monsieur Isidor!" murmured Pitou; "I was sure of
that."

He then felt as if the horseman and the horse were
weighing on his poor heart, and trampling him under foot.

He then felt in all his limbs the immense fatigue of the
race he had run, and which doubt, mistrust, and jealousy
had urged him to during a whole hour.

The two young people had each let fall their bridle, and
had grasped each other's hands, and remained thus, mute
and smiling at each other, while the two horses, no doubt
accustomed to each other, were rubbing their noses together, and pawing the green turf by the roadside.

"You are behind your time to-day," said Catherine,
who was the first to speak.

"To-day!" exclaimed Pitou to himself; "it seems
that on other days he was not behind time."

"It is not my fault, dear Catherine," replied the young
man, "for I was detained by a letter from my brother,
which reached me only this morning, and to which I was
obliged to reply by return of post. But fear nothing;
to-morrow I will be more punctual."

Catherine smiled, and Isidor pressed still more tenderly the hand which had been left in his.

Alas ! all these proofs of affection were so many thorns which made poor Pitou's heart bleed.

"You have, then, very late news from Paris ?" she asked.

"Yes."

"Well, then," continued she, smiling, "so have I. Did you not tell me the other day that when similar things happened to two persons who loved each other, that it is called sympathy ?"

"Precisely ; and how did you receive your news, my lovely Catherine ?"

"By Pitou."

"And who do you mean by Pitou ?" asked the young nobleman, with a free and joyous air, which changed to scarlet the color which had already overspread Pitou's cheeks.

"Why, you know full well," said she. "Pitou is the poor lad whom my father took into the farm, and who gave me his arm one Sunday."

"Ah ! yes," said the young gentleman, "he whose knees are like knots tied in a table-napkin."

Catherine laughed. Pitou felt himself humiliated, and was in perfect despair. He looked at the knees, which were, in fact, like knots, raising himself on both hands and getting up, but he again fell flat on his face with a sigh.

"Come, now," said Catherine, "you must not so sadly ill-treat my poor Pitou. Do you know what he proposed to me just now !"

"No ; but tell me what it was, my lovely one."

"Well, then, he proposed to accompany me to La Ferte-Milon."

"Where you are not going ?"

"No ; because I thought you were waiting for me here ; while, on the contrary, it was I who almost had to wait for you."

"Ah ! do you know you have uttered a royal sentence, Catherine ?"

"Really ! well, I am sure I did not imagine I was doing so."

"And why did you not accept the offer of this handsome cavalier ? he would have amused us."

" Not always, perhaps," replied Catherine, laughing.

" You are right, Catherine," said Isidor, fixing his eyes, which beamed with love, on the beautiful girl.

And he caught the blushing face of the young girl in his arms, which he clasped round her neck.

Pitou closed his eyes that he might not see, but he had forgotten to shut his ears that he might not hear, and the sound of a kiss reached them.

Pitou clutched his hair in despair, as does the man afflicted with the plague in the foreground of Gros's picture, representing Bonaparte visiting the soldiers attacked by the plague in the hospital at Jaffa.

When Pitou had somewhat recovered his equanimity, he found that the two young people had moved off to a little distance, and were proceeding on their way, walking their horses.

The last words which Pitou could catch were these :

" Yes, you are right, Monsieur Isidor ; let us ride together for an hour ; my horse's legs shall make up the lost time. And," added she, laughing, " it is a good animal, who will not mention it to any one."

And this was all—the vision faded away. Darkness reigned in the soul of Pitou, as it began to reign over all nature, and, rolling upon the heather, the poor lad abandoned himself to the overwhelming feelings which oppressed his heart.

He remained in this state for some time ; but the coolness of the evening at length restored him to himself.

" I will not return to the farm," said he ; " I should only be humiliated, scoffed at. I should eat the bread of a woman who loves another man, and a man, I cannot but acknowledge, who is handsomer, richer, and more elegant than I am. No, my place is no longer at the farm, but at Haramont—at Haramont, my own country, where I shall, perhaps, find people who will not think that my knees are like knots made in a table-napkin."

Having said this, Pitou trotted his good long legs toward Haramont, where, without his at all suspecting it, his reputation and that of his helmet and saber had preceded him, and where awaited him, if not happiness, at least a glorious destiny.

But, it is well known, it is not an attribute of humanity to be perfectly happy.

CHAPTER XXXI.

HOWEVER, on arriving at Villers-Cotterets, toward ten o'clock at night, after having the long run we have endeavored to describe, Pitou felt that, however melancholy he might be, it was much better to stop at the Dauphin Hôtel and sleep in a good bed, than to sleep canopied by the stars, under some beech or oak in the forest.

For as to sleeping in a house at Haramont, arriving there at half-past ten at night, it was useless to think of it. For more than an hour and a half every light had been extinguished, and every door closed in that peaceful village.

Pitou, therefore, put up at the Dauphin Hôtel, where, for a thirty-sous piece, he had an excellent bed, a four-pound loaf, a piece of cheese and a pot of cider.

Pitou was both fatigued and in love, tired out, and in despair. The result of this was a struggle between his moral and physical feelings, in which the moral were in the first instance victorious, but at length succumbed.

That is to say, that from eleven o'clock to two in the morning, Pitou groaned, sighed, turned and twisted in his bed, without being able to sleep a wink; but at two o'clock, overcome by fatigue, he closed his eyes, not to open again them till seven.

As at Haramont every one was in bed at half-past ten at night, so at Villers-Cotterets everybody is stirring at seven in the morning.

Pitou, on leaving the Dauphin Hôtel, again found that his helmet and saber attracted public attention.

After going about a hundred paces, he consequently found himself the center of a numerous crowd.

Pitou had decidedly acquired an enormous popularity.

There are few travelers who have such good luck. The sun, which, it is said, shines for the whole world, does not always shine with a favorable brilliancy for people who return to their own native place with the desire of being considered prophets.

But also it does not happen to every one to have an aunt crabbed and avaricious to so ferocious a degree as Aunt

Angelique ; it does not happen to every Gargantua, capable of swallowing an old cock boiled with rice, to be able to offer a half-crown to the proprietor of the victim.

But that which happens still less often to returning persons, whose origin and traditions can be traced back to the "Odyssey," is to return with a helmet on their heads and a saber by their sides ; above all, when the rest of their accouterments are far from being military.

For we must avow that it was, above all, this helmet and this saber which recommended Pitou to the attention of his fellow-citizens.

But for the vexations which Pitou's love encountered on his return, it had been seen that all sorts of good fortune awaited him. This was undoubtedly a compensation.

And, immediately on seeing him, some of the inhabitants of Villers-Cotterets, who had accompanied Pitou from the Abbé Fortier's door in the Rue de Soissons to Dame Angelique's door in the Pleux, resolved, in order to continue the ovation, to accompany him from Villers-Cotterets to Haramont.

And they did as they had resolved ; on seeing which, the above-mentioned inhabitants of Haramont began to appreciate their compatriot at his just value.

It is, however, only justice to them to say, that the soil was already prepared to receive the seed. Pitou's first passage through Haramont, rapid as it had been, had left some traces in the minds of its inhabitants ; his helmet and his saber had remained impressed on the memories of those who had seen him appearing before them, as a luminous apparition.

In consequence, the inhabitants of Haramont, seeing themselves favored by this second return of Pitou, which they no longer hoped for, received him with every manifestation of respect and consideration, entreating him to doff, for a time, his warlike accouterments, and fix his tent under the four linden-trees which overshadowed the little village square, as the Thessalians used to entreat Mars on the anniversary of his great triumphs.

Pitou deigned the more readily to consent to this, from its being his intention to fix his domicile at Haramont. He, therefore, accepted the shelter of a bedroom, which a warlike person of the village let to him ready furnished.

It was furnished with a deal bed, a palliasse, and a mattress, two chairs, a table, and a water-jug.

The rent of the whole of this was estimated by the proprietor himself at six livres per annum—that is to say, the value of two dishes of fowl and rice.

The rent being agreed upon, Pitou took possession of his domicile, and supplied those who had accompanied him with refreshments at his own charge ; and as these events, without speaking of the cider he had imbibed, had somewhat excited his brain, he pronounced a harangue to them, standing on the threshold of his new residence.

This harangue of Pitou's was a great event, and consequently all Haramont was assembled round the house.

Pitou was somewhat of a clerk, and knew what fine language was ; he knew the right words by which at that period the haranguers of nations—it was thus Homer called them—stirred up the popular masses.

Between M. de Lafayette and Pitou there was undoubtedly a great distance ; but between Haramont and Paris the distance was greater still—morally speaking, it will be clearly understood.

Pitou commenced by an exordium with which the Abbé Fortier, critical as he was, would not have been dissatisfied.

"Citizens," said he, "citizens—this word is sweet to pronounce—I have already addressed other Frenchmen by it, for all Frenchmen are brothers ; but on this spot I am using it, I believe, toward real brothers, and I find my whole family here in my compatriots of Haramont."

The women—there were some few among the auditory, and they were not the most favorably disposed toward the orator, for Pitou's knees were still too thick and the calves of his legs too thin, to produce an impression in his favor on a feminine audience—the women, on hearing the word family, thought of that poor Pitou, the orphan child, the poor abandoned lad, who, since the death of his mother, had never had a meal that satisfied his hunger. And this word, family, uttered by a youth who had none, moved in some among them that sensitive fiber which closes the reservoir of tears.

The exordium being finished, Pitou began the narrative, the second head of an oration.

He related his journey to Paris, the riots with regard to

the busts, the taking of the Bastile, and the vengeance of the people ; he passed lightly over the part he had taken in the combats on the Place Vendôme, the square before the Palais Royal and in the Faubourg St. Antoine. But the less he boasted, the greater did he appear in the eyes of his compatriots ; and at the end of Pitou's narrative, his helmet had become as large as the dome of the Invalides, and his saber as long as the steeple of Haramont Church.

The narrative being ended, Pitou then proceeded to the confirmation, that delicate operation by which Cicero recognized a real orator.

He proved that popular indignation had been justly excited against speculators ; he said two words of Messieurs Pitt, father and son ; he explained the revolution by the privileges granted to the nobility and to the clergy ; finally he invited the people of Haramont to do that in particular which the people of France had done generally —that is to say, to unite against the common enemy.

Then he went on from the confirmation to the peroration, by one of those sublime changes common to all great orators.

He let fall his saber, and, while picking it up, he accidentally drew it from its scabbard.

This accident furnished him with a text for an incendiary resolution, calling upon the inhabitants of Haramont to take up arms, and to follow the example of the revolted Parisians.

The people of Haramont were enthusiastic and replied energetically.

The revolution was proclaimed with loud acclamations throughout the village.

The men from Villers-Cotterets, who had remained at the meeting, returned home, their hearts swelling with the patriotic leaven, singing in the most threatening tones toward the aristocrats, and with savage fury :

> " Vive Henri Quatre !
> Vive ce roi vaillant ! "

Rouget de l'Isle had not then composed the " Marseillaise," and the Federalists of '90 had not yet reawakened the old popular " Ça Ira," seeing that they were then only in the year of grace 1789.

Pitou thought that he had merely made a speech. Pitou had made a revolution.

He re-entered his own house, regaled himself with a piece of brown bread and the remains of his cheese, from the Dauphin Hôtel, which he had carefully stowed away in his helmet, then he went and bought some brass wire, made some snares, and when it was dark, went to lay them in the forest.

That same night Pitou caught a good sized rabbit, and a young one about four months old.

Pitou would have much wished to have set his wires for hares, but he could not discern a single run, and this proved to him the correctness of the old sporting axiom, "Dogs and cats, hares and rabbits, live not together."

It would have been necessary to have gone three or four leagues before reaching a country well stocked with hares, and Pitou was rather fatigued; his legs had done their utmost the day before, for, besides the distance they had performed, they had carried for the last four or five leagues a man worn out with grief, and there is nothing so heavy as grief to long legs.

Toward one in the morning he returned with his first harvest; he hoped to gather another after the passage in the morning.

He went to bed, retaining within his breast remains of so bitter a nature of that grief which had so much fatigued his legs the day before, that he could only sleep six hours consecutively upon the ferocious mattress, which the proprietor himself called a shingle.

Pitou, therefore, slept from one o'clock to seven. The sun was, therefore, shining upon him through his open shutter while he was sleeping.

Through this open shutter, thirty or forty inhabitants of Haramont were looking at him as he slept.

He awoke as Turenne did on his gun-carriage, smiled at his compatriots, and asked them graciously why they had come to him in such numbers and so early?

One of them had been appointed spokesman. We shall faithfully relate this dialogue. This man was a woodcutter, and his name Claude Tellier.

"Ange Pitou," said he, "we have been reflecting the whole night; citizens ought, in fact, as you said yesterday, to arm themselves in the cause of liberty."

"I said so," replied Pitou, in a firm tone, and which announced that he was ready to maintain what he had said.

"Only, in order to arm ourselves the principal thing is wanting."

"And what is that?" asked Pitou, with much interest.

"Arms!"

"Ah! yes, that is true," said Pitou.

"We have, however, reflected enough not to allow our reflections to be lost, and we will arm ourselves, cost what it may."

"When I went away," said Pitou, "there were five guns in Haramont—three muskets, a single-barreled fowling piece, and a doubled-barreled one."

"There are now only four," rejoined the orator, "one of the fowling-pieces burst from old age a month ago."

"That must have been the fowling-piece which belonged to Désiré Maniquet," said Pitou.

"Yes, and by token when she burst she carried off two of my fingers," said Désiré Maniquet, holding above his head his mutilated hand: "and as this accident happened to me in the warren of that aristocrat who is called Monsieur de Longpré, the aristocrats shall pay me for it."

Pitou nodded his head to show that he approved this just revenge.

"We, therefore, have only four guns left," rejoined Claude Tellier.

"Well, then, with four guns you have already enough to arm five men," said Pitou.

"How do you make that out?"

"Oh, the fifth will carry a pike. That is the way they do at Paris; for every four men armed with guns there is always one man armed with a pike. Those pikes are very convenient things; they serve to stick the heads upon, which have been cut off."

"Oh! oh!" cried a loud, joyous voice, "it is to be hoped that we shall not cut off heads."

"No," gravely replied Pitou; "if we have only firmness enough to reject the gold of Messrs. Pitt, father and son. But we were talking of guns; let us not wander from the question, as Monsieur Bailly says. How many men have we in Haramont capable of bearing arms? Have you counted them?"

" Yes."

" And how many are you ? "

" We are thirty-two."

" Then there are twenty-eight muskets deficient ? "

" Which we shall never get," said the stout man with the good-humored face.

" Ah !" said Pitou, "it is necessary to know that."

" And how s it necessary to know ? "

" Yes, I say it is necessary to know, because I know."

" What do you know ? "

" I know where they are to be procured."

" To be procured ? "

" Yes ; the people of Paris had no arms neither. Well, Monsieur Marat, a very learned doctor, but very ugly, told the people of Paris where arms were to be found ; the people of Paris went where Monsieur Marat told them, and there they found them."

" And where did Marat tell them to go ? " inquired Désiré Maniquet.

" He told them to go to the Invalides."

" Yes ; but we have no Invalides at Haramont."

" But I know a place in which there are more than a hundred guns," said Pitou.

" And where is that ? "

" In one of the rooms of the Abbé Fortier's college."

" The Abbé Fortier has a hundred guns ? He wishes, then, to arm his singing-boys, the beggarly black cap !" cried Claude Tellier.

Pitou had not a deep-seated affection for the Abbé Fortier ; however, this violent outburst against his former professor profoundly wounded him.

" Claude !" cried he. " Claude !"

" Well, what now ? "

" I did not say that the guns belong to the Abbé Fortier."

" If they are in his house, they belong to him."

" That position is a false one. I am in the house of Bastien Godinet, and yet the house of Bastien Godinet does not belong to me."

" That is true," said Bastien, replying, without giving Pitou occasion to appeal to him directly.

" The guns, therefore, do not belong to the Abbé Fortier," continued Pitou.

" Whose are they then ? "

"They belong to the township."

"If they belong to the township, how does it happen that they are in the Abbé Fortier's house?"

"They are in the Abbé Fortier's house, because the house in which the Abbé Fortier lives belongs to the township, who gives it to him rent free because he says mass and teaches the children of poor citizens gratis. Now, since the Abbé Fortier's house belongs to the township, the township has a right to reserve a room in the house that belongs to it, to put its muskets; ah!"

"That is true," said the auditors, "the township has the right."

"Well, then, let us see; how are we to get hold of these guns—tell us that?"

The question somewhat embarrassed Pitou, who scratched his ear.

"Yes, tell us quickly," cried another voice, "for we must go to our work."

Pitou breathed again; the last speaker had opened to him a door of escape.

"Work!" exclaimed Pitou. "You speak of arming yourselves for the defense of the country, and you think of work!"

And Pitou accompanied his words with a laugh, so ironical and so contemptuous that the Haramontese looked at each other, and felt humiliated.

"We would not mind sacrificing a few days more, should it be absolutely necessary," said the other, "to gain our liberty."

"To gain our liberty," cried Pitou, "it will be necessary to sacrifice more than a day—we must sacrifice all our days."

"Then," said Boniface, "when people are working for liberty they are resting."

"Boniface," replied Pitou, with the air of Lafayette when irritated, "those will never know how to be free who know not how to trample prejudices under foot."

"As to myself," said Boniface, "I ask nothing better than not to work; but what is to be done, then, with regard to eating?"

"Do people eat?" cried Pitou, disdainfully.

"At Haramont they do so yet. Do they no longer eat at Paris?"

"They eat when they have vanquished the tyrants," replied Pitou. "Did any one eat on the 14th of July? Did they even think of eating on that day? No; they had not time even to think of it."

"Ah! ah!" cried some of the most zealous, "the taking of the Bastile must have been a fine sight."

"But," continued Pitou, disdainfully, "as to drinking, I will not say No; it was so hot, and gunpowder had so acrid a taste."

"But what had they to drink?"

"What had the people to drink? Why, water, wine, and brandy. It was the women who had taken this in charge."

"The women?"

"Yes, and handsome women, too, who had made flags of the front parts of their dresses.

"Can it be possible?" cried the auditors, with astonishment.

"But, at all events," observed a skeptic, "they must have eaten the next day?"

"I do not say that they did not," replied Pitou.

"Then," rejoined Boniface, triumphantly, "if they ate, they must have worked."

"Monsieur Boniface," replied Pitou, "you are speaking of things without understanding them. Paris is not a hamlet. It is not composed of a heap of villagers, accustomed to think only of their bellies—*obedientia ventri*, as we say in Latin, we who are learned. No; Paris, as Monsieur de Mirabeau says, is the head of all nations; it is a brain which thinks for the whole world. The brain, sir, never eats."

"That is true," thought the auditors.

"And yet," said Pitou, "the brain, though it does not eat, still feeds itself."

"But then how does it feed itself?" answered Boniface.

"Invisibly, with the nutriment of the body."

Here the Haramontese were quite at a loss; the question was too profound for them to understand.

"Explain this to us, Pitou," said Boniface.

"That is easily done," replied Pitou. "Paris is the brain, as I have said: the provinces are the members; the provinces will work, drink, eat, and Paris will think."

"Then I will leave the provinces and go to Paris," rejoined the skeptical Boniface. "Will you come to Paris with me, my friends?"

A portion of the audience burst into a loud laugh, and appeared to side with Boniface.

Pitou perceived that he would be discredited by this sarcastic railer.

"Go, then, to Paris," cried he, in his turn, "and if you find there a single face as ridiculous as yours, I will buy of you such young rabbits as this at a louis apiece."

And with one hand Pitou held up the young rabbit he had caught, and with the other made the louis which remained of Dr. Gilbert's munificence jingle in his pocket.

Pitou this time had the laugh in his favor.

Upon this Boniface became positively purple with rage.

"Why, Master Pitou, you are playing the insolent to call us ridiculous."

"Ridiculous thou art," majestically replied Pitou.

"But look at yourself," retorted Boniface.

"It would be but to little purpose," replied Pitou. "It might see something as ugly as yourself, but never anything half so stupid."

Pitou had scarcely said these words, when Boniface— at Haramont they are almost as passionate as in Picardy— struck at him with his fist, which Pitou adroitly parried, but to which he replied by a kick in the true Parisian fashion.

This kick was followed by a second, which sent the skeptic flying some few feet, when he fell heavily to the ground.

Pitou bent down over his adversary, so as to give the victory the most fatal consequences, and all were already rushing to save poor Boniface, when Pitou, raising himself up:

"Learn," said he, "that the conquerors of the Bastile do not fight with fists. I have a saber, take another saber, and let us end the matter at once."

Upon this Pitou drew his sword, forgetting, or perhaps not forgetting, that the only saber in all Haramont was his own, with the exception of that of the rural guard, at least two feet shorter than his own.

It is true that to establish a more perfect equilibrium he put on his helmet.

This greatness of soul electrified the assembly. It was agreed by all that Boniface was a rascallion, a vile fellow, an ass unworthy of being admitted to share in any discussion on public affairs.

And consequently he was expelled.

"You, see, then," said Pitou, "the image of revolution at Paris, as Monsieur Prudhomme or Loustalot has said— I think it was the virtuous Loustalot who said it—yes, 'twas he, I am now certain of it :

"'The great appear to us to be great, solely because we are upon our knees ; let us stand up.'"

This epigraph had not the slightest bearing on the question in dispute, but perhaps, for that very reason, it produced a prodigious effect.

The skeptic Boniface, who was standing at a distance of twenty paces, was struck by it, and returned to Pitou, humbly saying to him :

"You must not be angry with us, Pitou, if we do not understand liberty as well as you do."

"It is not liberty," said Pitou, "but the rights of man."

This was another blow with a sledge-hammer, with which Pitou a second time felled the whole auditory.

"Decidedly," said Boniface, "you are a learned man, and we pay homage to you."

Pitou bowed.

"Yes," said he, "education and experience have placed me above you ; and if just now I spoke to you rather harshly, it was from my friendship for you."

Loud applause followed this ; Pitou saw that he could now give vent to his eloquence.

"You have just talked of work," said he, "but do you know what work is ? To you, labor consists in splitting wood, in reaping the harvest, in picking up beech-mast, in tying up wheat-sheaves, in placing stones one above another, and consolidating them with cement. In your opinion, I do not work at all. Well, then, you are mistaken, for I alone labor much more than you do all together, for I am meditating your emancipation, for I am dreaming of your liberty, of your equality. A moment of my time is, therefore, of more value than a hundred of your days. The oxen who plow the ground do but one and the same thing ; but the man who thinks surpasses all the strength of matter. I, by myself, am worth the whole of you. Look at Monsieur Lafayette, he is a thin, fair man, not much taller than Claud Tellier. He has a pointed nose, thin legs, and arms as small as the back joints of this chair. As to his hands and feet, it is not worth while to mention them. A man might as well be without. Well, this man has carried two worlds on his shoulders, which is one more than Atlas did, and his little hands have broken the chains of America and France.

" Now, as his arms have done all this, arms not thicker than the back railing of a chair, only imagine to yourselves what arms like mine can do."

And Pitou bared his arms, which were as knotty as the trunk of a holly-tree.

And, having drawn this parallel, he paused, well assured that he had produced, without coming to a regular conclusion, an immense effect.

And he had produced it.

CHAPTER XXXII.

THE greater portion of events which happen to man, and which confer on him great happiness or great honors, are almost always brought about from his having fervently desired, or much disdained.

If this maxim were duly applied to events and to men cited in history, it would be found that it possesses not only profundity, but also truth.

We shall, however, content ourselves, without having recourse to proofs, with applying it to Ange Pitou, our man and our history.

In fact, Pitou, if we are allowed to retrograde a few steps, and to return to the wound which he had received straight to the heart—Pitou had, in fact, after the discovery he had made on the borders of the forest, been seized with a withering disdain for the things of this nether world.

He who had hoped to find blossom within his heart that rare and precious plant which mortals denominate Love—he who had returned to his own province with a helmet and a saber, proud of thus associating Mars and Venus, as was said by his illustrious compatriot, Demoustier, in his "Letters to Emilie on Mythology," found himself completely taken aback and very unhappy on perceiving that there existed at Villers-Cotterets and its neighborhood more lovers than were necessary.

He who had taken so active a part in the crusade of the Parisians against the nobility, found himself but very insignificant in opposition to the country nobility, represented by M. Isidor de Charny.

Alas! so handsome a youth, a man likely to please even at first sight, a cavalier who wore buckskin breeches and a velvet riding-coat.

How would it be possible to contend against such a man?

With a man who had long riding-boots, and spurs on the heels of those boots—with a man whose brother many people still call monseigneur.

How was it possible to contend against such a rival? How could he avoid at once feeling shame and admiration? two feelings which, to the heart of the lover, inflict a double torture—a torture so frightful that it has never yet been decided whether a jealous man prefers a rival of higher or lower condition than himself.

Pitou, therefore, but too well knew the pangs of jealousy, the wounds of which are incurable and fertile in agony, and of which up to this time the ingenuous heart of our hero had remained ignorant—jealousy, a plant of marvelous and venomous growth, which springs up without seed being sown, from a soil that had never seen germinate any noxious passion, not even self-love, that evil root which chokes up even the most sterile lands.

A heart thus tortured stands in need of much philosophy, in order to regain its habitual calmness.

Was Pitou a philosopher? He who the day following that on which he had experienced this sensation, could think of waging war against the hares and rabbits of His Highness the Duke of Orleans, and the day after that, of making the long harangues we have reported?

Was his heart, then, as hard as flint, from which every fresh blow draws a spark? Or did it possess only the soft resistance of a sponge, which has the quality of absorbing tears and of mollifying, without receiving a wound, the shock of every misfortune?

This, the future will indubitably testify; therefore, let us not prejudge, but go on with our story.

After having received the visit we have related, and his harangues being terminated, Pitou, compelled by his appetite to attend to minor matters, set to work and cooked his young rabbit, regretting that it was not a hare.

But, in fact, had the rabbit been really a hare, Pitou would not have eaten, but would have sold it.

That would not have been a very trifling concern. A hare, according to its size, is worth from eighteen to twenty-four sous; and although he was still the possessor of a few louis given to him by Dr. Gilbert, Pitou, without being as avaricious as his aunt Angelique, had a good dose of economy, which he had inherited from his mother. Pitou would, therefore, have added eighteen sous to his treasure, which would thus have been increased instead of diminished.

For Pitou had justly reflected that it was not necessary for a man to make repasts which would cost him one day half a crown, another eighteen sous. He was not a Lucullus; and Pitou said that with the eighteen sous his hare would have brought him, he could have lived during a whole week.

Now, during that week, supposing that he had caught a hare on the first day, he might very well have taken three during the six following days, or, rather, the six following nights. In a week, therefore, he would have gained food for a month.

Following up this calculation, forty-eight hares would have sufficed for a year's keep; all the rest would have been clear profit.

Pitou entered into this economical calculation while he was eating his rabbit; which, instead of bringing him anything, cost him a sou's worth of butter and a sou's worth of lard. As to the onions, he had gleaned them upon the common land.

"After a repast, the fireside or a walk," says the proverb. After his repast, Pitou went into the forest to seek a snug corner where he could take a nap.

It is scarcely necessary to say that as soon as the unfortunate youth had finished talking politics and found himself alone, he had incessantly before his eyes the spectacle of M. Isidor making love to Mlle. Catherine.

The oaks and beech-trees trembled with his sighs; nature, which always smiles on well-filled stomachs, made one exception in regard to Pitou, and appeared to him a vast dark desert, in which there remained only rabbits, hares, and deer.

Once hidden beneath the tall trees of his natal forest, Pitou, inspired by their cool and invigorating shade, became more firm in his heroic resolution, and this was to disappear from before the eyes of Catherine—to leave her altogether free, and not to affect himself extravagantly as to her preference of another, that he might not be more humiliated than was necessary by invidious comparison.

It was a highly painful effort to abstain from seeing Mlle. Catherine; but a man ought to be a man.

Moreover, this was not precisely the case in question.

The question was not exactly, that he should no more see Mlle. Catherine, but that he should not be seen by her.

Now, what was there to prevent the contemned lover from carefully concealing himself and catching a glance of the cruel fair one? Nothing.

From Haramont to the farm—what was the distance? Scarcely a league and a half—that is to say, a few strides—that was all.

Although it would have been base on the part of Pitou to have continued his attentions to Catherine after what he had seen, it would be so much the more adroit in him to continue to ascertain her acts and conduct, thanks to a little exercise, which could not be but favorable to Pitou's health.

Moreover, that portion of the forest behind the farm and extending toward Boursonneville abounded in hares.

Pitou would go at night to lay his wires, and the next morning from the top of some high hillock he would cast his eyes over the plain and watch Mlle Catherine's doings. This he had the right to do; this, to a certain point, was his duty, being the authorized agent, as he undoubtedly was, of father Billot.

Thus having consoled himself, and, as it were, in spite of himself, Pitou thought he might cease sighing. He dined off an enormous slice of bread he had brought with him, and when the evening had closed in, he laid a dozen wires and threw himself down upon the heather, still warm from the sun's rays.

There he slept like a man in utter despair—that is to say, his sleep was almost as undisturbed as that of death.

The coolness of the night awoke him; he went to examine his wires. Nothing had been taken; but Pitou calculated always more upon the morning passage; only, as his head felt somewhat heavy, he determined on returning to his lodgings and looking to his wires the following day.

But this day, which to him had passed by so devoid of events and intrigues, had been passed in a very different manner by the inhabitants of the hamlet, who had employed it in reflecting and in making combinations.

It might have been seen toward the middle of that day which Pitou had passed dreaming in the forest—the woodcutters, we say, might have been seen leaning contemplatively upon their hatchets; the threshers, with their flails suspended in the air, meditating; the joiners stopping their planes upon a half-smoothed plank.

Pitou was the first great cause of all this loss of time; Pitou had been the breath of discord, which had stirred these straws which began to whirl about confusedly.

And he, the occasion of all this agitation, had not even thought one moment on the subject.

But at the moment when he was going toward his own lodging, although the clock had struck ten, and usually at that hour not a single light was to be seen, not an eye was still open in the village, he perceived a very unaccustomed scene around the house which he resided in. He saw a number of men seated in groups, a number standing in groups, several groups walking up and down.

The aspect of these groups was altogether singular.

Pitou, without knowing why, imagined that all these people were talking of him.

And when he passed through the street, they all appeared as if struck by an electric shock, and pointed at him as he passed.

"What can the matter be with them all?" said Pitou to himself. "I have not my helmet on."

And he modestly retired to his own lodging, after having exchanged salutations with a few of the villagers as he passed by them.

He had scarcely shut the door of his house, when he thought he heard a slight knock upon the door-post.

Pitou was not in the habit of lighting a candle to undress by. A candle was too great a luxury for a man who paid only six livres a year for his lodgings, and who, having no books, could not read.

But it was certain that some one was knocking at his door.

He raised the latch.

Two of the young inhabitants of the village familiarly entered his abode.

"Why, Pitou, you have not a candle," said one of them.

"No," replied Pitou ; "of what use would it be ?"

"Why, that one might see."

"Oh ! I see well at night ; I am Nyctalops."

And in proof of this he added :

"Good evening, Claude ! Good evening, Désiré."

"Well ! " they both cried, "here we are, Pitou ! "

"This is a kind visit ; what do you desire of me, my friends ?"

"Come out into the light," said Claude.

"Into the light of what ?   There is no moon."

"Into the light of heaven."

"You have, then, something to say to me ?"

"Yes, we would speak with you, Ange."

And Claude emphasized these words with a singular expression.

"Well, let us go, then," said Pitou.

And the three went out together.

They walked on until they reached the first open space in the road ; Ange Pitou still not knowing what they wanted of him.

"Well ?" inquired Pitou, seeing that his two companions stopped.

"You see, now, Ange," said Claude, "here we are, Désiré Maniquet and myself.   We manage to lead all our companions in the country.   Will you be one of us ?"

"To do what ?"

"Ah ! that is the question.   It is to——"

"To do what ?" said Pitou, drawing himself up to his full height.

"To conspire," murmured Claude in Pitou's ear.

"Ah ! ah ! as they do at Paris," said Pitou, jeeringly.

The fact is that he was fearful of the word, and of the echo of the word, even in the midst of the forest.

"Come, now, explain yourself," said Pitou to Claude, after a short pause.

"This is the case," said the latter. "Come nearer, Désiré, you who are a poacher to your very soul, and know all the noises of the day and night, of the plain and of the forest, look around and see if we have been followed; listen whether there be any one attempting to overhear us."

Désiré gave an assenting nod, took a tolerably wide circuit round Pitou and Claude, and having peeped into every bush and listened to every murmur, returned to them.

"You may speak out," said he, "there is no one near us."

"My friends!" rejoined Claude, "all the townships of France, as Pitou has told us, desire to be armed, and on the footing of National Guards."

"That is true," said Pitou.

"Well, then, why should Haramont not be armed like the other townships?"

"You said why, only yesterday, Claude," replied Pitou, "when I proposed my resolution that we should arm ourselves. Haramont is not armed, because Haramont has no muskets."

"Oh! as to muskets, we need not be uneasy about them, since you know where they are to be had."

"I know! I know!" said Pitou, who saw at what Claude was aiming, who felt the danger of the proceeding.

"Well," continued Claude, "all the patriotic young fellows of the village have been consulting together to-day."

"Good!"

"And there are thirty-three of us."

"That is the third of a hundred less one," added Pitou.

"Do you know the manual exercise?" inquired Claude.

"Do I not!" exclaimed Pitou, who did not even know how to shoulder arms.

"Good! And do you know how to maneuver a company?"

"I have seen General Lafayette maneuvering forty thousand men at least ten times," disdainfully replied Pitou.

"That is all right," said Désiré, tired of remaining silent, and who, without intending to presume, wished to put in a word in his turn.

"Well, then, will you command us?" said Claude to Pitou.

"Who—I?" exclaimed Pitou, starting with surprise.

"Yes, you—yourself."

And the two conspirators intently eyed Pitou.

"Oh, you hesitate?"

"Why——"

"You are not, then, a good patriot," said Désiré.

"Oh! that, for example——"

"There is something, then, that you are afraid of?"

"What, I—I, a conqueror of the Bastile—a man to whom a medal is awarded?"

"You have a medal awarded you?"

"I shall have one as soon as the medals have been struck. Monsieur Billot has promised to apply for mine in my name."

"He will have a medal. We shall have a chief who has a medal!" exclaimed Claude, in a transport of joy.

"Come, now, speak out!" said Désiré; "will you accept the appointment?"

"Do you accept?" asked Claude.

"Well, then, yes; I will accept it," said Pitou, carried away by his enthusiasm, and also, perhaps, by a feeling which was awakening within him, and which is called pride.

"It is agreed: from to-morrow morning you will be our commander."

"And what shall I command you to do?"

"Our exercise, to be sure."

"And the muskets?"

"Why, since you know where there are muskets——"

"Oh! yes, at the house of the Abbé Fortier."

"Undoubtedly."

"Only it is very likely the Abbé Fortier will refuse to let me have them."

"Well, then, you will do as the patriots did at the Invalides—you will take them."

"What—I, alone?"

"You will have our signatures, and, should it be necessary, you shall have our hands, too. We will cause a rising in Villers-Cotterets; but we will have them."

Pitou shook his head.

"The Abbé Fortier is a very obstinate man," said he.

"Pooh ! you were his most favorite pupil ; he would not be able to refuse you anything."

"It is easy to perceive that you do not know him !" cried Pitou, with a sigh.

"How! do you believe the old man would refuse ?"

"He would refuse them even to a squadron of the Royal Germans.   He is dreadfully obstinate, *in justum et tenacem*.   But I forgot, you do not even understand Latin," added Pitou, with much compassion.

But the two Haramontese did not allow themselves to be dazzled either by the quotation or the apostrophe.

"Ah ! in good truth," said Désiré, "we have chosen an excellent chief, Claude ; he is alarmed at everything."

Claude shook his head.

Pitou perceived that he was compromising his high position ; he remembered that fortune always most favored those who possess some audacity.

"Well, be it so," said he ; "I will consider it."

"You, then, will manage the affair of the muskets ?"

"I will promise to do all I can."

An expression of satisfaction was uttered by his two friends, replacing the slight discontent they had before manifested.

"Ho ! ho !" said Pitou to himself, "these men want to dictate to me, even before I am their chief ; "what will they do, then, when I shall be so in reality ?"

"Do all you can," said Claude, shaking his head. "Oh ! oh ! that is not enough."

"If that is not enough," replied Pitou, " try you to do more ; I give up my command to you. Go and see what you can make of the Abbé Fortier and his cat-o'-nine-tails."

"That would be well worth while," said Maniquet, disdainfully. "It is a pretty thing, indeed, for a man to return from Paris, with a helmet and a saber, and then to be afraid of a cat-o'-nine-tails."

"A helmet and a saber are not a cuirass ; and even if they were, the Abbé Fortier would still find a place on which to apply his cat-o'-nine-tails."

Claude and Désiré appeared to comprehend this observation.

"Come, now, Pitou, my son," said Claude. (My son is a term of endearment much used in the country.)

"Well, then, it shall be so," said Pitou; "but, zounds! you must be obedient."

"You will see how obedient we shall be," said he, giving a wink to Désiré.

"Only," added Désiré, "you must engage with regard to the muskets——"

"Oh, that is agreed upon," cried Pitou, interrupting him, who was in truth extremely uneasy at the task imposed upon him; but whom, however, ambition was counseling to venture on deeds which required great daring.

"You promise, then?" said Claude.

"You swear it?" said Désiré.

Pitou stretched forth his hand. His two companions did the same.

And thus it was, by the light of the stars, and in an opening of the forest, that the insurrection was declared in the department of the Aisne, by the three Haramontese, unwitting plagiarists of William Tell and his three companions.

The fact is, that Pitou dimly foresaw that, after all the perils and troubles he would have to encounter, he would have the happiness of appearing gloriously invested with the insignia of a commander of the National Guard, before the eyes of Catherine; and the insignia appeared to him to be of a nature to cause her to feel, if not remorse, at least some regret for the conduct she had pursued.

Thus consecrated by the will of his electors, Pitou returned to his house, meditating on the ways and means by which he could procure arms for his thirty-three National Guards.

CHAPTER XXXIII.

THE whole of that night, Pitou was so absorbed in reflecting on the great honor which had befallen him, that he forgot to visit his wires.

The next morning he donned his helmet and buckled on his great saber, and set out manfully toward Villers-Cotterets.

It was just striking six o'clock when Pitou reached the square before the château, and he modestly knocked at the small door which opened into the Abbé Fortier's garden.

Pitou had knocked loud enough to satisfy his conscience, but gently enough not to be heard from the house.

He had hoped thus to gain a quarter of an hour's respite, and during that time to summon up some flowers of oratory wherewith to adorn the speech he had prepared for the Abbé Fortier.

But his astonishment was great when, notwithstanding his having knocked so gently, he saw the gate at once opened; but his astonishment soon ceased, when, in the person who had opened it, he recognized Sebastian Gilbert.

The lad was walking in the garden, studying his lesson by the sun's first rays—or, rather, we should say, pretending to study; for the open book was hanging listlessly in his hand, and the thoughts of the youth were capriciously wandering after those whom he most loved in the world.

Sebastian uttered a joyous cry on perceiving Pitou.

They embraced each other. The boy's first words were these:

"Have you received news from Paris?"

"No; have you any?" inquired Pitou.

"Oh, I have received some," said Sebastian. "My father has written me a delightful letter."

"Ah!" cried Pitou.

"And in which," continued the lad, "there is a word for you."

And taking the letter from his breast-pocket, he handed it to Pitou.

"P. S.—Billot recommends Pitou not to annoy or distract the attention of the people at the farm."

"Oh!" said Pitou, "that is a recommendation which, as it regards me, is altogether useless. There is no one at the farm whom I can either annoy or amuse."

Then he added to himself, sighing still more deeply:

"It was to Monsieur Isidor that these words ought to have been addressed."

He, however, soon recovered his self-possession, and returned the letter to Sebastian.

"Where is the abbé?" he inquired.

Sebastian bent his ear toward the house, and, although the width of the courtyard and the garden separated him from the staircase which creaked beneath the steps of the worthy priest :

" Why," said he, " he is just coming down-stairs."

Pitou went from the garden into the courtyard, and it was only then that he heard the heavy footsteps of the abbé.

The worthy professor was reading his newspaper as he came down-stairs.

His faithful cat-o'-nine-tails was, as usual, hanging by his side.

With his nose close to the newspaper—for he knew by heart the number of steps and every inequality in the wall of his old house—the abbé almost ran against Ange Pitou, who had assumed the most majestic air he could put on, in order to contend with his political antagonist.

But we must first of all say a few words as . to the position of the Abbé Fortier, which might have appeared tedious in any other page, but which here find their natural place.

They will explain how it was that the thirty or forty muskets which have been so much talked about happened to be in the Abbé Fortier's charge ; which muskets had become the object of the ambition of Pitou and of his two accomplices, Claude and Désiré.

The Abbé Fortier, who had formerly been the almoner or sub-almoner of the château, as we have already had occasion to explain elsewhere, had, in course of time, and, above all, with that patient fixity of ideas inherent in ecclesiastics, become sole intendant of what in theatrical language is called the properties of the château.

Besides the sacred vases, besides the library, he had received in charge all the hunting apparatus of the Duke of Orleans, Louis Philippe, the father of Philippe, who was afterward called Egalité. Some of this apparatus had been in the family as far back as the reigns of Louis XIII. and Henri III. All these articles had been artistically arranged by him in one of the galleries of the château, which had been allotted to him for this express purpose. In order to give them a more picturesque appearance, he had formed them into stars, the center being shields, surrounded by boar spears, hunting-knives, and short muskets, richly inlaid, and manufactured during the time of the League.

The door of this gallery was formidably defended by two small cannon of plated bronze, given by Louis XIV. to his brother Monsieur.

Besides these there were about fifty musketoons, brought as trophies by Joseph Philippe from the battle of Ushant, and had been presented by him to the municipality of Villers-Cotterets; and the municipality, as we have said, having furnished the Abbé Fortier with a house free of rent, had placed these muskets, not knowing what to do with them, in the collegiate house.

Such was the treasure guarded by the Dragon, named Fortier, and threatened by the Jason, named Ange Pitou.

The little arsenal of the château was sufficiently celebrated in the country to make people desire to obtain possession of it at little cost.

But, as we have said, the abbé, being a vigilant Dragon, did not appear disposed willingly to give up, to any Jason whatsoever, the golden apples which his Hesperides contained.

Having said this much, let us return to Pitou.

He very gracefully bowed to the Abbé Fortier, accompanying his bow with a slight cough, such as we use to attract the attention of persons who are naturally absent, or who are preoccupied.

The Abbé Fortier raised his nose from the newspaper.

"Well, I declare," said he, "'tis Pitou."

"To serve you, should I be capable of doing so," courteously replied Ange.

The abbé folded up his newspaper, or, rather, closed it, as he would have done a portfolio, for in those happy days the newspapers were still small pamphlets.

Then, having folded up his paper, he stuck it into his belt on the opposite side to his cat-o'-nine-tails.

"Ah, yes; but in that lies the misfortune," replied the abbé, jeeringly, "seeing that you are not capable."

"Oh! most worthy abbé."

"Do you hear me, Mr. Hypocrite?"

"Oh, good abbe!"

"Do you hear me, Mr. Revolutionist?"

"Come, now, this is good; for before I have spoken

even a single word, you get into a passion with me.   This is but a bad beginning, abbé."

Sebastian—who well knew what the Abbé Fortier had, for the last two days, been saying to every one who came near him about Pitou, thought it better not to be present during the quarrel which must necessarily ensue between his schoolmaster and his friend—stole away as quick as he could.

Pitou observed Sebastian's escape with a certain degree of sorrow.   He was not a very vigorous ally, but he was a youth of the same political communion with himself.

And, therefore, when he perceived him stepping through the door, he could not avoid uttering a sigh—then, turning to the abbé :

"Come, now, Monsieur Fortier," said he, "why do you call me a revolutionist ?   Would you insinuate that I am the cause of the revolution ?"

"You have lived with those who are carrying it on."

"Good Monsieur Abbé," said Pitou, with supreme dignity, "the thoughts of every man are free."

"Ah, indeed !"

"*Est penes hominem arbitrium est natio.*"

"Why, really," cried the abbé, "you know Latin, then, you clown ?"

"I know what you taught me of it," modestly replied Pitou.

"Yet revised, corrected, augmented, and embellished with barbarisms."

"Good again, Monsieur Abbé—barbarisms ! and who is there who does not commit them ?"

"Vile fellow !" cried the abbé, evidently wounded by this apparent tendency of Pitou's to generalize.   "What, do you believe that I am guilty of barbarisms ?"

"You would commit them in the eyes of a man who was a better Latin scholar than yourself."

"Only hear that !" cried the abbé, turning pale with anger, and yet struck with the reasoning, which was not devoid of point.

Then, in a melancholy tone :

"There, in two words, is the system of these vile wretches ; they destroy and degrade, and who profits by it ?   They know not even themselves—it is to the profit of the unknown.   Come, now, Monsieur Dunce, speak out freely—do you know any one who is a better Latin scholar than I am?"

"No; but there may be many, although I do not know them—I do not know everything."

"Zounds! I believe you."

Pitou made the sign of the cross.

"What are you doing there, libertine?"

"You swore, Monsieur Abbé, and I crossed myself."

"Why, rascal, have you come here to tympanize me?"

"To tympanize you!" repeated Pitou.

"Ah! good—now again you do not comprehend——"

"Oh! yes, I understand it well enough. Ah! thanks to you, I know the roots of words—tympanize—*tympanum*—drum; it comes from the Greek *tympanon*, drum or bell."

The abbé appeared perfectly astounded.

"Root, *typos*, mark, vestige; and, as Lancelot says, in his garden of Greek roots, *typos*, the form which impresses itself, which word evidently comes from *topto*, to strike. There you have it."

"Ah! ah! rascallion," cried the abbé, more and more dumfounded. "It seems that you yet know something, even what you did not know."

"Pooh!" ejaculated Pitou, with affected modesty.

"How did it happen that during the whole time you were with me you could not answer me as you have now done?"

"Because, during the time I was with you, Abbé Fortier, you brutalized me—because, by your despotism you repelled my intelligence, imprisoned within my memory all that liberty has since brought forth from it. Yes, liberty," continued Pitou, becoming more energetic as he proceeded; "do you hear me?—liberty!"

"Ah! rascal."

"Monsieur Professor," said Pitou, with an air which was not exempt from threat, "Monsieur Professor, do not insult me. *Contumelia non argumentum*, says an orator; insult is not reasoning."

"I think that the fellow," cried the abbé, in great fury—"I think that the fellow imagines it necessary to translate his Latin to me."

"It is not my Latin, Monsieur Abbé, it is Cicero's—that

is to say, the Latin of a man who assuredly would have thought that you made as many barbarisms in comparison with him, as I do in comparison with you.".

"You do not pretend, I hope," cried the Abbé Fortier, somewhat shaken on his pedestal—"you do not pretend, I hope, that I should discuss with you."

"And why not? If, from the discussion, light is to proceed—*abstrusum versusilicum.*"

"How! how!" exclaimed the Abbé Fortier; "why, really, the fellow has been in the revolutionary school."

"How can that be, since you yourself have said that the revolutionists are fools and ignoramuses?"

"Yes, I do say so."

"Then you are making a false reasoning, my worthy abbé, and your syllogism is badly founded."

"Badly founded! What say you? I have badly founded a syllogism?"

"Undoubtedly, Monsieur l'Abbé. Pitou reasons and speaks well—Pitou has been to the revolutionary school—the revolutionists consequently reason and speak well. There is no getting out of that."

"Animal! brute! simpleton!"

"Do not molest me by your words, Monsieur l'Abbé. *Objurgatio imbellem animum arguit*—weakness betrays itself by anger."

The abbé shrugged up his shoulders.

"Answer me," said Pitou.

"You say that the revolutionists speak well and reason well. But tell me the name of any one of those wretches who knows how to read and write."

"That is blinking the point in discussion; but I will answer you, nevertheless. I can read and write," cried Pitou, with assurance.

"Read—I will admit that—and yet, I know not—but as to writing——"

"Writing!" cried Pitou.

"Yes, you can write; but without orthography."

"That is to be seen."

"Will you lay a wager that you will write a page under my dictation without making four blunders?"

"Will you lay a wager, you, that you will write half a page under my dictation, without making two?"

"Oh! that, for example——"

"Well, let us to work. I will pick you out some participles and reflective verbs. I will season you up all these with a certain number of thats which I know of. I accept the wager."

"If I had time," said the abbé.

"You would lose."

"Pitou! Pitou! remember the proverb, *Pitonius Angelus asinus est.*"

"Pooh! proverbs! there are proverbs made for everybody. Do you know the one which was sung into my ears by the reeds of the Wualu as I passed by them?"

"No; but I should be curious to know it, Master Midas."

"*Fortierus Abbas forte fortis.*"

"Sir!" exclaimed the abbé.

"A free translation—the Abbé Fortier is not in his forte every day."

"Fortunately," said the abbé, "accusing is of slight importance; it is the proof that condemns."

"Alas! good Monsieur Abbé, that would be perfectly easy; let us see, what do you teach your pupils?"

"Why——"

"Allow me to follow up the argument. What do you teach your pupils?"

"Why, what I know."

"Good! remember that your answer was, 'what I know.'"

"Well, yes, what I know," said the abbé, somewhat shaken; for he felt that during his absence this singular combatant had learned some unknown thrusts. "Yes, I did say so; and what then?"

"Well, then, since you teach your pupils what you know, tell me what it is that you do know?"

"Latin, French, Greek, history, geography, arithmetic, algebra, astronomy, botany, and numismatics——"

"Anything more?" inquired Pitou.

"Why——"

"Try to find something else."

"Drawing."

"Go on."

"Architecture."

"Go on."

"Mechanics."

"A branch of mathematics—but that matters not—go on."

"But tell me, what are you aiming at?"

"Simply at this : you have stated pretty largely the account of what you do know ; now state the account of what you do not know."

The abbé shuddered.

"Ah !" said Pitou, "I clearly see that to do this I must assist you. Well, then, you do not know either German, or Hebrew, or Arabic, or Sanscrit, four mother languages. I speak not of the subdivisions, which are innumerable. You know nothing of natural history, of chemistry, of physics——"

"Monsieur Pitou——"

"Do not interrupt me ; you know nothing of rectilinear trigonometry ; you are ignorant of medicine ; you know nothing of acoustics, of navigation ; you are ignorant of everything that regards the gymnastic sciences."

"What say you?"

"I said gymnastics, from the Greek *gymnaza exercœ*, which comes from *gymnos,* naked, because the athletes were naked when they exercised."

"And yet it was I who taught you all this !" cried the abbé, almost consoled at the victory of his pupil.

"That is true."

"It is fortunate that you even acknowledge it."

"And with gratitude? We were saying, then, that you are ignorant of——"

"Enough. It is certain that I am ignorant of much more than I know."

"Therefore, you acknowledge that many men know more than you do."

"That is possible."

"It is certain ; and the more a man knows, the more does he perceive that he knows nothing. It was Cicero who said this."

"Conclude."

"I conclude——"

"Let us hear your conclusion ; it will be a fine one."

"I conclude that in virtue of your relative ignorance, you ought to be more indulgent as to the relative knowledge of other men. This constitutes a double virtue ; a duplex virtue, which we are assured was that of Fénélon,

who assuredly knew quite as much as you do ; and that is
the Christian charity of humility."

The abbé uttered a perfect roar of anger.

" Serpent ! " he exclaimed, " you are a serpent ! "

" You insult me, but do not answer me ; this was the
reply of one of the seven wise men of Greece ; I would
say it in Greek, but I have already said it, or something
nearly to the same purpose, in Latin."

" Good ! " said the abbé, " this is another effect of revolutionary doctrines."

" And in what way ? "

" They have persuaded you you were my equal."

" And even should they have persuaded me of that, it
would not give you the right of making a grammatical
error."

" What say you ? "

" I say that you have just made an enormous fault,
master."

" Ah ! that is very polite, indeed—and what fault did
I commit ? "

" It is this : You said, ' revolutionary principles have
persuaded you you were my equal.' "

" Well—and what then ? "

" Well—were is in the imperfect tense."

" Yes, undoubtedly."

" It was the present you should have used."

" Ah ! " cried the abbé, blushing.

" Only translate the phrase into Latin, and you will
see what an enormous solecism the verb will give you in
the imperfect tense."

" Pitou ! Pitou ! " exclaimed the abbé, imagining that
there was something supernatural in this astounding erudition—" Pitou, which of the demons is it that inspires you
with all these attacks against an old man and against the
church ? "

" Why, my good master," replied Pitou, somewhat
moved by the tone of real despair in which these words
had been pronounced, " it is not a demon who inspires
me, nor do I attack you. Only you treat me as if I were
a perfect fool, and you forget that all men are equals."

The abbé was again irritated.

" It is that which I never will permit ; I cannot allow
such blasphemies to be uttered in my presence. You—

you the equal of a man whom God and study have taken
sixty years to form ? "

" Well, then, ask Monsieur de Lafayette, who has proclaimed the rights of man."

" Yes, yes ; cite as an authority an unfaithful subject
of the king—the torch of all this discord—the traitor ! "

" Hey ! " cried Pitou, horrified. " Monsieur de Lafayette an unfaithful subject ! Monsieur de Lafayette a
firebrand of discord ! Monsieur de Lafayette a traitor !
Why, it is you, abbé, who are blaspheming. Why, you
must have lived shut up in a box during the last three
months. You do not know, then, that this unfaithful
subject of the king is the only one who serves the king—
that this torch of discord is the pledge of public peace—
that this traitor is the best of Frenchmen ? "

" Oh ! " exclaimed the abbé, " could I ever have believed
that royal authority would fall so low ? A worthless fellow
like that "—and he pointed to Pitou, " to invoke the name
of Lafayette as in ancient times they invoked the names
of Aristides and of Phocion."

" It is very fortunate for you, Monsieur l'Abbé, that
the people do not hear you," said Pitou, imprudently.

" Ah ! " exclaimed the abbé, with triumph, " you at
length reveal yourself—you threaten. The people—yes,
the people who basely murdered the king's officers—the
people, who even tore out the entrails of their victims.
Yes, Monsieur de Lafayette's people—Monsieur Bailly's
people—Monsieur Pitou's people. Well, then, why do
you not instantly denounce me to the revolutionists of
Villers-Cotterets ? Why do you not turn up your sleeves
to hang me on the first post ? Come now, Pitou *maete
animo*. Pitou, *sursum—sursum*, Pitou. Come, come,
where is your rope ? where is your gallows ? There is the
executioner ; *maete animo generare Pitoe !* "

" *Sic itur ad astra*," added Pitou, muttering ; but solely
with the intention of finishing the line, and not perceiving
that he was making a pun worthy of a cannibal.

But he was compelled to perceive it by the increased
exasperation of the abbé.

" Ah ! ah ! " vociferated the latter, " ah ! that is the
way you take it ! ah ! it is thus that you would send me
to the stars, is it ? Ah ! you intend me for the gallows,
do you ? "

"Why, I did not say that," cried Pitou, beginning to be alarmed at the turn the conversation was taking.

"Ah! you promise me the heaven of the unfortunate Foulon, of the unhappy Berthier."

"Why so, Monsieur l'Abbé?"

"Ah! you have the running-noose prepared—sanguinary executioner. It was you, was it not, who, on the square before the Hôtel de Ville, ascended the lamp-iron, and with your long, hideous, spider-like arms drew the victims to you?"

Pitou uttered a perfect roar of horror and indignation.

"Yes, it was you; and I recognize you," continued the abbé, in a transport of divination, which made him resemble Joab, "I recognized thee—thou art Catiline."

"But really," exclaimed Pitou, "do you know that you are saying abominable things to me, Monsieur l'Abbé? Do you know that, in point of fact, you are insulting me?"

"I insult you?"

"Do you know that if this continues, I will complain to the National Assembly? Ah! but——"

The abbé laughed with a sinistrously ironical expression.

"Lay your information," said he.

"And that punishment is awarded to ill-disposed persons who insult the good?"

"The lamp-post!"

"You are a bad citizen."

"The rope! the rope!"

Then he exclaimed, as if suddenly enlightened, and struck with a movement of generous indignation:

"Ah! the helmet! the helmet!—'tis he!"

"Well," said Pitou, "What is the matter with my helmet?"

"The man who tore out the still smoking heart of Berthier—the cannibal who carried it still bleeding, and laid it on the table of the electors—wore a helmet; that man with the helmet was you, Pitou—it was you, monster that you are! Avaunt! avaunt! avaunt!"

And each time that the abbé pronounced the word avaunt, which he did with much tragic emphasis, he advanced one step toward Pitou, who retreated in the same proportion.

But on hearing this accusation, of which the reader

knows Pitou to be perfectly innocent, the poor lad threw far from him the helmet, of which he was so proud, which rolled over upon the pavement of the courtyard, with the heavy, hollow sound of copper lined with pasteboard.

"You see, wretch!" cried the abbé, "you acknowledge it."

And he assumed the attitude of Lekain,* in Orosmanes, at the moment when, after finding the letter, he accuses Zaire.

"Come, now," said Pitou, completely taken aback by so horrible an accusation, "you are exaggerating, Monsieur l'Abbé."

"I exaggerate—that is to say, that you only hanged a little—that is to say that you only ripped up a little, poor, weak child!"

"Monsieur Abbé, you know full well it was not I, you well know that it was Pitt."

"And who is Pitt?"

"Pitt the second—the son of Pitt the first—of Lord Chatham. He who has distributed money, saying, 'Spend it—you need not give any account of it.' If you understood English, I would tell it you in English, but you do not know that language."

"You know it, then, you?"

"Monsieur Gilbert taught it me."

"In three weeks? Monsieur Impostor!"

Pitou saw that he had made a false step.

"Hear me, Monsieur l'Abbé," said he, "I will not contend with you any further. You have your own ideas——"

"Really?"

"That is but right."

"You acknowledge that? Monsieur Pitou allows me to have my own ideas! Thanks, Monsieur Pitou."

"Good! There, you are getting angry again. You must comprehend that if this continues I shall not be able to tell you the object which brought me here."

"Wretch! You had an object in coming here, then? You were deputed, perhaps?"

And the abbé laughed ironically.

"Sir," said Pitou, placed by the abbé himself upon the footing in which he wished to find himself since the com-

* A great French tragedian.

mencement of the discussion, "you know the great respect I have always had for your character."

"Ah! yes, let us talk of that."

"And the admiration I have always entertained for
your knowledge," added Pitou.

"Serpent!" exclaimed the abbé.

"What, I?" cried Pitou, "that, for example!"

"Come, now, let us hear what you have to ask of me?
That I should take you back here? No, no; I would not
spoil my scholars. No; you would still retain the noxious
venom; you would infect my young plants: *Infecit, fabula
labo.*"

"But, good Monsieur l'Abbé——"

"No, do not ask me that; if you must absolutely eat—
for I presume that the hangers .f Paris eat as well as
honest people. They eat, oh, God! In short, if you require that I should throw you your portion of raw meat,
you shall have it. But at the door, on the spatula, as at
Rome the masters did to their dogs."

"Monsieur l'Abbé," cried Pitou, drawing himself up
proudly, "I do not ask you for my food; I have wherewith to provide food, God be thanked! I will not be a
burden to any one."

"Ah!" exclaimed the abbé, with surprise.

"I live as all living beings do, and that without begging,
and by that industry which nature has implanted in me;
I live by my own labor; and more than that, I am so far
from being chargeable on my fellow-citizens, that several
among them have elected me their chief."

"Hey!" cried the abbé, with so much surprise mingled
with so much terror that it might have been thought that
he had trod upon a viper.

"Yes, yes; they have elected me their chief," repeated
Pitou, complacently.

"Chief of what?" inquired the abbé.

"Chief of a troop of freemen," said Pitou.

"Ah! good Heaven!" cried the abbé, "the unfortunate boy has gone mad!"

"Chief of the National Guard of Haramont," concluded Pitou, affecting modesty.

The abbé leaned toward Pitou, in order to gain from his
features a confirmation of his words.

"There is a National Guard at Haramont?" cried he.

"Yes, Monsieur l'Abbé."

"And you are the chief of it?"

"Yes, Monsieur l'Abbé."

"You, Pitou?"

"I, Pitou."

The abbé raised his outstretched arms toward heaven, like Phineas, the high priest.

"Abomination of desolation!" murmured he.

"You are not ignorant, Monsieur Abbé," said Pitou, with gentleness, "that the National Guard is an institution destined to protect the life, the liberty, and the property of the citizens."

"Oh! oh!" continued the abbé, overwhelmed by his despair.

"And that," continued Pitou, "too much vigor can not be given to that institution, above all, in the country, on account of the very numerous bands——"

"Bands of which you are the chief!" cried the abbé; "bands of plunderers, bands of incendiaries, bands of assassins!"

"Oh, do not confound things in this manner, dear Monsieur l'Abbé; you will see my soldiers, I hope, and never were there more honest citizens."

"Be silent! be silent!"

"You must consider, on the contrary, that we are your natural protectors, and the proof of this is, that I have come straight to you."

"And for what purpose?" inquired the abbé.

"Ah! that is precisely it," said Pitou, scratching his ear, and looking anxiously at the spot where his helmet was lying, in order to ascertain whether in going to pick up this very necessary portion of his military equipment he would not place himself at too great a distance from his line of retreat.

The helmet had rolled to within some few paces only of the great gate which opened on the Rue de Soissons.

"I asked you for what purpose?" repeated the abbé.

"Well," said Pitou, retreating backward two steps toward his helmet, "this is the object of my mission, good Monsieur l'Abbé; permit me to develop it to your sagacity."

"Exordium?" muttered the abbé.

Pitou backed two steps more toward his helmet.

But by a singular maneuver, and which did not fail to give Pitou some uneasiness, whenever he made two steps nearer to his helmet, the abbé, in order to remain at the same distance from him, advanced two steps toward Pitou.

"Well," said Pitou, beginning to feel more courageous from his proximity to his defensive head-piece, "all soldiers require muskets, and we have not any."

"Ah, you have no muskets!" cried the abbé, dancing with joy. "Ah! they have no muskets! Soldiers without muskets! Ah! by my faith, they must be very pretty soldiers!"

"But, Monsieur l'Abbé," said Pitou, taking again two steps nearer to his helmet, "when men have not muskets they seek for them."

"Yes," said the abbé, "and you are in search of some?"

Pitou was able to reach his helmet, and brought it near him with his foot. Being thus occupied, he did not at once reply to the abbé.

"You look, then, for some?" repeated the latter.

"Yes."

"Where?"

"In your house," said Pitou, placing the helmet on his head.

"Guns in my house?" asked the abbé.

"Yes. You have many."

"Ah! my museum; you come to rob my museum. Only fancy the cuirasses of old heroes on the backs of such creatures! Pitou, I told you just now that you were mad. The swords of the Spaniards of Almanza, the pikes of the Swiss of Marignon were never made for such a troop as yours."

The abbé laughed so scornfully that a cold shudder ran through Pitou's veins.

"No, abbé," said Pitou; "the Spanish swords and Swiss pikes would be of no use."

"It is well you see it."

"Not those arms, abbé, but those capital muskets I cleaned so often when I studied under you.

"*Dam me Galatea tenebat,*"

added Pitou, with a most insinuating smile.

"Indeed," said the abbé, and he felt his few hairs stand

erect as Pitou spoke.   "You want my old marine muskets ?"

"They are the only weapons you have without any historical interest, and really fit for service."

"Indeed," said the abbé, placing his hand on the handle
of his hammer, as the soldier would have seized his sword.
"Back ! now the traitor unveils himself."

"Abbé," said Pitou, passing from menace to prayer,
"give me thirty muskets——"

"Go back."   The abbé advanced toward Pitou.

"And you will have the glory of having contributed to
rescue the country from its oppressors."

"Furnish 'arms to be used against me and mine ?
Never !" said the abbé.

He took up his hammer :

"Never, never ! "

He wielded it above his head.

"Monsieur," said Piton, "your name shall be placed
in the journal of Monsieur Prudhomme."

"My name in his paper ?"

"Honorably mentioned."

"I had rather be sent to the galleys."

"What, you refuse ?" asked Pitou.

"Yes, and tell you to go !"

The abbé pointed to the door.

"That would be very wrong, for you would be accused
of treason.   Monsieur, I beg you not to expose yourself to
that."

"Make me a martyr hero ; I ask but that."   And his
eye glared so that he looked more like the executioner
than the victim.

So Pitou thought, for he began to fall back.

"Abbé," said he, stepping back, "I'm an ambassador
of peace, a quiet deputy."

"You come to rob my armory, as your accomplices did
that of the Invalides."

"Which was most laudable," said Pitou.

"And which will here expose you to the risk of the end
of my hammer."

"Monsieur," said Pitou, who recognized an old acquaintance in the tool, " you will not thus violate the law of
nations ?"

"You will see."

"I am protected by my character of ambassador."

The abbé continued to advance.

"Abbé! abbé! abbé!" said Pitou.

He was at the street-door, face to face with his dangerous enemy, and Pitou had either to fight or run.

To run, he had to open the door; to open the door, turn.

If he turned, Pitou exposed to danger the part of his body the least protected by the cuirass.

"You want my guns? you want my guns?" said the abbé, "and say, 'I will have them or you die!'"

"On the contrary, monsieur, I said nothing of the kind."

"Well, you know where they are. Cut my throat and take them."

"I am incapable of such a deed."

Pitou stood at the door with his hand on the latch, and thought not of the abbé's muskets, but of his hammer.

"Then you will not give me the muskets?"

"No!"

"I ask you again."

"No—no!"

"Again?"

"No—no!"

"Then keep them!" and he dashed through the half-open door. His movement was not quick enough to avoid the hammer, which hissed through the air and fell on the small of the back of Pitou, and great as was the courage of the conqueror of the Bastile, he uttered a cry of pain.

Just then many of the neighbors rushed out, and to their surprise saw Pitou running away with his sword and helmet, and the Abbé Fortier at the door brandishing his hammer as the angel of destruction wields his sword of flame.

CHAPTER XXXIV.

WE have seen how Pitou was disappointed.

The fall was immense. Not even Satan had fallen from such an eminence when from heaven he was thrown to hell. Satan fell, but remained a king, while the Abbé Fortier's victim was only Ange Pitou.

How could he appear before the persons who had sent him ? How, after having testified such rash confidence, could he say that he was a boaster and a coward, who armed with a sword and a helmet, had suffered an old abbé to put him to flight.

Pitou was wrong in having boasted that he would triumph over the Abbé Fortier, and in failing.

The first time he found himself out of view, he put his hand on his head, and thought.

He had expected to annihilate Fortier with his Latin and Greek. He thought that by kind words he would soften the old Cerberus, but he had been bitten, and all had been spoiled.

The abbé had great self-esteem, and Pitou had relied on it. What most offended the abbé was Pitou's finding fault with his French—a thing he cared more about than he did about the muskets, which he had sought to take from him.

Young people, when good, always think others as good as they are themselves.

The abbé was not only an outrageous royalist, but also an outrageous philologist.

Pitou was especially sorry that he had excited him both on account of Louis XVI. and the verb *to be*. He knew and should have managed his friend. That was his error, and he regretted it, though too late.

What should he have done ?

By eloquence have flattered the abbé of his own royalism, and not have noticed his mistakes in grammar.

He should have convinced him that the National Guard of Haramont was opposed to the revolution.

He should have said that it would sustain the king.

Above all, he never should have said a word about the verb *to be*.

There was no earthly doubt but that the abbé would have opened his arsenal for the purpose of securing to the cause of the king such a leader and such a company.

This falsehood is diplomacy. Pitou thought over all the stories of old times.

He remembered Philip of Macedon, who swore falsely so often, but who was called a great man.

Of Brutus, who, to overcome his enemies, pretended to be a fool, but who is thought a great man.

Of Themistocles, who deceived his fellow-citizens, but who is called a great man.

On the other hand, he remembered that Aristotle would admit of no injustice, and that he, too, was esteemed a great man.

This contrast annoyed him.

He thought, though, that Aristotle fortunately lived at a time when the Persians were so stupid that one could act honestly and yet conquer them.

He then remembered that Aristides had been exiled, and that this circumstance acted in favor of the King of Macedon. He rather approved of Philip, Brutus, and Themistocles.

Descending into modern times, Pitou remembered how Gilbert, Bailly, Lameth, Mirabeau would have acted, had Louis XVI. been the abbé and they been Pitou.

What would they not have done to have armed the five hundred thousand National Guards of France?

Exactly what Pitou had not done.

They would have persuaded Louis XVI. that they desired nothing more than to preserve the father of the French; that to save him, from three to five hundred thousand guns were needed.

Mirabeau would here succeed.

Pitou then remembered the two following lines:

> "When you to the devil pray,
> Call him the giver of good."

He came to the conclusion that Ange Pitou was a perfect brute, and that to return to his electors with any glory he would have to do exactly what he had not.

Pitou determined then, either by force or by tricks, to get possession of the arms.

The first means were tricks.

He could enter the abbé's museum and steal the arms. Tricks!

If he did it alone, the act would be theft. If with companions, it would be simply a removal.

The very word theft made Pitou uneasy.

There were yet in France people enough used to the old laws to call the removal highway robbery.

Pitou hesitated.

But Pitou's self-love was excited, and to save it he was forced to act alone.

He set to work most diligently to seek some mode of extricating himself.

At last, like Archimedes, he shouted, "Eureka!"

The following was his plan:

Lafayette was Commander-in-Chief of the National Guards of France.

Haramont was in France.

Haramont had a National Guard.

Lafayette, then, was Commander of the National Guard of Haramont.

He could not, therefore, consent that they should be destitute while the rest of France was armed.

To reach Lafayette he had to appeal to Gilbert—Gilbert—Billot.

Pitou had, then, to write to Billot.

As Billot could not read, he, in the first place, wrote Gilbert, thus saving the necessity of at least one letter.

Before he did so he went secretly to Haramont, not, however, without being seen by Tellier and Maniquet.

They withdrew in silence, and each with a finger on his lips as a token of silence.

Pitou had entered on the prosecution of a full course of politics.

The following is a copy of the letter which produced such an effect on Tellier and Maniquet:

"DEAR AND HONORABLE MONSIEUR BILLOT.— The revolutionary cause in our part of the country every day gains.

"The people of Haramont has enrolled itself in the active National Guard.

"It is, however, unarmed.

"Arms may be procured. Certain persons have large quantities, the possession of which would prevent the expenditure of public money.

"If General Lafayette be pleased to order these to be seized and distributed, I will myself assure thirty muskets can be placed in the arsenals of Haramont.

"It is the only way to oppose the anti-revolutionary action of the aristocrats, who are enemies of the nation.

"Your fellow-citizen and servant,
"ANGE PITOU."

When this was done, he remembered that he had forgotten to speak of the farmer's wife and family.

On the other hand, he was too much of a Brutus to tell Billot about Catherine. He, however, opened his letter and wrote, with a sigh, this postscript:

"P.S.—Mademoiselle Catherine and all are well, and send their love to Monsieur Billot."

He thus compromised neither himself nor any one.

He sent the letter, and the answer soon came.

On the next day, a mounted express reached Haramont and asked for M. Ange Pitou.

All the members of the militia were on the *qui qive*.

The horse was white with foam, and the rider wore the uniform of the Parisian National Guard.

From the excitement he produced all may fancy how great was Pitou's agitation.

He approached, and not without trembling received the package which the officer gave him.

It was the reply of Billot, written by Gilbert.

He advised Pitou to be both moderate and patriotic.

He inclosed an order of Lafayette, countersigned by the Minister of War, for the National Guard of Haramont to arm itself.

The order was thus written:

"The possessors of muskets and sabers, in a greater number than one, will be required to place them in the hands of the commanders of the National Guards of the Commune.

"The present order extends to all the province."

Pitou thanked the officer, and saw him at once set out.

Pitou had reached the acme of glory, having received a message directly from Lafayette.

This message suited his ideas exactly.

To describe Pitou's impressions would be impossible, and we will not, therefore, attempt to do so. The sight, however, of the excited countenances of all the people, the great respect exhibited to him, would have made all think Pitou a most important personage.

All the electors requested to see and touch the ministerial seal, a favor Pitou kindly granted.

When none but the initiated remained, Pitou said:

"Citizens, my plans succeeded. I wrote to General Lafayette, who wished to form a National Guard, and had selected me as commander. Read the directions of this letter."

The dispatch had been directed:

"Citizen

"Ange Pitou,

"Commander of the National Guard of Haramont."

"I am, then, recognized in my rank, by Lafayette, as commander. You are recognized as guards."

A loud shout was raised.

"I know where we can get arms," said Pitou.

"You will at once appoint a lieutenant and a sergeant. Those two functionaries will accompany me."

All present seem to hesitate.

"What is your opinion, Pitou?" said Maniquet.

"The matter does not concern me. Meet alone and appoint the two functionaries. But appoint capable ones."

Pitou bid adieu to his soldiers, and remained in a state of solemn grandeur.

He thus remained in his glory, while the soldiers discussed the details of the military power which was to restrain Haramont.

The election lasted an hour. The lieutenant and sergeant chosen were Tellier and Maniquet, the last of whom was the subaltern. They returned and announced the fact to Pitou.

He then said:

"Now there is no time to lose."

"Yes," said an enthusiast, "let us begin the manual."

"Wait a moment, let us get guns first."

"True."

"But can we not practise with sticks?"

"Let us be military," said Pitou, who watched the military order with anxiety, but who did not feel himself qualified to teach an art of which he was utterly ignorant.

"It is a difficult matter to teach a raw recruit how to shoot a stick. Let us not be ridiculous."

"True. We must have muskets."

"Come with me, then, lieutenant and sergeant. The rest of you wait here."

All acquiesced respectfully.

"We have six hours' daylight yet left. That is more time than is needed to go to Villers-Cotterets."

"Forward !" said Pitou.

The staff of the army of Haramont set off.

When Pitou, however, read again the letter he had received, he discovered that he had overlooked one phrase.

"Why did Pitou forget to give Doctor Gilbert some information about Sebastian ?

"Why does not Sebastian write to his father ? "

CHAPTER XXXV.

THE Abbé Fortier was far from suspecting what danger he was in, prepared carefully for him by deep diplomacy. He had no idea of Pitou's influence.

He was seeking to prove to Sebastian that bad company is the ruin of innocence ; that Paris is a pit of perdition ; that even angels would be corrupted there, like those who went astray at Gomorrah—and, seriously impressed by Pitou's visit, besought Sebastian always to remember to be a good and true loyalist.

By those words the abbé meant a very different thing from what Dr. Gilbert meant.

He forgot that as long as this difference existed, he was committing a very bad action, for he sought to excite the son's opinions against the father.

He met, to tell the fact, with no great difficulty.

Strange to say, at a period when the minds of most children are, so to say, mere potters' clay, on which every pressure leaves a mark, Sebastian, in fixity of purpose, was a man.

Was that to be attributed to that aristocratic nature which disdains everything plebeian ?

Or was it plebeianism pushed to stoicism ?

The mystery was too deep for the Abbé Fortier. He knew the doctor was an enthusiastic patriot, and with the simplicity of mind peculiar to ecclesiastics, sought for the glory of God to reform the son.

Though Sebastian appeared to listen, he did not, but was musing on those strange visions which previously had taken possession of him under the tall trees of the park of Villers-Cotterets when the abbé took his pupils thither, and which had become, so to say, a kind of second life, so closely however allied to the natural existence, that in our prosaic days it would seem impossible.

All at once a loud knock was heard at the door in Soissons Street, and it at once opened and admitted several persons.

They were the maire, adjunct, and town clerk.

Behind them were the gendarmes, after whom came several curious persons.

The abbé went at once to the maire, and said:

"Monsieur Longpré, what is the matter?"

"Abbé are you aware of the new order of the Minister of War?"

"I am not."

"Be pleased to read this."

As he read he grew pale.

"Well!" said he.

"Well, the gendarmes of Haramont expect you to surrender your arms."

The abbé sprung forward as if he would devour the National Guard.

Pitou thought it time for himself to be his own lieutenant.

"Here are the gentlemen," said the maire.

The abbé's face was flushed.

"What, these vagabonds?"

The maire was a good-natured man, and as yet had no decided political opinions. He had no disposition to quarrel either with the Church or the National Guard.

The words of the abbé excited a loud laugh, and he said to Pitou:

"Do you hear how he speaks of your command?"

"Because the abbé knew us when children, he fancies we can never grow old."

"The children, however, have now grown," said Maniquet, reaching forth his mutilated hand to the men.

"And are serpents."

"Who will bite if they be trampled on," rejoined Maniquet.

In these threats the maire saw all the future revolution, and the abbé martyrdom.

"A portion of your arms are needed," said the maire, who sought to effect a reconciliation.

"They are not mine ?" said the abbé.

"Whose are they ?"

"The Duke of Orleans'."

"Well, that matters not," said Pitou.

"How so ?" said the abbé.

"We would ask for them."

"I will write to the duke," said the abbé, majestically.

"The abbé forgets that if the duke were written to, he would reply that not only the weapons of his English enemies, but of his grandfather, Louis XIV., must be surrendered to patriots."

The abbé knew this was true.

"*Circum dedsiti me hostibus meis.*"

"True, abbé ; but to your purely political enemies. We hate in you only the bad patriot."

"Fool," said Fortier, with an excitement which inspired him with a certain kind of eloquence—"fool, and dangerous fool ! which is the patriot ? I, who would keep these arms, or you, who would use them in rapine and war ? Which is best ? I, who cultivate the olive of peace, or you who would lacerate the bosom of France, our common mother, with war ?"

The maire sought to conceal his emotion, and nodded to the abbé, as if to say :

"Good !"

The adjunct, like Tarquin, cut down flowers with his cane.

Pitou was amazed.

The two subalterns saw it, and were surprised.

Sebastian alone was cool.

He approached Pitou, and said :

"Well, what is to be done, Pitou ?"

Pitou said :

"The order is signed," and showed the minister's, his father's and Lafayette's signatures.

"Why, then, do you hesitate ?"

His flashing eye, his erect form, showed clearly the two indomitable races from which he sprung.

The abbé heard his words, shuddered, and said :

"Three generations oppose me."

"Abbé," said the maire, " the order must be obeyed."

The abbé put his hand on the keys which were in the girdle that from monastic habit he yet wore, and said :

"Never! They are not mine, and I will not surrender them till my master orders me!"

"Abbé, abbé!" said the maire, who felt compelled to disapprove.

"This is rebellion," said Sebastian. "Master, be careful."

"*Tu quoque*," said the abbé, like Cæsar folding his robe over his bosom.

"Be at ease, abbé," said Pitou, "these arms will be in good hands for France."

"Hush, Judas! You betrayed your master. Why will you not betray your country?"

Pitou felt his conscience prick him. What he had done was not at the instinct of a noble heart, though he had acted bravely.

He looked around, and saw his two subalterns apparently ashamed of his weakness.

Pitou felt that he was in danger of losing his influence. Pride came to the aid of this champion of the revolution.

He looked up, and said:

"Abbé, submissive as I was to my old master, not unreplied to shall such comments be made."

"Ah, you reply!" said the Abbé Fortier.

"Yes, and tell me if I am not right. You call me traitor, and refuse me the arms I asked you kindly for, but which I now take in the name and by the strong hand of the law. Well, abbé, I had rather be called traitor to my master than, like you, have opposed the liberty of my country. Our country forever!"

The maire nodded to Pitou, as he previously had to the abbé.

The effect of this address ruined the abbé.

The maire disapproved.

So, too, would the adjunct, but the absence of the two chiefs would certainly have been remarked.

He then, with the gendarmes and Pitou, who was perfectly familiar with the locality in which he had grown up, proceeded to the museum.

Sebastian rushed after the patriots, the other children appearing amazed.

After the door was opened the abbé sunk, half dead with mortification and rage, on the first chair.

When once in the museum, Pitou's assistants wished to

pillage everything, but the honesty of the commandant restrained them.

He took only thirty-three muskets, for he commanded thirty-three National Guards.

As it might be necessary for him some day to fire a shot, he took, as a thirty-fourth, an officer's gun, lighter and shorter than the others, with which he could either kill a false Frenchman or a true Prussian.

He then selected a straight sword like Lafayette's, which had perhaps been borne by some hero at Fontenoy or Phillipsbourg. He buckled it on.

Each of his colleagues then placed twelve muskets on their shoulders, and were so delighted that they scarcely felt the enormous weight.

Pitou took the rest.

They passed through the park to avoid observation in going through the city.

It was also the shortest route.

Our three heroes, loaded with their spoils, passed rapidly through the park, and reached the rendezvous. Exhausted and heated, they took their precious prize that night to Pitou's house. It may be the country had been too hasty in confiding it to them.

There was a meeting of the guard that night, and Pitou gave them the muskets, saying, in the words of the Spartan mother:

"With them or on them."

Thus was the little commune, by the genius of Pitou, made to seem busy as an ant-hill during an earthquake.

Delight at possessing a gun among a people smugglers by nature, whom the long oppression of gamekeepers had incensed, could not but be great. Pitou, consequently, became a god on earth. His long legs and arms were forgotten. So, too, were his clumsy knees and his grotesque antecedents. He could not but be the tutelary god of the country.

The next day was passed by the enthusiasts in cleaning and repairing their arms. Some rejoiced that the cock worked well, and others repaired the springs of the lock or replaced the screws.

In the meantime, Pitou had retired to his room as Agamemnon did to his tent, brightening his brains as others did their guns.

What was Pitou thinking of ?

Pitou, become a leader of the people, was thinking of the hollowness of earthly grandeur.

The time had come when the whole edifice he had erected was about to crumble.

The guns had been issued on the evening before, and the day passed in putting them in order. On the next day he would have to drill his men, and Pitou did not know a single command of "Load in twelve times."

What is the use of a commandant ignorant of the drill ? The writer of these lines never knew but one so ignorant. He was, however, a countryman of Pitou.

He thought with his head on his hands and his body prostrate.

Cæsar amid the thickets of Gaul, Hannibal wandering on the Alps, and Columbus drifting over the ocean, never thought more deeply, and never so fully confessed themselves *Diis ignotis*, the fearful powers who hold the secrets of life and death, than did Pitou.

"Come," said Pitou, "time speeds, and to-morrow I must appear in all my insignificance.

"To-morrow the captor of the Bastile, the god of war, will be called by all Haramont an idiot, as I do not know who was by the Greeks.

"To-day I triumph, but to morrow I shall be hooted.

"This cannot be. Catherine will know it, and will think me disgraced."

Pitou paused.

"What will extricate me from this dilemma ?

"Audacity.

"Not so. Audacity lasts a second. To load in the Prussian time requires half a minute.

"Strange idea, to teach the Prussian drill to Frenchmen. I am too much of a patriot to teach Frenchmen any of their inventions. I will make a national drill.

"But I may go astray.

"I saw a monkey once go through the manual at a fair. He probably, though being a monkey, had never served.

"Ah ! I have an idea."

He began to stride as fast as his long legs would permit, but was suddenly brought to a stand by the idea.

"My disappearance will astonish my men. I must inform them."

He then sent for his subalterns, and said :

"Tell the men that the first drill will take place on the day after to-morrow."

"Why not to-morrow ?"

"You are fatigued, and before drilling the men I must instruct the officers. Be careful, too, I beg you, to do as I do, and to say nothing."

They saluted him *à la militaire*.

"Very well, the drill will be at half past four on the day after to-morrow."

The subalterns left, and as it was half after nine, went to bed.

Pitou let them go, and when they had turned the corner, went in an opposite direction, and soon was hidden in the thickest of the park.

Now let us see what Pitou was thinking of.

CHAPTER XXXVI.

PITOU hurried on for half an hour into the very depths of the wood.

There was in the undergrowth, beneath a huge rock, a hut built some thirty-five or forty years before, which was inhabited by a person who, in his day, had excited no little mystery.

This hut, half buried in the ground and surrounded by foliage, received light only by an oblique opening. Not unlike a gipsy hut, it was often to be detected only by the smoke which rose from it.

None but gamekeepers, smugglers, and sportsmen would ever have suspected its existence or that it was inhabited.

For forty years, though, it had been the abode of a retired keeper, whom the Duke of Orleans, father of Louis Philippe, had permitted to remain with the privilege of killing a rabbit or a hare a day.

Fowl and large game were excepted.

At the time we speak of the old man was sixty-nine years old. His name was Clovis originally, to which, as he grew old, the title Father was annexed.

From his residence the rock took the name of Clovis's Stone.

He had been wounded at Fontenoy, and consequently had lost a leg, and been treated kindly as the duke appears to have done.

He never went into great cities, and visited Villers-Cotterets but once a year for the purpose of buying three hundred and sixty-five loads of powder and ball. On leap years he bought three hundred and sixty-six.

On that day he took to the hatter, M. Cornu, three hundred and sixty-five or three hundred and sixty-six rabbit or hare skins, for which he received seventy-five Tours livres. He never missed a shot, and we are, therefore, able to be so exact.

He lived on the flesh of the animals, though sometimes he sold it.

With the skins of the animals he bought powder and lead.

Once a year Father Clovis entered into a kind of speculation. Father Clovis went through the neighboring villages, and through the intervention of the old women, that all the young women, who bought his hares, to come on St. Louis, should come thrice a year and slide down the declivity of the rock.

The first year many young women came, but none dared the attempt.

On the next year three tried to do so. Two were married during the course of the year, and Father Clovis said the third would have been married had she been brave as the others were.

The next year all dared the attempt.

Father Clovis declared that enough men could not be found for so many young women, but that the boldest would be married. He had brilliant success.

For thirty-five years Clovis lived in this manner. The country treated him as the Arabs do their marabouts. He had become a legend.

One thing, however, excited the jealousy of the guards on duty. It was said that Father Clovis had fired but three hundred and sixty-five times, but had killed the same number of hares.

More than once the nobles of Paris, invited by the Duke of Orleans, who had heard of Father Clovis, placed a louis or a crown in his broad hand, and sought to ascertain how any one could never miss.

Old Clovis, however, told them nothing more than that

with the game gun he never missed a man at a hundred
yards. If he could kill a man, it was far easier to kill a
hare.

If any smiled when Clovis spoke thus, he used to say,
"Why do you fire when you are not sure of the mark?"

"Could I have belonged to the men of Monsieur de Po-
lisse how could I ever miss?"

"But why did Monsieur d'Orleans, who is not at all
mean, grant you permission to fire but once a day?"

"Because he knew that one shot would be enough."

The curiosity of this spectacle and the oddness of this
theory brought at least ten louis a day to the old anchorite.

Now, as he gained much money by the sale of his hare-
skins, and the holiday he had established, and he purchased only a pair of gaiters every five years, and a coat
every ten, he was not at all unhappy.

On the contrary, it was said that he had a concealed
treasure, and that his heir would get a good thing. Such
was the singular person whom Pitou went to at midnight
when the brilliant idea of which we have spoken entered
his mind.

To fall in with Father Clovis, however, required much
address.

Like one of Neptune's old herdsmen, he was not easily
overtaken. He knew easily how to distinguish the useless man from one from whom he could make money.

Clovis was lying down on his bed of straw, made of the
aromatic plants which the woods produce in September,
and which would not require to be changed until the same
month of the next year.

It was about eleven months, and the weather was calm
and bright.

To reach the hut of Clovis, he had to pass through the
thickets of oak and underbrush so thick that his arrival
could not be unknown.

Pitou made four times as much noise as an ordinary person would have done, and old Clovis lifted up his head.
He was not asleep, but was on that day in a terribly bad
humor. An accident had happened which made him almost unapproachable. The accident was terrible.

His gun, which he had used for five years with balls,
and for thirty-five years with shot, had burst.

For thirty-five years he had not missed a shot.

The fact of the hare being safe and sound was not the greatest misfortune which had befallen Clovis. Two fingers of his right hand had been carried away. Clovis had bound up his fingers with bruised herbs.

Now, to procure another gun, Father Clovis would be under the necessity of appealing to his treasury, and even though he expended as much as two louis, who knew if the gun would not burst at the second shot?

Pitou came at an evil hour.

At the very moment Pitou placed his hand on the door, old Clovis uttered a groan which amazed the commander of the National Guard of Haramont.

Was it a wolf or some one substituted for Father Clovis?

Pitou hesitated whether he should go in or not.

"Well, Father Clovis?"

"What?" said the misanthrope.

Pitou was reassured. He recognized the voice of the anchorite.

"Ah, you are in," said he.

He then entered the hut and bowed to the occupant.

Pitou said, as he entered the room, quietly:

"Good morning, Clovis."

"Who goes there?" said the proprietor.

"I."

"Who are you?"

"I, Pitou."

"Who is Pitou?"

"Ange Pitou, of Haramont."

"Well, what is it to me who you are?"

"Ah!" said Pitou, "Clovis is not in a bad humor. I was sorry to awaken him."

"Certainly you were."

"What, then, must I do?"

"Go away as quickly as you possibly can."

"But let us talk."

"About what?"

"Of a favor you can do me."

"I want pay for all I do."

"Well, I pay for all I get."

"Possibly; but I am no longer of use to any one."

"How so?"

"I shall kill no more game."

"How so? You never miss a shot, Clovis. It is impossible."

"Go away, I tell you."

"But, Father Clovis——"

"You annoy me."

"Listen to me and you will not be sorry."

"Well, then, what do you wish? Be brief."

"You are an old soldier."

"Well?"

"Well, I wish——"

"Go on."

"Teach me the manual."

"Are you a fool?"

"No; teach me the manual, and I will pay you."

"The creature is mad," said Clovis. "What a soldier!"

"Father Clovis, will you teach me the manual or not? Do so, and I will pay you what you please."

The old man arose and said:

"What I please? Well, give me a gun."

"Bah! I have thirty-four guns."

"Thirty-four?"

"Yes. I have thirty-five. It is a sergeant's musket—the last, I mean, with the king's cipher on the breech."

"How came you by it? You did not steal it, I hope?"

Pitou told him the whole truth frankly and honestly.

"Well, I will teach you; but my fingers are hurt."

He then told Pitou what accident had befallen him.

"Well," said Pitou, "I will give you another gun. I cannot give you other fingers, for all I have I need myself."

He arose.

The moon shed a torrent of white life on the little opening in front of the hut.

Any one who had seen those two dark forms gesticulating at midnight could not have repressed some mysterious terror.

Clovis took up his burst gun with a sigh. He then placed himself in a military position.

It was strange to see the old man again become erect,

bent as he was from the habit of passing the bushes, but revived by the recollection of his regiment, his aiguillet, and brushed back his dark hair.

"Look at me," said he, "look at me; that is the way to learn. Do as I do, and I will correct you."

Pitou made the attempt.

"Draw back your knees. Square your shoulders. Give full play to your head. Give yourself a good foundation, your feet are large enough."

Pitou did as well as he could.

"Very well," said the old man. "You look noble enough."

If he looked thus after an hour's drill, what would he not be in a month? He would be majestic.

He wished to continue.

Father Clovis, however, wished to get hold of the gun first, and said:

"No, this is enough for once. Teach this at your first drill, and they will not learn it in four days. I must, however, tell you, that to-morrow night there will be no moon."

"We will go through the manual in your house, then."

"You will have to bring a light."

"And whatever else you want."

"Then bring my gun."

"You shall have it to-morrow."

"Very well. Now let me see if you recollect what I told you."

Pitou behaved so well that Clovis complimented him. He would have promised Clovis a six-pounder if he had asked for one.

When they had finished, it lacked but an hour of daylight, and he bid leave to his teacher, going, it must be owned, slowly toward Haramont, the whole population of which slept soundly.

Pitou sunk to sleep, and dreamed that he commanded an army of many millions of men, and waged war on the whole world, his army obeying in one rank the word of command, "Carry arms!"

On the next day he drilled his soldiers with an insolence which they esteemed proof positive of his capacity.

Pitou became popular, and was admired by men, women, and children.

The women even became serious when, in stentorian tones, he cried out :

" Be a soldier !   Look at me."

He was a soldier.

CHAPTER XXXVII.

OLD CLOVIS had his gun ; for what Pitou promised he did.

In two visits Pitou became a grenadier.   But, unfortunately, when Clovis had taught him the manual, he had taught all he knew.

Pitou bought a copy of the " French Tatician," and of the " Manual of the National Guard," on which he expended a crown.

The Haramont battalion made, thanks to Pitou, very rapid progress.   When he had reached the more complicated maneuvers, he went to Soissons, where, in one hour, from observing real soldiers drilled by real officers, he learned in one day more than his books would have taught him in a month.

He thus toiled for two months.

Pitou was ambitious and in love.   Pitou was unfortunate in his love.   Often, after his drill, which always followed midnight study, had Pitou crossed the plains of Largny, and . now and then   the whole forest, to meet Catherine, who always kept her appointment at Boursonne.

Catherine used every day to steal away from her household duty, to a little cot near the barn of Boursonne, next her beloved Isidor, who seemed always happy and joyous, even though everything around seemed dark.

How great was Pitou's unhappiness when he remembered how unequal a share of happiness was vouchsafed to different men !

He to whom the girls of Haramont, Taillefontaine, and Vivières made love, who also had his rendezvous, yet was forced to weep, like a child, before a door open to Isidor.

Pitou loved Catherine the more devotedly because he saw that she was his superior.   He also knew that she loved another, and though he ceased to be jealous of Isidor, who was noble, handsome, and worthy of love, Catherine, at least, sprung from the people, should not disgrace her family nor make him unhappy.

When he thought, therefore, he suffered very deeply.

" It was heartless," said he, " to suffer me to go. When I did so, she never asked if I was dead or alive. What would Billot say if he knew his friends were treated thus, and his business thus neglected ? What would he say if he knew that the housekeeper, instead of attending to his business, was making love with the aristocratic M. Charny ?

" He would say nothing, but kill Catherine.

" It is something, however, to have such a revenge in my grasp."

It was better, though, not to make use of it.

Pitou had observed that good actions, not understood, never benefit the actors.

Would it not be well to let Catherine know what he was about ? Nothing was easier ; he had only to speak to her some day at mass, and let fall something to inform her that three persons knew her secret. Was it not worth while to make her suffer a little, to quell her pride ?

If, though, he went to the dance, he must appear as the equal of the noble, a thing difficult to do when the object of comparison was one so well dressed.

The pavilion in which Catherine used to meet Charny, was in a kind of grove which was an appendant to the forest of Villers-Cotterets.

A simple ditch divided the property of the count from that of his neighbors.

Catherine, who was every day called for one reason or another to visit the neighbors, found no difficulty in leaping over this ditch. The rendezvous was certainly well selected.

The pavilion was so placed that through the loopholes, set with painted glass, she could overlook the whole grove, while it was itself so secluded that no one could see it, and three springs of a horse would put any one who sought to leave in the forest or in neutral ground.

Pitou had watched Catherine so carefully, that he knew whither she went, and whence she came, as well as the poacher knows the track of the hare.

Catherine did not return to the forest with Isidor, who used always to remain some time in the pavilion, in order to see that she was not annoyed, and used then to go in a contrary direction.

Pitou hid himself on Catherine's pathway, and ascended an immense tree which completely overlooked the pavilion.

Before an hour had passed, he saw Catherine come by. She tied her horse in the wood, sprung over the ditch, and went to the pavilion.

She dismounted just below the tree where Pitou was.

He had only to descend and lean against the trunk. He then took from his pocket the "Manual of the National Guard," and began to read.

An hour after, Pitou heard a door open. He heard the rustling of a silk dress, and saw Catherine look anxiously around as if to see if she was watched.

She stood within ten paces of Pitou.

Pitou did not move, and kept his book on his knees. He no longer, however, pretended to read, and looked at Catherine so that she could not misunderstand him.

She uttered a half-stifled cry, and then became pale as death. After another brief moment of indecision, he rushed into the forest and became invisible.

Pitou had arranged matters well, and Catherine was caught in the snare.

Pitou returned, half happy and half afraid, to Haramont.

As soon as he thought of what he had done, he saw that it might have many consequences which previously had not suggested themselves to him.

The next day was appointed for a military parade.

Being sufficiently instructed, in their own opinion, the National Guards had requested to be assembled in the presence of the public.

A few neighboring villages, excited by rivalry, and who had also paid attention to tactics, were to come to Haramont for a kind of contest.

A deputation from these villages was present under the command of an old sergeant.

The announcement of such a spectacle brought many persons together, and the parade-ground of Haramont early in the day was occupied by crowds of young children, and at a late hour by the fathers and mothers of the champions.

Four drums beat in four different directions, that of Largny, Ver, Taillefontaine, and Vivières.

Haramont was a center, and had its four cardinal points.

A fifth replied ; it preceded the thirty-three National Guards of Haramont.

Among the spectators was a portion of the aristocracy and of the bourgeoisie of Villers-Cotterets come to be amused.

There were also many farmers who had come to see.

Soon Catherine and Mme. Billot came. Just at this moment the National Guard of Haramont came from the village, headed by Pitou, a drum and a fife. Pitou was on a great white horse, which Maniquet had lent him for the purpose of making a representation of Marquis Lafayette *ad vivum* at Haramont.

Pitou grasped his sword and bestrode the huge horse. If he did not represent the aristocracy, he at least represented the bone and sinew of the land.

The entrance of Pitou, and of those who had conferred so much honor on the province, was saluted by loud acclamations.

All had hats alike, with the national cockade, and marched in two ranks in the most perfect order.

When it reached the parade, all approved of it.

Pitou caught a glance of Catherine and grew pale. She trembled.

This was the most exciting portion of the review.

He put his men through the manual, and every command excited much attention and applause.

The other villagers appeared excited and irregular. Some were half armed, others half instructed, and were completely demoralized by the comparison. The others became vain of their excellence.

Both were uncertain, however, as to cause and effect.

From the manual they passed to the drill.

Here the sergeant expected to rival Pitou.

In consideration of age, the sergeant had received the command, and marched his men to and fro by files.

He could do nothing more.

Pitou, with his sword under his arm, and his helmet on his brow, looked on with infinite superiority.

When the sergeant saw his heads of column become lost amid the trees, while the rear took the back track to Haramont ; when he saw his squares disperse, and squads and platoons lose their commandants, he was greeted by a disapproving sound from his own soldiers.

A cry was heard :

" Pitou ! Pitou ! Pitou !"

" Yes, Pitou !" echoed the men of the other villages, offended at an inferiority which they attributed to their instructors.

Pitou, on his white horse, placed himself at the head of his men, to whom he gave the right, and gave the command in such a tone that the very oaks trembled.

As if by miracle, the broken files united, the maneuvers were well executed, Pitou made such good use of his books, and of Father Clovis's instructions.

The army, with one voice, saluted him Imperator on the field of battle.

Pitou dismounted, and, covered with sweat, received the salutations of the crowd.

He did not, however, see Catherine.

All at once Pitou heard her voice. It was not necessary for him to seek her. She had sought him.

His triumph was immense.

" What !" said she, with an air in strange contrast with her pale face. " Have you become proud because you are a great general ?"

" Oh, no !" said Pitou. " Good morning, mademoiselle."

Then to Mme. Billot :

" I am happy to salute you, Madame Billot."

Turning to Catherine, he said :

" Mademoiselle, you are wrong. I am not a great general, but only a young man anxious to serve my country."

What he had said was borne through the crowd, and treated as a sublime sentiment.

" Ange," said Catherine, " I must speak to you."

" Ah ! at last, at last !" In a louder tone, he said :

" When you please."

" Return to the farm with us."

" Very well."

CHAPTER XXXVIII.

CATHERINE contrived to be alone with Pitou, in spite of her mother's presence.

Old Mother Billot had some gossips, who walked by her and maintained conversation.

Catherine, who had left her horse, returned on foot with Pitou.

Such arrangements surprise no one in the country, where people are more indulgent than they are in great cities.

It seemed natural enough for M. Pitou to talk to Mlle. Billot. It may be none ever noticed it.

On that day all enjoyed the silence and thickness of the woods. All glory and happiness seems to reside amid the primeval grandeur of the forests.

"Here I am, Mademoiselle Catherine," said Pitou, when they were alone.

"Why have you for so long a time not visited our farm? That is wrong, Pitou."

"But, mademoiselle, you know the reason."

"I do not. You are wrong."

Pitou bit his lips. It annoyed him to hear Catherine tell a falsehood.

She saw and understood his expression.

"But, Pitou, I have something to tell you."

"Ah!" said he.

"The other day you saw me in the hut?"

"Yes, I did."

"You saw me?"

"Yes."

She blushed.

"What were you doing there?"

"You knew me."

"At first I did not. I did afterward."

"What do you mean?"

"Sometimes one does not pay attention."

"Certainly."

Both were silent, for each had much to think of.

Catherine said at last:

"Then it was you? What were you doing there? Why did you hide yourself?"

"Hide myself!"

"Why?"

"Curiosity might have made me."

"I have no curiosity."

She stamped the ground most impatiently with her little foot.

"You were," said she, "in a place you do not visit often."

"You saw I was reading."

"I do not know."

"If you saw me, you did."

"I did see you distinctly; but what were you reading?"

"My 'Tactics.'"

"What is that?"

"A book in which I learned what I have since taught my men. To study, madame, one must be alone."

"True; in the forest nothing disturbs you."

"Nothing."

They were again silent; the rest of the party rode before them.

"When you study thus," said Catherine, "do you study long?"

"Whole days sometimes."

"Then you had been long there?"

"Very long."

"It is surprising that I did not see you when I came."

Here she told an untruth, but was so bold that Pitou was convinced. He was sorry for her. All her wants were due only to the want of circumspection.

"I may have slept. I sometimes do when I study too much."

"Well, while you slept I must have passed you. I went to the old pavilion."

"Ah!" said Pitou, "what pavilion?"

Catherine blushed again. This time her manner was so affected that he could not believe her.

"Charny's pavilion. There is the best balm in the country. I had hurt myself, and needed some leaves. I hurt my hand."

As if he wished to believe her, Ange looked at her hands.

"Ah!" said she, "not my hands, but my feet."

"Did you get what you wanted?"

"Ah, yes. My feet, you see, are well."

Catherine fancied that she had succeeded; she fancied Pitou had seen and knew nothing. She said, and it was a great mistake:

"Then, Monsieur Pitou would have cut us. He is proud of his position, and disdains peasants since he has become an officer."

Pitou was wounded. So great a sacrifice, even though

feigned, demands another recompense ; and as Catherine seemed to seek to mystify Pitou, and as she doubtless laughed at him when she was with Isidor de Charny, all Pitou's good humor passed away. Self-love is a viper asleep, on which it is never prudent to tread unless you crush it at once.

"Mademoiselle," said he, "it seems you cut me."

"How so ?"

"First—you refused me work, and drove me from the farm. I said nothing to Monsieur Billot, for, thank God, I have a heart and hands."

"I assure you, Monsieur Pitou——"

"It matters not ; of course you can manage your own affairs. If, then, you saw me at the pavilion, you should have spoken to me, instead of running away, as if you were robbing an orchard."

The viper had stung. Catherine was uneasy.

"Or as if your barn had been on fire. Mademoiselle, I had not the time to shut my book before you sprung on the pony and rode away. He had been tied long enough, though, to eat up all the bark of an oak."

"Then a tree was destroyed. But why, Monsieur Pitou, do you tell me this ?"

Catherine felt that all her presence of mind was leaving her.

"Ah, you were gathering balm," said Pitou. "A horse does much in an hour."

Catherine said :

"In an hour ?"

"No horse, mademoiselle, could strip a tree of that size in less time. You must have been collecting more balm than would suffice to cure all the wounds received at the Bastile."

Catherine could not say a word.

Pitou was silent ; he knew he had said enough.

Mother Billot paused at the cross-road to bid adieu to her friends.

Pitou was in agony, for he felt the pain of the wounds he had inflicted, and was like a bird just ready to fly away.

"Well, what says the officer ?" said Mme. Billot.

"That he wishes you good-day."

"Then good-day. Come, Catherine."

"Ah ! tell me the truth," murmured Catherine.

"What ?"

"Are you not yet my friend ?"

"Alas !" said the poor fellow, "you, as yet without experience, began to make love, through confessions which only the skilful know how to manage."

Pitou felt that his secret was rushing to his lips ; he felt that the first word Catherine said would place him in her power.

He was aware, though, if he spoke he would die when Catherine confessed to him what as yet he only suspected.

He was silent as an old Roman, and bowed to Catherine with a respect which touched the young girl's heart ; bowed to Mme. Billot, and disappeared.

Catherine made a bound as if she would follow him.

Mme. Billot said to her daughter :

"He is a good lad, and has much feeling."

When alone, Pitou began a long monologue, which we will omit.

The poor lad did not know that in love there is both honey and absinthe, and that Charny had all the honey.

From this hour, during which she had suffered horribly, Catherine conceived a kind of respectful fear for Pitou, which a few days before she was far from feeling toward him.

When one cannot inspire love, it is not bad to inspire fear ; and Pitou, who had great ideas of personal dignity, would not have been a little flattered had he discovered the existence even of such a sentiment.

As he was not, however, physiologist enough to see what the ideas of a woman a league and a half from him are, he went and sung a countless number of songs, the theme of which was unfortunate love.

Pitou at last reached his own room, where he found his chivalric guard had placed a sentinel. The man, dead drunk, lay on a bench with his gun across his legs.

Pitou awoke him.

He then learned that his thirty men, good and true, had ordered an entertainment at old Father Tellier's,—the old man was the Vatel of Haramont,—and that twelve ladies were to crown the Turenne who had overcome the Condé of the next canton.

Pitou was too much fatigued for his stomach not to have suffered.

Pitou, being led by his sentinel to the banquet-hall, was received with acclamations which nearly blew the roof off.

He bowed, sat down in silence, and even attacked the veal and salad.

This state of feeling lasted until his stomach was filled and his heart relieved.

CHAPTER XXXIX.

FEASTING after sorrow is either an increase of grief or an absolute consolation.

Pitou saw that his grief was increased.

He arose when his companions could not.

He made even an oration on Spartan sobriety to them when they were all dead drunk.

He bid them go away when they were asleep under the table.

We must say that the ladies disappeared during the dessert.

Pitou thought, amid all his glory and honor, the prominent subject was his last interview with Catherine.

Amid the half hints of his memory, he recalled the fact that her hand had often touched his, and sometimes her shoulder had pressed his own, and that he, on certain occasions, had known all her beauties,

He then looked around him like a man awakening from a drunken dream.

He asked the shadows why so much severity toward a young woman, perfect in grace, could have been in his heart.

Pitou wished to reinstate himself with Catherine.

But how ?

A Lovelace would have said, "That girl laughs at and deceives me. I will follow her example."

Such a character would have said, "I will despise her, and make her ashamed of her love as of so much disgrace.

"I will terrify and dishonor her, and make the path to her rendezvous painful."

Pitou, like a good fellow, though heated with wine and love, said to himself, "Some time I will make Catherine ashamed that she did not love me."

Pitou's chaste ideas would not permit him to fancy that

Catherine did aught but coquette with M. de Charny, and that she laughed at his laced boots and golden spurs.

How delighted Pitou was to think that Catherine was not in love with either a boot or a spur.

Some day M. Isidor would go to the city and marry a countess. Catherine then would seem to him an old romance.

All these ideas occupied the mind of the commander of the National Guard of Haramont.

To prove to Catherine that he was a good fellow, he began to recall all the bad things he had heard during the day.

But Catherine had said some of them. He thought he would tell them to her.

A drunken man without a watch has no idea of time.

Pitou had no watch, and had not gone ten paces before he was as drunk as Bacchus or his son Thespis.

He did not remember that he had left Catherine three hours before, and that half an hour later, she must have reached Pisseaux.

To that place he hurried.

Let us leave him among the trees, bushes, and briers, threshing with his stick the great forest of Orleans, which returned blows with usury.

Let us return to Catherine, who went home with her mother.

There was a swamp behind the farm, and when there they had to ride in single file.

The old lady went first.

Catherine was about to go when she heard a whistle.

She turned, and saw in the distance the cap of Isidor's valet.

She let her mother ride on, and the latter, being but a few paces from her home, was not wary.

The servant came.

"Mademoiselle," said he, "my master wishes to see you to-night, and begs you to meet him somewhere at eleven, if you please."

"Has he met with any accident?" said Catherine, with much alarm.

"I do not know. He received to-night a letter with a black seal from Paris. I have already been here an hour."

The clock of Villers-Cotterets struck ten.

Catherine looked around.

" Well, the place is dark ; tell your master I will wait for him here."

The man rode away.

Catherine followed her mother home.

What could Isidor have to tell her at such an hour ?

Love meetings assume more smiling forms.

That was not the question. Isidor wished to see her, and the hour was of no importance. She would have met him in the graveyard of Villers-Cotterets at midnight.

She would not then even think, but kissed her mother, and went to her room.

Her mother went to bed.

She suspected nothing, and if she had, it mattered not, for Catherine was a being of a superior order.

Catherine neither undressed nor went to bed.

She heard the chime of half after ten. At a quarter before eleven she put out the lamp and went into the dining-room. The windows opened into the yard. She sprung out.

She hurried to the appointed place, with a beating heart, placing one hand on her bosom and the other on her head. She was not forced to wait long.

She heard the feet of a horse.

She stepped forward.

Isidor was before her.

Without dismounting, he took her hand, lifted her into the saddle, and said :

" Catherine, yesterday my brother George was killed at Versailles. My brother Olivier has sent for me ; I must go."

Catherine uttered an exclamation of grief, and clasped Charny in her arms.

" If," said she, " they killed one brother, they will kill another."

" Be that as it may ; my eldest brother has sent for me ; Catherine, you know I love you."

" Stay, stay !" said the poor girl, who was only aware of the fact that Isidor was going.

" Honor and vengeance appeal to me."

" Alas ! alas !"

And she threw herself, pale and trembling, in his arms.

A tear fell from Charny's eyes on the young girl's brow.

"You weep ; thank God, you love me !"

"Yes ; but my eldest brother has written to me, and you see I must obey."

"Go, then : I will keep you no longer."

"One last kiss."

"Adieu !"

The young girl consented, knowing that nothing could keep Isidor from obeying this order of his brother. She slid from his arms to the ground.

The young man looked away, sighed, hesitated, but under the influence of the order he had received, galloped away, casting one long last look on Catherine.

A servant followed him.

Catherine lay alone where she fell, completely closing the narrow way.

Just then a man appeared on the top of the hill, toward Villers-Cotterets, rapidly advancing toward the farm, and he was very near treading on the inanimate body that lay in the pathway.

He lost his balance, stumbled, and fell, and was not aware of the body until he touched it.

"Catherine !" said he, "Catherine dead ?"

He uttered a cry of such agony that he aroused the very dogs of the farm.

"Who has killed her ?" He sat pale, trembling, and inert, with the body on his knees.

THE END.